The
Fire Service

# of Sachem City

a novel

Tom Trabulsi

The Fire Service of Sachem City
Copyright © 2024 Tom Trabulsi

Produced and printed by Stillwater River Publications.
All rights reserved. Written and produced in the United States of America.
This book may not be reproduced or sold in any form without the expressed,
written permission of the author(s) and publisher.

Visit our website at **www.StillwaterPress.com** for more information.

First Stillwater River Publications Edition

ISBN: 978-1-965733-34-9 (hardcover), 978-1-965733-35-6 (paperback)

Library of Congress Control Number: 2025906020

1 2 3 4 5 6 7 8 9 10

Publisher's Cataloging-in-Publication
Provided by Cassidy Cataloguing Services, Inc.

Names: Trabulsi, Tom, author.
Title: The fire service of Sachem City : a novel / Tom Trabulsi.
Description: First Stillwater River Publications edition. | West Warwick, RI,
     USA : Stillwater River Publications, [2025]
Identifiers: LCCN: 2025906020 | ISBN: 9781965733349 (hardcover) |
     9781965733356 (paperback)
Subjects: LCSH: Fire fighters—New England—Fiction. | Fire
     departments—New England—Fiction. | Hazardous occupations—
     Fiction. | Friendship—Fiction. | Financial crises—New England—
     Fiction. | New England—Economic conditions—21st century—Fiction. |
     LCGFT: Action and adventure fiction. | BISAC: FICTION / Literary. |
     FICTION / Action & Adventure.
Classification: LCC: PS3620.R323 F57 2025 | DDC: 813/.6—dc23

Written by Tom Trabulsi.
Interior design by Elisha Gillette.
Published by Stillwater River Publications, West Warwick, RI, USA.

*The views and opinions expressed in this book are solely those of the author(s)
and do not necessarily reflect the views and opinions of the publisher.*

Dedicated to
Kim Lima-Ritacco (8/11/1973 — 1/29/2018)
The First Fan

"*I love those who can smile in trouble, who can gather strength from distress, and grow brave by reflection. 'Tis the business of little minds to shrink, but they whose heart is firm, and whose conscience approves their conduct, will pursue their principles unto death.*"

—Leonardo da Vinci

TABLE OF CONTENTS

Battalion Chiefs

Capt. Fredrick McLoud – A-Shift Acting Battalion Chief. Politically adept sycophant.

Capt. Ronald Riggs – B-Shift Acting Battalion Chief. Straight arrow to the point of extreme.

Capt. Theodore Etchel – C-Shift Acting Battalion Chief. Master pranker, athlete, and card player.

Capt. Brigado Rossi – D-Shift Acting Battalion Chief. The Loose Cannon.

Mayor

Charles Houlinik – First term mayor. Beloved son of the city.

Fire Chief

Chief Allen Draper – Thirty-year FD veteran and former Marine. Five years as Chief of Department.

Assistant Chief

A.C. Leo Fishbakke – Thirty-five-years on the job, four years as A.C.

IAFF Local 121 Union President

Lt. William Ahearn – Engine 2. 42-years-old. Eighteen-year veteran.

President of the Association of Rhode Island Firefighters

Capt. Vincent Szceriack – Twenty-years on Central Falls.

CHARACTERS

Fire Academy Class 61

Brian Fonseco, a.k.a. "Fonzie" – 22-years-old. 6'4", 240 pounds.

Jimmy Rowdell, a.k.a. "Row" – 38-years-old. Carpenter and logger.

Lenny Rialto, a.k.a. "Cheeseburger" – 26-years-old. Local boy.

Franklin Muscatelli, a.k.a. "Super-Wop" – 28-years-old. Two-tour Marine Corp Bomb Disposal Technician.

Glenn St. Pierre, a.k.a. "Yoda" – 28-years-old. Brilliant ex-teacher.

Roger Harrow, a.k.a. "Pus" – 29-years-old. Super-hooter from Coventry.

Duarte "Donnie" Da Rocha, a.k.a. "Grimace" – Ex-Teamster.

Tagir Taymaskhanov, a.k.a. "T-Bag" – 36-years-old. Former roofer and cook from Watertown, Massachuessetts.

Training Division

Lt. Robert McCarrick – Twenty-two-year veteran and fourth generation firefighter. In charge of the Division of Training before being promoted to Captain of Engine 2.

Private Kelly Michaels – "Chuckie" Not known for his patience.

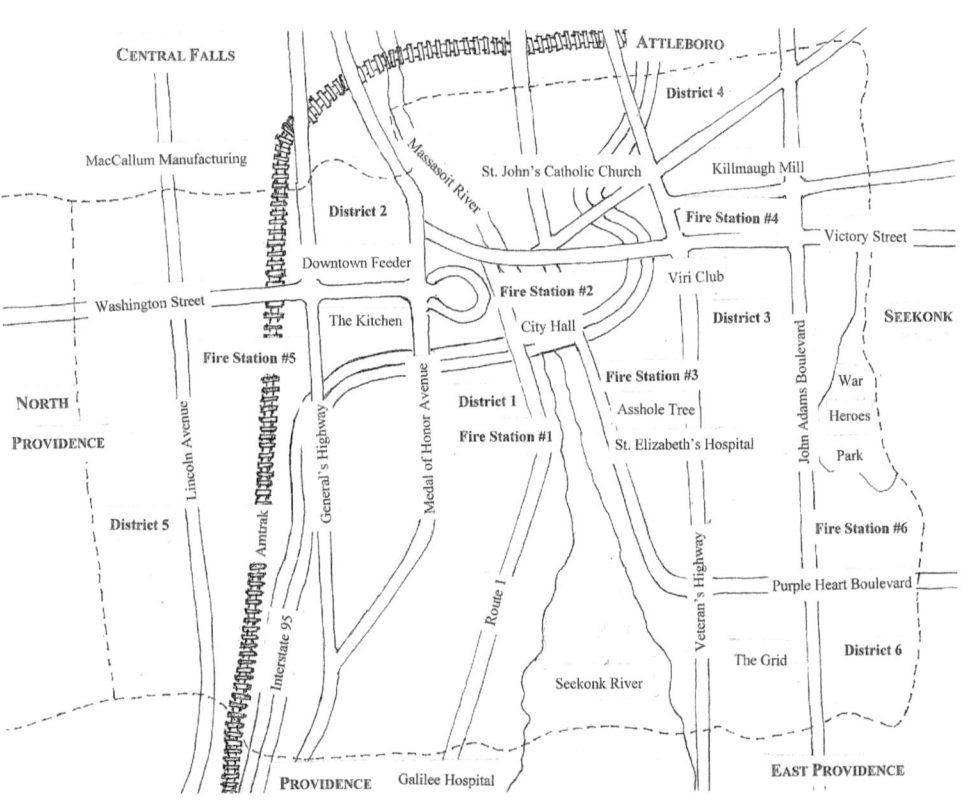

Map of Sachem City

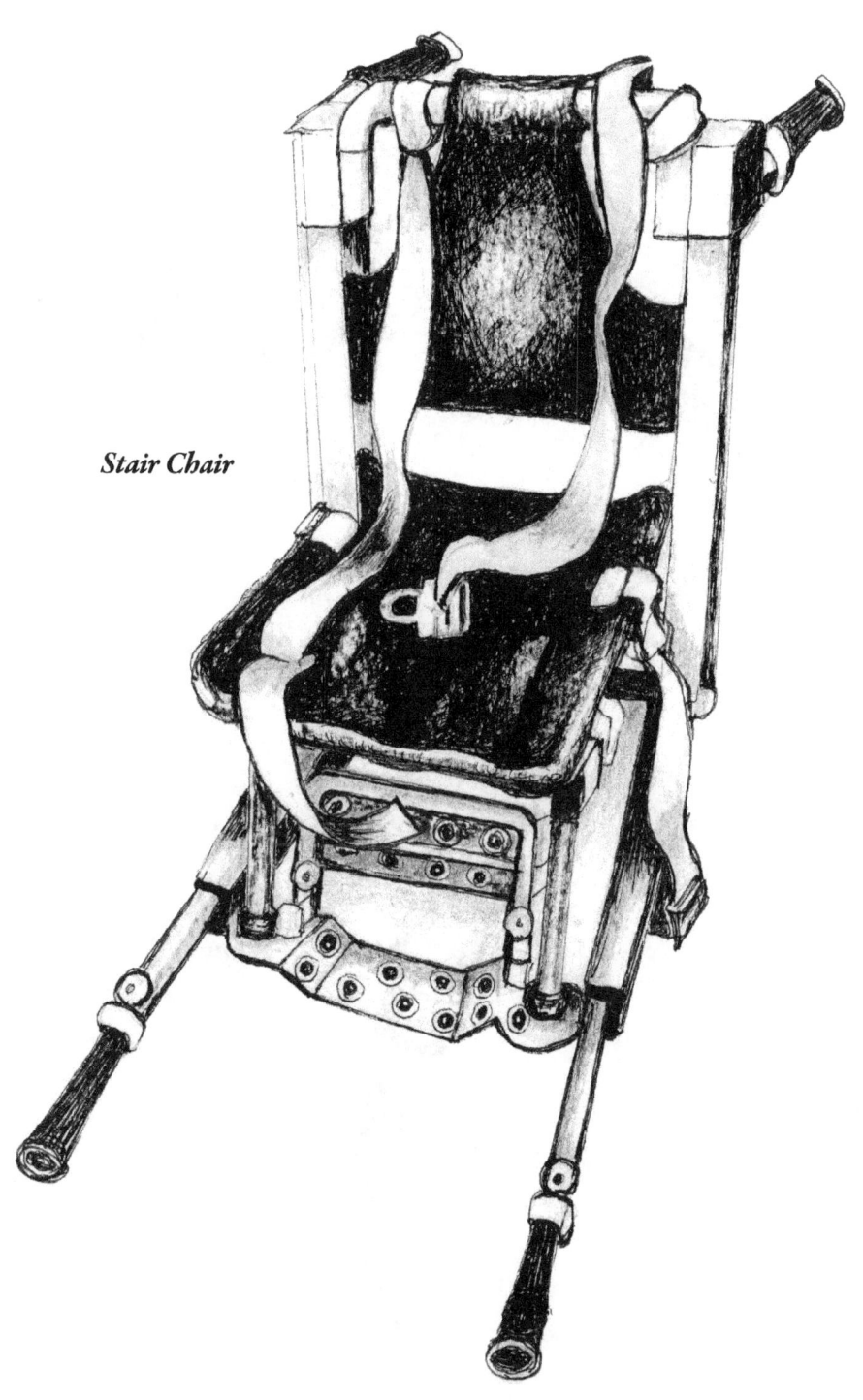

Stair Chair

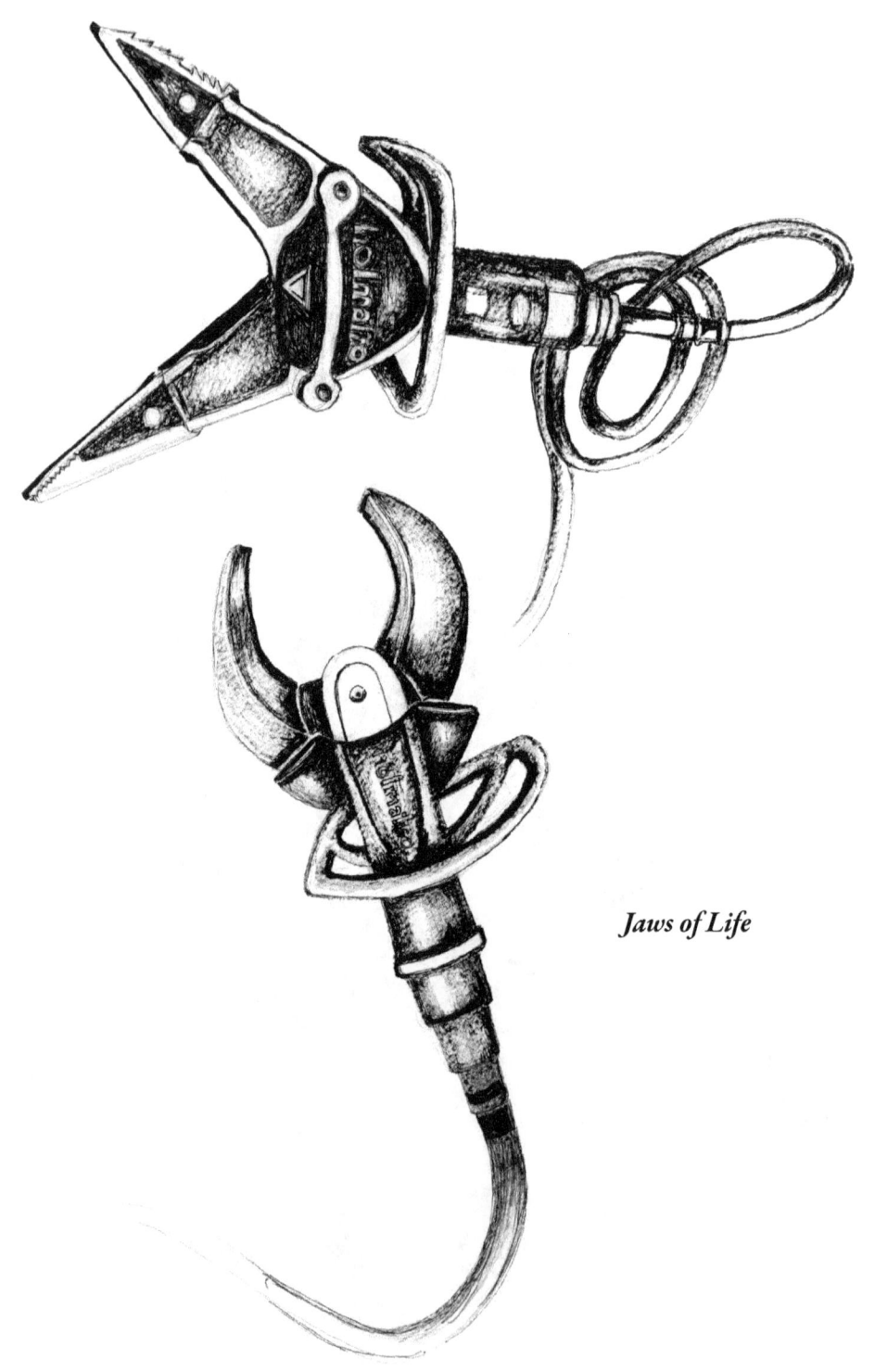

Jaws of Life

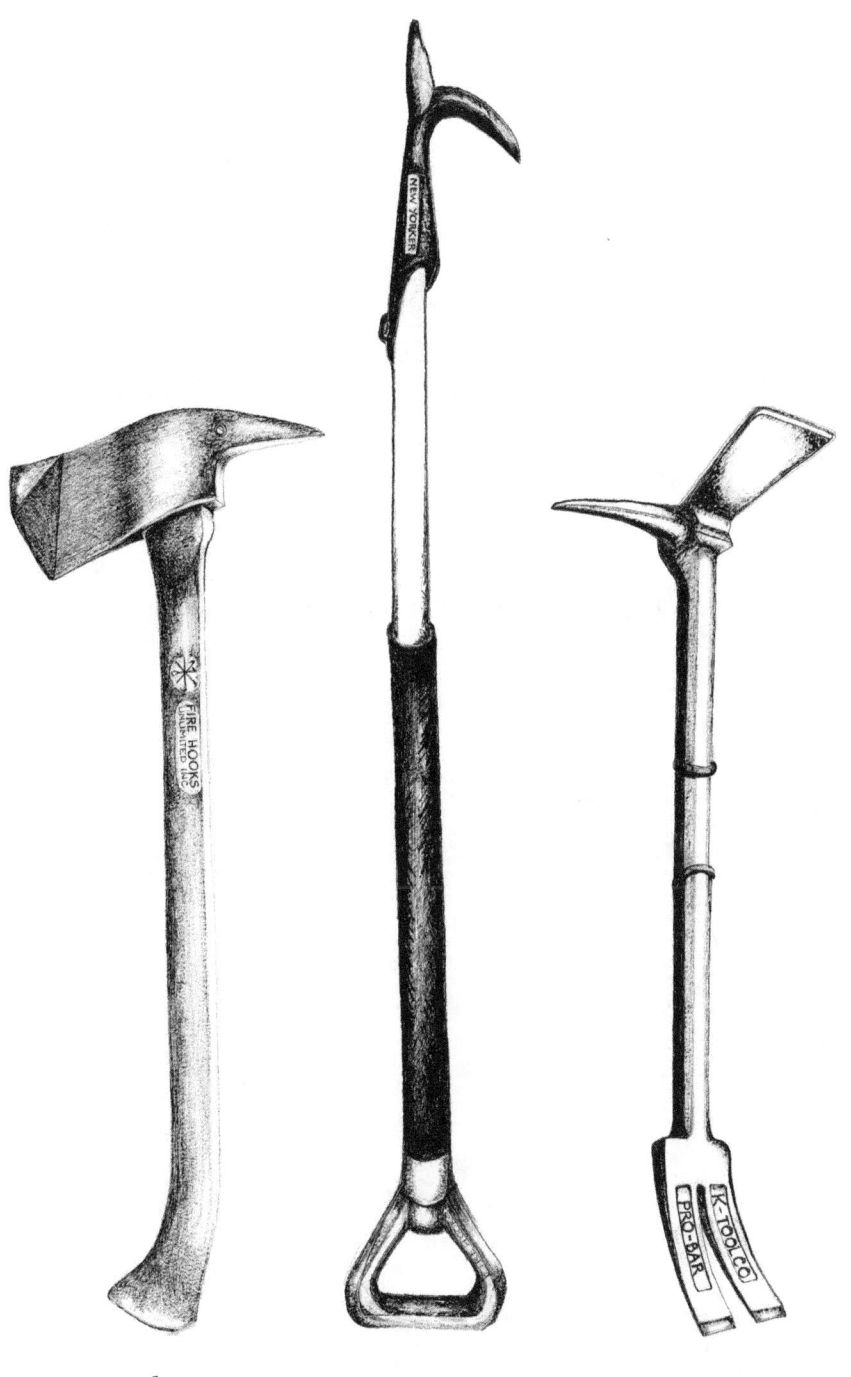

Pickaxe   **New York Hook**   **Halligan tool**

*Inspired by the men and women who have
served in the fire service of Pawtucket, Rhode Island since 1801.*

*All characters are fictitious. Any resemblance to
anyone alive or dead is unintentional.*

This is not biographical or autobiographical.

Receiver

Arthur Tillinghast Esq.– Retired Supreme Court Justice.

Governor

Marissa Carvalho – Daughter of legendary Rhode Island Governor. Master of old school machine politics and retribution. Undefeated in every election.

LINE FIREFIGHTERS

Rescue Division

Rescue Capt. Charles LeClaire – Rescue 1. 58-years-old. Vietnam Combat veteran. Thirty-four-years on Rescue 1.

Rescue Lt. David Killmoor, a.k.a. "No Stress EMS" – Rescue 2. 53-years-old. Twenty-eight-years on rescue.

Rescue Lt. Salvatore Giametti, a.k.a. "Psycho Sal" – Rescue 1. Used to be called "Straight-line Sal."

Rescue Lt. Franklin Gracey, a.k.a. "Cadillac Frank" – Rescue 1. Lead singer for "The Schemers."

Rescue Lt. Gabriel Herrein, a.k.a. "Doom" – Rescue 2. Ex-corrections officer from Auburn Correctional Facility.

Rescue Lt. Pelly Monet – Rescue 2. Army veteran. Fifteen-years on the job.

FIREFIGHTERS

Line Officers

Capt. Gary Romine, a.k.a. "Bullet Head" – Engine 5. Twenty-six-years on the job. Blunt to the extreme.

Lt. Russel Brodie – Engine 5. 6'7" with a seven-foot wingspan and blonde toupee. Recovering alcoholic on his third divorce.

Lt. Enrique Salamanca, a.k.a. "Baby Token" – Engine 2. Son of one of the first Hispanic firefighters. Weight-lifter and family man.

Lt. Cody Stokes, a.k.a. "The Dude" – Engine 1 before bidding to Engine 4. Twenty-year veteran. Master chef. Highly regarded.

Lt. Paul Kaczermarek, a.k.a. "Kaz" – Ladder 1. Cerebral and respected, considered a rising officer who might make B.C. one day.

Lt. Tim Hurst, a.k.a. "Apocalypse" – Ladder 1. Officer with a rumored death wish.

Privates

Charles Carrigan, a.k.a. "Dutch" – Engine 2. Thirty-eight-year veteran. Widely considered the best firefighter on the job.

Michael Doneen – Engine 4. 29-years-old. Eight-year veteran. Work ethic has made him a rising star amongst the old-school.

Chris Fullerton, a.k.a. "Slipknot" – Engine 4 with Mikey Doneen and Lt. Stokes. Death-metal aficionado and momma's boy.

Abel Hirsch, a.k.a. "Berserker" – Engine 1. 40-year-old ex-AHL enforcer. Nice guy with a résumé filled with violence.

Brian Klesko, a.k.a. "The Kid" – Ladder 1. Loquacious ladies' man, never stops talking.

Scotty Dumas, a.k.a. "Beef" – Ladder 1. No-neck ball-buster.

Henry Paulson, a.k.a. "Chunks" – Engine 3. Alcoholic, twenty-five-year veteran.

Margaret Duquesne, a.k.a. "Ma Dukes" – Department secretary since 1975. 56-years-old, hired when she was just 22.

Fire Alarm Bureau– 911 dispatch room in Station 2 in the City Hall complex. Two firefighters assigned twenty-four hours a day.

MISCELLANEOUS

Car 1 – Chief of Department.
Car 2 – Assistant Chief.
Car 3 – Fire Marshal.
Car 4 – Safety Officer/Training Officer.
Car 7 – Hazmat.
Car 9 – Lead Mechanic.
Car 32, 33, 35, 37 – Fire Prevention/Inspectors.

A-Shift – First Battalion.
B-Shift – Second Battalion.
C-Shift – Third Battalion.
D-Shift – Fourth Battalion.

Side-one – Front of building.
Side-two – Left side.
Side-three – Rear.
Side-four – Right side.

Truck Positions

Engine 1A – Officer.
Engine 1B – Backstep.
Engine 1C – Chauffeur.

Codes

Code Red – Transmission from first-due company if smoke or fire is present. Triggers an immediate second-alarm.
Code Yellow – Cancels multi-company response and leaves first-due engine on-scene to rectify situation.
Code Blue – Cancels a response if no patient or situation is found.

Code 99 – Person down/pulseless.
Code Brown – Defecation.

Lou – Slang for Lieutenant.
I.O.D. – Injured On Duty.
Still Alarm – 911 call to Fire Alarm.
Box Alarm – Alarm triggered by smoke or heat detectors hardwired to the Vision 21 system in Fire Alarm.

First Alarm – Three engines, one ladder, Battalion Chief.
Second Alarm – One engine, one ladder, one rescue.
Third Alarm – Two engines and one rescue.
Fourth Alarm – Out-of-town companies.

Engine Company – One officer, two privates. 750 gallons of water. 1600-feet of three different diameter-sized hoses.
Ladder Company – One officer, two privates. Forty-five-feet long and has a four-tier telescoping ladder that reaches 110-feet. Also contains 14, 24, and 35-foot extension ladders, a roof ladder, and a full complement of forcible entry tools and saws.
Rescue Company – Advanced Life Support Ambulance. One officer and one private.

Stations and Apparatus

Station 1– Engine 1 and Rescue 1. District 1 includes swaths of ghetto and triple-deckers. Rescue 1 is responsible for the entire east side, including Districts 1, 2, and 5.
Station 2– Engine 2, Ladder 1, Marine 1, and the Battalion Chief. District 2 covers I-95 North and South, has most of the high-rises in the city. Widely considered both the busiest and worst district. Ladder 1 is responsible for the whole east side.
Station 3– Engine 3 and Marine 2, a twenty-four-foot rescue boat

with twin 375 outboard motors. District 3 includes St. Elizabeth's Hospital, two housing projects, trucking companies, and the minor league baseball stadium.

Station 4– Engine 4, Ladder 2, Rescue 2. District 4 is the largest in the city. Covers I-95 South from the Massachusetts line, and large swaths of triple-deckers and mill complexes. Ladder 2 and Rescue 2 are responsible for the whole west side, which includes Districts 3, 4, and 6.

Station 5– Engine 5. District 5 includes I-95 North from exit 25 in Providence. It has a mixed residential and business base, a vast housing project, and clusters of mills that once made the west side a manufacturing powerhouse.

Station 6– Engine 6 and Marine 3. District 6 includes the zoo, vast strip malls, the country club, the last remaining portions of the middle-class, and the World War II generation living out their retirements.

MASTER BOARD
Set up at 0700 and 1700 shift changes.

Battalion Chief		
Engine 1 Officer	Engine 1 Senior Private	Engine 1 Junior Private
Engine 2 Officer	Engine 2 Senior Private	Engine 2 Junior Private
Engine 3 Officer	Engine 3 Senior Private	Engine 3 Junior Private
Engine 4 Officer	Engine 4 Senior Private	Engine 4 Junior Private
Engine 5 Officer	Engine 5 Senior Private	Engine 5 Junior Private
Engine 6 Officer	Engine 6 Senior Private	Engine 6 Junior Private
Ladder 1 Officer	Ladder 1 Senior Private	Ladder 1 Junior Private
Ladder 2 Officer	Ladder 2 Senior Private	Ladder 2 Junior Private
Rescue 1 Officer	Rescue 1 Chauffeur	
Rescue 2 Officer	Rescue 2 Chauffeur	
FAB—Senior Private	Junior Private	

BOOK ONE

CREATION

JUNE 2008 TO JULY 2009

FIRE ACADEMY CLASS 61

Sachem City, Rhode Island
June 12, 2008
Second of Twelve-Week Academy

"Incredible. Have you ever seen a bigger group of fuck-ups?" Lieutenant Robert McCarrick snapped his cigarette butt into the mud. He was a giant man with a beer gut and a massive handlebar mustache. As a fourth-generation firefighter, there had been a McCarrick on the Sachem City Fire Department since before World War I. But this legacy was not treated as a given. During his twenty-two-year career, he had so far climbed to lieutenant in both the rescue and firefighter divisions. This was also why he now watched the recruits with outright disgust. "Honestly, look at these idiots."

Kelly Michaels, his subordinate in the two-man Division of Training, loved seeing the twenty-five recruits struggle with the hose-lines. The exact physical opposite of his boss, Michaels was a small chunk of man with a hilariously explosive temper. Nicknamed "Chucky" after the murderous doll from the "Child's Play" movie franchise, he chomped his gum with an evil vigor, looked up at his boss, and said, "If they're having this much trouble with the inch-and-three-quarter, I say we charge a couple of deuce-and-a-halves and really watch these piggies sweat."

"I fucking love you."

Sachem City engine companies carried three 1¾-inch attack lines, a single 2½-inch line for blitz attacks, and a four-inch monster for either master-stream appliances or to tie the hydrant to the truck. Water was dead weight, so a fully charged 200-foot-length of 1¾-inch canvas attack line could weigh as much as 250 pounds. Altogether, there was over 1600 feet of hose on every truck.

Lt. McCarrick stuck two fingers into his mouth and let fly a piercing whistle. "Okay, morons! Disconnect those lines and get me four deuce-and-a-halves fully stretched out. I want to see a wall of water raining down. Move it!"

They were in the rear parking lot of a long-abandoned mill. Once the epicenter for the Industrial Revolution, many of Sachem City's seventy mills were now shuttered or already burnt away. Some had not seen use in thirty years. Others had only recently been renovated into high-end condominiums with brick exteriors, fourteen-foot ceilings, massive exposed beams, and refurbished wood floors. A hundred years before, these four and five-story, acre-sized behemoths produced thousands of jobs and goods shipped worldwide. But now they were vacant death traps filled with toxic waste, the homeless, the addicted, and the lost. Over the previous century, the city averaged one mill-fire every five years, so when one ignited, firefighters from around the region converged to spend days battling the flames and protecting neighborhoods.

With Sachem City's jobs gone and the middle-class destroyed, the 80,000 residents left behind were either elderly living in homes they had owned for fifty years, or the working class and immigrants just trying to survive. Fiscally, the city faced perpetual bankruptcy. There was never money for a full-time Fire Academy, so recruits showed up for free on Tuesday and Thursday nights after working their civilian jobs to receive three hours of harassment and classroom instruction. The term classroom was a stretch because the room itself was connected to the city garage and filled with lawnmowers and spare parts. They also spent eight hours every Saturday cutting up cars, dragging hoses, and wrecking condemned homes. Their mismatched gear, torched and ill-fitting, was literally taken off the backs of those recently retired.

Since the city had no funds to provide masks and regulators, they had to share, which meant repeatedly smearing someone else's sweat and spit across their own face.

Lt. McCarrick asked, "Are you seeing this?"

"Pathetic. How long before they realize simple math?"

"Idiots!" Lt. McCarrick screamed. "Are you kidding me? First of all, one truck can't run four deuce-and-a-halves without adapters or a manifold. Second, how in the hell is a two-and-a-half-inch hose-fitting gonna screw into a three inch out-take without a fucking adapter? Did anybody think to look for one? Everybody! Packs on and start humping!"

Twenty-five groans echoed across the lot. They shouldered their forty-five-pound Self-Contained Breathing Apparatuses (SCBAs) onto their backs, masked up, secured their helmets, and started jogging. In the ninety-degree heat, the combined weight of their bunker gear, boots, and air-packs neared sixty pounds. That was before adding in the axes or any other tools they carried.

"Faster! You look like a pack of drunk turtles!"

Chucky added to their pain by screaming, "Where's Number One?"

Being ranked Number One going into the academy might have seemed like a blessing, but no one cared who Number Twenty-Five was.

A slump-shouldered man in the middle of the pack raised his hand.

Chucky exploded, "Are you trying to piss me off on purpose? Gentlemen, there's been a fire department in this city since 1801. That's a two hundred-and-seven-year history now destroyed by this pathetic loser of a leader slow-speeding you all into more laps than I can count." Chucky was now in Number One's face as his mask filled with stress and sweat. "You better get your ass to the front or I will personally pop out your eyeballs and skull-fuck you until you die!"

Number One dug deep and pushed his way to the front. Ten seconds later, Chucky appeared again. "Are you kidding me? You just left your men behind? This is the fire service! No one ever goes anywhere alone.

But I get it. You're Number One. I guess the rest of us don't mean shit, right?"

It was the kind of fuck-fuck games the instructors loved. They leapt onto the weak, the strong, the privileged, the arrogant and the stupid until everyone was equally destroyed—including Number One, who was currently coming unglued.

Chucky screamed in his face, "Number One's a pile of shit! You're a disgrace. I'd eat my own ass before I ever pulled you out of a fire!"

Twenty minutes later, as guys started dropping from the heat, Chucky gleefully yelled, "Just think. Two more hours dragging hoses and then you get to break for lunch. Stay hydrated, ladies, because we're gonna be dancing all day long!"

Then he halted the run and dropped them for more push-ups.

***

Candidates were initially ranked out of necessity. Unlike bigger cities that could afford to hire everyone at the end of an academy, in Sachem City, as one man retired or died, another replaced him off "the list." Legally viable for two years, this list provided an official order for hire. But as the academy wore on, the weekly tests, instructor evaluations, and final exam could alter these rankings dramatically. However, one thing never changed—academy classmates were forever bonded. They would serve together and watch each other get married, raise families, get promoted, and later retire one-by-one. Class 61 was no exception. It contained guys from smaller departments looking for more action, blue-collar workers from the trades, ex-military continuing to serve, sons of established firefighters, and political sycophants enticed by the financial security and benefits.

Besides Lt. McCarrick and Chucky, other firemen off the line taught in the academy as well.

"Your reputation began the second you arrived," Lt. McCarrick had told them that first night. "By tomorrow morning, guys on the line will already be hearing about the hard workers or the deadbeats, about the guys who respect tradition, or the bags of shit just looking for the bennies. You want a pension? You want health insurance? You'll get it. But you're also gonna get hurt or even die. This job will poison and cripple you before the city forgets you ever existed. In the state of Rhode Island, all 911 calls are answered by fire departments. That means medical emergencies, car wrecks—everything. So you'll be on the rescues, engines, and ladders. But don't fool yourselves. As of now, you're nothing. You're "wannabes" entitled to absolute zero. You become probationary firefighters after you are sworn in. Six months after that, "probies" become "newbies" after they're voted into the union. Remember that, because if you screw up during that probationary period you will be dismissed without prejudice. How many of you are married?"

Twelve out of the twenty-five hands went up.

"Great. Get ready to be divorced. You're gonna miss holidays, birthdays, weekends, and your wife will be raising your kids without you while blaming you the entire time. You'll see some of the worst shit imaginable. Babies killed by their parents, abused kids, old people left to die in their own shit because their family couldn't care less. Men beating women, women addicted and whoring for cash. You'll be walking into beautiful homes filled with awful people, and utter pigsties you wouldn't let a dog live in. When I was on rescue, we had a run for a 16-month-old not breathing. Turns out he had been raped by the boyfriend and internally hemorrhaged because 16-month-olds aren't designed for anal sex with monsters. You'll see people cut in half after motorcycle accidents—"

"You ready for that?" Chucky suddenly jumped into the face of Number One and lost his mind. "You know what a guide-wire is? That diagonal support cable bolted from the telephone pole to the ground? Well, one night two guys flipped a motorcycle. The guy riding bitch had his legs ripped off by the guide-wire. The driver lost his head. The guy with no legs also had his guts ripped out. They were slung across the street. He was trying to sit up and talking to us calmly because he was in shock. The next day, two out of the three guys that responded with me on Engine 1 retired. Some guys have a threshold and some do not. What's your threshold, Number One? What qualifies you to be here?"

"I just want to help and serve—"

"Shut up. You scored high on a test and became Number One but you're still a bitch-ass stockbroker. What the fuck are you doing here?"

"Instructor—"

"Firefighter Michaels is my name. And just shut your mouth. You're making all of us dumber." He turned to the others. "How many of you went to college?"

Half the class raised their hands.

"Wow. Lucky us. Imagine that. You all got educated and were still so bad at what you did you decided to sweep up bodies for a living instead. For the record, I hate college boys. Bunch of privileged ass-clowns that know how to read books, so what? Go fuck yourselves."

Lt. McCarrick chuckled and asked, "How many of you have fathers on the job here or elsewhere?"

Five hands went up.

Lt. McCarrick said, "You might be the dumbest of all. You watched this job destroy your home, your parents' marriage, maybe turn your dad into an alcoholic and look—you just can't wait to sign up. Wanna know why? Because it's the greatest job in the whole world. It's up to you. Every day is someone else's worst day ever. It's your job to make it better, and if not, to just suck a little less. And you're gonna need each other to do it. How is it possible to enter a triple-decker with fire blowing out every window? Because the guy beside you, in front of you, and behind you is about to do the same damn thing. That's it. It's that simple. The kind of idiot that volunteers to face the worst shit imaginable has to be surrounded by idiots just like him, right?"

Twenty-five guys nodded.

"In this business," Lt. McCarrick continued, "you've never seen it all. Remember that. Remember that every time you walk through that door it might be the greatest or worst day of your career. And most important... have fun. There are few better places to do that than inside a raging inferno."

FIRE ACADEMY WEEK THREE
June 17, 2008

"One of you already quit." Lt. McCarrick looked at the anxious class. They all wore blue tactical pants, blue T-shirts, and black boots. A few had shaved heads, but since they needed to maintain an airtight seal between their mask and skin, none were allowed to grow beards until they retired. This did not apply to mustaches because they were contained behind the mask. All were male but some were not even 21-years-old.

Jimmy Rowdell was a late bloomer to the fire service. After high school, he spent fifteen years logging in Oregon and working construction in Colorado. The only reason he had returned to Rhode Island was because his uncle got sick. A longtime distance cyclist, Rowdell was startled to see he was in better shape than most of the 20-year-olds even though he smoked Marlboro Reds and drank too much whiskey. Half of these kids had barely ever held a job, and the other half never had a career doing anything.

At 38-years of age, Rowdell was the oldest, and Donny Da Rocha, a lifelong Teamster, had just turned 37. Da Rocha was third-generation Portuguese, a National Guard veteran, and a world-class ball-buster unafraid to speak truth to power. A decade later, Da Rocha would be a heralded union president, but for now he was just another newbie trying to survive. The youngest was Danny Ferguson, a 19-year-old legacy with an older brother and father already on the job. He was so young it was easy to misjudge his intelligence, which was formidable. He was pursuing a combined bachelor/master degree in nursing, and would later become the youngest captain in department history. In total, twenty-five hopefuls jockeyed for position—actually twenty-four, since someone had already quit.

It did not take long for cliques and friendships to form. Even though Rowdell was sixteen-years older than Brian Fonseco, their work ethic and blue-collar backgrounds made them instantly symbiotic. At 6'4", "Fonzie" was a 22-year-old wiser than his years.

The military guys coalesced around a former Bomb Disposal Technician named Frankie Muscatelli. Nicknamed "Super-Wop" after ending his sentences with the word 'Capiche' one too many times, Super-Wop was a ball-busting wise guy and no stranger to all-male environments. He was a two-tour Marine and natural leader whose former job revolved around disassembling car-bombs, suicide vests, and improvised explosive devices. He had a shaved head and patriotic sleeve tattoos that blanketed both arms.

Ultra-competitive, the place was packed with alpha males. Since "the list" was only good for two years, the candidates who finished the academy near the end were guaranteed nothing. And if the mayor did not get re-elected, the new mayor could just junk the whole list at any point for any reason. Politics never changed, so the people on that new list would then surely owe his honor their allegiance.

The recruits wore the standard "bunker gear" of boots, thick pants, and jackets. The gear itself consisted of three layers—an outer shell to withstand direct fire and heat, a moisture barrier to allow perspiration to escape while also preventing liquid penetration, and an internal thermal barrier that provided up to 75% of all thermal protection. The materials used were mixes of Nomex and Kevlar amid other synthetics, and all three layers were coated in fire retardants and forever chemicals like Polyfluoroalkyl Substances, or PFAS. Rated to withstand direct fire contact and temperatures that could reach 1600 degrees Fahrenheit, this outfit did not exactly translate well with summer conditions, so everyone was already drenched in sweat. Beneath the bullying and constant harassment, they were assembling and disassembling their SCBA's repeatedly.

"These Scotts are your lifeblood." Lt. McCarrick walked up and down the line. "They're called 'Scott packs' after the company that makes them. If you were in boot camp, this would be your M-16. You need to master every valve, knob, and hose. Since you must know how to activate your emergency PASS device blindfolded in the dark, guess what our next evolution is?" Lt. McCarrick singled out Super-Wop. "Hey, Stugats, tell us what a PASS device is."

"It stands for Personal Alert Safety System, sir. It's connected to our air-packs and emits a 95-decibel shriek so people can find us."

"Wow. It's amazing you actually listened to something. Now, for the rest of you, we've designed a maze inside this mill. We're going to blackout your masks with tin foil so you can't see anything. Then we're going to torture you and your air-pack, twisting hoses and throwing lumber and worse on top of you to simulate collapse conditions as you crawl through. Any questions?"

Engine 2 suddenly pulled in. The Sachem City Fire Department had six engines, two ladder trucks, and two ambulances protecting a dense urban population of 80,000 people squeezed into nine square miles. With the city broken into six districts, each one had a "district engine." These engine companies were responsible for all 911 calls within their zone of responsibility.

The city itself was shaped like a rectangle laid lengthwise on top of Providence. In 1956, when Interstate 95 was continued from Connecticut to Maine, it cut through Rhode Island and severed Sachem City. Each half was now covered by three engines, one ladder, and one rescue. Engine 2 was the busiest and responsible for District 2, which had stretches of ghetto, high-rises, massive mills, and all of I-95. It was a prized truck coveted by hard-chargers who liked action and little sleep. As it came to a stop in the yard, the recruits watched the instructors and even Lt. McCarrick fawning over one of its firemen.

"Dutchy!"

"What's up, Dutch?"

"Hey, Dutch, how they hanging?"

Super-Wop squinted. "Who's that?"

"Charles Carrigan." Glen St. Pierre was a 28-year-old former teacher who had quit his job in disgust. He cycled up his air-pack to make sure it worked. Nicknamed "Yoda" because he seemed to know everything, Yoda was considered the smartest member of Fire Academy Class 61. Since his intelligence was not only factual but circular, his 360-degree perspective made quick work of any problem-solving or debate. He, too, would one day serve as another union president under duress in turbulent times, but as for now he was just another wannabe fighting to survive. "Dutch's a monster. Been on the job for like forty years."

"I can't believe that's him."

Charles "Dutch" Carrigan was a short man with the scrunched face and log-thick forearms of a Norse dwarf. Since there was no higher compliment than being called a "fireman's fireman," or "a good Jake," Dutch Carrigan's reputation was second to none. He was one of the last smoke-eaters before the air-packs became standard issue in the 1970's. Before that, they just jammed wet sponges into their mouths and made entry. A gregarious man loved by all, he was also widely regarded as the best firefighter on the job. Still, his humble nature left no room for idle boasts. The fire service was not an easy culture to break into, so in an environment where "probies" and "newbies" were completely harassed and destroyed at the bottom of this hierarchy, Dutch walked straight over to the line of sweat-drenched wannabes, shook hands, busted balls, and told them all how lucky they were to just hit this lottery.

"Dutch, you sexy bitch." Lt. McCarrick, nearly a foot taller and a hundred pounds heavier, wrapped him in a sweaty bear hug. "I fucking love you."

"Jesus, Bobby, not in front of the kids."

"I have no shame. I fucking love you."

"Gross!" Dutch was laughing and trying to squirm away. "Put me down, Bobby, your mustache tickles!"

"Huh." Super-Wop grinned. "Guess those guys are pretty close."

"He usually only licks people's faces after he's been drinking." Yoda was smaller and thinner than most of the recruits, but tactically no one was more on point. "He's a serious alcoholic."

"Who isn't?" Rowdell continued stacking air bottles.

"T-Bag!" Lt. McCarrick abruptly screamed. "Get all the axes, sledge-hammers, TNT tools, and Halligans over to the mill. We're doing forcible entry next."

Unfortunately for Tagir "Tony" Taymaskhanov, Lt. McCarrick could not pronounce his last name. During roll call on the academy's first night, Lt. McCarrick called out, "Tiger Ta—Tayma—aw fuck it, you're T-Bag."

Once the laughter died down, the murderous look never left Tay-maskhanov's face, and once Lt. McCarrick saw how pissed off he was, he called him T-Bag a hundred more times that night.

"I'll help." Rowdell joined him in lugging the onerous tools. He, too, was from the trades, and in that world where guys barely knew each other's last names much less their histories, calling anyone a name like T-Bag could get that joker killed. But on the fire department there was no such thing as personal space, decency, or privacy. And the nicknames, unlike Hollywood depictions, were never cool or heroic. There was no one called "Axe" or "Bull." Instead, there was "Itchy," who had horrific dandruff, "Wrong Way," who caused a head-on collision taking a left down a one-way street, "Drano," who was so boring one would rather consume drain cleaner than listen to him, "Dead End," who was such a deadbeat, his career was considered over the day he got sworn in, "Berserker," who was an ex-AHL enforcer suffering from decades of concussions, "Diaper," who once shit himself at a fire, "Cesspool," whose personal hygiene was abysmal, "Small Pox," who was constantly sick,

"Captain Chaos," who lost his mind at every fire, and "Toe-Tag," widely regarded as one of the worst EMT's on the job.

"Row's the only one helping T-Bag?" Lt. McCarrick suddenly roared. "This is the Fire Service! Does anyone ever do anything alone?"

Realizing they had just been set up, the other twenty-two recruits shared a look of horror and shouted, "No, sir!" Everyone immediately dropped their water bottles and air-packs and started lugging tools. But Lt. McCarrick was not done. "Oh, you slugs are gonna have great careers. Let me catch you watching me work at a fire and I will drop a K-12 right through your fucking head. Row! T-Bag! I guess the workers know what it means to really work, huh? Just for that, you two don't have to roll up anymore hose today. And T-Bag?"

"Yes, lieutenant."

"I fucking love you. You got a problem with that?"

"No, sir."

"So I can love you even if I'm not gay?"

"I can't blame you for having good taste, sir."

"Fucking A."

The recruits did not have radios but the instructors did. The tones suddenly hit as Fire Alarm announced, *"Attention Engines 1,2,5, Ladder 1, Battalion 3, 165 Waltham Street, reported structure fire..."*

"Let's go, boys!" Even with thirty-eight years on the job, Dutch Carrigan was the first one to the truck. "Nothing like a Saturday morning weenie roast!"

The probies watched Engine 2 fly out of the mill with sirens screaming.

Lt. McCarrick pointed to the column of black smoke suddenly chugging into the sky and yelled at the recruits, "It's about time you shitballs saw the real thing. Get in your cars and get over there, but don't kill anyone doing it. And don't clusterfuck the street, park a block back. Do not, I repeat, do not put on your gear. You are not firefighters. Move!"

The recruits stripped out of their soaked bunker gear and jumped into their cars.

Lt. McCarrick, who was also the Safety Officer, fired up the lights and sirens on his department suburban. He grabbed the radio and growled, "Car 4 responding."

"Car 4 responding at 0914."

Waltham Street was only a mile away, so traffic was light at ten o'clock Saturday morning. As the recruits pulled up, Ladder 1 was already swinging for the roof.

Lt. McCarrick gathered up the class and asked, "What's the significance of the dispatch order?"

One of the recruits raised his hand. He had a bad case of acne, so Lt. McCarrick said, "Okay, Pus, enlighten us."

"Pus" was Roger Harrow, a super-hooter from a small town near the Connecticut border. Hooters were extreme fire buffs that were addicted to their scanners. Some just listened, but others grabbed cameras and actually went to document the fire ground. "Sir, since Engine 1 leads the dispatch, that means it's their district. They're first-due with the attack line. The second-due engine, Engine 2, hooks the hydrant up to Engine 1 before they run out of water. Upon arriving, third-due Engine 5 grabs another attack line off Engine 1 and backs them up."

"Excellent job, Pus. How much water do our trucks carry?"

"750 gallons. With one line running at 150 PSI it'll be emptied out in five minutes."

"What's the ladder doing?"

"Searching for life. After that, they head to the roof and cut a hole."

"And why do ladder trucks cut holes in perfectly good roofs, Pus?"

"So the super-heated gasses and smoke can vertically exit the structure."

"Are you telling me smashing out every window ain't gonna make a difference?"

"Gasses and smoke need to rise. They don't move horizontally unless forced to."

"Well, goddamn, Pus, you just scored a hundred out of a hundred. Maybe you should be a Battalion Chief."

"I'm pretty sure that's not possible, Lieutenant."

"Dare to dream, Pus, dare to dream."

They watched Engine 5 pull up, don their Scott packs, grab an attack line off Engine 1, and disappear into the smoke. Bystanders on the sidewalk wore mixed looks of uncomfortable excitement and disbelief.

A third-floor window, unable to withstand any more heat, abruptly exploded and filled with fire. The Battalion Chief calmly toggled his microphone and said, "Command to Fire Alarm. Strike me a third alarm."

"Roger, Command." The tones hit again. *"Attention Engine 3 and Engine 6, Special Signal. Fill in on a Code Red. 165 Waltham Street..."* The dispatch was repeated twice more according to protocol but unnecessary since every station was already monitoring the fire.

Across the street, the recruits had wide eyes. They watched Dutch and the guys from Engine 2 race to hook the hydrant up to Engine 1 before it ran out of water.

The Battalion Chief screamed out, "Engine 2! Get me a search of that third-floor!"

"Roger, Chief." The Engine 2 captain toggled his mic. "Engine 2 to Fire Alarm, conducting a primary search of level three."

"Roger. Engine 2's searching level three."

More trucks arrived but it was not enough. The three companies working inside would be running out of air soon and coming out to switch bottles. The Battalion Chief studied the smoke and saw it changing colors for the worse. Usually, with two lines going, good progress would have been judged by a lightening in color. Instead, ugly black smoke chugged from every blown open window. "Command to Fire Alarm, be prepared for a fourth alarm of out-of-town companies."

"Roger, Chief."

The sound of a chainsaw ripped the air. Since Ladder 1 was inside searching for people, the recruits watched two men from Ladder 2 climb the stick as the smoke washed across them in waves. After they cut a 4'x4' hole in the roof and smashed it clear with an axe, they punched a ten-foot Pike pole through the drywall ceiling below. The chimney effect was immediate. Any smoke that had been venting from a window got sucked back in as if the house was inhaling, and then it exploded through the hole. Fire leapt out as well, so the roof team retreated for the ladder.

"Ladder 2 to Command."

"Command's on."

"The lid's off the lobster pot, Chief. You want another hole? We can swing to the other side..."

"Only if you cut it from the ladder. I don't want anyone on that roof again. The third-floor just flashed and the attic's probably ripping."

"Roger."

The 100-foot ladder swung to the other side with two guys hanging on at the tip. The lieutenant grabbed the chainsaw off the guy behind him and checked his footing. Poised, he fired the blade and then dove it straight into the roof. This time, he barely had one side of the four-foot box cut before fire ripped through the seam.

"Command to Ladder 2. Abort. Repeat, abort."

"But Chief—"

"I said that's it. Get out of there. The whole roof might collapse."

By now every truck in the city was on-scene. Guys were dragging hoses everywhere. Engine 1 had three lines in use as its nervous chauffeur stood at the pump panel and monitored water pressure. News trucks started arriving and setting up cameras. The electric and gas companies terminated the power and gas at the street.

As the initial crews ran out of air, they emerged from the building soaked and steaming from the heat even though it was summer. The last-due companies took their place inside.

"Stokes!" The Battalion Chief waved at the lieutenant of Engine 1. "How we looking in there?"

Lt. Cody Stokes was a twenty-year veteran on Engine 1. With more first-due fires than any other truck in the city, Engine 1 crews were considered reliable and seasoned. Stokes was no exception. His older brother was already a captain, so tradition ran deep. Nicknamed the "Dude" because that's how he started most sentences, Lt. Stokes was a hardworking, chain-smoking, nice guy that was also one of the best cooks on the whole job. Selfless and humble, he also did not suffer the fool if someone was not pulling their weight.

Lt. Stokes approached with air hissing from his dislodged mask. "I don't know, Chief. Every wall we punched had fire in it."

"We gonna lose it?"

"It'll be damn close."

The chief watched the smoke growing blacker. "I ain't losing somebody for a house with no people in it." He toggled his mic. "Command to Fire Alarm. Have both ladder trucks get set up for master-streams."

Lt. Stokes was covered in debris and coughed out black phlegm. "You pulling everyone out, Chief?"

"Not yet, Dude, but close."

"Chief!" The lieutenant of Ladder 1 pointed at the fingers of flame now poking through the ridge. "Think we might be losing it!"

"Command to Fire Alarm. Clear all companies from the second-floor. Repeat. Clear the second-floor."

Since the ladders were unable to pump their own water, they were hooked up to engines connected to hydrants. The "master-stream" was a nozzle at the tip of the ladder capable of raining down 1500 gallons a minute. This defensive attack was called "surround and drown" and put no one at risk. Still, no self-respecting firefighter wanted to lose a house. Master-streams equaled failure and turned them into "foundation-savers," a term that was also said with some disdain.

The roof started collapsing.

"Command to Fire Alarm, clear the building. Have the ladder trucks start the master-streams."

"*Roger.*"

The Evacuation tones hit the airwaves as guys fled the building. Then the ladders began dumping a combined 3000 gallons a minute into the house, taking down the roof and third-floor within minutes.

Across the street, the overwhelmed recruits watched in awe. Hoses were spaghettied everywhere. Civilians snapped pictures and pointed. News crews panned cameras that captured their shiny reporters through the smoke. And because of the June heat, residents took pity and brought water to the exhausted firemen.

With the master-streams now doing all the work, guys had a chance to dress down. They dropped their air-packs and tools, shed their bunker coats and helmets, and then knelt like dogs panting in the street.

LIEUTENANT ROBERT McCARRICK

Later that day, Lt. McCarrick headed home. After his divorce, he could only afford a two-bedroom ranch house on the city's east side. Even though his neighbors were behind fences, they were only twenty-feet in each direction, so everyone knew everyone else's business. And while having a seasoned and decorated firefighter next door might serve as a source of security, the curfew-less blowouts he often hosted sullied that visage. But like everything else, with no middle gears, he existed at 1000 MPH or not at all. And while this allowed him to excel and attack his career, it also destroyed almost everything else around it, including his marriage. Some people joined the fire department looking for a job, but the zealots, once immersed, were never the same. Already at work for days on end, they ground through birthdays, holidays, and then, like junkies still jonesing for a fix, took even more shifts. They joined the Honor Guard, marched in parades, attended funerals, ran for the union executive board, the state association, or became delegates for the annual International Association of Firefighters conference in Washington, D.C. They arranged fundraisers, attended conferences on emerging threats to the fire service, organized charity events, and visited schools to lecture on fire safety. Even worse, when they were not at work, they sat by their scanners at home and listened as their co-workers continued the fight without them. This was also why the divorce rate was astronomical.

When Lt. McCarrick pulled into his driveway after work, he could already hear Dixie barking. Named after the indefatigable nurse on the classic TV show "Emergency," Dixie was a 6-year-old pug that loved two things—bacon and Lt. McCarrick's more than ample lap. He threw open the front door and yelled, "Dixie!"

Dixie was bouncing up and down and completely inconsolable until Lt. McCarrick scooped her up with one hand and hugged her. One of his elderly neighbors had a key and took Dixie whenever he was working. Dixie licked his face as he laughed and said, "I hope you behaved yourself at Mrs. Abernathy's today."

Dixie barked repeatedly in answer, so he set her back down. He immediately turned on the "blower," which was slang for scanner, so he could listen to the dispatchers and call them up and scream at them if they screwed up in any way. Dixie, knowing his routine, led him into the kitchen where he mixed the first of a half dozen vodka tonics. In the bedroom, she watched him change out of his uniform and then she followed him to the back porch for a smoke. When she was finished with her business, she went back inside and, because she knew what was coming next, hopped up and settled onto the sofa next to where Lt. McCarrick always sat. He already had the remote control in his hand and, when he looked down at Dixie, his giant mustache stretched into a grin. He scratched behind her ears and said, "What do you think, kid? Hill Street Blues or Emergency?"

Dixie barked and Lt. McCarrick said, "I totally agree. Emergency it is."

Like a museum, his living-room walls contained rows of framed pictures and newspaper clippings of fires his father and grandfather had fought going back as far as 1915. That was when the first McCarrick swore an oath that 90 years later his grandson still honored. Grandsons and great-grandson, to be exact, because Lt. McCarrick's younger brother, Michael, was a lieutenant on Engine 4, and his son Robert was already on another job. Their whole family, including Lt. McCarrick's father, a former Chief of Department, had battled these furious conflagrations together. Frozen in time, in some of these pictures it seemed half the city was ablaze. Ancient men in black coats and helmets swung axes and aimed hose-lines while seemingly trying to hold back hell itself. As always, the church and mill fires stole the show. Because both were built with massive timbers and an ocean of hardwood over vast empty spaces, once ignited these structures turned into the perfect bellows. Interspersed among the infernos were pictures of Lt. McCarrick's career. There, twenty-five years younger and sixty-pounds lighter, his right hand was raised as the mayor issued him the oath. Another picture showed him as a dispatcher in Fire Alarm in the mid-1980's, when the whole city seemed to be alive with fire. There were other photos of him in his turnout gear and covered in soot at dozens of fires over the ensuing decades. But at the very end of the last row, in the corner, were three small photos of his ex-wife and two children. In consequence, this was also why he was divorced. As his ex-wife had packed up her and the kids' belongings, she had finally arrived at the end of their marriage and told him she might as well have spent the last fourteen years alone.

"Your mistress is the fire department," she had said, and with that, decided it was time to move on with her life. He did not blame her nor try to stop her because he knew she was right. At every chance, at all opportunities, he always chose the job over his family. Which also explained why he was sitting alone on his couch chain-smoking and drinking until eventually he would pass out and wake up to do it all over again. And, incredibly, he still would not have changed a thing.

FIRE ACADEMY FINAL WEEK
August 11, 2008

The "Burn House" was a state-owned building in the middle of nowhere. It was a three-story block of concrete and steel. Designed to be stuffed full of mattresses and wood pallets, it was where fire departments trained to extinguish infernos.

The remaining twenty-four men of Class 61 were broken into four squads of six. Each squad had three Sachem City firefighters in charge of their safety. As always, everything about the recruits was being strictly evaluated. All summer, the veterans had been hearing about who was lazy, who was not, who was stupid, who was crazy, and who worked hardest. Now, as graduation approached, 122 firefighters were awaiting the new twenty-four like a pride of lions gathering for a feast. Since the city's unification in 1874, a graduation picture of every fire department class was hung in the basement of Station 2.

Lt. McCarrick stood in front of the class chain-smoking in his burnt-up turnout gear. He said, "The reputation of this academy is pretty shitty. I think we got three firemen, ten maybes, and eleven fucking guys who should be working at Wendy's. It's embarrassing, which makes me look bad, and I don't enjoy that. Since this is our first live-fire exercise, the rules are simple. We've packed this place with everything flammable.

We're gonna crank this fucker up to 900 degrees at least, so if you pull off your mask you will die. Does everyone understand that? There will be two evolutions. In one, all of you will be put in the basement on your knees as we ratchet the heat up. Then, later on, we will split into four squads and rotate through the upper floors practicing search and rescue. All of it will be live fire. Guys, this is no shit—if you pull off that mask inside, not only will you fail the whole academy, you'll suffer extreme inhalation burns and die. Our last line of duty death was in 1993, and that's exactly what happened on Oak Street. Bobby ran out of air, pulled off his mask—game over. Get comfortable with being uncomfortable. The gear is cumbersome, the air-packs are heavy, the heat is intense, and wearing the mask under duress makes people do very stupid things. If, *for any reason*, you feel the need to exit this building, you will raise your hand to signal for an instructor. You will not exit alone. Does everyone understand that?"

Twenty-four nods.

"Remember, panic equals air-supply. We talked about skip-breathing to extend your tank. Take a breath, do not exhale, take another breath, exhale. This is where you practice that. Are we clear?"

Twenty-four nods.

"All right. Two guys from this department have gotten on Boston. Obviously, their training budget allows them to do some pretty cool shit, so these sleeper agents keep us abreast of any new techniques. They're here today. Oscar Ramirez and Anthony Babineaux."

Two men in black gear stepped forward. Like their Sachem City peers, all of it was singed and scarred. Even their helmets were scorched. Babineaux was tall and had a facial tick. Ramirez was stocky and wore a full handle-bar mustache.

Anthony Babineaux introduced himself and said, "Be warned, because I'm a total super-hooter. A member of my family has been on the SCFD since before 1921, so leaving this department after eight years and breaking that chain was hard. But fire is fire, guys. What you're being taught here, I can tell you firsthand, you will use every day of your career. Worcester, New Bedford, Fall River, Sachem City, Providence, Central Falls—these are old cities with a ton of mills and triple and quadruple-decker houses built with balloon-frame construction. I'm sure your instructors have already taught you this. American home construction has three distinct periods—timber, balloon, and platform. Timber-framing existed until the 1850's, ballon-framing came next, and then platform-framing. From the 1940's to the present day, builders have used platform-framing, which essentially means each floor is an independent entity. This newer construction serves as a direct firestop because the floor system rests on top of the wall. But back in the 1800's, ballon-framing was considered revolutionary because suddenly they had milled wood, which was cheap and fast. You didn't need skilled craftsmen anymore because any simpleton could stand up a thirty-foot 2x4. But ballon-framing meant they hung the floors *off* the walls, so now all those empty bays in the walls fill with fire. This means if the fire starts in the basement or first-floor, it will race straight up the outside walls to the roof instead of having to burn through each floor system. As we know, once the roof gets involved, game over. The master-streams will then dump 30,000 gallons of water and wreck every square inch of that place and everything in it. After the two evolutions Lt. McCarrick spoke about, we're gonna light up the second and third-floor and practice some entry techniques. Speed and effort guys. The reason Sachem City and Central Falls have the reputations they do is because if they don't get a quick knock-down, neighboring houses or a whole block might go up. No one is more aggressive or effective with less. In Boston and New York they got four or five men per truck and a ton of guys to lessen the pain. Here, three-man companies and thirty guys on-shift eat it all. Be proud of that because I certainly was. Next door in Central Falls, those guys have even less. They ride with two-man companies. Two engines and one ladder, and if the rescue is on a run, that means six guys are fighting a house fire alone until you guys get there.

"Boston had volunteer firemen as far back as 1680. Cincinnati became the first paid full time career department in 1853, New York 1865, and

Sachem City was 1874. The entire fire prevention business started here because of the mills. Everything was made of wood. Before organized departments, fires here or in Boston used to take down half the city. In 1872, the Great Boston fire burnt up 776 buildings. Imagine that? Sachem City lost 50% of downtown in 1842. You have to remember, fire was used for everything. Cooking, heating, and with candles used for light, it was a constant threat. Every resident was required by law to have full buckets of water in their house ready to go. Fire Wardens inspected homes and fireplaces and issued fines. Neighborhoods formed their own brigades and companies. Pride led to competition and scoring free booze from nearby tavern owners grateful their businesses hadn't burnt down. I told you all I was a super-hooter. My family has lived here for a hundred and fifty years. The city ain't like it was in the 1920's when the tycoons owned the mills. Back then everyone had a job. Now? Half the city is unemployable and the other half is waiting to die. It's a hard town now. All the barons and debutantes are gone. It's still a great place, but only because the people have always been resilient. As for today, myself and Firefighter Ramirez have also been asked to show you some search and rescue scenarios we stole off the guys in Chicago. Lieutenant? The floor's yours."

"All right..." Lt. McCarrick pointed. "Everybody into the basement. Let me tell you this. If any of you haven't checked your Scott pack and mask, and it doesn't work when we fire it up in there, I'm gonna personally turn your life into one long endless hemorrhage. Move out!"

The recruits marched into the basement.

"On your knees!"

In the shadowy dark, they obeyed. The walls were blackened and burnt from a thousand fires. Even the air tasted like ash. Twelve Sachem City firefighters surrounded them with a pair of charged hose-lines just in case.

Using a blow torch, Lt. McCarrick lit up a cigarette before scorching the hay bales, mattresses and pallets that were stacked to the ceiling. "Masks on! Control your breathing!"

A minute later it sounded like three-dozen Darth Vaders breathing in a vacuum.

"Turn on your helmet lights!" Lt. McCarrick stood before them with no mask despite the growing smoke. "As we know, a fire doubles in size every thirty seconds. You hear my voice?" He snapped away his cigarette and slipped on his mask. Through its tiny amplifier, his voice now sounded like a tin-filled echo. "At the ceiling, the heat can reach 1600 degrees or worse. But along the floor the temperature reduces, sometimes to a barely survivable 150 to 250 degrees."

Smoke rose, hit the ceiling, spread across it, and then banked down because it had nowhere else to go. The fire kept growing behind Lt. McCarrick like a spreading tree. Pallets snapped. Mattresses spontaneously ignited. The heat inched up.

"This ain't Hollywood, guys. No one walks into a fire—they crawl. No one enters without a mask or with their jacket wide open because they'd be unconscious or dead in seconds. If you're on the hose and get lost or turned around, find the hose and follow it back out. If you find the hose but are confused about which direction to go, find a coupling. The female side always leads to the exit. If you're a ladder guy searching for life with no water and no hose to follow out, keep your right hand on a wall and search for windows. Search for doors. Activate your PASS device and hit the mayday button on your radio. Make noise and yell to help others find you."

The fire raged and started licking the ceiling.

Lt. McCarrick consulted a hand-held Thermal Imaging Camera and yelled, "400 degrees!"

The firemen knelt with the probies. The fire entranced them all as it licked up the front wall and started rolling across the ceiling.

"Ain't it beautiful?" Lt. McCarrick screamed above the growing roar. "Who else has a fucking hard on? 600 degrees! Now, can someone tell me why basement fires are so deadly?"

One of the probies yelled, "There's only one way in or out!"

Another shouted, "They're packed with tons of shit!"

Yet another, "No windows!"

"Fucking A!" Incredibly, Lt. McCarrick was still standing and silhouetted by the fire behind him. "Remember, basements are a concrete kiln. The stairway becomes a chimney. Because of this, entering or leaving must be done very quickly because of the intense heat and smoke. Even if you find a window you're still fucked because you're not gonna fit through it. A lot of guys die in basements. I've almost been killed three times, so I fucking hate basement fires. If you get lost, remember, stairways are only in two places—the middle or on an outside wall. Most are in the middle, so check there first. Stay low, don't panic, and search for the stairs or the hose-line. 700 degrees!" The heat became a fist pushing all of them down. "800 degrees! Everybody, on your feet!"

Standing was immediately brutal. Guys started squirming and panting, but nothing got by Lt. McCarrick. "Control your breathing! You start sucking air and you will drain your tank. Keep skip-breathing."

Visibility was now zero except for the ominous orange glow growing larger and larger behind Lt. McCarrick. "Say hello to six minutes. It's now 900 degrees. In the real world, six minutes is what you'll be walking into. And that's if you're hauling balls. Want to imagine what eight minutes feels like?" He waited, sensing their pain. "Everyone, flat on your bellies!"

The temperature difference was drastic. Incredibly, there was also a six-inch window of visibility.

"1000!"

Their bodies fought the heat by dumping sweat into their gear and masks. This physical duress forced an increase in blood pressure and pulse rate.

Lt. McCarrick shouted, "Embrace it! All twelve weeks comes down to this! Ain't this what you signed up for?"

No one wanted to reveal the true toll the heat was taking, but several turned back to look for the door just in case. For those in the first row, the fire was now practically in their faces.

"That's it!" Lt. McCarrick finally yelled. "Everybody out!"

They emerged one by one and ripped off their masks. Their faces were red and purple from the strain.

"Change out those bottles! Hurry up! We're going right back in to put this fucker out!" As guys scrambled for fresh tanks, Lt. McCarrick yelled, "Remember what we talked about. When making entry, you *never* pop a door without a charged hose-line. Start blasting at the ceiling first because you want to cool it down before it flashes. You also don't want the fire crawling over or behind you. Stay low. Back up the nozzle man and pull the line. Only one guy gets to be the hero, so if someone ever offers you the tip you better take it. Otherwise, you hump hose like everyone else. Charged attack lines can weigh 250-pounds, so use your body as leverage. One of you is about to be lucky as hell. Who wants the nozzle?"

Twenty-four hands went up.

"I know some of you are lying, which makes me want to puke. Where's the Cheese?"

Like T-Bag, Lenny Rialto had caught his nickname on the first night of the fire academy. At roll call, Lt. McCarrick had called out, "Rialto, Leonard!" After he saw who it was, Lt. McCarrick laughed and said, "Bet you never met a cheeseburger you didn't love."

Though somewhat overweight, Cheeseburger's work ethic was never in doubt, and more importantly, his classmates and instructors knew it. Since he treated every training evolution with a dire seriousness, he was the first to volunteer for everything and never complained. His quiet disposition was left-over from all the bullies who had tortured him growing up, but this also made him resilient. At twenty-six, he had been trying for years to make the Sachem City Fire Department.

"I'm fat too," Lt. McCarrick joked. "But I'm old. Get over here, ya sloppy fuck."

Cheeseburger hustled to the door, fumbled with his air-pack, but quickly geared up. He knelt and grabbed the nozzle. Behind the door the fire sounded like a freight train in a box. "T-Bag! Row! Back him up! Fonzie, grab a Halligan and pop that door!"

The Halligan, created in 1948 by FDNY Deputy Chief Hugh Halligan, was a forcible entry tool that had a fork on one end, and a pick and adze on the other. It was three-feet long, continuous poured high carbon steel, and weighed fifteen pounds. Made for prying, twisting, punching, or striking, seventy-years later every fire truck in the country still carried one or more of these formidable tools.

Fonzie drove the adze-end of the Halligan into the doorjamb by the knob and looked at T-Bag to show he was ready. With the back of a flathead axe, T-Bag smashed the Halligan deeper into the jamb.

Lt. McCarrick shouted, "Stay low, advance the line, and do not let that fire get behind you! Ready? Pop it, Fonzie!"

Fonzie was a 6'4" 260-pound monster. Of Polish and Portuguese descent, he had each country's coat-of-arms tattooed down either forearm. He leveraged his weight, and when the door popped, a sudden hell roared out of the concrete kiln. The velocity of flames was scary enough, but the blast of heat was scorching. Cheeseburger levered open the nozzle's bale as the fire reached straight for them. On their knees, they inched toward the inferno.

"Ain't this better than porn?" Lt. McCarrick screamed. "Get in there, get in there!"

Rowdell and T-Bag pulled the line before disappearing behind Cheeseburger into the smoke. Three firefighters stood at the door with a charged line in case things got out of hand. Three others followed the recruits with flashlights and thermal imaging cameras.

The smoke changed from black to gray as the water vaporized into steam. Cheeseburger was in total awe. He hit the ceiling and then did a figure eight towards the seat of the fire. He kept repeating these two things until Lt. McCarrick suddenly appeared on his shoulder, shouting through his mask, "What temperature is flashover?"

Cheeseburger, who was taking a beating despite kneeling, could not believe Lt. McCarrick was still standing. He also thought this was a hell of a time for a pop quiz. The hose was at 150 PSI, and even with Rowdell and T-Bag backing him up, Cheeseburger battled against the writhing backpressure. "Anywhere from 1100 to 1500 degrees, sir!"

"And what happens at flashover, Cheese?"

"Everything not already on fire spontaneously combusts!"

"Then how come you ain't on fire right now?"

"Because our gear is rated for 1600 degrees!"

"Yeah, for about fifteen fucking seconds it is. You see a 1,000, you either put it out or start running. Don't forget that. Goddamnit, watch out on the right! It's getting away from you!"

When the fire leapt to escape the water it found new life. Cheeseburger saw it and smashed it into the corner.

"Back! Get back to the ceiling!"

Ignored for even a second, the inferno resurged.

"Fuck yeah, Cheese, figure-eight that shit!"

Rowdell smiled while advancing the line. He was sweating and getting hammered by the steam and smoke, but it was a glorious feeling. T-Bag wore an even goofier expression. He hauled line while sneaking peeks back at the fire like a lunatic on a new high. Above them, Lt. McCarrick was completely unglued.

"My God, Cheese, are you the luckiest motherfucker in the *whole world*?"

Cheeseburger clenched his teeth, fatiguing on the bucking nozzle. "Yes, sir!"

"Advance that line, ladies, this shit ain't gonna put itself out!"

The three of them heaved ahead.

"Closer! Stop being cunts! There won't be time for this on the line!"

Cheeseburger's eyes went wide when Lt. McCarrick just stepped forward and disappeared into the smoke and flame. Cheeseburger did not want to hit him with the hose, but neither could he abandon the attack. "Who just walks into a fire?"

T-Bag, pulling line behind him, yelled through his mask, "Old fat guys with bad mustaches and nothing to live for!"

Cheeseburger grinned until Rowdell shouted, "Watch the ceiling!"

"Roger that."

Minutes later, they cornered the last of the fire by the concrete stairway and killed it on the landing. As the smoke cleared, they saw Lt. McCarrick standing four steps up. His thick gloves did a slow clap through the smoke. "Unchecked aggression is some sexy shit. In the real world, what would happen next?"

Cheeseburger said, "We would open up the walls with axes, right? Pull down the ceilings to see if it was extending for the roof?"

"My God, Cheese, you are one fat sloppy god of fire. The three of you, get some water. Strong work."

Outside, twenty-one jealous faces awaited.

ROWDELL

2006

Eighteen months before the academy began, Jimmy Rowdell was sitting in a bar, totally soaked. The rain had blasted his jobsite all day long. Having worked construction through brutal Rocky Mountain winters, Rowdell was well acquainted with meteorological discomfort. He was a squat man with scarred hands and a weather-beaten face. His shaved head still had sawdust on it. He had thick eyebrows and a permanent five o'clock shadow. He was not handsome but had a piercing gaze that never wavered. Intellectually oblivious, his hands created his life and were the only thing he truly believed in. His mother, who spent a lifetime worrying about her oldest son, always lamented the fact that he was still single at 36-years-old.

Someone abruptly said, "Holy smokes, is that Jimmy Rowdell?"

Rowdell turned and stared until the recognition dawned. "Matty B. Of all people..."

Mathew Brazo was moving in for a hug until Rowdell held up a hand. "I'm soaked, dude, and covered in sawdust."

"So what?" Brazo embraced him. He was a tall man with a white smile and blue eyes many women considered attractive. "Man, I ain't seen you since high school."

"I hear ya."

After a round of shots, Brazo asked, "When did you get back?"

"Couple of years ago."

"What brought you home?"

"I..." The full truth was too painful for an impromptu bar reunion, so he told him half the story. "I was working construction out west, a little logging too. I'm a carpenter now, rough framer. I wasn't planning on staying here either, just came home to help with my uncle and see family. Next thing you know I lost the last of my money on the Super Bowl and had to get a job."

"You don't sound too happy to be back."

"I am. But I miss the mountains. It's like this place with the ocean. Missed that too."

"Little Rhodey. Loved it so much I never had to leave."

They toasted as Rowdell asked, "Whatever happened with you and T?"

"Tara? I fucking married her, bro, got two kids and a dog."

"No shit?" Rowdell smiled. "It was inevitable. Probably the only chick on the planet that could keep you in line."

"What about you?"

"Came close once, but she flaked out. Took the dog and headed for Vegas."

"Now who would take a man's dog?"

"Right? It was just as well. I ended up moving to Montana and then Utah. Chasing the money, you know?"

"The vagabond life of a carpenter."

"How's work? You still with the fire department?"

"Just made lieutenant. Actually, my new crew should be here any minute. Great guys."

"Congrats." Rowdell ordered more shots. "Lieutenant Brazo. Good for you, man, the pride of Warwick."

"I love it, dude, every second of it. Greatest job ever."

"Wish I could say the same, because I'm getting ready to put my head across a sawhorse and drop a skillsaw through my neck."

"That bad?"

"I'm just burnt out. Like everything else, people ruin everything. Chasing money every Friday even kills the joy of working outside, which I love."

"You ever think about signing up?"

"No offense, dude, but I'm not the military type."

"I'm talking about the fire department, dumbass."

"The *what?*"

"You already use all of the tools. You know building construction, and if you're working on roofs all day, you clearly have no fear of heights. With your work ethic, you'd make a great fucking ladder guy."

"Huh."

"I'm serious, bro."

"What about my age? I'm thirty-six."

"So what? Look at the shape you're in. Half these 20-year-olds are absolute bags of shit."

Rowdell coughed up his beer and laughed. "It's not an insane thought."

"Not at all."

"But what do you do all day? If I don't stay busy I'll go crazy."

"Are you kidding? It's the second most densely populated state in the country and has 300-year-old buildings. There's a million people squeezed into a place that could fit into Texas 220 times. Imagine if 220 million people lived in Texas? Believe me, there's shit to do."

"I don't know, man."

"Just come for a ride-along. I'm on the Hazards, Station 8. Come by for a shift and we'll play fireman."

Rowdell showed up two nights later expecting to see a bunch of fat guys in recliners doing nothing. Instead, he barely had time to say hello to the six guys split between Engine 8 and the Special Hazards before they were immediately toned out for a car versus pole with possible entrapment. Wide-eyed, Rowdell put on the headphones in the back-step so he could listen as Brazo explained from the front passenger seat, "As a hazards truck, we carry everything except water."

"What does hazards mean?"

"Basically, we're a giant toolbox. You've heard the term Jaws of Life? That's actually two different hydraulic tools—the cutters and spreaders—that tear apart vehicles. We're talking 10,000 PSI. We handle gas leaks, trench rescues, industrial accidents, ropes and rappel, confined space rescues, and at house fires we pretty much do whatever hairball shit the chief needs done."

As they flew down Route 1, panicked drivers cleared a path for the screaming trucks. When Lt. Brazo turned, he took one look at the absolute awe on his friend's face and knew he was already hooked. He had also grown up with Rowdell, so he felt compelled to add, "Remember, after we get on-scene, you can't do anything. If you get hurt out here, I'm fucked."

Minutes later, Rowdell watched them cut the roof off a Porsche as the driver, whose legs were shattered, actually complained that they were wrecking his car. The "cutter" was three-feet long and resembled a giant lobster claw. It easily sliced through all four roof posts like scissors cutting through straws.

They were headed back to the station when a call came in for an elevator emergency at a hotel near T.F. Green airport. Electricians and a repair crew had spent an hour trying to fix the stuck car but finally called 911 when those trapped inside ran out of patience. Usually the doors could be opened with a universal drop-key, but this one would not budge. Not even with a Halligan being smashed by the back of a flat-head axe. After Lt. Brazo forced the door on the floor above, they were able to reach down and pop open the roof hatch. The people looking up at them clapped and cheered. One of the firemen dropped down into the car and helped everyone climb out one by one.

Through all of this they missed dinner and ordered pizza hours later.

Rowdell, who knew nothing about close-quarter camaraderie, watched six guys mercilessly busting each other's balls and fell in love.

The next day he called up the Community College of Rhode Island and began the arduous road to becoming a certified EMT-Basic, the first step for any potential wannabe.

CONNOLLY'S REVENGE

September 2008

Connolly's Revenge was a pub founded by two retired Sachem City firefighters in 1949. It was named after James Connolly, one of the seven leaders of the 1916 Easter Uprising in Ireland. A staunch opponent of religious bigotry, he was Commandant-General of the Dublin forces. Even grievously wounded, Connolly remained defiant. Too injured to stand for his own execution, he made the British firing squad carry him into a courtyard on a stretcher, tie him to a chair, and kill him sitting down. His son, Eamon, fled Ireland and landed in the mills of Sachem City. Five years later, in 1921, Eamon Connolly was on the Sachem City Fire Department.

For forty-years, Connolly's was packed with off-duty firefighters every night. They went from the station to the bar and from there became a citywide party patrol. Legendary characters forged bonds closer than family. Guys drank together, gambled together, chased girls together, and then went to each other's weddings, christenings, and, eventually, funerals. Outsiders were never trusted but tolerated, and the Fireman's Ball, a yearly tradition, was a black-tie event those not working always attended. So it went for decades until everything blew apart. At some point, the epic camaraderie devolved into something malevolent, incestuous, and by 1989, things finally turned nasty and violent. Suddenly, buried ghosts and past injustices tore everyone apart. Even the union Executive Board was dissolved after a golf outing turned into a head cracking beat-down between all seven members. Distrust and innuendo danced alongside awful rumors that guys unleashed on one another to sabotage promotions. And as everything imploded, Connolly's Revenge got left behind. Now, instead of forty guys on a Friday night, only a handful were in attendance. The walls of the bar, covered in patches from over 1,000 fire departments, were yellowed from time. The mirrors, stained by a million cigarettes, had not been cleaned in years. The bathrooms stunk, the carpet was ripped, and the televisions that worked were 30-years-old. Yet things began to change. As the old-school retired, and a new generation got sworn in, the viscous lava of hate had time to cool. It did not disappear, because the guys in their fifties and sixties who had lived through the war as newbies themselves still told the younger guys all the awful stories. What they failed to understand was that some of the newbies they were now trying to taint were not even born in 1989, the year the bloodletting began, and had no idea who this guy fucked over or that guy ratted out and did not really care. These kids ate vegetables, did not smoke cigarettes or eat bacon, and sat for hours contemplating their phones and gadgets. Some of the older guys openly despised them, calling them "corporate raiders" or just plain cunts. Outside of guys like Rowdell and T-Bag, blue-collar workers that came from the trades, the majority of the "kids" had actually gone to college, a development the older smoke-eaters could not fathom. Why anyone would spend the money and time for college and end up a firefighter was preposterous. The older guys had even worked side jobs to send their kids to college just so they would not have to watch people die a thousand horrific ways. Throughout the 1970's, the job was so disregarded, so far from its glory days of the 1860's through the 1960's, the city could not give it away. Guys worked seventy-two-hour weeks—three dayshifts, three nightshifts, three days off—and got paid $130 dollars before taxes. That roughly translated to $1.60 an hour.

When the recession hit in 1971, and the mills were finally pushed to the economic brink, the city's financial footprint started to crack. With the jobs gone, the only remaining mills closed one by one. In 1972, the final death blow arrived when Callahan Tool and Dye, built by a city founder in 1826, closed for good. The day the last worker punched out, the doors closed on a glorious 150-year ride. The old people knew it, knew what the young took for granted—mainly history and jobs. Children of the Great Depression never forgot those lessons, and this new generation was about to be fed a fifty-year ride to irrelevancy.

But the fresh blood from ensuing academies finally breathed life into moribund institutions. The Honor Guard, formed in 1848, was now back and fully staffed. A few guys even took lessons to learn the bagpipes, no easy feat. Charity drives for muscular dystrophy and other illnesses were taken up again. And the black-tie "Fireman's Ball," placed in a self-induced coma for fifteen years, made a triumphant return. Slowly, piece by piece, the job stitched itself back together until Wall Street, no stranger to creating economic destruction, pulled the trigger again in 2008.

The revival of these old traditions included Connolly's Revenge. On this Friday night, fifteen firefighters were shooting pool or pumping quarters into 1980's vintage video games. A few locals and die-hard alcoholics rounded out the crowd.

Mikey Doneen, a private on Engine 4, bought a round for himself, Jimmy Rowdell, T-Bag, Yoda, and Fonzie. Doneen had gotten sworn in before he could legally drink and now, at 29-years-old, was considered a rising star. He had a shaved head, pretty-boy face, and no-nonsense reputation with his fists. He also despised cliques, which meant he did not care about all the dirty looks the older guys now gave him for drinking with the newbies. The fire department was a hierarchal institution that put no stock in its young. "Probies" were probationary guys that had not earned a thing. As wannabes in the academy, they were explicitly told to stay away from Connolly's until they got sworn in. Anyone with less than five years was also told to avoid the twenty and thirty-year guys at all costs. As they had for 170 years, newbies did not dare read the newspaper, drink coffee in the kitchen, or offer an opinion on anything because no one cared. Instead, they checked and cleaned every inch of the truck, studied their map books, drilled each other on EMS protocols, and had to complete a long list of station chores.

Harry Paulson swayed as he approached them. A twenty-five-year veteran, Paulson was nicknamed "Chunks" because he was an alcoholic who could not hold his liquor. He was rail thin, had Brylcreamed hair, and always squinted like his glasses no longer worked.

"Da fuck, Mikey?" Paulson's Sachem City accent was a hard cross between South Boston and Staten Island. "Da fuck you doing drinking with these clowns?"

"What're you talking about, Chunks?"

Paulson drunkenly squinted. "There ain't supposed to be no fucking wannabes in—"

"They're not wannabes. They got sworn in weeks ago, ya drunk fuck."

"They did?" Paulson was so inebriated he could barely stand up. "They *did?*"

"Yeah, man."

"Who're you?" Paulson asked, poking one of them in the chest.

"Glenn St. Pierre." Yoda stuck out a hand which Paulson did not shake. "But these sick bastards call me Yoda."

"Why? Are you gay?"

"Yoda wasn't *gay*—"

"What'd you do before you got here?"

"I was a teacher. I taught sophomore English—"

"Now that's gay. Da fuck you doin' here then?"

"Well, turns out kids today have no supervision, manners, discipline—"

"Da fuck..."

"I just couldn't take it anymore."

"You're boring me. Besides, I hate the French." Paulson turned to

Fonzie who, at 6'4", towered above him. "Jesus Christ, look at the size of this one. What's your story, Godzilla?"

For a 22-year-old, Fonzie was mature. Because of this, during the academy, he found himself more aligned with Rowdell and T-Bag, both in their mid-thirties. Fonzie's father was a concrete contractor who never missed work for any reason. Likewise, he also raised his two sons and daughter under a regime of hard work and discipline. Uncannily, father and son had the same face, but Fonzie's was stuck on top of a massive body with hands the size of dictionaries. Given his stature, being the bully would have been easy had it been in his nature.

"I'm Brian Fonseco," Fonzie stuck out his hand. "It's nice to meet you, Harry. Heard a lot about you."

His forthright demeanor seemed to stun Paulson. "Da fuck, kid, you're the size of a bank vault. I want you backing me up!" When he laughed and spilled warm scotch on the dirty bar, the silence was otherwise deafening. "I've been on this job twenty-five years. Last few academies have totally sucked. You guys better not suck."

"Harry..." Mikey Doneen sipped his beer. "Just say congratulations and then fuck off."

Jimmy Rowdell smiled at that. A lifetime of logging and carpentry had left him in top shape. He did not have any physical anomalies or done anything stupid, so everyone just called him "Row."

"You think that's funny?" Paulson asked him. "Fucking newbies shouldn't think—"

"Didn't Mikey just tell you to fuck off?" T-Bag maliciously grinned. In many ways, once Lt. McCarrick had labeled him T-Bag and destroyed his reputation, he was able to cut loose from any reverence or respect and just speak his mind. He had worked in kitchens and as a roofer and, despite hating authority or being told what to do, took to these new brothers with a zeal that even shocked himself. Like Rowdell, he was deeply appreciative of the job, because where they came from there were no such things as sick days, vacation days, pensions, or health insurance, and in exchange they got to spend decades racing to some of the worst things people would ever see.

"I've heard about you," Paulson said, almost spitting. "Da fuck kind of name is *T-Bag*? You some kind of rapist?"

"Wow. A guy named Chunks talking shit. You really are a sloppy mess, even more than your daughter, who I've heard—"

"Okay, okay." Mikey Doneen stepped in. "Night's young, boys."

Paulson swayed and frowned. "Get some time on the job, kid, before you talk like that. And what's with those stupid sideburns? Show some respect."

"Blow me."

"Come on, man." Rowdell took out a pack of smokes and pushed T-Bag towards the door. "Let's pull a tube."

Paulson drunkenly turned back to Mikey Doneen. "He's got some mouth."

"Well, I think we've all had a few too many." Fonzie clapped him on the back. "Can I buy you another drink, Harry?"

"Seven straight up. At least you got some respect."

"When did you get on, Harry?"

"1983. Greatest year of my life. Got married the same year..."

Paulson's life history spilled out as Fonzie politely paid attention.

Just as Mikey Doneen left to play Space Invaders, the front door smashed open. Two guys hit the floor in a whirl of fists as people yelled and fled.

"Sal, no!" Doneen ran over. "Sal! Frank! Stop! Come on, guys!"

But Psycho Sal and Cadillac Frank were beating each other across the floor. Salvatore Giametti was a fifteen-year rescue lieutenant who should have bid to an engine or ladder truck years ago. Since the rescue ran non-stop, guys like Sal, for better or worse, got addicted to the action. The best rescue guys were highly skilled and compassionate. But the ones who had seen too much or could not compartmentalize anymore eventually went down in flames. For the first decade, Sal had a blast, out all day and up all night. He loved the hardcore trauma but was also adept at putting up with the nonsense, like people calling 911 for toothaches at three in the morning even though there were no dentists at the hospital. The rescues were two-man companies, and most of Sal's partners loved him. But that was before 2005, where over a two-month stretch he had a 10-year-old girl who hung herself, a single mom stabbed 49 times, two dead babies, and a carful of teenagers turned into hamburger after smashing into a bridge abutment at 70 MPH. He started putting away the ghosts with alcohol and soon after his first marriage blew apart. By 2006, his nickname went from "Straight-line Sal," because of his attention to detail, to "Psycho."

The way the shifts coincided, Lt. Frank Gracey was Sal's relief at five o'clock. Only two shifts covered every twenty-four-hour cycle—the 7 A.M. to 5 P.M. dayshift, and the 5 P.M. to 7 A.M. nightshift—two days, two nights, and four days off. But Gracey was always late. On an engine or ladder truck that was no big deal. If someone caught a late run, unless it was a fire, they were usually back in the station ten minutes later. But on the rescue, late relief was a death offense. The rescue was already so busy, oftentimes guys got stuck doing continuous runs straight through rush hour, or until they managed to stop the truck just long enough to leap off with their gear and swap crews like a NASCAR pit team. Since all Sachem City firefighters were EMT-Cardiacs and could be sent to the rescue if needed, the rescue guys carried their helmets, tools, and bunker gear just like everyone else.

Gracey was called Cadillac Frank because he drove a blacked out 1972 Cadillac Coup Deville. Like a 1950's hipster, he had slicked back hair, rolled up sleeves, and a cigarette constantly tucked behind his ear. His partners learned to love Chuck Berry, Buddy Holly, and Sinatra because that's all he played in the truck. He also fronted a tribute band called the "The Schemers," so he was constantly late for work.

After crashing to the floor again, Cadillac Frank ended up on top. He repeatedly close-fisted Psycho Sal until Mikey Doneen and Fonzie pulled him off. Rowdell and T-Bag ran in just in time to grab Sal before he attacked again.

"Fuck you, you hipster douche!" Psycho Sal's broken nose spewed blood. "You fuck!"

Mikey Doneen asked Rowdell, "What happened out there?"

"Nothing. Frankie just pulled in and Sal started punching him through the window. He's totally wasted."

"Fuck you too, newbie!" Psycho Sal writhed and lunged.

"Sally..." Doneen grabbed him and steered him towards the door. "Come on, man, let's go. Let me drive you home."

"This ain't over, motherfucker!" Psycho Sal pointed at Cadillac Frank. "See you at four forty-five tomorrow, bitch!"

Cadillac Frank smirked, retrieving his cigarette pack off the floor. "More like five-thirty, Sally boy!"

"Da fuck is going on?" Harry Paulson stumbled over. "You cunts can't even handle your booze. Corporate cunts!"

Doneen pushed Sal through the door, heading for his pickup. "Where am I taking you, Sal?"

"Home, bro." Sal climbed in. He reclined the seat to try and stop the bleeding. He was so drunk he could barely stay awake.

"Sal..." Doneen did not know how else to say it. "Didn't she kick you out?"

"She'll let me sleep it off. She's good like that. She'll bounce me in the morning. But thanks, Mikey, you're a good bro."

"Just don't bleed on my truck, okay?"

Psycho Sal passed out before Mikey Doneen even started the engine.

T-BAG

In 2006, two years before the fire academy, Tamir Taymaskanov's second-floor apartment quickly filled with smoke. He lived in a five-story Boston tenement in Kenmore Square. During the night, a massive fire had started in the kitchen of an Indian restaurant on the first-floor. The single working smoke detector barely woke him up, so he only had time to grab a pair of jeans and his two roommates before the smoke killed them all.

"Fire! Fire!" T-Bag coughed and pounded on doors down the long hallway. "Fire! Get out!"

This was just another moment added to a so far thirty-six-year debacle. Because of his father, a legendary character that ran his own roofing company, T-Bag learned to persevere from day one. He had no choice, especially not after his dad fell thirty-feet at work and landed on a picnic table. Left a quadriplegic in need of constant medical attention, his father never complained or lost his sense of humor.

T-Bag was 13-years-old when the accident happened, and he had to quit school so his mom could support them. For her, a nursing home was out of the question, so T-Bag got tutored at home so he could help care for his dad. As the nurses came and went, he became proficient with all the devices keeping his father alive, chief among them his ventilator, feeding tube, and colostomy bag. He also bathed him, changed him, and spent the next three years by his side. Since roofers were colorful people, they filled the day listening to blues records while his dad told inappropriate stories and made him laugh. Before the accident, six-day work weeks meant dad missed many of his son's events. With a crew of four on the books, every Friday became a stress-fest just to make payroll. He had always regretted being gone so much, which was no longer a problem since they were now finally made inseparable.

One of T-Bag's earliest memories was watching his dad climb up a seemingly endless extension ladder with an eighty-pound pack of shingles across his shoulder. It seemed like such a crazy place to work, up there on a pitched tabletop with the sky as the ceiling to his office. His father, unlike most of his own employees, loved the actual work. Roofing was a hard, repetitive series of physical tests with sudden death or horrible injury always a hazard. It also did not pay very well, so the allegiance his out-sized personality created was unusually cult-like. So much so that when word of his accident spread, heartbroken friends and rivals alike gathered to make his home more accessible. It was only a duplex in Watertown, Massachusetts, but they built long ramps up to the front and back doors, built a wrap-around porch for his wheelchair, took down walls to add space for the machines and mechanized bed, and installed a state-of-the-art audio system to play his beloved blues.

Nevertheless, death came at the end of three long years. When it was over, there were too many lessons crammed into too short a life for T-Bag to process. The shy kid found no solace in the platitudes spoken by others at these times. Instead, he decided to maximize every second and made a million wrong decisions through a haze of teenage indestructibility. After moving down the road to Boston, he got a job as a bar-back in a punk rock club and became a functioning alcoholic. But his father's work ethic, genetically ingrained, saved him from catastrophe. No matter how late or long the party went, T-Bag never missed work.

As a bar-back or cook, his income meant nothing because he always lived below his means.

His poor mother, when she heard he took a job roofing, almost had a stroke. She knew those with something to prove rarely listened to common sense, especially when anger and vengeance took hold. Since a roof had killed his old man, a roof is where he would now make his stand. T-Bag drank too much, drugged too much, worked too much, and took incredible risks up there on that tabletop in the sky. He never wore a safety harness or cared about living, so he became one of the fastest shingling machines in the city. Co-workers, lest they get bumped off into the abyss, learned to give him a wide berth.

After mom wore him down, he took classes and got his GED. To keep the ghosts at bay, he also got addicted to open water swimming and 100-mile century rides on his bike.

This was his life until his apartment burned down. That night, he stood shirtless in Kenmore Square and watched waves of Boston firefighters sweeping in and out of his building. The ladder trucks pulled people out of windows. But the hum was what he remembered, that whirring combination of idling diesel engines, chainsaws, roaring flames, people crying and screaming, and handlines dousing flames. It was the sound of a building dying as T-Bag watched everything he owned get blowtorched into the night.

Now homeless, he couch-surfed with friends but could not shake it. His mother, who had moved to Sachem City to care for her aging father, begged him to move in. "If you really want to be a fireman," she had said, "you're gonna have to go to school. Besides, you might be safer in a burning house than spending the next thirty years on a roof. I can't handle that again." Grandpa's house was a triple-decker with lots of room, so T-Bag would even have his own floor.

In the state of Rhode Island, one had to be a nationally registered EMT-Basic before any department would accept an application. T-Bag was enrolled in the six-month program at Community College of Rhode Island the day after he unpacked his things.

THE GREAT RECESSION BEGINS
October 16, 2008

After the academy ended in July, some of the newbies were barely sworn in before the entire economy crashed. Over the course of September and October, Fannie Mae and Freddie Mac were taken over by the federal government, Bank of America bought a failing Merrill Lynch for $50 billion, Lehman Brothers filed for bankruptcy, AIG accepted an $85 billion federal bailout, Wall Street lost 778 points in its worst one-day drop ever, Ford, Chrysler, and General Motors applied for bailout funds, and the collapse of the Washington Mutual Bank became the greatest bank failure in U.S. history.

The layoff talk started immediately. Since the entire fire department was run by seniority, the rule of "last-in/first-out" certainly applied.

So far, six of the twenty-four probies had been sworn in and immediately assigned to Fire Alarm, the two-man dispatch room at Station 2. In Rhode Island, all 911 calls first went to a central dispatch center in Providence before being re-routed to individual cities and towns. From there, police and fire departments ran their own dispatch. In Sachem City, two men were in Fire Alarm twenty-four hours a day. Since no one wanted this job, the probies got shoved in there until a spot opened on the line. But openings were only created when someone retired or died, so guys could be in Fire Alarm for weeks, months, or many years. The record was five-and-a-half years completed by Thaddeus Wright, a guy widely considered to be the Nelson Mandela of the Sachem City Fire Department.

No one became a firefighter to sit in a box answering phones, so everyone hated Fire Alarm. For the younger probies it was no big deal. But for guys like Rowdell, T-Bag, and Grimace, ex-Teamster Donny Da Rocha, the place was filled with everything they had spent their entire adult lives avoiding—mainly computers, phones, and dealing with the public.

Built in 1886, the City Hall complex was a massive stone monolith that housed, from left to right, the fire department headquarters, the mayoral and municipal government offices, and the police department headquarters. Engine 2, Ladder 1, and the Battalion Chief were downtown, so at least the probies could sniff the gear when guys returned from a fire.

Fire Alarm was also where the indoctrination began. Guys on Engine 2 and Ladder 1 would hang out in there and re-tell the same stories that had been told to them about epic fires and EMS runs gone horribly wrong. This oral history was also how the job got passed down. Because the department was filled with Type-A personalities, no one was better than anyone else, and anyone who tried to be was immediately busted back in line. There was no faster way to lose all credibility than by talking about yourself or any supposed exploits. That was the job of the guys beside you, in the back of the rescue or on the fire-ground, the eyewitnesses to what you did. And if it was truly hilarious, heroic, or horrific, everyone found out about it anyway. Rumors could spread across the entire job in a matter of minutes, so the 19th century axiom of "telegraph, telephone, tell-a-fireman," was not far from the truth. Guys spent so many hours together over so many years, nothing was sacred or secret.

Fire Alarm was also where the probies learned the rhythms of the job. The second it started raining, the oil and rubber on the road got raised up to the surface and started causing accidents, especially on the highway. The government checks arrived on the first of the month, so people bought groceries and other necessities like alcohol, drugs, and guns. And since no one wanted to go to the emergency room on the weekend, Medical Monday was always busy with those trying to dodge work. Most days, from 3 A.M. to 7 A.M. the elderly called 911 for ailments encountered during the night, 7 A.M. to noon was busy with the morning commute, 12-3 P.M. a little slower, and then it got busy again after kids finished school and people left work. It died down by 9 P.M. and then became sporadic. Of course, major incidents or fires were sprinkled across this daily schematic. Both rescues were usually up all night, as were a handful of engine companies in the busier working-class sections. The ladders rolled on anything big, or if the district engine was tied up on a different call.

To train for dispatch, Lt. McCarrick held class around the kitchen table at Station 2. In between screaming at the probies and calling them morons, he instilled the art of dispensing information.

"Don't make anything up or embellish." He tapped his temple. "Use your heads. People are gonna call up screaming and yelling. Remain calm. Your job is to get the address, phone number, and then ask why they're calling. Both guys stay on the phone. One talks while the other enters the run into the computer. The 911 Center in Providence stays on the line as well. They can run an instant GPS to tag someone's location within fifteen feet. Sometimes the people calling are from out-of-town and have no clue where they are. Or they're so freaked out by what's happened they might forget the name of a street they've walked down a million times. Remember, if you hang up but then have a question, call 911 back. They have access to databanks that search out phone numbers and business information. Like us, they record everything, but they also have the original call, and there might be more info there. Most important—be fucking professional. No laughing. Guarantee some guy's gonna call up after jamming something up his ass. They always do. Flashlights, soup cans, spoons, you name it, they jam it up their ass.

But you can't laugh. And don't get shitty with people because nowadays everything ends up on the news. On that note, always remember we are broadcasting on public airways. The fire department actually has its own radio frequency mandated and overwatched by the FCC. All their rules apply, so if any of you fuckheads get caught saying something stupid, look out. Remember, this is the shit that gets played in court. Don't be that guy."

In front of each probie was a six-inch binder that contained all the department protocols. The budget was so bad, the probies actually had to pay for their own copies. This massive binder also contained a list of every street in the city. The accompanying eighty-page map-book had been created a hundred years before cellphones and GPS made everything easy.

Lt. McCarrick said, "Turn to page twenty-one. This is the precise way you dispatch runs. Medical runs require an engine company and a rescue unless it's something simple, like the flu, then it's just a rescue. Anything involving smoke, fire, fire alarms, gas leaks, etc., gets three engines, a ladder, and the Battalion Chief right off the jump. Don't worry. I know you're all too stupid to figure this out. Once you type in the address and reason for the run, the computer will assign the appropriate companies. Now, let's practice. A call comes in for chest pain at 170 Hancock Street. Is it an apartment? A triple-decker? A duplex? A single-family home? A business? It's never just 170 Hancock Street. Also, every dispatch gets repeated three times. Instead of blurting out too much too fast, add information each time. Hit the Alert Tone and say 'Attention Rescue 2 and Engine 3, Still Alarm. 170 Hancock Street.' Pause five seconds, let the guys get up and moving, and then say, 'That's Rescue 2 and Engine 3, respond to 170 Hancock Street third-floor, apartment two, for chest pain.' Pause five seconds. 'That's Rescue 2 and Engine 3, respond to 170 Hancock Street on the third-floor, apartment two, for chest pain. Patient has a cardiac history. Time out, 1315.' Everything gets a time stamp. You're a parrot. You repeat anything they say and time stamp it. You idiots following this? I see a lot of stupid looks right now."

They were too intimidated to ask questions.

Lt. McCarrick was disgusted. "We'll see who knows everything momentarily, believe me. Now if you catch a fire, one guy runs it on Channel 2. The other guy stays on Channel 1 dispatching any incoming 911 calls. These moments are where you'll be tested. Running a fire is serious shit, guys. Write down where everyone is. Most important is who's pumping the fire and who's responsible for the hydrant. So dazzle me, class, how would I know that information right off the bat?"

Cheeseburger raised his hand. "The order of dispatch, sir."

"I fucking love you, Cheese, break it down for me."

"Well, if it's Engines 4, 3, 6, Engine 4 is first-due, so the driver is pumping. Second-due Engine 3 hooks the hydrant up to Engine 4, and Engine 6 grabs a line off Engine 4 and backs them up."

"That's some sexy shit, Cheese. But the most important thing is to listen. For everything, especially anything involving *water*. When the lieutenant of Engine 4 says charge the line, *make sure his pump man hears it*. When someone calls for water, they better fucking get it. They've probably popped the door and are now staring at a wall of flames. Same thing for the hydrant team. When they ask Engine 4's pump man if he's ready for the hydrant, *make sure he hears it*. Without water, guys, we're just a bunch of fucktards watching someone's shit burn up."

Super-Wop, the former Marine Corp bomb tech, raised his hand.

Lt. McCarrick pointed. "Yes, paisan?"

"Say we have a question before we dispatch a run. Who do we talk to?"

"The Battalion Chief. But don't fuck around. If you can't find him in fifteen seconds, like if you call his office or cell and no one answers, dispatch someone. Anyone. Remember guys, 90% of this job is just getting companies on the scene in a timely manner, because if shit goes sideways, the first thing the lawyers look for are what time the call came in, when it got dispatched, who went, and what time they got there. It's also why we send engine companies on just about all rescue runs. Besides the fact that people now routinely weigh 500 pounds, the lawyers look at the medical protocols and target if enough personnel were sent to ensure patient care. Okay. Let's check out the room where some of you unlucky bastards might be staying for a long long time."

They left the kitchen and walked five feet to a door marked fire alarm personnel only. Inside was a pair of identical workstations. Each had two phones, three computer screens, and plenty of anxiety.

"Even if nothing's going on," Lt. McCarrick said, "remember, the worst day of your career is only one phone call away. These two guys right here caught a mill fire last December and had to keep track of twenty-three out-of-town companies for a day and a half."

Rowdell suddenly looked sick. Even T-Bag, no stranger to pain, glanced around the room with dread. As if on cue, the 911 phone rang with a loud annoying bell.

"Sachem City Fire Department, Firefighter Moran, can I have your address please?... Phone number?... What's going on?... Is he still there, ma'am?... Does he have any weapons?... Okay, sit tight. We're on the way."

They both hung up at the same time. The other dispatcher already had the run typed into the computer. He hit the Alert Tone and said, *"Attention Rescue 1, Engine 1, Still Alarm. 135 Merrit Avenue..."*

Rowdell whispered to Yoda, "I know I'm supposed to know this, but what does 'Still Alarm' mean?"

"That it came in by phone. A 'Box Alarm' is an actual triggered fire alarm received on that panel." He pointed at a large cabinet-sized alarm box stationed between the dispatchers. It had rows of blinking lights and occasionally beeped and chirped. "That's the Vision 21 he's been talking about. Every master box in the city's connected to it."

The dispatcher continued, *"That's Rescue 1, Engine 1, respond to 135 Merrit Avenue on the third-floor for a female victim of assault. Stage for police. No weapons reported. Time out 0840."*

A minute later the radio crackled, "Engine 1 responding, 135 Merrit."

"Engine 1 responding at 0841."

"Rescue 1 responding."

"Rescue 1 responding at 0841."

Lt. McCarrick turned to the recruits. "There's been a Sachem City firefighter manning this room since the first phone lines were connected to the city in 1885. So show some fucking pride, guys, because few departments are cross-trained like ours. You know who doesn't combine dispatch, EMS, and fire like we do? New York, Boston, Washington D.C., Chicago... no one does more with less. Our members are trained to do every single job in this whole department."

Currently, nobody was taking pride in anything because the 911 phone rang again. Then again a second later. At the same time Engine 1 called on-scene, suddenly three runs were happening simultaneously. The dispatchers juggled phones and microphones and even coordinated with the police next door. Eight minutes later it was over. Ambulances took the sick to the hospital, and engine companies called back in service. One of the dispatchers turned to the newbies. "Any questions?"

Everyone laughed.

"Wow." Rowdell shook his head. "That was crazy."

"That was nothing," the other said. "One day we had a fire going on Channel 2, so I had to handle ten 911 calls alone in two minutes. We had rescues coming in from freaking Warwick. I was scared to death, because missing or forgetting a run either gets someone killed, you fired, or both. When it comes in waves, stay calm and make sure *you write down every run*. It's easy to get distracted. Also, pick a job. It's a lot safer if one guy does the computer while the other handles the microphone. Unless all hell breaks loose. Then you're just fucked."

Lt. McCarrick was staring at the disgust on T-Bag's face and pounced. "Just remember, before you start bitching like a twat, New York City gets 30,000 911 calls a day. You still got something to say?"

"Yeah. How long do we have to stay locked inside this nightmare? I didn't sign up to be a freaking secretary."

"You're right. Why don't we just skip all this bullshit and make you a lieutenant?"

"Now that's a great—"

"Shut the fuck up, T-Bag. But you do have a sexy voice. I can't wait to hear it on the blower. I got a scanner at home, too, so even off-duty I can call you up and tell you what a stupid fuck you are."

"Thanks, L-T."

"Now the rest of you, get ready. We're all gonna take turns putting out live runs, so don't fuck this up."

Guys scrambled to get their protocol books.

Inside Fire Alarm, the 911 phone was ringing again.

YODA

Glenn St. Pierre wondered if he was a horrible person. Could someone stare out at a classroom full of 15-year-olds and honestly detest them? He had been waging this inner battle for the last four years. That's all it had taken to smash his planned thirty-year teaching career into dust. After high school, he spent six years and $150,000 to earn his Master's, but in the end even that did not matter. Neither did the pension, benefits, or having summers off. He hated it so much, at 28-years-old, he walked out the door and never looked back.

The students... they were either coddled, spoiled, neglected, or abused. Economic means made no difference with zero parenting at home. Half the kids barely did their homework and the other half treated school like a giant daycare. They did not respect him, themselves, or their own futures. And since Yoda was a polite, slender guy, some kids were quick to take advantage. With four older brothers, Yoda tended to disappear in a crowd. His whole family was French-Canadian, and with the exact same black hair and eyes, the five sons were eerie different-sized replications of one another.

Three generations of Yoda's family had worked as teachers in Sachem City, including two of his brothers. Even after the entire region fell into decline, and the long-suffering schools took a turn for the worse, Yoda still thought he could make a difference. Walking out on his whole future was not easy, but neither was admitting he was not cut out to be a teacher. Granted, the schools had been decimated by a shrinking tax base caused by the flight of the middle-class, but as he and his co-workers went out of their own pocket for basic supplies for other people's kids, he wondered how this situation had been allowed to get so bad. The schools themselves were over a 100-years-old and in serious disrepair, but no one seemed to care. Least of all the parents, who either worked multiple jobs just to make ends meet or did not have a job at all. When Yoda listened to retired teachers describe a level of parental involvement that no longer existed, he wondered where the pride had gone? This new generation seemed to exist only to drain resources, the same resources every city department now waged war over. And as he witnessed the waste of funds and weaponization of the school board to pursue personal agendas, Yoda felt his liberal leanings burn away. It was one thing to offer someone assistance, but without accountability and time frames, he found no one voluntarily gave up anything that was free.

Then one day he was standing in line at the bank when a guy near the front collapsed. Those next to him gasped and stepped away. A woman screamed. But as a former lifeguard at a city pool, Yoda had received training in basic skills. He rolled the guy over but could not find a pulse. "Someone call 911!"

He started compressions and felt ribs crack. Instead of helping, he saw people recording the event on their phones. He lost track of time until the fire department arrived. They brusquely thanked him and pushed him out of the way. One firefighter dropped a tube down the throat to secure the airway, while another sunk an IV into the elbow. A third stuck pads to his chest for the AED, a fourth did CPR, and the fifth drew up epinephrine before pushing it through the IV line. They shocked him twice but never restored a rhythm, and Yoda was completely enthralled.

Later, he learned that Rhode Island fire departments handled all

EMS responsibilities. While he was no huge fan of fire, he spoke to a buddy on the Providence Fire Department and discovered one could make a career staying on rescue if so desired. Long intrigued by the human body and all its systems, Yoda thought he had finally found his niche.

Like everyone else, it took him six months to earn his EMT-Basic. Class was two nights a week and Saturdays were spent training with various fire departments. After he finished at the top of his class, he got a job on a private ambulance company to make himself more attractive for hiring departments. Since private ambulance did not handle any 911 calls, it was basically patient transport from nursing homes to medical appointments or dialysis. Fortunate to have always been healthy, Yoda had no idea how sick America really was. People weighed 400 pounds for no reason, had high blood pressure, high cholesterol, heart conditions, and rampant diabetes. The typical dialysis patient needed a treatment every three days. The ambulance ride each way was $500 and the treatment itself $2500, which meant taxpayers were on the hook for $35,000 a month for one dialysis patient alone, and there were thousands. The sheer plague of bad health pierced every stratum of society. 12-year-old kids weighed 350 pounds because parents fed them garbage and let them sit inside all day on their devices. People smoke and drank too much, ate too much, and sat at work until their hearts exploded. As far as job security, Yoda knew the failing health of his fellow citizens would not be improving anytime soon.

His wife, Cindy, was a nurse that never stopped helping others. Neither did her father, a longtime Providence firefighter. Even after blowing out a knee and hurting his back, he always said he loved the job so much he would have done it for free.

Yoda took written tests with five departments before Sachem City sent him his acceptance letter. Out of 421 applicants for twenty-five spots, Yoda had scored number two on the written exam. So he started working out and getting ready for the biggest challenge he had so far faced.

THE INAUGURAL SHIFT
October 2008

A week later the probies were officially put on-shift and paired off in Fire Alarm. Fortunately, Rowdell and T-Bag got computer savvy young guys as partners. Job-wide, the daily ball-busting was never-ending. Case in point, when T-Bag showed up in Fire Alarm that first day, he found Grimace had left a set of brass testicles hanging off the microphone directly over a steaming cup of tea.

Jimmy Rowdell got Fonzie as a partner, and despite the sixteen-year age difference, as always, they were on the same page from day one. They did their jobs and showed respect, asked questions, and cleaned everything they could. Since they wanted to learn, someone off the engine or ladder would sit in Fire Alarm so one of them could go through the trucks on the apparatus floor. There they were taught in finer detail the real differences between ladder and engine work. Both trucks did EMS runs, but since there were only two ladders covering the entire city, it was tactically important to have them free in case a fire came in. Consequently, the ladders only rolled on medical runs if the district engine was otherwise occupied.

The engine crews did a lot of work for little reward. They dragged hoses across snowy streets and up tight, twisting stairwells built in the

1800's. There were no such things as building codes or safety back then, so the stairs were steep and serpentine to save room inside the massive triple and quadruple-deckers built to house thousands of workers. The stairwells themselves were death traps stacked with whatever people could not fit inside their apartments. On EMS runs, when they carried people down in stair-chairs, it was dangerous enough. But during a fire, blinded by smoke banking down off the ceiling, guys tripped and stumbled on everything. Ankles sprained when they rolled on charged lines, and knees buckled when stairs were missed inside these blacked-out voids.

Again, they reviewed the ladder's primary responsibility, which was search and rescue in dangerous places with no water. They were taught how to maintain contact with the wall, counting lefts or rights in case they had to stop and reverse direction in order to find their way out. Staying on the wall, they were also taught how to reach out with hooks and axes to probe the center of the room for unconscious victims in blackout situations. If the searches came up empty, they went to the roof with chainsaws and axes, cutting holes to vent the fire. Because of these highly visible operations, it was usually the ladder guys who ended up on the news.

Most of the probies quickly adapted. There were a few horrendous screw-ups, like confusing Lynch Avenue with Lynch Street, or dispatching the wrong trucks on multi-company responses, but no one died and no one got fired. The probies also found an age-old cliché quickly proven true—shit did indeed roll downhill. No matter what went wrong, Fire Alarm got blamed for everything. In addition to the 911 phone, they also manned the department mainline and had to transfer all incoming calls to the appropriate extensions in the main office upstairs.

Luckily, T-Bag got partnered with Yoda, the former teacher, whose experience handling emotionally volatile teenagers came in handy when T-Bag lost his mind. Since he provided such an endless stream of quotable profanities, Yoda bought a notepad to write all of them down. His personal favorite was "Everything comes in this room to die," which proved uncannily accurate. The 911 phone rang with people screaming about shootings, stabbings, car wrecks, heart attacks, strokes, or old people waking up dead. Citizens died, but so did the careers of dispatchers fired when things went awry. Other personal favorites were "I'm not a fireman, I'm just a cunt with a microphone," or "Stop trying to think—you're making me dumber." Even worse, he was also inordinately intrigued by the inner workings of serial killers and mass murderers, so Yoda found himself watching way too many documentaries about some of the worst people in the history of the world. Still, it was a small price to pay compared to the hours of free entertainment T-Bag provided. Since the fire and police dispatchers requested various resources from each other all day long, T-Bag was barely professional. The strait-laced police dispatchers, of course, loved the abuse. It broke up the monotony of all the horrific things people did to each other before someone finally dialed 911 to make it stop.

Nonetheless, Yoda had to intervene at times when T-Bag forgot who he was speaking with.

"Yo, police, it's fire. Can you send a cruiser to 23 Langley? We got a real fuck-fuck going on."

"Excuse me? Did you just say fuck-fuck?"

"Yeah, some moon-bat is chasing his mom around with a broom."

"What's a *moon-bat*?"

Yoda clipped in on the call. "Police, it's fire. Emotionally disturbed man is making threats toward his mom with a broom."

"Well, we'll get right over there to protect you heroes," the dispatcher busted back.

Yoda, for his part, just tried navigating them through every shift hoping they did not get fired.

THE GOVERNOR
November 2008

."These are not the phone calls I enjoy receiving." Governor Marissa Adelina Carvalho stood up from her desk and headed to the window. The governor's office was located in the statehouse in downtown Providence. This massive stone building contained the House of Representatives, the State Senate, and the offices of state officials and cabinet members. Opened in 1901, it was made from 400,000 cubic feet of marble and 15,000,000 bricks supporting the fourth largest marble dome in the world. Atop that stood "The Independent Man," an eleven-foot tall, 500-pound, gold-leaf statue that resembled a soldier of Sparta standing guard over them all.

"Madam Governor." One of her aides stepped forward. "What if their numbers are off, even by a fraction, and this projected collapse—"

It was a surprising misstep, because the governor's inner circle was supposed to be just like her—all female, brilliant, and completely ruthless. The political press on Smith Hill had even taken to calling this posse the Dirty Dozen because, like the governor, they had perfected asymmetrical and phalanx warfare to the point where Governor Carvalho had yet to lose any election she had ever entered. The oldest daughter of a legendary Rhode Island governor who played political hardball with old school pain and suffering, Marissa Carvalho had studied at the feet of a grandmaster. She began by amassing information and rumor on her opponents, and then dipping into this cache to cut their throats behind the scenes as needed. A skilled and merciless tactician, her Portuguese roots also helped her in a state with sizeable Azorean, Brazilian, and Portuguese populations. She was 44-years-old, in great shape, and a brunette who knew how to tastefully use her looks. So far scandal free, even her enemies considered her magnanimous and polite until the doors closed, and then all bets were off.

It said something about the innate level of fear, that even those who worked closely with her on a daily basis, could be cutoff midsentence after realizing they were now dead meat in an open field.

The aide was flushed and penitent. "Madam Governor—"

"Please." Carvalho did not even turn around. "I hardly have time to consider the utterings of someone so completely ignorant of situational awareness." When she did turn, her black eyes withered the aide until she just stepped back into the shadows. "Now can someone with a functioning IQ please tell me our path forward through this gathering disaster?"

A ballpoint pen clicked in the silence but no one answered. Governor Carvalho returned her gaze to this view of Providence she had fought so hard to attain, achieve. Across the vast concrete pavilion before her, she could almost see the bodies of every slain opponent in all the races she had ever won. She asked, "Where are we financially with this new information?"

The General Treasurer, Fiona Womack, had graduated from Vassar and Carnegie Mellon, but when it came to politics, she wisely stuck to the facts since the governor only cared for opinions when asked. "Madam Governor, as of this point the state is sound, but there are considerable potential liabilities lurking. Of significant concern are the various pension funds that were heavily invested in Wall Street. Obviously, this crash is still ongoing, so until we hit bottom, an accurate forecast is hard to predict. We can say we are in the process of trying to determine the exact numbers, percentages, and potential legal exposure."

"What about the cities and towns?" The governor's gaze latched onto her chief of staff. "Talk to me, Macy, where are we?"

Micaela DeSousa was a pure fashionista nicknamed "Macy" after the department store where she spent the majority of her income. Her outfits were a finely coordinated presentation to the world, but she was always careful not to upstage her boss. Having grown up together, Macy DeSousa was the only survivor of the governor's many purges. Like the best consigliere, Macy was the gatekeeper between her boss and the rest of the world, so she kept the governor's goals, promises, and strategic vision at the forefront of any advice she offered. DeSousa also had dozens of spies and agents burrowed into the various political factions seeking access to the governor, greased all the powerbrokers and fundraisers, and was on a first name basis with every political reporter and talk-radio host that mattered. She said, "Well, as of now we have four communities on our radar—Providence, Central Falls, Woonsocket, and Sachem City. Not only are they our poorest communities per capita, they are also the most dependent on state aid for everything from schools to roads to even garbage collection. For all intents and purposes, we, the state, are their safety net. So long as the state stays fiscally solid..."

"Great." In front of the window, Governor Carvalho's gaze now seemed to glow. "This is not how it's going to end for me. Not after everything I've done to stand right here, right now, only to face down a tsunami no one else saw coming either." She returned to her desk and stood behind it like a captain on a vessel headed into unknown waters, and looked at every single woman in the room. "Some of you may ask what is our goal? And I would answer survival. Survival at any cost. We must be ahead of our rivals, and on top of any federal aid or programs or grants that come forward because, and mark my words, I will cut the throats of every other governor in New England to ensure our survival."

She took the answering silence to mean they understood.

"All of you," the governor said, "in whatever department or entity you represent, make sure we are kept abreast of every development, rumor, and potential advantage, or it might be you answering for any missteps along the way. Are there any questions?"

No one said a thing.

"Fine." Governor Carvalho sat at her desk and opened some folders. Then she looked up as if surprised they were still there, until they were not, and only Governor Carvalho and Macy DeSousa remained.

"So," the governor asked, "do you think I got my point across?"

"Permission to speak freely?"

"Of course."

"You said survival enough times to ensure that they will be thinking about yours as much as their own."

"Perfect." Governor Carvalho smiled for the first time all day. "My father used to always say, make them crave the taste of blood and they will never say no again..."

DUTCH CARRIGAN

It was a windy day when the tones struck at 9:43 A.M. on April 13, 1988. Dutch Carrigan, as always, was on Engine 2. He was in his sixteenth year, the fifteenth on his beloved Big Deuce. It was a truck for the hard-chargers because it was the busiest in the city, the second busiest in the whole state behind only Providence Engine 3. This was also why its turnover rate was constant. Some people, especially new lieutenants and captains with no seniority, got forced there because there was nowhere else to bid, or wherever they were coming from was bad enough to volunteer for this beating. But for the true-believers, Engine 2 was nirvana. They constantly trained and kept abreast of industry developments, and looked down on some of the outlying engine companies that did not. They watched fireground videos from around the world and trained with zealots from other departments. Dutch Carrigan was a true-believer, but he only truly cared about two things—the fastest way to the fire, and beating everyone else up the stairs with the nozzle first-due.

Twenty years before the 2008 Great Recession, Dutch was a 38-year-old bachelor when he met his future wife on one of the worst days of her life. Born and raised in Sachem City, Dutch had a personality that was so genuine and sincere he should have run for office. More than anything else, he loved meeting new people, and by this point had turned wrenches with half the mechanics in the city. He also, somehow, seemed to know everyone. This was no exaggeration, and probies for generations would tell the same story of riding backstep as Dutch drove Engine 2 through downtown and waved as people on nearly every block called out his name. At his funeral in 2017, thousands of firefighters marched out of respect, but so many civilians showed up for his wake they had to move it to the high school gymnasium. But on that day back in 1988, he was just a private on Engine 2 screaming towards what was being dispatched as a building collapse. There was confusion from the scene, so no one really knew what was happening until Engine 2 peeled around the corner. A vast dirt lot was filled with a long pile of cinder blocks. But the people waving and screaming implied something much worse. Workers and civilians alike had already formed into conveyor belts to remove the blocks. When the firefighters jumped in as well, they were informed the construction plans had called for the rear wall of the new Super Max grocery store to be built first. It was a hundred feet long and twenty feet high. Apparently, the engineers overlooked the fact that what was being built was essentially a massive sail that, improperly braced, toppled on top of three workers who had sought shelter from the wind while on break. One was cut in half, another had his head squashed like a pumpkin, and the third was barely alive. It was quite a spectacle on John Adams Boulevard, so word of the disaster traveled fast. There were certain sounds and smells that firefighters came to instantly recognize, and the sound of a suddenly widowed woman was one of them. One of the dead workers' wives, Laurie Pembroke, had rushed over after her friend called and told her about the accident. When Dutch heard the piercing scream, he was exhausted and covered in sweat and dust. But the pain and sounds coming from her were awful enough to propel him back onto his feet. When Dutch got there, she was on her hands and knees in the dirt and completely inconsolable. He may have been physically small in stature, but his sheer strength allowed him to simply lift her onto her feet. Her arms sprang closed around his sweaty neck as she just cried and cried. It was incredibly hard to be around that level of sorrow, especially that of a perfect stranger, so when the wife's friend arrived, Dutch quietly handed her off without saying anything else.

Six months later he was wrenching a new transmission into a '76 Camaro when the front door bell to his shop chimed. "Shop" was a strong word, because Dutch's garage had basically two lifts, a wall of tools collected over a lifetime, and a pile of tossed away car parts. He was covered in grease when he heard someone call out hello, so he scooted out from beneath the Camaro on his creeper and shouted back, "Can I help you?"

"Yes." When Laurie Pembroke stepped into the garage, Dutch had no idea who she was. She said, "My friend recommended you..."

He backhanded sweat and grease from his face as she told him about her check engine light. Then she abruptly stopped when she saw the Sachem City Fire Department jacket on the chair. "Are you a fireman?"

"Yes, mam."

She realized he was waiting for an answer as to why she had asked the question. "I really appreciate what you guys do. Being surrounded by all that grief must be hard."

"Aww, not to me. I love it. Not the grief, the job." Dutch finally stood up and that was when her face froze.

"It's you."

"Who?"

"You don't remember." Laurie Pembroke was known as a no-nonsense woman. So much so, she had only begrudgingly gotten married and, at 46-years old, had no children. After her emergency hysterectomy, she did not figure any man would have her anyway, so she wielded a fierce disposition. She had long brown hair, brown eyes, and was, at 5'6", the same height as Dutch. It was impossible to know they were about to spend the rest of their lives together, so she said instead, "You were there the day my husband died."

"I'm sorry to hear that." Dutch wiped his grease-smeared hands on a grease-smeared rag.

"He was a construction worker," she said. "You helped pull him from the rubble at the Super Max."

"Oh, Jesus Christ. That's right. I remember you now."

"Do you?"

"Yes, mam."

"What do you remember?"

"Well, I remember it was a miracle we even pulled one of those guys out alive."

"And what else?"

"Well." Dutch pushed his glasses up his nose. "I remember you."

"You poor man."

"It's never fair. You know?"

She frowned, sadly, and then said, "I wish we had never met..."

Months later they rented snowmobiles and vacationed in New Hampshire. But even though they were already in love, something worse was happening. Dutch spent his days-off riding his motorcycle and consorting with other bikers and even 1%ers, like the Hells Angels. Dutch knew everyone, including the Angels' sworn rivals, the Mongols, but Dutch hung out with them all. He also partied into the dawn at strip clubs and bars. Legendary characters still roamed that scene, and Dutch was one of them. But when it began to threaten his relationship with Laurie, she finally threw down the gauntlet. He could choose between her or his lifestyle, but a choice would have to be made. It took him two days to realize he could not live without her, so he quit everything for good. He still rode his bike and hung out with the fellas, but he never drank another drop of alcohol. She may or may not have saved his life, but one thing was certain, there was only one woman on the planet strong enough to corral Dutch Carrigan, and Laurie never left his side again.

NUMBERS NEVER LIE

Three months after the newbies started in Fire Alarm, between 9 A.M. and 5 P.M. on January 26, 2009, 40,000 people got laid off nationwide. It was one of the worst single-day job losses since the Great Depression. Across the country, 2.6 million jobs disappeared in 2008. One year later, that number would top 8.6 million. Even worse, the housing market completely imploded. By year's end, foreclosures were up a record 81% as millions lost their homes. Another 3 million houses were at risk for 2009.

In places like Sachem City, where economic survival was already a daily bloodsport, these foreclosures created block after block of boarded up homes. No people meant no property taxes or car taxes, so the beleaguered tax base and city coffers were put under even more duress.

Unfortunately for Charles Houlinik, he had been elected mayor in November 2008 just as the economy collapsed. Sworn in January 4, he had been mayor less than three weeks before realizing his entire administration was already doomed. He was a portly man with a cherubic face and cheeks some elderly women voters loved to pinch. He looked like the actor Phillip Seymour Hoffman, and since his boy next door demeanor disarmed even his fiercest detractors, he had yet to lose an election. His grandfather, Royce Houlinik, had been a beloved mayor, and, on a local scale, spawned a Kennedy-esque political dynasty. Like his grandfather, Charles had that same charisma and rare talent of turning even the most pedestrian and random encounters into a celebration of the people themselves. This also made his constituents immediately consider him part of their family. A two-term city councilor, he ran for the city's highest office thinking he could shepherd his beloved hometown through this gathering catastrophe. Originally, he had big plans for the ailing schools and worn-out infrastructure, but that was now an impossible fantasy.

He chose Laurence Timms to be his Budget Director because he was an outsider of city politics. Almost immediately, Timms started warning of an approaching crisis. The pension system, long underfunded, was nearing critical mass. None of the numbers were adding up. And the deeper he dug into the city's finances, the worse it got. Previous mayors, only concerned with their own re-election every four years, had been playing a dangerous shell game with city money for decades. Instead of raising taxes to keep pace with inflation and the unfunded liabilities, they only paid the bills they had to. Then at election time they turned to the voters and claimed success because there had been no tax increase. Nevermind long-term planning and infrastructure. Those were dirty words with no sex appeal. City workers, who paid into their own pensions every week, started hearing rumors the city had not met its obligations in years. The pension was supposed to be a fifty-fifty split, so by now it was in total arrears. Even worse, old school Rhode Island cronyism had placed the pension funds into risky Wall Street investments. Then everything crashed.

Mayor Houlinik's office overlooked the mighty Massasoit River, the same river that had powered the Industrial Revolution and Sachem City's subsequent rise.

Laurence Timms, an accountant by trade, pointed at the reams of paper on the mayor's desk and said, "So I've finished the forensic exam."

"Your expression is telling me a story, Laurence."

"Mr. Mayor—"

"What's the number?"

"It's still a preliminary calculation, sir, so it might change if we find more—"

"What is it?"

"Well, sir..." Timms fidgeted. "From what we've been able to ascertain, the unfunded portion of the pension, the city's responsibility, is $98 million."

Mayor Houlinik blinked. "But that's double the original prediction."

"Yes, sir. You should know it could get worse. The city is also delinquent on $4 million owed to various vendors and contractors, most of it from the snow removal budget after last year's marathon winter."

"Our budget for the upcoming year is $220 million. Where are we on revenue?"

"Depending on how much further erosion there is to the tax base, combined with the growing foreclosures and failed businesses, we're looking at $215 million."

Mayor Houlinik rubbed his temples. Cities and towns were not allowed to run deficits. "Minus $4 million for the vendors, and what's the minimum pension payment?"

"$15 million."

"So $215 million minus $19 million leaves us at $196 million."

"It would've..." Timms squirmed. "But Billy Casper at State literally called ten minutes before I walked in here. They just concluded an emergency budget meeting at the Statehouse. They're running a huge deficit. He's now saying the governor's going to cut all state aid to cities and towns."

"They can't just do that! Out of nowhere?"

"Sir, if that happens, the good news is that every mayor in the state is going to raise holy hell. The bad news is that cut adds another $10 million..."

"My God... we're $34 million short?"

"Sir..."

Even the mayor's legendary upbeat disposition could not withstand those numbers. "So I need to cut almost a fifth of the budget, which is a complete impossibility..."

"I wish I had better news, sir, but it only gets worse. Wayne Douglas in Housing sent an email predicting no quick bounce-back either. In fact, another 150 homes are in jeopardy of foreclosure next year as well."

"I could summon the union presidents, but I think we both know what will happen if I ask for $34 million in cuts."

But that is what he did. The next day, in a conference room with resplendent woodwork and portraits of city founders long dead, he sat across from the presidents of the six major municipal unions—the Sachem City Fraternal Order of Police, Lodge 19, the Sachem City Teacher's Union, NEA Local 198, Sachem City Firefighters, IAFF Local 121, and the Department of Public Works, the Department of Sanitation and the Department of Transportation were AFSCME Locals 1024,1025,1026 respectively. Gone was the pre-contract posturing ubiquitous to every negotiation. Mayor Houlinik handed them all a simple two-page document of what the numbers were compared to what they needed to be and said, "It doesn't get any more serious than this. We are at a crisis point reached by the neglect of previous administrations. By law, the city can't fall below the projected budget without cuts. Period. So we either make the necessary cuts, find additional revenue or..."

The president of the Teacher's Union skeptically grinned. "You really expect us to believe that if we don't open up all the contracts and let you gut them that the city will go bankrupt? There hasn't been a municipal bankruptcy in the history of the state."

"Make no mistake about it." Mayor Houlinik pointed at his budget director for back-up. "We will be the first. Which means Chapter 9. It also means a state-appointed receiver will come in here and fire me. The City Council gets dissolved next and all of your contracts will be declared null and void."

"Bullshit!" Major Landis, the president of the police local, was a former sailor in the merchant marine. "The state will never let that happen."

"Major, I just spoke with the governor last night. In fact, she's actually *cutting* all aid to cities and towns. We're about to lose $10,000,000 more. Besides us, Providence, Woonsocket, and Central Falls are all on the brink as well. She told me in no uncertain terms that all of us can't be saved. And since our shortfall is statistically nearly double everyone else's, I'll let you do the math."

The whole room was in denial. Union presidents yelled at each other until Mayor Houlinik shouted them down. "July 1 is our fiscal death date. If I don't go to the governor before then with an airtight plan to keep the city solvent, we all face extinction. Your membership, after their contracts get ripped up, will no doubt need someone to blame once they find out you did nothing to help stop this."

No one wanted to hear it. Lieutenant William Ahearn, the newly elected president of the city firefighter's union, was a no-nonsense man shaped like a series of stacked cinderblocks. He had a beer belly, a shaved head, and a blonde old-school fireman's handlebar mustache dyed yellow from a million cigarettes. He was 42-years-old and had two small children and elderly parents as dependents, so he knew firsthand any talk of pay cuts or layoffs was not something many in the union could survive. A skilled tactician, he never wasted words, so the ones he said always made people pay attention. "This city can't just be handed over to the state. Let me get with the chief and see what kind of numbers we can come up with."

Mayor Houlinik paused, taken aback. But the other union heads were not so altruistic. Donny Teagues, president of the DPW workers, turned to Lt. Ahearn and said, "What makes you think you can trust this? Could be their own accountants playing with the numbers again."

"Donny's right." The teacher's union president pointed at the other side of the table. "We caught the last guy in a bed of lies. What makes you think this is any different?"

"Because." Lt. Ahearn swiveled his massive head. "Last time we weren't facing the sequel to the Great Depression."

They all seemed skeptical and terrified simultaneously.

Someone's phone rang and it was quickly silenced.

Lt. Ahearn said, "In good faith, I'm willing to do a sit-down with the Chief, but I gotta be honest. With a budget of $23 million, we're already underfunded, understaffed, and overwhelmed. We're carrying fourteen vacancies. I don't know what else we can safely cut."

"Manpower." Major Landis smiled at the mayor like he knew what the game was. "Ain't that right?"

The president of the teacher's union added, "Didn't you just run a whole campaign on that, Mr. Do-More-With-Less?"

Mayor Houlinik did not take the bait. "Political rhetoric aside, I'm asking for solutions. I'm asking for help. The city has never faced a crisis like this. No doubt I'll be crucified first, but after my head rolls, who do you think they're coming for next?"

Lt. Ahearn asked, "What kind of cuts are we talking about? Realistically?"

"It's right there on the paper. $34 million."

"I mean seriously. How can any city, much less one with no money, cut nearly a fifth of its operating budget?"

Budget Director Timms said, "It's actually 15.4%."

"Forget this nonsense." Donny Teagues, the president of the DPW union, stood up. Unfortunately, the pattern of his baldness created a Bozo the Clown rim of curly brown hair around only the lower portion of his head. He was a smart guy with a short fuse, and as a young man had failed different phases of the Fire Department boards three different times. "Do whatever you want, 'cause you will anyway. Besides, we all know where those cuts will be coming from, and it sure as shit ain't gonna be from the sacred cows."

"Sacred what?"

He sneered as he held up three fingers. "Police, fire, and the teachers."

"Oh, come on, Donny." Mayor Houlinik tried to stop him at the door. "Attacking each other won't solve anything."

But Teagues could not be dissuaded. "Police and fire are public safety, and the teacher's union is stronger than the mob. The fucking school system already gets sixty cents out of every dollar. Us and Sanitation, that's who's gonna pay in blood."

"Donny—"

The door closed behind him.

Mayor Houlinik looked at the police and fire presidents. "Public safety has to be our top priority, but don't confuse that message. The cuts will still have to come from every department. There's no other way."

"Sixteen percent of the entire budget..." Lt. Ahearn looked at his hands. "I don't even know how that's gonna be possible."

"It's either that or bankruptcy."

"Tell me how this country isn't screwed?" Major Landis gathered his notes. "Wall Street's destroying everything in sight while normal people lose their jobs, homes, and pensions."

Lt. Ahearn asked the mayor, "When are you going public with those numbers?"

"Well, considering the details of this meeting will leak, we're going to stay ahead of this story. Probably hold a press conference this afternoon."

"All hell's gonna break loose."

"I agree. It's going to be a dark day filled with news no one wants to hear." Mayor Houlinik looked at the remaining union presidents. "I wanted you all in the loop. Figured you might be more willing to have a say in your own futures before we have to make decisions no one walks away from."

The room emptied, leaving only the mayor, Laurence Timms, and an uncomfortable silence.

Mayor Houlinik said, "Never thought I'd be a one-term mayor."

"Honestly, sir..." Timms did not know how else to say it. "You'll be lucky to even last that long."

In the strained silence, they watched the rain-swollen Massasoit River twisting by the window.

CHEESEBURGER

After high school, Lenny Rialto spent six years trying to get on the fire department. It was the only job he ever wanted. His dad, who was not exactly the best motivator, told him he was too fat to pass the state-run Physical Performance and Assessment Test. Without this certificate, no department in the state would even accept an application. Even worse, it was only offered twice a year, so failing it meant basking in six months of regret. Six evolutions had to be completed in under eight minutes—ladder carry, equipment carry/stairclimb, forcible entry, hose advance, ceiling breach and pull, and victim rescue. Eight minutes did not sound like a long time, but wearing a fifty-pound weight vest to simulate the weight of the gear made everything worse. The first time Cheeseburger took the test he did not even make it to the hose advance. The second time he got all the way to the victim rescue but timed out before he could drag the 200-pound dummy the required 100 feet.

Failing twice was bad enough, but listening to his father's laughter a second time made him mad enough to drop fifty pounds and train even harder. He was still heavy but jogging five miles every other day soon shed inches off his waistline. After he got sick of the kids at the track making fun of him, he started running different loops around the city.

This did two things at once—got him in shape, and more intricately familiarized him with the city he one day hoped to work for. Even though this was where he was born and raised, he still did not know all the streets, especially on the west side.

He and his mother lived on Cambrose Street. It was a modest home in the rundown northern part of District 4. His mom, Janina Adomatis, was a Lithuanian with the same fair skin and blue eyes as her son. His father, who had moved out ten years before but still visited, was a master plumber. He was also a mean drunk and usually only stayed long enough to belittle and verbally abuse them. Since mother and son were both 230 pounds and six-feet tall, in one breath he would tell them he loved them, and in the next called them fat and stupid.

After Cheeseburger passed the PPA Test and got his EMT-Basic, he tested with every department that came open. In Rhode Island, individual departments had to post a notice of a hiring window, but every city used a different test. Some were math oriented. Some were focused on reading and comprehension. Good at neither, Cheeseburger studied even harder. Gradually, his scores improved. Then he took Sachem City's exam alongside 400 other hopefuls and finally found his sweet spot. This test was a blend of math and comprehension. There were also thirty questions based on a map they could only study for five minutes before the proctors removed it. For some reason, Cheeseburger had always been good with maps. This one was drawn like a generic city containing rail lines, factories, airports, schools, hospitals, etc. The questions tested one's ability to absorb and retain information on the fly and he crushed it. He did not have any family on the job, had no political connections or influence, so his score of 91 put him eighth overall. But the written test guaranteed nothing. There was still a Bureau of Identification background check, credit check, a vetting of all references and previous employment, and a formal interview with the City Solicitor, Chief of Department, and an outside Chief brought in for fairness. One month later, Cheeseburger opened a letter from the city, found out he was ranked 15th, and immediately hugged his mom.

The city gave the probies four weeks to get their job schedules adjusted and personal affairs in order. Cheeseburger was so excited he could barely sleep. He kept working out and studying everything he could. But his enthusiasm almost died on the first night of the academy. After Lt. McCarrick played games with the roll call, his nickname stuck. But unlike T-Bag, who looked like he wanted to beat Lt. McCarrick to death with his own shoe, Cheeseburger embraced it. He even put a patch of the McDonald's Hamburglar on his helmet the day they issued him his gear.

He got sworn in by Mayor Houlinik on a cold January day. Economically, no one yet knew how bad things would get, so Cheeseburger was just happy to have a job. Once on shift, if he had any downtime, he cleaned the trucks, the apparatus bay, the bathrooms, the kitchen, took out the trash, and made sure there was always fresh coffee. He studied his protocols and map-book and kept his mouth shut. He only spoke to the senior guys if he had a question about the job, their individual career, or any advice they had for a new guy. Otherwise, he wisely steered clear. He had heard about what happened when Super-Wop got flip with Johnny Swistak, a 62-year-old with thirty years on the job. Swistak's biceps were imposing enough, but half his right ear had been chewed off in a bar fight twenty years before. He just grabbed Super-Wop, a combat Marine, by the throat and lifted him off his feet, saying, "No one here gives a fuck what you think about anything."

Cheeseburger was at his home cleaning the garage when his father's plumbing truck appeared. The elder Rialto usually started cracking beers at work after 3 P.M., so by the time he rolled in Cheeseburger saw he was already wrecked.

"Hey, pop."

"What're you doing?"

"Stacking and re-stacking. Can't seem able to keep this place clean."

"Where's your mom?"

"Upstairs."

Cheeseburger went back to work as his father stumbled up the steps.

The door banged closed. As always, Cheeseburger hoped it would be a normal visit until the screaming started. Then he ran inside. When he got upstairs, he saw his father had her backed against the wall.

"How many times do I have to tell you to stop accessing my accounts without asking?"

"It's not just your money, Phil, how else am I supposed to pay the bills around here?"

"You ask *me* for the money. You got that? If I see you messing with the money again, you're gonna get it."

"Dad—"

"Shut up. And what the fuck is wrong with you? I got a son with Cheeseburger as a nickname. Have you knocked out anyone for that yet?"

"Everybody's got one, dad. They even say if you don't have a nickname, no one likes you enough to even give you one."

"*Cheeseburger*? Where's your self-respect?"

His father pushed him out of the way and left the house. Tears started rolling down his mother's cheeks.

He said, "Come on, ma. Let's go downstairs. I think I hear the oven timer."

She looked haunted. "I'm sorry he's such a monster."

"Don't you ever apologize for him."

"We used to be in love."

"Stop." Cheeseburger flinched at the image. "I'm sorry."

He took her by the elbow as his father's truck screeched down the block.

THE ONCE AND FUTURE KING

Arthur Tillinghast

For those with means, the Ocean State offered many high-end luxuries and activities. Powerboats and yachts of every type sailed the coastal waters before docking at homes the size of small castles. On a sunny day at one of these homes, five men drank cocktails on a deck after just sailing back from Bermuda. Even though it was February, the temperature rarely dipped below 30 degrees and snow was scarce. A fire had been lit in the stone pit in the center of the 100-foot mahogany deck. From there, a staircase led down to the shore where they had docked a 2006 Westport Motor Yacht. At 130-feet long, it cost $15,000,000 and was crewed by a team of eight.

"It's too bad about Jacobs. I thought he had a real chance. Shame on me." The boat and house were owned by Cristos Drakos, the CEO of Azore Aquatics. As the leading builder of America's torpedoes, he was worth $3.6 billion. Theofylaktos Drakos, his father, had made a fortune in transatlantic shipping during the recession ravaged 1970's Europe. The family moved to Newport in time for Cristos, the eldest son, to enter high school. After graduating Oxford University, he earned a master's in underwater engineering from Texas A&M, got a job with LR5 Dynamics in their submersibles division, and then took all he learned back home to his father at Azore Aquatics. Once installed as CEO, Cristos doubled the company's value with billions in new Navy contracts. His Greek accent was long gone when he said, "Next time we will have to use a better polling company. Jacobs was never five points ahead. In Greece, we call that *mátso skatá*—a bunch of shit."

"It certainly was a blown calculation to be sure. And it cost us millions." Austin Almonte ran Spinnaker Jack, which made sails for half the sailboats in the country. "I mean how does this happen? Especially here. How does a freaking Democrat lose here?"

"Seriously, even Republicans become Democrats just to get a taste of power." Drakos sounded disgusted. "I heard the governor almost had an aneurysm when she received the news."

"That part is true." Vincent Piastre passed hand-rolled Cuban cigars amongst the group. He was already a legendary personal injury attorney who went from a single Cranston office to a near monopoly across southern New England. "Our fearless leader spent an awful lot of political capital in this defeat. What about you, Arthur? Ever thought about a run for office?"

"Me? Oh my, that's very flattering, but I would not know where to begin." Arthur Tillinghast was always meticulously groomed, his full head of silver hair perfectly in place. So was his smile, which was filled with impossibly white teeth even though he was 58-years-old. As a retired Supreme Court Justice and Superior Court Judge, he was not nearly as wealthy as his companions, but in Rhode Island's legal community no one wielded more power or connections. Like Drakos, Almonte, and Piastre, Tillinghast came from old money in a new design. Forty years earlier, all four had been high school classmates at the prestigious St. Theodore's Academy where tuition costs were now $50,000 per year.

As a former Supreme Court Justice, Tillinghast was well versed in the law but a total newbie when it came to politics. Still, like most men already exposed to power, he was instantly intrigued. "Indeed, for a senate run or something at that level to be successful, I would need vast amounts of everything."

Piastre nodded. "And exposure. That's the key. No one can vote for someone they don't even know exists."

"And nobody," Drakos added, "outside of One Exchange Terrace, knows who you are. That would be our greatest hurdle."

"Or strongest asset." Almonte shrugged. "Remember, he doesn't have a twenty-year voting record to defend."

"True enough."

"Let's play the long game." Almonte clipped off the end to his cigar. "This cycle is toast, so we begin the process of getting our dear friend here known."

"I got everybody." Piastre was not bluffing. His ubiquitous law commercials on radio and television were widely considered both annoying and amazingly effective. His representation of both the nefarious and virtuous meant he was owed favors from them all. "When our esteemed Madam Governor needed assistance, who do you think she called? Fundraisers, consultants, boots on the ground—I'm statewide, baby."

"It's probably wise," Almonte added, "to start off at the local level, gain that exposure, gain some trust, and then when Casper's seat comes available next cycle, who knows?"

"So where would we start?" Bruce Irwin threw another log on the fire even though four waiters tended to their every need. That was because Irwin was no stranger to hard work. He might have been worth $900,000,000, but he was originally from western Kentucky and grew up poor. That was until he used the last of his savings to buy up shares in a company no one thought would turn into the number one audio speaker maker in the world. Even now, he never lost touch with his Kentucky roots. In flannel shirts, jeans, and boots, his outfits rarely varied. "He hasn't even been on a city council, so running for mayor without ever holding office would be a stretch."

"That would definitely be a hard sell." Almonte fired up his cigar. "But let's see what happens. There is so much economic carnage still occurring, who knows where and how bad the fallout will be? Also, don't forget about scandal. If our politicians have taught us one thing above all else it's that they have a predilection for vice and self-destruction just like everyone else. Sudden opportunities and acts of God may provide a window for those ready to strike."

"Then it's dual paths to the same destination," Irwin said. "We plan for the next election while waiting and hoping for a political catastrophe to strike one of our esteemed officials."

Everyone laughed.

"To the future." Arthur Tillinghast raised his glass. "I love how we just brainstormed my way to congress. Flattering indeed, but if it does come to fruition, a long and arduous road ahead now awaits."

Drakos said, "Next month, Carvalho is attending an event down here at our alma mater, the esteemed St. Theo's. I say we get you in. It's $15,000 a plate, but everyone will be there. It will be perfect."

"I've known Governor Carvalho for twenty years." Tillinghast nodded. "And what a ringside seat it's been. In my court, when she was District Attorney, I watched her disembowel the guilty and the vicious. A voracious ally to have, no doubt, but a fearsome and unforgivable enemy when provoked. We must be very careful with her. There are so no such things as empty promises or safe redoubts where she's concerned."

"Gentlemen." Drakos raised his glass. "To our dear friend Arthur, the once and future king."

They toasted again as knots in the burning logs exploded embers like fireflies into the winter sky.

THE BEGINNING OF NIGHT

February 7, 2009

DPW union boss Donny Teague's words proved prophetic. The mayor did not wait. City layoffs started with the Department of Public Works, spread to the Departments of Sanitation, Transportation, and then through all non-essential administration personnel. Police and fire, already understaffed, remained immune, as did the teachers, whose union was by far the strongest.

The Fire Department contract was set to expire on July 1. As the financial chaos settled in, the new contract was so frighteningly uncertain that anyone with twenty years on the job had to consider retirement. Rumors of drastic cuts to the Cost-of-Living Adjustment and Blue Cross healthcare made Russian Roulette seem far safer than gambling one's retirement on a new contract in the middle of a fiscal meltdown. In consequence, over the next four months, thirty to fifty guys might walk out the door. On top of the existing fourteen vacancies, the department might be down another 25% by July 1, a staggering number on a 136-man job.

The February union meeting was a general bloodletting on all sides. The six-man Executive Board stood beside the president, Lt. Ahearn, as things got heated. Twenty-year guys were anxious and loud, wondering why no one on the board knew anything definitive on what cuts the new contract would likely contain. Some guys could not retire even if they wanted to. Bad divorces or college-aged kids made that impossible. Their only hope was to survive for three more years and pray the economy rebounded enough to make the next contract less devastating. But one thing was certain. If enough old guys did not walk out the door, the layoff talk for the new guys would only recommence.

"I ain't never seen it like this." Dutch Carrigan was sitting in Fire Alarm with Jimmy Rowdell. Rowdell's partner, Fonzie, was sleeping on the floor on a mattress behind the computers. Fonzie was so big his feet hung off the mattress. In Fire Alarm, one dispatcher slept from 11 P.M. to 3 A.M., the other from 3 A.M. to the 7 A.M. shift change. They only woke each other up if things got chaotic or if there was a fire.

Dutch Carrigan was a horrible sleeper. Thirty-eight years of jumping in and out of bed had destroyed the night. Some guys could lay their head down and be asleep in minutes, but others became insomniacs haunting the stations. Especially the rescue guys, who some nights did not even have time to make a bed.

At midnight, Rowdell brewed a pot of coffee. The wall-mounted television threw shadows around the darkened room. The computers and alarm systems hummed a dangerously sleepy white noise lullaby. Rowdell asked, "How old are you, Dutch?"

"Fifty-nine, my friend, believe that? I can't. Fucking incredible, really."

Rowdell smiled. "Ain't none of us getting any younger. How old were you when you got on?"

"Twenty-one. My old man was on this job, and he begged me to join. I was a mechanic, still am. I've always loved wrenching on cars. Anyways, this was like 1970. The war was on, the economy was in the shitter, and I was sick of living day to day. I fell in love with this place the second I walked through the door."

"I've heard some pretty sick stories. Someone told me you're one of the last sponge guys."

"That's right." Dutch's laugh, after all the fires and cigarettes, was a wheeze-filled series of gasps and coughs. "My first day, old man McGonnaghy cut me off a piece of sponge. Told me to wet it down before I went in."

"Jesus Christ. No one would ever believe it. Breathing through a sponge? Didn't you guys have air-packs back then?"

"We did, but not everybody had them. They were brand new and cost $1200. That's like $20,000 in today's money, so the officers were the only ones who had them. You'll see it too, don't think you won't. We're usually ten to twenty years behind every advancement, so we take a beating because we're always broke. Anyways, a lot of the older guys, the guys who had been eating smoke their whole careers, they hated the air-packs. Especially the masks. Some of them got claustrophobic and refused to wear them. You know how that goes. They'd been putting out fires without them for a hundred years, so why start being a pussy now?"

They both laughed at that. Dutch sipped his coffee. He had only recently acquired a belly. For a man still widely considered to be the best firefighter on the job, his reputation was a thousand times larger than his actual physical stature. And his taste in dress, which right now consisted of knee-high white socks, slippers, shorts, and a wrinkled Engine 2 T-shirt, left little to the imagination. "Anyway, the sponge was brutal. You could only go in so far before the heat turned the water inside the sponge into steam and cooked your throat."

"Oh God..."

"Those were some hard men. Hell, we didn't even have real pants. Just those old-school three-quarter rubber waders. Nowadays, the gear is better, everyone has their own radio, we all have a Scott on and can breathe, so we go in farther. But even back then, we had guys who could literally eat the smoke around them. Jimmy Hayes was one of them. He was an old school lieutenant on Engine 1. We would be on the floor puking from the smoke, and Jimmy would be standing there sucking down a tube in the middle of the fire."

"A cigarette? You're joking, right?"

"Nope. He's still alive, too. He's in his eighties, lives over near Bishop's Corner. Wanna know the craziest part? He still walks like eight miles a day."

"So you've been here for thirty-eight years. That's kind of incredible."

"I love this job. From the day I walked through the door. I max out at sixty-five, which's when everyone has to go. But believe me, they'll have to drag me out of here."

"Guess I don't have to ask if you're gonna retire before July 1."

"Save your breath. Retire and do what? I still wrench at the shop on my days off, so why not keep doing both?"

"But what about the contract—"

"Listen, I didn't take this job for contracts or benefits and what all. And any fool who does is risking his life for all the wrong reasons."

"Fucking A."

"Only place I ever felt more at home was in the saddle of my old Indian. Don't tell my wife I said that."

Rowdell chuckled and said, "I heard you were a biker. Used to run with the Angels."

"Man, you ain't no kid. Don't believe everything these clowns tell you."

"That's not a denial."

Dutch grinned. "I've been lucky, Jimmy, you know? Riding motorcycles, wrenching cars, and putting out fires were my favorite things to do. Some people go their whole lives working jobs they hate. If you hate this place you shouldn't be here. A lot of the old guys are cranky and whiney. A lot of the new guys, too. Hell, I was eighteen-years into my career before some of these clowns were even born."

"Amen. A bunch of TV babies. Half of these guys never even had a real job."

"Different times, Jimmy. This place too, nothing stops, right? Everyone thinks they're irreplaceable until they walk out that door, and then the job just grinds on without them."

"I've heard some crazy stories about the old days."

"I'm sure you have. It ain't like it was, that's for sure. Back then, after a job, the B.C. would send the junior guy to the packy and he'd come back with cases of cold beer. We'd be pounding cold ones while rolling up hose."

"That sounds delicious."

"To this day, there ain't never been anything I enjoyed more than a cigarette and a cold beer after a good fire."

"When did all that stop?"

"Late 80's. The whole job changed. Everything became more professional, especially the EMS stuff. The old saying used to be 'you call, we haul, that's all.' When I got on, we literally threw you into the back of a station wagon and hauled balls for the hospital. Nowadays, we almost have to be doctors. And for what? Half the shit people call us for is completely ridiculous. Believe me, if someone dialed 911 in 1973 complaining about a stomachache at two in the morning, they'd be lucky not to get their ass beat. Besides, people used to be tougher. You'll see. The World War II crowd never want to call 911, but their grandkids call us for seasonal allergies and anxiety."

"It's embarrassing."

"It is. But just be nice. That's what I always did. Never had a problem or a complaint. Never. You know what? It doesn't matter why they called you—it's your job to go. What's an emergency to me and you won't be the same for a 70-year-old lady. Just be nice. Some of these guys forget these people are our neighbors. They pay our salary..."

"I hear ya. When I was a taxpayer, I used to think firefighters were a bunch of leeches doing nothing."

"And now that you're here?"

"It's true. I really had no idea. But I guess it makes sense. It is a city. There's something going wrong all day long. And if the cops can't solve it, arrest it, or shoot it, the fire department goes. On everything. Elevators, boiler back-fires, burst pipes, gas leaks, car wrecks, smoke alarms, fire alarms, carbon monoxide alarms, medical alarms..."

"Fucking A."

"But not us. T-Bag's right. We're just a pack of cunts with microphones."

"Not for long. We've all done this job. This room blows a bag of dicks, but you'll be out of here soon enough. Believe me. Once the old guys start leaving all of you will get paroled. We were thirty guys down in 1976. Back then, when you went to work, you stayed for days. The younger guys got held, because it's still a paramilitary organization. Thirty-one guys have to be here no matter what. But rank and seniority didn't mean shit because the holds ran right up to the officers as well. It was crazy."

"Can I ask you something? In all this time, how come you never made lieutenant?"

"I was never a good test taker. Never. My old man used to say we were life smart but book stupid."

They both jumped when the 911 phone abruptly shattered the darkness. Rowdell swiveled and grabbed the phone in one motion so Fonzie did not wake up for a second ring. "Sachem City Fire Department, Firefighter Rowdell. What's your address?... Phone number?... Okay, miss, what's going on?... Asthma?... Okay, and how long's this been going on?... How old is he?... Sixty-six? Okay, miss, we're on the way." Rowdell turned to Dutch. "You're up. 152 Long Wharf, asthma attack."

"You got it. I can't believe it ain't even one o'clock yet."

"When you get back..." Rowdell madly typed into the computer. "We'll finish our trip down memory lane."

"Absolutely." Dutch headed for the door.

After 10 P.M., the stations switched their main radios to "Night Mode." From 10 P.M. to 7 A.M., Fire Alarm toned out individual stations so everyone did not have to wake up for someone else's run. But if it was a multi-company response, Fire Alarm hit the "All-Call." This triggered lights and bells in all six stations so everyone knew what was going on. On medical runs, Fire Alarm phoned the rescue directly before toning out the station of whichever engine company was responding with them.

Rowdell called Rescue 1 and a sleepy voice answered, "Rescue 1."

"Hey, Lou, 152 Long Wharf. Sixty-six-year-old male, asthma attack."

"152 Long Wharf. Roger."

Rowdell hung up and clicked the Station 2 icon on the dispatch monitor. Since Dutch had left the door open, Rowdell saw the lights suddenly pop on across the apparatus floor. He heard the tones and bells and then his own voice. *"Attention Rescue 1, Engine 2, Still Alarm. 152 Long Wharf, apartment 9, asthma attack..."*

Upstairs he heard doors slamming and the scurry of feet. The ceiling banged open as two men dropped down the pole.

Rowdell heard Dutch's uproarious laughter before Captain Fawkes yelled, "That must've been some sexy shit, right?"

"You having a mid-life crisis, Cap?"

"Sixty ain't mid-life, Dutchy, least I hope not. What sick fuck wants to live to be 120?"

"I keep telling you we're too old for that fucking pole."

"I know you don't believe that. You of all people?"

"We ain't done yet, right, Cap?"

"Fucking A. Just now when the tones hit, I heard 66-year-old male and cursed, 'this old fuck,' until I realized I'm only six years younger."

"Ah-ha-ha-ha!"

The truck doors slammed closed. The garage door ascended as the Detroit diesel engine growled to life.

"Engine 2 responding. 152 Long Wharf."

"Engine 2's responding at 0102."

After they left, Rowdell smelled the exhaust and stared at the computers and phones with a sudden burst of hate.

THE DIRTY GAME
February 15, 2009

One week after the mass layoffs began, a party was held in the maritime city of Newport. For generations, this port housed whaling crews, merchant vessels from Europe, and slave ships from Africa. It was also a world-renowned party town where the super-rich still maintained 10,000 to 130,000 square-foot mansions on properties so vast they looked like golf courses overlooking the Atlantic Ocean. The Vanderbilt estate alone was valued at over $150,000,000. Most were built in the Gilded Age of the 1890's. Others resembled opulent country estates built by the French aristocracy before the guillotine changed their world.

Fairfield Abbey was a 50,000 square-foot mansion. The cars in the parking lot were worth more than most people's homes. The back wall was pure glass and showcased the Atlantic Ocean. Women in expensive dresses and men in $10,000 tuxedos milled across the marble floor.

As a lifelong litigator, retired Supreme Court Justice Arthur Tillinghast knew the importance of preparation. Ever since their clandestine meeting on Cristos Drakos' deck last month, Tillinghast had been researching and gathering intelligence. Tonight, he had a list of players and powerbrokers he intended to corner, but as for now only one truly mattered.

At the bar, he ordered two extra-dry martinis while scanning the crowd. As always, his silver hair was impeccably groomed. His smile of bleached teeth was almost distracting. Finding his target and her accompanying retinue, he cut diagonally across the room. He smiled and nodded at a few familiar faces, but not wanting to lose momentum, did not stop to say hello.

As a judge, he had faced down murderers and rapists, mafia hitmen and biker captains, but no one scared him like Governor Marissa Carvalho. After he witnessed firsthand what she had done to her opponents as District Attorney, he knew those who made the mistake of not fully appreciating her expert skillset often met with a violent and bloody end.

"You still remember." She put away her phone, took the proffered martini, and dismissed the handful of aides around her. "My father always said you had a memory like a vice, Arthur."

"Extra-dry, two olives." He raised his glass. "To old friends."

"Old friends." She clinked his glass. She was wearing three-inch heels and a dress blacker than coal. Her suit jacket revealed smooth skin down to her cleavage. Dark-complexioned, her intense gaze intimidated the unsuspecting. This also helped explain her 98% conviction rate when she had been Bristol County District Attorney. "You must tell me your secret, Arthur, you never seem to age."

"A clean diet and a good night's sleep goes a long way, Madam Governor."

"It must be your tan. Even in the coldest depths of February, you maintain a George Hamilton-like hue."

"A genuine compliment, to be sure."

"So, tell me a story, Arthur. What brings you down to the "City by the Sea" this evening?"

"The company of others and this fine charity, of course. Afterall, it is my alma mater. What an erstwhile fundraiser."

"Is it?" She forked an eyebrow. "I almost didn't come. The optics, of course, could be misconstrued as borderline racist."

"How so?"

"St. Theodore's, where tuition costs $50,000 a year for high school, is raising money so under-privileged youth can learn to sail this summer? Seriously?"

"No good deed goes unpunished, I guess."

"Blame it on the times we live in." She sipped her drink. "I was with Speaker D'Amato last week. He seems to think you might be eyeing a run for office. Which one, he would not divulge."

"Oh, not to worry, Madam Governor, my ambitions are very modest. Start small, end big, so to speak."

"Wise counsel, considering you've never run for office."

"I've got to start somewhere, right?"

"Your résumé is impeccable, Arthur, but no one knows who you are."

"Exactly my point. Which is why I've been following the developments in Sachem City. Are conditions as dire as they appear?"

"Off the record?" She checked her perimeter and lowered her voice. "Without a miracle, Chapter 9 is all but guaranteed."

"A tragic turn of events, no doubt, but I believe given the chance, I could turn things around."

"And what kind of leader would I be if I unleashed Arthur Tillinghast on the poor people of Sachem City?"

"I am—"

"I know you, Arthur. I know *all* about you." Governor Carvalho smiled hollowly. "What I just said was only half in jest."

"I am not that man anymore—"

"I'm not sure that would matter. Especially if those rumors ever found their proof."

"Those were dark days many years ago... Besides, you'll need someone on the inside you can trust if they indeed go bankrupt. I could be invaluable to you."

"Me? I thought the Receiver was being appointed by the Federal Court?"

"And I'm sure you remember which state we live in, and how and when the real business gets done."

"Indeed I do. The politics at the top can be excruciating."

"All I'm asking for is your consideration when and if Chapter 9 is declared. As you said, my résumé just needs to see the light of day. Then it will stand alone."

"How prescient. Because that will be exactly what happens if anything goes awry. Afterall, with great opportunities comes great risk."

"I won't disappoint you."

"Let's just say I'll keep your proposal under consideration and leave it at that."

"I ask nothing more."

"Enjoy the rest of your evening, Arthur, I hear the dessert course is to die for."

"You as well, Madam Governor. Thank you for your time." Turning to leave, he made sure not to sigh with relief but certainly felt like doing so.

ROWDELL

He lived in a one-room converted garage. It was in the coastal town of Wickford, twenty-eight miles south of Sachem City. If Rowdell could not stack it or hang it, he did not own it, so the only visible possessions were his clothes and various tools.

Last week, the phone rang with horrible news. Today, something even worse arrived. He sat at a simple kitchen table he had built out of spare 2x6s and plywood. The coffee added steam to the cigarette smoke eddying across the table. Since he had been up all night at work, he could still hear the sirens spinning through his mind. In his blue work khakis, he was shirtless, his chest and arms still shredded from his former life.

There was a small cardboard box on the table. The return address was familiar. With the cigarette dangling from his lips, he grabbed a knife off his belt and sliced it open.

"Hey, Beth..." he said to her picture. It was the first of many. At Grand Teton National Park, she and Rowdell had spent a month camping in the backwoods. He saw himself in many of the pictures. Also in the box was an envelope with someone else's handwriting.

"*Dear Jimmy,*" it read, "*by now you've probably heard the news you and I had always expected would arrive at any moment...*"

How many nights had Rowdell and Lisa, Beth's mom, canvassed the Oregon night for Beth? Even at her worst, Beth would try and stay in touch, but when she did not, they worried.

"It's been a while since we last spoke, Jim, so I hope you are enjoying your new career. I always said you had a heart of gold, even though you went to great lengths to never show it..."

Beth stared at him from one of the pictures taken right before her addiction roared completely out of control. They had gone out for ice cream. Beth's cone was melting faster than she could eat it, and she was madly licking at it to keep up as it dissolved. Rowdell remembered that roadside shop outside Klamath Falls, Oregon. And while the picture was hilarious, her eyes were not. She might have been smiling and laughing, but this was near the end of their relationship, and pretenses, at least for her, were hard to keep up. By now, her allegiance belonged elsewhere. Out of money, and with Rowdell finally cutting her off, she started having sex with strangers to fund her habit. Two months later Rowdell was in Rhode Island.

The night before he left, he tracked down Lisa, Beth's mom, outside of Corvalis. Rowdell had been working on one of the remaining logging crews up north. His pickup was already packed for the trip back east.

Lisa made him coffee and they relived the good times. Rowdell and Beth had been together for four years, and while neither one spoke of marriage, it certainly seemed in order.

"Can't say you didn't try," Lisa had said, and that's when he gasped. The nightmare of the last year crumbled as he cried and leaned into her shoulder. He told her he was sorry for leaving, and that's when she cried as well. Together, they had endured Beth's slow decline and now knew they were on their own.

"I've had this letter written in my mind, in one form or another, since you left Oregon three years ago. Doesn't it seem like a different lifetime? You and Beth always brought such joy to my heart, Jimmy..."

Rowdell inhaled on the cigarette and blinked back the tears. Poor Lisa. Like every mom the world-over, nobody suffered more. This was the last thing he wanted to deal with after working thirty-eight hours straight, but he could not sleep. He searched for a cell number he had not called in years.

"Holy shit," the person said, "you must either be in jail or need a kidney. Fucking A, Jimmy, how you been?"

"Good, Rabbit, existing, you know what I mean?"

"I do. Fucking A, I do."

Rowdell got the story Lisa could not tell him. He knew Beth's habit went off a cliff after he left, but of course the worst was yet to come. She became the old lady of a biker captain in the Mongols MC and got passed around from there. But as her looks and sex appeal quickly faded, she got left behind.

Rabbit said, "The last time I saw her it almost broke my heart, dude. It was like last month or so ago. She was covered in scabs and looked like she hadn't eaten in weeks. They found her..."

Rowdell stopped listening. If Lisa had sent these photos, it meant she could not look at them either.

Rabbit asked, "Yo, Jimmy, where you at?"

"Rhode Island."

"Still? There ain't no logging out there."

"I'm a firefighter now."

"A what?" Rabbit laughed. "Well, I guess that's better than being a cop."

Rowdell thanked him and said good-bye.

Then he put Beth in her box and locked it all away.

CHEESEBURGER DROPS THE BALL

February, 2009

"Oh my God, L-T, it's cut in half!"

"Jesus Christ." Lieutenant Brodie grabbed the microphone. As a recovering alcoholic going through his third divorce, his patience was non-existent. He was a lanky 6'7" and had arms with a seven-foot wing-span. He also wore a horrible blonde toupee that he never groomed, so it always looked like a startled chipmunk stuck to his scalp. "Engine 5 to Fire Alarm."

"Go, 5."

"Advise Rescue 1 we have a car versus telephone pole. It's torn in half. Unsure on injuries. You better start another rescue just in case."

When Engine 5 stopped behind the rear half of the car, a body was hanging out of the smashed back window.

Lt. Brodie yelled, "New guy! Grab the trauma and airway bags!"

Cheeseburger, who worked in Fire Alarm, was only on the line today because he had switched shifts with another private needing the day off. Since this was his first shift ever on a fire truck, it was disconcerting to find out that even after six months of EMT school and a twelve-week fire academy, he really had no idea what he was doing. Panicked, he just grabbed every bag he could carry and took off after the lieutenant and senior private.

The body hanging out of the back of the wrecked car was a female. Her blond hair was splashed in blood. Lt. Brodie felt for pulses but found none since her neck had been ripped open. When he lifted her head and saw her face was gone, Cheeseburger gagged.

Lt. Brodie looked over to the front half of the car thirty feet away. "Scotty! Whaddaya got?"

Scott Hagan had climbed into the front seat where a man's body was unnaturally wedged beneath the dashboard. "No seat belt, but he's alive!"

"Hey fatso!" Lt. Brodie yelled at Cheeseburger. "Get the fuck over there and help him!" He toggled his mic. "Engine 5 to Fire Alarm."

"Go, 5."

"Advise rescue we have a deceased female and a severely injured male. We're checking for more bodies."

As Scotty Hagan and Cheeseburger packaged up the man, Lt. Brodie quickly checked under parked cars and sidewalks for any further victims.

Two police cruisers arrived and Lt. Brodie yelled to them, "Look for more ejections!"

The cops, who as a rule never went near horribly injured people, were always good at finding bodies.

Rescue 1 came screaming around the corner. Private Tim Gale was chauffeuring Captain Charles LeClaire, another legend on par with Dutch Carrigan. A Vietnam combat veteran, LeClaire was 58-years-old and had been high school classmates with Dutch. And while Dutch had spent the majority of his thirty-eight-year career on the bustling Engine 2, LeClaire had done most of his thirty-four years on Rescue 1, one of the busiest ambulance companies on the entire east coast. Quiet, humble, and tough, LeClaire was at the tail end of a four-decade beating he could have mitigated by just bidding to an engine or ladder truck years before. But after the war, still chasing the action, he got addicted to the chaos true rescue guys embraced. Polite and courteous, he treated everyone with respect even when they did not return the favor.

Rescue 1 slid to a stop next to the front half of the car. Nonchalantly, Capt. LeClaire snapped on his rubber gloves as he approached. "Whatta we got, fellas?"

Scotty Hagan was sweating and had blood all over his gloves and arms. He had just finished applying a tourniquet to a half-torn right arm, which looked like a shorn roast beef. "Hey, Cap. Mid-twentyish male, unconscious when we got here. He's got a welt to his right temple and pupils are un-reactive. Broken right humerus, broken left forearm, and then there's this—" When he picked up the right leg, it bent the wrong way.

Femur fractures were a hard sight for the uninitiated, so Cheeseburger finally vomited. With the leg twisted ninety-degrees, the human body became a cartoon gone horribly wrong. Cheeseburger puked again.

"Jesus Christ, kid." Lt. Brodie was disgusted. "You've got to be joking."

"I'm sorry—"

"Let's get him boarded," Capt. LeClaire calmly stated. They applied a neck collar and strapped him to a backboard. They traction-splinted the right leg to reset the femur before it tore up the blood vessels and tissue around it. After he was loaded into the truck, they cut off his bloody clothes and searched for more injuries. LeClaire started large bore IVs in both arms above the breaks to try and replace all the blood. Tim Gale, his private, hooked him to a BP cuff and EKG. The pulse was steady, but once they got a blood pressure of 80/50, Capt. LeClaire said to Lt. Brodie, "Need one of your guys to drive in case he codes."

"Roger that. Let's go, kid, back-step man drives the shitbox."

Cheeseburger, who had never driven an ambulance, still looked sick. "I... uh... Ocean State Hospital?"

"Are you sure you're a fireman?" Lt. Brodie turned to Scotty Hagan. "You drive—"

"No." Cheeseburger swallowed twice. "I got this."

"Hey, kid." Capt. LeClaire smiled. "It won't be your first time every time. 95 South, exit 21, bear right, and the ambulance dock is up the ramp on the left. We'll get there."

"Okay." Cheeseburger climbed into the driver's seat as Scotty Hagan leaned in and pointed with a bloody hand. "Sirens are here, horn is there, lights are here, radio is there. Tell Fire Alarm when you're going and when you arrive. Watch your corners and speed, otherwise you'll throw them all over the place back there. And hey..."

"Yes?"

"Don't fuck this up or I'll make sure you never live it down. You had six months to learn where the fucking hospital was. Like Cap said, exit 21, bear right, look for the ramp on the left."

"Okay."

"You got this, Cheese." Hagan punched his shoulder and then slammed the door.

Cheeseburger stared at the glowing dashboard like a pilot in an unfamiliar cockpit. He grabbed the microphone and said, "Rescue 1 transporting to Ocean State Hospital with one man from Engine 5."

"Rescue 1 to OSH with one man from the engine. 1134."

As terrified as he had ever been, Cheeseburger absorbed his humiliation and mistakes into a lesson he swore never to re-learn. Then he threw it into gear and hit the sirens.

LIEUTENANT RUSSELL BRODIE

After that fatal car wreck, Lt. Brodie arrived home to find a police car parked in front of his house.

"Russ!" the cop yelled. "Don't do it!"

"Do what?" Lt. Brodie smirked. "You telling me I can't enter my own house?"

"Please don't do this." The cop's name was Leo Wilbur and he had known Lt. Brodie since they were kids on Claymore Avenue. All the Wilburs and Brodies had grown up together, and they were now sprinkled throughout the civil service, whether it be in city hall, the post office, the schools, the police and fire departments, or even the Parks Department/Buildings and Grounds.

When Lt. Brodie got out of his car, his blonde toupee was in such disarray that he wore a SCFD baseball cap to hide it. At 6'7", his incredible wingspan had made him a basketball legend in high school. Because he was talented and usually the only white kid on the team, he got paid the highest respect of all after being nicknamed "Sour Cream." He even scored a scholarship to a Division II school but promptly partied his way to failure. Those days, however, were long gone. Now, Sour Cream was twice divorced, had three kids, and a third wife who was currently on track to becoming ex-wife number three. As Lt. Brodie saw her in the house moving from room to room, he was about to lose his mind on Officer Wilbur, lifelong friend though he might be.

"You see this?" Lt. Brodie held up what looked to be some kind of court decree. "I get half this shit too, you know?"

"Russ." Leo Wilbur just shook his head. "This is the third time you're getting cleaned out. I mean is there really anything left to take?"

"If you weren't my friend, Leo, I'd tell you to go fuck yourself."

"But I am your friend. And I'm telling you in the strongest wording possible, you cannot enter that house until she's gone."

"But—"

"No but, Russ. The last thing you need, especially with your job, is an arrest for trespassing and harassment."

"Oh, that would be just the beginning, believe you me."

"Please don't say stuff like that in front of a sworn peace officer."

The door banged closed and the ex-wife-to-be stalked down the steps with a large cardboard box. The movers had already left with everything else. As she approached, her face twisted into a sincere snarl. "Fuck you, Russ."

"Nice. That's real nice. That would almost hurt my feelings if I had any left."

"Kind of like your hair?" She lunged for his baseball cap and pulled both it and his wig off simultaneously. "Ha-ha!"

"Gimme that back, you bitch!"

She skipped towards her car, laughing.

Lt. Brodie, now bald, turned to Officer Wilbur and said, "Dude. Come on, man. Have a heart."

"She might be doing you a favor."

"Leo!"

The cop called out, "Mrs. Brodie—"

"Don't call me that!"

"Please give back the toupee and hat. This has gone too far already, for both of you, please act like adults. Do the police really need to be here to babysit you?"

"Yes," they answered together.

Leo Wilbur just shook his head. "Honestly, this country is doomed."

She tossed his hat into the street, but ground the toupee against her crotch.

"Ugh," Lt. Brodie said. "Here come more STDs."

"Fuck you!" She tossed it at him. "You're a shitty lay and an even worse person!"

"No shit. I got stuck with you, didn't I? Isn't that punishment enough?"

"Fuck you!" She jumped into her car.

"It's been a great three years, babe. Seriously, the pleasure has been all yours."

She gave him the finger one last time before she peeled out in a cloud of smoke that floated over the long-time friends.

"Well..." Leo Wilbur adjusted his police hat. "Guess that takes care of that."

As they watched her car flee into the distance, Lt. Brodie turned to his old friend and said, "Is it me? Honestly, you can tell me. I mean, each marriage seems to be getting worse, right?"

"I think it would be safe to say, Russ, that you would be far better off single."

"It—"

"Like forever. Please, for all of us, don't ever get married again."

"I can't believe I quit drinking for this."

"Um, you quit drinking because you were a raging alcoholic."

"No, Leo, I quit drinking because beating that cheating whore actually began to seem like a good idea."

"Um, yeah, except beating women is never a good idea."

"Huh." Lt. Brodie looked at his open front door. "Guess I should go see what's left."

"Are you talking about your belongings or your life?"

"Right?"

"As a wise man once said, half of nothing is still nothing."

"Boy, you're a real morale boost."

Leo Wilbur patted him on the back while heading for his cruiser. "Remember what I said."

"I ain't going near her again, believe me. The clap she gave me just cleared up."

"Gross, Russ."

"Have a great day, officer!"

Leo Wilbur just shook his head, seemingly aghast at his selection of friends.

FONZIE

Fifteen-year-olds were not supposed to bury their mothers. But Margaret Fonseco's long battle with alcoholism was about to end.

Just home from school, Fonzie was making a snack for his 12-year-old brother and 10-year-old sister. They heard a crash in the family room and knew she had either fallen or knocked something over. But when Fonzie turned the corner, blood was everywhere. She was vomiting torrents of it. Her shocked eyes found his as if pleading with him to help her make it stop.

"Mom!"

On her knees, she hemorrhaged from her mouth and nose. She gasped, puked more blood, and collapsed clutching her throat. Since she averaged a bottle of scotch a day, her cirrhotic liver was all but shut down. Pressure from all the backed-up blood it could not process had thinned out the surrounding vein walls in her esophagus until it finally ruptured. This was how she died, gurgling and drowning in front of her own children.

Growing up, Fonzie was small for his age and got picked on by others. His escape became reading about history and hanging out with his grandfather, a decorated World War II veteran. He told Fonzie stories of catastrophic European combat in the Battle of Monte Cassimo and, later that year, the Battle of the Bulge. In both battles, a total of 388,000 men had been killed or injured, but his grandfather somehow emerged unscathed.

It was one thing to read about these epic confrontations, but to hear his grandfather's eyewitness narration left Fonzie in awe. That a whole generation could march off to save the world and return home and work for fifty more years was nothing short of remarkable. This appreciation was also why Fonzie did not fit in. His classmates made fun of him. They called him a dork and chased him home from school. They waited for him in the bathroom or the playground and jumped him like a pack of wolves. They took his precious World War II books and, after his mother died, taunted him by singing, "Fonzie lost his momzie! Fonzie lost his momzie!"

To toughen him up, his father, a thirty-year concrete contractor, had Fonzie on the jobsite after his twelfth birthday. Since no one could pour concrete in the winter, that's when they plowed snow and shoveled out clients. Fonzie kept to himself at school until a strange thing happened—he turned sixteen and started growing. At seventeen he was almost six-feet tall, and by senior year he was a 6'4" retribution machine. All the bullies, any of his tormenters, received justice delayed. On the football field, he became a one-man wrecking ball. He got thrown out of school twice for fighting and eventually charged with assault. Even his dad, no lover of weakness or empathy, grew concerned. But he was not the first to notice that his first born was turning into a monster. Fonzie's grandfather had finally seen enough. He had a bad left leg, so he limped after Fonzie like the old grunt he used to be, calling him a thug and a criminal on his way to jail. After he told Fonzie he was ashamed they shared the same last name, that changed the game forever. More importantly, for his grandfather to say something that horrific, meant Fonzie was on the wrong side of history.

Born into a Polish/Portuguese mix, Fonzie was all Polish in appearance. The close-cropped blond hair and light blue eyes were framed by a square jaw filled with white teeth. His arms were logs attached to hands big enough to palm a basketball, and tattooed down either forearm were the Polish and Portuguese coats-of-arms.

As his grandfather aged and wore down, Fonzie checked in on him once a day. They went through old photo albums and visited places still fresh in his grandfather's mind. But the inevitable could not be delayed. One morning Fonzie showed up with coffee and donuts and found his grandfather on the floor.

He called 911 because he did not know what else to do, and that bothered him most of all. By chance, one of the responding firefighters was also an old high school friend. They met for drinks a week after the funeral and Fonzie was blown away. Having never known what the fire department actually did, the future became reborn.

In EMT school, Fonzie's instructors were impressed by his intuition and patient skills. He knew his protocols, and obviously had no problem with any physical task put before him. When other students had trouble, he was quick to lend a hand. Through this transformation, his nickname went from "Baby Monster" to the "Big Easy" because of his genuine demeanor. Fonzie had already played the brute. Now, he found himself drawn to axioms perfected by his grandfather's by-gone generation—no one should die alone, and when people needed help you helped them.

Six months later, the Sachem City Personnel Office notified him that he had made the list. Three weeks after that, he lined up alongside the twenty-five men in Fire Academy Class 61.

COUNTING THE BEANS

At 9 A.M., on February 20, 2009, Mayor Houlinik convened a meeting with his six department heads. He had given them three weeks to come up with a cost cutting plan. $34 million divided equally meant almost $6 million per department. But because of public safety, they all knew that could never happen. $6 million was more than a quarter of the police and fire's individual budgets through fiscal year 2009.

Budget Director Timms thumbed to the last page of all six reports and added up the proposed cuts. He wrote the number down and slid the paper to the mayor, who then said, "Well, I appreciate the effort, gentlemen, but $21 million is nowhere near our bottom line for solvency."

"I spent a week going line-by-line through our entire budget." Fire Chief Al Draper's thick gray hair was shaved into such a perfect flat-top his head looked like a box. While he had been Chief of Department for only the last three years, he had spent the last three decades watching politicians come and go. Most were a danger to the taxpayers because of their utter cluelessness when it came to public safety. But not this one. Mayor Houlinik knew enough to admit he knew nothing about public safety and did not pretend otherwise. Chief Draper actually liked Mayor Houlinik. He was a son of the city who just had the bad misfortune of being elected captain of the Titanic. No stranger to bruising city politics, Chief Draper was savvy enough to know a power grab when he saw one, but so far this did not appear to be the case. He said, "Out of our 23.4-million-dollar budget for 2009, we could only find $3.2 million in cuts, which guts everything but manpower. That's cancelling the next academy and putting off the purchase of two new engines. That's also cancelling the training budget for the entire year, maintenance to the stations, cancelling equipment and gear upgrades, holiday pay, uniform pay, promotional tests, computer equipment and software upgrades."

The other department heads then listed their proposed cuts as well but it made no difference.

The mayor thanked them all and they took the hint. Alone again with his beleaguered Budget Director, Mayor Houlinik said, "Guess I should call the governor."

Then he left the room.

SUPER-WOP

Super-Wop never claimed to be the sharpest knife in the drawer, so this evening's dinner disaster was not on him alone. His wife, Rose, held two master's degrees and was studying for a doctorate in Advanced Developmental Adolescent Psychology. So the fact that she also never saw this fiasco approaching made it even more hilarious.

On a previous cruise to the Bahamas, they met a couple from New Hampshire. In their thirties and childless as well, the husband was an IT salesman and she was a lawyer. The couples hung out at the pool and had dinner every night. They even left the ship together on port calls. At the end of the trip, contact information was exchanged and promises made to remain in touch.

Two months later, Super-Wop and Rose drove north to New Hampshire for a reunion. The four of them drank wine and ate dinner. They drank more wine. Super-Wop and Rose were sitting on a massive sectional that took up half the living room. They drank more wine. Nonchalantly, the wife sat next to Super-Wop, the husband next to Rose. Then in perfect synchronization, the wife placed her hand on Super-Wop's crotch at the exact moment her husband groped Rose's breast. Instinctively, she yelped and punched him so hard his nose broke. He rolled off the sectional backwards and bled on the floor.

After Super-Wop burst out laughing, he lifted the wife's hand off his penis and said, "Watch out or you could be next."

Rose stood up and the husband immediately flinched. Blood poured through his fingers. She grabbed her purse and said, "What is wrong with you people?"

Outside, Super-Wop started the car and said, "Guess we were dessert."

"That's not funny."

"It's a little funny."

"No. It's not." Rose had curly black hair and dark eyes that currently bored into her husband. She was a tough woman with a soft spot for her special needs students and that was it. Loyal to a fault, it took years for her to figure out that this cut both ways. Before Super-Wop, it made her the emotional victim in multiple relationships. Being unable to say no even when it came at her own expense made her feel used. Now, she had Apollo, a boxer rescued from Texas, and Super-Wop, rescued from 1st Explosives Ordnance Company, 1st Marine Logistics Group, 1st Marine Expeditionary Force. The "Spiderheads" were the ones called when massive IEDs threatened half a city, or when some poor kid showed up at a checkpoint in a locked vest loaded with explosives that had malfunctioned. Six years and three tours later, patriotic tattoos on Super-Wop's arms told these stories wrapped around the names of his dead friends.

He pulled away from the curb just as the couple appeared at the door trying to wave them back.

"Fuck this." Super-Wop punched it. "Good thing they didn't roofie us."

"Oh dear God."

Super-Wop took her hand. "Guess you're not into swinging and swapping."

"Gross. That is so gross. I'm an Italian Catholic, for Christ's sake.

What would make them think that it was okay to just *grope* us?" She paused, horrified. "Do you think that's the message we're sending?"

"I grope you all the time, babe."

"I'm glad you think this is funny. We just got sexually assaulted. Another man had his hand on my breast."

"I know. And you knocked him the fuck out."

They stopped for coffee to sober up since there was still two more hours to go.

Back in the car, the dashboard light painted her green as she asked, "You ever regret marrying me?"

"Seriously? What kind of ambush is this?"

"It's not an ambush. It's an honest question."

"I love it when you sound like Marissa Tomei."

"Can't you be serious for one second?"

"Why would I regret marrying you? Because you don't want to be groped by strangers?"

"No. Because I can't give you any babies."

"Stop it. How do you think we got this far? No other woman would ever survive this."

"You're making progress—"

"Not enough." He pulled his hand away from hers and stared through the windshield at the white lines snapping by. "It's the only thing I hear in my head sometimes. That silence. The just pure and absolute silence. Like it'll even be in my dreams. Tick, tick, tick—"

"The V.A.—"

"Screw the V.A. They got a thousand guys like me lined up at the door, and another thousand behind them. A million broken soldiers."

"You're not broken..."

He frowned because as a rule he did not like to be lied to. "I know what I signed up for. Of course you don't really know what the fine print means until it's too late."

"Who could ever..." She shook her head.

"Who could ever what?"

"It's the one thing I've always meant to ask you. I mean disassembling bombs and watching your friends die... who could return the same after something like that?"

"I've been thinking... You know how much I hate my job, right?"

"Yes."

"I was thinking about applying to the FD. Trading in my handcuffs and pepper spray and saying good-bye to the D.O.C. forever."

"I think it's a great idea except you hate blood."

"I wouldn't say hate—"

"And urine."

"Now, okay, urine's gross."

"Feces."

"Um."

"And vomit."

"Okay, alright. Touché. I'll just have to figure it out."

"On the other hand, fifteen more years jailing men convicted of the worst crimes in the state couldn't be good for anyone's long term mental health."

"So, you don't care if I walk out after just five years? I can cash out the pension, roll it into a 401k?"

"Babe, I just want you to be happy. Forget about the money. That can't fix a broken mess."

"Well, when you put it like that..."

"Rapists, murderers, molesters... I mean how much more psychic abuse do you want to absorb?"

"None. No mas. I'm done." He squeezed her hand as they crossed the Massachusetts border. "I'll start applying."

"Where would you work? Providence? Cranston?"

"I need a place more desperate than that."

"What about Central Falls? Or Sachem City..."

"Perfect." Super-Wop kept the car aimed towards home. "Time to turn the page."

THE DAILY GRIND
March, 2009

It had been a month since Mayor Houlinik had asked for the $30 million in cuts, but inside Fire Alarm none of that mattered.

T-Bag was trying not to lose his mind and failing. "If that phone rings one more time I'm gonna light myself on fire."

Jimmy Rowdell ignored him. The 911 phone had rung five times in as many minutes and the radios were going crazy. Rowdell's normal partner, Fonzie, was on vacation, so T-Bag was working overtime. Since neither he nor Rowdell were particularly proficient with the computers, Rowdell got stuck with them after losing a coin toss.

T-Bag said into the mic, *"Fire Alarm to Engine 6."*

"Go ahead, Fire Alarm."

"East Providence Rescue 3 is responding to your location." Mutual Aid was an agreement between surrounding cities to share resources when their own became overwhelmed or unavailable. Because Sachem City only had two rescues but needed four, out-of-town rescue crews were in the city doing runs all day long.

"Engine 3 to Fire Alarm. We're on-scene."

"Roger, Engine 3's on-scene at 0914."

"Engine 1 to Fire Alarm."

"*Go Engine 1.*"

"Advise incoming rescue, 62-year-old male, history of heart. Complaining nine out of ten on chest pain. Claims his pacemaker is misfiring."

"*Roger. Fire Alarm to Rescue 1?*"

"Rescue 1 copies that, Fire Alarm, you can show us on-scene."

"*Roger. Rescue 1's on-scene at 0915.*" T-Bag turned to Rowdell and said, "This is about as much fun as having anal sex with a chainsaw." The outside line rang. "Sachem City Fire Department, Firefighter Taymaskhanov. How can I help you?"

"Yeah, it's Providence. You guys got any rescues available?"

"Ex-squeeze me? Is this a crank call?"

When the Providence dispatcher finished chuckling, he said, "Right? Why the hell am I calling you guys? Had to try though. We already drained Warwick and Cranston."

"What else is new? You guys are a soul-sucking blackhole."

"Hey!"

"Ha-ha! See ya!"

"Engine 4 to Fire Alarm."

T-Bag hung up the phone and hit the mic. "*Go Engine 4.*"

"We have what looks to be a transformer fire. Call National Electric and tell them it's pole number 1651. Corner of Wayne and Babbet."

"*Roger that. Flaming pole at the corner of Wayne and Babbet.*"

"Central Falls Rescue 1 to Sachem City Fire Alarm. Transporting one to Women and Infants."

"*Roger, C.F., transporting to Women and Infants at 0917. Thank you for the assistance.*"

"Engine 5's in service."

"*Roger, Engine 5, back in service at 0917.*"

"East Providence Rescue 3 to Sachem City Fire Alarm. You can show us on-scene."

"*Roger that. East Providence's on the scene with Engine 6 at 0917.*"

On the dispatch console, Rowdell clicked companies on-scene, in service, or off at the hospital. Then, abruptly as it began, the rush ended.

The guys from Engine 2 spilled into the room and took seats facing the wall-mounted television.

Lt. McCarrick, their former academy instructor, had just been promoted to Captain. This allowed him to return to his beloved Engine 2 with Dutch Carrigan. At the tail end of their careers, they handled this reunion like a couple of kids causing trouble in the back of the classroom. Dutch's old boss, Captain Fawkes, had decided to finish his career on Engine 6, the slowest truck in the city's only remaining middle-class neighborhood. Since the job ran by seniority, when someone retired or died, a mass bid was held downtown. In this auction, seniority was the only currency accepted. If a captain retired and no other captain wanted that spot, the lieutenant getting promoted to captain had to take it. Then that lieutenant's spot was put up for bid and so on all the way down the line. At some bids, only one or two guys switched trucks or shifts. At others, dozens of guys might be packing up their gear and emptying lockers.

"Captain McCarrick." T-Bag swiveled his chair to face him. "What an honor and a pleasure it is to see you again."

"Fuck you, T-Bag, you lying fuck. You couldn't make a pimple on a fireman's ass."

"Uh, no offense, but that's not exactly an insult."

"You suck as a dispatcher. You suck at life."

"Now that's an insult."

"You ain't gonna cry, are you?"

"No. Actually, I'm just gonna jump up and down on your diabetic feet until they explode like jelly donuts."

Dutch Carrigan spit out the Coke he was drinking before erupting into his trademark belly laugh. "Jesus Christ, you are a mess."

"Ain't he though?"

"I'm talking about you, Cap." Dutch pointed at his feet. "The kid's right. If you don't start taking better care of yourself, they *will* explode like jelly donuts."

"And then they'll cut them off." T-Bag made a scissor with his fingers and went snip-snip. "Hola, Stumpy."

"Ah-ha-ha-ha!"

Captain McCarrick smirked, able to take it. "The fuck you laughing at, Dutchy? The other day when you squatted to get into your night-hitch, your balls hung ten inches out of the bottom of your boxers."

"I know. At fifty-nine, it's game over."

T-Bag snapped his wrist. "You should whip that shit like a lasso, Dutch."

"Ah-ha-ha!"

"Like at dinner, just smack the old lady with it. 'Woman, pass me the salt!'"

"All right, okay." Rowdell was grinning. "I think we need to draw the line at scrotum lassos."

"Why?" Capt. McCarrick said. "Don't be such a pussy."

"Yeah, Row, lighten up." T-Bag pointed at Dutch. "Or you might just get meat-leashed by Dutch."

Dutch turned to Rowdell. "You need to get out the book."

Rowdell pulled the notepad out of a drawer. He wrote down the quotes about diabetic feet and exploding donuts and Dutch's meatleash. He glanced at some of the other more horrifying quotes and shook his head. "Man, this book is your ticket to prison."

Dutch said, "You really are a sick prick, you know that? By the way. What kind of name is T-Bag?"

"My father was Chechen."

"Oh great," Capt. McCarrick said. "A fucking terrorist."

"Coming from you? Didn't the I.R.A. invent terrorism a hundred years ago?"

"Maybe." Capt. McCarrick forked an eyebrow. "But has anyone ever asked you the most important question of the fire service?"

"No."

Capt. McCarrick's pause let the moment swell in importance. "Do you eat ass?"

T-Bag flinched, offended. "Of course I eat ass. I eat ass, I eat pussy, I eat the whole damn thing."

"Me too. As a matter of fact, I keep a bottle of Scope on the night-stand for when I'm done."

"What a gentleman."

The 911 phone shattered the room.

"Sachem City Fire Department, Firefighter Rowdell. What's your address?"

"Sachem City this is 911. We just had a caller state their house was on fire. 3-1-6 Weller Avenue. Be advised we're receiving multiple calls on this."

"Oh shit." Rowdell flinched. "I'm sorry. We'll send someone right over."

Rowdell and T-Bag hung up the phones. Rowdell started typing in the run as T-Bag turned to Engine 2. "Structure fire, 316 Weller Avenue, multiple calls."

"Fucking A!" Dutch slapped Capt. McCarrick's shoulder. "See? You brought us back the good juju!"

Capt. McCarrick smiled as they hit the door. "I hope the whole place is fucking ripping."

"Me too."

T-Bag hit the All-Call. *"Attention Engines 2, 1, 5, Ladder 1, Battalion 3. Still Alarm. 316 Weller Avenue, possible structure fire. Be advised, 911's reporting multiple calls..."*

Even listening to the dispatch got Rowdell excited. In the other stations, those not immediately dispatched would hit the bathroom just in case. Then they would meander to the apparatus floor and monitor Channel 2, the fire-ground channel, and await the verdict. Many times it was not a fire at all. Food left unattended or boiler backfires were the usual culprits. But when 911 reported multiple calls, that meant neighbors and strangers alike were all seeing the same thing.

With the siren wide open in the background, Capt. McCarrick yelled, "Engine 2 to Fire Alarm!"

"Go Engine 2."

"Three-story wood frame, we've got fire blowing out of the 1-2 corner on both the first and second floor. Code Red."

"Roger, Engine 2. Fire Alarm to Battalion 3, receive?"

"Battalion 3 receives that. On-scene and establishing command on side-one. Strike me a second alarm."

"Roger, Command." T-Bag hit the All-Call and waited for the bells and tones to end. *"Attention Engine 3, Ladder 2, Rescue 1... 316 Weller Avenue. Fill in on a Code Red."*

From this point, T-Bag owned the fire and Rowdell handled any additional 911 calls. People did not stop crashing their cars or having heart attacks just because the fire department was busy.

"Command to Fire Alarm."

"Go, Command."

"Get me Car 4, Car 7. Also roll me the electric and gas companies. We've got significant exposure issues with both."

"Engine 2A to Engine 2C!" Capt. McCarrick shouted through his mask. "Charge my line!"

"2C receive! Here comes the water, Cap!"

"Engine 1 to Engine 2C."

"2C!"

"You ready for the hydrant?"

"Roger!"

"Here comes the water."

"Make it wet."

"Command to Fire Alarm."

"Go, Command."

"Have Ladder 2 come in from Reno Avenue. I want them providing egress on the 3-4 corner for Ladder 1."

"Roger. Fire Alarm to Ladder 2?"

"Ladder 2 receives that. We're two minutes out."

"Car 1 is on the air to 316 Weller Avenue."

"Roger, Chief, on the air at 0929."

"Ladder 1 to Command! Second-floor is clear!"

"Okay, let's get up to that roof. Looks like you can cut a hole right above the chimney."

"Roger."

"Engine 5 to Command. We are entering with the backup line."

"Okay. Command to Fire Alarm."

"Go, Command."

"Have Engine 3 take an attack line up the back stairwell."

"Fire Alarm to Engine 3?"

"Engine 3 receives that! Three minutes out!"

"Command to Fire Alarm."

"Go, Command."

"Strike a third alarm and then backfill our stations with mutual aid companies."

"Roger, Chief." T-Bag hit the All-Call and dumped the rest of the city. *"Attention Engines 4, 6, Rescue 2, fill in on a Code Red..."*

Now, with every truck in the city dedicated to the fire, Rowdell phoned surrounding departments to come and stand by at their stations to answer Sachem City's other 911 calls.

"Fire Alarm to Command."

"Command, go."

"Command, we have East Providence Engine 3 at our Station 6, Central Falls Engine 1 and Providence Ladder 6 downtown, and North Providence Engine 3 covering Station 5."

"Received. Command to Engine 2A."

When Capt. McCarrick hit his microphone button, the sound of rushing water and Dutch Carrigan screaming something in the background filled the air. Capt. McCarrick shouted through his mask, "Go, Command!"

"How we looking?"

"We got the bulk of it knocked down! But we also have holes in the floor! Second-floor, side-two."

"Command to Fire Alarm. Put out an Urgent Message about holes in the floor, second-floor, side-two."

T-Bag hit the Urgent Message tone and said, *"Attention all companies operating at Weller Avenue. From Command, there are holes in the floor, second-floor, side-two. Repeat. Holes in the floor, second-floor, side-two. Use caution."*

When events occurred that depleted resources, the department flexed into an all hands on-deck mindset. Those who worked as inspectors and marshals in the Fire Prevention Office upstairs were all veteran firefighters, so they grabbed their gear and joined the Central Falls engine and Providence ladder. "Bird-dogging" was the practice of one local firefighter riding along with out-of-town companies unfamiliar with the city or its buildings.

Minutes later, the out-of-towners were in Fire Alarm monitoring the fire and checking directions in case they were the next companies called to the scene. As if on cue, the 911 phone exploded.

Rowdell hit the Alert Tone and said, *"Attention East Providence Engine 3, Still Alarm. 141 Ballston Way, difficulty breathing..."* And then, *"Attention Central Falls Engine 1, Still Alarm, 275 Third Avenue, chest pain..."* and after that, *"Attention North Providence Engine 3, Still Alarm. Motor vehicle accident. Corner of Champlain and Owen Drive."* Then he had to find out-of-town rescues for every run while answering the phone and giving directions if the out-of-town companies got lost. The mainline rang and Rowdell said, "Sachem City Fire Department, Firefighter Rowdell. How can I help you?"

"Hey, it's Channel 9 News. We're monitoring the scanners."

"Miss, I'm kind of busy—"

"I know. I'm sorry, just wondering if there are any injuries at the fire?"

"Call back later." Rowdell hung up and cursed.

T-Bag said, "You need a hand with anything? These guys are on cruise control now."

"Need a rescue for the North Providence engine."

T-Bag called Lincoln and Central Falls but they had nothing

available. Neither did Attleboro or North Attleborough, but Plainville did. Their dispatcher laughed. "Talk about a road trip. Hope it ain't serious, cause we're twenty minutes out."

"I hear ya. Just start them rolling this way. If anything closer comes available we'll cancel you guys."

"Roger that."

"Fire Alarm to North Providence Engine 3. You're gonna have a Plainville rescue."

"North Providence receives that."

"Jesus Christ..." Rowdell's heel was jack-hammering the floor. "This sucks."

"Is it wrong for me to want to kill everything in this room, myself included?"

"Have at it. I got an artery right here."

"Command to Fire Alarm."

T-Bag said, *"Go, Command."*

"Fire is under control at this time. Overhaul operations are beginning."

"Roger that. Command is reporting fire's under control and overhaul is beginning at 0955." He turned to Rowdell. "Five o'clock is still hours away, bro."

"Well, after it gets here, I'll race you to the bar."

"Hell yeah."

Rowdell pushed away from the console. "Guess I can release my sphincter now."

But after the 911 phone rang again, they both went back to work.

SACRIFICES MUST BE MADE
March, 2009

Interstate 95 was 1,919 miles long and ran from Florida to Maine. It cut through fifteen states and was consistently ranked in the top five most dangerous highways in America. There were many hazardous sections, but none deadlier than a series of curves cutting directly through Sachem City. Nicknamed "Blood Alley," these sudden S-curves had been specifically designed to circumvent two Sachem City institutions—St. John's Catholic Church, a massive ornate brick structure that could seat a thousand people, and the Viri Autem Civitatis Club, which was Latin for "Men of the City." Founded in 1851, the Viri Club was a closed society home to Sachem City's elite. The mill owners and industrialists all built mansions in the adjacent Crescent Side neighborhood. In keeping with the club's name, there were no women allowed, either as guests, members, or employees. Within these walls, businessmen and politicians carried on many illicit activities and made deals that affected local citizens for 120 years. "Blood Alley" was one of them. By 1956, in order to complete the 43.3 miles of highway that was about to vertically bisect tiny Rhode Island, the design team originally drew up plans for I-95 to cut directly through the Viri Club and, a half mile further north, St. John's Church. But when club members and the archdiocese got wind of this proposal, influence and favors rained down on the politicians until the highway got magically bent around the Viri Club. It swung sixty degrees, swung back sixty degrees the other way, straightened out briefly, and then another S-curve flung motorists around St. John's Church. So far, this redesign became a decision paid for in blood for sixty years.

The Viri Club was still there, but its windows had been boarded up after the last member died in 1972. St. John's, auctioned off to help pay for the Catholic Church's pedophilia scandal, was bought by a developer that went bankrupt five months later, so the abandoned building was now a haven for drug addicts, the homeless, and those that preyed upon them.

But inside the S-curves the massacre continued. Whole families had been killed out there. When tractor-trailers misjudged velocity and physics, they jackknifed or flipped over completely, flattening anything in the next lane. Cars slammed into the Jersey barriers and then shot across four lanes, taking out other cars before crashing again. Some vehicles got launched over the divider into oncoming traffic, and that's when the decapitations and real horrific injuries occurred.

In case it was not dangerous enough, twelve bridges kept the suddenly bisected city connected above the highway, but their three-story concrete abutments created human soup and fireballs when vehicles smashed into them at 70 MPH. When accidents like these became catastrophes, the entire highway could be closed for hours. Stuck in this ensuing parking lot, people had asthma attacks, panic attacks, or even went into labor and had to be rescued from their cars. With the highway impassable, this had to be done from the other side of the Jersey barrier with traffic whipping by at 60 MPH.

In the rain, snow, or ice, the fire department might respond to this stretch of road so frequently it could look like a union meeting had spontaneously convened on the highway. Three engine companies covered the 6.1 miles of I-95 through Sachem City. Since people often gave 911 faulty information, protocol called for two engines—one to sweep the northbound lanes, the other southbound. Callers to 911 had good intentions but were sometimes startled eyewitnesses with a bad sense of direction and location. Engine 2, in the center of the city, responded on every highway run. If they headed south, Engine 5 came north from the Providence line. If Engine 2 headed north, Engine 4 responded southbound from the Massachusetts border.

On a normal stretch of road, rubberneckers were mere annoyances, but in the S-curves they caused accidents of their own. People snapped pictures or filmed as they passed by with their phones hanging out the window. Some of the older guys told the newbies the highway was even more dangerous than house fires. Incredibly, the drunks, mesmerized by the flashing lights, were drawn in like inebriated moths smashing into fire trucks, tow trucks, and State Police cruisers. Because of this, Sachem City had to replace two engines and one rescue in the last five years.

When the All-Call tones went off at 8:45 A.M., Fonzie was only riding on Engine 4 because, as the most junior member on-shift, he got held in a line spot the Battalion Chief could not fill. His brand-new gear was stiff, clean, and bright yellow when compared to the veteran's soot-smeared and battered pieces. Eager to learn, he had been out on the apparatus floor going through every inch of the truck since the 7 A.M. shift change.

Mikey Doneen, the other private on Engine 4 that day, was answering his questions. If a newbie showed up at a station and just threw his gear on the truck, grabbed a coffee, or read the newspaper, his reputation was promptly destroyed. Likewise, if an older guy approached a newbie and asked if he had any questions about the truck, the newbie that answered no was in for a long shift. Ten-year guys might turn a blind eye, but the real old school, the guys broken in thirty years ago by the World War II guys, considered this a complete lack of respect. Depending on the gravity of the offense, for some newbies it was a reputation killer only reversed by years of hard work.

Mikey Doneen was only 29-years-old and already had eight years on the job. He was watching Fonzie practice donning his gear and SCBA in a timely manner and said, "Jesus Christ, kid, how tall are you?"

"Six-foot-four."

"You are a monster."

"Why is my name machined into the manufacturer's tag inside my jacket?"

"All fire gear is custom made. It's also so they can identify your body if you get fried."

"Oh."

"Remember to keep your shoulder straps—"

The All-Call tones hit. *"Attention Engine 2, Engine 4, Rescue 2, Still Alarm. 95 South, in the vicinity of Exit 29..."*

After Doneen hopped behind the wheel, Lt. Stokes, "The Dude," jumped in beside him and said, "Sorry, dudes, I was right in the middle of dropping a heater."

"Hope you showed that turd who's boss."

"Damn straight."

Behind them, Rescue 2 already had its lights spinning.

Lt. Stokes grabbed the mic. "Engine 4, Rescue 2 responding."

"Roger that, Station 4 companies responding at 0846."

By protocol, Engine 4 entered the highway in Massachusetts and swept south from Attleboro. They were on the highway ninety seconds after leaving the station and hit a wall of traffic, either from the morning commute or accident or both.

"Fuck me." Lt. Stokes pointed to the right shoulder. "Take this, Mikey. I'll see if Fire Alarm has a better location. We might have to get over to that other shoulder if it's in the high-speed lane."

"Roger." Doneen punched it down the breakdown lane while Lt. Stokes pinned the siren pedal to the floor. Behind them, Rescue 2 rode in their wake. "Engine 4 to Fire Alarm. Do you have a lane for this accident?"

"Negative. But just received a second call from State Police requesting you to expedite."

"Fuck yeah." Doneen was pumped. "Grab extra gloves, Fonzie. When the cops say expedite you know it's gonna be a bloody mess."

Fonzie jammed rubber gloves into his turnout gear. From the back-step, he looked over their shoulders but could only see four lanes of dead stop traffic whipping by.

"Engine 2 to Engine 4."

The Dude said, "Go ahead."

"Yeah, Lou, we just passed it. You got a sedan on its roof. Middle two lanes. Might be another two cars involved. They're against the Jersey barrier beyond the first car."

"Roger that." Lt. Stokes motioned. "Mikey, get us over in front of the rollover." He toggled the mic. "Engine 4 to Engine 2, after you swing around, take the two cars against the barrier. The cops are all around the rollover flagging us down."

"Roger."

"Engine 4 to Fire Alarm, companies on-scene."

"Engine 4, Rescue 2 on-scene at 0850."

To provide them protection, Doneen parked diagonally to block two of the three lanes.

Lt. Stokes yelled, "Fonzie! Trauma and airway bags!"

"You got it, Lou." Fonzie put on his helmet, grabbed the two bags from the side compartment, and tried not to be overwhelmed. They had been taught in moments of extreme stress to revert to the basics—airway, breathing, and circulation. The ABC's kept people alive. He saw Doneen and Lt. Stokes rushing for the car until they abruptly stopped. When Fonzie turned the corner, he found out why and almost puked. A woman had been ejected. As the car rolled, it came to rest on her head. Otherwise, the rest of her seemed perfectly fine. The car had landed on the top part of her skull and squeezed all kinds of things out of her mouth, nose, and ears.

Mikey Doneen winced. "Are those her brains?"

Lt. Stokes said, "I don't know, man, but she's still moving."

Her arms and legs were shot straight out like a twitching starfish. When the red blood crept across her black skin it made it shine.

Lt. Stokes grabbed her wrist. "She's got a pulse." He turned to the cops. "Push the car so we can pull her out!"

The rescue guys appeared with the stretcher and more gear. Engine 2 screamed by heading for the two cars ahead.

"On three!" The cops rolled the car just enough to allow the firemen to yank her out. From the forehead up, she was crushed.

Lt. Stokes said what they were all thinking. "Just two more inches..." He blocked it from his mind but saw her wedding ring before he could turn away.

The rescue guys collared, boarded, and strapped her down. They all loaded her onto the stretcher and sprinted for the rescue.

"Dude!" Lt. Stokes yelled to Fonzie. "It's leaking gas. Stretch the trash-line in case it lights up!"

"You got it, Lou." Fonzie opened the front bumper and pulled the smaller trash-line. When he knelt and looked inside the car, he instantly regretted it. There she was, the collected parts of her life. Because of the rollover, everything was on the ceiling. Her briefcase and laptop were next to her purse. Shattered glass was everywhere. Her travel mug was still loaded with coffee for her ride to work and now leaking. Upside down, there were pictures of her kids attached to the dashboard. Fonzie realized that six minutes ago she was just another commuter on her way to work before this moment arrived to steal her life. Firefighters were not allowed to declare anyone dead unless they showed injuries incompatible with life, so if the patient had a pulse, they got the full work up despite likely non-survivable injuries.

The back doors of the rescue flew open and Lt. Stokes yelled, "Fonzie! Back-step dude drives the squad to OSH! Hurry, she's about to code."

"Roger that." Fonzie waddled over in full gear. He tossed his helmet onto the passenger seat and quickly scanned the dashboard. He had this. No sweat. "Fire Alarm, Rescue 2 is transporting with two men from Engine 4 to Ocean State Hospital."

"Roger that, Rescue 2, headed to Ocean State with two men from the engine at 0858."

The rescue lieutenant in the back of the squad toggled his mic. "Rescue 2 to Fire Alarm. Advise OSH we have a 38-year-old female with a severe crush injury to her head. Fixed pupils. She is unconscious, BP is 230/180, pulse 140, we have an airway but it's anatomically compromised. Two 16-gauge IVs established. We're eight minutes out."

"Message received, Rescue 2."

Fonzie put the pedal on the floor and, because of the closed highway, ate up the empty road.

THE EMBERS EXPLODE
June 13, 2009

With only seventeen days before the July 1 deadline, panic and rumor were ripping apart City Hall. In every department, civil servants were in disarray while readying their résumés in case the worst came true.

Nationwide, the economic carnage was slowing down by June, but that meant little to those barely hanging on. With 700,000 people a month still losing their jobs, the sea of foreclosures was a swelling tide. In most cases, people went peacefully when the constable's door-knock meant they were minutes away from becoming homeless. But others refused to leave. Some got violent, and that's when the SWAT teams got the call. No one enjoyed throwing people into the street, especially people with kids. But because it became so routine and machine-like, the worst of humanity collided one morning on Clyde Street.

Eugene Hennaman was the last remaining white man in a neighborhood that through the decades saw a sizeable increase in Hispanic and black-owned properties. Generations of Eugene's family had lived in the same house since 1886. It was a triple-decker with the stacked front porches as rundown as the rest of the place. In the 1970's, when everyone else left for the suburbs, the Hennaman clan remained.

The new neighbors got used to the obstreperous and, at times, outright racist nonsense coming from the house at 22 Clyde Street. Eugene, like an ignorant Don Quixote, became regarded as a neighborhood oddity, a source of amusement since one delusional man could not face down an army. He was not respected, but people at least knew where he stood. Usually, they just rolled their eyes every time he revealed the worst instincts a man could possess. But after Eugene's mom died and his sister finally moved out, a strange thing occurred. Eugene got lonely. At 56-years-old, this was the first time he had ever lived alone. He had never cooked a meal or even washed his own clothes. He became raggedy and thin and wore the same outfit for days on end. But one afternoon, as he watched a woman exit the bus and struggle with her baby and groceries, he offered to help. Since her apartment was on the fifth floor across the street, she accepted his offer while clearly unsettled. A recent Cape Verdean immigrant, she was still learning English, but her neighbors had already told her all she needed to know about the crazy white man that lived at 22 Clyde Street. As nervous as she was, together they climbed to her apartment.

Once inside, Eugene snuck a peak at beautiful pictures of her island homeland. She offered him iced tea as a thank you, and over the next half-hour, Eugene rediscovered his humanity. He found out her name was Adelma Almeida, and that she was a single mom far from home. He told her about himself. When she heard he could not cook, she sent him home with a container of fish and rice and beans. She spoke to the other neighborhood women, and, while some thought him pitiful, a few decided to help. Soon, Eugene Hennaman received cooking lessons from the same people he despised. They taught him how to make oatmeal, omelets, boil pasta, and how to assemble a monthly budget. They laughed when he told them how thankful he was that he did not have to eat another bologna sandwich.

Gradually, Eugene appeared on his front porch and, instead of hurling awful racist bombs at passersby, drank cold beer and waved hello. Unsure of what to make of this, some neighbors doubted this supposed transformation. Especially the men. The ones that had previous run-ins with Eugene usually restrained themselves from unleashing whatever justice he had coming. But for the ones that did not, Eugene earned their grudging respect by taking his beating and never calling the cops.

The constables from the Providence County Sheriff's Office showed up at 22 Clyde Street at 7:23 A.M. on Monday, June 13. In Rhode Island, people were given a thirty-day notice of eviction. Twenty-nine days could come and go but on that last day one thing was certain—whoever remained would be gone, either escorted off the property, forcibly removed, or arrested.

After the constables were greeted by an irate Eugene brandishing a gun, they retreated and called for backup. City cops quickly arrived and, after another attempt at communication was met with Molotov cocktails thrown from an upstairs window, the SWAT team got the call.

"1886!" Eugene tossed out another flaming bottle. "It ain't gonna be that easy!"

Negotiators had a phone thrown through a first-floor window so they could beg him to stop. They even brought his sister to the scene, but she immediately left in tears after Eugene called her a traitor for leaving him behind.

The neighborhood gathered at the barricades. Some were curious and some were angry. Camera phones live-streamed the escalating conflict so more people joined in. Once the SWAT team unleashed the gas grenades and crashed the door, those behind the yellow caution tape grew belligerent. They started launching bottles and rocks until the police were under attack from both Eugene and the crowd. More Molotov cocktails lit up inside the house because Eugene was not ever going to leave. The cops shot him in an upstairs hallway before the fire reached the rest of the gasoline and the upstairs bedroom exploded. They fled the house just as it turned into a full-scale conflagration and emerged into a scene of chaos. With the poor and working class under economic siege, 22 Clyde Street became the Alamo of the soon-to-be foreclosed upon. The police pushed back against this growing riot until both sides saw Eugene stagger out of his front door fully engulfed in flame. He still had the gun and raised it. People screamed and pointed. Eugene went to his knees, melting, and then face-planted into his lawn after the police shot him again. The ensuing gas-fueled fire took out two neighboring houses because the fire department could not get through. Trapped in the traffic, they came under attack as well.

The next day, as the city simmered, the damage had been done. When senior private Ian McCallum, who had been on the job for thirty-nine years, put in his retirement papers, the flood gates imploded. Within a week, as the July 1 expiration of the contract approached, McCallum became the first of the eventual thirty-two firefighters who walked out the door over the next two weeks. By July 1, the Sachem City Fire Department had forty-six vacancies, and the worst was yet to come.

THE GHOSTS INVITE THE DEVIL
July 1, 2009

The mayor's office was located on the top-floor of City Hall. It occupied a fifth-floor corner suite with views of both the Massasoit River, and the long-shuttered grandeur of what downtown used to be. From the 1860's through the Second World War, the mighty mills fueled the fortunes that turned downtown into a baby Manhattan. Grainy footage from the first motion picture cameras in the 1890's showed bustling avenues filled with restaurants, opera houses, vaudeville shows, and eventually the nation's first movie theaters. Finely dressed women strolled beneath parasols carried by men in suits and top hats. Horse drawn carriages and packed trolleys shared the road alongside the country's earliest automobiles. On side streets, merchants and tradesmen provided goods and services to sustain the boom. In southern Rhode Island, men with last names like Vanderbilt and Astor built extraordinary mansions that turned Newport into a playground for the rich. It was a high time for celebration until glitzier locales like the Hamptons and Palm Beach stole the show.

Mayor Houlinik was in his best suit, the one he was convinced made him look slimmer. He thought of this and smiled. In the early days, when he told his campaign staff of this suit's magic powers, they obediently nodded. Then he won the primary when no one thought he could, won the general election even though pundits said he was too young, and took office on the proudest day of his life. All his victory speeches had been made in this same suit.

He knew what was coming because Governor Carvalho's office had been courteous enough to call the day before. They offered not to notify the media until afterwards, and to have the convoy of state officials quietly ushered around the back of City Hall. But Mayor Houlinik would have none of it. This was not his fault and he refused to hide. On the wall was a picture of his wife and two kids. It was the last thing he shoved into the cardboard box containing his personal belongings.

On his desk was a single sheet of paper. Within the last week, as the storm roiled and gathered, he decided on one final act of defiance. There were ten remaining fire recruits on the list waiting to be hired. The city also had a public safety grant set to expire in September. Since there were no exceptions to federal grant money or how it could be spent, he signed off on the hiring of the ten even as the retirements flooded in.

At exactly ten o'clock, he watched the caravan of black government SUVs sweep down Blackstone Avenue. The media, camped on the sidewalk, swarmed the vehicles. Because threats had already been made, the state police had two cruisers stationed in front of City Hall.

Mayor Houlinik watched state officials, lawyers, and accountants flee the SUVs and scurry to the front door below. Cameras flashed. Reporters shoved microphones into their faces. State troopers let the officials through before blocking the door to City Hall. The media was informed that a press conference would follow soon after.

A moment later, the mayor's phone rang. It was Laurence Timms, his soon-to-be ex-Budget Director. "Sir, they're in the Finance and Tax offices. They're securing all the computer systems."

"That's to be expected. Make sure no one deletes anything, Laurence, and fully complies."

"Sir—"

"They're gonna make their way up one floor at a time. Why don't you come on up and help me enjoy this view one last time?"

"I..." Laurence Timms became resigned. "Yes, sir."

Over the past week, Mayor Houlinik had been quietly letting people go before Sachem City hit the iceberg. His chief of staff and most other executive branch personnel were already gone. The door opened. Laurence Timms awkwardly approached. "Sir, I just want to say—"

"All of our ghosts..." Mayor Houlinik was at the window staring out at the three-story Blackstone Mill, the first one built in the city. It was now a national landmark and museum, but in 1793, it had been state of the art. The original massive waterwheel that harnessed the power of the Massasoit River was still attached. Mayor Houlinik said, "Turns out they never left. They just waited in the shadows."

"This took decades, sir. They planted landmines without ever once thinking about the future. Our future."

Three knocks hit the door.

Mayor Houlinik yelled, "One second!" He shook Laurence Timms' hand. "Thank you. I know how much you gave up to take this position. And for only seven months..."

"It was an honor, sir. Do you... should I let them in?"

"Yes." Mayor Houlinik turned back to the view. Behind him he heard, "Good morning, Mr. Mayor."

Mayor Houlinik turned and saw people spilling into the room. He recognized the Secretary of State and the State Treasurer, and was then introduced to the governor's representatives, forensic accountants from the IRS and the State Police, lawyers from the Attorney General's office, and forgot all their names a minute later.

"Mayor Houlinik, my name is Arthur Tillinghast." A man with crisp white hair and a long-practiced frozen smile stepped forward. "I'm a retired Supreme Court Justice. I apologize for the unfortunate nature of this visit, but rulings by Judge Lorio in the Chapter 9 declaration end your role here. If you have everything gathered, the marshals are waiting in the hallway."

And that was it. They had him sign papers relegating him to a consultant's role. His pay was cut from $85,000 to $12,000, and all his benefits were stripped.

He was the first mayor in the 219-year history of the city to be removed from office. He would not be the only one to lose his job.

KILLSHOT

Two days later, on July 3, Fire Chief Al Draper stared at the memo on his desk. Ex-judge Arthur Tillinghast, the newly appointed Receiver, was wasting no time. The fire department budget for 2009 was $23,464,231. The Receiver was demanding $6.1 million in cuts. Chief Draper was stunned. He and Lt. Ahearn, the union president, had run the numbers a dozen times last February and came up with $3.2 million that could be squeezed without affecting the safety of the city or his personnel. But $6.1 million changed the game. The only way that would be possible was by breaking minimum-manning and closing trucks.

The National Fire Protection Association was a self-funded non-profit, non-partisan organization comprised of scientists, engineers, and insurance companies. Formed in 1896, its only concern was eliminating deaths, injuries, and monetary loss due to fires. Highly regarded nation-wide, its recommendations affected everything from fire department staffing levels to insurance rates. Depending on demographics and other myriad intangibles, it usually called for two firefighters per 1000 thousand people. Sachem City, with the recent vacancies, was now down to two per 1800. By contract, twenty-eight firefighters, two dispatchers, and one Battalion Chief always had to be on duty. To seek another $3 million in cuts meant not filling spots and closing trucks. That turned a four-minute response time into a six-minute minimum for the next closest truck. If that truck was already on a run, the third-due company might not arrive until eight to ten minutes after the initial 911 call.

The Receiver was "recommending" dropping minimum-manning from twenty-eight firemen and two dispatchers to twenty-two firemen and two dispatchers, meaning two engine companies would be closed before any spot could be filled with overtime. It was a risky proposition. Rolling blackouts had been tried in other cash-strapped cities. Nationwide, house fires had dropped in the previous two decades due to augmented fire codes and strict enforcement. But playing those odds was a dangerous game. Taxpayers, who might initially appreciate saving money, would be the first ones calling for someone's head if people died in preventable catastrophes. And with the mayor now gone, Chief Draper knew whose neck would be first inside that noose.

He stared at the memo like an impossible lie he could not correct. It was sheer insanity. If he rubber-stamped this proposal and someone got killed, that would be horrific enough. But if it was one of his own men who died, he knew the guilt would kill him.

One did not rise through the ranks to become Chief of Department without knowing how to play the game. Chief Draper was a politically adept survivor who realized saying no would cost him his job. The memo was a "proposal" that also doubled as a GPS locator to see exactly where he stood. It was not bad enough they had forty-six vacancies and guys would be forced to work round the clock. Now they would be even busier with two engines closed. It was a disaster in the making, and Chief Draper wanted nothing to do with it.

Lt. Ahearn, the union president, had requested this meeting. Once upon a time, Lt. Ahearn had been a private on then-Captain Draper's truck. They had much in common, so Ahearn paid attention to everything Draper did. He spent six years learning on Draper's truck before the captain became Battalion Chief and, one year later, Chief of the Department. Now, when their current positions made them enemies, they never let it get personal. Even still, Lt. Ahearn had so much respect for Chief Draper, it made it hard to currently say, "If you sign off on that memo, people will die."

"It's an impossibility. It means I believe we can still fulfill our S.O.P.'s."

"It also means Tillinghast can hang you out to dry. 'Well, the fire chief assured us these cuts would not affect public safety.'"

"Either way I'm fucked."

Lt. Ahearn carefully chose his words. "Do you think you would resign, or make them fire you?"

"I've never quit anything in my life. Ever. So abandoning my men is off the table."

"What's your play?"

"Public safety. I'm gonna write a refusal to this memo stating forty-six vacancies makes rolling blackouts a death wish. Then I'm gonna leak it to the press."

"They're gonna take that as an act of war. Even if they were thinking of keeping you on, the leak signs your death warrant."

"Well, this needs to be stopped."

"The union could do a simultaneous release stating the same thing, maybe deflect some of the heat off you."

"Do whatever you need to do. At least you'll get the union's objection on record."

"This is some pretty hideous business."

"It could get even worse, right?"

Lt. Ahearn could not disagree. "That's too awful to even contemplate."

RESCUE 1
July 5, 2009

Four days after the bankruptcy, real life kept on rolling. It was three o'clock in the morning when Jimmy Rowdell panicked and spilled Albuterol all over the floor of the rescue. He and Rescue Captain Charles LeClaire were tending to a 74-year-old black female asthmatic. Her breathing was so distressed she was gasping and clutching her chest.

Capt. LeClaire, who had been on Rescue 1 for thirty-four years, calmly told her, "We're setting up the nebulizer, darling. A few puffs on that and you'll be good as new." He turned and saw Rowdell fumbling with the mask. Since it was Rowdell's first shift as LeClaire's chauffeur, he was not about to air him out. It just was not in his nature. "Pour another one in, Jimmy, no sweat."

"Sorry, Cap, I feel like a moron." Rowdell dumped another ampule of medication into the tennis ball-sized chamber connected to the mask. Once he turned on the oxygen, it passed through the liquid-filled chamber and created an aerosol mist. He put the hissing nebulizer mask over her mouth and nose as she greedily gasped.

Capt. LeClaire caught Rowdell's eye and nodded toward the monitor. They watched her oxygen level slowly climb—78%, 82%, 87%.

"Wow." Rowdell saw it hit 94% before she gradually relaxed. The bronchodilator was opening her lungs. Relieved, she slowly savored every breath. She looked up at Capt. LeClaire and said through the mask, "Thank you, thank you, thank you. It's never been this bad. Usually, my inhaler works every time."

"It's really humid out, dear." When Capt. LeClaire squinted and spoke, his raspy voice reminded Rowdell of Clint Eastwood if Clint Eastwood was shorter and nicer. LeClaire, a sturdy six-footer with a slight paunch, had gray hair he had only recently started to lose. He painted houses on his days off, so his face was weather worn and wrinkled. He looked at Rowdell and said in that patented rasp, "Wanna start the line, kid?"

"Yes." Rowdell ran the sequence through his mind since he had not started an IV since testing for his Cardiac license. All the vacancies were now forcing the Fire Alarm guys onto the line. Rowdell sat on the benchseat next to the stretcher. With the tourniquet tied off mid-bicep, he sterilized her elbow with an alcohol swab and searched for a vein. He took the standard 20-gauge needle, looked her in the eye, and said, "Here we go."

"Why'd you say it like that?"

"Because it's my first one."

"Oh Lord..."

"That's not true, darling." Capt. LeClaire patted her shoulder. "He's done it in the hospital. You need ten sticks to get your license. It'll be fine. He's the best."

She said, "Guess I'll be the judge of that whether I like it or not, right?"

Rowdell was all business. He lined the vein up like a pilot entering a gun-run downrange. He put the needle on the vein and slowly eased it in. He felt the skin pop, the membrane beneath give way, and finally the vein shot blood back inside the catheter. He was in.

"Nice shooting, kid." Capt. LeClaire was on his shoulder, his voice a graveled whisper. "Now retract the needle, advance the catheter, attach the line, and we're good to go." He looked at the woman. "Smooth as silk, right?"

"Not bad," she said.

Rowdell was so proud he could not peel the goofy expression off his face. "Where we headed, Cap?"

"Galilee."

"Roger." Once up front, Rowdell grabbed the microphone. "Rescue 1 transporting to Galilee Hospital."

"Rescue 1 transporting to Galilee at 0315."

Once they arrived and transferred care to the ER nurses, Rowdell watched them interacting with the captain. All night, at every hospital they visited, nurses, doctors, and other firemen paid respect. After decades of transporting tens of thousands of patients to local Emergency Rooms, Capt. LeClaire was about as well-known as Elvis. Humble, tough, and genuine, he was setting an absurd standard. Most guys on rescue eventually crashed and burned, but not LeClaire. He was one of a handful of men that became so immersed in the job it was hard to tell where the job stopped and they began. Like Dutch Carrigan and Capt. McCarrick, this put Capt. LeClaire in rarified air.

Per agreement, rescue crews re-stocked at the hospitals. As Capt. LeClaire finished writing up the run report, Rowdell hit the supply room and got a nebulizer mask, IV set-up, and breathing medications.

Back in the truck, Capt. LeClaire toggled the mic. "Rescue 1's in service."

"Roger, Rescue 1, back in service at 0331."

Even though it was the middle of the night, Rowdell was amazed at how many people were on the streets. Alongside the hookers, drug addicts, and drunks, deliverymen, cabdrivers, and third-shift workers all shared the predawn darkness. It was an alternate universe filled with exhaustion and very bad decisions.

They had not been to sleep yet, so they got coffees and parked the rescue overlooking I-95 above the S-curves. Capt. LeClaire said, "How you holding up?"

"Good." Rowdell sipped his coffee. His shaved head was a blue glow in the dashboard light. "I certainly can't bitch about not sleeping to a guy who hasn't slept in thirty years."

Capt. LeClaire chuckled. "When you put it like that, I get exhausted just thinking about it."

"Seriously, you're a monster."

"Well, it's you young guys who're taking the beating now." He was referring to all the vacancies. In the last week, junior guys spent their regular shifts in Fire Alarm and then got ordered to stay if no one else wanted to work. And no one did. Guys were already pulling sixty hours away from home. Overtime costs were exploding, but that was set to change. The rumor mill said the Receiver was about to officially void all the contracts. If that happened, the Receiver could do whatever he wanted—lower minimum-manning, lower salaries, lower the overtime rate, or remove it altogether. Fire departments were paramilitary organizations that operated outside all labor laws and protections. There was no such thing as an eight-hour day or forty-hour work week. Before the current chaos, they worked forty-eight hours but only got paid for forty-two. Now, they could be ordered held indefinitely and spend days on end at work. Capt. LeClaire said, "This is just not sustainable. These guys got families, other jobs too. They can't be ordered to just give up their whole lives."

"I don't know how any of this works. I've never been in a union. All I know is federal law prohibits firemen from striking, which basically means we're at the mercy of the city."

"That's why collective bargaining agreements were created. What should happen is that, while a new contract is negotiated, the city operates in good faith under the old one. Period. End of story."

"You ever seen it this bad?"

"The job or the economy?"

"Both."

"No." Capt. LeClaire reached for his coffee. "After I got back from

Vietnam, the economy was in the shitter but it wasn't freefalling like this."

"How long were you over there?"

"Too long. Twelve months? Wanna hear a funny story?"

"Sure."

"Just before my nineteenth birthday, they came out with the first draft lottery. My birthday was drawn number nine. It was the only lottery I ever won."

They laughed.

Capt. LeClaire said, "Within a month I had my draft notice, had my physical, and two months after that I was in Basic Training."

"What year was this?"

"1970. I was inducted into the army January 8, 1971. Went to Vietnam in August of '71 as an 11 Bravo Infantryman. I was in the Central Highlands, saw some action, but not a lot compared to what others went through in other places, and at earlier times during the war. I came home in September of '72 and somehow they gave me an early out instead of having to do the full two years. I wasn't even twenty-one when I got discharged."

"Holy shit."

"It was eye opening, being on the other side of the world. Before that, I had never even left New England."

"Vietnam must've been some shit."

"Like I said, others had it much worse."

"You're being modest, but I can tell you don't want to talk about it."

"Not particularly. The good part is that it allowed me to use the GI Bill to sign up for accounting classes at CCRI. There, I ran into some Providence firemen taking classes, and talking with them kind of put the idea in my head."

"When did you get on here?"

"1975. I was twenty-four. It was a different world back then. EMS was virtually non-existent. We had one rescue, which was basically a station wagon with oxygen and bandages. That's it. We didn't even transport people. Private ambulances did that after we triaged what we had."

"Dutch says this generation is a bunch of pussies calling 911 for earaches and shit."

"Well, that's true. But people are a lot sicker these days, obese, diseased."

"Incredible, really. I also heard there were fires all the time."

"There were. Smoke detectors didn't even come around until the late seventies, and back then *everybody* still smoked. Couches, mattresses, recliners, porches—cigarettes ignited everything. At least once a cycle we were throwing a mattress out the window. On top of that, when I-95 was cut through the city, whole blocks were condemned. It was a real mess. We're talking about entire neighborhoods literally torn apart. They used to call it Plywood Alley because of all the abandoned homes. The feds, city, and state argued for years about who would pay to tear everything down. In the end it didn't matter. We're talking about 6 miles of worthless buildings. We had fires for twenty years."

"There was a story Dutch told me, about two guys drinking in a bar. The building next door caught fire and they ran inside to help...?"

"Oh yeah. Dexter Street. It was March 1989. Early in the nightshift, maybe six or seven o'clock. Dark out. Rain mixed with sleet, cold, miserable night. We got a call for a fire at 167 Dexter Street and I knew the building well because it was an old tenement, three-decker cut into one-room jobs, like a rooming house with a bathroom at the end of the hall. Bottom of the economic ladder kind of people. A lot of them were drinkers, druggers... Anyway, it was right next door to the B and D Tavern. When we pulled up, there was fire pouring out of the second-floor windows in the front side of the building. There was fire showing in six windows. At least. There were two guys hanging out of the third-floor window on the Dexter Street side. Well, actually one guy and, uh, there was a fire escape. So we threw a ladder up to the escape, ran up to the third level, and meanwhile the fire is coming out of the second-floor underneath us—"

"And rolling up the fire escape."

"Right. So somebody had to put water in the second-floor window to keep us from roasting. This guy was still conscious, but he seemed disoriented, and we're trying to pull him out, and there's all this hot smoke pouring out of the window behind him. All of a sudden it lit up. The smoke turned to flame—"

"It flashed over."

"Yup. The room flashed and at that point he collapsed. As I grabbed his belt to try and pull him through the window, everything came apart in my hands because he was burning up. And that's when I noticed there was a second guy behind him, wrapped around his legs. He was trying to escape too but was already unconscious and clinging to his buddy. We didn't know it at the time, but they had run from the bar next door to try and help get people out."

"Those were the two guys who went in to help?"

"Yup. They got trapped on the third-floor and the fire came up the stairwell behind them and rolled into the room, flashed it over, and they died right in front of us."

"Dear God..."

"I remember his fingers, the skin was melting off. Same thing with his face. It was right in front of us. And it was horrible because we were right there but couldn't do anything to help. Then we realized he was more or less being held by the dead guy locked onto him."

"And all they did was try to help."

"Yup. Their keys, their drinks, their cigarettes—they were all still on the bar waiting for them to return. I'll never forget that image."

"Jesus, that's awful."

"This job will humble you."

"It must be hard, watching people die."

"How old are you, Jimmy?"

"Thirty-eight."

"At least you got some life experience to bring to the table. Some of these young guys... they have no idea how life works. What'd you do before you got here?"

"Construction mostly, carpentry and framing houses, but I also did a little logging out west."

"So this is your first exposure to the job?"

"Yes."

"Wait until you see it, the real hardcore trauma. It's an adrenaline rush like no other, just like a good fire."

"What's some advice for a new rescue guy?"

"Be nice."

"That's exactly what Dutch said."

"Well, there you go. Throughout your career, you'll find them—learn from the good ones. And always be nice. Until it's time not to be nice. But that's a different story. Until then being nice solves a lot of problems. And diffuses situations. Another thing is that if someone climbs into the back of the rescue and says they feel like they're gonna die, get ready, because they probably will."

"You're busting my balls, right?"

"Nope. That impending doom thing is real."

"What're the worst runs?"

"Kids. Always remember, their youth means their bodies can compensate longer than adults. But once they crash the race is on, because they're harder to get back than adults."

"That must be awful."

"It is. I've had kids push through screens and fall three-stories and die, and I've seen them survive without a scratch on them."

"Incredible."

"We had a kid one time, 2-months-old, coming down I-95 from Boston. Mom had taken the kid out of his seat to feed him, and they crashed in Blood Alley. The kid went out the back window with nothing on but a diaper and a T-shirt, and he bounced down the highway like a basketball. Now it's a *baby*. The plates in his skull haven't fully formed yet. As we approached, I thought, 'Man, this kid's gonna die.' He had a mouthful of glass, and we cleaned all that out, and he started screaming and I thought, 'He might just make it.'"

"That's absolutely crazy."

"Kids are tough. Sometimes they have to be. One night a guy came home drunk, beat his wife to death, and during the night—she died in the chair—her toddler, a daughter, crawled into the dead mother's arms. And that's where we found her the next day."

"I heard domestics are the worst."

"They are. The women… it's heartbreaking. They just keep coming back for more until they end up murdered. We had one woman, off Claymore Avenue. The ex-boyfriend beat, strangled, and stabbed this girl with a 2-year-old daughter in the house, so the 2-year-old spent the whole day with the dead mother."

"Gross."

"I was with a new guy. He was horrified. But that poor kid, all day long just hanging out with her dead mom."

"Lemme ask you something. You ever think you've seen too much?"

"No. But speaking of having seen too much, we delivered a baby one time. Mom's in a room with three guys. The baby came out inside the placenta, which I had never seen before, so at first I looked and said, 'What is this?' Then it dawned on me—the baby's still in the sack. So I got the scalpel, cut the kid out of the sack, and the cord was wrapped around his neck three times. He was as blue as your pants. So we got him breathing, all pinked up, wrapped him in a blanket, and I says, 'Who's the lucky guy?' And they're all going, 'Not me, not me.' Well, it turns out she was a prostitute and was servicing these guys when she went into labor."

"*What?*"

"Yep. And the junkies… some will break your heart. They overdose over and over until they die. Especially when they enter that death spiral. We had a girl one time OD three times in 24 hours. The hospital kept releasing her because it's not a jail, right? Anyway, we told the family to say good-bye now because she wasn't gonna be around much longer.

They were frantic. Searching everywhere in the house for her stash but they couldn't find it. Sure enough the next day she was dead for good." He saw Rowdell's reaction and said, "What's up?"

"I... I'm familiar with that. My ex..."

"I'm sorry to hear that, Jimmy."

"Toward the end, like you said, it became unstoppable. I loved her, man, I really did. I mean we had been together for years. She just started fucking around with it one day and partying and the next thing you know, you're bailing her out, you're getting phone calls, people are talking, and then the overdoses start... one night I came home and found her on the shitter. Totally blue. Just leaning against the wall."

"My God."

"Yeah. Let me tell you, me and her mom did everything we could, and in the end it was just the end, you know? After I got the call, I felt so guilty at finally being relieved that it was over...? I hated myself for that." Rowdell blinked and blinked again. Then he smiled sadly. "That kind of heartbreak never goes away, does it?"

"I don't think so, Jimmy."

"Fire Alarm to Rescue 1."

Capt. LeClaire reached for the microphone. "Rescue 1."

"Start responding to 484 Vance Street. Man with a headache."

"Roger." LeClaire hung the mic on its dashboard hook. "You and I been gabbing so long I almost forgot we were working."

"Fucking A."

"That's the sign of a good partner."

"You've probably trained half of this department." Rowdell hit the lights and lit up the night, saying, "Shall we?"

"Absolutely. Every run's a drama. Every shift a chapter."

"Fucking A."

Rescue 1 headed off into the dawn.

AWAY FROM SACHEM CITY

July 8, 2009

When T-Bag was on-shift, he stayed for free at his grandfather's triple-decker in Sachem City. But on his days off, he lived in Newport, which was forty miles south. In Rhode Island, the West Bay was connected to the East Bay by crossing two massive bridges in succession. The Jamestown Verrazzano Bridge landed on tiny Connanicut Island, and a mile later the Newport Bridge, built high enough to accommodate any vessel of the United States Navy, soared 200-feet above the water for 1.6 miles.

In Newport, he shared a two-bedroom apartment with Louise Taylor, an accomplished chef who certainly did not mind living alone for half the week. Louise had grown up in Newport and, like generations of Aquidneck Islanders before her, never left. The middle-class was tiny, so the beyond-super-rich created jobs for the working-class that included lawncare, homecare, childcare, hotel jobs, and work inside some of the finest bars and restaurants on the entire east coast. But the greatest gift of all were the yacht people. Local marinas were filled with some of the best and most expensive boats in the world, and companies that designed, engineered, or assembled these vessels had vast docks and hangars filled with state-of-the-art equipment and personnel. On top of that, the presence of the United States Naval War College meant the defense contractors responsible for America's torpedoes, underwater submersibles, and submarines all maintained massive compounds along the water.

While most of T-Bag's co-workers lived in Sachem City, Rowdell was just across the bay in Wickford. Together they were preparing for the annual "Save the Bay" swim, a 1.7-mile fundraising event from Newport to Connanicut Island. Jamestown, the only town on Connanicut island, was another enclave of the exclusive and wealthy.

On the Newport side, after T-Bag illegally parked at an abandoned beach on Navy property, they walked down to the water. Daily, seven rivers dumped 2.1 billion gallons of water into Narragansett Bay. The bay contained over thirty islands and covered 147 square miles. Most of the islands were small chunks of uninhabitable land, but others were owned by the super-rich.

The place was totally empty because the "beach" had no sand and was instead filled with sharp shells and jagged rocks.

"I'm not gonna lie," T-Bag said. "Getting in and out really hurts. I usually just crawl."

"Awesome. What're you doing?"

"Taping these to my ankle just in case." He tore off some duct-tape and wrapped two packets of energy gel around his ankle. "Depending how long we're out there you might need some sugar to get back."

"Are you being serious?"

"No, Row. I always tape shit to myself for no reason."

"Is this whole thing really a good idea?"

"Come on, man. Two miles in a pool is like less than a mile in the ocean. Out here you're fighting the wind, the waves, and the current. We're talking zero visibility, spacial disorientation, and waves crashing over you when you breathe. If you don't at least practice you probably shouldn't do the swim in August."

"Okay, alright, you don't have to shame me."

"Dude. It's a free country. Sign on or sign off."

Rowdell took the gel packs and tape. He watched T-Bag get on his hands and knees and crawl into the surf. Stubborn as ever, Rowdell tried walking in until it hurt too much, so he crawled in as well.

They waded out thirty feet and put their goggles on.

Treading water, T-Bag said, "Since you can't switch-breathe—"

"What's that mean?"

"Alternating your breathing, left-side then right-side. If you could, you'd be able to stay on course easier. So, I need to show you how to stay in a straight line. If we were going south, you could just follow the coastline, right? That's why we're going north. When you can't see underwater, you lose your bearings. It's not like the pool with a line painted on the bottom. You have to find a marker. Like the sun. Every time I take a breath, I check its location. I adjust myself in the water to keep it at the same angle. In the same spot. Kind of like turning your head into a compass. Otherwise, you have to lift up every couple of strokes to make sure you're not veering off-track, which fucks up your momentum."

Rowdell nodded and glanced around Narragansett Bay. Sailboats and motorboats crisscrossed the picturesque horizon. He said, "How are we not gonna get clipped by a boat?"

"I don't know." T-Bag grinned. "I'm kidding. There aren't any boats this close to shore. Besides, jet-skis are way more dangerous because they're usually driven by drunk morons. But look around. There isn't another human being for miles, bro."

"Why is that?"

"Because this is Navy property. All the marinas are south or north of here. Look at that boat over there." He pointed at a motorboat roaring across the far-off distance. "Dunk your head. Sound is the only human sense enhanced by water. You'll be able to hear that engine even from here."

"I can't believe I agreed to do this without someone in a boat behind us. You don't even have a dive buoy."

"Who cares? I do this all the time."

"Alone?"

"No, Row, my imaginary friends swim with me."

"When was the last shark attack in Rhode Island?"

"Nineteen-fifty-blow-me!" T-Bag dove and then broke the surface pulling freestyle.

Immediately, Rowdell discovered the difference between playing in the ocean and swimming through it. He tried doing too much at once and got confused. T-Bag screamed at him twice after he unknowingly veered ninety degrees off course.

They halted and tread water.

T-Bag said, "Let's try this. We'll stay side-by-side. I'll be on the outside. When you breathe, look at me, look at the sun, and it'll all click together. Remember the compass. It will keep you on the same heading."

Rowdell made the adjustments. Using the sun for positioning definitely helped. Eventually he trusted himself enough to pull away, so T-Bag dropped back, let him take the lead, and took up position on his inside flank.

Time disappeared into the rhythm. Rowdell caught a few waves to the mouth and quickly figured out it was far safer to breathe in the trough before the upswell. Finished with the initial stages of exhaustion, he found his fear had yet to ebb. They were only thirty feet off the coast, but the thought of what might lurk below made him feel uncomfortably defenseless. It was not hard to imagine his soft belly being ripped open and his bloody guts spilling out into the water. Still, like a thief that had yet to be caught, this unknown created its own elation.

They headed north toward Portsmouth. The coast was still Navy owned and overgrown but otherwise undisturbed. A rusting World War II rail line, eaten by time, was gradually collapsing into the sea.

T-Bag slapped Rowdell's ankle to get his attention. "Watch out. Scallop farm's coming up."

"What?" Rowdell gasped as he treaded water. His years in construction had created a muscular physique rendered completely useless when it came to distance swimming. He was stunned that T-Bag was not even breathing hard.

"Just follow me around it." T-Bag reset his goggles. "Watch out for the posts. I've kicked them before and it fucking hurts. You can't even see them."

"I'm getting kind of tired."

"I've got us mapped for 1.5 miles. You wanna head back? Just let me know."

"You mean we haven't even gone a mile yet?"

"Nope."

"Oh, man. What the fuck. Why does it feel so far?"

"I told you. Everything is harder. In a pool, 1.5 miles equals 108 lengths, but out here that's more like 150."

"Jesus..."

"Dude. This ain't prison. We can head back."

"Where's the turnaround?"

"Beyond that bend are the main electric lines. The first tower is .75."

"Let's go." Rowdell reset his determination. "I already paid $250 to enter this damn thing."

"Thank you for not making me call you a total pussy."

Rowdell gave him the finger and took the lead.

At the halfway point, T-Bag said, "How you feeling? Need some sugar yet?"

"No."

"Like I said, the effort is double and triple out here. Don't let it get away from you."

Their pale arms rose and fell out of the dark green water. The sun splashed a million pictures of itself across the shimmering bay.

At the three-quarter mark, T-Bag saw Rowdell lagging and called a halt. He peeled the tape from his ankle and handed Rowdell a packet. "Suck it down."

Treading water, Rowdell swallowed the goo. "Thanks."

"You good?"

"Yeah, man."

"No littering. Gimme that and then let's do some side-stroke. Break it up a little bit."

They scooted side-by-side down the coast.

"It is amazing," Rowdell said between breaths. "If the Navy sold this land it would be worth millions."

"Way more than that, bro." T-Bag kept the pace. "Never happen though. I heard most of its too contaminated to ever sell."

"Contaminated from what?"

"There used to be warships stationed here, dude. Like the whole main Atlantic fleet before they relocated to Virginia. That might just look like trees and woods back there, but there are also massive fuel tanks and bunkers loaded with God knows what leaking God knows what for decades."

"Awesome."

"Whatever. I hope they never sell it. We've got our own private gym right here."

"How in the hell does a guy from Boston end up a distance swimmer?"

"A thousand broken dreams, my friend."

"Where did you swim up there?"

"Revere Beach and north. Swampscott, Marblehead..."

"Such a strange obsession."

"A gross one, too. You wouldn't believe some of the shit I've come across."

"You ever been bitten by anything?"

"Jesus, what is wrong with you? You trying to jinx us?"

"No—"

"I ain't answering that." T-Bag was freaked out. "Let's go. That tiny speck over there is the car."

Their arms rose and fell again.

BOTTOM FEEDER

Eight days post-bankruptcy, on July 9, Fire Chief Al Draper responded to Receiver Tillinghast's request for $6.1 million in cuts in an email that was promptly leaked to the Sachem City Gazette. In it, he stated delayed response times for 911 calls, as well as the safety of his men, put saving money above the security of the city. The next day, the front page of the Gazette screamed, "FIRE CHIEF CLAIMS CUTS COULD JEOPARDIZE SAFETY."

It did not take long for the Receiver to respond. Citing irreparable policy differences, he asked for the Chief's resignation. Twenty-four hours later, when he did not acquiesce, Chief Draper was fired.

With the department about to be decimated by budget cuts, Receiver Tillinghast realized finding a quality replacement would be next to impossible. Besides, while Tillinghast would never admit it, a quality replacement would not agree to these cuts either. So he aimed his sights a little lower.

***

The Assistant Chief's position, which was largely ceremonial, had been occupied by Leon Fishbakke since 2005. Because of patronage, family ties, and seniority, he had spent most of his career skating by on his formidable political connections. The men on the line would have followed ex-Chief Draper off a cliff, but not A.C. Fishbakke. "Leo the Fish" usually worked a half-day and then completely disappeared. Other than his wife and people who knew no better, no one respected him.

He was ten minutes early for his meeting with Receiver Tillinghast. He had made sure his Class A dress uniform was dry-cleaned and spotless. His white officer's hat was tucked under his arm when he entered the mayor's office—the new home for Receiver Tillinghast.

"Good morning, sir." A.C. Fishbakke wished he had checked himself in the mirror one last time before walking next door to City Hall.

"Good morning, Chief." Receiver Tillinghast was the perfect contradiction—his manicured hand had a fisherman's crushing grip. "Thank you for coming over on such short notice. Have a seat."

"No problem, sir." As A.C. Fishbakke sat down, nervous sweat beaded his brow. From years of drinking, his Norwegian skin was a pale mosaic of burst capillaries. His blue eyes were still watery from last night's hangover, so he hoped his breath did not stink of gin.

Receiver Tillinghast closed the folder he was reading. As always, he was impeccably dressed, his hair an upswept silver wedge glued perfectly in place. "I suppose you're wondering why I've summoned you here."

"If this has anything to do with Chief Draper's letter, I can assure you I had no knowledge of its contents until it made the papers."

"Yes, that was rather convenient, don't you think?"

"What was?"

"The leak."

"Sir, as I said, I had nothing—"

Tillinghast held up a polished hand. "I take you at your word. It is unfortunate that Chief Draper and I could not form a better working relationship. As you know I've been handed an awfully big mess to clean up."

"Yes, sir."

"The math of all this is quite daunting, but the only way to get this city back onto a firmer financial foundation is through painful sacrifices we all must make together. All of us. This is not a popularity contest. The politicians who thought that are why we are now poised above this abyss."

"Yes, sir."

"Chief Draper knew this, but he chose otherwise."

A.C. Fishbakke said nothing. He would have been waiting to get fired if he was not still protected by the union. Line firefighters up to and including the Assistant Chief were in the union, but the Chief of Department was not and served at the pleasure of the mayor.

"You've been a loyal public servant for thirty-five years." Receiver Tillinghast consulted an open file. "In the last four years as Assistant Chief, you've overseen your duties with the utmost discretion. But a new day has arrived. And hard decisions need to be made. So I've asked you here to see exactly where you stand on these important issues, to see if you're a man that I, and more importantly the city, can trust. Going forward, everyone must be on the same page, share the same strategic vision so to speak. The new Chief of Department must be pragmatic, but also optimistic, because this city will rise again."

A.C. Fishbakke tried not to look stunned since a job interview was the last thing he thought this meeting would turn into. Caught off guard, he went to a default preset, which centered on himself and his now re-ignited ambition. Chief of Department Fishbakke. It had a nice ring to it. Even his old man had only made Battalion Chief. It also came with a better parking spot, a more expensive city-leased vehicle, and more vacation time. Having spent four years as Car 2, Car 1 was now in his sites. Department-wide, his detractors that considered him a joke would now have something to truly fear. It was a no-brainer, so he carefully said, "This city can't survive with leakers sabotaging mandates and agendas. Our differences must be put aside for the good of the city. So if you're asking me if I can support your plan for salvaging the place

I grew up in and love, I can only say yes, I certainly do. Sacrifices, as you said, must be made by all. The fire department can be no exception."

"Do you think you can deliver on this? It's a pretty high number."

"I do." A.C. Fishbakke thought about what this bump in pay was going to do for his pension. "I certainly do."

"You're going to make a great Chief." Receiver Tillinghast stood up. They firmly shook hands. He said, "Congratulations. My office will be in touch. We should announce this together. I'll have my people put aside time tomorrow for a press conference. Acceptable?"

"Yes, sir." A.C. Fishbakke was still sweating but felt like giggling. Hard work and perseverance were worthy characteristics, but so was being a politically adept survivor. He exited the mayor's office and, on the way out of City Hall, could not help eyeballing ex-Chief Draper's brand-new blacked out department SUV.

THE ASSAULT AND COUNTER ATTACK
July 12, 2009

Two days later, Receiver Tillinghast brought down the hammer at a 10:00 A.M. press conference. The same Federal Bankruptcy court that had appointed him Receiver, had just officially declared Sachem City bankrupt. Chapter 9 meant the City Council was immediately dissolved, and all union contracts were null and void. He now had the power to cut the fire department's minimum-manning and the union could do nothing to stop it. By contract, minimum-manning meant thirty-one firefighters had to be on-shift. Receiver Tillinghast wanted that thirty-one dropped to twenty-five, which meant more than six people would have to be out before overtime was called. The end result of this was "rolling blackouts." Two out of the six engine companies would be closed depending on how many guys were out sick, injured, or on vacation.

At the podium, Receiver Tillinghast gathered the attention of the room. His appearance, as always, was impeccable. He told a roomful of reporters, "Now I know a memo got leaked this week. *Ex*-Fire Chief Draper claimed these cuts could not be implemented without jeopardizing the safety of both the citizens and the department. But the new Chief, Chief Fishbakke, has assured me that is not the case.

We're trying to save money, not imperil this municipality. To this end, effective immediately, minimum-manning of the fire department will be dropped to twenty-five firefighters. There will be no more overtime. Firefighters will be paid for forty-two-hour-weeks but expected to work fifty-six hours before they will be paid 10% above their salaried rate. Citizens of this city can rest assured that the brave men and women of the Sachem City police and fire departments remain on call and ready to respond to any and all emergencies.

"Now, when we entered this process, everyone understood that in order to put this city back on a firmer financial footing, painful steps would have to be taken, sacrifices made. As of right now, I am completely dissolving the Department of Sanitation. Going forward, garbage and recycling will be handled by private contractors. I wish to tell all sixty-one members of the sanitation department that your dutiful service will not be forgotten. Please understand no one takes any pleasure in these cuts. Indeed, putting even more people out of work will only strain city coffers further, but in the long-term this hard decision will return to the city $18.4 million in annual savings.

"As for the Department of Public Works, it will survive but not without drastic cuts. Its seventy-one employees will be trimmed to twenty-nine. Again, I want to reiterate that myself and my team take no pleasure in removing people from the very jobs that support themselves and their families, but we frankly have no choice. The $34 million shortfall has left us with only bad and worse alternatives. To this end, the Department of Transportation will also see staffing cuts of fifty percent, from sixty-two to thirty-one members.

"Early retirement packages will be offered to all eligible employees. This will hopefully enable us to retain the younger members of these departments, thereby allowing for a certain amount of continuity.

"Concerning the Department of Education, many factors came into play. Sub-standard educations are not acceptable, and the youngest members of our society should not be persecuted for the crimes of their parents. We looked at staffing levels, student performance, test scores, and graduation rates. Poor results in three of those four categories prevented us from reducing staff. However, we will be instituting across the board salary cuts for all teachers, regardless of seniority. The final numbers will reset somewhere between fifteen and twenty percent.

"I would also, at this time, like to caution all remaining city employees—expect significant increases in your monthly health insurance responsibilities. We're still working through the numbers, but some employees will see increases of twenty to thirty percent. Yet even this is not the worst news. I've saved that for last. And it brings me no joy to say this. But unfortunately, our retirees will be affected as well. Although the city always told you your pension was sacrosanct, regrettably, over the decades, certain obligations were allowed to lapse. This gross negligence created a massive shortfall, which, after the collapse of Wall Street, has now turned into a $94 million disaster. Originally, the pension was supposed to be a fifty-fifty split between the city and its employees, but that was rarely the case. The city used that money for other projects instead of keeping its word, which is why I'm now forced to inform all retirees that they might see thirty to fifty percent reductions in pension payments."

Even a few reporters gasped as they furiously scribbled out their notes. The press conference had been hastily called for a reason—to prevent all hell from breaking loose. There were no union representatives, retirees, or current employees to explode in anger. Instead, a dozen reporters raised their hands and shouted questions, but only one got through. "Doesn't that seem, well, unconscionable? On the one hand you're offering early retirement packages, but if the workers do indeed take them, they could lose half their pensions walking out the door?"

"I'm not prepared to comment on what's conscionable—"

Another reporter asked, "Are you saying the unions have been informed of these decisions?"

"For the most part, yes."

"That doesn't sound too committal."

"Listen, this is an unprecedented event. Before today, no city or town in the history of Rhode Island has ever declared bankruptcy. We are in unchartered waters. This week it was Sachem City. Next week it could be Central Falls, Providence, or Woonsocket—"

"Is this why Sachem City was allowed to declare bankruptcy? To serve as a kind of break wall to protect the rest of the state?"

"No one's ever said that—"

A third reporter asked, "Getting back to the retirees, how are people in their seventies and eighties expected to survive? Doesn't this seem especially pernicious? I mean it's not like they can go back to work..."

"This country's work ethic is second to none."

"That doesn't answer the question."

"Sir," another reporter said, "Is that thirty to fifty percent just a stopgap until the city rights itself? Or is that a permanent cut?"

"As of now, regrettably, for the foreseeable decade at least, there is no other way." More whispers and murmurs filled the room. "So yes, I'd say it's permanent."

"Sir—"

"Thank you." Receiver Tillinghast left the podium as the reporters rose to their feet shouting questions left unanswered.

***

The press conference ended at 10:23 A.M. By eleven o'clock, as word spread, so did the outrage. While everyone knew Chapter 9 might be on the horizon, no one was prepared for what it actually meant, so what started out as a tropical storm quickly exploded into a Category 5 hurricane.

Downtown at Station 2, which was connected to City Hall, retired firefighters began appearing. Still salty, men in their 60's, 70's, and 80's started losing their minds. Members of the union's Executive Board arrived, hoping to head them off before things got worse. Which is exactly what happened after Fubar Freddy roared up on his 1963 straight-pipe Harley. He was wearing a denim vest as a patched in Viking, and his biceps still looked like rocks covered in tattoos. While the years had scalped the top of his head into a horse-shoe patch of baldness, his remaining hair was gathered down his back into a two-foot silver ponytail. Age may have worn down the harder edges of his physique, but his chest was still as big as a table, his blue eyes so bright they seemed to glow inside his skull. He parked right in front of Engine 2 and grabbed a baseball bat off the back of his bike.

"Sir," one of the new guys said, "you can't park that—"

"Get the fuck out of my way." Fubar Freddy was a 62-year-old former Force Recon Marine. He had been awarded the Navy Cross for extraordinary heroism in the Battle of Hué, a house-to-house operation that cost the lives of 668 Marines and wounded an additional 3,707. With his platoon pinned down and running out of ammunition, Fubar traveled a quarter mile in each direction under such intense incoming fire, the citation read, "those who witnessed it would later claim the jungle around him seemed to be shredding itself." But he also had a long jacket filled with too much aggression and close-calls, so after the Marines let him go, he returned to Sachem City with something to prove. To get on any fire department in the state, "wannabes" had to pass the Physical Performance Assessment, a torture-fest that included hose carries, axe swings, stair climbs, dragging charged hose-lines, and a 200-pound dummy drag. Wannabes had an eight-minute time window to complete the course. The average was seven minutes, but no one had ever broken four until Fubar crushed a time of 3:30. He practically laughed in the faces of those proctoring the test, asking, "That's all you got?" Outside, he found other just-finished wannabes gasping and puking.

He did most of his twenty-five years downtown on Engine 2. But this was no reunion. He pushed past all the guys yelling out greetings and kicked open the kitchen door. He had sat at this same table for a quarter of a century. The place was packed with the Executive Board and twenty retired guys already screaming when the door banged open.

"I want my job back." The baseball bat was an extension of Fubar's right arm that was pointed directly at Union President Lt. William Ahearn. "You tell the city I'm reporting for active duty."

"Freddy—"

"Fuck yes I am!" Fubar pointed the bat at the other retirees. "And if you guys are smart, you'll do the same. This wasn't part of the deal."

"Fubar's right." Big Al Frisky had only gotten bigger in retirement. But unlike Fubar, most of it was in his waist. Still, he was called "Risky Frisky" after a series of hairball grabs made over a three-week period in 1978 when the whole city seemed to be on fire. "If all the rules to the game have been suspended, who's left to say no?"

"Fuck yeahs," echoed around the kitchen.

"Guys..." Lt. Ahearn sounded like the only adult in the room but meant no disrespect. Seniority carried into retirement because the older guys had already toed the line. "Believe me when I tell you this union is going to fight every inch of today's decision. We're gonna file so many grievances their fucking heads are gonna spin. But with all due respect to each and everyone of you, this can't be your fight again. I don't even know where we would begin. You're not even in the union anymore."

"Begin what?" Fubar glistened. "You heard him! There ain't no fucking rules no more!"

"Here, here!" others yelled.

"Let me tell you this..." Fubar lowered the bat but everyone still watched it. Fubar, after all, was not a nickname that allowed for less. "I'm not gonna let anyone flush away everything I worked for. What *we* did. All the shit—the birthdays, holidays, and all the Christmases that got half-assed along the way. Naw, man, fuck that. That ain't gonna be part of the program."

Lt. Ahearn said, "Freddy, please—"

The bat came back up. "No one's stealing from me! You got that? No one! Half that money's mine! With interest! Period, end of story! Make me whole or cut my throat, either way those thieves next door ain't taking nothing off me!"

Someone yelled, "Fuck yeah, Freddy!"

"Fu-bar! Fu-bar! Fu-bar!"

Lt. Ahearn digested the moment. Realizing this was not a fight he could win at the kitchen table, he tried to meet halfway. "Let our lawyers start to eat. Guys, that's why they're on the payroll. Let them pick this shit apart because that's what they do. If Freddy's right, if there's no contract and no hiring practices exist, then let them make the case. Let them reference the other cities that collapsed before us. And if they say we have a fight, then let us meet them at the gates."

Applause and cheers filled the kitchen. The battle might have been joined, but things were about to get worse.

***

An hour later, like gathering armies, the sidewalk in front of City Hall was where the disaffected made their stand. Now jobless, the sixty-one people from the Department of Sanitation stood alongside other city employees also losing their jobs. Outraged retirees from every municipal department numbered in the thousands, so all of Blackstone Avenue in front of City Hall had to be closed. The police were having a hard time maintaining order since retired cops were looking for a piece of the Receiver as well. Because of this, the State Police sent four cruisers that quickly called for backup. That was even before Fubar Freddy scaled a mailbox and raised the bat like a sword, calling for the Receiver's head.

Lt. Ahearn, the president of the fire union, was heading around back to the rear entrance of City Hall when he ran into Donny Teagues. The President of the Department of Public Works union was twitching and almost purple with rage. As he kept pace alongside Lt. Ahearn, his index finger kept pointing like a dagger. "What did I fucking tell you?"

"Not now, Donny, the fucking Receiver's trying to start a riot."

"Fuck him. And fuck you too. Backstabbing fucks, the whole lot of you."

"That's constructive."

"I told you this would happen. We've been left for dead!"

"Who hasn't?" Lt. Ahearn disappeared into the back door of City Hall instead of taking the bait or knocking him out. Upstairs, in the mayor's old office, he found staff and advisors in an anteroom quickly hushing each other the second he rounded the corner. "I need to speak to the Receiver."

A tall thin man stepped forward, saying, "I'm afraid that's not going to be possible. His schedule is booked—"

"Have any of you looked out that window?" Lt. Ahearn's blond handlebar mustache formed into a frown. He was a broad-shouldered man with a belly and fence posts for arms, but his words were never wasted. "Who rolled this out? Which genius advisor was too stupid to understand what Tillinghast was unleashing?"

"Excuse me?" A smart looking woman looked up from her laptop. "And who might you be?"

"Seriously? As Chief of Staff, you're not off to a very good start, Miss Williams. I'm Lieutenant Ahearn, President of IAFF Local 121. Come look at this."

He stepped to the window and pointed. Still on top of the mailbox, Fubar was coming unglued in front of a very receptive audience. The police that were trying to remove him ran into a ring of retired cops giving no quarter. Lt. Ahearn said, "Best case he gets arrested. Worst case, hundreds of pissed off retirees force those troopers to make some really ugly decisions. So unless you want those guys"—he pointed at the news crews scurrying about—"filming the State Police clobbering senior citizens in front of City Hall, I'd suggest someone with a working brain stem get me in with Tillinghast ASAP."

"I think he might have a two o'clock open—"

Lt. Ahearn pushed past and threw open the door to the mayor's office.

Behind a large mahogany desk, Receiver Tillinghast raised his eyes above the reading glasses on the end of his nose. "Well, Mr. President, that was rather abrupt."

"We don't have time for this."

An aide said, "Sir, he just barged—"

"It's all right. Close the door." Tillinghast motioned. "Have a seat."

"I'm all set." Lt. Ahearn held up his phone and hit play. Receiver Tillinghast came to life at the press conference as the reporter asked, "'Have the unions been informed of these decisions?'"

"'For the most part, yes.'"

Lt. Ahearn hit pause. "Seriously?"

"You were all told this was a possibility—"

"Exactly. A possibility. If I remember correctly, there were many possibilities discussed, but nothing had been formerly decided upon. This was supposed to be a good faith negotiation."

"It was. Until our numbers didn't add up." Receiver Tillinghast peeled off his glasses and tossed them on the desk. "Do you realize if this city was a business, lieutenant, it would have been closed and sold for scrap?"

"Well, it's not a fucking business. It's home to 80,000 people suddenly wondering about their safety, their schools, and if someone's even gonna pick up the trash. Guess you got an 'F' in public relations."

"They didn't teach PR in law school, lieutenant, we had many other pressing matters."

"My bad. I didn't know stealing from old people was a class. Guess you got straight A's in that fucking thing. Let me ask you this. What're you gonna say at the next press conference, after all those retirees get manhandled by the troopers live on CNN? Because guess what's coming next."

"You do have a flare for the dramatic."

"I've also been burdened with common sense. Guess you missed that class in law school too."

"As well."

"As well what?"

"Grammatically. That's how that sentence should end. 'Guess you missed that class as well.'"

"Go fuck yourself." Lt. Ahearn banged open the door and stepped past everyone suddenly scurrying as if they had not just been caught eavesdropping. He descended six flights to the basement and went down a little used hallway. In a far back office, he found ex-Mayor Charles Houlinik. Now a mere consultant that worked from 9 A.M. to noon three days a week, Houlinik smiled at his guest even though he sensed Lt. Ahearn's deteriorating disposition.

Through it all, ex-Mayor Houlinik remained upbeat. Politically, if he was concerned about his future, he should have resigned outright. Instead, he was making $12,000 working part time for the same city he used to run. The insult was as obvious as the fact that he had been fairly elected, still in fact considered himself as such, the leader of a proud but ailing people. His political calculus was all wrong but nothing would change his mind. His cherubic face, the same one the old ladies loved to pinch when he was on the stump, lit up nonetheless. He motioned at the cinder block walls and said, "I know this new office lacks the opulent views—"

"Have you seen what's going on outside?"

"I... I've heard about the crowd, yes."

"If you love this place as much as you say you do, now's the time to show it."

"As what? As who? Because we both know my role here has been subsumed."

"That idiot upstairs is on the verge of inciting a riot."

"William, I am not in charge. Nor could I be seen committing such an overreach. You know that."

"I also know these people elected a mayor. Whether or not you've already forgotten that I would, if I were you, exploit this opportunity to its fullest."

"And afterwards I'd be escorted off the premises."

Lt. Ahearn looked around the tiny cement office. "I'd say that's already happened, wouldn't you?"

***

Fubar Freddy was still screaming from the mailbox when his audience suddenly abandoned him. The roaring applause confused him until he turned and saw ex-Mayor Houlinik at the top of the steps.

Shocked by the greeting, Mayor Houlinik tentatively waved at the crowd. But as the applause grew, the showman returned.

"Citizens of Sachem City!" he screamed. "We are a proud and resourceful people! We invented the machines that invented this country! We manned the mills that made this place the center of the industrialized world for over one-hundred-and-fifty-years! We have welcomed immigrants from across the globe, and since 1776, our sons and fathers have served in every war this great country has ever fought! For generations, we have always answered the call!"

The crowd roared again.

"But sometimes this rich history hides the sordid affairs of unscrupulous men, and there comes a time when the sins of the past can no longer be avoided. These will be the times where we will be tested. Where we will be asked to bear a burden, unfair though it may be. And it is inside these moments of turmoil that we must fight! As citizens of a city in a republic that may be experiencing a comeuppance none of us has asked for, is responsible for, but in fact must now shoulder. I'm begging all of you to try and find a way to vent your frustration without forcing the ugliness of this day to turn us against one another. Afterall, that's what *they* want!" His arm shot like an arrow toward his old office in the mayor's corner suite, and the crowd cheered back. "We will not be divided, we will not stand alone, and we will not be defeated!"

Beneath an overcast sky, and for however briefly, the desperate cries of the dispossessed finally found their voice.

PAYBACK

Hardball politics and payback for the impromptu rally started the following day. After the overtime numbers for the police and fire departments were mysteriously leaked to the Sachem City Gazette, the front page screamed, "THE HUNDRED THOUSAND DOLLAR MEN." Names and salaries became the headline without context. There was no mention of how both departments had been woefully understaffed for years. While some worked around the clock by choice, others were ordered and forced to stay. Salaried firefighters, whose base pay was $51,000, were making anywhere from $70,000 to $85,000, and their officers were even higher. It did not matter that some firefighters, especially the newer ones who were getting held nearly every other shift, were never home.

The public did not care. They were losing their homes and jobs faster than at any point since the 1930's and needed someone to blame. Absolutely no one wanted to read that a firefighter, officer or not, was making over $100,000. So whatever goodwill and sympathy the Chapter 9 debacle created for the unions and retirees disappeared barely twenty-four hours later. With one email, Receiver Tillinghast and his staff effectively destroyed the union's entire case with the public.

With both sides now at war, someone with connections to the federal court leaked out a startling number that Lt. Ahearn immediately seized upon. He was with the other union presidents holding a press conference when a reporter asked about the overtime numbers, so Lt. Ahearn pulled the triggers on both barrels.

"This is a man who published the names and salaries of first-responders for political gain. It's a tactic as old as politics itself—if you can't win fairly, fight dirty. Did a rescue captain on our job make a $109,000? You bet he did. He also worked an average of sixty-five hours a week to do it. His name is Charles LeClaire, a combat vet who served in Vietnam before coming home to ride Rescue 1 for thirty something years. And instead of saying thank you, the Receiver wants to smear this guy's reputation?" Lt. Ahearn held up a sheaf of papers. "I printed out an accountability for every shift he's worked from July 1 to July 1. Now, when we take this job, we understand we're gonna miss certain occasions. No big deal. But if I told you that you would have to miss Thanksgiving, Christmas Eve, July Fourth, and the birthdays of both daughters, would you still think he was stealing? On the rescue? Seriously, those guys barely have time to eat, much less sleep. We only have two. We've been pleading for a third for years, but the city never listened. Run numbers go up every year. Providence has seven and can't even keep up. We actually need four. The rescue guys are being ridden like mules, and when they go down from injury and exhaustion, guys off the trucks have to take over, creating even more stress on the system. So I know it's easy just to release a bunch of salaries and throw everyone under the bus, but do you know what gets rid of overtime five seconds from now? Properly staffing the job. Overtime would be zero. We currently have forty-six vacancies on a 136-man job. Do the math. Nonetheless, we're not gonna sit here and be anyone's punching bag—especially not from a guy making $275,000 courtesy of me and you, the taxpayer."

The place erupted with questions, but Lt. Ahearn specifically pointed at a reporter from the Sachem City Gazette. "Yes?"

"How has that salary been justified?"

"You tell me. Honestly, as a city taxpayer myself, I'm slightly horrified that a glorified accountant would be paid a quarter of a million dollars to rescue a city he just got declared bankrupt. Believe me, his salary ain't helping either. And as for his staff, there must be half a dozen PR people and professional handlers upstairs collecting salaries for doing God knows what. So while Local 121 will continue doing everything we can to make sure this job keeps running, I just want people to know we are here for you no matter what. Politicians come and go, but your sons and daughters have been answering the bell since the unification of this department in 1874. Nothing will ever change about that. Thank you."

Questions were shouted. Cameras snapped. But it was a done deal. In the ensuing days, the public vented anger at the Receiver, the unions, and filled the newspaper and talk radio with a growing hatred of their public institutions.

No one knew who to trust any longer.

THE BID

July 18, 2009

After the telephone was invented, the first phone lines strung through Sachem City were the ones connecting all the fire stations with a central dispatch. Since then, two unfortunate souls had been locked inside Fire Alarm every second of every day for the last hundred years.

Once the newbies could bid out, they either went to the rescues or transfer pool, because spots on the engines and ladders were impossible to score. Transfer guys had no home. They could be shipped to any truck on their shift, but usually ended up right back where no one wanted to be—Fire Alarm. However, for those newbies that wanted to learn the job, and EMS had certainly become the majority of it, the smart ones took spots on the rescues.

When the mass retirements happened July 1, forty-six vacancies were on the board. The ten new guys created by the grant meant a "bid" held to be held. By contract, this auction had to be held within thirty days of any death or retirement. This allowed guys to jump to wherever their seniority carried them. But the new Fire Chief, Chief Fishbakke, knew what would happen if he held a bid—everyone would abandon Fire Alarm and the Transfer Pool for line spots. Even the rescues might empty. This only meant all the junior guys would be forced to rotate back to their old spots since, as the old saying went, the job had to run. Just because no one was bid to Fire Alarm did not mean Sachem City was closing down its 911. As with everything else, seniority determined one's fate.

In order to avoid this chaos, Chief Fishbakke sent out an email stating a bid would indeed be held, but only for the rescue division and below. Basically, he walled off the line. People could bid to Fire Alarm, the Transfer Pool, or the rescues, but above that no one was going anywhere.

Anyone with enough seniority to leave the rescues immediately bitched. This move also held up the promotions of those next up to be made lieutenants, captains, and Battalion Chiefs. But all the ensuing unrest amounted to nothing. Chief Fishbakke simply rubbed it in by saying since there was no contract, all bets were off.

If he was not already hated, this arrogance pushed those wavering over the edge. As the leader of a workforce that widely considered his entire career an elaborate fraud, Chief Fishbakke's reputation had been destroyed years before. One of his newer, kinder nicknames was "Rapunzel," because he rarely left his second-floor office. But for his fellow academy classmates and others that had served beside him for thirty-five years, he had long been labeled a "bag of shit" and openly derided.

Since 1874, notice of a bid had to be posted at every station seven days prior to its occurrence. This was still the case, but technology also notified everyone by email. On that specific date at 10:30 A.M., the bid always occurred downtown at headquarters. Engine 2, Ladder 1, and the Battalion Chief's SUV were pulled onto the front apron to make room. A card table was set up with two seats—one for the chief and the other for Ma Dukes, the secretary for every chief since 1975. Her actual name was Margaret Duquesne, but she had been called Ma Dukes for decades. She got hired as a 22-year-old flower child and thirty-years later was a revered figure. She loved the job so much, in 1986 she even tried to become the first female Sachem City firefighter. However, the 200-pound dummy drag evolution during the Physical Performance

Assessment test eliminated her three different times. Thousands of firefighters had come and gone under her watch, so Ma Dukes knew all the legends. She might have started off a hippy, but her work ethic was as old school as the guys who came out of the mills or returned home from Vietnam. She was not afraid to take sides or call people out and was the only civilian allowed to do so. She also served as a direct line to the chief, so messing with her created a needless nightmare for those who did not realize where the true power resided. She handled so many administrative tasks upstairs, when she missed a month for an emergency gall bladder operation in 1985, no one got paid for two weeks.

Bids were like mini-reunions. Off-duty guys started showing up alone or, if their wives were working, with their kids and dogs. Those who rarely saw each other or worked opposing shifts, slapped hands and busted balls. Old partners, especially old rescue partners, formed a bond that never died. When people started dying in the back of the rescue at three in the morning, or when an engine company pulled up on a rollover with multiple fatalities, those ties lasted even into retirement. Some stories became part of department lore and retold a thousand times. Horrific tales or hilarious incidents became part of the oral history passed down generation to generation. Which is exactly how most bids ended up. Classmates from individual academies usually clustered together and remarked how fast time was going by. Today was no different. Super-Wop, Cheeseburger, Rowdell, Fonzie, Yoda, T-Bag and the rest of Class 61 were in front of the same gear-lockers installed when the place was built 123 years before. The history was everywhere. As were the jokes, because guys were always doing awful things to each other's lockers. When a certain lieutenant called out sick on Christmas—a near-death offense since that ruined someone else's Christmas—he came back to find his turn-out gear duct-taped around a Christmas tree and a Santa cap super-glued to his helmet.

On-duty guys started arriving by 10:15 A.M. Since Station 2 was in the center of the city, most companies could respond to their respective districts in a timely fashion. Even if guys were not bidding to another truck, they usually showed up to watch the drama. Some were on the fence about leaving their current spot, so they attended in case the unexpected happened. Everyone had a dream truck or crew they wanted to work with, and bids were unpredictable. Nonetheless, seniority was the cash money of the fire department. When certain trucks became available and twenty hands shot into the air, only the most senior won.

Already under siege, the job had sealed off the politicians and outside noise. Forty-six vacancies meant only ninety people remained. More importantly, for their own safety, they all knew it. In a show of support, sixty of them were now here for the bid even though only the very bottom guys were in the mix.

Ma Dukes came downstairs first and guys called out greetings. It was hard to tell her age because of how well she took care of herself. That was not the case for many 55-year-olds. Then Chief Fishbakke descended amid an undercurrent of murmurs and boos. He smiled and could not have cared less. His lapels, after all, were finally pinned with the golden Chief's medallions. He sat down with a cup of coffee and a sheaf of papers, calling out, "All right! Let's come to order!"

He was ignored for a full minute while guys wrapped up their conversations.

"Hello! Let's come to order!"

Voices trailed off. Ma Dukes smiled and waved at all the familiar faces.

Chief Fishbakke said, "Believe me, this won't take long."

The unnecessary dig about the abbreviated bid did not win him any fans. Guys stared at him with complete disinterest or outright disgust. Incredibly, he smiled into the face of it and said, "Let's start at the bottom. Fire Alarm, B-Shift!"

No one wanted it, so a transfer guy would just get sucked back in. When the chief got to Rescue 2 A-Shift Chauffeur, Yoda's hand shot into the air along with six others.

Chief Fishbakke said, "I don't even know who the new guys are. Which one of you is senior?"

"I am." Yoda seemed relieved. He wanted to learn the city and the job, and the rescue provided a PhD in both. Not only was he going to an awesome spot, but being on rescue also prevented him from getting suctioned back into Fire Alarm.

The SCFD had six autonomous divisions—Battalion Chiefs, Fire Alarm, rescue chauffeurs, rescue officers, line officers, and "the Line," which was the largest division and contained seventy other firefighters and the transfer pool. No one could work spots outside of their division unless they were covering someone else's shift as a favor.

Chief Fishbakke asked, "Who are you?"

"St. Pierre, sir." Yoda was psyched. Two years before this moment he had watched that man die at the bank. He was so stoked he turned to Rowdell, Fonzie, and T-Bag and high-fived all three.

Chief Fishbakke called out, "Rescue 2, D-Shift Chauffeur!"

Fonzie's hand went up. His smile echoed how happy he was to be released from the Transfer Pool and Fire Alarm. Some guys were here to do the job and make an impression, and Fonzie considered himself one of them. He was a "worker," a term of some significance. Certain skillsets were intrinsic among the best. Between the engine, ladder, or rescue, some were good at one or two of these disciplines but rarely all three. A few were afraid of heights and wanted nothing to do with climbing eighty feet to a roof that may or may not collapse. Likewise, others shunned the claustrophobia of interior operations and the brute struggle of hauling 200-pound charged hose-lines around an inferno. Beyond that were the rescue guys, who pretty much represented the department everywhere they went. Interfacing with the public, the hospitals, the police, and patients' families were just a few of the responsibilities they shouldered outside of the life and death decisions that took place some days on an hourly basis. Hiding on a fire truck was easy, but on the rescue no such thing existed. Those lacking skills were exposed at the speed of light. As chauffeurs, the newbies responsibilities included checking the truck for everything. Stair-chair, arm splints, leg splints, HARE traction for broken femurs, neck collars, backboards, the main

3,455-liter oxygen tank, turn-out gear, Scott packs, and that was just the outside compartments. Inside was a portable pharmacy/medical clinic. There were dozens of different sized bandages, gauze pads, needles, and breathing masks. Combat tourniquets and Quik-Stop clotting dust had been perfected and brought back from the battlefields of Iraq and Afghanistan. Bullet-proof vests, restraints, and forcible entry tools were beneath the bench seat. In the racks above were dozens of drugs to counter cardiac arrest, heart arrythmias, diabetes, allergic reactions, drug overdoses, asthma, COPD, emphysema and dozens more. The batteries for the Lifepack 12 Cardiac Monitor and their portable radios also had to be changed every shift. In addition, four portable jump-bags containing everything listed above, had to be accounted for as well.

By contrast, the rescue officer only had to check one thing—the drug safe with the morphine and valium. As Schedule II and IV narcotics, they were directly monitored by the DEA. Because of this, the logbook in the drug safe had to be signed by the officer of every shift. Felony charges, if any drugs went missing, were a career-ender. Felonies invalidated EMT licenses, and without those no one could be a firefighter in the state of Rhode Island.

Chief Fishbakke called out, "Rescue 2, C-Shift Chauffeur!"

More hands went up.

"Who's senior?"

"I am." T-Bag was ecstatic.

"Who are you?"

"T-Bag!" two dozen guys abruptly shouted. As always, just saying the name brought an instant smile to everyone's face. But Chief Fishbakke was so disconnected from his own rank and file, he did not even know it was a nickname. Instead, he thought he was being personally attacked. "There's a lady present!"

Laughter broke out everywhere as Ma Dukes smiled and whispered to the Chief, "That's him. That's T-Bag."

"Good Lord, what kind of name is *that*?"

Everyone laughed except Chief Fishbakke, who called out, "Quiet down! Next up, Rescue 1, C-Shift Chauffeur!"

Rowdell's hand shot up. As a transfer guy on C-Shift, he was already working with Capt. Charles LeClaire, but it would now become his permanent home.

"Rescue 2, B-Shift!"

"Here, sir." Super-Wop raised his hand. Unlike the others, he did not want the rescue, but he *really* did not want Fire Alarm.

With the line sealed off, the bid was over. The newbies now went to find their new bosses. It was customary to approach an officer *before* bidding to his or her truck. Without that blessing, just bidding over could be suicidal. Some guys did not like one another or trust their skills or reputations. Or maybe their work ethic did not match up. If someone liked sleep, they did not bid Engine 4 or Engine 2, because they were usually up all night. If the highway instilled fear, Engine 5 was avoided. Likewise for Code Reds, because Engine 1 responded to more first-due fires than any other truck in the city.

But for a bid like today, the rescue officers could not be asked before-hand. Half the rescues were vacant, so it was hard to know where anyone would end up. Besides, the rescue lieutenants and captains were used to turnover. Hardly anyone stayed on rescue, but the ones who did treated it as a religious calling. On the road all day and awake all night, they chased down the dawn like ghouls. Some guys got off on the pain of getting pissed on, puked on, bled on, and shit on, in more ways than one. In contrast, the sleep deprivation of Fire Alarm was only about surviving the slow death torture of forcing oneself to stay awake just to answer the phone. But on the rescue the line between life and death got straddled twenty-four hours a day.

T-Bag went to find his new boss. The officer on Rescue 2 C-Shift was Lt. David Killmoor. Twenty-eight years ago, Killmoor had been a rookie chauffeuring Capt. LeClaire on Rescue 1. Together, they shared an epic ride during the violence of the Cocaine Cowboys in the early

1980's. Now, Capt. LeClaire and Lt. Killmoor were the officers in charge of Rescue 1 and 2 on C-Shift respectively.

A gregarious people-person with a laid-back personality, "No Stress EMS" was Lt. Killmoor's moniker. The worse things got, the faster he slowed them down. Good rescue guys could keep someone alive during transport, but the great ones yanked people back from death. They shoved their fingers into bullet holes or whole hands into knife wounds trying to stop the bleeding. Comparatively, being on a fire truck was easy. But a rescue officer could make more life and death decisions in one four-day cycle than most line officers would in a month. Like drug addicts, Capt. LeClaire and Lt. Killmoor got strung out on the constant action, and before either one knew it thirty years had come and gone.

"Lieutenant Killmoor." T-Bag approached with an outstretched hand. "Hope you don't mind me just bidding over."

"Great to have you aboard." Lt. Killmoor was fighting with an outdated cell phone. "This goddamn thing..." Carrying stair-chairs and lifting stretchers for three decades had created a furniture mover's physique. He was bald up top but gray everywhere else—even his handle-bar mustache. His blue eyes were surrounded by the pink skin of someone who should not have been in the sun but played there anyways.

Lt. Killmoor stopped messing with his phone long enough to shake hands. T-Bag, like the rest of the newbies, wore the sweet smile of blessed freedom. With the Transfer Pool and Fire Alarm officially behind them, their real careers could now begin.

"Do you mind?" T-Bag held up his phone. "I just want a pic to remember this day."

"Sure." Lt. Killmoor grinned. "Fire Alarm's that bad, huh?"

"Oh God, I'm so psyched."

"That's what my last partner said and he only made it two months before bidding off."

"Yeah, well, no way the rescue could be worse than Fire Alarm. I never want to see the inside of that hellhole again. Dude"—T-Bag handed his phone to Fonzie— "can you snap a pic of us?"

Lt. Killmoor and T-Bag threw an arm around each other's shoulders and smiled for the camera. Within sixteen months, one's career would be over while the other's would be destroyed by injury. But for that moment, they were just two guys smiling at a camera downtown at Station 2.

PLAYING HARD
July 20, 2009

Two days after the bid, a caravan left Sachem City and headed for the beach. For a state that was only thirty-seven miles wide and forty-eight miles long, Rhode Island had over 400 miles of coastline. The public beaches charged for parking and admission and were always jammed. But for those seeking solitude and isolation, secret spots existed. T-Bag had found this one on the north side of Aquidneck Island while swimming up the coast.

Half of the twenty-four graduates of Fire Academy Class 61 were now gathered on this empty beach. They had coolers of beer and food. For those who just came off shift at 7:00 A.M., umbrellas provided shade for a quick nap. Only eighteen of the original twenty-four became Sachem City firefighters. Pus got hired by Coventry where his father was chief, two others went to Providence, one got a D.U.I., and the remaining two went to fire departments in East Greenwich and Woonsocket. Some just did not want to wait on the list and never get hired. But the economy crashing solved all that. Now there were openings everywhere.

For all the newbies, they worked their normal dayshifts, usually got held one or both nights, and then might get held again on the dayshifts between their nightshifts. This did not happen all the time. If enough guys volunteered for the now meager overtime rate, people went home. But because of the summer vacation schedules, some shifts never had enough guys.

For a brand-new newbie coming on shift, there were many adjustments, but none rivaled sleep. Most never had jobs that forced them to stay awake in a place like Fire Alarm or jump in and out of bed on the line. The rescue was even worse. On bad nights, they might not even get one hour in the rack. So these abrupt disruptions did funny things to people's sleep. A few could still fall asleep at a moment's notice, but others, after being woken up enough times during the night, just laid in bed and stared at the ceiling. Some never slept right again, even at home. Others awoke and stayed awake in the pre-dawn hours for no reason. After working four nights in a row, most newbies spent their first day off in a shattered haze of pain.

Joining them on the beach were six Emergency Room nurses from Ocean State Hospital. The groups had met while tailgating at a Kid Rock concert two weeks prior. Inevitably, random romances occurred. Fonzie quickly paired off with a tiny woman whose overwhelming personality counter-balanced his quiet disposition. He was 6'4" and Molly Bish was barely 5'0" and weighed 90 pounds. She had long blond hair, green eyes, and was always smiling. Skilled and highly regarded, she seemed carefree until the hardcore traumas rolled through the door.

T-Bag got pulled into Hayley Erskine's orbit because of her sarcasm and incredible tattoos. Both arms were full sleeves, and her back had twin mesmerizing Irezumi dragons that wrapped her shoulders and ended at her neck. Her black hair was shoulder length but always pulled into a ponytail. As a respiratory therapist who oversaw the care of patients with emphysema, COPD, and severe asthma, she was no fan of T-Bag's cigarette addiction. But she was no angel either. They shared the same reckless tendencies that at times hampered sound decisions. Their first date was supposed to be for coffee until a half-dozen tequila shots created a naked free-for-all on her kitchen floor.

Since neither one was particularly gifted with restraint, they were now crawling all over each other in the surf which, thankfully for those present, was deep enough to cover their antics.

Super-Wop, the Marine Corp bomb-tech, screamed out, "Get a room!" He was so in love with Rose, his wife, and Apollo, his dog, that he never went anywhere without them. Rose, like Super-Wop, had no problem dealing out the truth. "Pervs!" she yelled, and everyone hooted and clapped. Apollo barked in concurrence from his own blanket. Rose was a Special Education teacher well versed in the needs of the mentally challenged. Super-Wop jokingly swore this was the only reason their marriage had survived. Childless, they spent so much time at the gym, their wardrobes were primarily lycra and body descriptive. She was Italian and loud and unafraid to waste the unsuspecting, so Super-Wop just laid back and loved it all. He leaned in for a kiss and said, "I love it when you talk dirty."

"Don't push me, honey."

Yoda was there with his wife Cindy. She was a nurse in Galilee Medical Center's Oncology Unit. They were an intelligent couple wise enough to keep their own counsel, no small feat as far as the fire department was concerned.

"Yeah, Cheese!" T-Bag screamed from the water. "Get some!"

Cheeseburger guzzled from a handle of Jack Daniel's whiskey. Since he had started drinking even before they left Sachem City, he puked when they arrived, passed out for an hour, and was now back for round two. The sun was already turning his face and belly pink.

T-Bag could not get enough. "Cheese! Cheese! Cheese!"

"Stop it!" Haley was straddling T-Bag's lap, arms around his neck. Like the others, she was just a pretty girl in a bikini on a summer day. "Someone needs to stop him."

"Hell yeah, man, he's a fucking mess. Ha-ha! Cheese! Cheese! Cheese!"

She punched him as he just laughed and laughed. He held up a hand. "Row! Beer me!"

Jimmy Rowdell fetched one from the cooler and made a perfect lob. Then he sat back down next to Annie Sadler. She was a 32-year-old trauma nurse and respiratory therapist. Physician's Assistant was her ultimate goal but that was years away. Recently divorced, she originally wanted time alone until the Kid Rock concert knocked her off course. She only noticed Rowdell after he sprang into action when another tailgater gashed open a palm on broken glass. Once he peeled off his shirt to wrap the person's lacerated palm, Annie's baser instincts caught the hard-chest and striated veins webbing his forearms. That night, they made small talk and eventually disengaged from the others. She thought he seemed simple but entirely genuine. Including today, they had been on four dates, but Annie was not giving anything away for free. Still adjusting to the single life, she told him point blank she was in no rush to make any more mistakes.

The guys started grilling hamburgers as the afternoon wore on. Narragansett Bay was a summer painting of blue sky and sailboats. Rhode Islanders were an aquatic people who utilized every second of good weather before the endless New England winters returned.

As they ate, they talked shop. The nurses were no strangers to long days and overnight-shifts, but even they were appalled by what was happening in Sachem City. Sixty to eighty-hour work weeks seemed inhumane. Once guys went on shift, there was no telling when they would be home. Babysitters, petsitters, parents, or kind neighbors had to be drafted on short notice. The Battalion Chiefs set the board for the 7:00 A.M. dayshift at 6:00 A.M., and the 5:00 P.M. nightshift at 3:00 P.M. That left the newbies an hour or two to find coverage for their pets, kids, or second jobs. "The Master Board" was a spreadsheet document available on every station computer. It was an official roster for the upcoming shift. Starting from the Battalion Chief down, every truck position was listed horizontally. Engine 1 officer, Engine 1 senior private, Engine 1 junior private, all the way down through the rescues.

Hayley Erskine, seated next to T-Bag, said, "It would be one thing if you were still in that place, what did you call it?"

"Fire Alarm."

"Yes, in there. At least you could rest. But all of you are now on the rescue, right?"

"No. The bottom eight guys are in Fire Alarm, and the first ten of us are either on the rescue or transfer guys sent anywhere. It just depends."

"Well..." Annie Sadler handed Rowdell the rest of her hamburger. "I have to say, in all honesty, if I call 911, I don't want some zombie that's been working for eighty hours straight showing up at my house."

"I hear ya." Rowdell chased the burger with a swig of her beer. "But together an engine and a rescue means five guys show up. The officers don't get held at all, and the privates with enough seniority only get ordered to stay after all of us newbies get held first. So someone will be awake."

"Great." Annie shook her head. "Must be awesome entering a burning building after working sixty hours straight."

Super-Wop was slathering himself in oil. Even his eyeballs seemed tan. He tossed the oil to Rose. "Babe, lube my back?"

"Lube it!" T-Bag immediately screamed.

"Who wants to do more shots?" Cheeseburger hoisted the handle. He was a big boy who was turning from pink to red in the hot sun. Usually shy, the alcohol changed all that. And since he had spent the last two cycles driving for Capt. McCarrick on Engine 2, he needed to blow off steam. Screamed at, stressed out, and tortured, public toilets saw less abuse than Cheeseburger on Engine 2. Dutch Carrigan tried to shelter him as much as possible, but Capt. McCarrick only accepted perfection. Nothing was sacred. Cheeseburger could not drive right, do chores right, or exist in any way without Capt. McCarrick's constant disapproval.

"I'm down, Cheese." Rowdell reached for the whiskey.

"Me too, please." Hayley Erskine squeezed T-Bag's bicep. "Wanna play?"

"Absolutely."

They both swigged off the whiskey before running back into the surf.

Later, they played volleyball, women against men, which the women promptly won. Twice. Once the sun began to set, they piled everything into the cars and headed for Newport. Now was the time, because once on-shift tomorrow, none of them knew when they would be home again.

RESCUE 2

July 22, 2009

The good news for all the newbies who landed spots on the rescues was that they now had a permanent home. Rescue 1 was housed at Station 1, Rescue 2 at Station 4. Arriving newbies got assigned two sets of lockers. One was for their fire gear on the apparatus floor, the other was in the dorm for their uniforms and personal items. Lacking seniority, they got assigned the worst of everything and took whatever was offered.

Two days after the beach party, T-Bag showed up at Station 4 on his first day with the exuberance of a kid handed a new toy. With an engine, ladder, and rescue, Station 4 was the biggest in the city. There were eight people on shift, four shifts altogether, so thirty-two firefighters called the 4's home. In comparison, a single engine company house with four shifts had a total of twelve people.

Existence at Station 4 was a blood-sport. With so many outsized personalities, newbies walked a fine line between slow acceptance or immediate ostracization. The smart ones kept their heads down, mouths shut, studied their map-books, and cleaned everything they could. One thing they did not do was make a coffee, sit at the kitchen table, and run their mouth. Those who chose that path instantly had thirty guys labeling them a "bag of shit," an unfortunate turn of phrase that became the main drain through which many careers quickly dissolved.

T-Bag arrived with his gear, two uniforms, and a pillow. He was so happy to be out of Fire Alarm he would have slept on the floor if ordered. He made sure he walked up to everyone, introduced himself, and shook hands. It was a superfluous gesture because his nickname meant the whole department already knew everything about him, but it showed respect.

T-Bag found Lt. Killmoor in the kitchen drinking coffee, so he said, "Morning, Lieutenant. I'm gonna start the truck check unless you need anything."

"Sure. You can start by checking my locker and throwing my gear on the truck." Then he smiled. "Just kidding. Have at it. Don't forget the batteries."

"Roger that."

"And one more thing..."

"Yeah?"

"No Stress EMS."

"If you say so. Right now, I'm psyched but also pretty freaked out."

"Why?"

"Lt. Stokes told me all about his first day on the rescue."

"The *Dude*?" Lt. Killmoor winced at the mere mention of the name. "Are you trying to *hex* us?"

"I've never heard anything like it."

"You've been transferred to the rescue before, so technically speaking this is not your first day. Don't *do* that shit to us, man."

The Dude, Cody Stokes, was a twenty-year veteran who got on the job at 19-years-old, so he was now only a few years older than the oldest newbies. Stokes' first day on the line was spent as chauffeur on Rescue 1, and the rest became part of department lore. While both rescues did well over 5,000 runs a year each, Rescue 1's half of the city had more "quality runs," which meant they contained a fair measure of everything bad. Both halves of the city were working-class, but the crime and gangs were worse on the west side. So in the span of Stokes' first ten-hour dayshift, he started with a Code 99, then had a fatal car wreck, a riot at a funeral, a suicide, and a 9-year-old girl hit by a bus who literally died right on their stretcher. When he went home that night he thought about quitting but got addicted instead. He did five years before flaming out and jumping to Engine 1 and Engine 4 respectively.

To allow for drive-through access at Station 4, there were three twenty-foot-high garage doors on either side of the building. The engine and ladder went out the front, the rescue out the back, and reserve trucks were stored in the other bays.

T-Bag started the "truck check." For the rescue, this could take upwards of an hour. But he did not even have time to put his gear on the squad before the tones hit and Fire Alarm announced, *"Attention Rescue 2 and Engine 6. Still Alarm. 135 Ballan Avenue."*

"Jesus Christ!" Panicked, T-Bag jammed everything into the soot-smeared gear compartment, including his extra uniforms and pillow.

Lt. Killmoor strolled out with his coffee and, after seeing his new partner having a stroke fumbling through a map-book, said, "I think I know where Ballan Avenue is."

"No." T-Bag found the page. "It's my job as chauffeur."

"Okay." Lt. Killmoor was amused because they went to 135 Ballan Avenue sometimes three or four times a day. It was where Pete DeAngelis lived. Hit by a drunk driver twenty years prior, DeAngelis suffered partial paralysis of his entire left side. He could only shuffle/walk with the use of a cane. One hand was retracted into a claw that never moved, and the other twitched from overuse. The left half of his face was permanently frozen from the head injury, so everything he said slurped out of the right side of his mouth. Incredibly, his house, which was purchased as part of the $3 million DUI settlement, was spotless. He would have been a sympathetic figure except for the fact that he took unbelievable satisfaction in torturing the police and fire departments. Home all day, he just sat in his garage chain-smoking and calling 911 for no reason.

"Ha-ha, ya cocksucker!" he called out once the rescue came to a stop.

Lt. Killmoor yelled out the window, "Morning, Pete. Do I even have to get out of the truck? I know it's not professional, but medically speaking, you look pretty good from here."

"Ha-ha! Lazy cocksucker! I know you. I know you!"

"Jesus." T-Bag threw it into park. "What the fuck is wrong with this guy?"

"Everything. Time for a meet and greet. You're gonna love this." Lt. Killmoor grabbed the mic. "Rescue 2's on-scene. You can cancel Engine 6."

Fire Alarm answered, *"Roger, Rescue 2, on-scene at 0715. Engine 6 receive?"*

"Engine 6's in service. Thanks, 2." The engine roared by them and honked its airhorn, appreciative of being freed from this nonsense.

"What's going on, Pete?" Lt. Killmoor slowly approached. "We gonna play nice today?"

"You sons of bitches!" Because of his half-frozen face, everything became a sneer. His one good eye followed their movements. "Ya dirty sons of bitches! I know you, but I don't know you!" He jabbed his cane at T-Bag. "I'll break you yet, ya bald cocksucka!"

"Dude..." T-Bag could only grin. "You can't do this, man."

"Do what?"

Lt. Killmoor said, "Insult someone nicknamed T-Bag."

"*T-Bag?*" Pete DeAngelis' one good eye grew wide. "Ah-ha-ha! Outstanding, ya dirty cocksucka!" He chanted with glee, "T-Bag! T-Bag! T-Bag!"

A police cruiser came to a stop. The officer, watching Crazy Pete yell something awful as two firemen hysterically laughed, could only shake his head. Brendon Haggerty was a two-tour Army veteran on the downside of a failing marriage. "For the love of God, Pete..." Haggerty slammed his door. "We're not doing this all-goddamn day."

"T-Bag!"

"What'd you call me?"

"That's him!" Pete pointed with his cane. "That cocksucka right there! T-Bag! T-Bag!"

"You can't insult public servants!"

Lt. Killmoor was having too much fun, so he said, "Naw, man, that's his name."

"Jesus Christ. You firemen really are a bunch of freaks." This sideshow, at seven in the morning, was clearly not appreciated. "Listen, Pete. You got three choices. You can go inside, you can go with them to the hospital, or you can come with me to jail for abusing 911."

"I'm abused!" he slurped. "I know my rights!"

"Jesus Christ—"

"Haggs..." Lt. Killmoor waved him off. "We got this."

"You sure?"

"Yeah. As much as I want to see him go downtown, he could still bail out and get home, which means I'll be back again this afternoon. But if I take him all the way to Ocean State Hospital, he'll be totally f—"

"I'll go inside! Ya cocksuckas! I'll go inside!"

"You sure?" Lt. Killmoor tried to sound sincere. "We'll still take you to the hospital if—"

"I'll go inside, ya cocksuckas!" Pete stood up and wobbled. Lt. Killmoor and T-Bag each grabbed an arm and helped him inside. They made sure he was back in his wheelchair before Lt. Killmoor pointed at the phone. "Pete, the next time you dial 911 and it's not a legitimate emergency, forget about OSH, because I'm driving you all the way to freaking Westerly. By the time you get home from there I'll be on my days off. Capiche?"

"Yes! Ya gray cocksucka! Ya old bag of shit!"

"Okay." Lt. Killmoor patted his shoulder. "Just so we understand each other. Have a nice day."

"Fuck you, cocksucka. T-Bag! T-Bag! T-Bag!"

"Nice to meet you, Pete."

They closed the door and found the cop still trying to restrain himself. "This is gonna be some kind of fucking day all right."

"You living the dream?" Lt. Killmoor asked.

"Barely." Officer Haggerty frowned and got back into his cruiser. "Those died long ago."

***

They returned in service and stopped for ice coffees. Back inside the truck, Lt. Killmoor opened the steel contractor case that contained the blank run reports. Then he took out four pictures and put them on his visor. He smiled at them in greeting before seeing T-Bag's curious expression, so he said, "My girls and my son. My wife and two daughters."

"Oh yeah?"

Unbeknownst to T-Bag, from this point until their partnership abruptly ended in disaster, this was a ritual completed before every shift.

T-Bag asked, "Your wife work?"

"She's a nurse." Lt. Killmoor sipped his coffee. "My daughters are finishing college, and my son's in the Marine Corp."

"Nice."

"What about you? Got any kids?"

T-Bag burst out laughing and switched lanes after barely looking. "Oh God, that's too horrific to even contemplate."

"So's your driving. Do you even know what a blinker is?"

They got dispatched to a car accident as the morning rush hour commenced.

Once on-scene, Lt. Killmoor was instantly disgusted. "It's a gross new day, alright." They were at a rear-end crash so low-speed the airbags in both cars did not even deploy. There was also no visible damage to either car, not even the bumpers. But all four people in the front car were claiming neck and back pain. As they pulled out the stretcher, Lt. Killmoor said, "We call this a trial lawyer's delight. Not to mention four ambulances are about to be tied up for the next hour for no reason."

T-Bag said, "No wonder car insurance costs so much."

They headed to St. Elizabeth's Hospital. The "Big E" or "Easy E" was the same hospital that had existed in one form or another since 1846. Back then it was in a converted triple-decker. Now it was a community hospital with a 300-bed capacity and a full ER that handled everything except major trauma. Those went directly to Ocean State Hospital's Level One Trauma Center eight miles south of Sachem City. In between was also Galilee Medical Center, a renowned facility that specialized in strokes and cardiac events.

In matters of life and death, state protocols called for patients to be transported to the closest hospital. Emergency Rooms were expected to have the capability even if they did not have the expertise, so they got tasked with keeping people alive until they could be transported to a more appropriate facility. The exception were children. Unless they had an obstructed airway and would otherwise die, all of them went to Hasbro in Providence.

From the car wreck, the four rescues, two from Sachem City and two from out-of-town, caravanned to St. Elizabeth's because no one was hurt enough to justify a trip to OSH. Lt. Killmoor and Capt. LeClaire finished their run reports before joining chauffeurs T-Bag and Rowdell in the ambulance bay.

Lt. Killmoor said, "Bet you young-ins didn't know me and the good captain here used to be partners. He was my boss many moons ago."

"Too many moons." Capt. LeClaire chuckled. "So many moons I lost track."

"He broke me in right, even though I drove him nuts. In the beginning, I sometimes left the auxiliary battery on by mistake, and we'd go out to the truck for a run and it would be totally dead. The good captain here would never get mad. He'd just shake his head as we hooked up the jumper cables, saying, 'Davey, Davey, Davey.'"

"What about the time you ran out of gas?"

Lt. Killmoor loudly laughed. "That was a good one. I forgot about that."

"That was real low stress EMS, all right."

"Sure was."

Rowdell said, "One night when we were in Fire Alarm trying to stay awake, we did the math. Each rescue does something like 5500 runs a year. Divided by four shifts times thirty-years turned into something like 80,000 people transported between you both."

Lt. Killmoor said, "Your math is off. The good captain's been on the squad longer than me. Thirty-three years?"

"Thirty-four. Thanks for making me feel even older."

Dispatch interrupted them. *"Fire Alarm to Rescue 2."*

Lt. Killmoor toggled his shoulder mic. "Rescue 2."

"Status?"

"Clearing the Big E momentarily. You gotta run for us?"

"That's a roger."

"Send it."

"25 Linwood Street for a panic attack. Do you want an engine company?"

"Negative. It's a frequent flyer."

"Roger."

Capt. LeClaire said, "Isn't 25 Linwood Shaky Eddy?"

"It sure is." Lt. Killmoor clapped T-Bag's shoulder. "Good thing we already stopped for coffee. Ready to make a difference?"

"Roger that, boss. Run number three and we ain't even been on shift an hour."

A police cruiser went screaming past and that should have been omen enough. They hit the lights and sirens and followed the cop to Linwood Street. That was where a large white man in pajama bottoms and a wife-beater T-shirt yelled and swung a baseball bat at an old woman.

"Oh boy." Lt. Killmoor grabbed the mic. "Rescue 2 on-scene with police."

"Roger. Rescue 2's on-scene with police at 0805."

Lt. Killmoor quickly exited the truck. The Sachem City police were all professionals, but in matters of lethal force they were not bashful. Especially when guns and knives were aimed against them. Or some poor mom was about to get her skull bashed in with a baseball bat.

Statewide, over the past decade, five of the fourteen fatal police-involved shootings had occurred in Sachem City. But there were no protests. And there were no charges. By protocol, to remain transparent, the State Police and Attorney General's office were immediately called in to investigate after any police involved fatality. In line with its old school traditions, it was a sentiment consistently shared throughout Sachem City's racially diverse neighborhoods—nine times out of ten people who pulled guns on the police usually got what they deserved. As far as the fire department was concerned, having that kind of backup allowed them to do their jobs without fearing for their safety.

"Wait!" Lt. Killmoor ran by the cops. One held a taser and the other a gun pointed at the ground. "Eddy! Listen to me. You can't do this, man." Lt. Killmoor stood in front of the mom as she yelled to the police, "Please! He hasn't taken his meds! Please don't shoot him!"

Shaky Eddy circled right with the bat cocked on his shoulder. A longtime bipolar hallucinatory schizophrenic, Eddy Snell was supposed to be on a cocktail of drugs including Thorazine and Haldol, powerful anti-psychotics that usually left him in a tranquilized stupor. His twitchy hands were a side effect, hence the nickname Shaky Eddy. But when he refused his medications, all 6'3" of him became a legitimate threat. Recently released from a state psychiatric facility due to budget cuts, 43-year-old Eddy Snell was forced to move back in with his mom on Linwood Street.

Lt. Killmoor kept the mother behind him as all three now circled the yard. "Eddy, I know you're in there. You gotta put that bat down. Okay? You got everybody out here all excited."

"That's not what they told me."

"Excuse me?"

"He's been hearing voices all morning!" his mother gasped, heartbroken. She was crying hysterically because two more cops had arrived with drawn guns following this dangerous dance. "Please don't kill my son!"

"Ma'am, get back." One of the cops dragged her to safety.

"Eddy, it's me. Remember me?" Lt. Killmoor desperately searched

Eddy's eyes for any hope. "I've transported you before. Last time we were playing B.B. King on the way to the Easy E, remember? We talked about Lucille."

"I want my dog!"

His mother cried out, "Bosco's dead, Eddy, please! Put down the bat before they shoot you!"

Eddy Snell paused. He looked at the bat with a sudden confusion.

Lt. Killmoor held out his empty hands to show he posed no threat. "Can you just come with us to the rescue? We'll check your vitals."

"I'm... I..." Eddy seemed suddenly exhausted. He dropped the bat and started to cry. "What did I do? Where's my mom?"

"I'm right here, honey!" She waved from behind the cruiser. "I'm fine! You didn't hurt me!"

"I'm sorry, mom!"

"Eddy, please..." Lt. Killmoor extended a hand. "Please, man, I'm begging you."

Eddy went to his knees and sobbed. The police moved in and gently took him all the way down to search him. Once cleared, he followed Lt. Killmoor to the rescue. T-Bag was still in awe. "Some panic attack."

"Right? Guess I shouldn't have cleared the engine." Lt. Killmoor hopped in the back. "Let's just roll. I don't want to waste any time while he's calm."

"Roger that." T-Bag slammed the rear doors closed after Lt. Killmoor refused a police escort.

They arrived at St. Elizabeth's six minutes later. Shaky Eddy was a 280-pound man on a 150-pound stretcher, so pulling him out of the truck had to be done in one fluid motion. Thankfully, he was light compared to the four, five, and six-hundred-pound people that were now routine.

Shaky Eddy was so tired he was already nodding off. Since no one wanted to live in a drug induced prison, it was not uncommon for psychiatric patients to refuse their medications. Depending on the severity of their condition, abstaining could provide a brief return to lucidity, or turn into a terrible mistake that might end in a death spiral of hallucinations and bullets. Either way, no one took joy in using any type of force against someone so sick they did not even know what they were doing.

Like any newbie worth his salt, T-Bag was always on the hunt for helpful tips or new tricks. As he yanked out the stretcher, he saw Lt. Killmoor had utilized the straps as makeshift restraints without Eddy even knowing it.

Inside the ER, triage nurse Mary Durando waited. She was a twenty-year veteran who ran the whole shift. Arriving ambulance crews quickly learned that messing with her could prove highly unproductive. As the gatekeeper, Mary had the power to turn a five-minute patient exchange into a thirty-minute nightmare if so provoked. To remain on her good side, a medium iced coffee with two creams and sugar went a long way.

She was typing on her stand-up computer when they strolled in. "Hello again, Rescue 2, it's been what... a whole twenty minutes since we last saw each other?"

Lt. Killmoor said, "Any longer than that and I'll develop separation anxiety."

"Hello, Eddy." Mary appraised him over her bifocals. "Heard you refused to take your medications again."

"I don't like them." His sweaty, balding hair was stuck to his scalp like seaweed as he grew more agitated. "And this place has too many lights."

"Eddy, relax." Lt. Killmoor glanced at nurse Mary. "It might be nearing midnight for Cinderella..."

"Bed six. Security's already waiting."

"Roger that."

Afterwards in the truck, T-Bag was blasting Pantera before Lt. Killmoor got in and immediately turned it off. "Oh no, my friend, that is definitely not low stress EMS."

"What's good, baby? You probably like stuff with feelings, right?"

Lt. Killmoor acted insulted. "Human beings do have feelings."

Grinning, T-Bag slipped on his sunglasses. "Hall and Oates? Captain and Tennille?"

"How dare you. I am a child of the 70's."

"Gross."

They compromised on the Clash and headed back to the station. As they backed in, dispatch said, *"Fire Alarm to Rescue 2?"*

"Goddamnit." T-Bag stopped backing up and hit the lights. "I really need to take a piss."

Lt. Killmoor clicked the mic. "Go ahead, Fire Alarm."

"Are you available for a run?"

"That's a roger."

"Respond to Gilmont Park. Report of a man down."

"Roger."

Fire Alarm hit the Alert Tone and said, *"Attention Rescue 2 and Engine 3, Still Alarm. Gilmont Park."*

"Go take your piss," Lt. Killmoor said. "That's Asshole Tree, where all the drunks hang out and fight. Besides, I'm in no rush to see those guys."

"Who?"

"Do you know Lt. Cunty Conti? He and his privates are the worst shift at the 3's. What's so funny?"

"You just said cunty and privates in the same sentence."

Minutes later they screamed down Scarborough Avenue toward Gilmont Park, which was actually a boat dock where people had fished the Massasoit River since the first settlers in 1671. Others huddled in the shadows and drank and schemed. Diehard alcoholics were usually strewn about covered in some form of their own biological matter.

As Rescue 2 descended the hill toward the river, Lt. Killmoor said, "That's not good." He pointed at one of the guys from Engine 3 who was bent over puking. The other two were giving a prone figure a very wide berth.

"This is gonna be bad." Lt. Killmoor grabbed the mic. "Rescue 2's on-scene."

"Rescue 2 on-scene at 0930."

T-Bag parked next to the engine and saw a figure writhing in the dirt.

Lt. Conti and the remaining private who was not vomiting looked very much like they wanted to.

Lt. Killmoor said, "It's the Chin."

"Who?"

"Robert Lowell. DOB 8-13-61. SSN 188-34-3467. Allergies to sulfur and latex. Used to be a mechanic in the Navy. I've picked this guy up so many times he might as well be family."

"Why's he called 'the Chin?'"

"Because he's got no teeth and a massive under-bite."

As they approached, T-Bag smelled it from twenty-feet away. Like meat left out in the August sun, it was a stench those who smelled it never forgot. And listening to someone else's stomach emptying mere feet away did not help.

"So..." Lt. Killmoor glanced at Lt. Conti. Opinions on Paul Conti rarely varied. A hard-charger at the beginning of his career, after he blew out his knee at a fire and returned to work sixteen months and three surgeries later, his attitude was never the same. For guys that got hurt and missed two or three weeks, it was no big deal. But the badly injured were often set adrift on an ocean of red tape and humiliation. As payback, after his recovery, Paul Conti returned to work determined to do nothing for the rest of his career. And like one sour apple attracting two others, his privates were awful EMTs nicknamed "Useless" and "Toe-Tag." Together, the three of them were widely considered to be the worst engine crew in the city. Like the U.S. military, Congress, the police department, City Hall, and any other massive bureaucratic institution, the fire department had places for the uninspired to hide. It was a story as old as the world and never to be altered. Wherever there was one there was another, and on and on and on.

Lt. Killmoor said, "Since you guys got here first, what's the assessment?"

"Gee, I don't know, Dave." Lt. Conti all but laughed. "It's the Chin. I'm guessing he's completely fucked up."

"Yeah, but what's that stench?"

The drunks usually reeked of feces or urine or both, but this smell killed them all. It was what dead bodies smelled like. But the Chin was very much alive. Lt. Killmoor rolled him onto his back and immediately winced. Open belly wounds appeared to be moving. Lt. Killmoor looked closer and saw maggots crawling in and out like busy commuters. The tissue that was not infected was necrotic and filled with a gangrenous stench. Lt. Killmoor fought the rational instinct to puke and flee but said instead, "Congratulations, Chin. In twenty-eight-years I've never been left speechless."

With no teeth, the Chin gummed something unintelligible through his massive under-bite. He was so drunk he moved in slow, crab-like movements, so slow that he looked like an injured sloth. His clothes were a collection of stains and stink, his patchy beard filled with dried vomit.

Lt. Killmoor saw that T-Bag was more fascinated than horrified, which was definitely a good sign. But he could not say the same for the guys on Engine 3, who were absolutely no help standing thirty feet away. Knowing they were a do-nothing crew with a horrible reputation, Lt. Killmoor could have cut them loose, but now he wanted to punish them instead. "Get the stretcher and some sheets."

They returned with the requested items as Lt. Conti said, "I'm not touching this fucking guy."

"Paul—"

"Naw, man, fuck that. He did it to himself."

"Huh. Kind of sums up your whole career."

T-Bag, stunned, watched the rage do funny things to Lt. Conti's face. Since the fire department lived on the serve and volley, comebacks were expected. But Lt. Conti could only stammer, "Fuck you, Dave." He motioned his guys toward the truck. "And fuck this nonsense. Let's go."

"Was it something I said?" Lt. Killmoor high-fived T-Bag. "Let's roll him onto the sheet and lift him to the stretcher."

"You got it."

"How come you ain't puking yet?"

"I used to empty my dad's colostomy bag three times a day. Ready?"

"Yeah. On three. One, two, three."

When they rolled him onto the sheet, it released a whole new odor.

"Oh man." T-Bag winced. "Code Brown, yo."

"Code Brown. Jesus, Chin, you're a godawful mess today, buddy."

The Chin grinned and slowly gummed something no one understood. They hauled him to the rescue. T-Bag hoisted the stretcher, Lt. Killmoor lifted its wheel-rack, and T-Bag shoved it inside. They were a new team, so this procedure had to develop into one flawless motion.

Once inside the truck, the stench banked down in concentrations too pure not to comment upon. Or gasp against, which T-Bag futilely did. He hit the switch that fired the evacuation fans but nothing happened. "Shocking."

"Yo, you gotta see this." Lt. Killmoor pointed at the Chin's ruined abdomen. In the light, maggots crawled through the wounds and tubes of intestines leaving muculent trails. "Chin, how did this happen?"

The Chin took twenty seconds to gum out, "In...glec...shun..."

"What?"

"Infection." T-Bag flinched like someone caught wondering what it might feel like to be eaten alive by maggots.

"Dear Jesus..." Resigned, Lt. Killmoor finished assessing the Chin. "Let's get vitals, an IV, blood sugar, and then it's off to OSH. Saint E's can't handle this."

"Roger."

"Wet down a trauma dressing. Let's at least cover this mess up."

To start an IV, T-Bag sat on the bench next to the stretcher. At this close range, withstanding the malodorous assault became an epic test. "It's like a gumbo of shit, piss, puke and pus."

The Chin and Lt. Killmoor both laughed. The Chin was slowly rolling his head side-to-side like an inebriated Stevie Wonder. His slitted eyes flared open as he mouthed something no one understood.

"At least he has a sense of humor." When T-Bag pushed up the Chin's sleeve for the IV, maggots fell to the floor. "Gross." He popped them beneath his boot and stared at the unwashed arm. He cinched a tourniquet above the elbow, searching for a vein through the smear of pure filth the alcohol swab created. "This is gonna be the fastest IV in the history of the world."

"Don't jinx yourself." Lt. Killmoor collected the BP, pulse, and SpO2. "Stick that thing and let's roll."

"Roger that." T-Bag sunk the 18-gauge and ran a bag of saline to counter the dehydration. He then deposited a drop of blood from the needle onto the glucometer strip. "Blood sugar's 117."

"Incredible. BP is 110/70 and pulse is 72. He's got better vitals than I do."

"He feel hot to you?"

"Good point. Get a temp."

T-Bag jammed the thermometer into the Chin's ear and waited for a beep. "101."

"Seriously, with all he's got going on, that's nothing. A true infection would be jacking up anyone else's pulse with a temp through the roof."

"Maybe there are unseen benefits to chronic malnutrition, alcoholism, and homelessness. You ready to jet?"

"Yes, sir."

T-Bag toggled his shoulder mic. "Rescue 2 transporting to OSH."

"Roger, Rescue 2, transporting to OSH at 0952."

Lt. Killmoor speed-dialed the triage nurse at Ocean State Hospital and said, "Good morning, Kathy. This is Sachem City Rescue 2. We are transporting a 47-year-old male, known alcoholic, with an advanced infection on his stomach. This infection is now an open wound with visible intestines. And maggots. Lots and lots of maggots."

"Is that you, Dave? Are you busting my chops?"

"It is and I am most definitely not. Wait till you see it. You'll be able to tuck this image away and think about it, like I never will, even after you retire."

"Thanks. You're always looking out. ETA?"

"Six minutes. My partner's got the pedal on the floor out of consideration for myself."

"Great."

"He's also a Code Brown on top of everything else."

"Code Brown?" She chuckled when she figured out the meaning. "Good Lord, see you soon."

Lt. Killmoor ended the call and yelled, "Partner! The sequel to the Code Brown just arrived!"

"I'm going as fast as I can, bro!"

"I'm not sure which is worse—your reckless driving or the current state of the Chin's undergarments."

T-Bag grabbed the mic. "Rescue 2 is off at the State."

"Roger, Rescue 2, off at Ocean State at 0957."

"Five minutes!" T-Bag shouted, reversing the squad into the bay. "That's gotta be some kind of record."

Rescues from six different cities clogged the ramp. As an acute care facility, OSH had an 800-bed capacity and was the largest hospital in the state. They wheeled the Chin into the ER which, as always, was completely overrun. The ER at OSH processed a daily average of 420 patients. But no one had a problem with the Chin jumping to the front of the line. His stench, for the unprepared, was so bad it already had multiple people gagging twenty seconds after the doors closed.

Nurse Kathy came right over. She was a mid-fortyish woman with a strong stomach, but nothing could prepare her for what was happening beneath the dressing that Lt. Killmoor peeled back. She immediately covered her mouth so she did not gasp inappropriately. "They're waiting for you in CC2."

Critical Care 2 housed millions of dollars of equipment designed to handle the worst traumas and multi-system life threats. Dr. Aguilar Dosroyo was already gloved and masked up. Same with the other P.A.'s and nurses.

"Lieutenant Dave." Dr. Dosroyo was the son of high school sweethearts who fled Honduras forty years earlier. As the lead trauma surgeon in the only Level One Trauma Center in the state, Dr. Dosroyo was the last face many people saw before they died. This carnage created a dark humor he only shared with people he trusted, like Capt. LeClaire and Lt. Killmoor. Two months prior, when Lt. Killmoor had wheeled in a dying gunshot victim, Dr. Dosroyo only had time for one thing—cracking open the man's chest with a bone saw right in CC1. As he did, he turned to Lt. Killmoor and said, "You ever do open heart massage?"

"Uh, no."

"Well, get ready. Today's your lucky day."

A bullet had bored a perfect hole through the heart which, incredibly, was still beating. They shocked it into asystole so Dr. Dosroyo could quickly stitch it up around the cadence he kept for Lt. Killmoor, "Squeeze... squeeze... squeeze..."

Dr. Dosroyo now said, "What'd you bring us today, Dave?"

"Hey, Doc. This is Robert Lowell. He's a 47-year-old male with a long history of alcoholism. He's currently homeless. Allergies to sulfur and latex. BP 110/70, pulse 72, BG 117, temperature 101. He's got an eighteen-gauge IV KVO in the left AC. Developed a skin infection on his stomach that went untreated, so it's turned into this..."

"Oh my..." As Dr. Dosroyo tried to corral the escaping maggots, onlookers winced and gasped. "Let's sedate him please."

5 mg of Midazolam was pushed through the IV.

Dr. Dosroyo looked at Lt. Killmoor and said, "Watch this." He poured hydrogen peroxide into the Chin's open wounds which immediately began to bubble. The maggots did not care for this because they began streaming out of the intestines in protest.

"Guess I'm not eating lunch today," one of the nurses quipped.

"Are you joking?" T-Bag leaned closer. "In some cultures, they're considered a delicacy."

Lt. Killmoor laughed. "Come on, junior, before you horrify anyone else."

"You sure? A little lemon and cocktail sauce could really get this party started."

"Ugh," Nurse Kathy said. "Your new partner leaves quite a bit to be desired."

"You don't know the half of it."

Dispatch interrupted them. *"Fire Alarm to Rescue 2."*

"Go ahead, Fire Alarm."

"Are you available for a run?"

"Negative. Clearing the State momentarily."

"Roger."

"Come on, partner," Lt. Killmoor said. "Let's grab supplies in time to save the world."

***

With the morning rush hour ended, I-95 was wide open.

Lt. Killmoor sipped his coffee. "You ever listen to Chuck Berry?"

"What was the Depression like, grandpa?"

"Asshole." Lt. Killmoor inserted a compact disc. Seconds later the opening riff to Johnny B. Goode filled the rescue. Lt. Killmoor grabbed the dashboard mic. "Rescue 2 to Fire Alarm. We are back in the city, back in service."

"Roger, Rescue 2, back in service at 1027."

Lt. Killmoor looked at his ringing phone. "It's Mikey back at the 4's." He answered it. "Yes, Michael."

"Hey, L-T. You guys in on lunch? We're thinking about doing tacos."

Lt. Killmoor looked at T-Bag. "You in on tacos?"

"Absolutely."

"Yeah, Mikey, we're both in. That's if we ever make it back to the station."

"No shit. You guys are getting your dicks kicked in and it's not even eleven o'clock."

Lt. Killmoor ended the call and told his new partner, "For your information, Chuck Berry invented rock and roll."

"Have I said a thing? I'm actually enjoying it. It would sound even better if Slayer did it as a cover."

"*Slayer?* God help me. The only thing worse than your taste in music is your driving."

"Ah-ha-ha!"

Dispatch said, *"Fire Alarm to Rescue 2."*

"Go ahead."

"562 Pasquale Street. 26-year-old male with flu-like symptoms."

"Roger. Responding from 95 North."

"Rescue 2 responding at 1035."

"You ready to make a difference?" T-Bag flipped on the lights and sirens and punched the gas. "Hang on, Flu-boy, here we come!"

"God help me."

Pasquale Street was in a former Italian neighborhood now inhabited by a sizeable Caribbean population.

T-Bag squinted at the rundown houses. "You got an address over there?"

"Just passed 502. It'll be on my side any second."

"Roger."

"Rescue 2 to Fire Alarm. On-scene."

"Rescue 2's on-scene at 1041."

"You think that's him?" Lt. Killmoor exited the truck and yelled, "You call the rescue?"

"Yes, I did."

"What's going on? They said you got the flu?"

"Yes, I think so." The young white man was wearing tight jeans and a T-shirt with a cat on it. "It started last night."

T-Bag came around the corner of the truck. "Nice cat. This him?"

"Yes."

"Who's that?"

"My friend," the man said. "He's gonna meet me at the hospital."

"He has a car?"

"Well, yes."

"Then why didn't—"

"Here we go." Lt. Killmoor helped him up into the rescue. He said to T-Bag, "Let's just roll. I'll grab vitals on the way."

"Roger that." T-Bag triggered his shoulder mic. "Rescue 2 transporting to St. E's."

"Roger, Rescue 2, transporting at 1043."

***

They cleared St. Elizabeth's at 11:15 A.M. and made it back for lunch. T-Bag was finally conducting the truck check five hours into the shift when Fire Alarm hit the Alert Tone.

"Attention Rescue 2 and Engine 6. Still Alarm. 172 Eagle Street. Elderly female with a possible prolapsed uterus..."

After they got in the truck, Lt. Killmoor made the mistake of asking, "Have you ever seen one of these?"

"Who hasn't? Don't you watch porn?"

"Trust me, this is nothing pornographic. It only occurs in older women. Basically, the pelvic floor muscles and ligaments weaken and collapse. Sometimes the uterus protrudes from the vagina."

"Ex-squeeze me?"

"Any physical activity or rubbing, obviously, can create ulcers."

"Maggots and vaginal ulcers, what a day..."

"In this case, compassion, empathy, and consideration are the only treatments we have to offer, so please keep that in mind."

"We park our cars in the same garage, my friend." T-Bag hit the gas. "Hang on, Grandma, here we come!"

Since District 6 was the last middle-class area, Engine 6 was the slowest truck in the city. Residents either had health insurance or good-paying jobs or both. This was also where the World War II generation was slowly dying off. Most of the houses were capes or single-story ranches with small, pristine yards.

"Fire Alarm, Rescue 2's on-scene."

"Roger, Rescue 2, on-scene at 1220."

Lt. Killmoor knocked on the front door. "Hello! Fire Department!"

"Please come in!" a faint voice called. "In here, I can't..."

They heard quiet sobbing as Lt. Killmoor led the way. "Where are you?"

"Upstairs." More sobbing. "In the bathroom."

T-Bag glanced around the immaculate house.

Upstairs, Lt. Killmoor found an elderly white female sitting on the edge of a bathtub.

"I'm so sorry," she said. "I'm so embarrassed."

"Honey, stop it. Don't worry."

She was wearing a nightgown hoisted to her waist. Her bright gray hair and homely face could have made her anyone's grandmother, except for her hands. They were shaking as her terror-filled eyes stared at the bloody towel laying over her crotch.

"Miss, what's your first name?"

"Roberta." Her tear-streaked face looked up at Lt. Killmoor. "Roberta Parlou."

"Okay, Roberta, you're gonna be fine. Would you mind if I take a look? How long have you been diagnosed with the prolapse?"

"It's only been a month but it's getting worse. I can't hardly walk. Or urinate." Ashamed, she turned her head and lifted the towel.

Lt. Killmoor leaned in and saw a bulging mucus-covered membrane protruding from her vagina. It was the size of a small fist and visibly irritated. "Roberta—"

"I'm so sorry you have to see me like this."

"Stop. We do this all day long. Believe me, there ain't nothing we haven't seen a hundred times before."

"You poor man."

Like any situation involving intimate female issues, whether benign medical calls or horrific beatings and sexual assaults, the presence of extraneous men never helped.

Lt. Killmoor turned to T-Bag. "Stair-chair and a stretcher. I'm cancelling the 6's."

"Roger."

"Rescue 2 to Fire Alarm. Cancel Engine 6."

T-Bag returned with a stair-chair and a white hospital bed sheet. The stair-chair was the primary means of carrying people down from upper floors. It had collapsible arms at its feet and shoulders.

T-Bag set up the chair with a sheet. Roberta took a seat before they cocooned the sheet around her. Two shoulder harnesses crisscrossed her body to lock her in. She apologized again for the inconvenience.

"Are you kidding?" Lt. Killmoor joked. "We just had tacos and refried beans. We should be apologizing to you."

"Yeah, darling." T-Bag squatted and grabbed the handles. "It's gonna be a long, pain-filled afternoon."

She laughed before catching herself, and finally just relaxed.

T-Bag looked up at his boss. "Ready?"

"Roger that."

"Okay, Roberta, here we go. Keep your hands in and don't grab anything. 1-2-3."

They lifted her as T-Bag carefully stepped backwards with the front end of the stair-chair. He looked over his shoulder to line up the stairs since he would be going first. Then he called out, "Good to go?"

"Roger that."

They began the descent in total synchronization. Stair-chairing people was awkward and dangerous. The person on the bottom handles carried most of the weight, while the person on top tried avoiding a horrendous back injury while bent with the chair hanging between their legs. Luckily, she only weighed 120 pounds. The real career-gambles came with people who weighed 300, 400, or worse.

Once outside, they lifted her onto the stretcher and loaded her into the truck. T-Bag grabbed a bottle of wipes and cleaned the vaginal blood and urine off the stair-chair. In the truck, they started an IV, took vitals, and then headed for Galilee Medical Center.

***

"Rescue 2 to Fire Alarm. Did you say 516 Columbia Drive?"

"That's a roger."

An hour after dropping Roberta at Galilee, Rescue 2 tore across the city. Lt. Killmoor said, "This is Sergeant Slaughter."

"Who?

"Delmar Higgins. We're getting him a lot now. Kid's a local hero. After 2001, he and seven other seniors enlisted. Three went into the Army, and the other five shipped off to the Marines on Parris Island. They called them the "Sachem City Five" because they all ended up in the same division. I think it was the 1st Marines. They pulled a bunch of deployments. Invasion of Iraq, the Battle of Baghdad, and both Battles for Fallujah. By the end of 2006, two of the five were dead, one was dishonorably discharged after some kind of drunken nonsense in Germany, the fourth tested for the SEALs, and the fifth, Delmar Higgins, retired to become a cop."

"Incredible."

"When he first got back, he was working construction and taking classes at night. Since his grandfather was one of the first black cops in the city, and his father's currently a captain, all he had to do was finish school and he was pretty much guaranteed a spot in the next academy. But six months after he got back his PTSD went crazy. The battles returned. Then came the insomnia."

"Jesus."

"When the NyQuil failed, he switched to booze and drugs. He lost his job, quit school, and bounced in and out of programs at the Providence VA. Now, whenever he gets overwhelmed, he just grabs a bottle of booze and heads to his roof." As they turned the corner, Lt. Killmoor nodded and said, "There he is. I was hoping we'd get here before he climbed up there."

"What's with the roof?"

"He used to be a sniper."

Two police cars were parked out front.

"Rescue 2's on-scene with police."

"Roger, Rescue 2, on-scene with police at 1301."

"What's the plan?" T-Bag asked.

"That guy, his asshole neighbor, makes everything worse. They've been beefing for weeks. He torments him by blasting machine gun noises from his stereo."

"You've got to be shitting me."

They joined the four cops speaking with the irate neighbor who was yelling and pointing up at Delmar Higgins.

Lt. Killmoor asked, "What's the problem?"

"Problem or *problems*?" the neighbor scoffed. "As usual, he's up all night, banging around his goddamn garage, talking to ghosts, drinking—"

"You know what, man, what's your name again?"

"Justin Radcliff."

"You know what, Justin? You're a real piece of shit. That guy's a combat vet whose brain is fracturing into smaller and smaller pieces every day. Now, I know for a fact that you two have been beefing for weeks. Last time I was out here you were blasting off fireworks just to torture the poor guy."

"That's not true—"

"It is true because I was here." Lt. Killmoor pointed at the cops. "How many of you guys are vets?"

Two out of four raised their hands.

Lt. Killmoor looked at Radcliff and said, "Any idea what happens to vet-hating pieces of shit after they've been arrested?"

"For what?"

One cop said, "How about disturbing the peace?"

"Or battery," another added, "and you're also creating a public nuisance."

"What about him! He's getting cocked on his fucking roof!"

"Is he becoming hysterical?" Lt. Killmoor asked the police. "Because altered mental status means we might have to put him into protective custody for his own safety and the safety of others."

"Sir, turn around."

"Are you kidding me? Do you know who my uncle is?"

"Sir, please turn around."

"What if I don't comply?"

"Ultimately, that is not an option."

"Man, fuck that guy!" Radcliff looked up at the roof and screamed, "You hear that you crazy fuck? Fuck you!"

"That's it." The cops took him down. "Stop resisting!"

"I'm calling my uncle! He's an assistant D.A.!"

"Even better. Hopefully he'll be the one filing charges against you at your arraignment."

"Come on." Lt. Killmoor grabbed T-Bag and headed for the ladder. "Heard you used to be a roofer."

"I was."

"Good. You go first. I hate ladders."

"Roger that." T-Bag started climbing.

Up top, Delmar straddled the ridge. He was average height but still in shape, his hair high and tight. His Jamaican blood made him look blacker than the shingles he sat on.

T-Bag rested his hands on the roof and said, "Hey, man."

"You thirsty?" Delmar smiled, swigging off the bottle. "Funniest part is that I always hated whiskey."

"I'm gonna pretend I didn't hear that blasphemy."

"Be careful, man, that gutter's loose."

"I gotta climb up there, dude. My boss is right behind me and you and him need to speak. Cool?"

"That's fine. But no one comes near me."

"Fair enough." T-Bag scampered up to the ridge like a lemur through a forest.

Delmar said, "Some view, ain't it?"

T-Bag scanned across the sprawling triple-deckers and mills and said, "It's got a funky kind of beauty, all right."

"Hello again, Delmar." Lt. Killmoor poked his head above the gutter, but the rest of him would be going no further.

"Afternoon, lieutenant. I'm really sorry about all this. I know how much you hate ladders."

"All in a day's work, right? You know that better than anyone else. But just the same, how about next time you shut the garage door and drink in there instead?"

"Deal." Delmar took another swig. "Believe me, every day I wake up I hope there is no next time. But it never lasts. And no one knows how to make it stop, neither. None of them."

"You taking the meds they gave you?"

"Nope. They make me anxious."

"Yeah, well, having this conversation thirty feet in the air is making me anxious. But not him." He nodded at T-Bag. "He used to be a roofer, so this ain't nothing to him."

Delmar nodded. "I knew something was up when dude came scurrying up here like a monkey." He glanced at T-Bag. "Ain't it liberating? To have no fear of heights?"

"My pops used to say working at height was even more fun because you could die at any moment."

"Spoken like a true nut-bag." Delmar raised his bottle out of respect. "Part of my job was providing over-watch with the long gun. They always had me as high up in the sky as I could climb."

"Death from above."

"Fucking A."

"Excuse me," Lt. Killmoor said, "I hate to break up this disturb-a-thon, but the cops cuffed and stuffed your neighbor, so you won't be seeing him anytime soon."

"Ain't it something?" Delmar asked, disgusted. "It was for assholes like that..."

"I know. I hear ya. But ain't nothing ever gonna change about that though, right?"

"Man..."

"This has to be about you. End of story. Screw that guy. Now please come down. Okay? We'll take you over to the VA, get you checked out."

Delmar paused. He took another guzzle before offering T-Bag the bottle.

T-Bag said, "I can't, dude, I'm on duty." But then he winked and took a pull nonetheless.

Lt. Killmoor shook his head. "Didn't your dad die from falling off a roof?"

"Yup."

"Well, wasn't that an important lesson?"

"It sure was. Enjoy the fuck out of what you're doing because the next second might be your last."

"Amen." Delmar looked relieved. "Thank you."

"Let's get out of here."

They followed Lt. Killmoor down the ladder.

***

"Fire Alarm, send two additional companies and the B.C."

Fire Alarm hit the All-Call and announced, *"Attention Engine 1, Engine 2, Battalion 2... Special Signal. Assist Rescue 2 on-scene at 438 Wilkinson Way..."*

"I don't know what to say." T-Bag was as amazed as he was disgusted. "How is this even possible?"

"Welcome to the Rescue Division."

They waited at the truck for reinforcements. Upstairs on the second-floor, 600-pound Jasper Voitjchek was basically an invalid.

Lt. Killmoor said, "You ever hear of Big Oscar Rodriguez? He's been on Oprah a bunch of times. Anyway, he's our biggest customer. Weighs 1,100 pounds and the same thing happened to him. Didn't leave the second-floor for years and before anyone knew it, he couldn't even fit down the stairwell. We had to cut a ten-foot hole in the second-floor wall and lower him on the basket of Tower Ladder 1."

"Dear God. This is some country. How is it acceptable to be so fat you can't even fit down your own stairs?"

"It's the families, man, they just keep feeding them. You just met the mom. Ain't she the sweetest little thing you've ever seen?"

"She's five-foot nothing and weighs ninety pounds. And Jasper's as big as a Toyota. Did you smell that room? The milk jugs filled with piss?"

"Brutal. She says he knocks them over all the time. He can't even fit in the bathroom."

"That poor lady. Imagine speaking to your own mom like that?"

The engine companies rounded the corner. The Battalion Chief pulled up next. No one wanted to be there.

"Whaddaya got, Dave?" Acting Battalion Chief Brigado Rossi was actually the captain of Engine 4. He did not want to be a Battalion Chief and so never took the eligibility test, but because of seniority and all the vacancies, he was forced into the B.C.'s position nonetheless. Outside of being responsible for the whole shift and 80,000 residents, the Battalion Chiefs handled a myriad of administrative tasks few enjoyed.

"Hey, Briggs." Lt. Killmoor had known Acting B.C. Rossi since they were kids on Gallston Avenue. In 1987, Brigado Rossi had entered department lore after one long night on Engine 1. A knife-wielding rapist created a hostage situation in The Kitchen, a violent neighborhood, which then escalated into a four-hour marathon of fruitless negotiation. Tired of waiting, Rossi consulted with his boss, Lt. Elmore, a Vietnam veteran crazy enough to have volunteered for one of the most dangerous jobs of the entire war—clearing tunnels filled with VC. But that night in The Kitchen, the two of them snuck a deuce-and-a-half beneath the window. In unison, one smashed the glass at the same second the other fired the hose into the chest of the would-be murderer. Getting hit with a garden hose was one thing, but taking a fully charged deuce-and-a-half through a smooth bore nozzle at 150 PSI did uncontrollable things to the human body. Smashed and pinned into the corner, the rapist virtually drowned before the cops crashed the door.

Currently, Lt. Killmoor said, "Upstairs we have Jasper Voitjchek. I believe in the business they call it 'failure to thrive,' but for all intents and purposes he weighs over 600 pounds. I know you're an east-sider, but we deal with this guy a lot. A month ago, Engine 1 showed up and two of the guys dragging him down the stairs got hurt. He's a cripple-fest. Last time, the family was told by the Fire Marshal that he had to be kept on the first-floor, no exceptions."

"Goddamnit. I'm trying to set up the board for the nightshift and now I have to deal with saving Shamoo?"

"There is no easy way to do this. Since he's been lying in bed for God knows how long, his legs atrophied. We either bust out the saws like we did for Big Oscar, or we drag his ass down the stairs again. That's it. Those are the options."

"Pretty fucking grim, L-T."

"I know. But just because he made these decisions doesn't mean our guys have to pay for them. Personally? I'd drop a K-12 into that wall in a second if his mom wasn't so nice. Besides that, she's old. Having her second-floor torn apart is gonna be traumatic."

"So what're you telling me, Dave?"

"We drag him to the stairs and then he slides down them on his ass. No carrying. He can probably still fit."

"Done. What happens when he makes the landing? The stretcher can't handle that kind of weight."

"I told Fire Alarm to call around for a bariatric truck. If not, we toss the stretcher and just wedge him on the floor. If that fails, we'll put him on a flatbed like we had to do with Oscar."

"Do whatever you have to. I can't believe this job's turning into some kind of wildlife rescue." He turned to T-Bag. "You want OT tonight? If not, no offense, but you're probably getting held."

"Okay, Chief. I'll go wherever."

"Excellent." Chief Rossi glanced at Lt. Killmoor. "I'm going back downtown. Shout if you need me."

"Roger."

Back upstairs, eight firemen winced at the stench.

"Two things," the Engine 1 lieutenant said. "How much does he weigh? And will he fit through the door?"

"680 pounds and he did last month." Lt. Killmoor twisted a bed sheet lengthwise until it morphed into a taut, pseudo cable. "Let's twist up two more of these. We'll put them under his knees, butt, and shoulders. With six guys—three per side—we should be able to land him on the floor."

"Excuse me!" Jasper said. "I'm laying right here, I'm not invisible. Stop speaking about me like a piece of meat!"

Lt. Killmoor kept his composure. "What were you told last time, Jasper? You were told to stay on the first-floor."

"I don't have to—"

"You were told that if this place ever caught fire, and you were on the second-floor, you were as good as dead. Remember that conversation?"

"My mom talked to them, not me—"

"You're lying. Now listen to me. You called us for help. And we're gonna get you out of here. But all of these guys have a right to go home to their families uninjured. We need to do this so it's safe for you and us. Roger that?"

"Yes, okay, all right."

Jasper Voitjchek's boxer shorts were stained and large enough to wrap around a gas grill. The rest of him was unwashed and covered in grease. They worked the sheets beneath his five-foot width. His armpits, breasts, and chins had formed a cheesy substance between the skinfolds, which, once disturbed, released a sour milk odor. His feet were purple blocks cemented to swollen calves that no longer worked.

"Here's the plan," Lt. Killmoor said. "We lift him to the floor. Three guys standing, three guys on the bed. Questions?"

There were none because the stench was close to unbearable. Three guys stepped up onto the soiled bed and grabbed the rolled-up sheets. Their boots sunk into the mattress, which had been turned into a giant diaper long ago. Three guys stood ready beside the bed.

"On three. One, two, three!"

Voitjchek hit the floor with a thud. "Ouch! Easy!"

"Are you hurt?"

"Not yet."

"Great. Because here comes challenge number two."

They wrapped his legs with two sheets and dragged him out into the hallway. His purple feet were dangling over the stairs as Lt. Killmoor stood above him and said, "This next part you have to do alone. You're gonna inch down step-by-step. One at a time."

"I can't do that."

"I don't think you get it. You *have* to do that. We can't even fit guys in this stairwell to help you. It's either this or we wreck your mom's house for no reason except for the fact that her 46-year-old son has given up so badly he can't even walk downstairs anymore."

"You don't have to be so mean!"

"Come on, Jasper. Help us help you, man. Okay? That's all we're asking."

"All right, all right!" He slowly raised up to his elbows but could barely support his own weight. "Here we go."

It took him ten minutes to make it to the first-floor.

Lt. Killmoor toggled his mic. "Rescue 2 to Fire Alarm. Any luck with that bariatric truck?"

"That's a negative, Rescue 2. We called three companies and their trucks are tied up. Closest E.T.A. was two hours."

"Roger, thank you." Lt. Killmoor turned to everyone else, including Jasper. "Time for Plan B."

T-Bag yanked out the stretcher and set it aside. Then he backed the rescue up to the front door. After adding a fourth sheet, all eight guys carried him straight out the door and into the squad.

Municipalities could not afford to man bariatric trucks for the morbidly obese. Instead, private ambulance companies had stretchers as big as single beds inside ambulances the size of milk trucks. When none were available, alternate actions had to be taken.

The fire trucks caravanned to St. Elizabeth's. In the ambulance bay, two orderlies pushed an oversized bed directly up to the rescue. Together, ten of them hauled Jasper onto the bed. When its digital scale read 702 pounds, no one could disagree.

Once Lt. Killmoor and T-Bag were back in their truck, neither knew what to say.

T-Bag threw it into gear. "I wish I could erase that last hour of my life."

"You too?"

"Fire Alarm to Rescue 2."

"Perfect." Lt. Killmoor grabbed the mic. "Go ahead, Fire Alarm."

"Report to the city garage for a changeover. Per order of Car 2."

"Roger."

"Changeover for what?"

"We been so busy I forgot to tell you. This thing's been leaking oil for a week. Apparently, they waited until four o'clock to fix it."

"Interesting."

They headed to the city garage.

***

The Department of Transportation operated out of two giant airplane hangar-sized buildings in the industrial part of town. Decimated by the recent layoffs, the mechanics that remained were like characters from the bar in Star Wars located on the planet Tatooine. A dozen guys had nicknames like Peanuts, Jughandle Johnny, Slim, Puddin' Head, and Sad Sam, who was the lead Fire Department mechanic. A colorful group, they all wore oil-smeared jumpsuits and chomped cigars, busting balls all day long.

The lack of mechanics meant the acre-sized parking lot was jammed with dump trucks, salt trucks, excavators, vans, pick-ups, loaders, pavers, police cars, fire trucks, and the trash trucks waiting to be sold now that the Department of Sanitation had been dissolved. The backlog of injured trucks was so great the mechanics only laughed when department heads called up inquiring about the in-service date of their broken vehicles. But the rescues were different. They had to be kept on the road. Sachem City had two reserve rescues held together with third-hand parts. The day and night pounding, hard city driving, and rapid accelerations and braking, all of it combined to wreck the transmissions and suspensions. Most people only found out too late that the most jarring ride of their lives was about to happen during a medical emergency on the way to the hospital. As run numbers went up every year, these trucks had to be replaced every three years and cost $300,000.

"There she is." Lt. Killmoor pointed at the old Rescue 2 waiting at the garage bay doors. "That old destroyer carried me through many battles."

"Park next to it?"

"Yeah. For now. Let me track down Sad Sam and see what the deal is."

Inside the hangar, greetings were shouted towards Lt. Killmoor. Like him, the mechanics were sons of the city now tasked with keeping it running. Even though it had 80,000 people and a dozen schools, most who grew up here knew somebody who knew somebody else who knew that same person. It was in this way that people made their name.

"Sammy!" Lt. Killmoor waved across a slew of vehicles on lifts or in some other current state of dis-assemblage. In case fixing the vehicles was not enough work, there were also rows of lawnmowers, tractors, weed-eaters, and chainsaws waiting to be repaired.

"What's up, Dave?" Sad Sam wiped his hand before greeting Lt. Killmoor. His disposition and hound dog face rarely varied. "I'm sorry about the changeover but that thing's gotta go to Geldspar in the morning."

"No worries. I'm out at five anyway, so this ain't nothing, my friend."

"Appreciate it. Gotta keep the line moving, right?"

"How long are they talking?"

"Who knows? They're gonna pull the engine and give the drive train a thorough going over. Best case, four days. Worst case, who knows."

"Okay, I'll take everything just in case." He shouted to T-Bag, "Dump the whole truck!"

"Roger that!"

"Rescue 2 to Fire Alarm. Put us out of service for a changeover."

"Roger. Rescue 2's out of service at 1615."

Changing over a fire truck was relatively painless. But the rescues took much longer. Every different sized needle, bandage, and dozens of drugs had to be accounted for. They started at the front and worked their way through every compartment. Forty minutes later, they finished and called back in service just in time to catch a late run at shift change.

"Gilmore Street's right on the way," Lt. Killmoor said. "Swing by the station. Maybe our relief is already there."

Station 4 was at the intersection of two main boulevards, so as they made the turn, they saw the nightshift officer and private already standing in the driveway waiting with their gear. With the speed of a NASCAR pit team, one crew jumped off while the next jumped on, and thirty seconds later Rescue 2 was back on the street.

Lt. Killmoor grabbed his turnout gear and headed for the station. "Not bad for your first shift, partner."

"Right? We had fun, right?"

"We did."

"I wonder what's gonna happen tomorrow."

"Where are you tonight?"

"Engine 3."

"If Cunty Conti's there when you get there, tell him I said he's a bag of shit. Stay safe."

"Later, L-T."

"See you in fourteen hours."

BOOK TWO

WHO WE ARE

JULY 2009 TO DECEMBER 2009

INNOCENCE DESTROYED
July 24, 2009

"Jesus Christ!" Psycho Sal braced against the dashboard. "What did I tell you about the fucking brakes? They never work right."

"I'm sorry, Sal." It was only Yoda's second day on A-Shift as chauffeur of Rescue 1, and he had almost just T-boned a car. His boss, Lt. Salvatore Giametti, was easy to read since he pretty much existed on the edge of a perpetual meltdown. Yoda knew all the stories, how Sal, formerly known as "Straight-line Sal" because of his attention to detail, had his rescue career blown apart after a string of horrendous runs he could no longer process. There was the single mom stabbed forty-nine times, the 10-year-old girl that hung herself in her own closet, two dead babies, one murdered, the other killed by SIDS, and a carful of teenagers turned into ground beef when their car hit a bridge abutment at 70 MPH. This was over a two-month period in 2005, and after that he was never the same.

But Yoda was determined to stay positive. He said, "It's kind of incredible how poorly these trucks are maintained."

"Welcome to the Rescue Division." Psycho Sal lit a cigarette. His disheveled black hair and chiseled cheek bones would have made him attractive, but his eyes ruined everything. They were always bloodshot and filled with a blatant skeptical hostility. "Hope you enjoy getting your nuts punched in all day long."

"How old is this truck?"

"2006."

"It's only three years old?"

"I thought you were supposed to be some kind of genius? Guess your big brain can't wrap itself around the fact that these trucks run day and night."

"Guess that's true."

"Besides, the Receiver shit-canned most of the mechanics."

"Fire Alarm to Rescue 1."

Psycho Sal grabbed the mic. "Rescue 1, go."

"Start responding to 516 Cantwell Street for a possible overdose."

"Roger." Psycho Sal turned to his new partner and said, "Ten gets you twenty we play Jesus and raise the dead."

"No bet. Sounds like you've been there before."

"And we'll be going back again. Place's a total shooting gallery, so watch out for everything—needles, blood, guns, knives..."

Fire Alarm hit the Alert Tone and announced, *"Attention Rescue 1 and Engine 1, Still Alarm. 516 Cantwell Street, apartment 2, for a possible overdose..."*

Yoda fired up the lights and sirens while fumbling with his phone. Mobile GPS had just been made available to the public, and he had no idea where Cantwell Street was.

"Are you kidding me?" Sal puffed on the cigarette. "Put that phone down before you kill us both. Take a right."

"I'm sorry—"

"You better learn your goddamn streets, newbie. This ain't Fire Alarm."

Yoda tried not to be discouraged. Despite hitting every IV and three flawless runs so far today, he felt all of it had been erased in the last two minutes. He tried not to cough through the fog Sal's chain-smoking produced.

"Take a left." Sal leaned forward, scanning the block. "Just passed 421. It's gonna be on your side."

Yoda's pulse was pounding. He tried avoiding parked cars on either side of the tight road while hunting for the address. "I think that's—"

"Watch out!"

A police car responding to the same call blew the stop sign. After Yoda slammed on the brakes and sent Sal into the windshield, his cigarette exploded in a burst of sparks. "He's not even using his siren!"

Yoda struggled to maintain his composure. "That was close."

A block later, Sal had his door open before they even stopped. He went straight to the cop's window and said, "That was some great driving, superhero, you almost killed us!"

"Don't be so dramatic—"

"Didn't you hear our siren?"

Yoda grabbed the First-In bag, which was a backpack stuffed with an oxygen tank and every conceivable breathing attachment—nasal cannulas, non-rebreather masks, bag-valve masks, nebulizers, and steroid ampules for treating asthmatics or anyone with COPD. There was also a glucometer for diabetics, oral glucose, stethoscope, blood pressure cuff, pulse and SpO2 gauge, epinephrine for allergic reactions, Narcan to reverse opiate overdoses, and various-sized needles to administer both.

516 Cantwell was a bombed-out triple-decker in the worst part of District 1. Home to the city's open-air drug market for cocaine, heroin, and crack, there were whole blocks of foreclosed triple and quadruple-decker homes. Built a century before to house thousands of workers who had once flooded the mills, these massive homes were now vacant nightmares filled with the worst things people could do to themselves and one another. Zombie junkies and tooth-grinding meth-heads scavenged for cash and schemed. Female addicts transformed into bedraggled prostitutes that stepped out of shadowy doorways at night. Nicknamed "The Kitchen," this ghetto straddled the border of both the "Knock Out Kings" and the "Fifth Street Vatos." They shared a fortified

DMZ along Claiborne Avenue where atrocities, traded in an endless cycle of provocation and retribution, were only a part of doing business.

As Psycho Sal and the cop argued, Yoda shouldered the First-In bag and took the stairs two at a time. There was no front door, and the dark hallway was strewn with garbage and used diapers tossed outside the door of apartment two.

"Fire Department!" Yoda banged on the door. The ripened stench, in the July heat, was overpowering. "Hello! Open the door!"

"Hello?"

He tried the handle. "Fire Department!" He slowly pushed open the door. A thin white man and woman sat at a filthy table in a fetid kitchen. Their arms were bruised pathways tattooed by the needle. The woman was barely awake and had a long drool oozing from the corner of her mouth. The man, a lesion-filled mess, cackled loudly at her expense. He had leaky brown eyes inside hollow and emaciated sockets. He was wearing dirty boxers and a stained T-shirt. He said, "I woke up first and thought she was sitting there dead!" He cackled again. "Guess I was wrong."

"Sir." Yoda did not know where to begin. "Have you both been using drugs today?"

The man laughed even harder. "Naw, she's all right. She's a tough old goat. But I won't let her shoot no more today."

"Ma'am. Can you tell me what day it is?"

As she turned her head, the long drool let go and splashed across her deflated breast. "July?"

"Long as you're here..." The man jerked a thumb over his shoulder. "It's been awful quiet. I think there's something wrong with the baby."

"What baby?" Yoda was confused. "There's a baby here?"

"Yeah. She's in that room right there. She's been sick."

Convinced the man was just high, Yoda kicked aside beer cans and trash. He pushed open the bedroom door. He saw the empty crib and stepped closer. "There's no baby in here."

"You're a funny guy. No baby..." The guy laughed.

As Yoda left the room, something in the bathroom across the hall caught his eye. He took another step and then dropped the backpack and screamed, "Sal!"

"Who's Sal?"

Yoda dove at the tub and pulled out a toddler. "Sal! Oh Jesus." He desperately searched for a pulse. "Come on, kid. Sal!"

"What's going on?" The junkie appeared in the doorway. "Oh no. Oh shit! Linda was gonna take a bath—"

"Get out of the way!" Yoda was doing CPR on the still warm child. He ran out the door and straight for the truck. "Sal!"

Sal and the cop stopped threatening each other long enough to register the panic on Yoda's face as he sprinted by. Then Sal blinked. "Was that a *baby*?"

Inside the truck, Yoda laid the kid on the stretcher, doing CPR one-handed while hooking up the pediatric-defibrillator pads. He turned on the monitor as Sal jumped in and said, "What the fuck is going on?"

"I don't know, man! There were two junkies just sitting at the table and the kid, the kid was in the tub—"

"Gimme that." Sal applied the pads in case the monitor called for an electric shock. "Stop CPR."

They both watched the screen and saw the flatline crawl across the screen. The monitor's soothing voice said, *"No shock advised. Continue CPR."*

"Fuck me, man." Sal ripped open the IV drawer. "Keep going with the CPR."

"We should be able to get her back if she just drowned, right?"

"Do you know how long she was down for?"

"No. That junkie—"

Psycho Sal turned to the cop. "Go in and get that fucking guy."

The cop was all cop and tore off for the house. Sal, reminiscent of the gifted medic he used to be, somehow found a tiny vein and sunk the IV while CPR continued. Yoda, pumping away, was in awe.

"Where's the epi?" Sal spun for the med-drawer, did some quick math to draw up the appropriate pediatric dose of epinephrine, and had it going into the IV-line thirty-seconds later. Next, he cranked back the kid's head and tried to intubate her, but her tiny trachea made this impossible. Instead, he used an OPA to keep her tongue out of the way, hooked up a bag valve mask, and pumped pure oxygen into her tiny chest. "Where the fuck is the engine?"

"Didn't you have your radio on? They called responding from Lester Street. They were on a Box Alarm."

"Of course they were." Sal drew up another dose of epinephrine and toggled his mic. "Rescue 1 to Engine 1."

"Engine 1, go."

"Approximate 18-month-old, Code 99. Expedite."

"Roger that."

"I don't think so..." Sal pumped the bag-valve mask every three seconds. "That's not how this is gonna go down today, little lady."

Engine 1 tore around the corner. Three men jumped down and ran for the rescue. Lt. Walls got there first. "Whaddaya got, Sal?"

"Looks like a drowning. I need one man back here with us to run the code and one to drive. Like right fucking now."

Lt. Walls said, "Bugsy, you drive. Finn, do what you do."

Kevin Finnegan was no ordinary twenty-year guy. The first five years of his career had been spent on Rescue 1 working for Capt. LeClaire. The next five he rode with Lt. Killmoor to learn the other side of the city. Since he was taught by both department pioneers in EMS, Finnegan was widely regarded as one of the best rescue guys on the job. But one day at 135 Eddings Street finished that for good. A mother shot her three kids in the head and then herself. At the time, Finnegan had two small kids of his own and bid off because he knew he was drowning in the ghosts. He said, "What do you need, Lou?"

"Can you get another epi ready?" Sal pumped the bag-valve mask. "Talk to me, Finn, what're you thinking, bro?"

"Nothing, man. You got the line, the tube, the epi, the BG, the CPR... I can't think of anything else except some good pavement medicine."

"Bugsy!" Sal screamed. "Let's roll, dude!"

"Roger that!"

Sal toggled his mic. "Rescue 1 to Fire Alarm."

"Fire Alarm's on, Rescue 1."

"Advise St. E's we're coming in with an approximate 18-month-old female found face down and unresponsive in a bathtub. Unknown on time. She's currently asystolic. We have a twenty-four gauge IV in the left AC, two rounds of epi are on board, and we're about to drop a third. Kid's intubated, CPR's in progress, we're two minutes out."

"Roger."

Rescue 1 was barely parked before its back doors shot open. Yoda hopped out and grabbed the stretcher while Finnegan continued CPR and Sal pumped the mask. Ideally, they knew Hasbro Children's Hospital in Providence would have been better suited to handle this situation, but the lack of a confirmed and stabilized airway made St. Elizabeth's the only option. The ER doctor on call wore an expression that seemed to reflect this, that he was about to become the wrong man in the wrong place at the worst possible time.

"Doc, we got an approximately 18-month-old female found face down in a bathtub." They wheeled her into Critical Care Room 1 where an army awaited. Sal continued his report, "She's been asystolic, no shocks. Don't know how long she's been down. Four rounds of epi on board. No vomiting of water or stomach distension, twenty-four in the left AC."

The nurses motioned that they were ready for the transfer, so they moved the child from the stretcher to the bed. As they did so, the mask moved. The doctor approached. "Halt CPR."

"What?" Finnegan was pounding out a steady rhythm.

"Look at this." The doctor pulled away the mask and pointed at her tiny light-blue lips. Then he motioned toward her mottled skin. "Was she found face down?"

"Why?"

"Look at her belly. Lividity is already present—

"You're wrong. She was still warm! Blue lips could mean she's hypoxic."

"Lieutenant—"

"You ain't calling it." Sal made it sound like a threat. "You haven't even done anything!"

"Sal..." Yoda tried to step in. The anxious room did not know what to do.

"I'm sorry, lieutenant. Our protocols are pretty explicit."

"You're a piece of shit." Sal seemed to think of it. "It's a little girl, man."

"Lieutenant—"

"You ain't even gonna *try*?"

Finnegan said, "I'm continuing with CPR. Screw this guy."

The doctor said, "The water probably kept her warm, guys. You don't even know how long she was down for. Asystolic the entire time...?"

"So you just..." Sal deflated. "A little fucking girl, man?" He shrugged. "I'm all filled up. This one's on you, med-school."

Then he left the room.

***

When Yoda got home that night, his wife knew something was wrong because she immediately asked, "What happened?"

"Cindy..."

"Are you kidding me?"

"Honestly, it's better if you don't know."

"Good plan. Internalize it. Say nothing and see where that gets you. Where are you going?"

"I'm changing out of this stuff. God only knows what I'm covered in." He stripped out of his clothes and showered. He stared up at the shower head until he saw her dead face appear again, then he closed the water.

He grabbed a beer and ignored her in the kitchen. On the back deck, he watched the sun fading behind the trees. Their combined salaries allowed them to live on five acres thirty miles from Sachem City. Their closest neighbor was a mile away, and this isolation allowed them to decompress. Between her shifts and overtime, Cindy averaged fifty-hour weeks in the oncology unit at Galilee Medical Center.

The door opened and she joined him with a glass of wine. They stared out across the back lawn to where the forest rose in a sea of pine. The sky was a smear of purple and pink in the dusk.

He said, "I found a little girl drowned in a bathtub."

"Oh dear God..."

He told her the story and finished it by saying, "The ER doc didn't even work her. I thought Sal was gonna punch the fucking guy."

"How awful..."

"Day two on the rescue..."

"You'll get used to it. What do the older guys say?"

"It gets easier. Find a way to deal with it. Don't be a pussy. Blah, blah, blah." He sipped the beer. "That little girl showed up in this life and had zero chance."

"That's so awful. What's your boss say?"

"*Sal?* Honey, he's a complete time bomb. He's like the Exxon Valdez of PTSD."

"Awesome."

"I know we talked about having kids, but I don't know if I can let them live amongst these monsters."

"If and or when that happens, you're gonna make a great dad." She reached over and took his hand.

Yoda finished his beer and stood up.

Cindy said, "I grab your hand and you recoil?"

"This can't be about you right now, okay? Besides, I need another brew."

He left her outside on the deck and did not return.

LIEUTENANT DAVID KILLMOOR

Lt. Killmoor and T-Bag caught multiple runs through rush hour, so Lt. Killmoor was running late. He lived in a modest two-story cape in District 6. It had a small yard and above ground pool his now-grown kids had once used every summer day. He and his wife, Penelope, had been married for thirty-one years. In this same house, they had raised two daughters and a son. For a nurse and career firefighter, they had prospered, and, because of their jobs, knew how fortunate they were to raise three healthy kids while dodging any true misfortune.

Until today.

When Lt. Killmoor got home, he exited his beloved 1976 green Ford Ranger pick-up truck and banged open the door with the same greeting he had given Penelope since the day they had first moved in three decades before. But she did not respond. He found her in the kitchen seated at the counter. She had been crying but was now too proud to meet his gaze. When he asked her what was wrong, she could only push a piece of paper across the counter. In all the time he had known her, she might have put on a few pounds and added some wrinkles, but she was still the same girl he had fallen in love with. And to see her crying scared him because she only did that when something was really wrong.

He grabbed the paper and quickly scanned it. "Oh, man."

Penelope's face was circular and had two tear-swollen brown eyes that spilled over again. They had always made a good couple. She was serious, he was not. He was the good-time, she was the disciplinarian. She also handled the family finances because he was awful with money. Now, when he hugged her, she finally sobbed.

Six months ago, after she started tripping and dropping things for no reason, she was initially oblivious to what was occurring. Then her hands got weak at work and she found herself slurring words. All of this may have started subtly, but now none of it could be hidden. They were both healthcare professionals, which made this moment even more devastating.

Because of his nature, he wanted to be optimistic and never stop fighting. "Okay, so they say it's ALS. We're gonna get a second opinion."

"For what?" And when she did smile, it was more a hopeless sneer that almost killed his resolve. "I don't want to be one of those people."

"What people?"

"The ones who shop from doctor to doctor until they hear whatever lie they are seeking. My symptoms..."

"Honey—"

"Stop. If I don't say this to you now, I don't know how we can continue. If this thing takes me—"

"We don't even know for sure..."

But her look finished him in his tracks. He gave up because he knew she was right. The worst part of their jobs was knowing how badly most lives ended. There would now commence an all-out attack on the nerves that controlled her muscles. And as each muscle died one by one over a three-to-five-year stretch of unimaginable indignity, finally she would be left in a diaper in a wheelchair until even those deep postural muscles got extinguished. Then she would be placed in a bed with a Foley inserted into her bladder as even the muscles that allowed her to breath failed and died. Left a prisoner inside a body that no longer spoke, swallowed, stood, laughed, or cried, she would be forced to await this final suffocation entombed in silence. Like being buried alive in front of her own family, the shovels of dirt could not be stopped.

As they embraced, she may have cried and wondered at the fairness of this death sentence, but she would never ask why. There was no why, because nothing was ever fair.

LEFT FOR DEAD
August 10, 2009

Engine 4 was screaming down Veteran's Highway. Fire trucks did not have FM radios, so Slipknot, the back-step man, had Skinlab blasting on an old school boom-box like a metalized Radio Raheem. His real name was Chris Fullerton, but he was called Slipknot because of his tattoos, piercings, dyed black hair, and death metal obsession. In his late twenties, his humongous size was invaluable when it came to brute force or dealing with the obese. But his forbidding appearance was mainly a charade since he spent most off-days with his dog and widowed mother.

At the wheel was Mikey Doneen. He had only been on the job for eight years but had already established a solid reputation. Some young guys got hired and treated the place like a fraternity instead of a way of life. But Doneen did not need to be taught the difference. Since he came from two generations of masons, he had grown up on jobsites. His grandfather, father, uncles, cousins, and brother were all master stone workers. They mixed eighty-pound bags of mortar and carried a thousand bricks a day. It was a hard life made impossible without work ethic, something that proved invaluable after Sachem City hired him. He spent the first hour of every shift going over every inch of whatever truck he was on. He explored all the bags and compartments and even crawled over the hose bed to double-check the jump-lines and nozzles. It was the kind of effort that made the old schoolers consider him one of their own, a descendant. His head was always freshly shaved and shiny, and he had layers of muscle from stacking stone. Despite his blue-collar disposition, his inquisitive mind was never idle. Quick with his fists, he was also unafraid to use them.

Their boss was Lt. Cody Stokes. The Dude's first day on the line had since become part of the oral history of the job. He survived five-and-a-half years on both rescues before flaming out and jumping to Engine 1. He was such a nice guy, when his wife threw him out because she did not want to be married anymore, he just packed up his stuff and left. Eventually, he got custody of his two young sons and loved being a dad. He was also a great cook, so in-between chain-smoking Marlboro Lights, the Dude made some of the best meals on the job.

"Dudes..." Lt. Stokes pitched his cigarette out the window. "This is gonna be a mess."

"I remember her." Mikey Doneen took a right on Calderon Street. "What number we looking for?"

"1-6-1."

"Here we go."

They stopped in front of a run-down triple-decker. Lt. Stokes grabbed the mic and said, "Engine 4's on-scene."

"Engine 4's on-scene at 1015."

A 400-pound white woman stood wheezing in the doorway. Her dress was more like an extra-large tablecloth, and without a bra, her massive breasts made her look like she had three stomachs. She gasped, "She's in here."

They followed her through a cluttered apartment. The July heat filled the place with various odors. There were empty Girl Scout cookie and pizza boxes on the floor. Dirty dishes were stacked a foot-high on the counter. The place smelled like rotten food in a summer dumpster, but the bathroom was worse. The woman's sister, who weighed even more than she did, had fallen off the toilet and was now wedged between it and the bathtub. The bathroom, also, had not been cleaned in years.

"Please," she panted. "I can't breathe."

"Hang on, miss." Mikey Doneen climbed into the slime-smeared tub so he could better appraise the situation. The way she had crumpled left all her weight crushing her chest. "Dear, are you hurt anywhere, or do you just need us to lift you up?"

"Please get me out of here! I can't breathe!"

Doneen said, "Yo, Slip, grab a sheet off the bed."

Slipknot returned with a stained sheet. Doneen had him wedge it beneath her shoulders and feed it through to him. "On three."

Slipknot and Doneen deadlifted 450-pounds and got her onto the toilet. That's when it hit them. The morbidly obese were oftentimes unable to wash themselves. Deposits between the skinfolds, once disturbed, stunk like rotten eggs. Slipknot winced, but Doneen had spent four years on Rescue 1 and smelt much worse.

"Okay," he said, "now we're gonna stand you up, okay?"

Lt. Stokes said, "Dudes, let me get in there and help."

"There's not enough room."

She panted and cursed. "I can't stay in this bathroom."

Lt. Stokes said, "Where do you want to go, dear?"

"Just get me out to my wheelchair."

They lifted her again. Even though her legs were the size of trees, they nearly caved in from the weight. She shuffled to the bedroom and collapsed into her chair.

Mikey Doneen asked, "How do you feel? Do you want to go to the hospital?"

"No, no. Just leave me be."

Lt. Stokes toggled his shoulder-mounted mic and said, "Engine 4 to Fire Alarm. Clear the rescue. This is a lift assist only."

"Roger. Fire Alarm to Rescue 2?"

Lt. Killmoor answered, "Rescue 2 receives that direct. Back in service."

"Fire Alarm to Engine 4? Are you available for a run?"

"Momentarily."

"Start responding with Rescue 2 to 168 Withrow Road for a diabetic emergency."

"Roger."

"Rescue 2 to Fire Alarm. We will have a delayed response. Stopping for equipment re-supply at Station 4."

Slipknot had taken care of his grandmother at the end of her disease, so he was always extra attentive with the elderly or infirm. He helped the woman slide into her dismally worn-out slippers and said, "You all set? You need anything else?"

For the first time since their arrival, the woman shared a smile. "I'm all right now, thank you. Thank you all."

Outside, they hopped into the truck as Doneen said, "I think my nose died."

"Dude," Lt. Stokes said, "if there's ever a fire in that place, those two are definite goners."

"Withrow means the 6's must be on a run," Slipknot called out from the back. "We're not used to that kind of real estate."

"Right? The lifestyles of the rich and famous."

"Whoa," Mikey laughed. "Let's not get crazy."

District 6 was a middle-class spread of ranch homes, schools, and strip malls. It was also where the remainder of the World War II generation were content to live out the rest of their retirement. Because people still had good jobs with healthcare, it was also the slowest district in the city.

Withrow Road was long and curvy and bordered a golf course. The homes were large colonials with spacious yards. Since District 4, their home district, was the exact opposite and filled with the working-class, Lt. Stokes said, "It's only three miles away, man, ain't that incredible?"

168 Withrow was a two-story 2500 square-foot house with a tennis court and pond in the backyard. Slipknot killed the screaming guitars and grabbed the medical bags. They walked across the manicured yard.

A white middle-aged woman who was nicely dressed appeared in the door and said, "She's in the garage."

"What's going on, ma'am?" Lt. Stokes asked as they walked.

"You tell me. Isn't that why you're here?"

"Um..."

"I'm no doctor, but I think her blood sugar's low? She's a horrible diabetic."

Lt. Stokes looked past her attitude and said, "So she went out to the garage and collapsed? How old is she?"

"She didn't really collapse."

"What do you mean?"

When Slipknot pushed open the garage door and looked inside, his confusion was apparent. "What is... is she on a mattress?"

"Well, she's between nursing homes at the moment. Medicare—"

"Why is she on a mattress?"

"Because this is where she lives?"

"Excuse me?" Lt. Stokes saw an elderly white woman with dual below-the-knee amputations laying on a filthy mattress. Delirious, she kept reaching for them as she cried.

"What's that on the..." Mikey Doneen squinted. "Is that piss and shit on that mattress?"

"Well, we haven't yet had a bathroom installed—"

"Lady, *who* is this?" Lt. Stokes was losing his sense of humor.

"She's my aunt."

"And you keep her on a mattress in the freaking garage?"

"How dare you—"

"Please help me," the old lady said.

"Are those sores?" Mikey Doneen pulled on his gloves and tried lifting the stumps. "Lou, she's stuck to the freaking mattress."

"That's it, dude." Lt. Stokes hit the mic. "Engine 4 to Fire Alarm. Send me the police."

"I've never smelt anything like this." Slipknot knelt to get her vitals. "I know, dear, I'm sorry, just bear with us."

"Police?" The niece was aghast.

"For what?" A college-aged man had abruptly joined her. He was six-foot and wearing a Temple Lacrosse T-shirt.

"Who're you?" Lt. Stokes asked.

"That's my great-aunt." His hostility was only overshadowed by his outright disdain. "Mom, what's going on?"

"And this seems normal to you people?" Lt. Stokes asked. "Seriously, barn animals don't even get treated like this."

"You got some nerve!" The son let fly a cocked fist that got intercepted by Mikey Doneen's straight-cross, which put the kid to sleep before he even hit the floor.

"Chaz!" the woman screamed. She knelt and cradled her son's head as blood poured from his nose.

"Goddamnit." Doneen reached into the trauma bag and tossed her some gauze. "He'll be fine."

"How dare you!"

"He made a move—"

"I want all of your names! I'm suing the city, the department, asking for your jobs and prosecution!"

"Ma'am..." Lt. Stokes shook his head. "You're the only one going to jail today. I've been a fireman for twenty years and seen my share of horrible things, but this is some next level type of shit. Shame on you."

"Shame on *me*?" She stood up. "Shame on *you*, sir, for assaulting my son!"

"Self-defense is not assault."

"Hey," Slipknot said. "BP 80 over 60, pulse 111, blood sugar is 34."

"Those are some terrible numbers, dude. Let's go, lady, we need to treat her." Lt. Stokes took the woman by the arm and steered her outside.

"This is my property!" she yelled.

"Tell it to the cops." He slammed the door and locked it.

Slipknot used a stethoscope to listen to her lungs. He did a thorough assessment, telling her, "It's okay, we're gonna get you—ma'am, can you see my hand?"

"I'm blind, honey."

"Jesus Christ," Lt. Stokes said, "Is this really happening?"

Mikey Doneen was setting up for an IV. He wrapped a tourniquet around her bicep and began searching for veins. He had to breathe through his mouth because the stench was incongruent with the sweet old lady it came from. Since diabetics had bad or nonexistent vascular access, he asked her, "Where do they usually stick you, dear?"

"Here." She pointed to a spot below her right wrist.

He zeroed in with the 18-gauge needle. It was a pressure shot in a tough, bony spot. Blowing through it would mean their access to quick interventions would be lost. He lined up the needle, applied pressure, felt the skin pop and, after he saw the flash of blood backfill into the catheter, knew he was in. He advanced it a tiny bit more before retracting the needle. He screwed in the intravenous D-10 dextrose drip and ran it wide open. As the sugar flooded her system, she instantly transformed, blinking, relaxing. As she became more conscious, she got chatty despite all she had been through. Mikey Doneen was holding up the IV bag with one arm when he asked, "What's your name, dear?"

"Priscilla. Priscilla Spitzer."

"Okay, Priscilla Spitzer, how old are you?"

"Eighty-one, but I feel like I'm twenty-nine."

"Me too." Doneen smiled. "But that's because that's my actual age."

"Oh, cherish it. You must cherish it. It is such a wonderful ride, but you can never replace those years."

"Oh yeah?"

"I was one of the first female buyers on Seventh Avenue. Back then, that made me an exotic fruit."

"Different day back then, right?"

"It surely was. But Manhattan will never change. That's what makes it such a magical place."

"Priscilla," Slipknot said. "What's your date of birth?"

"A lady never tells."

"I promise to be discreet."

"In that case, 2/21/1928."

"Do you have any other medical problems?"

"Too many to list but nothing major until they started sawing off parts of me. That was two years ago and I've not been the same since."

"Any heart problems?"

"Other than being broken a few times, no."

"No offense, but your niece is a real piece of work."

Priscilla's unseeing milky brown eyes filled with tears. She felt for Slipknot's hand and squeezed it. "To think that this would be the way it ends..."

"Not today." Slipknot turned to Lt. Stokes who was heading for the door. "What's up?"

"Rescue's here." He unlocked the door, careful to let in only Lt. Killmoor and T-Bag. Outside, the niece was still raging.

Lt. Killmoor read the scene and said, "Seems like a real friendly lady."

"Oh yeah, dude," Lt. Stokes said. "She's a real treat."

"So, what do we have here? A diabetic emergency that turned into someone else suffering a sudden, violent narcolepsy? I'm guessing that was Slipknot."

Lt. Stokes chuckled. "Not this time. This dude suffering from the sudden narcolepsy is the son of that awesome lady outside."

"Shocking."

"This, however, is Priscilla Spitzer, one of the first female buyers on Seventh Avenue back in the day."

"Is that right, Priscilla?"

"It is." She smiled, but her teeth had not been brushed in months. "Fashion Week was my domain."

"I want to hear all about it. And we're gonna talk about all that on the way to the hospital, okay? But for now just bear with us." He looked back to Lt. Stokes. "What else?"

"She's diabetic and a dual amputee whose nice family has seen fit to store her out here in the sweltering heat on a freaking mattress. Apparently, she's in-between nursing homes."

"With no toilet, wheelchair, water, or anything else." Slipknot stood up and handed Lt. Killmoor a piece of paper. "Her vitals when we arrived are on the left. Just took them again and the new ones are listed on the right. Sugar went from 34 to 160, so we just DQ'd the D-10 drip so we don't send her too far the other way. BP is now 130/80. I'm running saline wide open because of her severe dehydration. 18-gauge in the right wrist."

Lt. Killmoor frowned at the paper. "Guess that nice, air-conditioned house is too good for her."

"In July, dude, in a freaking garage." Lt. Stokes was standing right there and still could not believe it.

Neither could T-Bag, who had taken care of his paralyzed father for years. "How long has she been in here?"

"To tell you the truth, dude, I was afraid to ask. Double-murder would not look good in my jacket downtown." He glanced at Priscilla. "Dear, how long have you been in here?"

"You said it was July?"

"Yes, ma'am."

"I left the last nursing home in February."

"February... Dear God..."

A cop knocked on the door. They allowed him in and gave him their report. The story was bad enough, but the visual evidence was way worse.

"My God." Altarr Fredrickson was an Army veteran with a plow-shaved afro that made his head look like a Coast Guard cutter. He was quick to the point and never suffered unnecessarily. "I guess the address doesn't matter when it comes to being a monster."

Lt. Killmoor said, "She's going directly to OSH. Those wounds on what's left of her legs need to be debrided. She's been laying in her own waste... Hey, guys, we need to roll her."

Mikey Doneen did not know how else to say it. "She's welded to this thing, L-T, like I've never seen before."

Lt. Killmoor stepped up for a closer examination. "Priscilla, I'm guessing you've been on that mattress for quite some time. Do you remember the last time you were off it?"

"Honestly, I have no idea. A week ago?"

They tried a variety of things to free her, even pouring out a bottle of saline to try and loosen the seal, but her skin tore off every time they tried to move her.

"You know what?" Lt. Killmoor said. "Who's got a knife? We'll cut the mattress around her."

The son on the floor did not think anyone had seen him wake up, but T-Bag was standing right beside him. When the kid tried to lunge at Mikey Doneen, T-Bag's boot found his chest and pinned him back to the floor. "Nice try, zippy."

"What's going on?" He squirmed beneath the boot. "I'm the one who's been assaulted!"

"You're going to jail," Officer Fredrickson said. He was still writing on his notepad. "Right now, it's attempted assault on a first responder, battery, unlawful imprisonment, torture, elder abuse, disturbing the peace, kidnapping, and wherever else the whim takes me. Now rollover."

"I want my lawyer—"

"We're not there yet, little fella. Rollover, put your hands behind your back, and if you even twitch in my direction you're getting tazed. Do you understand that?"

"Just get this over with. By the time my attorney's done with you, you'll be a security guard in a mall somewhere."

"Don't threaten me with a good time. Rollover." Officer Fredrickson cuffed him. "Good thing I carry two sets, because mom's going next. Why split up such a nice family?"

More police arrived to secure and document the scene. The firefighters lifted her off the cut apart mattress and carried her out. In the fresh air she had not felt in so long, Priscilla Spitzer smiled as she aimed her sightless eyes toward the warm sunshine.

CAPTAIN RICHARD LECLAIRE

When Capt. LeClaire returned from Vietnam, he was still only 20-years-old. It was 1970 and the country was tearing itself apart over the war. He had heard horrible stories of returning veterans being accosted and assaulted by ungrateful crowds after surviving the horrors of combat on their behalf, but as was his nature, he always ignored the bad and dedicated his life on Rescue 1 to helping as many people as possible. Sometimes, he would even take multiple patients to the hospital even though it was illegal to transport more than one at a time. Often, he would be taking the next run before they had even arrived at the hospital to dump their current patient, an act that irritated the endless line of chauffeurs who would drive him on the tens of thousands of runs he had completed over the last thirty-four years. Turning and burning, Rescue 1 on C-Shift never stopped moving. And neither did Capt. LeClaire. When he was not at the firehouse, he painted houses as a side gig. An accomplished tradesman, he had all the gear and experience. He even, at one point, ran multiple crews, but that became too stressful. Now he worked on his own and basically had no days off. Even after staying awake all night on the rescue, he painted the whole day before returning for his night shifts. It was the kind of quiet work ethic that created the level of old-school respect Capt. LeClaire had earned without ever raising his voice or, more importantly, at the cost of anyone else. He was never in a bad mood and treated every single patient as if they could be part of his extended family.

His pick-up truck was a lot like him—beat up and covered in paint. When he got home, Lois, his wife, was at the door with a smile. She was a wide woman with a cherubic face, but her quiet disposition was the glue that kept their family together. Between the fire department and his painting business, LeClaire was barely home at all, so Lois got tasked with raising their three daughters. She was strong, unyielding, and did not like television, bad grades, or excuses for poor performance.

"Hey, babe," he said with that trademark Clint Eastwood-rasp. He pulled open the screen door and gave her a kiss. "My dogs are already barking and it's barely lunchtime."

"I made you a sandwich."

"Thank you." He took off his boots and followed her into the kitchen. They had met thirty-five-years before at Rocky Point, an amusement park that generations of Rhode Islanders frequented in the warmer months until it closed for good in 1995. She was a quiet girl who came from a prominent South County family, but Capt. LeClaire was Sachem City blue-collar all the way, so at first their union wreaked havoc with her family. Yet as was the case with every future pattern in his life, he just kept his head down, went to work, treated everyone with respect and dignity until even her father, who was not easily deceived, finally recognized the indelible qualities of the suitor standing before him.

Because he was always covered in paint, Capt. LeClaire's splattered appearance never made his wife flinch. Lois placed a tuna fish sandwich on the table next to a glass of milk and bag of chips. She had made the sandwich with capers and extra mayonnaise just the way he liked it. On the walls of their home were pictures of their three grown daughters time-lapsed through the years. Kelly was a dentist, Denise was an engineer, and Sammy was a social worker. They were all married and had kids of their own, so the LeClaire house was usually filled on the weekends.

Even though he had seen the devastation of drownings over and over at work, he still bought a pool so the grandkids had even more reason to hang out. He had survived combat and decades of trauma on the rescue, but nothing stressed him out as much as that backyard pool. And while it was behind a double-locked six-foot fence, he always thought of the pool as a life-destroying event just waiting to happen. How many times had he rounded the corner of someone's home as one parent or the other held a lifeless blue body while crying and making sounds of such unimaginable anguish that Capt. LeClaire never forgot them. Those parents' lives were now over as well, they just did not yet know it.

He finished his sandwich, thanked his wife, and headed back to work. This afternoon he was helping Lt. Killmoor finish painting his own house. When he pulled up in District 6, T-Bag and Rowdell were already there.

"Well, well," Capt. LeClaire said, "looks like I'm not the only one who got roped into this on their day off."

"Guilt," T-Bag said, "should never be underestimated."

"How you doin, Cap?" Rowdell shook his boss' paint-covered hand. "Looks like you've already been hard at it today."

"Ah, just finishing up a job on Ellis Street. Seems like I've been there forever. Either that or I'm just getting so old it feels that way."

"Captain." Lt. Killmoor appeared carrying more cans of paint from the garage. "How nice of you to join us."

"How could I turn down such a blatant invitation?"

"Or threat, right?" Lt. Killmoor was smiling around the giant cigar clinched between his teeth. "Let's head around back."

As they got set up, T-Bag was putting on music, so Lt. Killmoor instantly called out, "Please, for the love of God, no Anthrax!"

Rowdell and T-Bag, as the junior guys, climbed the ladders to paint the second-floor while their bosses worked below.

The high sun splashed across all four as they chomped cigars and got to work. But just like the firehouse, to pass the time, they shared stories. It was called "smoking and joking" and had been done the same way since the dawn of man.

T-Bag asked his boss, "What year did you get on, Lou?"

"1980." Lt. Killmoor loaded more paint onto his brush. "Coincidentally that was the same year Rescue 2 got created."

"How did they do that?"

"By closing Ladder 3."

"Bet that caused some problems."

"That," Capt. LeClaire added, "is the understatement of the century."

Lt. Killmoor added, "Guys, especially the senior ones, fought like hell to keep Ladder 3. It got ugly. I was brand new and headed to the rescue anyway, so I didn't care either way."

Rowdell said, "Then you never left."

"Yup. Twenty-eight years. A bunch of them with that guy right there as my boss. But when I first got on, just like you guys, I was sent to Fire Alarm where I dispatched the good captain here for an officer involved car wreck."

Even after all this time, Capt. LeClaire could only shake his head. "Peanut."

"That's what they called my sister," Lt. Killmoor said. "Even though she was tiny, like five-foot-nothing and weighed a hundred pounds, she was tough as nails."

"Wait a second." Rowdell looked down. "Are you saying you dispatched the captain to your own sister's death?"

"Yes. She was brand new, too. She looked so young, when she first got on the job, they had her working undercover in the Providence high schools. They had a big drug problem back then. She was also the third female ever hired by the Sachem City PD."

"What happened?" T-Bag asked.

"Well," Capt. LeClaire did not seem to like re-opening this wound. "She got a call for a man with a gun/possible robbery. She was chasing him up Chatham Avenue when her car went through a construction zone, hit a patch of sand, and lost control. Now remember, this is in the

1980's. There were no airbags and no one wore seatbelts. She hit the leg of a back-hoe which ricocheted her into a telephone pole. Incredibly, even with no seatbelt, there wasn't a scratch on her. When we got there, coincidentally, a priest who had been passing by was tending to her. He said she just got out of the car, brushed off the broken glass, and then collapsed."

"Not a mark on her," Lt. Killmoor said. "But she whacked the back of her head hard enough to throw her into a seizure that she never woke up from. The good captain here transported her to St. E's, because this was even before the advent of trauma centers. So they shipped her up to Boston, but they pulled the plug on her six days later. Total brain death."

"Jesus Christ," T-Bag said. "That's awful. But she sounded like a bad ass chick."

"She was." Lt. Killmoor pointed north. "Off John Adams, there's Killmoor Baseball Field named after her."

"That's crazy."

Capt. LeClaire said, "He comes from a family of cops. Sister, brother, hell, his father was the Chief of Police, and instead he ends up doing twenty-eight years on the rescue."

"Yeah," Rowdell said. "How'd that happen?"

"It's like I always say," Lt. Killmoor answered. "Cops would make horrible firemen, and firemen would make horrible cops. In case you haven't noticed, I'm not too big on authority."

"Me either." T-Bag climbed down to get more paint. "What'd you do before you got here?"

"Believe it or not, I was a French-trained chef."

"Seriously?"

"Yup. I loved cooking, but I just got sick of working in restaurants."

"Me too." T-Bag re-ascended his ladder. "That's how I ended up on a roof."

"What about you, Cap?" Rowdell asked his boss. "What'd you do before you got here?"

"After Vietnam, I worked for my uncle's construction company. I was also taking classes at CCRI on the GI Bill, and that's where I ran into a bunch of Providence guys. They were already on the job and sold me on the whole idea pretty quickly. I started applying immediately."

"It's true," T-Bag said. "Before this place, I had no health insurance, sick days, vacation days, personal days... hell, if you wanted to go on vacation, you just quit your job and got another one when you got home."

Rowdell laughed at that. "True story."

Capt. LeClaire asked, "Either one of you got kids?"

"No." Rowdell moved his ladder over. "I can't imagine that level of responsibility. And God forbid if anything bad happened. How do you survive that?"

The silence was so awkward that Rowdell had to add, "What's wrong?"

Lt. Killmoor looked at Capt. LeClaire and said, "It's okay if you don't want to tell them."

T-Bag was too nosey. "Tell us what?"

"It's okay." But Capt. LeClaire's usual smile and cheerful disposition could not hide it. "When I got back from the war, I met Lois and got married. We tried like hell to have kids. Like for years. Even went to specialists with all the bells and whistles. And then finally, miraculously, Lois somehow got pregnant. We had all but given up. We were psyched. Got the baby's room all good to go, brought our new baby son home..." Capt. LeClaire ashed his cigar. "I had taken a few vacation days to finish up a painting job I had going on in South County. Nice sunny day just like this one. Now, you gotta remember, this is way before cell phones. I had no idea what was going on until a police car pulled up out front. This guy—" he nodded at Lt. Killmoor. "He called the Narragansett PD. They came and told me my baby boy was dead."

Rowdell looked at Lt. Killmoor. "*You*? You were on that run?"

"I was. Worst run I ever had."

"Man oh man," T-Bag said. "You two are like the angels of death."

Rowdell asked, "What happened to the baby?"

"SIDS." Capt. LeClaire shared a wry smile. "Worst day of my life."

"That's awful, Cap." Rowdell just shook his head. "What a terrible story."

"It gets worse," Lt. Killmoor said. "He even pulled a code on his own mother-in-law."

"Seriously?" T-Bag asked.

"Yup." Capt. LeClaire ashed his cigar. "Thanksgiving Day, 1996. We were having it at my house, so I went to pick her up. Poor lady got in the car, said she wasn't feeling well, and then she just keeled over."

"Holy crap," T-Bag said. "You did CPR on your own mother-in-law?"

"Did she live?" Rowdell asked.

"Yup. Seekonk Fire showed up really quick. Those guys did a great job. We got a pulse, got her all pinked up and moving air, and transported her to Saint E's."

"One thing the rescue has taught me," Lt. Killmoor added, "is that there is no rhyme or reason to life. It comes and goes. I had a guy one time, 30-years-old. Dude never drank, never smoked, ate right, and exercised. And that's where we got the call, for a man down at Bailey's Gym. We got there and there he is, dead as hell, right on the freaking treadmill. They were even doing CPR, so it wasn't like he went a long time pulseless. In fact, there happened to be an off-duty Galilee ER nurse there, and she said she was doing CPR within twenty seconds of him hitting the deck. Out of any code I've ever had, I thought for sure we'd get this one back. Nope. Asystole the whole time. Couldn't even get him into V-Fib. Nothing. I could not believe it. Just could not believe it. I was with Slipknot. We must've broken every rib in that guy's chest, pushed half a dozen Epi's—nothing. It was the most disheartening run ever."

"Boy," T-Bag said. "Hanging out with you dudes is really depressing."

"Seriously," Rowdell concurred. "Is it too early to start drinking?"

T-Bag laughed. "No such time exists. As a matter of fact, I got a coffin-sized Coleman cooler loaded with ice-cold Miller High Life."

Lt. Killmoor rolled his eyes. "Who knew he was such an aristocrat?"

Capt. LeClaire chuckled. "For some reason, members of this newest generation seem intent on rolling back the clock to 1975. With all these wonderful independent breweries and IPA's, it's a damn shame."

"We fought the fight but lost the war." Lt. Killmoor looked up at T-Bag on the ladder. "Well? That beer ain't gonna serve itself."

Minutes later, the cooler was exhumed and opened.

RACE DAY

August 14, 2009

"Does this make any sense?" Haley Erskine, T-Bag's girlfriend, watched T-Bag and Rowdell disappear into the crowd. "Can you imagine swimming two miles after working for forty-eight hours straight?"

"No." Annie Sadler drove away from the beach where 400 swimmers were readying for the 1.7-mile trek from Newport to Jamestown. Participants with signed affidavits certifying they completed two miles in a pool in under an hour did not have to be escorted by a kayaker for safety. Since the route followed the Newport Bridge, the Coast Guard had the entire east passage shut to all boats from 6:45 A.M. to 8:45 A.M. Annie said, "There's something seriously wrong with your boyfriend. You know that, right?"

"I hear ya. Met his mom the other day."

"Momma T-Bag?"

Haley smiled. "Momma T-Bag. She said the same thing. Said he's just a sad little boy still running away from everything."

"Aren't we all. Wow, look at all these people."

"There are some crazy bathing suits, right? Hey, look! That guy's wearing a lobster head!" Haley Erskine's full color tattoos crawled out of her tank top. Twin dragons crisscrossed her back, wrapped her shoulders, and faced each other above her breasts. Her unassuming dark eyes were hollow from the 4 A.M. wake-up. She and Annie were both respiratory therapists, but Annie was also a trauma nurse. She had two more years in Brown University's Physician Assistant program before she could return home to Maine. Together they made a strange duo. Conservative versus anarchy did not usually translate into friendship, but they had been best friends for years. They even shared a two-bedroom Providence apartment.

Annie said, "I think Row's getting sick of me."

"No way." Haley changed the radio station as they crossed the Newport Bridge. Built in 1966, this 1.9-mile expanse was the longest suspension bridge in New England. "So what if you're making him wait? Personally, I think it's lame, but if you're not ready you're not ready."

"I wasn't even looking for this. And what do you mean I'm *lame*?"

"I didn't say you're lame. I said that might be the way the situation is viewed, is all."

"Thanks." Annie parked a mile away from the beach where hundreds of families and friends awaited the arrival of the first wave of swimmers. A cannon fired in the distance. With the race now underway, the fastest swimmers would not be appearing for thirty minutes.

Annie Sadler said, "Divorcing freakshow Frank was bad enough. But I really just wanted to ride out the summer and finish the next two years of school. That's it. Then I'd be heading home to Maine."

"Oh my God. You've known this guy for a month. Who cares?"

"It's—"

"Can't you just enjoy anything without overanalyzing it? It's summer. Believe me, he ain't looking to get married either."

"How do you know?"

"You're a freaking headcase, you know that? You suck the life out of everything around you."

"That's not nice."

"Ha!"

"Come on, let's set up over there."

They chose a spot down the shore and spread out a blanket.

Annie Sadler was checking her phone after it pinged. "Listen to this. This is the email I just got from Kathryn. This is why she's the worst boss ever. 'In the future, all nurses are to submit fully completed B-109 schedules with their reports.' Why? Talk about a useless circle jerk. The main report already contains all of that information."

"Okay, new rule. No talking about work or boys."

"Agreed." Annie put away the phone. She looked up into the sky and closed her eyes. The sun, just beginning its day, was already making everything sticky and humid.

***

Rowdell ran headfirst into T-Bag and came to a stop. They treaded water as Rowdell asked, "What's going on?"

"I don't know, man, the fire department and Coast Guard are flying all over the place."

Boats were screaming toward the bridge.

Rowdell said, "Is it a shark?"

"What is it with you and sharks? The last shark attack here was 1955. Besides, there's 400 people out here. Don't be the slowest and you just might live!"

"Then why's the Coast Guard—"

"Who cares? Let's go!"

The quest toward Jamestown had been rejoined.

***

An hour after the start, they staggered out of the water. Exhausted swimmers were handed fruit, sandwiches, sport gels and water. Everyone searched the crowd for their loved ones.

T-Bag asked, "How you feeling?"

"Good." Rowdell was still catching his breath. "Surprisingly. Hey, there they are."

T-Bag and Haley hugged and kissed.

Rowdell and Annie shared an awkward hug.

"How was it?" Haley asked.

"Cool. Glad we did it." T-Bag pointed toward the bridge. "What the hell happened during the race?"

"The state cop said some guy killed himself."

"*What?*"

"Yup." Annie nodded. "Blocked both lanes on the bridge and just jumped off."

T-Bag laughed. "What an asshole. He couldn't wait until we were done? Did he land on top of anybody?"

"Not as far as we know. But the cop was pissed. Said the guy could've at least left the keys."

"Imagine that, Row?" T-Bag said. "And here you were worried about sharks."

"Right? Silly me. The real threat was dodging suicides."

"Where's our car?" T-Bag asked.

"About a mile that way." Haley pointed.

"You guys want to grab some breakfast? I'm freaking starving."

"I'm in." Rowdell took Annie's hand. "Wanna head to the beach after?"

"Sounds like fun," she answered.

"What about you?" T-Bag asked Haley. "Beach and a little day-drinking sound like a winning combo to you?"

"I'm in," she said.

Together, the four of them walked into the August sun.

CHEESEBURGER SAVES THE DAY
August 18, 2009

Four days later, in the basement of a triple-decker on Terrace Street, an electrical short in an overloaded power-strip ignited a box of papers next to a shelf filled with solvents. Within five minutes, the basement was roaring, and, because of the 1800's balloon-frame construction, the fire in the walls was already racing for the roof.

Out of seven apartments, three were illegal one-room cut-ins. On the first-floor, smoke began puffing out of door frames and window moldings before people started screaming. There was only one working smoke detector, but by the time it went off on the third-floor, it was way too late.

Citywide, the tones hit at 11:15 A.M. as Fire Alarm announced, *"Attention Engines 3,2,6, Ladder 2, Battalion 3. Stillbox. Possible structure fire, 284 Terrace Street..."*

It was actually Engine 4's district but the rolling blackouts had put them out of service. So Ladder 2, which was housed at the same station as Engine 4, arrived on-scene first-due with no water. Even worse, after a car T-boned Engine 3 at an intersection, they had to stop and help the injured. Without the first and second-due engine companies, third-due

Engine 2 turned the corner to find Ladder 2 pulling people out of windows.

"Engine 2 to Fire Alarm!" Capt. McCarrick screamed. "First and second-floor are fully involved! We got hangers in the windows!"

"Fire Alarm to Battalion 3. Did you receive that?"

"Roger. I'm on-scene establishing Command on side-one."

"Roger. Command established on side-one."

"Command to Engine 2. Assist Ladder 2 in rescue operations. Command to Fire Alarm."

"Go, Command."

"Engine 6 is the primary attack once on-scene."

"Roger. Fire Alarm to Engine 6?"

"Engine 6 receives that!" the lieutenant screamed over his whaling siren. "Two minutes out!"

"Command to Fire Alarm. Dump the city."

Fire Alarm hit the All-Call tones and sent every remaining truck.

Capt. McCarrick, Dutch Carrigan, and Cheeseburger grabbed axes, Halligans, and a 24-foot ladder.

The guys from Ladder 2 did not even have time to set up their aerial. They just grabbed ground ladders and threw them up to windows filled with terrified people.

"Command to Fire Alarm. Strike a third alarm with out-of-town companies and backfill our stations after that."

"Roger, Command."

Around back, Engine 2 found a black woman in a bathrobe frantically waving from a second-floor window. She coughed and choked as the smoke engulfed her. "Please help me!"

"Get up there, rook!" Capt. McCarrick footed the ladder for Cheeseburger. He climbed as fast as he could, trying to remember what he was supposed to do until the woman surprised them by suddenly yanking her children into the window.

"Ma'am, wait!" Cheeseburger dropped the axe because the mother, who could barely breathe, was now dangling two coughing kids by their feet.

Cheeseburger grabbed the first kid and hurriedly descended until Capt. McCarrick screamed, "Just drop him! I got it!"

Cheeseburger obeyed and was so panicked he did not even look down to see if the kid was okay. All he could think about was the woman. She was now on the verge of passing out and dropping her other son onto his head.

"Give him here!" He snatched the choking kid and dropped him because time was running out. The fire poured into the room at the exact second Cheeseburger yanked her headfirst out of the window.

Capt. McCarrick screamed, "Use your knee!"

Like muscle-reflex, Cheeseburger instantly remembered the move Capt. McCarrick had taught them in their academy. Since she was still half-conscious, he sat her on his knee and descended one rung at a time as she gagged and drooled in his face.

At the bottom, Capt. McCarrick tended to the victims while Dutch moved the ladder to the next window.

Capt. McCarrick toggled his mic. "Engine 2 to Fire Alarm. Get somebody around back. We got three pulled out needing medical attention."

Cheeseburger, still winded, now footed the ladder for Dutch. As he had for decades, Dutch Carrigan started climbing. He could not scamper up as fast as he once had, but he was a lot quicker than Capt. McCarrick.

The top of the ladder was right below the second-floor window. Dutch, already on air, screamed, "Watch out down there!" He let the axe fly and then used the handle to clear away any glass teeth still poking from the frame. Dense black smoke, chugging out as if pumped by an exhaust fan, swallowed Dutch completely.

Before Capt. McCarrick secured his mask, he said, "Engine 2 to Fire Alarm. Making entry on the second-floor of side-three in the 3-4 corner!"

"Roger. Engine 2's conducting a primary search of level 2, side-three, in the 3-4 corner."

Visibility was zero. Protocol called for both men to stay together in black-out conditions, but combined they had been doing this for sixty years. As one crawled left and the other right, they used axe handles to sweep the floor in-between for victims. They banged into each other at the door to the hall. Dutch put a glove on it and said through his mask, "It's pretty hot!"

"Pop it! If it's shitty we'll close it and bail!"

Eerily, the hallway was filled with incredible heat and even blacker smoke, but no flames. "Which way?" Dutch asked.

"Let's go left!"

They could not see a thing but knew this was how people died. Without a hose-line to follow out, one wrong turn and it was over. Capt. McCarrick kept clawing at Dutch's boots so he did not lose contact. Dutch crawled to the next door. "Ready?"

"Do it!"

The door opened on an inferno that immediately leapt towards them.

"Fuck me!" Dutch barely slammed the door in time. They continued crawling down the hallway until they hit the side-four wall. Doubling back on the opposite side of the hall was a sketchy gamble, but they got to check two more rooms before the hallway suddenly turned into a blast furnace. The heat was steam-filled because Engine 5 was climbing, battling, and pushing a giant ball of fire straight up the stairs.

"Holy Shit!" Lt. Anderson saw their helmet lights. "Who the fuck is that?"

"Dutch and Cap!" Dutch yelled back.

"Dutchy?" Lt. Anderson was laughing. "We almost killed you guys!"

Capt. McCarrick crawled around Dutch and stole the line from Lt. Anderson. "Enough with the chit-chat! We gotta fully involved room down here! Pull me some line!"

Lt. Andrews and Dutch dragged the line. At the door, Capt. McCarrick screamed, "Here we go, Dutchy!"

Dutch flung open the door as Capt. McCarrick braced and unloaded with the nozzle. The water met the fire in a stand-off of boiling vapor and exploding smoke. Debris flew everywhere. The fire hissed at the water, turning it to steam as a stifling punishment. Dutch ducked behind him to help advance the line into the room. Capt. McCarrick figure-eighted the nozzle, swinging it from the ceiling to floor and wall to wall.

"Aw fuck!" Capt. McCarrick's Vibe-Alert began rattling his mask. It meant he had 25% of his air remaining. Dutch's popped a minute later but both were having too much fun to leave.

Dutch yelled, "That corner!"

Capt. McCarrick swung the nozzle and blew the last of the fire out the shattered window. He dropped the line. "Let's go! We gotta go!"

They reversed back into the hallway where Dutch told Lt. Andrews, "Fire's out but we didn't search it!"

"Okay."

"We gotta go!" Dutch led them back to the ladder. Once on the ground, they ripped off their helmets and masks and panted in the smoke-filled air.

"I wish we did this every fucking shift," Dutch said.

"Me too." But Capt. McCarrick was wheezing and sweating. He saw the concern on Cheeseburger's face and said, "What the fuck are you looking at?"

"You, you sexy bitch."

Dutch burst out laughing. "Ain't that right?"

"Fuck you too, Dutchy." But Capt. McCarrick's soot-smeared face could not hide his smile. He clapped Cheeseburger on the shoulder and said, "I can't believe I'm about to say this, but that was some salty shit, junior. Now let's go change out bottles before someone else steals all our fun."

They grabbed their gear and tools and headed back to the truck.

SOUNDING THE ALARM

When newbies stepped across certain lines and found success, they gained a foothold into a whole new world. Still shy of total acceptance, it was more a nod from the veterans who knew the difference.

At a press conference the next day, union president Lt. Ahearn played footage from yesterday's fire. Bystanders with cell phones had caught the drama of Cheeseburger's triple rescue. Lt. Ahearn paused the footage and said, "Now remember, this was at eleven o'clock in broad daylight. The first two engines—one shut down from the rolling blackouts, the other involved in a crash on the way to the fire—were out of the picture. The third-due engine had to make rescues like these, so it was actually the fourth due truck that finally provided water. It is not an overstatement to say that if not for the heroic actions of the Sachem City Fire Department this story could have had a much more tragic ending. Sixteen people were inside at the time of the fire. Imagine if this was at midnight? People trying to find their way out of an inferno filled with darkness and smoke? With one working smoke detector all the way up on the third-floor, it would've been a massacre. The worst part is that it only took four weeks to see how short-sighted these manpower cuts truly are. The citizens of this city need to know we will move heaven and earth to help you but make no mistake. We are all now playing Russian Roulette with a revolver solely provided by Receiver Tillinghast."

One of the reporters shouted, "But hasn't the new Fire Chief signed off on the safety of these manpower reductions?"

"I won't pretend to know the new chief's motivations behind agreeing to these dangerous proposals. You'll have to ask him why the safety of his own men and women and the people of this city can be sacrificed in the name of fiscal responsibility."

Another reporter added, "Are you saying the new chief knows he's deliberately placing people in harm's way?"

"Yes."

Murmurs and scribbling filled the room. A third reporter asked, "Lieutenant, do you know the time it took for the fourth due engine to arrive at the fire?"

"Eleven minutes. A fire doubles in size every thirty seconds, so for anyone trying to escape this death trap, that would make it the longest eleven minutes of their lives. Let's not forget without an adequately staffed Fire Prevention office to make inspections and enforce the fire codes, who is going to make sure that there isn't one lone detector on the third-floor of a place filled with illegal apartments? I hope people are beginning to understand how lucky we got on Terrace Street yesterday afternoon. Hopefully, next time it won't end with someone's funeral."

ON DEAF EARS

Fire Chief Leo Fishbakke had spent the last few weeks transforming his new office after his promotion. The walls were freshly painted. His wife, ever the perfectionist, had even hung new drapes and family pictures. But her worst idea was the bowl of candies from which he could not stop eating.

His phone rang and Ma Dukes told him, "Lt. Ahearn's here to see you."

"Send him in."

Chief Fishbakke glanced around looking for anything out of place. He checked his tie and then wiped the sweat from last night's gin off his forehead.

"Good morning, lieutenant." Chief Fishbakke poked through a hastily opened folder. He motioned his reading glasses towards an empty chair and said, "Have a seat."

"If this is about yesterday you can save your breath."

"So much for pleasantries, right?"

"You're sitting in the same chair, of the same man, who actually had the courage to speak truth to power."

"I had nothing to do with Chief Draper's dismissal."

"Maybe not. But you certainly didn't waste any time stepping over his corpse to swear an oath you've already broken."

"How noble." Chief Fishbakke was annoyed. "And save me the indignation. The part you seem to be missing is that we don't get to tell them anything anymore, lieutenant, those days are gone."

"Is there a reason you called me in here?"

"The incendiary rhetoric, the need to throw the entire department under the bus at any one of the last half-dozen press conferences you've held... Accusing me of having secret motivations and not caring about the safety of my men? Who do you think you are? What gives you that right?"

Lt. Ahearn stood and pointed at the walls. "Usually, by the time someone reaches this office, these walls are filled with old newspaper clippings or photos from their career." He made his way to the door. "Guess pictures of the family are better than empty spaces, right?"

"Be careful, lieutenant—"

Lt. Ahearn slammed the door and nodded at Ma Dukes on the way out.

HISTORY REVEALED

August 22, 2009

Master Box 215 triggered in Fire Alarm at 10:15 A.M. on a Saturday morning. Rhode Islanders were likely at the beach or on the water most summer weekends, so downtown Sachem City was empty.

Fonzie, who normally worked on the rescue, had come in on his day off to work for a buddy on Engine 2. Besides, Fonzie loved Station 2. Little had changed in the 123 years since the City Hall complex had been built, and 100-year-old pictures still hung on its walls. Firefighters were frozen in time wearing the gear and uniform particular to their generation, but otherwise change happened at a glacial pace. Two-hundred years later, soot-covered men with outrageous mustaches were still photographed at scenes wielding axes and hooks like unhinged Vikings. The apparatus had gone from horse-drawn coal-fired steam engines to 600 horsepower Cummins diesels powering Hale pumps capable of throwing out over 1600 gallons of water a minute.

Because of his grandfather, Fonzie appreciated the stories and history from World War II. It was this same tradition of honor and sacrifice that made the fire department his newest obsession.

When the All-Call tones hit for Master Box 215, Fonzie had just finished playing with the industrial-strength airbags. They were pneumatic and used for lifting heavy objects, like cars. Since Sachem City could not afford to man a Special Hazard's truck, all the extrication equipment, jaws, and torches, were carried on Engine 2. Founded in 1814 by amending the village charter, Engine Company 2 was now, 198 years later, among the oldest continuous fire companies in the country. Yet it was not even the oldest in Sachem City. The formation of Engine 1 was the first act of a nascent city government. Created in 1801, "The Wild Ones" had just turned 208 years old. But Engine 2 was still the busiest truck, responding on over 3400 runs a year. Most of the guys who bid there were hard-chargers that spent their down time talking tactics and exploiting the lessons learned from other departments nationwide. They were junkies for training and new toys, so they always got the best equipment and gear before anyone else. This also, in a hyper-competitive environment, earned them no friends at the other stations.

"Attention Engines 2, 1, 3, Ladder 1, Battalion 3. Box Alarm, 136 Main Street..."

Engine 2, Ladder 1, and the Battalion Chief left Station 2 and headed two blocks north. The Augustus Theater was a five-story brick building built in 1889. During Sachem City's rise, the mill owners and businessmen from New York and Boston had required certain cultural amenities. To this end, they funded the arts and built regal theaters on par with their counterparts in more heralded places. There was the Paragon, the Strand, the Universal, the Music Hall, the Leroy, and the granddaddy of them all, the Augustus. Plays, musicals, vaudeville revues, and national theater companies always made stops in Sachem City. In 1893, the Augustus was the first theater to debut silent movies outside of Boston or New York. In 1928, Broadway productions and silent films were eventually replaced by "talkies," the first movies with dialogue and sound. Structurally, the five-story building went through many transformations, and to survive finally morphed into a dinner-theater before closing for good in 1973. Like many of the abandoned buildings citywide, owners were either hidden behind multiple LLC's or buried in red tape and bankrupt, so no one paid taxes on anything.

Fonzie knew none of this. He was born in 1987, fourteen years after they shuttered the windows and locked this history away forever.

Lt. Enrique Salamanca grabbed the mic and said, "Engine 2's on-scene. Five-story brick building, nothing showing." He was a squat man with a permanent five o'clock shadow. After his parents emigrated to Sachem City from Guatemala fifty-years ago, Salamanca's father became one of the city's first Hispanic firefighters. Nicknamed "Token" because of it, the elder Salamanca was a powerlifter, and he began training his son almost as soon as he could walk. After that, Enrique, or "Baby Token," spent most days in the gym with his dad. It paid off. Senior year, Baby Token was bench-pressing and squatting 400-pounds apiece. His arms, legs, and torso were different diameter-sized barrels. Within two years of joining the department, he was voted captain of the team that took down the police department at the annual "Guns and Hoses" weight-lifting tournament. The son of good Catholics, Lt. Salamanca did not drink or smoke or hang out in bars, and spent most days-off playing with his two small daughters. A stickler for the job, he expected the same from his crew. Fonzie knew this, so he was paying extra close attention to detail.

As always, the first-due truck's chauffeur stayed with the truck to man the pump-panel in case there was a fire, so only Lt. Salamanca and Fonzie geared up. The August heat, inside the mattress-like bunker gear, boots, and helmet, on top of the forty-five-pounds of air-pack and tools, made everything heavier.

The "Knox Box" was a small steel cube bolted into the exterior walls of all businesses, public buildings, high-rises, and any multi-unit dwellings. The fire department carried a master key that opened these tiny boxes. Inside were other keys specific to that building only. Alarms happened all the time, and not always in the middle of the day. Since no building could ever be left in full alarm, the Knox Box allowed entry without smashing doors and windows.

Lt. Salamanca swung open the hand-carved front door. The fire alarm panel was right inside the hallway. The Acting Battalion Chief,

Theodore Etchel, put on his reading glasses to examine the panel. He was actually the Captain of Engine 1, but since there had still been no promotions to fill the vacancies created by July's mass exodus, Etchel had been forced into the B.C.'s car on C-Shift. A thirty-year veteran, B.C. Etchel had been classmates with Dutch Carrigan, Capt. LeClaire, and Lt. Killmoor. He was 60-years-old and had a full head of shockingly white hair. He knew he should have retired before the contract expired but just could not pull the trigger. Life without his beloved Engine 1 was something he was not quite ready to envision. A superb athlete, he still played basketball, golf, and cards, and had emptied the pockets of many co-workers betting on all three through the years.

B.C. Etchel glanced at the panel and said, "Smoke detector, third-floor, rear hallway."

"Roger." Lt. Salamanca popped on his helmet light. Despite the sunny day, inside it was dusty and dark. They were sweating already. The guys from Ladder 1 joined them as everyone's lights swept the double-wide oak staircase. On the walls, ancient candelabras were filled with spiderwebs.

As their boots echoed in the cavernous dark, Fonzie swung his light to the left and said, "Holy crap."

"That used to be the main stage." Lt. Salamanca kept climbing.

Fonzie's 1000 lumen light pushed back the shadows. Hundreds of seats surrounded a full orchestra pit and three-story stage. Rows of lights hung like stalagmites in front of the thirty-foot tall curtain. The second-floor was only a U-shaped balcony of additional seating. The third-floor was a dining room with a 300-person capacity, and on floors four and five were luxurious hotel rooms. A century before, Fonzie could almost picture men in top-hats and elegant women selling the place out on a Saturday night.

Lt. Salamanca lead them into the third-floor dining room. In the rear hallway, the smoke detector was activated. He dug the shoulder mic out of his jacket and said, "Engine 2A to Battalion 3."

"Go ahead."

"We got the detector. No smoke or fire. Try for a reset."

"Roger that. Battalion 3 to Fire Alarm. Code Yellow for myself, Engine 2 and Ladder 1."

"Roger, chief." Fire Alarm hit the Alert Tone. *"Attention all companies operating at 136 Main Street. It's a Code Yellow for Engine 2, Ladder 1, and Battalion 3."*

The Code Yellow released the other two engine companies staging outside.

B.C. Etchel said, "Battalion 3 to Fire Alarm. System will not reset. We're gonna need a building rep down here."

"Roger. Standby."

"Battalion 3 to Engine 2A. Pull that detector and let's see if we can zone it out."

Lt. Salamanca looked up at Fonzie, who was eight-inches taller, and said, "Find a chair, big boy."

Fonzie pulled one over and popped the detector. He blinked, confused, because water splashed across his chest.

"Damn it." Lt. Salamanca triggered his radio. "Engine 2A to Battalion 3. Looks like we have a water leak. The detector's full of it."

"Roger."

"Fire Alarm to Battalion 3. Building representative will be on-scene within ten minutes."

"Roger that."

Lt. Salamanca helped Fonzie safely step down and said, "You make me feel like a dwarf, kid."

"Yeah, well, I don't know too many dwarves that can bench press four-hundred pounds."

By the time they trekked back down to the front door they were all panting and sweating. Lt. Salamanca and Fonzie dropped their axes and air-packs. They shed their helmets and jackets and then wiped away the sweat.

B.C. Etchel turned to the guys from Ladder 1 and said, "Do me a favor. Kill the water and then you guys can clear. We'll wait for the rep."

Fonzie was still in awe. "This place is incredible."

"Did you see the upstairs?" B.C. Etchel asked. "The tables?"

"I didn't. I guess I missed that."

"They're still set for dinner. That's how fast this place closed down."

"Creepy. Just walking up there I felt like I was surrounded by ghosts."

"This was the place, when I was a kid, it was *thee* place to be. There's a bar in the basement, and that's where all the men would hang out and play cards."

Lt. Salamanca said, "Guess that's where you learned how to fleece your co-workers."

"Absolutely." B.C. Etchel grinned, his teeth even whiter than his hair. "They took the wives to dinner upstairs, stayed for a show, and afterward hung out in the bar smoking cigars while the women took their martinis to the verandas. You see this?" B.C. Etchel pointed at a ticket window cut into the wall. "People must've been really small back then to sit in there."

Fonzie said, "It's amazing. I grew up here and never knew anything about this place."

"My father was drinking here the night 316 Main Street burned to the ground. Right down the street. It used to be an old rooming house. Packed with people, packed. They rented by the room. Anyway, a lady on the first-floor was using a hot-plate and lit her drapes on fire. She panicked and ran from the room. But she left the door open. The fire roared out and up the staircase. People were jumping out of the fourth-floor windows and dying in the street."

"Unbelievable."

"My dad was off-duty. He was on Ladder 1. I remember standing with him at this exact spot as the glow of the fire lit up the whole block. There were a bunch of off-duty guys here and they all left to get their gear. Fourteen people died that night."

"Really?"

"Yup. November 1961. Deadliest fire in the city's history."

The front door opened and silhouetted a small figure. He was old and thin and wore a Herringbone Ivy cap despite the heat. His cane was polished wood with a carved bone handle.

"Mr. Keys," B.C. Etchel said. "How you doing, Sherm?"

"Outstanding, Chief. Sadly, I would also say that I am doing far better than you all, considering what a mess everything is."

"You ain't kidding. It hasn't been this bad since the 1970's. You remember those days."

"Indeed I do."

B.C. Etchel turned to Fonzie and said, "This is Sherman Keisler. Long retired but not forgotten."

"From the very old school." Keisler's ancient parchment skin creased into a warm smile. His eyes looked like two brown buttons surrounded by wrinkles. "This new asshole Receiver and his rolling blackouts must be straining everything and everyone. It's a miracle this hasn't already ended in disaster."

B.C. Etchel patted his shoulder and said, "From your mouth to God's ears, my friend."

Fonzie asked, "Why do they call you Mr. Keys?"

Sherman reached behind his back and detached the biggest key ring Fonzie had ever seen.

B.C. Etchel said, "All these old buildings downtown, the closed down mills, Sherm's the caretaker. He served with my dad back in the day."

"That's right. We were on the rescue together when the rescue was just a station wagon with oxygen and bandages."

Fonzie asked, "What year was this?"

"Well, I was born in 1923. Got on the job in 1948, after the war. Rescue 1 came into service in 1955. I was one of the first six that manned it because back then there were only three battalions. Things, as you might imagine, were vastly different. There were no radios, so you'd get dispatched by phone. One ring was for the engine, two was for the rescue. And Box Alarms would be announced by bell. After it rang, the junior guy would have to go check the ticker-tape machine to see who was going and what the address was."

"Are you talking about the old pull-boxes on the street?"

"Yes. That's all there was back then. The 911 number was created later in 1968, so everyone in the neighborhood knew where their pull-box was."

"It's crazy that some of this stuff has never changed, like a century later they're still dispatching the same trucks in the same order."

"People..." Sherman Keisler smiled. "They're the only thing that changes. Buildings, highways—what's not alive can never die."

"Until it burns to the ground," Lt. Salamanca said.

"You're just like your old man. He came to work everyday praying we would get a fire."

"Fire Alarm to Battalion 3."

B.C. Etchel triggered his radio. "Battalion 3."

"Box 476 just came in. Are you in service?"

"Yes, I am. So is Engine 2."

Fire Alarm hit the All-Call tones and announced, *"Attention Engines 4, 2, 3, Ladder 2, Battalion 3. Box Alarm..."*

Sherman Keisler said, "What's the story here?"

Lt. Salamanca threw his gear back on. "Water leak in the ceiling. Third-floor, rear hallway. We pulled the detector and it was full of water. The ladder guys already killed the main."

"I'll get the plumber over here. And then the alarm company. Thank you, gentlemen."

"It was nice to meet you." Fonzie shook his hand.

Sherman craned his neck. "I think you're twice my height."

"For real." Lt. Salamanca grabbed his axe and helmet.

B.C. Etchel held the door open and toggled his shoulder mic. "Battalion 3 to Fire Alarm. Responding from 136 Main Street. A building representative is on-scene and has taken control of the building. He's been advised that there is currently no fire protection at this address."

"Roger, Chief. We have you responding to Box 476. Switch to Channel 2."

They piled back into their vehicles and headed for the east side in the summer sun.

***

Fonzie headed home after work. His grandfather's single-story ranch house had stayed in the family after his death, so Fonzie bought it off his dad and uncles.

Molly Bish's car was in the driveway. She already had a key and a toothbrush stored for overnight visits even though they had only been dating for two months. Fonzie found her dumping ice into a cooler and said, "How we looking?"

"Good to go." She slammed the lid and grabbed her purse. "Haley said not to bring any food."

"All right. I'll get changed and then we'll blast." He leaned down and gave her a kiss. She barely weighed a hundred pounds, so Fonzie lifted her up with one arm as she squealed, "Stop it!"

"My little bean." He smiled and kissed her before setting her back down. He put on shorts and a T-shirt covered in paint. He was such a large man the Coleman cooler looked like a shoebox in his hands.

Six-blocks later, they pulled into a dilapidated triple-decker with other triple-deckers tightly packed around it.

"The House of Bag." Fonzie killed the engine.

T-Bag was on an extension ladder with a paintbrush. Like his class-mates, who were all acquiring property or buying homes, painting was the one cost unskilled labor could complete for free. T-Bag's mom, Hilda, and girlfriend, Haley, were painting the low stuff. All of them waved at the new arrivals.

"Look at this crew." Fonzie set down the cooler by the painting supplies. "This must be the A-Team."

"Hell yeah, son, thanks for coming." T-Bag grabbed the side-rails of the ladder and skip-jumped it down the wall.

"Stop it!" Haley turned to Fonzie. "Please tell him to stop doing that. He's too lazy to climb down and actually move the ladder."

"That's not true." T-Bag skipped it again. "When I painted houses, climbing up and down wastes time. And wasted time costs money."

"Where do you want us to start?" Fonzie asked.

"Anywhere you want, bro, but you haven't even cracked a beer yet."

"Good point."

"Ma!" T-Bag called out. "You remember Fonzie's girl, Molly, right?"

"Of course. The world needs more nurses." Hilda Taymaskhanov put down her paint brush. She and her son had the same green eyes but she was much prettier. Her husband had been dead for twenty-years, but she never re-married. Her long black hair was streaked gray and lassoed into a ponytail. "Can I get either one of you a water? Something to eat?"

Haley turned to T-Bag. "You might as well tell everyone the menu."

"What?" He acted offended. "What's wrong with hot dogs and grilled cheese?"

"Nothing, if you're in second-grade."

Molly laughed as she poured paint into a plastic container and grabbed a brush. She and Fonzie were painting together when T-Bag called down, "You two make a good team. The elf gets the low stuff, and the giant gets the rest!"

"Hey!" Molly pretended to kick out his ladder. "You shouldn't insult the help, especially when the help is working for free."

"She has a point," Haley said. "And this is a big damn house."

"True story." T-Bag skipped the ladder as everyone yelled at him again. "Ma! Put on some tunes!"

"I'll do it." Haley fired up some reggae.

T-Bag gyrated on the ladder. "Fonzie! Beer me!"

"No!" girlfriend and mother yelled together.

Haley added, "You're doing enough stupid things up there as it is."

"Sorry, bro." Fonzie shrugged. "You just got shut down."

"Dude, where's the love?"

It did not get dark until 9 P.M., so they broke for dinner at 7:30 P.M.

"Okay." T-Bag emerged from the kitchen with a platter of sand-wiches. "I have something for everyone. Grilled cheese, grilled cheese and bacon, and grilled cheese and tomato."

"Wow, what a connoisseur," Haley cracked.

"Easy with the big words, Webster."

"Hey!"

He laughed and started grilling hot dogs. They were barely on the table before he said, "All right, people, eat with a purpose. We're losing daylight and I really need to start drinking."

Fonzie chuckled.

"Look at the Big Kielbasa." T-Bag pointed at Fonzie's plate. "Four grilled cheese and three hot dogs. That's a compliment, bro."

"Nobody makes grilled cheese like you."

"I fucking love you, man."

"Watch your mouth," Haley and Hilda said.

T-Bag asked Fonzie, "You like the potato salad?"

"I do."

"That's homemade, too."

"He's lying," Haley immediately said.

"I also made cupcakes."

"No, he didn't."

Everyone was laughing. He came out with the store-bought cupcakes and said, "All right, people, let's go. One hand can hold the cupcake while the other works the paintbrush."

They ignored him completely and kept eating.

DANGEROUS PLACES
September 15, 2009

A month later, summer was over and school had started. It was still a beautiful day when the nightshift at Pasco Papertube began at five o'clock. But at 6:58 P.M., a 911 call relayed news of a possible machine fire on the fourth-floor.

Fire Alarm hit the All-Call tones and stated, *"Attention Engines 2, 1, 3, Ladder 1, Battalion 1, Still Alarm. 1680 Addison Street. Possible machine fire..."*

Certain streets or businesses were known to be dangerous places, so this address sent a shudder through everyone working. Addison straddled the border between Sachem City and Central Falls. Concentrated in this six-square-block area were the biggest mills in either city. Ten thousand people once went to work in the six gigantic buildings that formerly comprised MacCallum Manufacturing. Now it was just 2,000,000-square-feet of ghost town ringed by a mile of chain-link fence. Pasco Papertube employed just fifty people and was the only business left in the one remaining operable mill.

Engine 5 was supposed to be the first-due truck, but they were tied up on a medical run. Capt. Gary Romine was not happy about this. He kept clenching his fist as they waited for the rescue. The call was for chest pain and totally legitimate, so by law they could not leave without the rescue on-scene. It was called "Transfer of Care," and violations like that got people fired.

Romine's two privates, Matt Biggio and Sylvester Keating, were taking vital signs. Biggio was an Air Force veteran with three small daughters. While some joined the fire department having never known anything or been anywhere else, others had traveled the world. In this latter class, Biggio had been a star college baseball pitcher before partying it all away. Despite a 98 MPH fastball, he got expelled from North Carolina State after a Spring Break gone horribly wrong. Fluent in three languages, he later scored a scholarship to the Sorbonne in Paris and studied Humanities at a world class level. He was also an accomplished saucier who made some of the best meals on the job. But his time exposed to European racing had also turned him into a mad speed addict, so twice a month he raced his Ducati motorcycle at New Hampshire Motor Speedway at 190 MPH. Three years before, he got pulled over on a deserted stretch of I-95 doing 170 MPH and nearly lost his job. The Rhode Island State Police found little humor in speeds like that, much less from a first-responder. He was going so fast he did not even know they were chasing him until the Connecticut State Police popped him at the border. And while his career would be saved and might yet be filled with future achievements, he would, like Ozzy Osbourne after the decapitated bat, be forever known for this one stupendous act.

This was also why Sylvester Keating was an important crew member. He wore thick glasses and had a seemingly intrinsic knowledge of all things electrical and mechanical. He studied textbooks on subjects concerning gas/air ratios of explosive chemicals, technical rescues, and anything concerning pump-operations. He had a fetish for the brute power required to move huge quantities of water, which weighed 8.1 pounds per gallon, so his head was filled with myriad pump theories and formulas. A natural worrier, he also played devil's advocate at crucial moments to reign in his ultra-aggressive boss and partner.

When Rescue 1 arrived, Capt. LeClaire could see Engine 5 was nearly having a stroke, so he said, "Head to Pasco. We got this."

"You sure?" Capt. Romine was already throwing on his gear and called responding on Channel 2. "Thanks, Cap. Maybe we'll see you there."

"I hope not. If you don't get a quick stop, we're all gonna be there for a week."

Biggio threw on his jacket and called out, "Cap, patient can ambulate. Vitals are stable. BP's 140 over 90, pulse 72. Chest pain started an hour ago with no cardiac history. Eight out of ten on pain."

"Roger."

Capt. Romine climbed into the truck and hammered the siren as they screamed away.

When Engine 5 rounded the corner, Capt. Romine could see two things. The first was Ladder 1 and Engine 1 smashing windows on the ground-floor, and the second was smoke pouring out of the fourth-floor on the complete opposite end of the humongous building.

"What the fuck're they doing?" Capt. Romine toggled the mic. "Engine 5 on-scene."

"Engine 5 on-scene at 1823."

"Bobby!" Capt. Romine shouted at the lieutenant of Engine 1. "What's going on?"

"Standpipes are dry. The box didn't even trip. Donut wants to run a line all the way from here."

"That's like a thousand feet and four stairwells away." Capt. Romine could not believe it. "We got five minutes before this whole place turns into an inferno. One-line ain't gonna be enough anyway. Where is he?"

"Donut? Down the alley around back."

When Capt. Romine turned and saw Ladder 1's Lt. Kaczmarek, he seemed relieved. "Kaz" was one of the lucky officers because his crew remained intact despite the mass vacancies. His privates were young, dedicated, and knowledgeable, but they were also relentless ball-busters. Scotty Dumas, nicknamed "Beef" because he was a chunk of man with a neck as wide as his head, provided the dry one-liners. His partner, "The Kid," was an impish character and legendary ladies' man who called everyone Kid. He also never stopped talking. They were both in their late twenties and called Kaz "Dad" just to torture him. While some crews could not stand each other, Kaz, Beef Dumas, and the Kid were nearly inseparable, even off-duty. The symbiosis created by this familiarity transformed them into one of the best ladder crews in the city.

Capt. Romine said to Kaz, "Yes or no. Can you back that thing down this alley?"

"Beef!" Lt. Kaczmarek shouted to his chauffeur. "Cap's wondering if you can make this alley!"

Beef Dumas barely smirked. "Does the Pope shit in the woods?"

"Perfect." Capt. Romine pointed. "Back that thing down the alley and put the stick up. Engine 1's gonna lay a feeder from here. We're gonna turn you guys into a standpipe. We can attach two attack lines into the pre-connects in the basket."

"Fucking brilliant." Lt. Kaczmarek turned to his guys. "You heard him."

"What about Donut?" the Engine 1 lieutenant asked.

"I'll handle him," Capt. Romine said. "Besides, he never met a good idea he wouldn't take credit for." He headed down the tiny alley between the two mills. This was the only way in since it was basically a cul-de-sac surrounded by the massive mill. Once he turned the corner, he saw Engine 2 and B.C. McLoud, a.k.a. Donut, looking up at the smoke chugging from a fourth-floor window.

Since all four Battalion Chiefs had retired en masse on June 30, the senior captain on each shift became acting Battalion Chief by default. Unfortunately for the men on A-Shift, that left Capt. Frederick McLoud in charge. Like Chief Fishbakke, Capt. McLoud had largely avoided his entire career by dodging the rescue, hiding out in the Division of Training, or on slower trucks acquiring no skills. Since he talked a big game in front of the same men who openly derided his rank, most would not follow him into a Dunkin Donuts, much less a burning building.

He was only 5'9" but weighed over 300 pounds, so he looked like an obese canary in his extra-large yellow turnout gear.

B.C. McLoud was monitoring the radio when he saw Capt. Romine appear. "Seems to be contained to one room on the fourth-floor—"

"Are you kidding me?" Capt. Romine checked himself. Nicknamed "Bullet Head" because of his shaved head and ultra-abrasive nature, he wielded a hard-earned edge with regard for no one. That was because in the 1970's, Capt. Romine's father, Chief Romine, made a slew of enemies. A recession had forced pay and benefit cuts, so the department was understaffed. It became a dangerous career no one wanted if they could make twice the salary working in the mills. Things got so bad the city could not give the job away, so necessity forced them to hire who-ever they could. Test scores were thrown out, standards were dropped, background checks went uncompleted, and soon the ranks became filled with bikers, brawlers, and small-time hoodlums. Parties raged at some stations on the weekends. Guys showed up for work drunk and fought each other, drank some more, and fought again.

Historically, discipline and authority were always enforced. The line grunts respected their officers and vigorously policed themselves. If someone got out of line or tried to rise above the good of the others, he or she was immediately smacked back in place. It usually began with guys dropping hints about the offending behavior, whatever it was, from not checking the truck to not cleaning or doing enough housework. The offender might get a week of subtle nudges, but behind the scenes, around kitchen tables at every station, impromptu courts were condemning suspects with or without their presence or testimony. And no one could evade this justice. If the offending behavior did not improve, all subtleties were dropped. Guys would just gang up like a pack of wolves restoring order. The accused could be hounded and harassed until they sometimes bid to a different station just to escape the abuse. The only problem was that one's reputation remained such a knotted, visible scar, no laser could ever remove it. And the new crew, by decree of the courts, were free to administer further torment if the offending behavior continued.

This was the kind of thing that went missing in the early 1970's. The pride was gone. They were working three dayshifts, three nightshifts, and had three days off. That translated to a seventy-two-hour work-week for $115 before taxes. Bad pay and no healthcare meant most had other jobs first and the fire department came second. Rogue actors and other department thugs started turning up in all the wrong places. Next door, the police were sick of making the arrests of firemen disappear. Meetings were held, the mayor informed, but nothing happened until the F.B.I. and State Police took down a cocaine syndicate running out of Station 3. Since the city's politics was so insular, a ring of powerful families had relatives working in City Hall, the District Attorney's office, and the Police and Fire Departments. Because of this, the F.B.I. and State Police kept the S.C.P.D. totally out of the loop for operational safety.

After the bust, the good old days were over. In the Fire Department's 208-year history, only one chief had ever been hired from outside the department—Chief William Romine. He was a retired Battalion Chief from Philadelphia who made his bones on Engine 7 on Kensington Avenue, an outpost in the Harrowgate neighborhood renowned for violence. At his job interview in 1975, he sat across from the Sachem City mayor and promised a radical transformation. He instituted a buy-out to nudge the older guys out the door, and then welcomed a brand-new class of forty tested recruits. Pay and benefits were increased, and random "lifestyle" checks were enforced at every station day and night. It took five years to reverse course, but when the department re-emerged in the 1980's, it had been re-forged.

However, memories were long when generations of firefighters from the same families carried on their fathers' wars. Chief Romine lasted long enough to see his only son get sworn in as a Sachem City firefighter. But by 1985, the chief got forced out by the new mayor, whose own father had been one of the corrupters Chief Romine chased off the job a decade before.

In hindsight, the chief should have gotten his son a job on the Philadelphia Fire Department instead. At first, Gary Romine was only ostracized, but after Chief Romine got fired, Gary became one man against 135. Everyone hated him. Most guys went their whole careers without ever getting "called to the basement." For generations, the basement was where perceived injustices or slights got settled. Afterwards, the two combatants would mop up their blood and shake hands like men. Not anymore. Gary Romine got challenged at every station. Guys he barely knew called him out the second he walked through the door. It got so bad he did not even want to go to work. Who his dad was would never change, so he did not know how to stop the abuse until, one day at Station 4, he smashed an elbow into Mean Sully's temple. Since there were so many Sullivans on the job, each one had a nickname. There was Drunk Sully, Dumb Sully, Stinky Sully etc. Mean Sully was a brawler with fists as big as a pit bull's jaw. A onetime amateur boxer, Sully's massive handlebar mustache looked like a dead ferret stapled above his lip and draped down each side of his mouth. He was twenty-years older than Bullet Head and no stranger to the basement. With an engine, ladder, and rescue at Station 4, eight guys were on-shift that night to watch a legend fall. Mean Sully caught that elbow across the temple and immediately crumpled. Romine, as stunned as everyone else, just jumped and pummeled him until the others pulled him off.

It turned out to be a statement beating. Once word spread of Mean Sully's violent de-throning, guys belatedly realized all their harassment had created a monster. Bullet Head was bench pressing 380 pounds and in the shape of his life. He knew he was a marked man, so he tried to be stronger, smarter, and tougher than everyone else. Guys had to be on the job for ten years before they could take the lieutenant's test, so Romine started studying at year eight. He got the highest score and became an officer. Two years later, once he became eligible for the captain's test, he crushed it, and two years after that scored number one on the Battalion Chief's test. But these lists were only good for two years, so without any retirements or movement up top, they got discarded.

He impatiently waited and tested three more times, but nothing came available. Even worse, after the contract expired and all four Battalion Chiefs retired, the Receiver came in and halted all promotions. Which is how Capt. Romine, who sat at number one, was now taking orders off Capt. McLoud, who, as the senior of two captains on-shift, was entitled to the B.C. spot instead.

"We don't have time for this." Bullet Head Romine couched his response. "Listen, with all due respect, instead of dragging a thousand-feet of hose through a cluttered nightmare, we can just use Ladder 1."

"Ladder 1? Are you crazy? That thing will never—"

"Here it comes now."

They heard the beeping as Beef Dumas, in a maneuver that would be talked about for years, did the impossible. With six inches of clearance on either side, he somehow cut the turn perfectly in reverse and slid the forty-five-foot tower ladder around the corner. This part of the alley was wider, so he was able to get the outriggers down and lift the truck off the ground. In the basket, Lt. Kaczmarek and The Kid were busy screwing 1¾ inch attack lines onto the pre-piped discharges. If needed, they could also blast 1500 gallons a minute through the master-stream canon hanging below the basket. Lt. Kaczmarek was already considering using it as a last resort.

On the fourth-floor, Engine 3, already on-air, smashed out two windows and waited as the swirling smoke spun around them.

Lt. Kaczmarek hit his mic. "How we looking down there?"

Capt. Romine's tiny figure gave him a thumbs up from the ground. Over the radio, he said to Kaz, "Hooking up the feeder right now. Should be going hot any second."

Six guys finished rolling out 250 feet of four-inch LDH from Engine 1 to Ladder 1. Engine 1's pump man already had the truck hooked up to a hydrant.

"Engine 1 to Ladder 1. We are good to go."

"Roger."

Beef Dumas swung the ladder toward the building. Lt. Kaczmarek and The Kid coughed through the chugging smoke. They handed the nozzles to Engine 3 even before the basket arrived at the engulfed window. Kaz triggered his mic and said, "Charge the line!"

The rushing water raced down the alley and snapped the large hose tight. It hit the pre-connect and shot up the ladder pipe where it slammed against the closed gates in the basket with a shuddering thud.

Engine 3 disappeared into the smoky room. The ladder guys fed them hose from the basket.

"Engine 3 to Ladder 1," the Darth Vader voice of the masked lieutenant called out. "Charge the lines."

Lt. Kaczmarek and The Kid spun open their gates. The attack lines snapped taut. The black smoke began turning gray after Engine 3 made entry and opened up with both nozzles. In the corner, a large paper rolling machine was engulfed in flame. The room was fully involved. Flames fueled by stacks of cardboard were itching to eat through the ceiling. Still, it was in a contained room and extinguished minutes later.

"Talk about anti-climactic." Lt. Kaczmarek was already busting balls. "Yeah, those Engine 3 guys are real heroes. Just so long as it takes half the department to get them a charged line while they sit in a window waiting like freaking Rapunzel."

"Right?" The Kid was loving it. "Which one's Kurt Russell gonna play when they make the movie?"

"Tom Cruise, Kurt Russell, Keanu Reeves... they'll still be no match next to the real thing. The legends..."

From inside the smoky window, someone said, "Knock-knock" one second before the attack line opened up. The helpless ladder crew had their helmets blown off in the massive soaking as anyone who witnessed it burst out laughing. But not B.C. McLoud. He triggered his mic and yelled, "Knock it off!"

Water rained down on him and others scurrying to find cover. The Kid curled into a ball on the floor of the basket as the onslaught continued. Lt. Kaczmarek swung them away from the building while getting pounded in the face for his troubles. He brought the four-inch canon hanging beneath the basket on target with the window.

As much as Capt. Romine would have loved to have seen this, it could not happen. Since no one listened to B.C. McLoud, he toggled his mic and said, "Ladder 1, stand down. You too, Engine 3."

People were still laughing. Ladder 1's Lt. Kaczmarek was totally soaked. He wiped off his face, yelling, "I hope you guys aren't too exhausted from that massive inferno to walk down four flights of stairs!"

Jokes were fine, but no one was under any misimpression. Five minutes either way and one of the biggest fires in the history of the city had just been averted.

As far as reputations were concerned, the men on A-Shift knew who the real boss was. Bullet Head had just climbed another notch.

LIEUTENANT DAVID KILLMOOR

The house was quiet now that their children and grandchildren had left for the evening. Lt. Killmoor was a large man with large hands and a chest as big as a table, so fortunately both of their daughters resembled their mother instead. Philosophically, even their son was more aligned with Penelope. Both were big men that looked alike, but politically and ideologically, they could not have been further apart. Still, they never let it get personal. The father wore Hawaiian shirts and professed old school peace and love, while the son was a two-tour combat Marine stationed in the Middle East. The daughters, like their mother, held that line as well. They might have been Democrats, but barely, like a purple mix of Republican and Democrat, the former especially in matters of foreign policy. Penelope may have married half a hippie, but she found no honor or safety in weakness. And if she had to send her only son into harm's way to prove the lengths of this belief, then so be it.

Early fall in Rhode Island still meant warm days and long hours before nightfall. Autumn was Penelope's favorite season, which is why Lt. Killmoor had built the fire pit in their backyard in the first place. As part of their nightly ritual, at dusk, they would start a fire, grab a bottle of wine, throw a blanket over each other, and cuddle against the chill.

Tonight was no different. Since each had known every part of the other for decades, he usually knew what she was going to say before she said it.

Penelope asked, "Do you think it was too much?"

"Nope." He almost bristled. "Do you think we raised three weaklings?"

She squeezed his hand and leaned against his shoulder as they watched the fire dance. They would notify their son who was deployed overseas by phone later that night. As for now, Penelope seemed resigned but stoic, as if what might come next had the distinct possibility of destroying their lives.

"Besides," he said, "you saw their reaction."

"Tough as nails," she concurred. "Whoever thought, you know?"

"How dare you." He lit up a cigar. "How could two exceptional parents such as ourselves not create two incredible women?"

He made her smile, however this time it did not linger. Penelope just stared into the flames. She usually liked the smell of his cigars but not tonight.

"Ugh," she said. "That thing is ultra stinky."

"Are you talking about me or the cigar?"

"Both." She squeezed his hand under the blanket and leaned on his shoulder again. "Can you promise me one thing?"

"Of course, my dear."

"No matter what happens, just promise me you'll wheel me out here so I can watch the fire?"

"You have my word." He heard her start to cry and that hurt most of all. "Hey, hey." He patted her head. "We're gonna fight this thing together."

"I don't want to die alone—"

"Trust me when I tell you that is never gonna happen."

Her tears would not stop and just kept rolling out of her eyes and down her face as if trying to escape. "We did a good job, didn't we?"

"Baby," he said, "we raised three of the greatest kids in the whole world. You're their mother. And you're my wife. And I wouldn't change a single goddamn second of the last thirty-one years."

She closed her eyes and smiled because he always knew what to say even if it was not true. She said, "I don't want to be a burden."

"You won't be. Unless you piss me off. Then I'll just wheel you into a corner and pretend you're not there."

She laughed while crying and then punched his shoulder. "Jerk."

"Honey," he said, "I'm planning on loving the fuck out of you until you throw me out." He did not want to cry either, but there was no controlling it now. "It's gonna kill us all, but I promise to keep this family together."

"No matter what?"

"No matter what."

"Please don't let all of this be in vain."

They were quiet for a time.

He said, "Did I ever tell you about the first time I saw you?"

"Are you talking about that day at the beach?"

"Yes. But I have a confession to make. I was originally attracted to your friend, so I stalked her until she met up with you."

"And then you stalked me?"

"Yup. Best decision I ever made."

"Me too."

A knot in the log exploded a shower of sparks into the sky. The silence became more comfortable, so they sat hand in hand and watched the flames.

THE VICE TIGHTENS
September 21, 2009

Things had only gotten worse in the two months since Sachem City's Chapter 9 declaration. A picket line was in front of City Hall every day from 9 A.M. to 5 P.M. Current and former teachers, policemen, janitors, garbage men, civil service workers, firefighters, and other unions from across the state took shifts carrying signs that were both inflammatory and informational.

When word spread that Receiver Tillinghast was holding a press conference, everyone marching took out their phones to watch it.

Lt. Ahearn, president of the union, positioned his so B.C. Etchel could watch the screen.

They watched Receiver Tillinghast step to the podium.

B.C. Etchel said, "As much as I hate him, the guy does know how to dress."

"How much do you think that suit cost him?"

"More than I make in three months."

"Ladies and gentlemen of Sachem City." Receiver Tillinghast, after years of public speaking, read from a prepared statement while dutifully making eye contact with everyone in the room. "As all of you know, recent events have called for immense sacrifice from our unions, our retirees, current public servants, and private citizens. Some have been asked to shoulder an unfair burden. Some have lost homes during this economic crisis. Others won't be able to retire when they originally planned. And none of this is fair. I wish it could stop here, but the new math dictates otherwise."

Lt. Ahearn smirked. "I think that's code for 'Lube up,' because someone's about to get porked."

"Right?" But B.C. Etchel could not leave it alone. "I mean look at his hair. It's perfectly in place. There's not a single hair out of place. Who lives like that?"

"You sound kind of jealous."

"Don't be hurtful."

Receiver Tillinghast continued, "We've already cut teachers' pay, privatized garbage and recycling pick-up, and removed minimum-manning from the fire department. But now even more is asked of us. As of tomorrow, the same will happen with the police department. By contract, there must be eleven officers on the street for both eight-hour dayshifts, and ten officers from midnight to 8 A.M. That will no longer be the case. That number will shrink to eight, eight, and seven. The Chief of Police assures me that this will not in any way endanger public safety."

"There it is." Lt. Ahearn knew what few others did—the police held all the secrets. When elected officials were caught behind the wheel at 2 A.M. after a night out drinking, or important businessmen got pulled over with their mistresses riding shotgun, the police knew it all. Which was also why most politicians were loath to poke this beast. Laying off cops and slashing their budgets meant there was nothing left to cut.

"In an effort to procure additional savings," Receiver Tillinghast said, "we have done an extensive cost/savings analysis. To this end, it also appears privatization of Sachem City's EMS responsibilities might save taxpayers millions more. This will also assist our beleaguered fire department."

"Excuse me?" B.C. Etchel blinked. "Did he just say he's handing our rescue duties over to private ambulance companies?"

"It looks like the Receiver wants a war." Lt. Ahearn was usually patient and measured, slow to anger. "This will destroy our job."

"How did they keep this under wraps? They leak like a sieve over there. You never heard anything about this?"

"Not a word."

"Jesus. That's even worse."

"EMS has become half of what we do. At least."

"That would also kill sixteen positions."

"That too." Lt. Ahearn looked grim. "Every department in the state just heard this. If we fall first, they're as good as gone." Right on cue, his phone exploded. He let all of it go to voicemail except one. "Hey, Vin."

"Billy, what the hell is going on over there?" Capt. Vincent Szceriack was the President of the Association of Rhode Island Firefighters. He was a twenty-three-year veteran of the Central Falls Fire Department and had an aggressive reputation. They all did. With nine guys on shift protecting one of the most densely populated cities in America, Central Falls was not a place for the easily daunted or discouraged. It was called "The Wild Mile" because of its square footage and penchant for violence. Since Sachem City responded to all fires in Central Falls on the first dispatch, this also meant the rolling blackouts put the guys in Central Falls at risk as well. Lt. Ahearn had known Vinny Szceriack for twenty years. They were both overweight, balding, and had no love for frivolous dispositions. They also abhorred surprises.

Lt. Ahearn said, "Your guess is as good as mine. We didn't hear a single word about this."

"What kind of chief is Fishbakke? Am I supposed to believe Tillinghast just did this without even consulting with the chief of his own goddamn department?"

"Let me call you back."

"Do that. I got every local in the state already blowing me up and I don't even know what to tell them."

Lt. Ahearn ended the call and looked at B.C. Etchel. "Is he upstairs?"

"Billy—"

Lt. Ahearn left the sidewalk and entered Station 2. Up in the administrative offices, he found Ma Dukes behind her desk listening to the same speech. "Hey, Ma. Is he in?"

"Yes. But the *Chief*—she rolled her eyes—"is on the phone."

Lt. Ahearn barged in. He closed the door and stood staring at Chief Fishbakke.

"No, those seats will be perfect." Chief Fishbakke held up one finger. "Yes, it's the same credit card number. Thank you!" He hung up and said, "Taking my grandkids to the ice capades."

"Is there any part of you that still gives a shit about this department?"

"I would be careful with your tone, lieutenant."

"You don't think privatizing the rescue is something you should consult with the rank and file about? The union? Your own freaking men?"

"Lieutenant, I am in meetings every day. Nowhere in my list of daily responsibilities is there any mention of having to brief the union president about every decision I'm tasked with."

"Is that a serious statement? As a matter of fact, if it concerns the workplace or the contract—"

"There is no contract, lieutenant, so I become the final arbiter."

"You? You haven't made a substantive decision in twenty years. No way this came from you."

"Do you think at some point you and the men you represent will understand the old way of doing business is now dead and gone? There's a new political reality, lieutenant. When the game changes, those who recognize this are the only ones who survive."

"That's one hell of a rallying cry from our fearless leader. Can I quote you?"

"Sarcasm aside, you're a political creature too, right? Men who attain power always are. They have to be."

"That has nothing to do with what's right."

"In the end, that's all a matter of interpretation. Which is entirely subjective."

"That seems like a fancy way of weaseling out of any responsibility. Decisions have consequences. If you think what happened today exists in some kind of vacuum, you couldn't be more wrong. Tomorrow, that picket line out there is gonna be filled with a thousand firefighters from around the state."

"They will do what they have to."

"I hope you have a plan." Lt. Ahearn turned for the door. "I guess that's what all good survivors do, right?"

"The smart ones, yes."

"Huh. Guess we all know where that—"

"I lobbed you a softball, lieutenant, the noble thing would be to ignore the obvious retort."

"Today wasn't softball, Chief. It was a headshot disguised as fiscal responsibility."

Chief Fishbakke frowned, but he had to tip his hat. He called out, "You always know how to make an exit, lieutenant!"

"The good ones always do." Lt. Ahearn nodded at Ma Dukes on the way out.

LIBERTY OR DEATH
September 22, 2009

At 8:30 A.M. the next day, it was 80-degrees and sunny. After the tourists went home, September in Rhode Island became a second summer for locals. Empty beaches and beautiful weather kept the party going until October warned everyone of winter's approach.

Once the buses started arriving, the picket line swelled with members from every fire department in the state. The bagpipes from the Rhode Island Professional Firefighters Pipes and Drums shrieked and sang.

After yesterday's rescue bombshell, Lt. Ahearn made phone calls and sent out an emergency job-wide email. The Association of Rhode Island Firefighters wanted a show of force for Receiver Tillinghast and any other city contemplating privatizing their EMS responsibilities. The presence of all off-duty Sachem City personnel was requested. So by 8:30 A.M., over 3000 retirees, teachers, firefighters, police, and other unions forced the shutdown of Blackstone Avenue from City Hall to Main Street.

Central Falls Capt. Vinny Szceriack, the President of the ARIFF, and Lt. Ahearn surveyed the crowd.

Lt. Ahearn said, "Not bad for twelve-hour notice."

"I hear ya." When Szceriack chomped his cigar, he looked like a bulldog with a mouthful of kibble. He had stumpy, powerful arms attached to a wheelbarrow torso. "Spoke with the head-shed again this morning. That contingent they're flying up from D.C. should be landing at Green by one o'clock."

"Sweet." Lt. Ahearn had only met the president of the International Association of Firefighters once before, but the presence of the IAFF was never trivial. As a labor union, it had over 340,000 members in 3500 locals across the United States and Canada.

B.C. Rossi, B.C. Etchel, B.C. McLoud, and B.C. Riggs joined Lt. Ahearn and Vinny Szceriack on the apron of Station 2. Formerly, the picket line had been a circular procession up and down the sidewalk in front of City Hall. But with this amount of people, it now crossed the street and cycled down the other sidewalk as well. There were old men and grey-haired women who thought the government takeover had reincarnated the communist menace of their youth. There were 60-year-olds afraid to retire and afraid not to, people in their forties with kids to put through college, and 30-year-olds afraid of everything. They were from every trade and job and marched together because there was no one left to turn to.

With people feeling scared and disobedient, old-timers began passing flasks back and forth. Alcohol and insurrection were nothing new to the Ocean State. In the 1700's, Rhode Islanders turned molasses and sugar into rum, smuggled it to the other colonies, and, until the British discovered this illegal bootlegging, paid taxes on none of it. When the crown enacted a host of unpopular acts to create additional taxation, residents stormed the "Gaspee," a British revenue schooner, and burnt it in Narragansett Bay. Two years later, on May 4, 1776, Rhode Islanders took it one unfathomable step further when they became the first colony in the empire to declare independence from the British crown. Yet after the war, it took fourteen years of negotiations and pleading until "Rogue Island" finally agreed to join this new republic.

As a maritime powerhouse founded on whaling and international trade, local ports were always crowded with fishermen. The U.S. Navy had maintained such a large presence, it built the Naval War College in Newport and from there war-gamed every naval confrontation of the twentieth century. These thousands of sailors and fishermen, in need of certain comforts, found Sachem City's saloons and speakeasies filled with the kind of women eager to make a buck. It was, after all, a capitalistic time.

With the whalers and fishermen eventually replaced by urban factory workers, the party rolled on until the mills started closing in the 1960's. Now, after the crash, it seemed the people of Sachem City were reconnecting with the Rogue Island of old and itching for a fight.

Perfectly timed, Fubar Freddy came roaring down Blackstone Avenue on his Harley Davidson. The American flag attached to the back was as flat as a postcard in the wind. He pulled right onto the apron and parked in Fire Chief Fishbakke's empty spot.

B.C. Etchel said, "Freddy—"

"Fuck Fish-head." Fubar killed the engine. "I got twenty years on that bag of shit." He grabbed the flag and a baseball bat and stalked right past the Battalion Chiefs. When he saw Szceriack and Lt. Ahearn, he shook hands and said, "Death before dishonor, right?"

"God love ya, Freddy." Szceriack appreciated the enthusiasm but did not necessarily want the mess. "We need you here, man. But please don't bash in any heads. This ain't the old days."

Lt. Ahearn held up his phone. "Too many cameras."

"We'll see." Fubar headed for the picket line. "I ain't making any promises."

Szceriack said, "Man, he hasn't given an inch. Not one. Still jacked, too."

"Right?" Lt. Ahearn chuckled. "Dude's in his sixties and he's still rocking the sleeveless-T with bowling ball biceps."

"Gunshow."

"Fucking A."

"Speaking of twenty years, that's about how long it's been since I've worked out."

"You definitely shouldn't wear any sleeveless-T." Lt. Ahearn saw who was approaching and said, "I guess all the crazies are out today, because here comes Bullet Head."

Capt. Romine crossed the street. He was in civilian clothes but bristled like someone very much on-duty. His shaved head glistened like an anvil. He did not drink or smoke or hang out with anybody, and never saw the need for useless chatter. He always knew what his responsibilities were and, regardless of rank, was never afraid to remind someone else of theirs. Which was also why he did not have many friends. He asked, "Anybody hear about Ray Tally?"

B.C. McLoud said, "No."

"I heard something," B.C. Etchel said. "Didn't want to believe it. Is it true?"

"Yup. Just ran into him. He's gone, as of today. Next in line to make captain, too. Believe that? There's been a Tally on this job since 1913."

They all knew the extent of this loss. In a hyper-critical place that was quick to judge, Raymond Tally had no enemies. His reputation as a hard worker and a bull on the fireground was earned and respected. Good lieutenants balanced two things—instructing the young and studying up to move ahead. As the direct link between the brass and the line, they had to know how to keep their people alive in situations where that was not always a guarantee. Unlike Capt. Romine, who was equally well-respected but not at all liked, Raymond Tally was loved by all.

Capt. Romine held up both hands, fingers spread. "That makes ten. Ten more fucking guys gone since July 1."

"That means we're back to forty-six vacancies." B.C. Etchel seemed stunned by his own words. "Isn't that incredible?"

"Imagine this?" Capt. Romine said. "They could've left three months ago with full pensions. That's how bad it's gotten working round the clock."

"Well, the Receiver whacked the pensions anyways, so..." B.C. McLoud shrugged. At 300 pounds, he stood out, especially next to the other B.C.'s who were older but still in shape. His shirt looked like a tent draped over a small car. "I guess it's six of one, half-dozen of another."

Capt. Romine, as always, seemed dismayed that this was his direct superior. "I don't even know what that means."

B.C. Rossi said, "Hard to fathom forty-six vacancies on a hundred-and-thirty-six-man job."

"Forget about that," Capt. Romine answered. "That's bad enough. But we got guys working eighty, ninety-hour weeks. Rescue guys that look like freaking zombies. We got privates as acting lieutenants, lieutenants as acting captains, and captains as acting B.C.'s. This whole job's out of position. Coupled with exhaustion and rolling blackouts, it'll be a miracle if no one dies."

"Dear Lord," B.C. McLoud said. "Way to cheer us up." When he turned to the others and waited for backup, the chanting crowd filled the vacuum instead.

"Hopefully," Capt. Romine said, "we won't be hearing these bagpipes at someone's funeral."

They watched him march over to a table filled with picket signs and join the crowd.

"Fucking Bullet Head," B.C. McLoud muttered. "There was a time when rank and respect mattered."

"What rank?" B.C. Etchel asked. "Believe me, I'm no fan. But he's right. We can only go so long until the wrong person gets plugged into the wrong position."

"I think Chief Fishbakke deserves a little more credit than that," B.C. McLoud countered. "After all, our safety is still his number one priority."

"Stop..." Lt. Ahearn seemed more disappointed than disgusted. "You're embarrassing yourself."

"Oh really..."

Someone called out, "Excuse me, Lieutenant Ahearn?"

They all swiveled and saw a woman reporter trailing a cameraman. "Hi again. Elizabeth Kraymore, WPLO. Can I ask you a few questions?"

"Of course. In case you two haven't met, this is Captain Vincent

Szceriack, President of the Association of Rhode Island Firefighters. They represent every local in the state."

"I know Liz." Szceriack's hand enveloped hers. "She plays a mean second base."

"Hope you guys aren't still holding a grudge," she said. "Our team was loaded last year."

"At least you beat the cops after us. That's all that matters."

"I'm glad you're both here. Saves time." Kraymore's long brown hair and pretty face were ruined by exhaustion. Becoming a heralded investigative and political reporter meant little sleep or time for self-care. "Any truth to the rumor that the president of the IAFF's making an appearance here today?"

"Yes," Lt. Ahearn said. "Last we heard, President Iannucci is gonna be here at one o'clock."

"This proposed privatization of the EMS must've riled some serious feathers."

"Not necessarily. What we have here is a battle between doing what's right and saving money. Sometimes those two things coexist. But not in this case."

"How so?"

"This is fool's gold. It's been tried before, and the cities that have done it are switching back to fire-based EMS."

"Then why would this be proposed by the new administration?"

"Because, in the short-term it might save money. But over time... look at it this way. If your house is on fire and you call 911, the fire department extinguishes it for free. It's part of your taxes. But not the medical. If you call for medical services, that ambulance ride is gonna cost anywhere from $500-3,000 depending on what treatments you need. That bill goes to the insurance companies or, if you're uninsured, your home address. If you don't pay, the city can lien your house. Do they? Not very often, if at all. Wanna know why? Because it's the cost of doing business. We don't leave people to die in the middle of the street, regardless of their insurance status. The homeless, the poor. If they need medical attention they're gonna get it. So the city takes a hit because the alternative is neglect to satisfy bottom lines. Once these private ambulance companies don't get paid, they will have to begin making up that loss by overcharging for everything else. After all, it's a private company with shareholders that have to hold them fiscally responsible. But remember, when these services are kept in-house, there's accountability. Our level of care isn't gonna suffer just because we're not turning a profit."

"Do you think the public knows this? These differences?"

Lt. Ahearn nodded at the picket line. "That's why they're all here. Why the president of the IAFF is flying in twenty-four hours after it was even announced. If Sachem City is allowed to fall, it will open the door to the rest of the state. Then everyone will suffer equally."

"But the IAFF is a huge union with far reaching power, who have far-reaching friends. Is that why the president is showing up? As a threat of force?"

"No, no, we are not there yet. Not even close."

"But theoretically, a city or town could save money if the number of insured versus uninsured met a certain threshold?"

"Possibly. Sachem City used to be that place forty years ago but take a look around. We have 21% unemployment, 40% have no health coverage, and nearly half the residents are on some type of government assistance. Any private company invited in here wouldn't survive the year. Then they'd pull out and we'd have to start all over again. Why? Why put everyone through this nonsense? The fire department has been providing these services since 1801. And you know what? There's nothing wrong with that. Some things exist because there is no alternative. That's the basis for our whole creation as a profession."

"Are you afraid people are going to hear that they'll be saving money, short term or not, and just say, 'Privatize it.'"

"I hope not. I hope people remember that one day it might be them or their loved ones riding in the back of that ambulance. And if that day comes, I'm sure they're gonna want well-trained and qualified EMS personnel delivering top-notch care."

"Thank you, lieutenant."

"My pleasure."

Elizabeth Klaymore made a slicing motion across her own throat, so the cameraman stopped filming.

"What do you think?" Lt. Ahearn asked her.

"On the record? I hope you guys survive." She finished rolling up the microphone cord. "Off the record, I don't think you have a chance in hell."

Vinny Szceriack said, "I told you she plays mean. Watch out, right?"

"I just think the whole thing's pretty sad," she said. "A lot of things are about to get a whole lot harder for people who have already suffered enough."

***

Later that day, like all great showmen, IAFF President Viterello Iannucci focused all of his innate charisma on the spasming crowd in front of City Hall. One did not get elected president of one of the largest labor unions in the country by blending in or playing nice. Hailing from Detroit, Michigan, Iannucci was a member of a department that per capita saw more fire than anyone else in the country. In fact, so many ruined and abandoned homes were burning in his broken city, the beleaguered department decided to stop risking their own lives for no reason.

Iannucci made his bones on Ladder 25 in the Belmont neighborhood. Judged one of the most dangerous parts of an already dangerous city, the crime rate in Belmont was 664% above the national average.

The second he wrapped up his speech, Iannucci hooked elbows with Lt. Ahearn and Vin Szceriack, saying, "I didn't come all this way, especially to friggin' New England, and not get some lobster. Gentlemen, lead the way."

After Rhode Island's industrial heyday died in the 1970's, it produced nothing of consequence other than world class chefs and restaurants. Since the only thing it could now offer was coastline and seafood, most of the state economy was based on some aspect of the tourist and hospitality trade.

"Hear that, Vin?" Lt. Ahearn asked Szceriack. "They always ask the fat guys where the best food is."

"Well, they certainly ain't gonna ask us how to get to the closest Whole Foods."

When Iannucci laughed it was so loud and full it always made people want to join in as well. Every part of him seemed infectious. Like Lt. Ahearn and Szceriack, Iannucci was balding and had a belly and could not stand small talk, passive aggressive people, or wasting other people's time. He was 5'10," still married to his high school sweetheart, and loved being president of the IAFF. This love was able to hide most of his ruthless nature, but one did not climb over 340,000 bodies to reach the top without a blackbelt in hand-to-hand combat. He made sure to put the union above everything, even himself, which was rare for a person of power. Because of his profession, he knew the troops would follow a fearless leader off a cliff, so he always took point at any picket line or protest.

At the East Bay Chowder House, on a deck overlooking Narragansett Bay, they ordered oysters and rounds of beers. The handful of aides and staffers that traveled with Iannucci got a table of their own.

"Talk to me, boys." Iannucci slurped down another oyster. His thick eyebrows formed a ridge above his eyes. "How do you think it went today?"

Lt. Ahearn said, "Judging by the crowd-size, the frenzy of your speech, and all the media, I'd say we got our point across. Over our dead bodies, right? Ain't that what you said?"

"I sure did."

"Fucking A."

"Exactly." Iannucci licked the mignonette sauce of his fingers before slurping down another oyster. "Power consists of two things—instilling fear in your opponent, and acquiring tons of cash to crush them if they dare fight back. We did both things today."

Vinny Szceriack was feasting on crab-cakes as he said, "So how far do you think that voice reached?"

"Statewide." Iannucci did not pause. "Going forward, that's our only goal, to make sure any mayor or city council that thinks privatization of EMS is a good thing will now reconsider. We call that creating a new flow-path." He laughed at the dangerous fire-term used in this derogatory way. "Politics, in its basest form, is a popularity contest. And there's nothing pretty about thousands of retirees and firefighters picketing and raising hell. That's bad business. So if the powers that be want to play fuck-fuck games, bring it on. We can make things very messy when called upon."

"Tillinghast is one thing," Lt. Ahearn said. "But what about Carvalho?"

Iannucci barely smirked. "What about her? There's a reason I flew up here not even twenty-four hours after Tillinghast made that ridiculous announcement. There's also a reason my visit contains no mention of her nor any plans to see or speak with her. We'll let this conspicuous silence deliver its own message."

"But what's our recourse if Tillinghast actually goes through with this proposal?"

"Gentlemen..." Iannucci seemed amazed at the question. "I didn't come to Rhode Island to make new friends or go to the beach. This was their last and only warning shot. Fuck around and find out. In public, we can all be smiles and *kum-ba-yah*. But behind the scenes? That's when the knives come out. Whoever survives that fight without bleeding to death wins." Iannucci winked at them. "Trust me. Tillinghast ain't shit. It's the Gov who controls all the levers. He's *her* bitch. He barks at us, we take a swipe at her, and whoever blinks first loses. And I don't fucking lose. At anything."

"Neither does she." Lt. Ahearn did not want to sound disloyal. "She's covered in more blood than a serial killer."

"Well then, game on." Iannucci raised his beer. "Now we fight."

CHEESEBURGER TAKES A HIT

September 27, 2009

"Attention Rescue 2, Engine 4, Still Alarm. 118 Cambrose Street for a possible stroke."

Cheeseburger was downtown at Station 2 doing the dishes and barely heard the dispatch.

"That's Rescue 2, Engine 4, respond to 118 Cambrose Street on the second-floor for a female, possible stroke."

"Yo, Cheese, ain't that your house?"

"What?" He turned off the water.

"... respond to 1-1-8 Cambrose Street..."

"Oh no." He grabbed a towel and headed into Fire Alarm.

Capt. McCarrick and Dutch Carrigan were in there hanging out with the dispatchers. McCarrick immediately pounced. "Those dishes better be done, ya sloppy fuck."

"That's my address. On Cambrose Street. I think that's for my mom."

"Aw, shit."

"Nice going, Bobby." Dutch was disgusted. "Come on, kid, let's go."

Even though Cheeseburger was driving, Dutch told him, "Hop in the back."

Capt. McCarrick said into the mic, "Engine 2 to Fire Alarm. Put us out of service on a detail."

They pulled up to Cheeseburger's house lights and sirens two minutes after Rescue 2 and Engine 4.

"Mom!"

"Dude." Lt. Stokes stopped him at the door. "She's fine, dude, they're bringing her down now."

Cheeseburger pushed past and went upstairs. EMTs had a standard field test to identify obvious signs of stroke, including facial droop, the inability to squeeze a hand, or hold an arm straight out. When Cheeseburger arrived, Cadillac Frank was administering these tests. But it only took one look at her at her face to know something was drastically wrong. Cheeseburger panicked. "Mom, it's me." He bent and kissed her face. "It's gonna be all right, these guys are the best."

She was staring straight ahead and turned to him but could not speak. His eyes filled with tears as he gulped and said to Cadillac Frank. "What is it, Lou? Is it a stroke? She has high blood pressure..."

"I don't want to get crazy, Cheese, but she did fail two out of three. Could just be a T.I.A. But let's get her to Galilee. Those people went to college, right?"

Engine 4 strapped her into a stair-chair and carefully carried her down. Cheeseburger saw his father lurking in the kitchen but so far lacked the nerve for conflict.

They all knew the clock was ticking as far as strokes were concerned, so no one was screwing around. They took her vitals, started a line, and that was it.

"See you at Galilee," Cadillac Frank called out.

"Love you, ma, I'll meet you at the hospital." Cheeseburger slammed the doors closed and said to Capt. McCarrick, "Gimme one sec."

He stalked back into the house and found his father in the kitchen. A pleasant expression was not exchanged.

Cheeseburger said, "What're you doing here, dad?"

"I'm not allowed in my own house? Who do you think pays for this—"

"248 over 180."

"Excuse me?"

"That's her blood-pressure. Which she's already struggling to control. You can't keep coming over here yelling and screaming—"

"You're gonna tell me what I can and can't do now?"

"You're gonna fucking kill her!"

"You watch your mouth!"

"Is there a problem, Cheese?" Capt. McCarrick and Dutch filled the doorway. "Seems like a pretty shitty thing to do to someone during a medical emergency."

The father yelled, "Why don't you mind your own business!"

"He is my fucking business. Especially since you don't seem too fucking concerned—"

"Fuck you!"

"Oh yeah? Fuck me?" Capt. McCarrick grabbed his face with one hand and squeezed it like a zit before he flung him into the wall. "Now do the right thing and just fuck off." He nodded at Cheeseburger. "Let's get you to Galilee."

They got back into Engine 2 and peeled out lights and sirens all the way to Providence.

***

As always, word spread fast. Within an hour Super-Wop, who never went anywhere without his wife, was at the ER with ice coffees for everyone. Rowdell and Fonzie showed up covered in dust from a demolition job. Yoda and his wife Cindy, a nurse who worked upstairs in the oncology unit, appeared after her shift. As requested by Cheeseburger, Cindy had been orchestrating things behind the scenes since his mom's arrival.

All of them were in an alcove outside the critical ICU awaiting further news when Cheeseburger said, "My father's a serious asshole, but he's claiming he found her like that. Which better be the truth, because I'm gonna ask her after this mess is over. Whatever the case, if he hadn't found her, she would've died or been a vegetable by the time anyone else did."

"Where is your pops?" Super-Wop immediately regretted asking the question.

Cheeseburger smirked and said, "Story of his life, right? Anywhere but here. He's probably three-deep at McMahon's already."

A tall man in a white jacket arrived and said, "I'm looking for Leonard Rialto?"

"That's me."

"I'm Dr. Chakrabarti. I'm the vascular surgeon that performed the neurothrombectomy on your mom. Can we speak in private?"

Freaked out all over again, Cheeseburger followed him like a condemned man resigned to whatever fate came next. His cheeks were flushed and his eyes red, but nothing compared to this anxious dread. It's all he felt even after the door closed and the doctor tried to make him feel that the whole world as he knew it was not about to end.

Dr. Chakrabarti must have sensed this because he asked, "Do you need some water?"

"No offense, doc, but I've already seen the awful ways this is gonna end."

"Whoa. Easy. Please, sit down."

"I don't really care about all the jargon, either. I just need to know who she's gonna be when she gets home. She is coming home, right?"

"Yes. Of course. According to what I've so far been able to ascertain, you left the house at 7:00 A.M. and your father got there in the vicinity of eight o'clock. So somewhere in that hour is when the event occurs. Considering we didn't have her on the table until 8:28 A.M., whatever damage that happened outside that golden hour is what we now must contend with. She might've gone down at 7:53, which means she beats the hour by plenty. But she also could've been stricken at 7:03."

"Great."

"It's a waiting game now. She came out of the anesthesia like a champ. You will be able to see her soon. But I should tell you. Preliminarily, there does appear to be some right-sided impairment. How bad? We don't yet know. Will rehabilitation correct these issues? That's always the hope."

"I just want to know if she's gonna walk. Gonna talk. Have a life again, you know?"

"That's what we're all pulling for, isn't it? Hopefully, we can find some answers sooner rather than later."

"I guess that means you have no idea."

"Exactly. Believe me, I wish I did."

***

While waiting for Cheeseburger, the inanity crossed over into the surreal. Cindy and Rose were speaking in hushed tones when they heard a sudden clamor.

"Where are the boys?" Rose asked. Like her husband, she always looked like she was coming or going to the gym, and her physique reflected this.

Cindy, who was still in her work scrubs, went searching for the noise. She and Yoda had so far maintained a healthy boundary between their relationship and the fire department, but those worlds abruptly collided when Cindy pushed open the supply room door and exclaimed, "Guys! What the hell? Glenn, Jesus Christ, what is in your *mouth*?"

Rose arrived and burst out laughing. "And he's supposed to be the smart one?"

Yoda guiltily removed the test tubes. "Honey, I won. No one else could stack fifteen of them in."

"Oh my God." Cindy was dismayed. "I don't know what's worse—the fact that you guys thought this was a good idea, or that you're actually responsible for saving other people's lives."

Cheeseburger appeared and said, "He basically told me they have no idea." Then he looked closer. "What's going on?"

"Nothing much." Super-Wop grinned. "Yoda jammed fifteen test tubes into his grill and thinks you ain't got shit."

"Oh yeah?"

"Oh my God." Cindy had had enough. "Cheese, your mom's in the freaking post-op ICU!"

"I know. I'm doing this for her."

The chant was instantaneous. "Bur-ger! Bur-ger! Bur-ger!"

"Please, God." Cindy shook her head. "People, I have to work here!"

"Cheese! Cheese! Cheese!"

"I'm doing this for mom!"

Cindy shoved him in and then locked the door. "Is nothing sacred?"

Rose wiped her eyes, laughing. "Apparently not."

"Cheese! Cheese! Cheese!"

LIGHT TURNS TO BLACK

October 10, 2009

By this point, most of the newbies had completed one year on the job. Part of their adjustment was dealing with the quirks and drama of those who outranked them. On Rescue 1, Psycho Sal and Cadillac Frank were at war again. Yesterday, things escalated to the point where Cadillac Frank, knowing he was inches away from another blowout, swapped shifts with "Doom" so he would not run into Sal at shift change.

Doom was Gabriel Herrein, a lieutenant on Rescue 2. He had curly blond hair and a tiny head. But most exotic of all was his voice. Already high-pitched, it flew into a screech the second he got excited. His bulging blue eyes twitched the angrier he got, and while his appearance was ripe for comedic abuse, no one dared try. Doom, after all, had been a prison guard at Auburn Correctional Facility, a maximum-security prison in upstate New York. His baggy clothing provided a deceiving camouflage beneath which lurked enough brute force to deflate even the craziest inmate's delusion. Overall, Doom was a nice quiet guy who minded his own business. Usually, it was only after someone put their hands on him or his partner that people received the wakeup call of their lives. He had a trademark move that was more of a violence-filled shoulder throw. Tossed and smashed flat on their backs, his victims gasped like fish before Doom pounced and finished them off.

Super-Wop, unlike his academy classmates, absolutely hated the rescue. It was not because of Cadillac Frank, who was a great boss and an even better partner. But as a lifelong germaphobe, Super-Wop flinched every time he saw blood, urine, puke or feces, and the rescue was filled with all of it. Patients climbed into the back coughing, wheezing, sneezing, hacking, and bleeding. They were dying of emphysema, cancer, or a thousand other diseases. People contracted bedbugs and scabies from rot-filled apartments, and people with Hepatitis C and HIV who needed IVs freaked him out even more. All he could think about was getting pricked by a contaminated needle and dying because of someone else's bad choices or misfortune.

While Super-Wop loved Cadillac Frank, working with Doom put him at ease when responding to assaults or other calls of violence. Currently, they were headed to 101 Mathews Street for a victim of assault. Job-wide, Mathews Street was well known. It was a five-block strip filled with triple-deckers in various stages of disrepair. There were no gangsters, just the extreme poor surviving.

When they turned the corner, Doom said, "Where are the freaking cops?"

"L-T." Super-Wop pointed up at a woman's silhouette in a window. "Third-floor, apartment two, right?"

"Yep." Doom grabbed the mic. "Rescue 1's on-scene. No police yet."

"Rescue 1 on-scene. No police. 2152."

After Doom cracked his door, Super-Wop said, "Whoa, man, I'm a gung-ho motherfucker too, but shouldn't we wait for the cops?"

"We should." Doom's high-pitched voice nearly screeched from the excitement. "But I couldn't live with myself otherwise. Besides, didn't you used to be a Marine?"

The streetlights bathed the surrounding squalor piss yellow. Because of the neighborhood's constant turnover, the sidewalk was strewn with everything people hastily dumped when escaping their own lives—mainly broken appliances, ruined furniture, and trash.

The front door of 101 Mathews had been jammed open. Inside, ten mailboxes barely hung on the wall. As they climbed the stairs, the sound of babies crying, people yelling, and televisions cranked way too loud provided a real-time soundtrack.

On the third-floor, they identified themselves and knocked on the door of number two. Both were smart enough not to stand directly in front of it in case a swarm of bullets crashed through.

"We should really wait for the cops," Super-Wop whispered. "This could be a domestic, man."

"Go away!" a woman shouted. "Nobody wants you here!"

Doom said, "It's the fire department, ma'am, not the police. We got a call for a victim of assault."

"Nobody's been assaulted, and nobody called you." She started crying. "Now just fuck off!"

"Ma'am—"

"I said fuck off!"

Boots clomped up the stairs until a female cop appeared. She was average height and co-owned an MMA gym, so she was totally squared away.

"Sorry about the delay, fellas, we just had a hit-and-run on Lenox." Officer Kayla Decker was one of ten women on the 162-member Sachem City Police Department. Known for her intuitive street knowledge and overall acumen, she was considered an expert of her district. Like the best cops, she built relationships throughout the neighborhood until she knew who all the players were.

"Well, this one ain't coming out." Doom knocked on the door again. "Miss, will you please just let us check you out?"

"Fuck you!"

"That's not nice," Super-Wop said. "As a matter of fact, that's very hurtful."

Officer Decker cracked a half-smile before stepping forward. "Sandra. It's me. Officer Decker."

"Fuck you, too, nigger!"

"Hey!" Doom kicked the door so hard the wall shuddered, but Officer Decker stopped him. She said, "Sandra, please. How many times, you think, until he finally kills you?"

There was silence.

"This is my fourth time getting dispatched here in the last two weeks. And that's just me."

"I never call you people!"

"I know. Your neighbors do after they hear you getting beaten and strangled in there."

"That's not true! That's not what happens!"

"Where is he? Where's Ramon?"

"He's not here. And I'm not coming out!"

Officer Decker turned to the firemen. "Frequent flyer, boys. It's still private property. Without probable cause or a warrant..."

"What?" Super-Wop was horrified. "We're just gonna *leave* her?"

"He's new," Doom told her. "It's just the same. You can't help some-one that won't help themselves."

Officer Decker knocked one last time. "Sandra, please, just let us see that you're okay and then we'll leave."

"No! No! No!" She was no longer sobbing. "Nothing happened, no one's here except me. I didn't call you, don't want to talk to you, so please, all of you just—Fuck. Off."

"Okay." Officer Decker slipped her card beneath the door. "You're the boss. But when the day comes that you change your mind, we'll be waiting. Okay? We've already talked about the battered-women's shelter."

"Go away! Stop harassing me!"

Officer Decker turned for the stairs. "This way, gents."

Outside, Super-Wop could not wrap his mind around it. This must have been obvious because Officer Decker said, "People have a right to refuse care. You didn't hear any active abuse or screaming when you arrived, right? We can't just break down doors because we feel something's wrong."

"Yeah, well, next time we catch this Ramon motherfucker on-scene we're gonna beat his ass."

"That's my job. Don't be poaching."

"She's the best." Doom patted her shoulder. "She really is."

"Fire Alarm to Rescue 1."

Doom clicked his mic. "Rescue 1, go."

"Status?"

"In-service from Mathews. Patient refused care A.M.A."

"Roger. In-service with patient refusing care Against Medical Advice. Start responding with Engine 2 to 336 Madison Street. Possible Suicide."

Officer Decker was receiving the same news from her own dispatcher and said, "Car 7 responding from Mathews." She looked at the firemen. "Wanna race?"

Super-Wop winced. "Not in this busted bucket."

336 Madison was a five-story brick building with thirty apartments. Inside, a distraught woman stood at the top of a staircase that led to the basement. She was quietly sobbing and pointing down into the darkness. "I live on the first-floor. I heard a scream and a thump..."

Officer Decker tried the basement light but it was broken. She grabbed the Maglite off her belt and led the way. The stairs, like the building, were old and groaning beneath their collective weight. The basement had two far away windows trying to spill gray light across the gloom.

"What the..." Her light found an unconscious middle-aged man strewn across the floor. He was in a National Electric uniform but still breathing. Doom checked his pulse and found it rhythmic and strong.

"Is that...?" Suddenly Officer Decker's light flashed across a girl in a Sunday dress hanging from a noose. She was attached to a rafter with a knocked over chair beneath her. "Oh my God..."

Doom sprang up and immediately cut her down with his utility knife.

He laid her out and feverishly searched everywhere for a pulse like a thief going through someone's pockets. Carotid, radial, femoral—he found none. Besides, she was cold, and her pretty brown eyes were opaque and tattooed with the 8-ball hemorrhages common in strangulations.

"Fuck me." Doom toggled his mic. "Rescue 1 to Fire Alarm. Cancel the engine. What's our on-scene time?"

"2215."

"Roger." Doom looked at Officer Decker. "2215 for the coroner. Looks like she may've been down here for only a couple of hours."

"What's his deal?" She nodded at the National Electric worker.

"Well, he's still got his tool belt on, so I'm guessing he was coming down here on business, turned the corner, and saw the worst thing he's ever seen."

"He fainted?"

"That's my guess. The lady upstairs said she heard a scream and a thump."

Super-Wop was already taking vitals. "120 over 80, pulse 70, blood glucose 113."

"It doesn't get any better than that." Doom could not take his eyes off the girl. "Imagine the kind of world we live in where little girls hang themselves?"

"I can't look at her anymore, man." Super-Wop began re-packing the First-In bag when the National Electric worker suddenly awoke and saw her again.

"Oh no, no, no!" He gagged and then nearly passed back out. It was only startling because this growing hysteria, for such a burly man, was completely incongruous.

"Sir, calm down." Super-Wop stepped in front of his view. "How do you feel? Did you hit your head when you collapsed?"

The guy checked his own skull, shaken. "No, I think I'm fine. Please, please tell me this is a practical joke!"

"Sir—"

"Please tell me that!"

Doom approached. "Let's get you back on your feet, buddy. You feel okay?"

"I-I-I think so."

"Here we go." Super-Wop led him back upstairs as the worker mumbled, "Had to be, right? Just a sick joke?"

"Watch your step, sir. And please don't puke on me. If you puke, I puke."

The guy was distraught. "Are you *serious*?"

Alone in the basement, Officer Decker and Doom stared at the body.

"Guess I should check her for ID," she said.

"Let the M.E. do that."

"I think I'm about to ruin someone's night…"

"Yeah." Doom had two sons and could not begin to imagine. "Their life basically ends tonight, too."

"Jesus…"

"I feel kind of sick."

"Me too."

"But I don't want to leave her down here alone."

"Me neither." Officer Decker clicked off her light. Side-by-side, they stood in the near dark like sentinels tending to the left behind. Upstairs, the world walked on.

***

Rescue 1 cleared St. Elizabeth's after midnight. They were backing into the station when Fire Alarm said, *"Fire Alarm to Rescue 1?"*

"Go ahead."

"Start responding with police for a male ETOH at Marshal Park."

"Roger."

ETOH was the chemical abbreviation for ethyl alcohol, the main ingredient that got people drunk.

"Great." Super-Wop hit the lights and sirens, smirking. "Another emergency, right?"

"You can blame the cops for this one. Public intoxication used to send people to jail, not the hospital. But diabetics with low blood sugar can appear drunk. Sure enough, Providence P.D. locked up a guy that was actually diabetic. He went into a coma and died. After that, all the drunks got sent to the hospital."

"What a waste. Can't someone just check their blood sugar and then lock them up?"

"No."

"Why?"

"Because that makes too much sense. So instead it costs a $1,000 for the ambulance ride, the ER visit bills out at three times that, and then as an added fuck you, they get new clothes before discharge. Eight hours later they're strewn out on a sidewalk somewhere covered in puke and shit and sent right back to the hospital."

"That's nuts. You know, in the military, I saw plenty of blatant wastes of taxpayer money. But nothing rivals the medical system. Everyone gets paid. At every step along the way. Emergency Rooms are filled with people who don't even need to be there. Wasting millions of dollars. Can I ask you something?"

"Yeah?"

"What's gonna happen with tonight? With me, I mean."

"What're you talking about?"

"That girl."

"What's it gonna do to you?"

"Yes."

"The same thing it does to everyone else. Forty years from now you'll see her face clear as day. For me, for some reason, I remember all their names."

"Awesome. Great news. Thanks for sharing."

"You'll learn how to process it. My first week on the job, I caught a stabbing. I mean this guy's intestines were hanging out of his belly like bloody snakes. An hour later the engine guys made spaghetti for lunch. It is what it is."

"I just can't figure it out. When I was overseas, dead Iraqis didn't bother me. It was just the cost of doing business. But I... I'm trying not to think about it but that ain't working."

"Suppressing it is even worse. Watch out!"

They nearly clipped a taxi slow rolling a stop sign. Marshall Park was named after the World War II general largely credited with organizing the Allied victory in Europe.

"Fuck me. It's Magic Mike." Doom grabbed the mic, disgusted. "Rescue 1's on-scene."

"Rescue 1's on-scene at 0019."

Super-Wop opened his door. "Who's Magic Mike?"

"A twice convicted child molester. Used to do magic tricks at kids' birthday parties before he got caught raping them."

"You're kidding, right?"

"He's been out for like four years. Now he just drinks."

"What a piece of shit."

Doom grabbed a flashlight and headed into the park. They stopped at a broken fountain with a ten-foot statue of General Marshall ruined by graffiti.

"Again," Doom said, "where are the goddamn cops?"

Super-Wop un-slung the First-In backpack. Magic Mike was barely conscious. He was propped against the fountain drooling. Beneath the grime smeared across his forehead was a fresh cut. His pants were filled with feces as Doom waved a hand to disperse the odor. "Code Brown."

"Aw, man..." Super-Wop could not stand the smell, sight, or even suggestion of bodily secretions.

"Mike!" Doom nudged him with a boot. "Hey, Mike, wake up!"

Magic Mike was in his late forties and balding. What hair remained was long and matted. He was wearing a stained winter jacket even though it was only October. He groaned and abruptly puked just as Doom held out a boot to nudge him again.

"Goddamnit!" Doom dragged his foot through the grass. "I love these boots!"

"Come on, Mike." Super-Wop extended a gloved hand. "Let's get you to the truck."

Magic Mike moaned but managed to stand. He farted and then his loose bowels pooled around his feet. He took four steps before suddenly attacking Doom from behind. After Doom grabbed Magic Mike's arm, the act of flipping him over his shoulder slung diarrhea out of Magic Mike's pants cuff. As this brown juice splashed across Super-Wop's chest, he had a second to gag in horror before violently puking.

On the ground, Doom straddled Magic Mike's chest and was close-fisting his head back and forth as he screeched, "Stop resisting! Stop resisting!"

Super-Wop, bent over vomiting, looked up in time to see this and somehow laughed while emptying his stomach. He ripped off his shit-covered shirt and was standing there bare-chested, Doom was beating Magic Mike senseless, and the cop who abruptly appeared behind them took it all in, saying, "What in the actual fuck is going on here, over?"

"Stop resisting!"

Smash.

The cop laughed. "Resisting? I think he's dying."

Doom's hand was cocked but did not fly again. "Fucking guy jumped me from behind. Now I'm covered in his shit."

"Me too." As Super-Wop continuously gagged, the sound was a disgusting mix of gas and moist belching. "His pants were like a jelly donut filled with shit."

"Unreal." The cop's flashlight washed across Magic Mike's face. His shirt was dislodged and feces was smeared all over his back and stomach.

Doom's crotch was soiled from the straddle. The stench was terrifying. He said, "Jesus Christ."

Super-Wop asked, "What do you want to do, boss?"

"Let's get the stretcher and extra sheets. Hopefully he won't wake up, because if he does, I'm probably going down for murder."

They used three sheets to wrap him up like a burrito. They tossed him onto the stretcher as the cop said, "You guys are like garbage men for people."

"Praise the Lord," Super-Wop said.

"You going to the hospital with no shirt on, Fabio?"

"If it's the cost of doing business. We decided earlier that's what life's about."

Doom said, "And the price keeps going up and up."

The cop laughed. "You two are a couple of freaks. I like that. Listen, you want to press charges? For the assault?"

"Naw. More trouble than it's worth. But write it up in your report. I'm gonna force them to test for STD's and everything else."

"You want a rider in the back in case he wakes up?"

"Fuck no. The less witnesses the better."

The cop chuckled as they loaded Magic Mike into the truck.

Doom hopped in and said to Super-Wop, "Let's take him all the way to Norwood. It'll take him a day just to get back here."

"Good thinking. By then, we'll be on our days off."

The cop suddenly pulled alongside and tossed out a police windbreaker. "Better put that on, Fabio. We don't need all those nurses stroking out when they see the gunshow." He sped off in a peel of tires.

"Rescue 1 to Fire Alarm. Transporting to Norwood."

"Roger, Rescue 1. Transporting to Norwood at 0029."

Super-Wop lowered the windows to dissipate the already awful stench.

"Fuck!" Doom punched cabinets in the back. "It fucking stinks!"

"Dude, I think I'm gonna puke again!"

"Do not stop this rescue! Punch it!"

Super-Wop hit the gas even harder and stuck his head out the window.

NIGHTMARE ON CAUSEWELL STREET

October 26, 2009

The 911 calls started pouring into Fire Alarm at 4:15 P.M. On Causewell Street, one of the main thoroughfares downtown, a four-story building was on fire. A domestic altercation had escalated into arson. 216 Cause-well, after all the mills and supporting businesses shut down, became transformed into a rooming house for the indigent. All four-floors had been cut into illegal one room boxes with a communal bathroom and kitchen at the end of the halls. Thirty-two people called it home. There were drinkers and drug addicts alongside immigrant families all shoe-horned into tiny claustrophobic spaces.

On the second-floor, Sophia Jimenez was beaten by her on-and-off again boyfriend. Tito Guillermo had met Sophia only two months prior after paying her $60 for oral sex. Soon, he found himself falling in love by mistake. Their last altercation got heated after she again refused to quit her job and told him to leave. Channeling this heartbreak, he punched her throat so she could not scream, and then beat her until her pretty face broke apart. He left and returned, doused the second-floor, the stairways, and all three exterior doors in gasoline. She was still alive when he splashed her with the last of it. Then he struck a match. By the time the smoke detectors did their job, there were only three ways to exit the building—running through the flames, finding one of only two fire escapes, or jumping out the windows.

On Rescue 1, Capt. LeClaire and Rowdell had just cleared the hospital when the All-Call tones hit. Suddenly they saw the roiling black smoke exploding over downtown. They arrived one minute later to find total pandemonium. Bystanders were running and pointing, yelling up to the trapped people screaming from the windows. First on-scene, Capt. LeClaire grabbed the mic and said, "Rescue 1 to Fire Alarm. Large multi-unit, second-floor is fully involved. People trapped. Code Red."

Rowdell was already throwing on his gear.

Capt. LeClaire did the same, grabbed an axe, and headed toward the building.

"Please! Over here!" People who had jumped from various heights were in the street with broken ankles, legs, and worse.

"I'm sorry." Capt. LeClaire forced himself to step past the wounded. At least they had made it out. Inside, people could be heard screaming and crying as fire quickly poured from every second-floor window. Black smoke was swirling and choking the unlucky people stuck frantically waving from the floors above.

In construction, Rowdell had walked the top-plate of exterior 2x6 walls forty-feet in the air, and as a logger dropped ninety-foot trees while running for his life. While those other jobs might have had chances for occasional danger, nothing compared to entering buildings filled with fire. The situation would have been overwhelming without someone else to follow, so Capt. LeClaire's nonchalance transformed the unacceptable into a rite of passage.

They had no hose-line and so could not approach the flaming front door. Instead, Capt. LeClaire smashed out a first-floor window and tossed himself through. Rowdell, just trying to weather the pure adrenaline dump, followed right behind him. Inside, it was smoky and hot, but a fog-like visibility remained. The one-room apartment had a mattress on the floor surrounded by stacks of cardboard boxes. They crawled to the door. Capt. LeClaire pulled off his glove and used his hand to check for heat. He turned back to Rowdell and said through his mask, "Ready? Stay on me." He swung open the door and found no fire in the hallway. He toggled his mic and said, "Rescue 1 to Command. First-floor hallway's smoky but still clear of fire." He stood up and began smashing open doors as he and Rowdell cleared each room. Inside the stairwell at the end of the hall, they climbed through the smoke and heard pockets of hysterical screaming. Capt. LeClaire felt the heat through the second-floor door but had to try it.

"Down! Get down!" On his knees, he cracked the door and saw the hallway was more like a throat filled with fire. But just opening the door introduced fresh fuel. The fire instantly lunged as black smoke exploded and swallowed them whole before LeClaire could close the door.

"Holy shit." Rowdell was trying to control his breathing through the heat-filled panic. "No one could live through that." Capt. LeClaire toggled his mic. "Rescue 1 to Command. Second-floor's fully involved. We're proceeding to level three."

"You guys have no water!" B.C. Rossi sounded upset. He was the captain of Engine 4 and disliked the Battalion Chief's job so much he had not even taken the test. But as the senior captain on D-Shift, all the vacancies and non-promotions forced him into the car nonetheless. He liked fighting fires, not standing around outside in charge of everyone's safety. Tonight was no different. There were at least a dozen people laying injured or burned in the street, so he was also triaging their evacuation as well. In the end, he told the arriving out-of-town rescues to just pick the worst patient and transport them.

The sheer fire-load on the second-floor concerned him. It would not be long before the heat and flames eroded the structural integrity of the floors above. From the street, he could see five people waving for help, and that was just in the front. Elsewhere, he was getting reports of people trapped and fire escapes impinged by flame. But with every truck in the city already on-scene, and a fourth alarm of out-of-town companies on the way, miraculous rescues began to take place. The ground ladders were only good up to the third-floor, so the ladder trucks were making grabs from the fourth-floor and roof. Determined engine companies popped doors and made entry through the flames. One of them was Engine 2. After Capt. McCarrick and Dutch Carrigan smashed in the front door, the fire leapt into the oxygen before Dutch threw open the nozzle. Punched by the water, the fire hissed and spit back steam and smoke, fighting them all the way in.

Capt. McCarrick, who was nearly a foot taller than Dutch, jumped behind and pulled hose. Together they faced an absolute wall of fire in the front stairwell. Even on their knees, the heat was unbearable.

"There!" Capt. McCarrick screamed, pointing over Dutch's shoulder to the first-floor door.

"I can't cover you at the same time!" Dutch was holding back the flames that filled the staircase going up the left-hand wall.

"I got it!" Capt. McCarrick cracked the door and saw the hallway was still free of fire, so he jumped back behind Dutch and all but forced him up the stairs. "We're good!"

"Jesus, Bobby!" Dutch screamed over the roar of everything burning around them. "I'm taking a beating!"

"Keep going!"

"You're gonna burn me up, ya sick prick!"

"You fucking love it!"

"I do." Dutch clawed up another two steps. "I really do."

They climbed to where the second-floor inferno awaited.

***

Mikey Doneen was driving Engine 4 with the pedal on the floor. They crossed the river with the siren wide open and screaming so loud cars a block away were scared enough to pull over. In the distance, ugly black smoke chugged into the sky. Lt. Cody Stokes went airborne after they hit the bump on Cerrano Street, braced against the dash, and grabbed the mic. "Engine 4 to Command. Where do you need us?"

When B.C. Rossi's mic triggered, people could be heard screaming in the background. "Engine 4, backside, side-three, we got fire rolling up and blocking the fire escape."

"Roger." He turned to Mikey Doneen. "Dude, Foster's one-way. Jump it and hit the alley."

"You got it." Doneen swung the wrong way down Foster. They turned into the alley and saw fire blowing out of every second-floor window. Trapped, the people at the top of the fire escape were choking and coughing through the smoke. "Shows you how bad it must be inside."

"Right?" Lt. Stokes pitched his cigarette, shouldered his air-pack, and grabbed his helmet. He turned to Slipknot, his backstep man. "Slip, stretch a line. I'm gonna check it out."

"Yup." Slipknot stacked the 1¾-inch line on his shoulder and sprinted down the alley. The fire escape was in the middle of the building, and beyond that Engine 1 was using their ground ladder to pull people out of third-floor windows.

Back at the truck, Mikey Doneen engaged the pump. He waited until he saw the Dude circle his index finger in the air before he charged the line. The water snapped the hose taught and raced to where Slipknot shot it straight into a second-floor window. Rolling up and out, the flames had the fire escape cut off.

"Keep hitting it!" Lt. Stokes yelled, already planning the rescue of those stuck above. "Engine 4 to Command. We almost have the fire escape back in action."

"Roger. Do you have anymore people in the windows?"

"Negative. Engine 1's pulling the last of them out of the third-floor as we speak."

"Roger."

"Mikey!" Lt. Stokes pointed to a hydrant twenty feet away. "Grab that plug."

"Roger!"

"Dude…" Lt. Stokes picked up his Halligan and made sure he had eye contact with Slipknot. "I'm going up. I don't give a fuck what happens down here, do not let that fire come back out of that window."

"You got it, L-T."

Lt. Stokes started climbing. Incredibly, the wrought iron fire escape was already hot through his gloves. In every academy for the last fifty years, newbies had been instructed to steer clear of all fire escapes. They were never inspected, and some had been hanging off the sides of buildings for a hundred years. As he climbed by and got blasted by the hose, he saw Slipknot was barely holding back the flames. The room was orange and shimmering like a furnace, completely filled with fire. He had no way of knowing this was the apartment of origin, and that the dead prostitute was right below the windowsill.

He kept climbing until he reached the line of people stacked up to the fourth-floor window.

"Let's go, people! Let's go, let's go!" He heard radio chatter about the fire eating into the first and third-floors while the panic-stricken civilians filed past.

Someone screamed, "Please, please help!"

He looked up and saw a woman in the fourth-floor window. "There's a man in a wheelchair down the hall!"

"What apartment?"

"4D!"

Lt. Stokes triggered his mic. "Engine 4 to Command. Fire escape's back in action but we have a report of a man in a wheelchair in apartment 4-Delta. Checking it out." After he helped the frantic woman out of the window, he knew he was going in alone.

A sudden explosion was followed by screaming. When Lt. Stokes looked down, he saw a first-floor window had showered Slipknot in glass. Without his hose-line, the fire surged back out of the second-floor window just as the last two people passed by.

As chauffeur, it was a cardinal sin to abandon the pump panel, but in a disaster rules did not matter. With Slipknot on the ground clutching his bloody face, the people on the fire escape were going to burn alive without water. Mikey Doneen corralled the writhing hose, smacked the fire back inside the window, and then shouted to Engine 1 for help.

Hysterical people dropped off the fire escape as Doneen handed the hose-line to Engine 1. "I gotta go! The Dude's upstairs alone!"

Two people had been badly burned in the blowback, so Engine 1 helped them, helped Slipknot, and took over pumping Engine 4.

Upstairs, Lt. Stokes pulled on his mask because the fourth-floor was suddenly filling with smoke. The radio was filled with yelling and chaos, so he had no idea Mikey Doneen was trying to catch up with him. He disappeared into the smoky fog. At times his light punched through to reveal a cluttered and garbage strewn hallway. Because of the tiny rooms, the hallway was where people illegally stacked their extra stuff. The electricity suddenly died. At 4D, he kicked in the door and found an incredibly obese man stuffed into an oversized wheelchair. He was clutching a picture and so relieved to see Lt. Stokes, he gasped through his tears, "Please help me!"

"Hang on, bud." Lt. Stokes grabbed his mic. "Engine 4 to Command. I have that victim."

The guy coughed and yelled, "We have to get out of here!"

"I hear ya, dude. Can you walk at all?"

"No." The guy panicked. "Please don't leave me!"

"That's not gonna happen, I can promise you that. What's your name?"

"John. John Bellmore."

"Okay, John Bellmore." Lt. Stokes sized things up. There was one window but no way to get him down an extension ladder. Even if there was an elevator, the loss of power killed that option. Besides, it would most likely open on the inferno ripping apart the lower floors. "We need a plan." When Lt. Stokes saw John's continuing panic, he tried to change the subject. "Dude, who's in that picture you're holding?"

"My mom, God rest her soul."

"Yeah, well, you ain't gonna be seeing her today. Listen, I gotta make a hole. Otherwise, that chair ain't gonna fit down the hallway." He wet a towel and wrapped it around John's head. "Hang tight, dude, and try to breathe through that, okay?"

"I'm not gonna die, am I?"

"Nope." Lt. Stokes was already in the hall dragging boxes out of the way when Mikey Doneen suddenly appeared.

Lt. Stokes said through the mask, "Thank God, dude, help me make a hole. His wheelchair is like four-feet wide."

"Better hurry. They're clearing the first and third-floor, man, we're losing the building."

"Fuck me."

They smashed in two doors and tossed everything they could into both apartments. The temperature was rising, and all the exertion was eating through their air. They still had thirty feet of hall to clear when the fire racing up the center staircase finally found the door and now danced like a demon taunting them just behind the glass.

Lt. Stokes said, "Fuck, dude, we gotta hurry!"

"I'm trying." Mikey Doneen smashed in three more doors as the frantic clearing continued.

"Command to all companies. Third-floor is now fully involved. Engine 4, are you still on level 4?"

"Roger, Chief." Lt. Stokes was dumping sweat into his mask, the heat increasing. "We can't get this guy out without making a path for the wheelchair."

"Can't you drag—"

"He's a big boy, Chief. 400 all day."

"Roger. I'm gonna try and get you some more help."

They were almost cleared to the fire escape when the door at the end of the hall flung open. Capt. LeClaire and Rowdell stepped out of the smoke like an optical illusion.

Lt. Stokes yelled, "Is that staircase fully fucked?"

"Yes!" Capt. LeClaire pointed. "It just burnt through the second-floor door."

"He's in 4D! Fire escape's down here!"

Capt. LeClaire and Rowdell found John crying with a towel clamped over his nose and mouth. Panting, he was already not getting enough oxygen and they were nowhere near the exit.

"Please," he said between coughs. "I'm sorry I'm so fat, but please don't leave me!"

With the hallway now clear, Lt. Stokes and Doneen hustled back to help them. They shone their lights back down the hall just as the fire started eating through the center staircase door. Even worse, every doorjamb was puffing smoke, meaning the fire was now in the walls around them as well.

"Twenty more feet!" Lt. Stokes said. It was a struggle to get all that weight down the tight hallway.

"It's breaking out!" Mikey Doneen pointed to the now flaming line where the wall met the ceiling.

Unfortunately, the open window at the fire escape was acting like a chimney. The temperature soared from all the energy and force building from everything burning below. In the wheelchair, John panted and rightfully panicked. "It's too hot!"

"Hang on, dude, we're almost there." But even Lt. Stokes was worried. Then he saw the size of the window. "Goddamnit!"

Mikey Doneen yelled, "What's up?"

"He's not gonna fit through the opening."

Capt. LeClaire tossed them his axe as the smoke streamed over them and out the window. John was coughing so hard he was just drawing in more smoke with every breath. The temperature kept climbing. He panted and coughed, his body drenching itself as he overheated.

With conditions deteriorating by the second, Lt. Stokes and Doneen axed out chunks of wall, but it was not enough. To make matters worse, Capt. LeClaire and Rowdell, who had been first on-scene, were now both running out of air. Their warning systems, which vibrated their masks and banged a shoulder-mounted bell, suddenly erupted.

"Command to Engine 4."

"Go ahead, Chief."

"Status report."

"We're at the window trying to get him through. Rescue 1 is up here too."

"Great. Neither one of you has any fucking water!"

The rolling blackouts had closed two engine companies for the dayshift.

"Command to Fire Alarm. Inform incoming out-of-town companies to report directly to the rear of the building. We have no more assets!"

"Roger, Command."

"Engine 4. I want to know the second you clear the building."

"Roger, Chief."

Capt. LeClaire and Rowdell tried to slow down their breathing. Already short on air, there was no way they could swing an axe.

"Please!" John was struggling. He was coughing so much he could not even breath anymore. "It's too hot!"

"You're doing great, John, keep that towel on your face." Capt. LeClaire knew the wet towel was useless, but the old schoolers used this trick to keep frantic people busy with their own survival. "We're gonna have you out of here in no time."

Ten seconds later, the smoke from both hallways funneled over them and out the window.

"Please!"

Visibility was reduced to random pockets, but the heat became too much.

"He's gonna pass out," Capt. LeClaire said. When he looked back, he tried not to panic. Then he glanced down the other hallway but it, too, was now filling with flames.

"I..." Cough. "I..." Cough. Cough.

"He's out!" Capt. LeClaire yelled, "Cody, we need to expedite!"

"I'm trying!" Lt. Stokes and Mikey Doneen had smashed out two feet of wall on either side of the window. "I'm gonna hop out onto the fire escape while you guys lift him out!"

They pushed the wheelchair over, put one man under each massive arm, but did not even budge him. They tried again and failed.

"Here comes the fire!" Rowdell yelled as both hallways met and now turned toward the window. "Oh God!"

Lt. Stokes jumped back in to help. "Last chance! On three. One, two, three!"

They lifted John enough to roll him out onto the fire escape. But it was then that Lt. Stokes realized the obvious—the fire escape had been built a hundred years before people weighed 400 pounds for no reason. Even if they could drag him down, he would not fit through any of its openings.

"Engine 4 to Command!"

"Cody, here it comes!" Mikey Doneen yelled. Trying to shield John, he, Capt. LeClaire, and Rowdell stood between the window and the advancing flames. The fire crawled over the walls and across the ceiling. The smoke banked down until a perfect blindness was created.

"Engine 4 to Command! We are unable to move the victim down the fire escape! We need a charged line up here or he's gonna roast!"

"Command to Engine 4. There is no one left to send."

"Fuck!" Lt. Stokes looked down at the guys from Engine 1. One was at the pump panel of Engine 4, a second manned the hose-line, and the third tended to the wounded. "We need a line!"

"We can't take much more!" Doneen did not need to look back because he could feel the fire licking at their backs. Sweating and trying to withstand 700 degrees, time became measured by the second.

"That's it!" Capt. LeClaire pushed Rowdell and Doneen even though they did not want to leave. The old-timers did not wear Nomex hoods, because once they felt their ears begin to melt, it was time to go. "Everybody out!"

They unceremoniously climbed over John whose unconscious body filled the entire window.

Lt. Stokes made room for those bailing out by descending the fire escape. Besides, if he did not get a hose-line John Bellmore was as good as dead.

The Engine 1 private tending to the wounded had heard him

screaming for a hose, so he was already dragging one over. Lt. Stokes slung it over a shoulder and said, "Don't charge it until I get up there!"

He was climbing back up when a jelly-like substance splashed across his forearm. He heard chaos above and looked up in time to see fire pouring out the window. Capt. LeClaire, Rowdell, and Doneen had pulled off their tanks and tried to shield John with their jackets, but it was already too late. With the volume of fire roaring out of the window, they had to retreat to the landing below. It was then that Lt. Stokes realized the jelly-like substance was fat and skin dripping off John's body. He climbed as fast as he could and handed the line up to Mikey Doneen. Horrifically, John Bellmore had somehow regained consciousness just as his face started to melt.

Doneen fought the flames. He climbed up to the fourth-floor landing and blasted water over John's body directly into the window. He told himself not to look down but did anyway and saw the front half of John had burned through to the bone.

Below him, Capt. LeClaire and Rowdell were covered in melted skin and flesh.

AFTERMATH
October 31, 2009

Within days, Capt. LeClaire knew something was wrong. With so many hours spent together, partners on the rescue could not keep secrets. Rowdell, like LeClaire, was a blue-collar worker. As a carpenter, Rowdell had said he had only missed one day of work in seven years. But the week after the Causewell Street fire, he called out sick both dayshifts for the first time since being hired the year before. He was too ashamed to answer the phone, so when Capt. LeClaire ran into Mikey Doneen and saw how awful he looked, he knew something malignant had been unleashed.

As for himself, he could not sleep. Mikey Doneen had diarrhea and could not eat. And when Capt. LeClaire called up Lt. Stokes, the Dude said he was watching John burn alive on an endless loop. He felt so guilty about the botched rescue, he had been nauseous for days.

Capt. LeClaire knew there was a recent fire service development called the Critical Incident Stress Debriefing. Before this, after particularly brutal calls, the old-timers would just get together, drink, and hope for the best. The profession as a whole was so averse to weakness, the idea of sitting down with psychologists or social workers at first proved to be a huge disaster. Their lack of relatability and understanding only got transformed after retired firefighters received the training required to host these sessions on their own. They, too, had seen people shot, stabbed, burned, torn apart in car wrecks, and, worst of all, knew the unique horror of doing CPR on a baby.

The meeting was held where everyone felt most comfortable—the apparatus bay at Station 4. Physically, it was the biggest station in the city. It was also where the monthly union meetings were held.

They pulled six chairs into a circle on the far side of Ladder 2. Those on duty ignored them.

Eddie Brzezicki was a retired captain on Providence Engine 3, one of the busiest engine companies in New England. He wore a Miami Dolphins sweatshirt in the heart of Patriots country, which pretty much summed up his arbitrary disposition. Unafraid to play the spoiler, he said what was on his mind and expected the same in return.

Joseph Jasso was a retired Boston firefighter who spent thirty-one years on Ladder 15 at Station 33 on Boylston Street. Like any good "truckie," he was happiest when conducting searches inside flame-filled buildings or climbing eighty-feet out to cut a hole in a roof. He never had any interest in becoming an officer even though he knew more than every boss he ever had, and stayed on the line his whole career.

They might have been in their late fifties, but talking shop never got old. They were also in awe that Capt. LeClaire was 58-years-old and still on Rescue 1. They busted his balls and told him this was actually a surprise intervention because he must have surely lost his mind.

Eddie Brzezicki eased them through the introductions and most of the fire. Then he said to Lt. Stokes, "What do you remember about the end?"

"That the whole thing couldn't have lasted more than ten minutes. That's what I don't get, because it felt like a fucking lifetime."

"Every second, right? You remember every one."

"Yes. He was... His name was John, John Bellmore, which kind of makes it worse, because I actually knew the dude's name, you know? It wasn't like I found him unconscious and just dragged him out like all the others. I mean he was crying and hugging a picture of his freaking mom when I found him."

"It is worse." Mikey Doneen was leaning back in his chair. "Like we were in it together with this guy and telling him we had his back, you know, and then we watched him fucking die, man, just burn up in front of our eyes, man, and there wasn't nothing we could do..."

"Politics and physics," Joe Jasso said, "That's what killed him."

No one said anything, so Jasso continued, "Two trucks were out of service that day. That erases six guys off the jump. You had a building filled with people and rescues taking place on every side of it. The elevator was fried and he couldn't even walk. Four-hundred-pound people that live on the fourth-floor of tenement houses have a 0.0 chance of surviving that kind of fire. He should've never been up there. Period. End of Story."

"You guys know..." Capt. LeClaire leaned forward. "You only have so many chances over your career to actually save someone's life, so it is, it's precious, right? Every one of those chances has to mean something or else why even do the job?"

"This wasn't a failure. Thirty-two people lived there. Twenty-four were home at the time. Ten jumped and thirteen were directly rescued. There was only one fatality and three people burned. That ain't a bad day at the office, fellas, it's a freaking miracle. In Boston, we'd have a hundred guys at something like that. You did it with twenty-three."

"You say that," Capt. LeClaire said, "and I know you're right. But in the end he still burns."

"Melts." Mikey Doneen looked at Jasso. "He woke up just in time to die, half of him burnt to the fucking bone, the other half perfectly intact."

Rowdell said, "And the skin, the melted fat—"

"Without any water we were gonna die if we didn't fall back..." Mikey Doneen looked out the window and saw it all again for the thousandth time. "Jesus Christ, we had to fall back..."

"He was all over us, even dripping through the fire escape," Lt. Stokes said. "Four-floors of that, man... all the way down..."

***

That night was Halloween, so Connolly's Revenge was packed. People bought rounds of drinks until everyone had a handful of chips to cash in. The jukebox was a blast furnace of screaming guitars. While the neighborhood knew who the bar belonged to, the dozen off-duty guys present on any given night also doubled as security just in case.

Forty-deep at the bar meant half of the department was present. Costumes varied from nothing at all to the extreme. "Sons of Anarchy" had debuted the year before, so there were plenty of bikers. The late Heath Ledger was also memorialized by a handful of demented Jokers. For the ladies, Sarah Palins and Taylor Swifts bedazzled, albeit in varying stages of undress.

Connie McIntyre, the de facto owner, fired out drinks alongside-two other bartenders trying to hold back the tide. After Eamon Connolly's death in 1976, the deed to Connolly's Revenge reverted to family interests back in Ireland. After consultation, Connie McIntyre, a cousin from South Boston, got appointed interim manager and forty-years later was still behind the bar. He had a love for obscene jokes, scotch-whiskey, and women who did not mind either one of these obsessions.

Job-wide, the exhaustion was only getting worse. Because of the ten additional retirements, the forty-six vacancies now overwhelmed the rank structure. Below the officer's grade, it no longer mattered what division anyone was in. Line guys were being transferred to the rescue and Fire Alarm and vice-versa. Bodies got plugged into whatever holes existed at the twice daily shift change. With people being held and ordered in from home on whatever days off they scraped together, the eighty-hour work weeks began to take their toll. Marriages already strained snapped in half. Such was the case for Lt. Pelly Monet, an officer on Rescue 2 D-Shift. A decade before, her five years on Engine

2 with Dutch Carrigan had cemented her reputation. An Army veteran, Lt. Monet was already familiar with the mostly harmless idiocy of an all-male culture, so becoming the first woman on the Sachem City Fire Department in 1995 was no big deal. At least for her. But for the old-schoolers unaccustomed to sharing a dorm with a 24-year-old female, this change was unnerving. One was so uncomfortable sleeping in the same room with a woman who was not his wife, he slept on the couch in the dayroom instead. Pelly did not care or ask for any special dispensations. She slept in boxers, a sports bra and T-shirt, and responded to the bell like everyone else. Her long brown hair and fit body would have been distracting had her no-nonsense demeanor rebuffed all potential suitors. Her husband was a computer programmer who had only recently succumbed to his anxiety, so her extended time away from home only made everything worse. This five-year marriage, already filled with conflict and despair, was now a crashing plane neither could escape.

She heard that one-of-a-kind laugh from the bar and pushed her way through the crowd. Old partners shared a bond beyond the regular job. It was how Dutch Carrigan became one of her favorite people. He had not touched a drop of alcohol in twenty years but held court at the bar as if he owned the place. When he saw her, he threw his arms wide open and said, "Come here, kid. Happy Halloween."

"Hey, Dutch." She hugged him. "Is Lori here?"

"Naw, she's at home. Wasn't feeling good. Why? What's up?"

"Well, I know she collects sea-glass." Lt. Monet handed him a Ziploc bag of broken glass scrubbed smooth by the ocean. "I found a new spot she's gonna love."

"Thank you, Pel." Dutch handed the bag over to Connie for safekeeping behind the bar. "Sit down, kid, what're you drinking?"

"Absolute Raspberry, rocks."

Dutch ordered another Coke and then smiled at her. "How's life on the box?"

"Do you have to ask?"

"Yeah, I know. You look tired."

"You're being very generous."

"You forget who I'm married to?" Dutch laughed. "She keeps me on my toes. An ounce of prevention, right?"

Their drinks arrived and they toasted old times.

Dutch said, "What's on your mind, Pel?"

"Nothing really... outside of my marriage imploding, everything's fine."

"Yeah, well, you got some catching up to do. I've lived with three women my whole life and still ain't learned no lessons."

"It's pretty miserable at home."

"My first one, I had to drink a six-pack just to walk in the door. Then we'd fight all night long. I tell ya, that one cost me years on my life. Brutal."

"When did you know it had to end?"

"That was it. A six-pack just to go home? I was drinking night and day. I was a real mess."

"Great."

"Unfortunately, until you know it's time to go, you learn to survive. Until you can't no more and then everything just turns to shit any-damn-way."

She smiled and pinched his cheek.

"Look at this!" Capt. McCarrick suddenly appeared. "Come here, you sexy bitch."

Any thought that this might be sexual harassment was quickly dispelled after Capt. McCarrick grabbed Dutch and abruptly licked his face.

"Ugh!" Dutch laughed and wiped his cheek on Capt. McCarrick's shirt. "Jesus Christ, Bobby!"

"You love it." Capt. McCarrick drunkenly swayed. "You're beautiful, you know that?"

"More beautiful than Pel?"

"Absolutely." He was about to lean in for another slurp but then suddenly yelled, "T-Bag! Come here, you beautiful fuck."

Johnny Cash's "Man in Black" started people singing along. But some refrained. At the end of the bar, Lt. Stokes, Mikey Doneen, Capt. LeClaire, and Rowdell were burrowed into the corner. They were done re-hashing and just wanted to enjoy their drinks. That was the plan until Harry Paulson joined them. "Chunks" was already intoxicated on bottom-shelf scotch. A twenty-five-year veteran, he always went out of his way to harass any newbie he could. However this time he made the mistake of only seeing Rowdell instead of the others he drank with.

"Da fuck," he said, squinting through his glasses. "What'd you think this job was?"

"Excuse me?" Rowdell blinked. "What do you mean?"

"Crying to a shrink barely a year on the job makes you kind of a pussy, don't ya think?"

"Harry—" Capt. LeClaire, as always, tried to be diplomatic.

"Dude..." Lt. Stokes did not have that same inclination. "You've got to be kidding me."

"Yeah, Chunks..." Mikey Doneen shot him a menace-filled glance. "You basically just called us all a bunch of cunts."

"Dis ain't got nothing to do with yous." Swaying, Chunks pushed his glasses up the bridge of his nose. "This kid ain't never gonna make twenty years if he's weeping already."

"First of all, he ain't no kid," Mikey Doneen said. "Dude's been a carpenter and logger and whatever the fuck else, man, shame on you."

"Yeah, dude." Lt. Stokes shook a cigarette from the pack. "It ain't like he spent the last twenty-five years at the 3's doing nothing."

"You got some nerve!" Chunks stepped closer. "You ain't nothing like your old man. He had respect!"

"Harry..." Capt. LeClaire put a hand on his shoulder. Chunks was so drunk he did not even notice he had been spun around and walked away until he was already gone.

"Sometimes," Mikey Doneen said, "I really hate this place."

"Anyone want to pull a tube?" Lt. Stokes held out a cigarette that Rowdell quickly poached. They headed outside as Mikey Doneen ordered another round of drinks.

A sudden commotion erupted further down the bar. Someone had challenged Cheeseburger to a game of Reaper. Six whiskey shots were quickly lined up for each contestant. Bets were exchanged.

"Bur-ger!" the chant began. "Bur-ger! Bur-ger! Bur-ger!"

Cheeseburger's pink cheeks glistened, his eyes focused. The other contestant was a civilian in work boots and dirty jeans and thought he had a chance.

"Ready!"

The competitors hunched over, hands poised above their first shot.

Connie McIntyre set the clock and yelled, "Go!"

Bang. Bang. Bang. Bang. Bang. Bang. Cheeseburger was finished ten seconds later. His competitor did not fare as well. After the fourth shot, his cheeks chipmunked with puke. But trying to choke it back only made him vomit again, this time exploding it all over the floor. People hooted and clapped.

Connie yelled, "There's the mop bucket, loser!"

Cheeseburger counted his winnings before slamming all $80 on the bar. "Line everybody up!"

"Bur-ger! Bur-ger! Bur-ger!"

By midnight the crowd was only growing larger. Rescue Lieutenant Doom showed up with Abel Hirsch. Hirsch was a private on Engine 1 who had played ten seasons in the AHL. A competent skater and decent defenseman, he also had an ornery disposition and hands the size of dumbbells. Once upon a time, he was barely hanging onto a roster spot when his coach saw him punch out a teammate and put him to sleep on his feet. That single punch transformed his whole career. He was subsequently turned into a feared enforcer and crowd favorite whenever he hit the ice. It was a juxtaposition for those who knew him, because otherwise he was just a nice guy with a really violent job. His nose had been broken so many times it looked like a piece of fruit had smashed into the center of his face at high speed. After he retired six years ago, he got on the job at 34-years-old and was now a balding ex-athlete with bad knees. But the fire department showed no mercy. He was promptly nicknamed "Berserker" after tossing his partner through a bay window at a fire on Buckland Terrace. Considering he had been in more fights than everyone on the job combined, this hurt his reputation. Subsequently, Berserker now tried to turn the other cheek whenever he felt his eyes deadening over.

"The Hebrew Hammer!"

"Hey, fellas." Berserker slapped hands with Beef Dumas and The Kid from Ladder 1 who, as always, were looking to bust balls. The music was so loud everyone was leaning in to speak. Berserker only drank Johnny Walker Black out of a snifter, so they quickly pounced.

Beef said, "You know where you're at, right? The bathrooms barely work in this place."

"Yeah, kid," The Kid said, "this ain't no cotillion."

Beef turned on his own partner and said, "You know how I know you're gay? You just used cotillion in a sentence."

"Okay, fellas." Doom handed out pink-colored shots. His high-pitched voice was torqued even tighter after an already long night out.

"What the hell is this?" Beef peered into the glass. "Are we about to get our periods?"

"Looks like Pepto Bismol to me, kid," said and raised his shot. "To all the homies that don't know me."

"Here-here."

Super-Wop and Cadillac Frank arrived with their wives after a Hank Williams III show in Providence. Normally, their appearance would not have raised any alarms except for the fact that Psycho Sal and Yoda were already bellied up to the bar. The longstanding blood feud and malice between Psycho Sal and Cadillac Frank was so bad it had forced their drivers to coordinate shift changes so neither boss ever saw the other. Their original beef had been about Cadillac Frank providing late relief for Psycho Sal, but like all uncontained disasters, its implosion was now like a black hole sucking in everything around it. So the second Yoda and Super-Wop locked eyes, the combined horror of this moment was so apparent their lieutenants immediately scanned the crowd like a pair of alerted dogs.

"That motherfucker!" Psycho Sal tore free from Yoda. It looked like he was swimming freestyle to get through the crowd.

"Pussy!" Cadillac Frank handed his drink to his wife before she realized what was happening.

"Frankie!" Super-Wop gave chase. "Come on, man, not now."

Anyone with more than six minutes on the job knew the situation, and no one wanted any part of it tonight, so Doom, Berserker, Fonzie, and Beef Dumas stepped into the breach.

"Fellas..." Beef was a thirteen-year guy whose words carried weight. "Let's not do this."

"Yeah, dudes," Lt. Stokes said. "Not tonight."

"Fuck that." Psycho Sal lunged again but all 6'4" of Fonzie was in the way.

Mikey Doneen appeared and said, "Sal, come on, man, let's get a drink."

"Mikey—"

"This ain't happening tonight." Doneen held the eye contact. "Time and place, bro, and this ain't neither one. Nobody wants this drama, capiche?"

"I'm buying." Beef threw an arm around Psycho Sal before steering/strong-arming him toward the bar.

"Fucking pussy." Cadillac Frank looked like he wanted to spit on the floor. "That's all he is."

"Come on, bro." Super-Wop punched his shoulder. "Let's get back to our ladies. You ready for another drink?"

By one o'clock, ten of them took off for the strip clubs in Providence. Others went in search of a diner to grab breakfast. But Capt. McCarrick was going nowhere. Incredibly, he was so drunk he was asleep on a bar-stool, his head against the wall. He was snoring so loudly he occasionally jerked himself awake to take a mouthful of scotch from the drink he somehow had not yet dropped.

"Fucking professional right there," Dutch said, and laughed.

"His blood sugar's probably 500." Lt. Pelly Monet took the scotch from his listing hand. "What're we gonna do with him?"

Dutch waved across the bar. "B! Can you and Fonzie give us a hand?"

Berserker and Fonzie each grabbed an arm as Capt. McCarrick snapped awake. "What're you doing?"

"Time to go, Cap." Berserker was trying not to laugh because Capt. McCarrick was smacking his lips like a drunk fish.

"I'm fine. Lemme go before I knock you out."

"You'd be the first." Berserker slung Capt. McCarrick's arm around his neck and stood him up. "Come on, Cap, we'll help you walk out."

Fonzie did the same with the other arm.

"You are a beautiful fuck, you know that?" Capt. McCarrick abruptly slurped Berserker's cheek.

"Gross!" Berserker could only laugh. "Oh God, that mustache is so moist and gross..."

"But you still couldn't make a pimple on a fireman's ass."

"Please don't lick me again. It feels like a wet mop."

"And you..." Capt. McCarrick turned toward Fonzie as they reached the door. "You're a fucking good Jake, you know that?"

"Thanks, Cap."

They got him through the door as Berserker said, "How come you didn't lick him?"

"Good point."

Fonzie laughed while trying to squirm away but got slurped nonetheless.

"I love you beautiful fucks, you know that?"

"Thanks, Cap."

They laid him in the bed of Fonzie's pickup and Dutch slowly drove them home.

NIGHT MOVES
November 2, 2009

The first time Rowdell and Annie had sex it was a disaster. Nothing went right. Once the mutual awkwardness humiliated them both, the night was pretty much over. They slept back-to-back and pretended neither existed.

It was worse in the morning. Rowdell stared at the ceiling and wondered if it was too early to leave. It got even more uncomfortable when T-Bag and Haley began tearing each other apart in the adjoining room. The headboard of their bed sounded like a battering ram coming through the wall.

"Jesus Christ." Rowdell could not take it anymore and got up. "You want coffee?"

"I guess so." Annie Sadler yawned. "It's still early. Not very considerate of them..."

"Those two have zero impulse control."

"Seriously. It's kind of a disaster in the making."

Rowdell pulled on his jeans. He went into the kitchen as the sounds of fornication escalated.

Both couples had gone out for drinks the previous evening, and since

T-Bag and Rowdell lived in South County and could not drive home, they all crashed at Annie and Haley's Providence apartment.

Rowdell brought their coffees out to the enclosed porch. Cypress Street was quiet on a Saturday morning. With nothing being said, the silence strangled the room.

Annie was apparently thinking the same thing, because she said, "I think we should talk about last night."

Rowdell did not say no, but he did not look happy. "I don't know what went wrong," he said. "Can I be honest?"

"Please."

"I don't know how to say this without sounding like a total douche. But it didn't feel right, did it?"

"Yes..." She stared into her coffee forlornly. Her face was still sleepy. She pulled her robe tighter against the chill. "I guess we have some things to work on."

"Do we? I mean I don't know everything, but I do know it's not supposed to feel like *that*."

"I guess I should tell you more about my ex..."

Her marriage to Frank had fallen apart after years of misery. She told Rowdell about how his depravity intensified. Frank barred her friends and took control of her life. His manipulation even extended into what she could or could not wear. Around the house, he made her outfits even more risqué. Their sex life changed as well. She became more of an object to abuse and demean. After he took control of her social media, he was able to monitor her like a parolee. Yet the most unsettling development was his sudden thirst for urine, her urine, which he kept bottled in the fridge. He claimed drinking it made her part of him, and that's when she finally started planning her escape.

"Urine?" Rowdell winced. "The wet arts."

"This isn't funny."

"No kidding." He stopped himself. "I'm sorry to hear about this. Your ex sounds like a real dick. I guess you're lucky to have gotten away without any more damage."

"I've put up a lot of defenses."

"I can see that."

"I'm still trying to take them all down. What's your excuse?"

"Don't know that I have one." He sipped his coffee. "If I tell you something, can you promise not to get mad?"

"No."

"Fair enough."

Nothing else was said for a full minute.

"I already know," she said. "You're in love with a ghost."

"I didn't think I still could be." Rowdell looked sick. "What're we gonna do?"

"I don't know. This is a first for me too."

"Doesn't it feel like we're screwed?"

"Kind of."

The activities in the back bedroom reached a volatile crescendo as the end for both had apparently arrived. A minute later, T-Bag threw open the bedroom door and strolled out buck naked before realizing he was not alone.

"Oh Jesus!" He grabbed a dishtowel to cover his junk. "I thought you two were still asleep."

"Asleep? Who could sleep through that?" Rowdell grinned and said, "Is it cold in here?"

"Very funny!" T-Bag ran back into the bedroom as Annie called out, "Nice ass!"

"You two are very abusive!"

Haley came out pulling on a bathrobe and rolled her eyes. "He's such an exhibitionist." She poured herself a cup of coffee and then left to get dressed.

Annie Sadler made sure they were alone again before she said, "You know that picture you have of her on your wall?"

"Yeah."

"I'm not telling you to take it down, because that would make me sound like a psycho..."

"Okay."

"But you should probably take it down."

"Annie—"

"Regardless of what happens to you and me, you'll never be able to move forward if you don't. And now that you've admitted you're still in love with her, how do you think this makes me feel?"

Rowdell opened his mouth but nothing came out. He stared at his coffee with an unpleasant expression.

"What're you thinking?" she asked.

Rowdell did not know how to lie. "I'm just sorry is all."

"About what?"

"About what we did. I just can't believe we waited four months to ruin it like that..."

"Neither can I. You're in love with someone else, and I'm completely unreachable."

He stood up, suddenly freezing with no shirt on. "You want more coffee?"

"No."

"I think I'm taking off. Is that okay?"

"Sure."

He saw her expression and said again, "I'm really sorry. In my mind, I must've thought about our first time a hundred times and it never ended like this."

"I know." She seemed devastated. "A part of me wishes we never had..."

THE BROTHERHOOD
November 3, 2009

In the five weeks since her stroke, Cheeseburger's mom made slow progress re-learning how to walk. But she could not return home from the rehabilitation facility until a wheelchair ramp got built.

On a cold afternoon, Cheeseburger invited his academy classmates over to help dig holes for the concrete footers. Fonzie's dad, who was a concrete contractor, was swinging by in the next half-hour to fill the cardboard tubes, so time was running short.

"Row!" Cheeseburger yelled. "Beer me!"

"Roger." Rowdell tossed him one from the cooler. Then he yanked a stringline from his worn leather toolbags. He attached one end to the first tube and walked it out to the last. "Dead-nuts. Straight as an arrow, bro."

Super-Wop said, "We got two more on this side and then we're done."

"What's this *we*?" Yoda cracked. "That shovel might as well be a post holding you up."

"Yo, this is him." Fonzie held up his ringing phone. "What's up, pop?... Yeah, twenty minutes works. 118 Cambrose... Cool, see you then."

Yoda kept digging before looking up at Super-Wop. "You spend two hours a day in the gym, and even with all that useless muscle, you can't even shovel for more than ten minutes?"

"Work smarter, not harder."

"Or not at all, apparently."

When T-Bag pulled up in his two-tone Buick Skylark, Super-Wop yelled out, "Nice ride, gramps."

"Yeah," Yoda added, "what time's your colonoscopy?"

"Right after I'm done banging your mom." T-Bag pulled a case of beer from the trunk. "Least I could do seeing as how I missed the shovel party. Believe me, I wish I was here because work sucked. We still on for Cadillac's show tonight?"

"Yes, sir." Fonzie took a beer. "He goes on at nine o'clock."

"Right on."

"What's in the bag?"

T-Bag showed him a dozen tequila nips. "Always be prepared."

"That's just good planning."

"I can't thank you guys enough." Cheeseburger raised his beer. "Cheers."

"When is she coming home?" Rowdell asked.

"They're saying two weeks."

"That's perfect. We'll let these set up and harden over the weekend. Then I'll have a lumber drop ordered for Monday. We should be able to bang it right out."

"Row, man, I never would've been able to do this without you. Or even afford to hire someone else."

"Stop thanking me. It's the least I could do. I don't mind buckling on the bags again if it'll help somebody out."

A roaring cement truck rounded the corner.

Arthur Fonseco hopped down from the cab. He was eight-inches shorter than his giant son, but they shared the same face. He was covered in dirt and dust and had a limp from forty years of labor.

"Hey, pop." Fonzie hugged him. "You know the boys. That's Row, Cheese, Yoda, Super-Wop and T-Bag."

"Sounds like rollcall at a psych ward." Arthur Fonseco took one of the beers and said to Cheeseburger, "I was sorry to hear about your mom. Me and her went to high school together a thousand years ago. I'll keep her in my prayers."

"Thank you. I really appreciate you coming over. Can I cut you a check—"

"For what? I just poured a foundation and this is the leftover. It's getting tossed anyway."

"You have to take some money—"

"Nope. Besides, we're running out of time. Let's get this poured before it starts to harden." He chugged half the beer and handed it to Fonzie. "Keep these guys clear. Me and you done this a thousand times."

The truck belched and lurched forward. The giant mixing drum groaned as it spun. Fonzie steered the discharge chute to the first hole and held up a fist. The truck stopped. Soon after the concrete came flowing down. Ten holes took ten minutes. Then Fonzie hosed the chute off as Cheeseburger kept trying to pay Arthur Fonseco.

"You work hard enough for your money, son. Keep it to help your mom." He turned to Fonzie. "You coming over for dinner? Your brother threw a ham in the oven at two o'clock."

"I am. But then we're headed to the Last Stand. Our buddy Cadillac Frank is in a band called The Schemers."

"Ain't none of you got a normal name, huh? Cadillac Frank sounds like a gangster."

"He's actually just the front-man for a mediocre cover band."

"Well, I gotta get rolling and get this pig dumped out before it sets up. I'll see you at the house." He waved to the others but shook Cheeseburger's hand. "You let me know if you need anything else."

"I will. But next time I'm paying."

"Buy me a beer at Connolly's and we'll call it square." He nodded at Fonzie. "Back me out, will ya?"

The cement truck heaved and spewed exhaust back down Cambrose Street.

***

Despite a legendary reputation, the Last Stand was a Providence night-club on the perpetual verge of bankruptcy. It was surrounded by strip clubs and liquor stores long banished to the waterfront.

The place looked ominous until the double-doors swung open on a hundred people drinking beer and dancing. Onstage, as always, Cadillac Frank's hair was slicked back like a 50's Greaser. A pack of cigarettes was rolled up into the left sleeve of his white T-shirt as he thrashed his Fender Telecaster.

"I want to thank you all for coming out!" he shouted. "Chuck Berry invented rock and roll. We only play it. One-two-three!"

His band, which also had a lead guitarist, bassist, and drummer, launched into Johnny B. Goode.

"My God," Super-Wop yelled to his wife. "He looks totally at home up there, doesn't he?"

"It's kind of incredible," Rose answered. "You'd never expect them to be this good, right?"

"That's why he's my partner!" Super-Wop started dancing very badly.

"Oh wow." Yoda winced. "That's absolutely horrific."

"Seriously." Yoda's wife, Cindy, finished her drink. "I wish I'd never seen that."

Fonzie and Molly Bish arrived and bought a round of shots. Even in boots she was still a foot shorter than Fonzie. Her blonde ponytail was so long it almost reached her buttocks.

"Hey, ladies." Molly hugged Cindy and Rose.

Conversation was nearly impossible as Cadillac Frank tore into "Great Balls of Fire."

"You shake my nerves and you rattle my brain! Too much love drives a man insane!"

When he pointed the microphone toward the crowd, it sang back, *"You broke my will, oh what a thrill. Goodness gracious great balls of fire!"*

People hooted and clapped.

When Rowdell and Annie Sadler walked in, Rose said, "Here come the Grim Twins."

Super-Wop added, "Remember Debbie Downer on SNL? This chick makes her seem like a ray of sunshine."

"That's not very nice," Molly immediately hissed. "The fire department is not the real world."

"Oh really? Want to see if that's a true statement? Hey Yoda? What do you think of me?"

Yoda, who had been speaking with his wife, did not miss a beat. "I think you're a total piece of shit. You drive around talking like some half-ass Guinea from Brooklyn. Meanwhile, you were born and raised in Coventry."

Rose was in mid-sip and almost spit out her drink.

"And those tattoos..." Yoda rolled his eyes. "We get it already, Captain Freaking America."

Everyone was laughing.

"And don't get me started on those eyebrows. What kind of man plucks—"

"Okay! Okay! We get it!"

"What's up, guys?" Rowdell and Annie shook everyone's hands. Row said, "I'm awful thirsty. Who needs one?"

Ten minutes later, when Molly Bish saw Cheeseburger staring at his phone alone at the back bar, she brought him a beer.

"Hey, Cheese." Molly was always upbeat. "What's going on?"

"Just chilling. It's a little quieter back here."

"You don't look happy."

"I'm definitely not happy. My old man... he's just relentless. He's cocked and texting me about this damn ramp I have to build... I'm trying to tell him that Row's a master carpenter. Pretty sure he can handle a stupid wheelchair ramp."

"How's mom?"

"Honestly? She's terrible. Her whole right side... I mean I still got hope, it's only been a month, but that's my mom, you know?" His bottom lip quivered, so he pounded his beer in an effort to regain his composure. "See? Here he is again. 'What're you doing about keeping costs down?' What kind of question is that? It costs what it costs to have it built in the next two weeks. Otherwise, what's the point?"

Molly said, "Tell him that."

Cheeseburger blinked and then started typing.

Molly raised her glass. "To mom's speedy recovery."

Cheeseburger did not even hear her. He was staring at his phone. "Am I really supposed to believe he's gonna help care for her in *any way*?"

Molly said, "She's gonna make a full recovery, just wait."

"And if she doesn't?"

"Cheese..." But her job had taught her the difference between useless platitudes and reality. "It's way too early to think like that."

"No, it's not. What if she needs round the clock care? She ain't going in no nursing home, that's for sure."

"Just get her home first. What else is going on? You look anxious."

"Nothing. It just sucks being on the other side of the healthcare system," he said. "This perspective totally blows."

"Ignore him and put your phone away, will ya?" Molly dragged him by the hand to rejoin the others.

From the stage, Cadillac Frank shouted, "It can't be about tomorrow when today ain't even over. Hit it, Stevie!"

The opening organ riff to the Kingsmen's "Louie Louie" got the crowd jumping.

"My man!" Super-Wop high-fived Cheeseburger and handed him a shot.

T-Bag and Haley arrived and together, Fire Academy Class 61 followed the Schemers into the dawn.

FONZIE MAKES HIS BONES
November 14, 2009

Two weeks later, Fonzie was completing the truck-check before his shift. As always, he paid attention to detail and took nothing for granted because newbies, in his estimation, did not have the luxury to operate any other way. It was this relentless work ethic and respect for the job that the older guys loved. Like Mikey Doneen eight years before, Fonzie was carving out a solid reputation. In-between runs on Rescue 2, he stocked and washed the truck, studied his medical protocols and map-book, or swept the apparatus floor if there was nothing else to do.

His boss was Lt. Pelly Monet. When he bid her truck last July, Fonzie had been anxious. He was 23-years-old and had never had a female boss. It was nerve-racking enough to be around the veterans, much less the only woman on the job. During one of their first runs, when Fonzie tried to be chivalrous by shouldering all the bags, she put an immediate stop to it by deadpanning, "What's next? You gonna hold the door for me too?"

Originally, Molly, Fonzie's girlfriend, was uncomfortable with him having an accomplished and attractive older woman as his boss. But Fonzie told her he had no interest in committing career suicide. Lt. Monet might have had a pretty face and fit physique from her years in the military, but Fonzie was too intimidated to even think of hitting on his boss. His co-workers, who kidded and asked for details of sexual exploits that never occurred, were always disappointed.

Like any new partnership, synchronization took time. Stair-chairing people down three-flights of winding stairs in the middle of the night, and lifting stretchers with 500-pound people on them had to be done in perfect symbiosis or someone would get hurt. Gradually, they settled into a routine that inspired confidence and trust. After that, Lt. Monet stopped worrying about his nascent skills and instead focused on sharpening them as fast as she could. He was hungry to learn and never squeamish, so she allowed him to do more and more. This was a pleasure compared to her last partner, "Toe-Tag," who only bid the truck to escape Fire Alarm. Widely considered the worst EMT on the job, Toe-Tag was bad at everything and did not even care enough to learn. The first two weeks he did not hit a single IV, refused to listen to any advice, and somehow got written up three times for civilian complaints of misconduct. After only a month, Lt. Monet informed him that at the next bid it might be best for him to bid off her truck before she strangled him, and the way she said it was not exactly in jest. And not without precedent. After another ex-partner on Rescue 1 spread lies about an incident to cover his own ass, she throat-punched him so hard he could not swallow solid food for days.

Nothing was worse than a bad partner on the rescue. Spending forty-eight hours a week alongside someone you detested was not survivable when other people's lives were at stake. Horrible attitudes and lack of skills became precursors to disaster. The primary responsibilities of a rescue private included re-stocking the truck after every run, knowing where all the hospitals were, and starting IVs. The fact that she never once had to mention or remind Fonzie of any of this only elevated his reputation even more.

He asked, "You want an ice coffee?"

"Sure."

They had just cleared St. Elizabeth's. Lt. Monet was finishing up her previous run report.

She clicked her microphone and said, "Rescue 2's in service."

The monotone of Fire Alarm echoed back, *"Rescue 2's in service at 1131."*

Fonzie parked and returned with ice coffees. He heard her on her phone saying, "What is the problem? You know what's going on at work. I'll be lucky to be allowed to go home tomorrow night, if at all."

She got out of the truck and finished her conversation walking in angry circles in front of the rescue. Her free hand shot out in occasional exclamation. Fonzie did not know all the particulars because Lt. Monet was exceedingly private. Anything job-related was fair game, but nothing personal. He knew she was an Army veteran and had spent five years with Dutch Carrigan on Engine 2 but that was it. He had never met her husband and, considering the current state of their relationship, figured that was probably for the best.

Once she ended the call, he knocked on the windshield and held up her coffee.

Frowning, she got back inside the truck.

"Thanks." She added cream to hers. "I really shouldn't drink this much coffee. I'm already torqued enough."

"Coffee's good for you. I hear health reports about that all the time."

She was scrolling her phone when dispatch said, *"Fire Alarm to Rescue 2?"*

Lt. Monet hit the mic. "Rescue 2."

"Rescue 2, start responding to 312 Roslindale Avenue for a diabetic emergency..." Fire Alarm hit the Alert Tone and said, *"Attention Rescue 2 and Engine 6. Still Alarm. 312 Roslindale Avenue for a diabetic emergency..."*

Every rescue crew on the east side knew this address. Once on-scene, they parked in front of a small cape with an even smaller yard. Each yard was a box next to other same-sized boxes stacked front to back. Built after the Second World War, this neighborhood was called "the Grid."

"I hate coming here," Lt. Monet said.

Fonzie could not disagree. It was a sad story. He grabbed the First-In backpack while Lt. Monet shouldered the diabetic bag. When people needed sugar, they either got it through an IV, an intramuscular shot, or sucking a syrupy-goo from a toothpaste-sized tube if they were conscious. Since every cell in the body used glucose for energy, especially the brain, diabetes was a life-threat on multiple fronts.

At the front door was a thin white woman in her 50's. Her red hair was pulled into a tight bun and her hazel eyes looked exhausted.

"Hi, Patty," Lt. Monet said. "Where is he?"

"On the kitchen floor. How've you been, lieutenant?"

"Living the dream, Patty, just like everyone else." Lt. Monet pressed her mic and said, "Rescue 2 to Fire Alarm. Cancel Engine 6."

"Roger. Fire Alarm to Engine 6?"

They made their way into the house. The family room contained pictures of a happier time. The McClatchy's had been a husband, wife, and three sons. The husband's diabetes had eaten him to death a decade before, and their eldest son died from the same disease soon after. The worst part was that none of them were obese, negligent, or disrespectful towards this condition. In fact, it was the exact opposite. But the middle son, Mike, had just turned 38-years-old and already had both legs amputated at the knees.

He was found unconscious on the kitchen floor. Because severe diabetics had awful circulation, his recent amputations were slow to heal. The stumps had soiled through the bandages, creating an unpleasant odor.

After Lt. Monet got a blood sugar of twenty-three, she had Fonzie spike a bag of D-10. She sunk an IV catheter into his forearm, waited for the flash of blood, and asked Patty McClatchy, "How long ago was the amputation?"

"Two weeks."

"He been keeping up with his wound care?"

"I've been trying. Bobby, my youngest, he's not doing too good either. So there's a lot to do."

"Where is Bobby?"

"Front room. I caught him in time, because he was just starting to nod off in front of the TV."

Lt. Monet had seen genetic anomalies in families before, but nothing this pernicious. Patty McClatchy did not even have diabetes, but it would soon be responsible for the deaths of everyone she loved.

Lt. Monet let the D-10 run into the son's system. She peeked beneath the bandages and said to Patty, "I don't see any infection, so that's good news. Maybe take the bandages off a couple of times a day to help dry up these wounds?"

"Okay. There's so much—"

"I know you have a lot to do. Where you get the strength from, I'll never know."

"Sometimes it feels like a dream, right? Like it must be someone else's life?"

"Hey, Mike." Fonzie gave him a sternum rub with his knuckles. Sugar, like Narcan with opioid overdoses, saved diabetic lives. With every cell crying out for it, Mike moaned as the concentrated glucose woke him up.

Fonzie said, "Hey, buddy, welcome back."

"Damnit." Mike rolled his head, taking everyone in. "Guess I passed out again, huh?"

"You're doing good, buddy. Let me check your sugar." Fonzie pricked his finger with a lancet. The glucometer sucked up the tiny drop of blood, processed it, and ten seconds later the display read 136.

"That's good enough for me." Lt. Monet disconnected the IV. "You need to eat, though, or it'll nosedive again."

Patty McClatchy pointed at two sandwiches on the counter and said, "I had just finished making them right before he passed out."

"You got any orange juice?"

"Sure." Patty went to the fridge.

Fonzie, still kneeling, propped up Mike's head so he could drink it. "How you feeling, bud?"

"Better." Mike smacked his lips. "I'm really sorry to bother you guys."

"How's your head feel?" Lt. Monet asked. "Did you hit it after you fell out of the wheelchair?"

"I'm fine." Mike tried propping himself onto his elbows. "I just don't want to waste anymore of your time."

Lt. Monet said, "Let's get him up."

Before she could even lean down to help, Fonzie had already lifted him back into his wheelchair.

Patty said to Lt. Monet, "Must be nice having a partner the size of a Mack truck."

"It certainly doesn't hurt."

"And he's easy on the eyes, too."

Lt. Monet did not answer that. She was busy filling out the run report before handing the clipboard to Mike for a signature.

"You know the deal," Lt. Monet said, "This is just a refusal saying you refused transport. Gets the city off the hook. If you change your mind, do not hesitate to call us back, okay?"

"You guys are the best," Patty said. "Thank you so much."

Lt. Monet poked her head into a room on the way out and said, "What's going on, Bobby, how you feeling?"

"Hey, Pelly. I'm a little tired." The youngest son was 32-years-old and always in considerable nerve pain from his degenerating vascular system. Even though all three sons looked exactly like Patty, their father's sabotaged genes were about to finish the McClatchy name for good.

Patty McClatchy walked them out. "Thanks again..."

"Good luck, Patty." Lt. Monet toggled her shoulder-mic and said, "Rescue 2 to Fire Alarm."

"Go ahead, Rescue 2."

"That was a treat no transport."

"Roger, Rescue 2, back in service with a treat no transport at 1215."

"What do you feel like eating?" Fonzie pulled away from the curb. "We did Mexican yesterday."

"I don't think I'm hungry."

"Roger that." Fonzie headed back to the station. "You know, every time we go there, I wonder how she—"

"There's no wondering," Lt. Monet said. "That's an occupational hazard. Business is business, right?"

"I guess..."

"Surviving this truck is hard enough, Fonzie. Don't make it any harder. You'll find compassion has its place until it turns you against the world."

"Okay." It did not matter that he did not want to believe her. He realized newbies, as always, could never afford that luxury.

***

"Attention Rescue 2, Engine 4. Still Alarm. 1515 8th Avenue, third-floor. Meet the police for an emotional male..."

"An emotional male?" Lt. Monet was not buying it. She joined Fonzie in the truck. "Sounds like an oxymoron to me."

"I don't know what that means but I think I agree."

"Rescue 2 to Fire Alarm," she said. "If police are on-scene, cancel Engine 4."

"Roger, Rescue 2, Engine 4's back in service at 1305."

8th Avenue was a long boulevard of buildings with "taxpayer" con-struction—the first-floor were businesses while apartments filled the floors above.

Lt. Monet saw three police cars in front of 1515 and toggled her mic. "Rescue 2's on-scene with police."

"Rescue 2's on-scene with police at 1316."

She turned to Fonzie. "Bring the First-In bag just in case."

There was a hardware store on the ground-floor. On the third-floor were three apartments. A policeman met them in the hallway and quietly said to Lt. Monet, "Kid's having a bad day. His mom passed last month and the uncle's a little overwhelmed."

"Geez. How old is he? It got dispatched as an emotional male and I just told my partner there's no such thing."

The cop laughed. "He's eight."

"Wow." If Lt. Monet had one hole in her game, kids were it. She barely had any motherly instincts at all outside of caring for her dogs, so she said, "Eight-years-old..."

"Yeah, he's a mess. We got him squared away in the kitchen."

She turned to Fonzie. "Can you grab the phone out of the truck? It has all the hospitals in it."

"We can use my cell—"

"Never use your personal phone for work. If something happens on a run, they can subpoena your phone."

The cop nodded. "She's right."

After Fonzie returned with the phone, they entered the apartment. The uncle, Guillermo Tatsana, had only recently become the guardian. He had straightened and cleaned his apartment, bought some toys, but the place still had the feel of a bachelor turned instant daddy. Tatsana was a 34-year-old machinist who greeted them by saying, "I apologize for this. I was just telling the police I didn't know who else to call. Last night he said he didn't want to eat dinner. He said the same thing this morning. I couldn't send him to school like this, so I called out sick again. At lunch, I begged him to eat something but then he said he just wanted to join his mom in heaven."

Lt. Monet looked completely out of her element.

Fonzie said, "Hey, Lou, you want me to talk to him? I lost my mom when I was fifteen."

"Jesus, Fonzie..." Lt. Monet now looked concerned for him as well. "I didn't know that. How awful."

"It's been a long time." Fonzie smiled. "I'm fine, L-T."

"You wanna give it a shot? Just get him to go to the truck. Tell him we'll let him flip on the lights and sirens. The kids love that." She turned to the uncle. "I'm gonna call Hasbro Children's Hospital. That's where they'll evaluate him, and if he needs some further psychiatric assistance, they'll send him to Bradmore."

"Okay."

Fonzie asked, "Which way's the kitchen?"

"Straight ahead."

In the kitchen, a small boy sat on a chair looking despondent. There were two cops standing on either side of him trying to appear busy. When the kid heard Fonzie's size sixteen steel-tip boots clomping across the hardwood floor, his gaze filled with awe.

"Hey, buddy." Fonzie's massive frame filled the doorway. "What's your name?"

"Eddy." The kid wiped his eyes. "Are you a fireman?"

"I am. We came by because we heard you were having a rough day."

Eddy looked down at the floor and did not say anything else.

"Your uncle told me about what's been going on." Fonzie knelt down to eye level since that is what he had been taught in EMT school. "I was fifteen when my mom passed away."

"Really?" Eddy seemed doubtful.

"Yup. In the beginning it was really bad because I missed her so much. But as time went by things got better, easier. I still missed her—still do even now—but I just wanted you to know you're not alone."

"I just miss her so much." He started to cry again. "Do you ever wish you could just see her one last time?"

"Everyday."

"What would you tell her?"

"The same things you would. That I love her. That I miss her. That I'm not gonna let her down just because she's not here anymore. She would never want that. And neither would yours, right?"

He slowly shook his head, sobbing.

"It's okay, buddy." Fonzie wrapped him in a hug. "How about you take a ride with us? Get you checked out. Let you talk to somebody if you need to, okay?"

Eddy peeled his face off Fonzie's shoulder and asked, "Am I gonna go in an ambulance?"

"You are. I drove it here. Wanna throw on the lights and sirens?"

"Yes!" He wiped his cheeks. "That would be so cool!"

"Let's do it."

He and Eddy walked past everyone else like they were not even there. Eddy asked, "How old were you when you became a fireman?"

"Twenty-three."

Eddy did the math on his fingers. "So I have to wait fifteen more years?"

"Nope. You can start applying after you turn eighteen."

"Sweet! That's only ten more years!"

Downstairs, Fonzie put him behind the wheel. Then he got in the officer's side and together they flipped on the lights and went through all the different sirens. Eddy's grin was so wide it looked like it would swallow his whole face. "*This is so cool.*"

"Isn't it? I get to do this all day long."

"I can't wait to be eighteen!"

"Hey, Eddy?" Lt. Monet poked her head through the small window connecting the cab to the back of the truck. "Wanna check out all the cool stuff we got back here?"

Fonzie looked at him and said, "She's right. There's some really sweet toys back there too."

"Okay."

Around back, Fonzie helped him climb aboard.

***

An hour later Fonzie heard a pop and saw white/gray smoke begin to pour from underneath the hood. "Um, lieutenant?"

"Yes?" Lt. Monet was exchanging increasingly hostile texts with her husband. When she looked up and saw the spewing smoke, she said, "Pull over. Incredible. Just incredible." She picked up the mic and said,

"Rescue 2 to Fire Alarm. We are out of service on Whitland Street. 2-5-9 Whitland Street. We need Car 9 here to evaluate the truck. It's currently undriveable."

"Understood, Rescue 2. 1441."

Lt. Monet grabbed her portable radio and said, "Pop the hood."

The rescues were always in rough shape because they ran day and night. After three years, the odometers might have only read 90,000 miles, but they were the hardest 90,000 miles any truck on the road withstood. Going lights and sirens from the station to the call to the hospital meant whipsawing the truck through rapid accelerations and sudden braking nearly every city block. This also quickly turned the drivetrains and suspensions into arthritic joints waiting to snap. Considering these frontline pieces only had a three-year life expectancy, and even though replacing them cost $300,000, at some point fixing and maintaining the older trucks became fiscally irresponsible.

The hood was hot to the touch. Since the rescue personnel carried their own bunker gear and air-packs like everyone else, Fonzie retrieved his fire gloves from his bunker pants and opened the hood.

Standing next to him, Lt. Monet looked like a dwarf. "You know anything about diesels?"

"Some. My dad's a contractor. I grew up tinkering with his stuff."

"Fire Alarm to Rescue 2?"

Lt. Monet answered, "Rescue 2."

"Car 9 is en route. Five-minute ETA."

"Roger. Thank you."

"1445."

"I think the radiator's blown." Fonzie did not want to open the cap to check the fluid because it was still too hot. He knelt and looked under the engine. He tapped a finger in a puddle of liquid and smelt it. "Yeah, it's the radiator."

"Great."

They saw a police car flying toward them lights and sirens and got nervous enough to step back onto the curb. But it was only the city's lead mechanic. Car 9 was Eddy Nazarian, a notorious wild man who oversaw the DOT garage where all the police cars, city cars, dump trucks, snowplows, and fire trucks got repaired. Stripped by budget cuts after the bankruptcy, the mechanics that survived the purge were overworked and exhausted.

"Hands up!" Nazarian yelled through the P.A. He pulsed the siren and then got out laughing. "Just finished fixing it so I had to take it for a spin."

"Officer Nazarian?" Lt. Monet said. "That's too horrific to even contemplate."

"Right?" His brown Carhartt pants and green shirt were splotched with grease like abstract art. His dark eyes and what remained of his black hair reflected his Armenian heritage. He was very happily married but also loved being shockingly inappropriate. "So what happened?"

"I think it's the radiator," Fonzie said.

"Wouldn't surprise me. Driving around with the hottest lieutenant on the whole FD, it was bound to overheat."

"Oh God," Lt. Monet said. "You are something else."

"I made you blush!" Nazarian looked under the truck and said, "The kid's right. Your radiator is an *adios* special. Guess you get to do a changeover. The old Rescue 1 is at the yard."

"Swell. But what about this hunk of junk?"

"It'll make it to the yard." He held up a pair of handcuffs. "Found these on the front seat, though. Wanna play bad cop/worse cop?"

"I don't think your wife would like that."

"I won't tell her if you don't."

"Gross."

"You can cuff me and read me my rights."

"You have the right to stop being a pervert. You have the right to act like a married man and not some total creeper..."

"I don't like those rights."

"You also have the right to remain silent."

"Why? Do you have a ball-gag?"

Fonzie chuckled even though he did not want to and Lt. Monet punched him. "Don't encourage him."

Nazarian flashed a grin and said, "I'll follow you guys back just in case it craps out."

"Roger that," Fonzie said. "Thanks, Ed."

Nazarian smoked a U-turn and waited behind the rescue.

Fonzie was concerned because the engine sounded rough. "It's only a mile, right?"

"If Pervy the Mechanic says it's okay to drive," Lt. Monet said, "whatever else happens from here is on him."

"Okay, boss." He pulled away from the curb. In the sideview mirror he saw Nazarian throw on the lights and start to sing over the P.A. Fonzie frowned. "Wow. That's terrible. What song is that?"

"'I Got You Babe,' by Sonny and Cher." Lt. Monet grimaced. "As if this day couldn't get any worse..."

***

Changing over the rescue with only two people could take anywhere from forty minutes to three hours. Because there was no one in charge of the rescue division, and supplies were always scarce, the reserve rescues were usually already looted of medicines and gear. Most municipal fire departments had a Battalion Chief in charge of their EMS division, but City Hall had so far refused to create and fund this position.

Once they finished stocking the reserve truck, Lt. Monet got in and shook her head. The frontline pieces were bad enough, but the reserves were held together with duct-tape and prayers. Some did not even have keys and got started by jamming screwdrivers into exposed steering columns.

Fonzie hit the ignition and a cloud of black smoke belched from the exhaust. He ran through the systems, checked the house oxygen tank, and circled the truck to see what lights worked. He got back in and said, "She'll run, but our truck radio doesn't work."

Lt. Monet grabbed the shoulder mic on her portable and said, "Rescue 2 to Fire Alarm."

"Go ahead, Rescue 2."

"We are back in-service running with Reserve Rescue 1. Be advised, we have no truck radio, so make sure we acknowledge everything by portable."

"Roger, Rescue 2, on portables only. 1546."

She turned to Fonzie. "How long have you been on?"

"Fourteen months."

"Once you hit eighteen, you're eligible to be put in charge of the rescue. Remember, if you don't say it over the air, it's your word against theirs. When we get to the emergency room, what do we usually do if our portables are busy? We turn them down, right? Out of courtesy? It's already chaotic enough in there. Now let's say we walk out to the truck that has no radio. If we forget to turn our portables back up, we miss a run. This is a zero-sum game. When things go sideways, the folks upstairs aren't gonna be the ones offered up to the Board of Health, bet on that."

"Good to know. Cover your ass."

"Maximum C.Y.A. at all times, Fonzie, never forget that. That brotherhood shit only exists on TV. Out here, people get sacrificed." Lt. Monet hit the mic. "Rescue 2 to Fire Alarm. Back in service running with Reserve Rescue 1. On the air for fuel."

"Roger. Rescue 2's on the air for fuel at 1550."

***

On the way back from the city pumps they got dispatched for difficulty breathing. Fonzie swung onto Elmwood Avenue with the sirens screaming. "What number is it?"

"Twenty-six. It's gonna be on your side. We just passed one-ninety-five."

Fonzie floored it. Two blocks further down they parked in front of a dilapidated triple-decker. Fonzie snapped on rubber gloves and grabbed the First-In backpack.

On the third-floor they found a morbidly obese man wheezing for air. Incredibly, he was smoking a cigarette while leashed to an oxygen tank by nasal cannula. On the table was a full ashtray.

"You've got to be joking." Lt. Monet snatched the cigarette and tossed it into the sink. "On pure oxygen? You trying to kill everybody in here?"

"Please..." Wheeze. "I can't breathe."

"We'll handle it." She turned to Fonzie. "Let's get an SpO2 on him."

Fonzie put the man's index fingertip into a tiny box-like device. It scanned the nailbed until numbers popped on-screen. "Pulse 115, SpO2 83%."

"Not good. Sir, what's your name?"

"George." Wheeze. "McTavish."

"I'm guessing COPD, emphysema...?"

"Everything." Wheeze. "Asthma." Wheeze. "Please help me. I can't breathe."

"We're gonna give you a breathing treatment." She was impressed because Fonzie was already mixing the Albuterol and Atrovent into the nebulizer mask. These bronchodilators would help open his lungs. Seconds later, George was desperately sucking down the humidified vapor.

Lt. Monet said into her mic, "Rescue 2 to Engine 3."

"Engine 3's on."

"Stair-chair and stretcher to the door."

"Roger. On-scene."

Boots clomped up the staircase. Engine 3 appeared with the stair-chair and placed a sheet on it. George stood and walked two feet and was instantly out of breath. Lt. Monet and Fonzie locked the straps into an X across his gelatinous chest.

Even though George weighed over 350 pounds, everyone on the job knew Lt. Monet well enough to not even offer. Engine 3 stepped aside. Lt. Monet and Fonzie got into position. One guy from Engine 3 left to make sure the hallway was clear and front door open. Another got behind Fonzie for safety since he would be walking downstairs backwards. Fonzie shouldered into the backpack that fed the oxygen mask on George's face. "Okay, George, here we go. Do not reach out or try to grab anything because that might tip us over."

"Okay." Wheeze. "Please hurry." Wheeze. "I still can't breathe."

They extended and locked the stair-chair's collapsible handles.

Fonzie knelt at the feet and locked eyes with his boss. "Ready?"

"Yup. On you."

Fonzie backed to the edge and said, "Up."

They lifted in unison and began the dangerous descent. The guy behind Fonzie called out the number of steps to the landings and any upcoming turns. It was a brutal carry down a twisting stairwell built a hundred years before the building codes made these steep, windy staircases completely illegal.

A fireman said, "Fonzie, second-floor landing coming up."

Fonzie's thighs and arms were screaming. He peeked over his shoulder before descending backwards again.

Lt. Monet was a foot shorter and a hundred pounds lighter than Fonzie but did not miss a step. She said, "How you making out?"

"Just ducky. You?"

"In it to win it." But she was running out of breath as well. The staircase was so tight they were bumping into either wall the whole way down.

"Ground-floor coming up."

They did not bother stopping because the front porch had six more concrete steps to reach the sidewalk. At the bottom, they put the stair-chair down next to the stretcher and tried not to show the exact toll this descent had taken. Engine 3 loaded him into the ambulance before Lt. Monet cut them loose.

In the truck, Fonzie was sweating. He affixed the blood pressure cuff and clamped the SpO2 gauge onto George's finger.

Lt. Monet said, "Let's square away his breathing and then go for a line."

"Please," George wheezed. "I can't breathe. I can't breathe!"

"We're working on it, George." Lt. Monet pointed at the monitor and said to Fonzie, "See that? Even if he needs another treatment his pulse is too high. The side effect of those breathing meds is that they spike the pulse. It was 115 before the treatment. Now it's 140."

"What do you want to do?"

"CPAP. You can hear the liquid, right? Grab that stethoscope."

Fonzie listened to George's edema filled chest.

Lt. Monet took out a different, more occlusive mask. "Remember when we talked about how uncomfortable this mask is? Some people really freak out, especially the claustrophobics. But just talk them through it, 'This is for your own good, blah, blah, blah.' You remember how to assemble it?"

"I think so." Fonzie grabbed it and put it together. The CPAP was a new item on an updated protocol, so everyone was still learning how to use it. He placed it over George's mouth and nose and cinched it by tightening the webbing at the back of his head. It always reminded Fonzie of the movie *Alien*, because there was now a hissing suction cup stuck to George's face. CPAP, Continuous Positive Airway Pressure, was only for people still spontaneously breathing. With every breath extra air got jammed further and further into the lungs, driving back the fluid.

"Watch this." She pointed at the SpO2, which began at 86% and started climbing. George became visibly relieved, which also dropped his pulse. He was almost breathing at a normal rate when he surpassed 94%. She said, "George, how're you feeling?"

"Better." His voice was muffled through the mask. Still panicked and sweating, he was gradually calming down.

Lt. Monet asked Fonzie, "With his high BP and difficulty breathing, if we have an IV established, what else can we do by protocol?"

"Um... nitro?"

"Yes, but Solucortef first. In extreme cases, epinephrine. But with his pulse rate, epi is the last thing I would try. And he'd have to be circling the drain for me to do it."

"What does that mean?" George looked nervous again. "Circling the drain? I'm sitting right here!"

"Just running through scenarios, George, I'm still brand new." Fonzie sunk the IV and hooked up the line.

"Nice job." Lt. Monet dialed the phone. "Hello, St. E's, this is Sachem City Rescue 2. We are inbound with a 56-year-old male, difficulty breathing. Positive for asthma, emphysema and COPD. One breathing treatment on board, IV established, he was 83% on room air and is now 96% by CPAP, pulse 100, BG 167, BP 190 over 90. ETA 6 minutes."

"We ready to go?" Fonzie asked.

"Yes, sir."

"Roger that." Fonzie jumped out and toggled his shoulder-mic. "Rescue 2 transporting to Saint Elizabeth's."

"Rescue 2's transporting at 1640."

***

As always, just getting off the rescue was a job in and of itself. They cleared St. Elizabeth's at 5:20 P.M. and, already twenty minutes past shift-change, caught a car wreck on Tidewater Avenue. Rush hour was in full swing, and Engine 4 had just cut an irate man from his own car. Miraculously, he appeared uninjured, but like most everyone else, claimed neck and back pain before demanding transport to the hospital. An attorney, he announced plans to sue the city over the placement of the utility pole he had just wrapped his car around. He was so obnoxious, the police threatened to go through his phone to see if he had been texting at the time of the crash. Lt. Monet was even more blunt. "I don't care who you are," she said. "By protocol, all MVA victims must have their C-spines stabilized. Which means you get backboarded and collared. Period."

"But it's very uncomfortable—"

"Sir, please..." Even Fonzie was growing aggravated. "We can get into big trouble if we wheel you into the ER with no collar. We could even lose our licenses. Besides, if something really is wrong with your neck, you could paralyze yourself by just turning your head."

Minutes later, as Fonzie got into the truck, he received a text and yelled into the back, "Hey, Lou, T-Bag and Killmoor are here for a jump-out."

"Whose *T-Bag*?" the attorney asked.

Lt. Monet ignored him and said, "Yes, please. The sooner the better."

As a courtesy, T-Bag and Lt. Killmoor had arrived on-scene in the latter's pickup truck. All four swapped out their bunker gear and tools.

"Whaddaya got?" Lt. Killmoor asked Lt. Monet.

"Oh, he's a real gem. Single car MVA. Car vs. pole but he's fine. Claiming neck and back but watch out, he's a lawyer."

"Great."

"I already filled out the report." She handed him the contractor case. "All you gotta do is get a signature."

"Roger that. See ya, Pelly." Lt. Killmoor hopped into the back and closed the door.

Fonzie briefed T-Bag by saying, "We did a changeover this afternoon but everything should be accounted for. You're on portables only, no truck radio. Whatever we used today we replaced."

"Good man. Where am I going?"

"Nonsense MVA, so we were taking him to Saint E's instead of Rhode Island. Careful, he's kind of an obnoxious prick."

"I'll make sure to hit every curb and pothole the whole way there." T-Bag grinned and jumped behind the wheel. "See you soon, sweet-tits."

With the shift change complete, Rescue 2 headed off in Reserve Rescue 1 for fourteen more hours of abuse.

RED VERSUS BLUE
November 18, 2009

It had been two months since Receiver Tillinghast proposed privatizing the rescue division. In the interim, Lt. Ahearn, the union president, organized the resistance. Once his sources inside City Hall revealed the exact date the ambulance companies would be presenting their plans and bids, he put out a call for help.

To head off privatization everywhere else, fire departments statewide had already volunteered to assist in this morning's protest. 900 firefighters surrounded City Hall. Every entrance was blocked. Employees were allowed through but no one else. This forced the police into engaging, and that was made even more awkward because police headquarters, attached to the right side of City Hall, had become part of this impromptu quarantine as well.

Fifteen policemen emerged at once and were immediately booed. Police Capt. James McAllistair, whose own father had been a city firefighter, took no joy when he shouted, "Come on, guys, you know you can't do this. No one can bar access to public buildings."

There were more boos and shouts, taunts, and accusations. A crowd was gathering at the base of the stone steps leading up to police headquarters. The daily picket line, still staffed by retirees, now drifted over as well.

Capt. McAllistair looked down at the growing crowd. He carefully chose his words after he spotted the news crews aiming cameras from across the street. He yelled, "This isn't gonna be blue against red. Aren't we all just trying to survive this nightmare together? Believe me, they're gonna take half my pension too, but I can't do anything about that when I'm wearing this." He tugged the captain's bars on his shoulder. "This isn't a costume. It comes with responsibilities. And let's be honest, the law didn't come looking for you today, you all ran into it on your own. But now that you're here, the law says no one has the right to bar access to public buildings, much less City Hall."

More boos and epithets rained down. When the crowd bulged forward, the policemen backing up Capt. McAllistair stepped closer. They began snapping on their helmets just in case.

Lt. Ahearn and Vinny Szceriack, the president of the ARIFF, were at the back entrance of City Hall when word of the confrontation reached them. As they tried to jog around front, Szceriack started laughing.

"What's so funny?" Lt. Ahearn asked.

"Oh nothing. Just a couple of fat guys jiggling around the block."

"I'm big-boned."

"Yeah, me too. Last check, my bones weighed 290-pounds." Szceriack did not even bother removing the cigar from his mouth.

As they rounded the corner, B.C. Etchel saw them jogging and yelled, "Talk about the wrong stuff!"

Someone else shouted, "Yeah, is there a donut shop on fire?"

Lt. Ahearn pushed through the crowd until he got to the front. There he found Big Al Frisky, the retiree known as Risky Frisky after a string of dangerous grabs in 1978, leading the heated exchange.

"I don't think so, Lou," Frisky said after Lt. Ahearn asked him to step back. He was surrounded by a phalanx of equally pissed off retirees. "I'm done standing down. Voiding contracts and stealing my pension's bad enough, but destroying the fire department? Naw, man, that ain't gonna happen. You young guys can thank us later."

Lt. Ahearn knew better than to smirk. After all, seniority was seniority. "We can move forward together or —"

"Or what? Starve to death? Because that's what me and my wife are getting ready to do. I raised two kids and worked two jobs but never budgeted on losing half my retirement. That's because I never thought I would be thanked for my thirty years on the line by being forced to move in with one of my kids or go homeless."

"Al—"

Big Al pushed back to the front and shouted up at Capt. McAllistair, "No one's getting through today! You hear me? Nobody!"

"I understand you're upset—"

"Please, Al." Lt. Ahearn tried grabbing his arm.

Big Al swung an index finger into Lt. Ahearn's face and hissed, "Leading from behind ain't leading at all."

He started walking up the staircase.

Capt. McAllistair shouted, "Please don't do this!"

"You ain't no brothers." Big Al kept climbing.

"You will be arrested!"

"So what? At least I can live for free in jail!"

A cheer went up. The crowd bowed forward. The cops stood fast. When there was no other option remaining, the nightsticks met the crowd and bodies started dropping. After it was over, twenty-six people got arrested. The ambulance companies, however, never appeared. They were told to email their bids instead.

MURPHY'S LAW
November 25, 2009

By chance, Thanksgiving fell on A-Shift but it did not matter because half of the shift was vacancies anyway. The young guys with no seniority on C-Shift got held in the morning, or D-Shift was ordered in from home to fill any remaining spots. By contract, no one could be held longer than twenty-four hours. But no contract meant Chief Fishbakke, fronting for Receiver Tillinghast, now increased this to seventy-two hours instead. Depending on who was getting held and who was going home, the remaining spots got filled by ordering the next due shift back to work early.

Firehouse menus on holidays were like everyone else's. Some stations had great cooks, but the ones that did not relied on wives, moms, or girlfriends to save the day. This year was different. In the five months since the bankruptcy flipped Sachem City onto its head, exhaustion and fatigue had cratered morale. It no longer mattered what day it was because they were now all the same.

Considering no one wanted to go to the hospital on a holiday, Thanksgiving morning was quiet for EMS. But the greatest part of working any holiday was entering people's homes and seeing how they celebrated it. Since it was a city of immigrants, this became a potentiality with a million variants but one—the American core of it all. And with everyone cooking, smoke detectors and heat sensors were going off all over the city. Inside of those apartments and homes, people were festive and apologetic for tripping the alarms while also trying to feed the firemen food from all over the world. Like the rest of the country, those on duty were waiting for football when the All-Call tones hit at 11:15 A.M. *"Attention Engines 6, 4, 2, Ladder 2, Battalion 1... Still Alarm, smoke in the building..."*

Since the usual causes for this were boiler backfires, food on the stove, or an electrical fire, no one took it seriously until Engine 6 turned the corner and abruptly blurted out, "6! Smoke! Code Red!"

Without promotions after the July exodus, Engine 6 on A-Shift had no official officer. The senior private in charge, Brian Creasie, was a nice guy but had spent ten years acquiring minimal skills on the slowest truck in the city.

The second-due truck should have been Engine 3, but the rolling blackouts had closed it and Engine 1 for the dayshift. Engine 4 was six minutes out and Engine 2 was even further. For now, Engine 6 was on its own.

At Station 5 on the other side of the city, Bullet Head Romine did not even wait to be dispatched. There was no one left to send except for him and Ladder 1, so he beat the tones out the door.

"Floor it, Matty, we got a road trip on our hands." Capt. Romine wailed the siren. "95 North to Exit 28 and then haul balls down Greenwich."

"Roger, Cap." Matty Biggio, the motorcyclist caught doing 170 MPH on 95 South, was the right man for the job. He swooped the twenty-five-ton truck in and out of traffic, lane to lane, and even caught air on the off-ramp.

Capt. Romine was monitoring the radios and heard, "Command to Engine 6."

No answer.

"Command to Engine 6."

"6!"

B.C. McLoud asked, "Whaddaya got in there?"

"Chief, it's... we think most of its out, but..."

"But what?"

"Awesome," Capt. Romine spat. "Creasie's a fucking idiot and B.C. Fatso ain't much better. Can't you drive any faster?"

Biggio tried to oblige but Greenwich Avenue was a one-lane road filled with sleepy drivers.

As Capt. Romine pulled on his Nomex hood and bunker jacket, he yelled to his backstep man, "Syl!"

"Yeah!" Sylvester Keating was already donning his jacket and air-pack.

"After we get there, while Matty gears up, grab the irons. I'll find B.C. Donut and figure out where we need to go."

"Is that the smoke?" Biggio pointed at a small gray stain smeared across the sky. "Boy, it doesn't look like much."

"Who knows what these idiots are doing." Capt. Romine grabbed the mic. "Engine 5 to Command."

Nothing.

"Engine 5 to Command!"

"Go 5!"

"Where do you need us?"

When there was no response, Capt. Romine was so disgusted he threw the mic onto the dashboard and said, "Just put us behind the deuce."

Ladder 2 was telescoping for the roof in case it needed to be vented.

Capt. Romine looked up at the triple-decker. He analyzed the smoke color, how it was puffing from the eaves on side-one and two but saw no visible fire. One handline was stretched through the front door, and another snaked around back. When B.C. McLoud waddled around the corner in his extra-expansive yellow bunker gear, Bullet Head called out, "Whaddaya got...?"

B.C. McLoud was trying not to look nervous. "Damnedest thing,

Gary. Creasie said there was visible fire rolling out the kitchen window on side-two, but they knocked it down quick..."

"So what the hell's going on?"

"We're trying—"

"That was a rhetorical question. Is anyone running a TIC around the walls yet?" He held up a Thermal Imaging Camera. Recently adapted from the military's Night-Vision technology, the TIC was a hand-held rectangle with a small screen that displayed the world through different heat signatures. It was an excellent tool for finding hidden fires or unconscious people through the smoke.

"We haven't," B.C. McLoud said. "Not yet. There hasn't been time. We've been stretching lines."

"We'll handle it."

Biggio and Keating caught up with Capt. Romine as he headed for the front door. "We're gonna TIC the walls, boys, mask up."

All three went on air. They popped on their helmet lights and stepped into the smoke.

Even though it was noon, inside it was dusky black. Visibility was a foot, but at least conditions allowed them to walk. They got to the blackened kitchen and Biggio said, "Feels hotter in here still."

"Sure does. They said it was rolling out this window." Capt. Romine pointed his light at the charred wood and said, "See that? They call this scaly kind of burn pattern 'alligatoring.'" The drywall above the stove had already been pulled down, the wall studs exposed. "I'm no brain surgeon, but I'm guessing the fire's in the walls above us."

"Are your feet hot?" Keating asked through his mask.

Capt. Romine ran the TIC across the floor and said, "Good call, Syl, there it is." He toggled his mic. "Engine 5 to Command."

"Go ahead."

"Fire burned into the floor system below the kitchen. Looks to be about a ten-foot square. It's crawling in the bays but not exceedingly hot yet. Four-hundred degrees on the TIC. Recommend stretching a line to the basement to chase it down. We're gonna head upstairs and scan the walls."

"Command to Engine 6. Get back in there and stretch that line to the basement..."

On the second-floor, Bullet Head ran into Engine 2 and asked, "You guys check the kitchen walls?"

"We just got up here," Lt. Salamanca said. With everyone still on air, they sounded like astronauts far from home. "Pretty smoky and hot if the fire's supposedly out, right?"

Because it was a triple-decker, the floor plans were all the same. In order to save money on plumbing and electric, the kitchens and bathrooms were always stacked on top of each other. Capt. Romine aimed the camera at the same kitchen wall as below and the screen immediately lit up. "Who has that other line?"

"The 4's. They're upstairs."

"We're gonna soak it from above. Get ready to smash open this wall."

"You got it, Cap."

"Engine 5 to Command. We've got extension inside the side-two exterior wall, second-floor. Going up to check out the third-floor now."

They had to move fast. Upstairs, it was even hotter and smokier, so Engine 4 was opening windows for ventilation.

"Close those windows before you feed this thing." Capt. Romine aimed the TIC at the same kitchen wall as below. Then he freaked everyone out by saying, "We've got two minutes before the roof catches and we lose the whole building."

They frantically smashed open the drywall. Like some insidious prank, the fire snapped and licked along each bay between the studs. This fresh oxygen allowed it to now lunge the last few feet towards the attic.

Capt. Romine yelled, "Hit that whole ceiling line right now!"

The Engine 4 private dug in, threw open the bale, and wrestled against the backpressure. The kitchen filled with smoke and steam as everyone took a knee and ducked to avoid both. The nozzleman kept blasting, running the line from wall to wall, soaking every bay and everyone else.

Capt. Romine exposed his microphone and shouted above the crashing water, "Engine 5 to Engine 2. Open it up. Think we got it."

Below, he could hear smashing and violence.

"Engine 2 to Engine 5. Keep soaking it. Looks to be out but just in case..."

"Roger." Capt. Romine leaned toward the nozzleman and yelled, "Keep hitting it! Sounds like we got it."

It was then, as things began to clear, that Capt. Romine saw it. The kitchen. The dining-room. Thanksgiving had been totally destroyed. Entering through the smoke, Engine 4 had flipped over the table, scattering and shattering the plates and silverware. Whatever food that had been prepared was now ruined by the water and smoke. It also had to be the same for the families on the floors below.

Across their radios screamed, "Ladder 2 to Command!"

"Go, Ladder 2."

"We got visible fire on side-three. It's breaking through the wall!"

Capt. Romine grabbed an axe and headed for the back wall. He aimed the TIC and the whole wall lit up. "You've got to be shitting me." He punched a hole through the drywall and fire leapt out. "Let's go, boys!"

There were two rooms on side-three. They opened every bay and dumped water straight into the basement.

Lt. Salamanca placed a hand on the side-four wall. "You're not gonna believe this." After his TNT tool smashed through the drywall, more flames flickered through.

"This is embarrassing." Capt. Romine smashed open more bays along the wall. "We suck."

"Engine 6 to Command!"

"Go, 6."

"I think it's traveling along the HVAC! It's still drawing air."

"They didn't even cut the power yet?" Capt. Romine had had enough.

"Engine 5 to Engine 6. You might want to shut down the electric since you're in the basement!"

Their low air warning systems began going off but no one cared. The bulk of the fire suppression was over, so they just pulled their masks and choked in the smoke and debris-filled air instead.

Capt. Romine said, "Let's go, boys, we're opening up every wall."

They dropped their air-packs and started demolishing walls.

***

By the time it was over, the third-floor interior walls on side-two, three, and four had no drywall. The fire had followed the HVAC system and piggy-backed through the house, so the ladder crews skewered the first-floor ceilings with New York Hooks and yanked all of them down.

"Incredible." Outside, Capt. Romine dumped water over his head. "We nearly burnt down a triple-decker over a stupid oven fire."

"We've been here for two hours," Lt. Salamanca said. "Dios mio."

"If we'd lost this house I would've had to quit in shame."

"Happy Thanksgiving, right?"

Capt. Romine followed his gaze and said, "Aw, man..." Across the street, three families, the former tenants, huddled with representatives from the Red Cross. "These poor people. Imagine dealing with this shit on Thanksgiving?"

"No." Lt. Salamanca chugged Gatorade off the "canteen truck." In Providence, intrepid civilian volunteers manned a pair of re-purposed food trucks twenty-four hours a day. Through good weather and bad, Rhode Island's small size allowed the canteen to appear at every fire in the state. Coffee and chili were fed to the same firefighters that financially supported these trucks out of their own pockets.

"You know what?" Lt. Salamanca said, "Jimmy DelFrisco's dropping off a feast downtown. Said it would be enough for two shifts."

"Yeah, we gotta lot of food too. Wanna combo it up downtown?"

"You? Sharing the Thanksgiving spirit?" It said something about Lt.

Salamanca's reputation that he could get away with busting Bullet Head's balls right to his face. "You getting soft in your old age?"

"Don't tell anyone else."

Lt. Salamanca grinned and headed over to the families to extend the invitation in Spanish. Appreciative of the gesture, they did not want to impose, but Lt. Salamanca would not take no for an answer.

"What'd they say?" Capt. Romine asked.

"I told them three o'clock. By the time we pack hose and clean up, that might even be cutting it close."

"Roger that. And Sal?"

"Yeah?"

"Snitches get stitches. This Thanksgiving secret dies with us."

Lt. Salamanca threw him a salute and headed over to help pack 600 feet of hose. For one oven fire, they had pulled three attack lines, run a feeder, dumped a thousand of gallons of water into the basement, and smashed open enough drywall to make the place uninhabitable. Unfortunately, inexperience and the rolling blackouts were poised to wreak more havoc.

A GHOST RETURNS

November 29, 2009

The monthly union meeting started badly and rapidly deteriorated. As always, it was at Station 4 on the east side. All the trucks were out on the apron. In the humongous apparatus bay, Lt. Ahearn sat with the six other members of the Executive Board facing the anxious crowd. They went over the minutes from last month's meeting before all hell broke loose. Regarding last week's Thanksgiving Day fire, people brought up safety issues, incompetency, and, most disturbingly, an overall lackadaisical fireground attack. Disrespecting longtime standards was acceptable to no one. Those not at the fire called out the ones that were, and those on the receiving end returned the favor. Off-duty members who had been drinking at Connolly's Revenge before the meeting only made everything worse. All the screaming built into a crescendo until both sides had to be divided.

"Good thing Bullet Head's not here!" Lt. Salamanca screamed. "None of you would ever have enough balls then!"

"Fuck him!" someone yelled, and Lt. Salamanca lunged again.

"That's enough!" Lt. Ahearn stood and pointed. "Everyone back up. Act like fucking adults, would you please?"

People milled and murmured until order got restored.

Lt. Ahearn took his seat and said, "This union has way more important issues to consider other than some burnt turkey in the 6's. Now, as we all know, events on the eighteenth show us two things. Number one—he's serious about privatizing the rescue. Number two—he's not afraid to unleash the police. While they were cracking the heads of 70-year-old men on the steps of police headquarters, that sick prick was probably watching from his office with a hard on. Imagine this? He's already stealing the retirements of every former member of this union. Forcing grandparents onto food stamps ain't exactly what we signed up for, is it? I just wanted this membership to know that we are keeping track of everything. All of it. To date, since the July 12th bankruptcy, we have filed over four hundred grievances regarding breach of contract. Do we have a contract? No. But all of this will be adjudicated somewhere down the road. What we're doing for now is creating and maintaining a written record of everything being done to this union. On a personal level, for the record, watching this job be torn apart because of politics and money makes me sick.

"As for the retirees, things are only getting worse. We're still holding raffles. We also have two more fundraisers set up for next month at Connolly's. As most of you know, Jasper Wychek, who's now 89-years-old, is facing foreclosure. Fellas, this guy was putting out fires before your fathers were born. He lives on Euclid Avenue and has for the past seventy years. But the banks don't care about that. The people of this city don't care about that, and Receiver Fuckface certainly doesn't either. But we do. I know its tough right now, but with the raffles coming up, try and sell more tickets. Dig a little deeper into your own pockets, too, because one day when you're eighty-nine and the city bends you over, you might need your younger brothers to help you survive."

People nodded.

"We've started gathering a list of retirees in need of assistance. Some are just odds and ends around the house—patching roofs, painting, you name it. If you're a plumber, a roofer, a carpenter, an electrician, please look at this list and see if there's anything you can do to help. I know

Robby McIntyre's back stairs are basically falling apart. Poor fuck can't even get down to his own deck. Fellas, these are the exact people we need to look out for. I was at Stop & Shop the other day and ran into Ray Dungeoness. But he wasn't buying anything. Poor fuck's bagging groceries. 76-years-old. Imagine this? These stories are becoming more common."

Murmurs punctuated the helplessness swamping everyone.

"No confidence!" someone shouted.

Heads turned to find the speaker. Ronnie Rondoulet was called "Two-Face" because of horrific injuries sustained in a 1987 backdraft that nearly killed him and his boss. On the second-floor of a triple-decker, they were dragging out an unconscious man when someone smashed out a window on the wrong side of the building. This introduced fresh oxygen into a fire already starving for fuel. The ensuing explosion hit the back of his boss, Lt. Elmore, and torched his neck. But Two-Face was not as lucky. He was carrying the victim's feet and facing the fireball. It was so intense it smashed into his face and fused the mask into his skin. At Ocean State Hospital, surgeons used scalpels to dissect the line between skin and the rubber gasket just to remove the mask. It, the mask, saved his features, which remained totally intact. But now, twenty-two years later, the third-degree burns that surrounded them had created a violent mosaic of scars and ruined skin.

After all the surgeries, Two-Face fought to return to work. He threatened to file suit against the city if they pensioned him off. But the city, like his doctor, was only trying to do the right thing. No one thought his return to work was a good idea. Desperate for one last chance to stay on the job, he consulted with a world-renowned dermatologist in Boston. This specialist told him, despite being a very lucky man, there was zero chance his patched over skin grafts would ever survive another blast of serious heat. The doctor told him to go home to his family and enjoy the rest of his life. So that's what Two-Face did, raising three kids while his wife went back to work. On a department where everyone existed as an equal or did not exist at all, Two-Face was amongst a handful of all-timers forever elevated into the rafters.

Now a grizzled 60-year-old, his welted skin twisted like thorny vines above his ominous blue eyes. As a retiree, he was no longer part of the union and should not have been allowed into the meeting at all, but no one said otherwise. "An old man once told me I was nothing special. He said he'd been doing the job before I was even born. Said there'd been many others before him that did the same, and that many more would come after. So there ain't nothing special about none of you either. I'm here to tell you that. I'm here to tell you that before you know it your careers are gonna be over. This small window of years, on this job, is precious. I'm here to tell you that too. Because after you retire and look back at all the memories and craziness, it will already be too late. Believe me, what you do here right now will end up being the best part of your lives. Don't forget what brought you here. And don't forget that without leadership this place is doomed. This ain't the Water Department, it's the *Fire* Department. And as far as the chief's position goes, there's only been one no-confidence vote in the last 200 years. The crash of '29 meant layoffs and budget cuts. Sound familiar? Guys died back then. So here we go again, reunited with the same men who faced the same end as all of you now."

"No confidence!" someone else yelled, and everyone cheered.

Lt. Ahearn said, "Are we really motioning to hold a no-confidence vote on the chief of this department?"

"Fuck yeah!" another shouted.

"I second that!"

"All right." Lt. Ahearn scribbled on his pad. "I believe the by-laws state there must be a two week notice of a vote. I'll double-check, but for now that makes December 12th the date. All in favor?"

A chorus of "Ayes" rang out and people cheered again.

Two-Face never heard it because he had already left the station.

BLOOD ALLEY STRIKES AGAIN
December 8, 2009

"Attention Rescue 1, Engine 6, Still Alarm. 135 Ballan Avenue."

At Station 1, Capt. LeClaire descended the steps to the apparatus floor. Rowdell was already out there waiting. He was limping so badly Capt. LeClaire asked, in that Clint Eastwood-like rasp, "Are you sure you're okay, kid?"

"I'm fine, Cap, just a little sore."

He squinted. "Looks like you can barely walk."

"Ain't that the truth. Those bike seats are rough. Winter forced me and T-Bag out of the ocean."

"Who bikes in the winter?" Capt. LeClaire joined him in the truck. "Heard that's how he gets to work from Newport. That true?"

"Not everyday, but yeah."

"How? I thought the Newport Bridge was closed to bikes?"

"It is. So he sneaks across the Mt. Hope Bridge instead."

"Good God. How far is that on a bike?"

"Thirty-eight miles."

"What a horrible idea. How far did you go yesterday?"

"I think forty?"

"It's thirty degrees outside. What is wrong with you guys?" Capt.

400

LeClaire grabbed the mic and said, "Rescue 1 responding. 135 Ballan Avenue."

"Rescue 1's responding at 1752."

Rowdell hit the lights and whooped the siren to clear the street. "We're gonna try and do a couple of century rides this winter."

"What's that mean?"

"A hundred miles."

"On a *bike*? I don't even want to drive a hundred miles."

"Me neither."

"Then why are you trashing yourself?"

"I don't know. I guess I like the challenge, right?"

"Just be careful. You were in construction for twenty years, so I'm not telling you anything you don't know, but on this job a healthy body is your most important tool."

They screamed across town to meet Engine 6. It was cold. Winter had arrived, so the rescue guys wore black leather department bomber jackets. Rowdell had a Sachem City Fire Department knit cap covering his shaved head. He said, "I wonder what this sick bastard has going on today?"

"One can only imagine."

Engine 6 was already on-scene when they pulled up. Pete DeAngelis, the DUI victim with the brain injury and left-sided impairment, pointed at them with his cane.

"Booooooo!" Pete yelled. "I don't want you cocksuckas, where's Killmoor?"

Capt. LeClaire nodded at the Engine 6 officer and said, "You guys can clear. I think we can handle this."

"You sure? Seems like a real emergency to me."

"Aren't they all. So what's up, Pete? Why'd you call?"

"T-Bag!" he chanted. "T-Bag! T-Bag! T-Bag!"

"Killmore and T-Bag are on a different run, Pete, so you're gonna have to settle for us."

"Boooo! You suck!"

"Pete—"

"Kill-moor! T-Bag!"

"They're busy, Pete. And I'm kind of hurt you're not cheering our names instead."

Pete pointed at Rowdell. "What's his name again?"

"You know Rowdell."

"Looks like a cock-face to me! Cock-Face! Luh-Clair! Cock-Face! Luh-Clair!"

"Geez." Rowdell grinned. "I know I have a big nose but isn't cock-face a little extreme?"

"Cock-Face! T-Bag! Kill-moor! Luh-Clair!"

"Pete—"

"I have chest pain!"

"Pete—"

"Difficulty breathing!"

"What—"

"Left-sided weakness!"

"What else?"

"T-Bag! T-Bag!"

"Come on, Pete, let's just go to the truck. Maybe T-Bag's at the hospital."

"T-Bag!"

They helped him step up into the back and laid him on the stretcher.

Capt. LeClaire, with his trademark patience, asked, "So why are we really here, Pete?"

Pete held up the shrunken claw his left hand had become. "It really hurts and I don't know why!"

"Saint E's," Capt. LeClaire told Rowdell. "All right, Pete, sit back and enjoy the ride."

"Rescue 1 to Fire Alarm," Rowdell said into his portable. "Transporting one to Saint Elizabeth's."

"Roger, Rescue 1, transporting to Saint Elizabeth's at 1758."

At the hospital, Rowdell swung open the back doors of the rescue just as Lt. Killmoor and T-Bag exited the ER with their empty stretcher.

"T-Bag!" Pete screamed with glee. The left side of his face was frozen, but the right was ecstatic. "T-Bag! T-Bag!"

"Excuse me?" A woman passing by at the same instant took immediate offense.

"Don't mind him, ma'am." Rowdell dragged out the stretcher. "He ain't shuffling with a full deck."

Pete DeAngelis looked directly at the woman and excitedly screamed, "Cock-Face! T-Bag! Kill-moor! Luh-Clair!"

"You're a filthy man!"

"Ah-ha-ha-ha!"

"Jesus Christ, Pete..." Rowdell quickly dragged him toward the ER. "You're gonna get us all fired, bro."

"Ah-ha-ha-ha!"

T-Bag high-fived Pete as he rolled by, yelling, "Merry Christmas, you cocksucka!"

"Ah-ha-ha-ha! Happy Hanukkah, you kike!"

"I'm not Jewish, Pete."

"Let's get out of here," Capt. LeClaire said, pushing the stretcher even faster. "Before we get charged with a hate crime."

"Right?" Rowdell punched in the code and yanked the stretcher into the building.

Twenty minutes later they were back on the street. As part of the city's circulatory system, the rescues rarely stopped moving. Capt. LeClaire grabbed the mic and said with his trademark wisp, "Rescue 1's back in service."

"Rescue 1's back in at 1818."

"You got any errands or anything?" Rowdell wheeled them through traffic.

"Naw, lets head back and see what the fellas got cooking for dinner."

"Fire Alarm to Rescue 1?"

"Guess not," Rowdell said. "Have you ever had a hot meal on this truck in thirty years?"

"Very few and far between." Capt. LeClaire toggled the mic and said, "Rescue 1's on, Fire Alarm."

"Start responding to Gilmont Park for a male, ETOH."

"Roger that."

"Would you like an engine?"

Capt. LeClaire knew that Engine 3 on C-Shift was manned by Lt. Cunty Conti, Useless, and Toe-Tag.

Apparently thinking the same thing, Rowdell said, "No thanks, man, fuck those guys."

Capt. LeClaire could not disagree. "Negative, Fire Alarm, we'll handle."

"Roger, sir, responding at 1819."

They descended towards the river. Past the boat ramp, Asshole Tree was strewn with cardboard shanties and filthy sleeping bags. Their headlights caught three homeless men pointing at a fourth laying on the ground.

"Look at this. The whole crew's here," Capt. LeClaire said. "Oscar, Tito, the Chin... who're they pointing at?"

"I can't see him."

"Damn. I think that's Paul." Capt. LeClaire picked up the mic. "Rescue 1's on-scene."

"Rescue 1 on-scene at 1823."

"Hey, fellas," Capt. LeClaire said, and they all called out hello in return. "How you doing, Chin?"

"Good." The Chin grinned and moved with his sloth-like slowness. His toothless under-bite left him smacking his gums.

"You look better, Chin, that belly wound must've healed up nice."

"No more maggots," he slurped, and rolled his head like Stevie Wonder.

"You guys be careful out here tonight. Hypothermia ain't nothing nice this early in the season." Capt. LeClaire knelt and felt for a pulse. "This is a shame. I heard he was doing good this time."

"What's his story again?" Rowdell asked.

"Paul Theroux. Used to be an ER nurse at OSH. Let's get a blood sugar on him." Capt. LeClaire took the glucometer. "He was the charge nurse for the whole ER. I was dropping off patients with him for over a decade. Long story short, ten years ago he and his wife buried their 3-year-old daughter."

"Ugh."

"Leukemia." Capt. LeClaire used the lancet to draw blood from Theroux's finger. Five seconds later the glucometer read 110. "After that, he and the wife couldn't be around each other without thinking about it, so their marriage fell apart. Hand me the BP cuff?" He wrapped it around Theroux's bicep. "Originally, he started drinking only at night, and then the nights turned into days and nights, and then both became forever. He lost his job. He's been in and out of rehab, but this time, he made it seem... you can only achieve this by really wanting it, you know?"

"That's an awful story."

"Always remember, you and me and everyone else, we're only one bad decision away from becoming this guy. BP's 180 by palp. Paul!" Capt. LeClaire propped open Theroux's dirt-smeared eyelids and saw the pupils retract. The alcohol and frozen nights had turned his face into a veiny tomato.

Capt. LeClaire looked up at the other homeless men and asked what happened.

"He just fell," Oscar said. "One minute we was drinking, the next he was on the floor."

"Get the gurney," Capt. LeClaire told Rowdell. "He's like me. He just needs a good nap."

"Don't we all."

They lifted him onto the stretcher and then loaded him into the truck.

Rowdell climbed into the cab and said into his portable, "Rescue 1 transporting to Saint Elizabeth's."

"Rescue 1 transporting at 1833."

It was not something Capt. LeClaire did all the time, but for an old friend, he slipped a twenty-dollar bill into Theroux's pocket. Then he watched him sleep.

***

Things calmed down after rush hour. They got back to the station and microwaved their dead dinners back to life. December in New England meant sunsets at four o'clock, so outside it was already cold and dark.

Rowdell went upstairs. Built in 1911, Station 1 was the oldest in the city and a registered national landmark. Like an old western brothel, the switchback stairs led up to a U-shaped second-floor. Individual bedrooms ran the circumference of the long banister around the stairs. In every other station, the officers were the only ones that had their own rooms, and the privates slept in dormitories. But Station 1 had private bedrooms for everyone, even if they were not much bigger than the single beds they contained. The woodwork, in keeping with the period, was intricate and never to be repeated. Rowdell, the construction worker, was always in awe as he drove around the city and saw what had been achieved with hammers and sweat before the machines took over. Station 1's fourteen-foot ceilings had double-layered crown molding installed forty years before the first power saw.

Also upstairs were the showers, bathrooms, and a day-room with a bookcase from the 1800's. Inside it were logbooks dating back to 1878. The books from 1801 to 1878 had, ironically, been lost in a fire at City Hall in 1881. Inside these leather-bound volumes, the officer in charge listed the shift hours, the men on the truck, the chores they did, any runs they had, and, since the city did not buy mechanized apparatus until 1910, the feeding times and care of the horses. The logbooks connected the modern era to a time when the written word preceded telephones, telegraphs, and telegrams. Every shift had perfect penmanship. These books became captured histories of every day station life. Situationally, it was startling to see how little things had changed. The nature of what they did meant certain eras suffered various hardships, but otherwise, substantive improvement in gear meant crews pushed interior attacks into even more dangerous places. This was also why the annual national average of one hundred line-of-duty deaths remained a constant.

The lights upstairs were individual wall sconces installed in the 1940's, half of which were broken, so the top of the walls and high ceiling disappeared into the permanent shadows. It was only nine o'clock, but Rowdell wanted to make his bed in case things got busy. Nothing was predictable. A payday Friday night could come and go with only a handful of runs, while a quiet rainy Sunday night could unleash a fifteen-run pounding into the dawn. The rescue played no favorites and showed no mercy.

Rowdell finished making his bed just as the All-Call tones hit and Fire Alarm announced, *"Attention Engines 2, 5, Ladder 1, Battalion 3... Still Alarm. 95 South before Exit 28. Reported rollover with ejections..."*

Capt. LeClaire might have been a thirty-year veteran, but he was still the first one to the truck. He said into the mic, "Rescue 1 responding 95 South."

"Rescue 1's responding at 2115."

Capt. McCarrick on Engine 2 called the same. As always, Engine 5 would sweep north from Providence just in case the caller got the north-south direction wrong. Friday night on the highway always combined a host of bad factors—late commuters from Boston, payday, date night, alcohol, and people arriving or escaping for the weekend. For the unsuspecting, impaired, or unfamiliar, Blood Alley became the worst roller coaster ride of their lives.

Capt. McCarrick called over the radio, "Engine 2 to Fire Alarm."

"Go Engine 2."

"On-scene. Multiple ejections. Looks to be a limousine that's been cut in half. Start me four rescues at least."

"*Roger.*"

In the cab of Rescue 1, Capt. LeClaire said, "That's not good news. Rescue 2's in East Providence mutual aid."

"Engine 2 to Ladder 1! Block off the low speed and middle lanes behind us right now! There are bodies all over the highway!"

"Battalion 3 to Fire Alarm."

"*Go ahead, Chief.*"

"Have Engine 5 swing around and park with Ladder 1 to shut down the highway. Inform the State Police we're shutting it down. Also, dispatch me three more engine companies."

"*Roger, Chief.*"

B.C. Etchel parked in front of Engine 2 and stepped into the carnage. He counted at least nine women and one man strewn between the front and back halves of a black limousine. Other drivers who had witnessed the destruction now staggered around trying to help but only got in the way. Capt. McCarrick screamed at them to return to their cars and wait to give statements to the State Police. He, Dutch Carrigan, and Cheeseburger were going body to body triaging the wounded. He said, "Engine 2 to Battalion 3."

"Go, 2."

"We have seven critical, three D.O.A."

"Roger. Battalion 3 to Fire Alarm. Send me a total of seven rescues and seven engine companies. Notify OSH we are declaring a Mass Casualty Incident. Inform the Staties they're gonna need the Medical Examiner out here along with their Accident Reconstruction Team."

"*Roger, Chief. 2121.*"

"Also, inform the Mass State Police they're gonna have to shut down the highway southbound at Exit 1. No one else is getting through here tonight."

"*Roger, Chief. 2122.*"

Cheeseburger, in the Transfer Pool on C-Shift, usually worked Engine 2 or Engine 5. Since both were highway companies, he was growing accustomed to dismembered bodies and crushed skulls. Pulling up, he saw one woman had been torn in half. The only thing connecting her was ten feet of glistening intestines. Eerily, the bodies and wounds started steaming in the winter air. As if guillotined, another woman was missing the top of her skull. The third fatality was the driver. His head was spun backwards, his limbs stuck at crazy angles from his destroyed torso. The scattered women who survived were either unconscious or in shock. One was talking to her dead friends while holding up the half of her face nearly torn off when she went through the back window. Her arm was also broken and missing its hand, so it was actually her torn stump holding up her face.

Some of the eyewitnesses to the crash were anguished or in shock. Others were just pointing and crying. But B.C. Etchel did not have the resources for additional casualties. "Back! Everyone get back! Let us handle this!"

Cheeseburger stumbled across the most critical woman. Her legs had bilateral femur fractures and rested at unnatural angles. She was a ragdoll with a shattered pelvis. Her left arm was broken into a question mark and her nose had been ground off skidding across the pavement. It said something about how far Cheeseburger had progressed because none of this mattered. He addressed one life threat after the other. He started a large bore 16 gauge IV with lactated ringers as a volume expander. He dumped saline on her torn open stomach, covered it in a trauma dressing, and was about to check for distal pulses in her ankles to see if her arteries had been cut or impinged when Rescue 1 pulled up through the stopped traffic. "What do you got, Cheese?"

"Cap! I need two H.A.R.E. traction splints. Oh Jesus!" He tried to laugh it off. "You scared me."

Somehow, her eyes had opened. They were green and expressive above the grated red bone where her nose should have been. He took her hand and said, "Can you hear me, dear? What's your name?"

"Moira," she whispered, blinking. Blood dribbled out of her mouth. "Where am I?"

"What's your last name, Moira?"

"Daniels."

"Okay, Moira. Listen, you've been in a car accident, okay?"

"Someone needs to walk my dog."

"Moira—"

"Will I be okay for the wedding next weekend?"

"The..." Cheeseburger put it all together. "Are—is this a bachelorette party?"

"Where's LaShonda? She's the bride."

Capt. LeClaire and Rowdell arrived with the stretcher, trauma bag, and traction splints. They started buckling her into them when Cheeseburger squeezed her hand and said, "Moira, I'm not gonna lie. This is gonna hurt, but we need to straighten out your legs, okay?"

"Morphine?" Rowdell asked his boss.

"Negative. BP is too borderline."

Cheeseburger said, "Moira, here we go. On three."

"I hope I'm at a good table."

"One, two, three."

They cranked the winch attached to her ankle and she immediately screamed. Cheeseburger was still learning how to hurt people in order to help them because none of this was easy. The traction stretched the broken leg back into position before the jagged bone ends severed everything around them, including her arteries. Cheeseburger did not have to warn her about the second leg because she had screamed herself unconscious. With both legs splinted and her neck collared, they carefully rolled her to check for posterior injuries. Finding none, they slid the backboard beneath her and then rolled her back. Strapped down, she had stabilizing blocks placed on either side of her head before they lifted her onto the stretcher. In the back of the truck, a dozen things began happening at once. Capt. LeClaire said, "Cheese, get some O2 on her and then cut off the rest of her clothes. Row, get me another IV with saline in the left arm above that break. We have no choice." He unlocked the narcotics box just in case. Her BP was 106/80, so she was borderline. If that top number fell below 90 no narcotics could be given anyway, so unless she woke up screaming, he would not be pushing it.

Dutch Carrigan jumped into the driver's seat and shouted through the access window, "Ready, Cap?"

"Just like the old days, right Dutchie?"

"Ha-ha-ha! Thirty years later and I'm back in the box with you again!"

Capt. LeClaire said into his shoulder-mic, "Rescue 1 to Fire Alarm."

"Go, Rescue 1."

"Advise Rhode Island we are inbound with a late-twentyish female with bilateral femur fractures. She is splinted and does have distal pulses. She has a left radial/ulna fracture, facial trauma, and partial evisceration of the lower abdomen. Vitals are—"

"Cap!" Rowdell pointed at the new blood pressure, which read 80/66 with a pulse of 120.

"What're we missing?" Capt. LeClaire double-checked her legs. As the back-up medic for his platoon, Vietnam had taught him many things about the human body. Like a hydraulic system under constant pressure, saving lives meant stopping blood-loss and injecting IV fluids to keep the system under pressure. The pulse in the right ankle was fine, but the left was fading. Without any pooling of blood in her leg, he became immediately alarmed. "It has to be in her belly." Ripping off the bandages, he saw the blood had soaked through them all. They hit the floor with a wet thump.

Rowdell grew concerned. "Cap, what're you doing?"

"She's gonna code if we don't stop the bleeding. Her pulse is going up because she's losing too much blood. Her cells are crying out for oxygen."

"We'll work her—"

"They don't work trauma codes at the State. If we roll her in there with no pulse she's as good as dead."

Rowdell tried one last time. "You're sure about this?"

"No. But I'm gonna need a scalpel and clamps. They're in the OB kit."

Rowdell tore it open and his bloody gloves were shaking.

Capt. LeClaire made one last terrain study of the exposed fatty tissue, muscle, and intestines. He ran the scalpel through the fascia to open up a nice clean line. He gently made additional passes to ease back more tissue. Since her left distal pulse was fading, he was guessing it might be the descending aorta or iliac artery that fed her leg. Also, as quickly as Rowdell suctioned out the blood more appeared. Problem was these arteries were buried deep next to her spine. Cheeseburger switched out the now empty first IV bag as Capt. LeClaire thrust both hands into her torso.

Rowdell winced. "Jesus Christ, Cap."

"If I find it," Capt. LeClaire said, "you're gonna have to clamp it."

"*Excuse me?*"

"Give me more suction. Who wants an anatomy lesson? The descending aorta splits into two iliac arteries that feed blood to both legs—"

"Cap!" Rowdell pointed at the newest BP which was 60/46.

"Slow it down, Row. Slow is smooth, smooth is fast. That's an old Navy SEAL motto." He pulled aside enough intestines until he saw blood spurting from a tiny torn smile. "That's it! More suction. Clamp it above the cut. Now!"

Rowdell did not think, he just reached into her abdomen and grabbed the slippery tube spurting blood. Dutch was flooring the rescue, so Rowdell missed twice with the clamps before finally securing it.

"Don't go crazy." Capt. LeClaire held back the organs and intestines. "Just tighten them enough to stop the bleeding."

Rowdell squeezed until the blood tapered off.

Cheeseburger, standing above them, was speechless.

Capt. LeClaire gently let the intestines reset around the clamps. Then he used his blood-smeared hands to squeeze both IV bags in order to speed-dump enough fluid into her system to keep her alive.

"Hang on!" Dutch yelled. "Off-ramp's coming up!"

"Look at that." Rowdell pointed at the new BP, which was 80/56. "You're almost a God, you know that?"

"We're backing in!" Dutch yelled.

They popped open the doors even before the rescue was parked. Inside, Critical Care One was already filled with a cadre of trauma personnel.

Capt. LeClaire delivered his patient's story covered in her blood. "This is Moira Daniels. She was a passenger in a limousine with ten ejections—three fatalities on-scene. Six others are coming right behind us. She has bilateral femur fractures, distal pulses, a broken left radius and ulna, facial trauma, and a ruptured left external iliac artery, which has been clamped off. BP was as low as 60/46 but after the clamp it rebounded to 80/56 backing in. No morphine onboard and unsure about medical allergies."

Moira Daniels was devoured by the medical team.

In the doorway, Rowdell and Cheeseburger watched the action.

"A year ago," Rowdell said, "I was banging nails on a roof."

"Are we gonna get in trouble for this?"

"Probably."

Dutch Carrigan appeared with a pair of plastic buckets filled with blood-soaked items. One contained her clothes and purse. The other had the torn packaging from everything they had used.

"Hey, Dutch..." Cheeseburger checked to make sure no one was listening. "Are we gonna get in trouble for this?"

"Only if she dies."

"Oh God."

"I'm kidding. Listen, if anyone other than Cap tried pulling that shit, I'd say they should be arrested for aggravated assault. Truth is, if she lives, it's for only one reason, right?"

"I guess."

"It's a game of inches, kid. Now stop obsessing and help me clean the box. It's a real mess out there."

***

On top of the usual Friday night madness, and with news that six more critical patients were inbound, the on-call surgeons activated by the Mass Casualty Protocol immediately brought extra hands into the ER Department.

One of the arriving doctors was lead trauma surgeon Dr. Aguilar Dosroyo. He was too busy triaging patients to get the full story, but he had known Capt. LeClaire for twenty years, so news of his extreme intervention was not a shock.

Even the security guards helped the half-dozen arriving rescues unload their patients. Inside, a medical maelstrom was occurring. Since human bodies were not designed to be thrown across the asphalt at 70 MPH, members of the X-ray, anesthesia, and airway teams wrestled over patients. With all of the operating rooms already occupied, orthopedic and trauma surgeons began bolting and stitching people back together. There were three Critical Care Rooms at Ocean State Hospital capable of handling six trauma patients at a time, but three beds were already filled with two shootings and a stabbing. So in order to remain within the proximity of the Trauma Department's equipment, impromptu surgeries were even occurring in the hallway. Those people with head injuries were the first ones loaded into the CT Scanner.

No catastrophe was worse than another, but the fact that it was a bridal party somehow changed the game. On the seven tables, young moms and professionals in the prime of their lives fought the odds. Two of the women and the driver were already dead but none of them knew it. That news would be held back until some other point for whoever survived the night.

Capt. McCarrick arrived with Engine 2 to pick up Dutch and Cheeseburger. They were inside Rescue 1 wiping blood off the benchseat and equipment. The Sani-Wipes, which were in a coffee-can sized drum, killed fungus, bacteria, tuberculosis, and viruses like Herpes, Hepatitis B, C, and HIV. The floor would have to wait until they could mop it with bleach back at the station.

"Cheese!" Capt. McCarrick pounded on the side of the truck. "Get out here!"

"Great." Cheeseburger still held a bloody wipe in his gloved hand as he opened the door. "Yes, Cap?"

"You..." But Capt. McCarrick could not keep a straight face. "God-damnit, I was gonna fuck with you. But you actually looked like a fireman out there."

"Whoa!" Dutch exclaimed. "An actual compliment? You stop at Connolly's on the way down here?"

"I wish." Capt. McCarrick's cigarette was half-disappeared inside his massive mustache. "If I had, I'd be licking your face right now, you sexy bitch."

"Ah-ha-ha-ha!"

Inside the ER, as Capt. LeClaire was finishing his run report, Dr. Dosroyo appeared over his shoulder and said, "Heard you were trying to steal my job?"

"I'm sorry about that, doc. Judgment calls aren't always appropriate, but she was gonna die."

"Still might, who knows, right?"

"That would be a real shame. They're too young for this."

"With that in mind, despite the fact that this is highly unethical, and could in fact jeopardize both our licenses, this impromptu laparotomy will be staying between you and I. If the Board of Health gets wind of this, despite your legendary reputation and status, there will be nowhere for either one of us to hide."

"I couldn't help myself."

"You think I've been asleep the last twenty years? We've been down this road a long way, my friend. Believe me, if it wasn't appropriate, we'd be having a very different conversation." He clapped him on the back. "Strong work though. There isn't a medical school in the whole world that teaches that kind of impromptu surgery in the back of a speeding ambulance with barely trained personnel. Incredible, really."

"Thanks, doc."

They went back to their assigned roles.

***

"Rescue 1 to Fire Alarm?"

"Go ahead, Rescue 1."

"Put us out of service for decon at Station 1."

"Roger, Rescue 1, out of service for decon at 2230."

"Hard to believe..." Rowdell pulled out the stretcher. "An hour ago we were just rolling up on the accident."

Capt. LeClaire was filling a mop bucket with water and bleach. "You'll find it'll be the same thirty years from now. Everything. I can re-play some runs like videos in my head."

Rowdell held out his wrist. "You should feel my pulse. It's banging like a crackhead." Rowdell climbed into the back and mopped out whatever blood was not already caked onto their boots. When he finished, he hopped down and tipped the bucket over the drain.

Capt. LeClaire said, "What're you staring at?"

"Nothing. Sorry. It's just weird washing someone's blood down the drain."

"You hungry? I could use a midnight snack."

"I'm so jacked up I'll never sleep anyway. Can we change our clothes first? I got blood on everything."

"Good idea."

They met back at the truck ten minutes later. Rowdell hit the door opener.

Capt. LeClaire said into the mic, "Rescue 1 to Fire Alarm. In service from decon and on the air."

"Rescue 1's back in service and on the air at 2245."

Rowdell asked, "Where to?"

"You like tacos?"

"*Sí.*"

"Taco King in C.F. has the best. It's on Dexter."

"Roger."

El Rey de los Tacos was a food truck with award-winning tacos.

Staying open late created hazards, especially in the state's most dangerous city. The owner, Fabricio Elizondo, dropped what he was doing when he saw Capt. LeClaire at the back of the line. He stepped out of the food truck and said, "*Vengo, hermano*. No lines for you."

"Fabricio, how are you?"

They hugged. Fabricio Elizondo was a balding Mexican immigrant who had worked fourteen hours a day for the last thirty years. In 1979, his father told him an honest man who worked hard could make it in America, so Elizondo jumped the border and never looked back. He was now 52-years-old, owned three food trucks, and employed nine workers. As a good Catholic and God-fearing man, he wore a gold crucifix, the same one he had on the night he met Capt. LeClaire.

"How's the family?" Capt. LeClaire asked. "Your wife feeling any better?"

"Abriala is fine, *El Capitán*, thank you for asking. She is making great progress."

Capt. LeClaire turned to Rowdell. "She had a stroke a few months back. Fabricio, this is my new partner."

"Row." Rowdell stuck out his hand. "Cap says you have the best tacos in the city."

"*Sí, el jefe conoce sus tacos*!" Farbicio laughed. "I hate to cut this short but we are very busy."

Capt. LeClaire said, "Just a six-pack then. The works. And two Cokes."

"No problem." He disappeared into the truck.

Rowdell said, "This guy loves you. You eat a lot of tacos or what?"

"They're the best. Wait 'til you taste them."

A minute later the back door swung open. Elizondo handed down six tacos and two Cokes and refused to take any money.

"Please." Rowdell held out ten dollars.

"You must be new." Insulted, Elizondo lifted his shirt. He had a hairy belly creased by a nasty six-inch scar. "*Su dinero no vale nada aquí*."

The door slammed closed.

Capt. LeClaire took the ten dollars off Rowdell and said, "That's why I don't come here more often."

"Why did that guy just show me his tits?"

"He got robbed. He was working with one of his sons. They shot the kid and killed him. But me and Capt. McCarrick, he was my private back then, which shows you how long ago we're talking. C.F. took the kid because he was already dying. We got Fabricio."

"They shot him too?"

"Yup. Stole $243, killed his kid, destroyed a nice family, which then made the father come back to this same spot every night for decades to prove them wrong. He could've made a fortune in a better, more prosperous location. But not Fabricio. He wasn't going anywhere." Capt. LeClaire snuck up to the window and jammed the ten-dollar bill into the tip jar. The dozen people on line did not appreciate the firemen jumping the line but no one said anything about it.

They got back into the truck and unwrapped their tacos.

"You weren't kidding," Rowdell said between mouthfuls.

"Fire Alarm to Rescue 1."

Capt. LeClaire answered, "Rescue 1."

"Rescue 1, start responding along with Engine 4 for a woman ill, dizzy."

"Fire Alarm, cancel the engine if she's only dizzy."

"Roger. That'll be 782 Knowlton, apartment three."

"On the way."

"Responding at 2318."

Rowdell smashed the last taco into his mouth. He lit the lights and whooped the siren to clear the curb.

The "Person Ill" on Knowlton normally would have been Rescue 2's run alone, but they were already on another call. Since it was an out of district rescue responding, Engine 4 had to as well in order to satisfy the legalese of 911 response times. "Person Ill" was the only EMS run engines did not respond on unless the district rescue was busy.

782 Knowlton was a stately old house cut into four apartments. The door to number three was ajar. Seated inside was Belleflower McIlroy,

an 83-year-old black woman. Even though it was nearing midnight, she was dressed in her Sunday finest because she knew she was going to see the doctor. She even wore a linen cloche hat with a yellow flower. She was five-foot nothing and did not weigh more than a hundred pounds.

"Good evening, gentlemen." She wore a bright smile despite the late hour. "I'm so sorry to bother you, but I just don't feel right."

"Dispatch said you were feeling dizzy?" Capt. LeClaire grabbed her wrist to take a pulse.

"Yes, I am."

"Do you have any medical conditions?"

"No. Just a little high blood pressure."

"Are you on medication for that?"

"Yes I am. Lipitor."

"Did you take it today?"

"Yes."

Rowdell wrapped the BP cuff around her other arm. He listened through the stethoscope and said, "140 over 80."

"That's not bad," Capt. LeClaire said.

"I know, but I'm just feeling so dizzy. And earlier tonight "Dateline" had a special on strokes. They called it the *silent killer*."

"It does sound scary. Strokes are dangerous but—"

"Do you think I'm having one now? My fingertips are tingling."

Capt. LeClaire smiled. "No, ma'am. But we can do a quick test. Can you smile for me?"

She did.

"Grasp my hands and squeeze as hard as you can."

She did.

"Close your eyes and hold your arms straight out."

She did.

"I'm pretty sure you're not having a stroke—"

"But you never know. You're right. Better to get checked out just in case."

"That's up to you entirely. We're not doctors..." Capt. LeClaire knew he was not about to dissuade her. Besides, if she did not go now there was a good chance she would just call back later. The elderly were very possessive of their health. "You ready to go, miss?"

"I sure am." She waddled to the door and killed the lights. Then she double-locked the door. "Kids these days have such idle habits."

He took her hand. "Watch your step, darling."

"Aren't you the perfect gentleman."

"Don't make me blush. I'm so old I might feint."

"Oh, hush up. You're a spring chicken compared to me."

Downstairs, they helped her step up into the truck.

Rowdell said, "Not as much adrenaline as the last run, right?"

"That," Capt. LeClaire said, "might be the understatement of all time. Saint E's."

"Roger that."

Rowdell jumped behind the wheel.

***

The rescue phone shattered the darkness. It was an old rotary phone with a bell so loud sleeping through it was impossible. Rowdell hated it so much he always tried to answer it on the first ring out of spite just so he would not have to hear it ring twice. Now, half-asleep, he said, "Rescue 1."

"Get up you lazy fuck."

Rowdell blinked, thinking he must still be asleep because it sounded just like Chucky. "No, it can't be."

"Oh it sure is, sweet-meat. Been a long time since the academy."

"How did you get into dispatch?"

"Pork-pie went home sick, that fat fuck. And I was the only one stupid enough to pick up the phone."

"Talk about desperation. If they're letting you out of your cage to interact with the public, we're totally screwed."

"Oh, it's way worse than that, butt-plug. I haven't dispatched in twenty years. Everyone dies tonight."

"Oh God."

Chucky emitted a horribly evil laugh. "You have no idea how happy it makes me to send you out in the middle of the frozen night for a lousy stupid earache."

"What time is it?"

"1:30."

What? He had been asleep for only fifteen minutes. "Fuck, I thought it was like five o'clock."

"Ha-ha! You wish! I am going to anally pound you all night long."

"No..."

"It's gonna be so deep and long you'll feel my tip poking into your stomach."

"Please, God..."

"Trust me, you're gonna need a fucking psychiatrist by the time this night is over."

Rowdell hung up, stunned. He felt like he had just been assaulted. He stared at the ceiling and wished he was dead. But he jumped when the phone immediately rang back. "What do you want, you evil dwarf?"

"I forgot to give you the address, fuckface. 523 Pleasant Street. Just like me. Ah-ha-ha!"

Rowdell hung up the phone and pulled his pants on in the dark. Both rescue rooms had phones, but Capt. LeClaire somehow always slept through his.

"Cap!" Rowdell pounded on the wall. "Cap! We gotta run. Pleasant Street."

"Okay. What for?"

"Earache."

Rowdell pulled on his shirt while stumbling for the stairs. Since Station 1 was a hundred-years-old, every floorboard creaked. The engine guys were asleep in their rooms so he did his best to be quiet.

Capt. LeClaire joined him in the truck and said, "I never should've gone to sleep."

"Right? That was only fifteen minutes ago."

"What's fifteen minutes compared to thirty years?"

"You're a madman."

Capt. LeClaire said into the mic, "Rescue 1 responding."

"Rescue 1's responding at 0135 for an EARACHE!"

Capt. LeClaire flinched. "Who's that?"

"Chucky." Rowdell eased the truck out with spinning lights only. He did not need the siren because the street was cold and empty. "Pork-pie went home sick."

Capt. LeClaire chuckled. "Great."

"Tell me about it. It wasn't exactly the most pleasant wake up call."

"I can only imagine."

They transported the 37-year-old white male with an earache even though he had two cars in his driveway, then they had a psych patient hearing voices, and after that a 40-year-old woman who had a panic attack at 3 A.M. because she could not sleep.

When they returned to the station at 3:40 A.M., Rowdell did not even bother getting undressed and just dove into bed. He was almost asleep when the rescue phone exploded. He said, *"What?"*

"Nothing." More evil chuckling. "Just checking to see if the phone still works."

"I hate you."

"Ah-ha-ha!"

The phone rang back twenty minutes later and Chucky only laughed and hung up. When it rang again later Rowdell was too tired to pick a fight and barely whispered, "Rescue."

"Wakey-wakey! Hand off snakey!"

"I am going to run you over with this truck, you evil fucking midget."

"GI bleed. 16 Kensington Court with Engine 5."

"Gross."

"Oh, enjoy. Sounds like granny's a real mess."

Rowdell hung up and pounded on the wall. "Cap! We gotta run!"

"Where to?"

"16 Kensington Court. GI bleed."

In the truck, Capt. LeClaire said, "Rescue 1 responding."

"Go get 'em, boys! Rescue 1 responding at 0445!"

Outside it was total winter darkness. The rescue lights spun across the buildings like an out-of-control disco ball. It was hard not to think of all the people sleeping in nice warm beds inside all the homes they passed.

Capt. LeClaire asked, "Have you had one of these yet?"

"GI bleed? Negative."

"They can occur anywhere from the mouth to the anus. Some are sudden and potentially deadly. Bright red arterial blood is the real emergency there. But the slower ones accumulate over time. The blood gets digested and turns into this coffee-ground-like substance called melena. Once enough builds up, you either vomit or shit it out. Besides decomposing bodies or gangrene, it's the worst thing you'll ever smell on this job."

"Thanks."

Sure enough, outside the front door of 16 Kensington Court, a firefighter violently vomited.

"That," Capt. LeClaire said, "is not a good sign." He said into the mic. "Rescue 1 on-scene."

"Rescue 1's on-scene at 0450."

"Engine 5 to Rescue 1. We're gonna need a stair-chair and a bunch of extra sheets up here."

"Roger."

Rowdell grabbed those items and followed his boss. They passed by Scotty Damatti, nicknamed "Stretch" because of one miraculous night on the Massasoit River. Stretch entered department lore after a woman had been washed downstream. They found her snagged on a branch as the river raged around her. From the bank, two firefighters reached out with a twelve-foot New York Hook hoping to grab her. They did, but the bank gave way. The first fireman would have been washed away as well until Stretch, spun backwards as he fell, and in an act of divine providence, somehow got his legs accidentally tangled in a tree root at the same second his arm got stuck in his partner's gear. Literally stretched as the water tried to drown them all, Stretch hung on until help arrived and all three got pulled to safety. Now, however, Damatti was dry-heaving off the stoop. Some guys had no problem with bodily secretions. Others were okay with blood and vomit but not feces, or feces and blood but not vomit. Damatti got sick from all of it. "It's bad up there," is all he said, and then he puked again.

Climbing the stairs, they heard gentle weeping. In the bathroom they found a half-naked elderly white woman standing in a pile of her own melena. It was still running down her legs as she cried. Lt. Brodie, the thrice-divorced recovering alcoholic, held her hands for comfort as he said, "Hey, Cap. This is Angela. She woke up thinking she had to have a bowel movement when this happened instead."

The stench was so bad Rowdell's eyes started watering. No one wanted to make her feel anymore uncomfortable than she already was but it was not easy.

"I'm so sorry," she said. "I'm so embarrassed."

"Angela." Capt. LeClaire gave her a warm smile. "This is nothing."

"But it smells so bad—"

"Trust me when I tell you we've smelt much worse. Now let's take care of you. We're gonna wrap you up in some sheets, put you in this chair, and carry you out."

"I'm mortified—"

"Please don't be. This is our job, darling, stop apologizing."

They mummified her inside two sheets and sat her in the chair. Her feet, covered in black tarry diarrhea, popped out of the sheets and smeared into Rowdell the whole way down the stairs.

Outside, Stretch was ash-faced. The return of the odor as she went by caused him to dry-heave again.

"That poor man," she said.

In the back of the truck, there was no escape even with the evacuation fan on high. Capt. LeClaire never blinked. He reassured her the entire time as Rowdell started a line and got the vitals. Once she was squared away, Capt. LeClaire said, "Okay, Angela, sit back and enjoy the ride."

Rowdell jumped out and gulped fresh air like a drowning victim suddenly revived.

***

At the hospital, they ran into Rescue 2. Lt. Killmoor and T-Bag had been running and gunning all night as well and looked it. Standing in the black dawn of the frozen ambulance bay, Rowdell and T-Bag had a smoke while waiting for their bosses to finish their run reports.

"How about Chucky?" T-Bag grinned. "Sick prick. I picked up the phone and he was blasting 'The Ride of the Valkyries' from Apocalypse Now."

Rowdell flinched. "Man, there ain't nothing right about that guy."

"Nothing."

"Hey, do me a favor?"

"What's up?"

"Do I have any of her bloody shit on my pants? I think I got most of it off."

"Gross."

"Dude!"

"I don't know, man, I can't see shit out here."

"Not funny."

With their paperwork finished, the officers joined them outside. Both rescues loudly idled just trying to survive the cold. At 5:34 A.M., it was 24 degrees.

"Well," Lt. Killmoor said, "this night has been one long kick in the dick."

"Whoa, the shift ain't over," Capt. LeClaire said. "Don't jinx us."

"I'm freaking starving," T-Bag said. "Anyone wanna grab breakfast? Or maybe we can just lick the bloody diarrhea off Row's pants."

Lt. Killmoor winced. "That is the most disturbing thing you've said all night. And that's saying quite a lot."

"*Fire Alarm to Rescue 2?*"

"So much for breakfast." Lt. Killmoor toggled the mic. "Go ahead, Fire Alarm."

"*Start responding to 37 Baltimore Road. Bloated male with painful gas and anal leakage.*"

"Chucky's on a roll." T-Bag headed for the truck. "He's probably begging his friends to shit themselves and call 911." "Back-to-back Code Browns," Rowdell called after him. "Hope this one doesn't geyser out on the way over."

"Say a prayer, babe."

It was 5:41 A.M. Shift change was still seventy-nine minutes away.

Anything could happen...

BOOK THREE

SEE YOU IN HELL

DECEMBER 2009 TO MAY 2010

THE VOTE

December 12, 2009

At Station 4, the voting process had been done the same way since 1927. Hours were from 2-8 P.M. so that the day and nightshifts could both attend. Injured personnel showed up on crutches or in slings to run the actual vote. This served two purposes. The first was getting them out of the house and back inside the circle, and the second was to remind those that were healthy that this could easily be them. Sadly, because of the eighty-hour weeks and accruing exhaustion, there were more than enough volunteers to choose from.

Inside the station, Danny Carillo and Ramos Gutiérrez stood guard at the dormitory door. "Stood" was a strong word since Danny Carrillo could barely stand up, but sitting was even worse. Thirteen months ago he herniated four discs stair-chairing a 371-pound woman down from a third-floor apartment. After she panicked and lunged, they fell, and both she and his partner rode Danny like a surfboard down into the second-floor wall. The dislocated shoulder and broken leg turned out to be the least of his problems and quickly healed. His back, however, remained a disaster. He had four fully herniated discs and severe nerve damage. The doctors wanted to fuse him but that would mean the end of his career, so he now existed in a pain-filled universe that, according to rumor, was about to cost him his marriage.

Ramos Gutiérrez was a lieutenant on Ladder 2. He tore a rotator cuff swinging an axe on a Diebold Street roof and was six months in on a nine-month recovery. He checked off the names of anyone entering to vote.

Inside the dormitory, Kenny Voitcheski handed out the ballots and pens. Budget cuts and decades of slack maintenance had caught up with Kenny by surprise. NFPA standards recommended replacing frontline pieces every seven years. Sachem City's trucks were anywhere from five to 30-years-old. After Kenny Voitcheski went flying out the door of Engine 6, a beloved but now dangerous 27-year-old Maxim, the doctors bolted his right leg back together and told him he would be out of work for six months. Since he was used to working two jobs and never being home, at first, he thought he would go crazy. That all changed when he found out how interesting his kids' lives really were. He was not allowed off the couch for five weeks, and when those five weeks came and went, he wished he could have stayed there even longer. He played video games with his 10-year-old son and read stories to his little girl. He put together puzzles with his 12-year-old daughter and helped them all with their homework.

He had a reputation as a hard worker, which was more than could be said of his fellow vote-minder. Les Green was a politically connected slacker who went out injured for one reason or another every year. His family had deep ties to City Hall and was even rumored to be distant relations with Receiver Tillinghast. Currently he was out of work for generalized body pain from fibromyalgia and high blood pressure.

When union president Lt. Ahearn arrived to check on the vote, he saw thirty off-duty guys waiting around to hear the results. Because it was snowing, everyone was inside the apparatus bay. He parked his car and immediately ran into Psycho Sal and Berserker. Sal was halfway through a hangover and a cigarette as he said, "No offense, Mr. President, but can you tell us why the fuck Lester the Molester is in there with the ballots?"

"Relax, Sal, they're in a locked box sitting right next to Kenny. I don't want that creepy fuck in there anymore than you, but I need him to scurry next door afterwards and let them know this vote was totally legit. Otherwise, we're just handing them more ammunition to use against us."

"That," Berserker said, "is some evil genius type shit right there."

"That's why you're paying me the big bucks, right?" Everyone knew the extra $350 a month was in no way commensurate to the daily grief dealing with a diverse union body at times entailed. "Besides, who better than Kenny to keep an eye on things?"

"Lieutenant!" someone yelled.

"Excuse me."

After voting, some people went to Connolly's for cocktails. Others shot baskets at the hoop inside the garage. Either way, by 8:09 P.M., the ballots had been counted. Lt. Ahearn called whoever was around to order and said, "After Two-Face brought up 1930, I did a little research. Back then, the government didn't know any better and did nothing when everything crashed. It wasn't like last year where all the car companies and banks and Wall Street pigs ran to the federal government for help and got it. As bad as the last two years have been, 1929 and 1930 were a fucking disaster. They couldn't pay anybody. People were starving and no one had a job. I guess the bright side would be we haven't sunk that far yet. Anyway, five guys were killed and eight seriously injured at three different fires between 1930-1932. Equipment failure. Lack of maintenance. The same shit we're dealing with right now is why they voted no confidence. It hadn't been done before and never since. We got more pride than that. No one around here throws anyone under the bus until the lives of others come into play. Terrace Street, Causewell Street, Addison Street... how many more close calls have we got left before someone dies? The vote tonight was eighty-seven to three no confidence in Chief Fishbakke."

The place erupted in cheers. Guys high-fived one another while already trying to figure out who the three dissenters were. Either way, the administration was about to be put on notice. Chief Fishbakke served with the support of only three other firefighters, Receiver Tillinghast, and no one else.

CHESS MOVES
December 13, 2009

Chief Fishbakke's informants notified him of the results minutes after the vote was announced. He was not shocked or hurt but, as always, considered self-preservation his only goal at any cost.

The next morning, he made sure his Class A uniform was neatly pressed. Upstairs in his office, he asked Ma Dukes to request a meeting with the Receiver.

An hour later he walked next door to City Hall. After he was left waiting for thirty minutes, his annoyance turned to concern once he realized what this might also mean.

The secretary hung up the phone. "The Receiver will see you now."

Receiver Tillinghast was seated behind the former mayor's desk. As usual, his suit was immaculate, and every grey hair was combed perfectly into place.

"Chief Fishbakke," he said, peering at him over the top of his bifocals. "It's great to see you. Can I interest you in a refreshment?"

"Okay." Chief Fishbakke suddenly started sweating.

"Well...?"

"Oh, water's fine."

"Helen, two waters please." Receiver Tillinghast was still taking notes when he said, "So to what do I owe the pleasure of this visit?"

"I just wanted to touch base with you, sir. Make sure there haven't been any new developments after last night's vote."

"Ah, yes, our pesky little firemen are at it again. They seem to be very good at two things—drinking and making my life exceedingly difficult. They send retired grandfathers up the steps of police headquarters to get their heads bashed in and then blame me."

The secretary dropped off the waters and left.

Chief Fishbakke said, "The vote was eighty-seven to three, sir."

"I know. At least you have three friends, right?" Receiver Tillinghast yanked off his glasses and leaned back. "Honestly, let them have their vote. Running a municipal fire department is not a popularity contest."

"I completely agree." Chief Fishbakke reacted on the fly. "I was about to say it's a badge of honor."

"Whatever you're doing has crawled right inside their heads."

"Reforms are never popular. It's a new day. A new way of doing business."

"And with change comes turmoil."

"You know, I will have to say something about all of this to the press..."

"Indeed." Receiver Tillinghast now followed his lead. "If it was me, I'd repeat what we just said. But really hammer the union. Get ahead of them, call them disloyal. To the city, the department, and its traditions. People are starving and losing their homes and these civil servants are just worried about their pensions? Blah, blah, you know the rest."

"I like that. Do you have a pen?"

"Yes." He slid one across the desk. "What're you writing on?"

"A receipt."

"Would you like a piece of paper, Chief?"

"Naw, I'm good. Just jotting down some highlights."

"Stress the fact that it smacks of cowardice, inciting a rebellion during a time of crisis."

"Maybe I will take that piece of paper."

"Of course. Here. And stress the word union with real disdain."

"Okay. How do you spell 'rebellion?'"

"Chief..." Tillinghast just gave up and spelled it. Then he said, "There is something else you should know. When I got word of this impending vote, I decided on a counter plan of action. It seems we might need a trusted outside voice to refute union claims of inadequate staffing, dangerous conditions, and the such. Someone to observe day-to-day operations, someone people will believe when the manpower issue gets examined closer."

"But couldn't that backfire?"

"Trust me, Chief, I've done my homework as to who may or may not be more malleable to the city's, and thereby the taxpayer's, point of view."

"Okay."

"The firm we've decided to employ—"

"We, sir?"

"Correction. The firm *I've* chosen is sending Clarence Fastow. He's a retired Battalion Chief who served thirty-one years in Baltimore. After that, he worked in the NFPA Compliance Division and has all the certificates. He is considered one of the pre-imminent experts in these matters."

"Okay."

"I want you to open the books for him, Chief. Let him see whatever he wants."

"Sure. Just let me know when—"

"Today."

"Excuse me?"

"He's here. Got here last night. He'll actually be in your office in an hour. We wanted to keep this under wraps. That picket line out front does not need any extra motivation."

"An hour..."

"It's no big deal, Chief. Besides," Receiver Tillinghast shared a knowing wink. "We already know what he's gonna say."

"Okay."

"Just give him a quick tour and call me this afternoon to let me know how it went."

"Yes, sir." Chief Fishbakke took the hint and stood up. He donned his gold leaf Chief's white dress hat. "Anything else?"

"No, that'll be all." Receiver Tillinghast put on his bifocals and went back to work.

***

Bullet Head Romine was seething. After he received a frantic text from one of the fire marshals who worked upstairs in the office, he learned about the arrival of ex-Baltimore Battalion Chief Fastow. Playing a hunch, Bullet Head parked his Jeep Wrangler across the street from fire headquarters and waited.

At 11:20 A.M., Fire Chief Fishbakke, B.C. McLoud, and ex-Baltimore B.C. and now consultant Clarence Fastow emerged from headquarters. Fastow was a large black man with a shaved block for a head. He was built like a linebacker but, now 58-years-old, moved a little stiffly. They got into the Chief's blacked-out department SUV and headed immediately for District 6. They went by nice homes in this, the only middle-class neighborhood left in the city. The golf course and zoo were also on the tour.

Capt. Romine stayed a few cars back and tried to maintain a low profile. He followed them through halfway decent parts of Districts 3 and 4 before they returned to headquarters downtown.

"Incredible." Capt. Romine parked across the street and was so mad he was twitching. An hour later, he saw Fastow leave City Hall.

Capt. Romine swung a U-turn and startled Fastow by stopping short. "Hey, Chief. Gary Romine. I'm captain of Engine 5. These jokers are playing you hard..."

Fastow was hesitant. He examined the union and department fire stickers on Capt. Romine's jeep. "What's your name again?"

"Gary Romine."

"And you're a captain?"

"Yes. And not in District 6, either. If you want a real tour of the city, hop in. Believe me, we won't be going by the fucking country club again."

"Jeeps and bad hips don't mix too good." Fastow carefully climbed in. He pointed at his suit. "Not exactly jeep-wear."

"We ain't going mudding, Chief." Capt. Romine shook his hand. "Sorry to meet you under these conditions. Heard you were a legend on Ladder 18 down there."

"Truck 1-8, baby, best years of my life. Hey, wait a second. How do you know—"

"One of our guys followed his wife's job to Maryland. He's on Baltimore now. So from one ghetto to another we go. This tour starts in The Kitchen." Bullet Head swung another U-turn and peeled down Blackstone Avenue. He honked his horn as they went by the picket line.

Fastow said, "I heard these are the retirees."

"Yup. Some of them lost half of their pensions."

"That is just incredible."

"Rumor has it that Central Falls is going to file Chapter 9 next. You know about that place? They got nine guys watching over 20,000 people squeezed into one square mile of triple and quadruple-decker houses. They call it the Wild Mile. God knows what'll happen to them in bankruptcy." He swung them onto the highway. "The S-curves are behind us, but they probably already told you—"

"What're the S-curves?"

"Seriously?"

They exited the highway and descended into District 1. Their surroundings deteriorated rapidly. Capt. Romine swung a left onto Claiborne Avenue and parked next to a burnt-out building. Ahead, junkies, dealers, and gang members watched the Jeep as if unsure of its contents or intentions.

"Look at them scuttling around," Fastow said. "For real? Do I see two different colors right across the street from each other?"

"Yup. They call this place 'The Kitchen' because something bad is always cooking. Claiborne Avenue is the DMZ between the Knock Out Kings"—Capt. Romine pointed to the left side of the block—"and the Fifth Street Vatos"—he nodded to the right. "This is strictly black versus brown down here, so the hate runs deep."

"The ghetto is the ghetto, right?"

"Never changes. It started with the Italians in the 1850's, then the Irish, then the Polish. Now it's the blacks and Hispanics. These guys aren't afraid to drop bodies in broad daylight either. They had a truce for years. The Knock Out Kings handled coke and crack, the Vatos moved the H. Everything was fine until the Kings saw the heroin market exploding and broke the deal. Now we got everything over here. Kidnappings, drive-bys, assassinations, take your pick."

"Somehow this got left off the itinerary."

"We're out of here. I got creepers coming up on the left." Capt. Romine shot from the curb and wheeled them through the wasteland. "This was a mill city for a hundred-fifty-years. Then the good times ended."

Fastow was peering around. "This is the home of the triple-decker, all right."

"Yup. Worcester, Sachem City, Fall River, Providence... they invented these humongous tenement houses. You guys got balloon-frame construction?"

"Some."

"Well, take a look around. Unless it was built after 1940, which ain't much because this place is so old, everything is balloon-frame. This right here, District 1, is the number one fire district in the city. It's also sandwiched between Districts 2 and 5, so it's the one most likely closed on this side of the river. Sound like a good place for rolling blackouts?"

The jeep headed across the highway.

Fastow said, "So what do they call you?"

"Bullet Head, but not to my face."

"Excuse me?"

"Some joker once said he'd rather take a round to the head instead of working with me. What about you?"

"Cuddles."

"What? Jesus Christ, that's horrible."

"I know."

"Wow. B.C. *Cuddles?*"

"Man, I caught overtime between my nightshifts. I was in the dorm on the phone with the wife and she was missing on me. So, I told her we would cuddle in the morning and someone immediately dimed me out."

"Oh, man."

"Yeah. That two-minute phone call brought me thirty years of pain. Wow. Look at the size of this place."

"This is MacCallum Manufacturing. This used to be the crown jewel. 10,000 people a day used to work in these mills. There are six of them jammed in here. 1.6 million square-feet of wood and toxins left abandoned. We had a machine fire here last month. Came within five minutes of losing the whole joint. This complex straddles Central Falls and Sachem City. We used to joke with the C.F. guys that if this place ever caught fire, whichever way the wind was blowing would determine which city got burnt to the ground."

"That's a lot of fire right there."

"Right? Sound like something twenty-three guys can handle on their own?"

"Twenty-three?"

"That's our new minimum-manning. Thirty-one guys on shift, with two guys in dispatch. That leaves twenty-nine for the trucks. But they don't fill six spots, which means they'll close two trucks before they call overtime."

"For 80,000 people?"

"I wish I was making this up. We had a mill that was a fifth of this size on the other side of the city. It caught fire in 2004. We ended up with something like fifty out-of-town companies helping us keep the whole east side from burning down."

Fastow stared at the massive complex. "This place in its hey-day must've been something to see."

"The whole city was like this. Industry everywhere, and everyone was making money. The owners, manufacturers, designers, engineers, workers, truckers, builders, suppliers... the table was set for generations."

"And then they hit the brakes."

"Everything went south. First it was to South Carolina, Georgia, and then Mexico became even cheaper. Bye-bye jobs. The end."

"Sounds familiar. Baltimore's lost a third of its population since World War II. We got 640,000 people and 1,700 firefighters. You got 80,000 people and what—they said ninety-nine left on duty?"

"Negative. We have ninety remaining."

"So if it was a role reversal..." Fastow worked the calculator on his phone. "I'd be protecting 640,000 with 680 firefighters."

"And you have four guys on a truck."

"True."

"If your family lived here, would you want to hear that some of the people charged with protecting them had been at work for the last seventy-two hours?"

"Zombie squad."

"You Baltimore born and raised?"

"Yup. I'm a legacy."

"Me too. My dad used to be chief here. Wish we'd stayed in Philadelphia though. He left there a B.C. like you. He was the only outsider ever hired as chief here. So your dad was on the job?"

"Yup. Engine 15 for most of his career. But he was from the trades. Left school early, so he could never pass the officer's exam. Said the same thing wouldn't be happening to me. Told me I was gonna go to college and that was it. Played defensive end for the Terps through college, took the fire test, and then waited for the phone call like everyone else."

"Greatest job ever, right?"

"Never hated a single day of it."

Capt. Romine backed them out of MacCallum Mills.

Fastow asked, "Where to now?"

"I'll save you the trip to the Amtrak and Providence/Worcester rail lines. The whole northeast corridor runs through here. We have Acela trains blowing by on their way to Boston at 120 miles an hour."

"That was left off the list."

"What about the electrical substation? One time, the electric company told us they had steam lines in there under so much pressure, a hole the size of a pin could cut someone in half."

"Like a laser?"

"Yeah."

"I gotta say, that would be kind of cool to see."

Capt. Romine swung them back onto the highway. "We're responsible for 6.1 miles of I-95. Hang on. These are the S-curves."

Fastow grabbed the roll bar as they swung one way, swung back, straightened out, and then switch-backed again. "That," he said, "was not very relaxing."

"Sometimes, if it's raining or snowing, we'll be out here all day. The southbound side is even worse because it has an incline, so all the water sits in the first curve. They hydroplane, hit the wall, and wake up in the back of the rescue having no idea what happened."

"You all must be awful good at cutting people from their cars."

"I'm just dreading the next disaster when, because of these ridiculous rolling blackouts, we don't get the right people out here in time. There are only two trucks that have the JAWS on them. If Engine 5's out of service for the blackout and Engine 2's tied up on a different run, what good is anyone else if they don't have the right equipment? You got kids?"

"Two. Boy and girl."

"I got two sons. God forbid I roll my car out here and watch my kids die because these stupid fucks are more concerned with saving money than people's lives. How old are your kids?"

"My boy, James, is thirteen. Keisha's ten."

"Mine are ten and eight and I'm already scared to death."

"I hear you. This job will do that to you, right? You just see too many bad ideas played out in real time."

Capt. Romine swung them back downtown and got off at Main Street. He said, "Fifty years ago all these buildings were full of businesses supporting the mills. Now, look at what's left behind. Homeless people and ghosts."

"Oh man, look at that." Fastow ran his eyes across the destroyed remains of 216 Causewell Street. "Talk about big fire."

"It's been two months since this place went up, but the city is now so dysfunctional, they're arguing in court over who the legal owners really are. No one wants to pay for the demolition and removal, much less millions more from the death and injury lawsuits. This used to be a supply house for machine parts back in the day, but twenty years ago a slumlord converted it into a giant rooming house with all kinds of illegal cut-ins. Last October, some piece of shit beat a hooker half to death, covered the entrances and stairways in gasoline, and struck a match. Remember, this is broad daylight. And because no one has jobs anymore, twenty-four of the thirty-two people living here were home. Before it was over we had one civilian fatality, thirteen grabs, ten people injured jumping from windows, and three badly burned."

"Talk about lucky. Look at this place."

"Total death-trap."

"Twenty-three guys..."

"The other rescue was at the hospital, so it was actually twenty-one."

"Incredible."

"Kind of important to see though, right?"

"I'm beginning to think the Chief and B.C.... I forgot his name."

"Who? Donut? He's another disgrace. Book smart, job stupid."

"Every department has them, right?"

"Same circus, different monkeys. Donut's only incompetent, but Chief Fishfuck is way worse. We just voted no-confidence on his ass eighty-seven to three."

"I saw that in the paper. He didn't even bring it up this morning, so

I had to. I asked him what the ramifications could be and he literally just shrugged. Didn't say a word. Damn shame, too. Anywhere else, that kind of vote could cost someone their job."

"Well, not here. These morons will probably elect him mayor."

Fastow chuckled until Capt. Romine said, "My spy might have told me who you were, but no offense, the city *is* writing your check."

"My check comes from Vulcan Corporation, Captain, and my report and evaluation will reflect that. To suggest otherwise is borderline offensive."

"That's why I kidnapped you. Your reputation down there was solid. I just wanted to know who you might've turned into wearing that suit."

"You really are a bullet to the head."

"Look, the Receiver's an attorney. Attorneys never ask questions they don't already know the answers to. And while I hate a lot of the guys I work with, I don't necessarily want to see them die. And your report could bury us for good. There's nothing safe about this place. I've been saying it for months—the whole job's out of position. We got privates as acting lieutenants, lieutenants as acting captains, and captains as acting Battalion Chiefs. These ridiculous blackouts put different trucks out of service every day. You know better than anyone else what happens when this kind of fuckery goes unchecked."

"It's not if..."

"Exactly. Receiver Fuckface doesn't get that. He's a glorified accountant handed the power of God, accountable to no one except the governor, and she couldn't give two fucks neither."

"It's because all of our friends are gone. That's what this destroyed economy has done. There's no money left for anything other than survival."

"This is the last place I'm gonna show you. 1520 Shore Road. See the river down there? This douchebag company was dumping its waste into it for a hundred years. We did a walk through here last year and determined conditions inside were so dangerous, we put out a standing S.O.P. stating that, when this place lights up, no one is allowed entry for any reason. Instead, we made evacuation plans for everyone downwind. We found dozens of thousand-gallon vats containing God knows what. It was never cleared out, so whatever was in this place the day they locked the doors in 1973 is still in there. It was an old metalizing mill, so we're talking about palladium chloride, tin chloride, chromic acid, sulfuric acid, aluminum oxide, and a dozen other toxic powders used in various processes. If that wasn't bad enough, the roof is falling in and the support beams for the fifth-floor are now corroding from this added weather exposure. We told the mayor that if big fire ever got a hold of those chemicals, we could be talking about the downwind evacuation of 70,000 people."

"That's all bad news."

"This isn't anything new, either. The entire fire-insurance industry began right here. When these mills caught fire back in the day the owners lost everything. So they started insuring each other. Here in Sachem City, there were fires in 1826 and 1837 that burned down dozens of homes and businesses. The Great Fire of 1846 nearly took out half the city, so the neighborhood fire brigades were no longer enough. Before 1874, Sachem City was on the left bank of the Massasoit River only. The right bank was part of Rehoboth before it got annexed. 1874 is when the fire department was brought in under a central command for the united city. Basically, since then we've averaged one mill fire every five years. And when these things go off, as you can imagine, we're on-scene for days. At one point there were seventy abandoned mills. Sound like good odds for twenty-three guys?"

"No."

"Chief Fishfuck has some nerve. He was gonna pull a total snow-job on you, jeopardizing the safety of his own men and everyone living in this city because his master told him to."

"Weren't we just talking about survival?"

"It's all he cares about."

They drove back downtown. Capt. Romine parked behind ex-B.C. Fastow's rental car and said, "I'm glad we talked. I won't lie, because it is, it's hard for me to believe he would hire any firm that might jeopardize his agenda. But then again, anyone nicknamed Cuddles can't be that bad a guy, right?"

"For the record, the Bullet Head tour was much more colorful."

"Go figure. How long you in town for?"

"I leave the day after tomorrow. I told the Chief I'd have a preliminary opinion completed by then."

"Roger that."

They shook hands.

"Good luck, Captain." Fastow exited the jeep.

Upstairs, in both fire headquarters and City Hall, curious eyes were always watching.

DAMAGE CONTROL
December 15, 2009

Two days later, Receiver Tillinghast read Clarence Fastow's preliminary findings. These were not the results the Receiver had been hoping for and, even worse, essentially promised. He had no idea who Bullet Head was, but one of Tillinghast's aides had sources inside the fire department who had seen something. She obtained video from City Hall cameras showing Fastow climbing into Capt. Romine's jeep the day before.

Clarence Fastow arrived at City Hall at two o'clock. Upstairs, he was shown into a conference room that had spectacular views of the Massasoit River. He made himself a cup of coffee right before the door swung open.

"Retired Battalion Chief Fastow." Receiver Tillinghast swept in and firmly shook his hand. "It's an honor and a pleasure to finally meet you. First of all, let me thank you for your service. I'm sure the people of Baltimore were far better off because of it."

"Thank you. I hear you wear many hats. Receiver, attorney, judge..."

"My friends call me Arthur and you should do the same." He fixed himself a coffee and then joined Fastow at the table. "Quite a view, isn't it?"

"They tell me this is the river that founded the Industrial Revolution."

"It is. The history of this place is quite amazing. A village of black-smiths, craftsmen, and artisans created the American dream. Blackstone Mill, one of the first ever built, was declared a national historic site in 1983. It's right next door and has an accompanying museum with original pieces of equipment."

"I'll have to check it out."

Receiver Tillinghast pulled a handful of papers from a folder and said, "I want to thank you for all your hard work and prompt turn-around. This preliminary information will help us when we decide to make these much-needed reforms."

"You have a great city here and a proud fire department. Professional-ism, despite the decimation to its ranks, is not a catch word around here."

"I'll have to pass that along to the Chief. I'm sure he'll be tickled to hear how his strong leadership has paid off."

"Of course."

"It was a thorough report." Receiver Tillinghast thumbed through it. "But I had some questions about a few of its summations."

"Okay."

"For instance, here on page seven, you write, 'these reductions in overall manpower have not been addressed, but long-term the combina-tion of exhaustion and injury will be precursors to a loss of preparedness and ultimately impinge upon morale.'" Receiver Tillinghast looked at him over his bifocals. "That seems to be rather subjective. As if you can foretell the future?"

"I guess my language wasn't strong enough. Your attrition rate, quite simply, will out-strip your current resources within a couple of months. Yes, you've recently gotten younger on the job, but there are still plenty of personnel with more than twenty years who can walk out the door at any second. If all they're being shown is a future filled with seventy-hour work weeks, the decision to walk becomes significantly easier."

"I have to say, I disagree. You just said it yourself—this department has a lot of pride. No matter what they have so far faced, they've con-sistently answered the bell."

"But that's not because of the city, it's in spite of it. Either way it's not sustainable."

"Agree to disagree. Another question I have is with this statement. 'The lowering of the minimum-manning number to twenty-three removes all margins for error. If even one engine company is on a run when a structure fire occurs, that now leaves only three engines and two ladders capable of responding.' I mean really, what're the chances of these events occurring simultaneously?"

"No offense, but is that a serious question? In a 200-year-old city, with 80,000 people, and a department that averages 15,000 runs a year?" Fastow frowned. "I should tell you, I was told one story before I arrived, but facts on the ground have made that previous calculus obsolete."

"I'd say."

"I hope you don't think I was being contracted to present only the best-case scenario. This is not a best-case scenario kind of business."

"I never said that. But I was under the impression that you'd at least be impartial. I have to be honest. When I read this, the first thing I thought was that it was written by the union president."

"The problem is in the approach. Political people love to play games with numbers. They think they can bend them and misuse them, but in the end a number is a fact. Even you must read these numbers and realize none of this is sustainable. Is it a good way to purge the old-timers and deadbeats out the door? Sure. But forcing ninety people to work the spots of 136 positions might exist only as a short-term solution. Look, let's be real. Nationally, municipal fire departments in the northeast average two firefighters per 1,000 people. If we use your full staff number of 136 before the attrition, that's already two firemen per 1200 people. And the ninety that now remain makes it a ridiculous two firemen per 2,000 people. Traditionally, we don't see high rates of success when numbers reach those heights."

"Again, that's totally subjective. Is it better to be full staff? Of course. But can the personnel who remain get the job done? I think that's already been proven true."

"What happens if five guys get hurt at the next fire? Now you're at eighty-five men. At some point this wagon's going to crash, and when it does there might not be enough people left to pick up the pieces. You don't even have finished recruits waiting to be hired, which means even if the academy started tomorrow, they'd still be nine months out."

"Again with the doom and gloom. Still, the most egregious statement to me is this one on page sixteen. Quote, 'In my five years employed by Vulcan Corporation, this might be the single most dangerous situation, for both first-responders and citizens alike, that I've yet to encounter.'"

"Doom and gloom would be the truth. I can't save you from that." Fastow shrugged. "And I'm sorry you feel that way."

"I just think we have a fundamental difference in opinion."

"Granted."

"But again, I want to thank you for visiting our humble city. Outside eyes and different points of view bring fresh ideas to the table and creates a new discussion." Receiver Tillinghast stood and shook his hand. "May I ask how many copies of this preliminary report exist?"

"My own and the attachments in the email I sent to you and Chief Fishbakke."

"Excellent. Please do not distribute it to anyone else."

"I'll show myself out." Fastow paused at the door. "I take it you're not going to release it."

"Not before I have time to decide what's in the best interest of our citizens. I would of course expect you to respect whatever decision occurs."

"It's your report." Fastow opened the door. "But I would strongly ask you to reconsider. Second chances when decisions like these get made rarely happen."

"Thank you again, B.C. Fastow. Enjoy the sites in our fair city."

***

Ten minutes later, Receiver Tillinghast was back in his office. He called out, "Karen, can you please connect me with Chief Fishbakke?"

She appeared in the door a moment later. "His secretary says he's gone for the day."

"The *day*? Good Lord, it's only two-thirty." Receiver Tillinghast squinted at her over his bifocals. "Two things. First, please get me his cell number. And secondly, I am going to need the current salaries of all the department heads."

"Yes, sir."

She got him the cell number.

"Chief Fishbakke," he soon said. "Arthur Tillinghast. How are you?"

"Fine, sir."

"I was planning on reviewing B.C. Fastow's findings with you, but I understand that you are gone for the day?"

"Uh, yes. I had a previous appointment."

"Of course you did. You know, after ascertaining the facts and weighing the relevant findings, I've concluded that releasing this report at this date and time might not be in the best interests of the citizens that we both serve. Have you had a chance to read it?"

"You know, it was on my list, but the day kind of got away from me."

"Of course it did. Any-who, B.C. Fastow said you and I were the only ones who received copies of his report. Until such a time arrives where these findings shall be released, I think it best if we—I—maintain a strict chain of custody. After all, if I have the only copy, there's no worry about unforeseen events or leaks tripping us up, correct?"

"Okay... so I guess you're asking me to delete my copy?"

"That's exactly right, Chief. In fact, you don't even have to read it. This way, I also won't have to question anyone's allegiance if any word of it appears outside the framework of our agreed upon arrangement."

"I can do that. I'm driving right now, so I'll have to make a note—"

"The sooner the better, Chief."

"Of course. I just don't want to forget. That's responsible leadership, right?"

"It sure is, Chief, we're lucky to have you. Listen, the fewer people that know about this report the better. Call me in the morning. We have other matters to discuss."

"Yes, sir."

"Good-bye for now." Receiver Tillinghast hung up and stared at the phone far longer than he should have.

THE MEAN SEASON

December 18, 2009

For most people, the period between Thanksgiving and Christmas was filled with excitement and expectation. For others beset by poverty, dysfunctional families, mental illness, or any combination of all three, there was no safe haven. Families that hated each other got together and poured too much alcohol across simmering grievances. People got assaulted in front of loved ones by their loved ones, further traumatizing everyone. For this reason, the guys on the rescue called this four-week period the Mean Season.

"Look at this mess." Psycho Sal grabbed the mic and said, "Rescue 1 to Fire Alarm. Where are the police?"

"Rescue 1, police are en route."

"Tell them to expedite. We've got a riot in the middle of Eddings street."

"Roger."

But when those fighting realized the flashing lights were not the police, they immediately re-engaged.

Yoda asked, "What're we gonna do?"

"Us?" Psycho Sal lit a cigarette. "You're looking at it. You got a gun, handcuffs, or pepper spray?"

"No."

"Me neither."

Yoda watched the shifting brawl. Men of various ages assaulted one another in the night. Even the women traded fists until there seemed to be ten different fights occurring simultaneously. Only playing the witness made Yoda uncomfortable, but not enough to challenge Sal's authority.

Someone pounded on Sal's window. He took a drag and tried to ignore whoever it was until they knocked again. He cracked the window. "Yeah?"

A Hispanic man's eyeballs were bulging. "Ain't you gonna do nothing?"

"What's the side of this truck say?"

"*Qué?*"

"Sachem City *Fire* Department, right? No *policia*."

"*Follate a tu madre!*"

"That's not very nice."

Yoda asked, "What'd he say?"

"Fuck my mother."

"Great." Yoda turned back in time to see a man punch out a woman before taking her to the ground. "That's it."

"Wait!" Sal yelled.

But Yoda was gone. He jumped out, grabbed the guy, and they both fell. The other man was faster and scrambled on top. Yoda could not buck him off, so Psycho Sal throttled the guy from behind.

More sirens screamed toward them. When the combatants saw that it was just another rescue, their fists did not even pause.

Lt. Doom and Super-Wop jumped out of Rescue 2. Doom shrieked in his high-pitched voice, "We just cleared Galilee! You guys okay?"

"Yeah." Psycho Sal was slowly choking his man out. "He's almost asleep."

"Piece of shit." Yoda bitch-slapped the guy before he passed out. "You like beating on women?"

Super-Wop and Doom wasted no time yanking people apart. After someone took an ill-advised swing at Doom, they became the latest victim of his infamous arm-bar/shoulder-toss. Doom then pounced, close-fisting the guy's head back and forth as he yelled, "Stop resisting! Stop resisting!"

Yoda yelled into his radio, "Rescue 1 to Fire Alarm! Where are the police! We're being assaulted!"

"Standby, Rescue 1—"

"Engine 1 to Fire Alarm. We are responding to Eddings Street to assist Rescue 1."

"Engine 1, standby—"

"Negative, Fire Alarm."

"Rescue 2 to Fire Alarm! On-scene with Rescue 1. Where are the cops?"

"Engine 2 to Fire Alarm. Responding to Eddings Street."

"Engine 2. Per order of the Battalion Chief—"

"Ladder 1 to Fire Alarm. Responding to Eddings Street."

Fire Alarm hit the Alert Tone and said, *"Attention all companies self-dispatching to Eddings Street. Per order of Battalion 2, you are to clear and remain in service."*

"Engine 2 to Fire Alarm. You're all broken up. Repeat?"

"All companies self-dispatching to Eddings Street—"

"Engine 3 to Fire Alarm. Responding to Eddings Street."

With no one listening, Fire Alarm just gave up.

"Battalion 2 to Fire Alarm. Responding to Eddings Street."

"Roger, Chief. Just got off the phone with P.D. They have an active shooter on Oak Street. There's no one left to send, so State Police and Providence P.D. are en route instead."

"Roger. Guess the Receiver was wrong about cutting manning."

"Engine 1's on-scene." Lt. Robby Fogle was a Vietnam combat veteran one year away from the mandatory age sixty-five retirement. Growing up in "The Kitchen," he became familiar with the worst parts of life at an early age. In 1963, to escape the wrath of an alcoholic father and endemic poverty, he enlisted in the army and served four tours with Kilo Company, 1st Brigade Combat Team, 82nd Airborne. Two Bronze Stars and three Purple Hearts later, a grenade killed his two friends and shattered his leg. He spent a year at Walter Reed Military Medical Center re-learning how to walk and then disobeyed his doctors by applying to the fire department. No one thought he should be there until he somehow passed all the physical tests and only got stronger.

"Stop the truck!" Lt. Fogle jumped out.

The crowd was still fighting itself as well as the four rescue guys. Lt. Fogle grabbed the first person he could and punched him directly in the face. "Enough! Break it up!" When Engine 2 and Ladder 1 arrived, the firefighters tried restoring order. Witnesses started piecing the story together as the first Providence Police cars pulled on-scene.

Lt. Fogle was speaking with an elderly Hispanic woman. He waved over one of the Providence policemen and said, "Okay. That guy"—he pointed at a bleeding man sitting on the curb—"apparently, he's an addict. His family banned him from coming around because he keeps stealing everything. They were having a family party when they caught him out here breaking into everyone's cars."

The cop was a light-skinned black man whose nametag read Gooding. "So why the riot?"

"Who knows. A few of his friends are with him, all gangbangers. Also, there's a separate family beef about the care their grandfather is apparently not receiving."

"What a fucking mess," the cop said. "As if we don't have enough shitballs in our own city?"

"Variety's the spice of life, sergeant."

The cop snorted and left to get the drug addict's side of the story.

More shoving erupted.

"Whoa! Easy!" a state cop yelled at Doom after he landed a devastating liver punch that instantly folded a guy in half, and left him motionless on the ground.

The State Police and Providence Police began handcuffing whoever else was getting arrested. This allowed the firefighters to switch hats and administer aid.

"Fire Alarm to Battalion 2."

B.C. Riggs answered, "Battalion 2."

"Chief, be advised, police are reporting at least one gunshot victim so far on Oak Street."

"I'm freeing up companies right now."

"And the rescues?"

"Standby." B.C. Riggs stuck two fingers in his mouth and whistled. "Sal! You taking anybody?"

"Yeah, the lady that got punched in the face."

"Doom! You tied up?"

"Yeah, Chief, we might even need another rescue. I got one guy with a possible broken wrist and another with a bum ankle."

"Sal! Dump the broken nose over here with Doom. We'll get more rescues. I ain't letting somebody die over a sprained ankle. Battalion 2 to Fire Alarm."

"Go ahead, Chief."

"Rescue 1 is clearing Eddings, heading to Oak Street. Have police secured the scene?"

"Not at this time."

"Hey, Chief!" Lt. Fogle called out. "That's our run. We're gonna head over there with Rescue 1 unless you need us."

"Listen to me, Robby. Do not cowboy this thing. Make sure no one goes in until the police secure everything. You got that? I'll be there in a minute."

"Roger."

Psycho Sal escorted the woman with the broken nose over to Doom. He yelled out to B.C. Riggs, "A riot and a shooting. The Mean Season rolls on."

"Yeah, Merry fucking Christmas." But B.C. Riggs, after twenty-seven years on the job, wondered how much more of this merriment he could take.

MOUNTING PRESSURE
December 21, 2009

Days later, the Sachem City Gazette got the story before anyone else. The banner read, "DATE SET FOR EMS PRIVATIZATION." LifeMed was the ambulance company awarded the contract. Boston-based LifeMed had been founded by two men—a former medical industry lobbyist, and a Wall Street venture capitalist. Starting off with transports to and from doctor appointments, nursing homes, and dialysis centers, they soon turned the company into a Fortune 500 behemoth. When Massachusetts allowed cities to privatize EMS services, LifeMed won the bids for Fall River and New Bedford, a pair of cities founded on whaling and, like Sachem City, filled with mills. But after two years, both contracts were forfeited once LifeMed could not turn a profit. Sachem City, they promised, would be different. After all, Rhode Island was the most generous welfare state in the country. It spent 31% of its budget on public assistance programs and was populated by just one million people. 200,000 of those were on some type of Medicare. At 13%, Rhode Island had the third highest unemployment rate in the country. 81,000 out of 499,000 possible workers were jobless.

When the phone rang, Lt. Ahearn, the union president, was drinking coffee at his kitchen table. His hangover was not abating. Between that and the newspaper headline, his morning could have used a reboot. He was wearing boxers and a wife-beater T-shirt that barely covered his belly. His bloodshot eyes saw that it was ARIFF President Vincent Szceriack calling. Vinny was his friend, but even that would not matter if things got too heated. The phone stopped ringing.

"Dad!" His son Ian came running into the kitchen. "Something's wrong with the toilet!"

"Excuse me?"

"The toilet, something's really wrong with it."

"What did you do?"

"It wasn't my idea. Colin thought it would be funny—"

"Which bathroom?"

"The one by the front door."

Lt. Ahearn got there in time to see his 12-year-old son Colin shutting off the water valve behind the toilet.

"Dad—"

"Seriously? What is going on?"

"There was this YouTube video—"

"Colin—"

"We flushed half a roll of toilet paper."

Lt. Ahearn looked at the water pooling on his new tile floor. "My advice to both of you is to get the wet-vac and clean this up before I lose my mind." He grabbed the plunger and went to work. Three pumps later he disgorged a giant wad of paper. His sons reappeared from the basement, so he said to Colin, "Scoop out that paper and then dry this up. Every drop of it."

"But dad, that's so gross."

"Consider it a life lesson, son. He who doesn't think gets to clean up the mess. Besides, you're the oldest. This nonsense falls directly on you." He left the bathroom and went back to his coffee. He heard the wet-vac fire up just as his phone rang again. Resigned, he said, "Domino's. Pickup or delivery?"

"Don't think you can hide from me."

"Sorry I missed your call, Vin, I was at the gym."

"Good one."

"I'm not kidding. I just jogged ten miles on the treadmill."

"You couldn't jog ten feet without stroking out."

"I think this might be considered fat-on-fat crime."

"So tell me. How's your morning going?"

"Great. Other than the hangover ripping apart my skull, my oldest son thought it would be a good idea to flush half a roll of toilet paper and flood the bathroom."

"Sounds exciting."

"I don't know what to tell you, Vin. I know as much as you do. Incredibly, this whole rescue business has been pretty much airtight. Which means it's coming directly from Tillinghast's office without even circulating through the chief. We got enough spies in the office upstairs to know that. Fishbakke's fucking clueless."

"Worst leader ever."

"I cannot disagree. I'm not even sure it can qualify as leadership."

"Pretty coincidental they announced it on the same day as Central Falls."

"Central Falls what?"

"Are you hungover or dead? You ain't heard? C.F. declared Chapter 9 twenty minutes ago."

Lt. Ahearn was stunned. "This is gonna fuck you guys hard. There's only nine of you on shift now as it is."

"Imagine what it'll be tomorrow?"

"Wow. I heard the rumor but I didn't think the governor would allow a second city to go down in flames. This will kill the bond rating for the whole state."

Szceriack said, "I wonder who they'll get to take us over?"

"Hopefully, whoever it is will use some grease."

"I got my whole job calling me up and I don't even know what to tell them."

"I just told you. Pray for the grease and grab your ankles like a man."

"Listen. It might be time to call our friend in D.C."

"Yeah..." Lt. Ahearn sighed from the hangover and everything else. "I didn't want it to come to this. No one did. But enough's enough."

"Right? Time to kick the fucking nest."

"I'll call him. I'll let you know what happens."

"Dad!" Colin yelled.

"Vin, I gotta go. My bathroom decon team is calling."

"Talk later."

"Roger that. Good luck today." Lt. Ahearn ended the call and stared at the wall.

***

An hour later, he was showered and on his second pot of coffee. The bathroom was spotless and his sons were upstairs cleaning their rooms as punishment.

When his phone rang, he saw it was IAFF President Iannucci, so he said, "Good morning, Mr. President, thanks for calling back."

"Talk to me, lieutenant, how are things in the Ocean State?"

"Well, let's see. My kid watched some stupid fucking You Tube video and flooded my bathroom, Central Falls declared bankruptcy two hours ago, and Receiver Dumb-Dumb just released the EMS date for when LifeMed takes us over. It's been a rough morning."

"When is it?"

"February 13."

"Jesus. Game on."

"Which is exactly why I was calling."

"You didn't even have to. Since my visit, I've been making phone calls and squeezing favors. Rhode Island might be the smallest state, but logistically that works in our favor. Pardon the pun, but we can put the whole fire out at once."

"What's the plan?"

"I'm gonna get Carvalho on the phone, try to be nice, and when that fails, we go to war."

"Roger that. The sooner the better."

"Which one? The phone call or the war?"

"Right? Not sure it makes a difference."

"I'll holler back when I get some news."

"Yes, sir. We'll be waiting."

"Keep the faith up there. Help is on the way."

When Lt. Ahearn ended the call, he thought of the last six months and how much those words now actually meant.

DECEMBER 24, 2009

Three days later, it was early evening when the phone rang. Governor Carvalho was staying late on Christmas Eve to prove a point. She was still burying the bodies from a recent scandal involving state employees caught leaving work early or skipping it altogether. There was a knock on the twelve-foot oak door that opened into her office with its sixteen-foot ceilings and ten-foot windows. Since it was the governor's favorite view, there she was again, framed by the long dark drapes pinned to the walls beside her. Outside it was cold and gray. Inside was not much better.

"Madame Governor—"

"Allow me to guess." She did not turn around because she was staring out over the vast snow-covered pavilion in front of the state house. "Is it our Italian friend again?"

"Yes, ma'am."

"Well, I've already ignored him for three days, so let's just get this over with."

"Line three, ma'am."

"Thank you. You can leave. And Pam? Merry Christmas."

"Thank you, ma'am."

Governor Carvalho waited for the door to close before she clicked on the speaker-phone. "I was wondering when you were going to crawl out into the daylight. I'm sure I can guess the reason why you've been haunting my office for the last week like the Angel of Death?"

Uncharacteristically, when Viterello Iannucci laughed, it lacked conviction. "It's nice to finally meet you too, Madame Governor. And a very Merry Christmas to you as well."

"Do you know there are few things I detest more than insipid and unctuous trade reps trying to hustle me?"

Iannucci chuckled, and this time it sounded genuine. "I assure you, Madame Governor, I am not some mere trade rep looking to become a speed-bump in your suddenly national aspirations. Isn't that what I heard? That you might be eyeing a run for senate?"

"Is that why you're calling? To offer election advice?"

Another chuckle. "Not for a woman with zero election defeats. That would be a waste of time, another pet peeve of mine, so allow me to shorten this dance."

"Please do. I'm already bored."

"I have two sets of numbers for you. 15,000, 2.4 million, 180 million. The second are 81,000, 96%, and as much PAC money as you can feast upon. There are currently 15,000 union members working on various infrastructure projects throughout your state, 2.4 million is the dollar figure you'd be losing a day through various slowdowns and stoppages, and 180 million is the cost to the surrounding economy. The second set is simple. We have 81,000 total union members statewide who can work for your next election, whether it be the senate or another term as governor, a 96% success rate in your state when we do, and a promise to extend this financial and voting support to you after your arrival in congress as the first female senator in your great state's history."

"Well, allow me to counter offer. Fuck off or I will turn your life into my own personal toilet. Your cheating wife, your mistresses, the vacations and gifts you think no one else knows about—"

"Madame Governor—"

"What balls," she hissed, "allows you to call my office with threats of strikes and slowdowns?"

"No one ever said strike—"

"Regardless. I will grow a dick before I take marching orders off some pervert in Washington D.C."

"I just—"

"And your various bank accounts and LLC's, does anyone know about them yet?"

"Governor Carvalho, please, do the jobs of sixteen proud and honorable EMT's warrant this level of vitriol? When they are only trying to serve their community?"

"Well, I don't know how they do things in Detroit—isn't that where you're from?"

"It is."

"You have my condolences."

"Truthfully, are these sixteen jobs worth all the bloodshed that will ensue from here?"

"Sixteen jobs," she nearly scoffed. "We're talking about the whole state after that, Mr. President, so your final offer, while simple and cute, will certainly have to reflect that."

"There is one other thing."

"Of course there is."

"In my various phone calls with the leadership of the other unions, a deal was struck. Ponham Rocks will be yours. The Teamsters, the steelworkers, IBEW, and everyone else, they have agreed to go-along to get-along. That's millions in future taxes, Madame Governor."

"Ponham Rocks..."

"And it will also help with your unruly Indian problem, I believe it's the Ninituck? They will love you forever along with every progressive and leftie in the state."

"That is an intriguing offer."

"What casino isn't? Imagine the permanent tax windfall?"

"I think we might be able to come to a deal, Mr. President."

"And wouldn't that be a fine gift on Christmas? To bury this rescue fiasco forever?"

"Please don't grease me on the way out. Do we have a deal?"

"Indeed we do. I want to wish you a Merry Christmas to you and your family."

"The pleasure was all yours. I'll be in touch after it's done." She clicked off the call and even now, despite the late hour, began ticking through the political cost and calculus, gains and losses, and decided it might just be a fine New Year after all.

***

When Lt. Ahearn answered his phone, he immediately heard President Iannucci screaming, "—how the fuck should I know? But she said it, the LLC's, the gifts—"

"Hello!" Lt. Ahearn tried cutting in. "Can you hear me?"

"Yeah, hey, how's it going?"

"You sound pretty heated."

"That fucking bitch. Boy, you weren't kidding. The Grim Reaper probably has more friends than that fucking cunt."

"I tried to warn you."

"What a piece of work. I hope she gets cancer and dies."

"You wouldn't be the first to say that."

"I just got off the phone with her...." He took a deep breath. "Listen, it's over. We spent a few minutes telling each other to fuck off, but in the end we cut a deal. Private EMS in the state of Rhode Island is officially dead and off the table and in return the unions are gonna step back and let the Ponham Rocks Casino go through."

"Holy shit."

"Yeah, it's a done deal. We bled a little bit but everyone gets their back scratched."

"I don't know what to say. Thank you seems pretty inadequate."

"Don't worry about thanking me. Just keep looking out for your membership. You're doing it right. Remember that."

"I really appreciate it. We all do."

"Call me if you need anything else. That's what we're here for."

"I will."

"Alright, I gotta go. I gotta call my lawyer. I don't know how the fuck this bitch knows all this shit, but I gotta be ready."

"Friendly advice? Pull down the periscope and just sink into the shadows. You got what you needed. She has levels of hell the devil doesn't even know exist."

"I wish that was in my nature."

"Live to fight another day, Prez, or you might not ever fight again."

"Jesus, she pulls that kind of weight?"

"If all the stories are even half-true, I wouldn't fuck with this chick from a mile away."

"Message received. Merry Christmas, lieutenant."

"Same to you. And, Prez? We owe you a lobster dinner. Next time you swing through..."

DECEMBER 25, 2009

It had been twenty-three years since anyone committed the cardinal sin of calling out sick on Christmas. Because of the four days-on, four days-off, eight-day work-week schedule, everyone knew a year in advance which holidays they would be working, so making someone else lose time with their family was considered extremely taboo. In 1986, a lieutenant named Al Raddison called out sick on Christmas morning and was promptly re-named "Al-bee," for "Al-bee Home for Christmas."

This year, Kevin Wilson had been stuck on Rescue 2 for 96 hours. When he finally walked out the door Christmas Eve, he woke up Christmas morning with diarrhea and a 103-degree fever. Another guy, Ray Latanski, was in year two of an ugly divorce. He would not be allowed to see his kids this Christmas, so he was at the end of a three-day bender when he showed up drunk for work Christmas Eve. The guys at Station 4 were not amused. They drove him right back home and someone else got held instead. But justice was not long delayed. Those on shift Christmas day promptly labeled them both "bags of shit" and immediately started torturing them by text.

The Alert Tone hit at 10:23 A.M. as Fire Alarm announced, *"Attention*

Rescue 2 and Engine 3, Still Alarm. 161 Belmore Drive for a man in need of assistance..."

"Sounds like my life story." Lt. Russel Brodie headed for the truck. He was usually on Engine 5 but got forced to Engine 3 on the dayshift between his nightshifts. Surviving his third divorce without alcohol was bad enough, but working round the clock was pushing some guys to the edge. A tall man with a seven-foot wingspan, his blonde toupee, as always, was as fascinating as it was disconcerting. His 6'7" height meant he barely had to pull himself up into the truck as he said, "Looks like I picked the wrong week to quit smoking." He was only half-joking. "Let's go, morons."

Useless and Toe-Tag were the usual privates on C-Shift, but Toe-Tag, the worst EMT on the job, had swapped out his Christmas shift. Filling in was Blister, ironically nicknamed because he had no work ethic. He was also a strident Yankees fan, so Lt. Brodie had even more reason to hate him. As far as crews go, Engine 3 on C-Shift led by Lt. Cunty Conti was the worst on the job. Lt. Brodie was just hoping to survive the shift without having to rely in any way on either one of the privates he commanded.

"Jesus Christ." He angrily pointed. "You just missed Belmore. This isn't even my fucking district and I know that."

"I always get that confused with—"

"Stop talking." Lt. Brodie said into the mic, "Engine 3's more or less on-scene."

Because of who he was with and what he had just said, laughter could be heard in the background when Fire Alarm answered, *"Engine 3's on-scene at 1029."*

They circled the block before stopping in front of a single-story cape. It had a long wooden ramp extending off the front porch. There was no snow on it because of the unseasonable forty-degree weather. At the front door, Lt. Brodie knocked and called out, "Hello! Fire department!"

A muffled return shout was unintelligible.

Lt. Brodie tried the door but it was locked. He heard on his radio, "Rescue 2 to Engine 3. Whaddaya got?"

Lt. Brodie answered, "Not sure yet. Still trying to gain entry."

"Roger. Two minutes out."

"Well don't just stand there!" Lt. Brodie yelled at Useless. "Check the windows, see if we can't get lucky and find one that's unlocked."

Useless' real name was Grant Ungerfelt. He was a cerebral sort and college graduate who held a physics degree from Yale. But that pedigree amounted to nothing without common sense or an intrinsic knowledge of anything medical or mechanical. Even worse, he did not care enough to learn.

Lt. Brodie saw Blister still wandering around the truck and screamed, "What're you doing?"

"I can't find the Sawzall!"

"Sawzall? Are you kidding me?"

As Useless half-heartedly checked the first-floor windows, Lt. Brodie cupped his hands around his eyes and looked through the back door window. In the center of the kitchen, he could see a man in a wheelchair.

"Please help me!" the man shouted. "It won't move!"

"All right! Hang on! You got a spare key hidden out here?"

"No!"

Lt. Brodie already had a plan in mind. Like deputized criminals, firemen were taught how to break into cars, homes, and all types of buildings, in all types of ways. They entered through windows, doors, vents, skylights, and, when necessary, straight through the wall, floor, or roof. When people locked their kids or pets in the car, they were often both relieved and fascinated to see how the fire department could break into someone's car without even leaving a trace.

Lt. Brodie pulled a putty knife from the pocket of his night-hitch and went to work on the lock. Most guys had pockets jammed with screwdrivers, knives, pliers, spanner wrenches, door-chalks, and everything else.

Blister's real name was Donny Aiello. Somehow, he was the

disappointing son of a legendary Battalion Chief. Considered a big-talker who accomplished little to back any of it up, it was hard for others to take him seriously. Like B.C. McLoud, and even Chief Fishbakke, Blister was a political creature focused on all the wrong things. Lt. Brodie, skeptical of anyone that rode the coattails of someone else's hard work, was no fan of Blister.

Once he got the window open, he intertwined his fingers into a basket and yelled, "Blister! Get over here. I'll boost you through."

"Me? Useless is the junior man—"

"I'll give you one choice. You can either climb through this window, or I get to kick you in the nuts."

"That's not really fair. By contract I don't think you—hey, wait!"

Rescue 2 pulled on-scene just as Lt. Brodie's boot landed squarely inside Blister's crotch, lifted him off his feet, and dumped him to the ground.

Lt. Killmoor spit out his coffee. "God, I'm so happy we were here to see that."

"Me too." T-Bag threw it into park. "Look. He ain't even moving."

They opened their doors in time to hear Lt. Brodie losing his mind. "You piece of shit! Get in the truck! You make me sick!"

"Merry Christmas, Russ!" Lt. Killmoor cheerily called out. "What're you guys doing? Auditioning for the next Jackass movie?"

"I might as well have come alone!" Lt. Brodie stepped back to the window and said, "All right, Baggy, in you go."

T-Bag stepped into the finger basket, grabbed the sill, and pulled himself through. He made sure to land on the toilet lid to avoid the urine-stained floor.

Lt. Killmoor shook Lt. Brodie's hand and said, "Where's your other private?"

"I don't know. Probably hiding around back? Just look to where there's absolutely nothing going on and I guarantee he'll be in the dead center of that."

"At least he's consistent."

"Are you trying to send me over the edge, Dave? Cause I'm real fucking close."

T-Bag threw open the back door.

Inside, the kitchen had one dim bulb. A man in a wheelchair was stuck inside its shadows. He was balding but had a ponytail and a look of total desperation. He said, "I've been stuck here for six hours. I really tried everything, but it's a new chair—"

"What's your name?" Lt. Killmoor asked.

"Buddy."

"Okay, Buddy. What's going on with you physically?"

"Nothing. I'm a paraplegic but I have enough use of both arms to live alone and steer this thing."

"So we're just here because the wheelchair doesn't work?"

"You see this?" He pointed to his shirt that said, Not As Lean, But Still a Marine.

"I'm a fucking veteran—"

"Whoa, whoa. I didn't mean it like that. I just want to make sure I know you're otherwise medically okay. That's all."

"I got no family left, man, believe me, I tried for six fucking hours—"

"Is this the battery?"

"Yes."

"You got a spare? Let's try that first."

Nothing worked. Thirty minutes later, they had booted, re-booted, and gone through the small phonebook-sized manual. Buddy must have realized this because he suddenly said, "Please don't leave."

"We're not going anywhere." Lt. Brodie scoured the manual for contact information. "But if we can't get this figured out, we might have to take you to the hospital."

"Please." Buddy's long dead legs were shrunken sticks. "I don't want to go to the hospital on Christmas for nothing."

"I know, dude, but we can't just leave you here like this."

"Then can you just put me into my bed?"

"Do you have your old chair?"

"No." He was crestfallen. "I had to give it up to get this one."

"Where'd you get it from?"

"Providence. Some distributor. Should be on the receipt."

"I got an idea." Lt. Brodie had Fire Alarm contact the Providence Fire Alarm to look up the contact information for Mobility Distributors. He was given three numbers. The first two went nowhere, but the third rang an answering service. A pleasant man said the offices were closed on Christmas but would re-open in the morning.

"That's not gonna work," Lt. Brodie answered. "I'm at the home of one of your customers—"

"This is just the answering service, sir."

"Be that as it may, I'm a lieutenant on the Sachem City Fire Department, and we're open twenty-four hours a day. This man is a decorated combat vet—"

"I was never in combat," Buddy quickly said. "I got hurt flipping an ATV in Colorado Springs on leave."

Lt. Brodie shushed him and continued, "I want to be connected with either the owner or a technician or someone who can fix this thing, because we're not leaving a paraplegic veteran stuck in the middle of his goddamn kitchen on Christmas just because your product is faulty."

"Sir, like I said, this is just an answering service—"

"I don't think you get it. This is not a negotiation."

"Hang on, please."

A series of phone calls finally produced a service technician on the line. Soon after, Buddy was back at full power and pulling celebratory donuts in his kitchen. He said, "I can't thank y'all enough!"

"No problem." Lt. Brodie stacked the manuals on the counter. "Call back if this thing shits the bed again, okay?"

"I really appreciate it, guys, you have a Merry Christmas." Buddy closed the door behind them.

"I can't believe it's only eleven o'clock." Lt. Brodie looked at Useless and Blister warming themselves in the truck. "I'm almost tempted to dump the entire hose-bed and force these two morons to repack every inch of it just for the fuck of it."

"Company drill on Christmas Day?" Lt. Killmoor smiled. "That would turn you into an instant legend."

"We'll see how the day goes. At the very least, they're cleaning all the bathrooms."

"Bring the pain, Russ."

"Yeah, merry fucking Christmas."

"Fire Alarm to Rescue 2?"

"Go ahead."

"Disposition?"

"We're getting ready to clear Belmore."

"Roger, sir. Start heading for 216 Morris Drive for difficulty breathing."

"Roger." Lt. Killmoor called out to Lt. Brodie, "I'm climbing back into my sleigh! Put out some cookies at the 3's and maybe I'll slide down the chimney!"

"No offense, Dave, but judging by your waistline, I'd say you're chimney sliding days are over."

***

Master Box 516 tripped in Fire Alarm at 2:13 P.M. At the same time, a 911 caller reported an explosion and a transformer fire on a pole in front of the same address. Citywide, the main electrical lines carried 13,000 volts. That kind of power could not be brought directly into homes and businesses without causing them to explode, so the transformers, shaped like four-foot-long soup cans, broke that number down to a more manageable 120 volts. The machinery inside these transformers ran on hydraulics, so when transformers caught fire and popped, they usually shot flaming oil onto anything close-by.

The All-Call tones hit before Fire Alarm announced, *"Attention Engines 5,2,3, Ladder 1, Battalion 3. Box Alarm. 1556 Washington Street. Edison Mills..."*

A hundred years ago, Washington Street was home to all the man-ufacturing on the west side. Many of the old mills had already burnt down or been converted into office space or condominiums. Such was the case for Edison Mills, a mixed-use facility that had businesses on the first-floor and condominiums on the floors above. It was five-stories tall, 500-feet long, and covered 250,000 square-feet.

"Engine 5 to Fire Alarm." Lt. Bodean "Bow" Ibrahim saw a thin column of black smoke rising into the winter sky, but the mill was not yet in sight. Lt. Ibrahim was the son of a Jamaican father and a mother from West Africa. He was one of five black men on the job. Like most fire departments, Sachem City was still playing catch up with the changing times, a feat made even harder since only 18% of the city was black. As far as standards and testing, thankfully no one was in favor of lowering anything since that's how people died.

Lt. Ibrahim was 38-years-old and one of the captains on the SCFD hockey team. In addition to Berserker, they had two ex-NHL players, a handful of ex-AHL players, and dozens of guys who had played in high school or college. One of them, Harold Raymar, was an old school NHL veteran talented enough to star on the 1984 Olympic hockey team, and even played alongside Wayne Gretsky at the end of his career in Los Angeles. Nicknamed "Shooter" because of a devastating slapshot, Raymer played for a decade, had a family, had a divorce, but never lost the itch. Hockey in New England was a lot like football in Texas or Pennsylvania—a rite of passage.

Lt. Ibrahim was lucky because he grew up with the white kids before anyone was taught to hate anyone else. His friends were white and black, his girlfriends the same. Post-graduation, he was planning on enlisting in the army until he got jumped and robbed one night on Union Street. Because of the coma, he spent half of senior year in rehab. His friends, including "the Dude," Lt. Stokes, handled the retribution. Back in the day, Stokes and Ibrahim's fathers were in the same fire academy, so their sons had pretty much grown up together. Known for his intensity and relentless work ethic, Lt. Ibrahim had bulging eyes, so he was also called "Mr. Peepers."

When they crested the hill, Edison Mills swung into view. A telephone pole was on fire in front of the mill, and some of the flaming oil had splattered on the eaves and roof.

Lt. Ibrahim nonchalantly said, "Engine 5 to Fire Alarm."

"Go ahead, Engine 5."

"Five-story brick mill building. It appears a transformer has caught the front of the mill and roofline. Slight smoke condition, Code Red."

"Roger. Engine 5's reporting a Code Red. Battalion 3 receive?"

"Roger. Strike a second alarm."

"Jesus, Bow." Scotty Hagan started braking. "What's the plan?"

"Forget the roof. Let the ladder get that. The front's all brick, so we ain't worried about that either. Put us by the stair-tower. We'll grab the high-rise gear and head up to the top-floor, see if any of this has spread inside."

"If it has..."

"If it has, we're gonna be here until next week." He said into the mic, "Engine 5 on-scene. We're heading up to level five to check for extension."

"Roger, Engine 5."

"Let's go, boys, time to hump them steps."

They geared up and grabbed forcible entry tools. Two of them shouldered 100-foot shots of hose, while a third carried the fifty-pound bag of nozzles, wrenches, and adapters to hook into the standpipe. All told, with their gear and tools, they shouldered a 100-pounds apiece.

Obviously, since it was Christmas Day, only the condominiums were occupied. People were still emerging in bathrobes, jackets and hats. Some held coffeecups while pointing their camera phones to where the transformer had blown flaming oil into an ascending "V" up the wall.

"Let's go, people, move with a purpose." Lt. Ibrahim pushed past those exiting. "Head across the street, please."

"Excuse me!" someone yelled. "There's a lady on the fourth-floor that's bedridden."

"What apartment?"

"I think it's 402."

"Thank you." Lt. Ibrahim triggered his mic. "Engine 5 to Fire Alarm."

"Go ahead, Engine 5."

"Advise Command that tenants are reporting a bedridden woman on the fourth-floor. Possibly number 402."

"Roger, Engine 5. Battalion 3 receive?"

"That's a roger," B.C. Etchel said. "I'll be on-scene in thirty seconds establishing command on side-one. The 3's are too far out, so have Engine 2 tag a hydrant for the standpipe. Have the 3's check the fourth-floor for that lady and any additional extension. Have Ladder 2 set up on the 3-4 corner when they arrive."

"Roger, Chief. Fire Alarm to all companies..."

The mill had a six-story enclosed brick stair-tower attached to the center-front of the building. That was where Engine 5 entered. By the time they reached the fourth-floor people descending were coughing and pointing above.

"Not a good sign." Lt. Ibrahim, like his men, was starting to labor beneath all they carried. When they opened the fifth-floor door, the hallway was charged with smoke. "Engine 5 to Command."

"Go, 5."

"We have smoke in the fifth-floor hallway. Gonna pull some ceilings."

"Roger."

Lt. Ibrahim slammed a New York Hook through the plasterboard and yanked down a section of ceiling. Smoke dumped out. A few flames flickered through. "Scotty, hook us into the standpipe and hit this shit. We'll check a little further in to see if its extending."

They walked twenty feet deeper into the building, in-line with the flaming telephone pole and their first hole, and then pulled more ceiling. Only a few tendrils of smoke crept out.

"Engine 5 to Command."

"Go, 5."

"We have some interior extension, mainly at the roofline, but that's it."

"Roger. Are civilians still exiting?"

"Affirmative, Chief. People are still stumbling out of the rear apartments. I guess some are ignoring the alarms."

"Roger. Command to Fire Alarm. I want Engines 3 and 6 going door-to-door clearing apartments. Top down, starting on five. Have Engine 4—"

"Command, there is no Engine 4 today."

Because of the rolling blackouts, Engine 1, the second-due company, and Engine 4 were out of service.

"Okay." B.C. Etchel did not want to panic, but he knew with a building this size he just did not have enough manpower. "Fire Alarm, strike a third-alarm with out-of-town companies."

"Roger, Command."

B.C. Etchel did the math. He could either clear the building but possibly lose the entire mill to a ridiculous transformer fire, or throw all his resources at stopping the fire before the asphalt roof ignited. That would be a game-over situation. It was the kind of decision he knew he should not have to make. The out-of-town companies were ten minutes away at best, and by then their fate would have already been decided. "Command to Fire Alarm."

"Go, Command."

"Forget clearing the building. I want all companies focused on suppression."

"Ladder 1 to Command."

"Go, Ladder 1."

"We just made the roof, Chief. We have fire in the eaves and some extension to the roof. The asphalt is starting to catch. We're gonna need a line up here double-quick."

"Well, come back down and grab some hose. We're gonna turn you into a standpipe. The 6's are gonna pump you. Command to Engine 6."

"We got that, Command, getting set up to pump Ladder 1."

Rescue 2 had just cleared the hospital, so T-Bag was taking corners like a driver at Le Mans.

"Easy!" Lt. Killmoor shouted. "You're gonna flip this thing!"

"Good. It's a shitbox anyway."

"What is your hurry? It's a stupid transformer fire."

"Dragging fat people around all day is really fun, L-T, but I ain't missing a fire."

Washington Street was already awash in fire trucks, police cars, and utility companies. A hundred people were in the parking lot across the street watching the firefighters crawl across their building.

"Watch out!" Lt. Killmoor screamed.

"Thread the needle!" T-Bag slalomed the rescue between two police cars and smoked the brakes.

"Hey, new guy!" B.C. Etchel yelled. "Ease up on the psycho."

"Sorry, Chief." T-Bag was already gearing up.

Lt. Killmoor was one of the most knowledgeable EMS guys on the job, but even he was the first to admit his firefighting days were all but over. He joined B.C. Etchel, who was surveying the scene with trepidation.

"Ladder 1 to Command."

"Go."

"We now have smoke coming out of the roof on the stair-tower."

"Roger." B.C. Etchel turned to Lt. Killmoor. "This is rapidly turning into a clusterfuck."

"Ladder 2's on the corner. We could back them up and stick the tower from there."

"But they're on the fifth-floor pulling ceilings."

"I'll set it up but I ain't climbing it."

B.C. Etchel heard a commotion and saw Engine 3 stumble out of the mill. Lt. Brodie was berating Useless and Blister for already blowing through their air supply.

B.C. Etchel whistled and shouted, "Brodie!"

"Yo!"

"Got a mission for ya." He explained the plan as the blood drained simultaneously from Useless and Blister's faces.

Lt. Killmoor backed the truck up, put the stabilizers down, and telescoped the ladder toward the roof. The rectangular stair-tower was seventy-feet high and six-stories tall, one more than the building to allow for walk-out roof access. Because of the angle, Lt. Killmoor had to extend full boom to 109 feet just to reach the edge of its roof.

Engine 3 ransacked Ladder 2 for axes, watercans, ropes, and ladder belts so no one would fall to their deaths. Lt. Brodie might have despised his crew, but he did not necessarily want to see them die. He said, "All right, boys, hope you ate your Wheaties. T-Bag, you go first—"

"Why him?" Blister asked, already straining beneath the weight of all the gear and tools. "I'm the senior private."

"Are you high? Two hours ago you said the same thing, but only because you didn't want to do anything. Now you want to be the leader on a hundred-foot climb?"

"I can do it."

"Forget it." Lt. Brodie climbed up onto the truck. "I'm going first. T-Bag, you bring up the rear."

They started climbing. Forty-feet later Useless came to a dead stop. "I can't do this."

"Kid, we got seventy feet to go." Lt. Brodie looked back and tried to encourage him. "You did this in the academy—"

"That was five years ago."

"So what?" Lt. Brodie snapped. "Goddamnit, are you a fireman or what?"

"You can do this, dude." T-Bag prodded him from behind. "Just climb the rungs like gym class."

Blister bristled. "Fuck you, new guy, get some time on the job—"

"We don't have time for this, you fucking morons!" Lt. Brodie started climbing again.

"Come on, guys, what the fuck." T-Bag was stuck behind them. "You're making us look like idiots."

"Oh, sorry, Backdraft, are we holding you up?"

T-Bag bit back his retort, because while Blister was just being obnoxious, Useless looked completely terrified. "Can you make it back down, bro? Do you need a hand?"

"I can get back down." Useless seemed relieved by that possibility. "Can you climb past me? I'm too freaked out to lean either way."

"Sure." T-Bag stepped past and then looked back. "You sure you're alright?"

"Yeah, man, I'll make it."

"Okay." T-Bag looked up at Blister. "Shall we dance?"

"I think I should help him back down."

"Are you serious?"

"Buddy system, right?"

"Gimme your gear." T-Bag took the water can off Useless and the ladder belts and ropes off Blister. He carefully stepped past Blister and started climbing.

As Lt. Brodie neared the tip, the ladder started bouncing up and down. He stopped climbing, knowing his and T-Bag's unsynchronized energy this far out was unleashing opposing forces. Then he made the mistake of looking down and saw the only thing between him and the street sixty-feet below were the inch-thick rungs he was looking through.

Lt. Brodie had an aggressive reputation, but even he was now staring at the tiny roof with a certain look that caused T-Bag to say, "Mind if I step past, Lou? I used to be a roofer."

"A what? Are you *kidding* me?"

"No, sir."

"Well, don't hate me, but I forgot to bring the chainsaw."

"No worries. Can you just hold all this *crap*?" T-Bag left him at the tip with the watercans, ropes, and belts. Then he examined the roof. It was a ten-foot by ten-foot square. Hip rafters from each corner met in the center providing a slight pitch to slough away any rainwater. Smoke was puffing out of the far-left corner. To make sure the integrity of the roof was not in doubt, T-Bag sounded it with the axe before stepping off the ladder. From there, he did not take a single step without first sounding the roof.

"I don't know about this," Lt. Brodie said. "Isn't it stupid to be standing on a roof that's obviously on fire?"

"I'm wondering how it's burning if there's no fire inside the tower?"

"The hydraulic oil caught the eave. Sound that edge with the axe."

"Command to Engine 3!"

"Jesus Christ." Lt. Brodie's hands were full, so he had to secure the watercans to the ladder before he answered, "Engine 3."

"Engine 3, why is he swinging an axe without wearing any fire-gloves?"

T-Bag could not believe it. "How can he even see me?"

Lt. Brodie looked over the edge and saw *everyone* staring up at them. "Oh great. As if this didn't suck enough."

"I can't swing an axe up here with those oven-mitts on. This thing slips out of my hands and someone down there is gonna die."

"What're you two cowboys doing up there?" B.C. Etchel was not done. "Where's his ladder belt?"

T-Bag said, "Turn your radio off."

"I can't do that, man, just put the fucking thing on."

As the roof burned, T-Bag stepped back to the ladder, put the belt on, and handed the other end of the rope to Lt. Brodie. T-Bag said, "These things are actually dangerous. You get tangled up or roll a boot on the rope and you're gone."

"Yeah, but at least you'll live."

"Great."

"Ladder 1 to Engine 3."

"Go ahead."

"We see visible fire in the eave facing the transformer."

"Well, no shit." But Lt. Brodie said into the mic, "Roger."

Oddly enough, in the fire academy they had been taught to smash through plywood roofs with the dull, or flathead, side of the axe. That's because the bladed edge often got stuck or snagged. But now the axe just bounced off the roof like a rubber toy.

"Something's wrong." T-Bag reached down and tore off a shingle. "Oh holy fuck."

"What is it?"

"2x4s. Tongue and groove instead of plywood."

"Are you shitting me? Who does that?"

"Someone who never wants to repair this roof ever again."

"I guess that makes sense. This ain't exactly accessible."

"Oh well." T-Bag flipped the axe and started chopping and spewing wood like an angry beaver.

Ladder 1, which was a tower ladder with a basket, chainsawed off any eaves on the main building still on fire. Engine 2 and Ladder 2 were on the football field-sized roof checking for extension but found nothing. Inside on the fifth-floor, Lt. Bodean and Engine 5 called an all clear after extinguishment. The fire seemed to be contained.

After ten minutes, Lt. Brodie yelled, "Come on, switch out. You must be exhausted."

"I'm almost through." Sweat was pouring down T-Bag's face. Minutes later, he said, "I'm in, L-T. Got a two-foot hole."

"Here. Hit it with the watercan."

When T-Bag triggered it nothing came out. "What the fuck!" Disgusted, he tossed it down to the main roof, took the second can, and fired it into the hole.

"Boy," Lt. Brodie said. "Talk about anti-climactic."

"Right?"

Since Ladder 1 was finished destroying the front eave of the building, they now swung into position on the stair-tower. They cut down whatever else was burning below where T-Bag was swinging the axe and blasted it with water. From the basket, Beef Dumas smiled up at him and said, "Bet you could use a ride down."

"Can't leave the L-T, bro."

"And I can't take both of you at full boom. Three's the max."

"No worries. Here, take this can down, will ya?"

"How we looking?" Lt. Brodie shouted from the other side.

"Good, Lou, the ladder got the rest."

Lt. Brodie triggered his mic. "Engine 3 to Command. Stair-tower roof is secure."

Down below, they began packing up the hoses and tools. Guys were never effusive with compliments or quick to celebrate individual actions, which is why T-Bag was confused. After another high-five, he said, "But I used to do this every day."

"What don't you get?" Lt. Killmoor was helping him roll hose. "I saw what was happening up there. Those weren't ladder guys. I've known Brodie my whole life. He would've done it if he had to, because that's who he is, but he didn't look too psyched to be operating out that far either."

Over the radios could be heard, "Command to Fire Alarm."

"Go, Command."

"Fire scene is secure. Marshals are on-scene. I'm terminating Command and returning in service."

"Roger, Chief. Washington Street Command has been terminated and you are back in service at 1533."

Four of the fifty condominiums were uninhabitable due to smoke and water damage, but everyone else returned to their Christmas celebrations.

ROADKILL

January 4, 2010

"Receiver Tillinghast? Governor Carvalho is on line two."

"Thank you, Karen." Receiver Tillinghast stared at his blinking phone. This call was not expected, and in politics, the unexpected rarely contained good news. Especially not when Marissa Carvalho was involved. His hand paused above the phone before he picked it up and said, "A belated happy holidays to you, Madam Governor. How is everything on Smith Hill?"

"Arthur, hello. Same to you. We had an excellent Christmas. Both Danny and Beth are home from school, so the house feels full again. What about you? How's Martha?"

"Oh, she's absolutely fantastic. Our kids are home as well, so Christmas was a joy."

"Crazy how time flies."

"It sure is."

"I wish I was calling for purely social reasons, Arthur..."

It was unusual for Receiver Tillinghast to squirm. "What can I help you with, Madam Governor?"

"Honestly, it's more along the lines of what we can do for each other? As you know, there has been public speculation about my long-term political ambitions. And while I have not decided as to whether or not a Senate run could be in my future, if that time comes and I am fortunate enough to win, that would leave my seat vacant. You and I have already spoken about your burgeoning political interests once your duties as Receiver have been completed."

"Oh, that's very flattering to say but—"

"Of course, at this level, broad coalitions are hard to form, much less maintain. But without my base, I can go no further. As Democrats, we have a long tradition and close alliance with organized labor. Indeed, they are the blue-collar backbone upon which we rely. Without their ground game and generous support, this picture begins to look a whole lot bleaker."

"I completely agree." He had no idea where this was going.

"Even worse, during these hard economic times, massive public works projects are one of the only vehicles driving employment. I need to keep people's bellies filled, Arthur."

"Are you speaking about the I-195 relocation project?"

"I'm talking about all of it. 195, the new convention center, the Providence Waterfront Redevelopment Authority..."

"Okay..."

"All of these projects are balancing acts. We're talking about the involvement of huge unions in these endeavors. The United Steelworkers, the International Brotherhood of Electrical Workers, the Teamsters, plumbers and pipefitters, carpenters, ironworkers, and two dozen more. These are the hardworking people that form our foundational supports as a political party. Without them, we lose. Period."

"A harsh reality, to be sure."

"All of these issues become intermingled. Enmeshed. It's hard to keep everyone happy, Arthur, and as you'll see, sometimes what's good for the many has to trump what's good for the few."

"Another harsh realization for how democracy works, but true."

"With that in mind, I have a favor to ask."

"Shoot."

"The IAFF is also one of these unions, and with 340,000 members in the U.S. and Canada, they have many, many friends. Some of these friends are in other unions, and their leaderships have begun reaching out. On behalf of their Sachem City *brothers*, they appear willing to make my life even more complicated than it already is. Job slow-downs lead to blown budgets, and blown budgets lead to layoffs. While they say they don't necessarily seek that outcome for these construction projects, that threat has certainly been implied."

"What can I help you with, Madam Governor?"

"Make this rescue thing go away. Bury it under a thousand feet of concrete and forget it ever existed, or I'm gonna have this problem in every city in the state."

"I see." He clicked his pen, nauseous. "I've already expended a tremendous amount of political capital on this. Backing down now would weaken me considerably."

"How so? Phrase it however you need to place the blame. Release a statement at midnight on a Saturday and say, 'We've decided, in these perilous times where people are truly hurting, that initiating a massive social experiment on this scale might not be a prudent idea, or in the best interests of the people of Sachem City.' It almost writes itself."

"I hear what you're saying—"

"Hearing isn't listening, Arthur. Listening means you can see what the bigger picture contains. These people, these friends, have long memories. And elections are where old scores get settled. In your political future, if there is to be one, you're going to want to end up on the right side of this math or you'll be stillborn in front of the world."

There was a long pause.

"So," she finally said, "is this something we can count on?"

"In the best interests of all involved, I can certainly adapt on the fly."

"Isn't that what nature dictates? Adapt or die? What a brilliant comparison, Arthur, you certainly haven't gotten to where you are without a keen intuition."

"Thank you, Madam Governor."

"Do take care."

"You as well."

Formalities complete, Receiver Tillinghast hung up the phone and thought he saw his own blood spilled all over the desk. The governor, after all, never took hostages.

THE DEATH OF HOPE

January 6, 2010

"Attention Rescue 1. Still Alarm. 178 Abbington Road. Woman ill..."

It was two weeks after Christmas and, at Station 1, Psycho Sal and Yoda had been watching 'Goodfellas.' No rescue guy who ever started a movie seriously thought he would actually finish it.

Downstairs in the truck, Psycho Sal said into the mic, "Rescue 1 responding."

"Rescue 1 responding at 1445."

Yoda said, "That might be the best movie ever made."

"You ever seen 'Raging Bull?'"

"No."

"'Taxi Driver?'"

"No."

"Then how can you say that?"

Woman Ill was no reason to blow through intersections and hurt people, so they were driving with caution. On top of that, four-inches of snow had fallen the day before, and driving was still treacherous. Rhode Island barely averaged twenty inches of snow a year, but the periodic Nor'easters sometimes created blizzards that shut down the whole state for days.

Psycho Sal lit a cigarette as the siren rose and fell. "For the longest time I was convinced it was 'The Godfather.' But shit like 'Raging Bull' is the reason why people make movies in the first place."

"What about 'Shawshank Redemption?'"

"Stop embarrassing yourself. No one gets near old school DeNiro and Scorsese."

"Isn't Abbington on the left?"

"Yeah. Two more blocks."

They took a left and saw a man frantically waving from a front porch.

"That's odd." Psycho Sal grabbed the dashboard mic, "Rescue 1 on-scene."

"Rescue 1's on-scene at 1448."

"Look at the stash on this guy." Sal said. "He and Saddam Hussein could be kissing cousins."

They barely had their doors open before the guy screamed, "Please hurry! It's my mother! She's in here!"

"Calm down, mister, we're coming."

"Something's very wrong!"

"If she's ill or has the flu, we'll take care of her—"

"She's not moving!"

"What?" Psycho Sal snapped on his gloves and picked up the pace.

Wails and screams exited the front door. Inside, the house was spotless. Black and white photographs of austere ancestors from a century before were hung in reverence on the walls. Cloth doilies were placed like lily-pads beneath anything that could scratch the fine wood furniture the family had passed down for generations. Everything was in its place except for the elderly woman on the floor surrounded by her hysterical family.

Immediately alarmed, Sal pushed people out of the way. "What happened?"

"She just dropped!" a woman said in a thick Middle Eastern accent.

Sal gave her a brutal sternum rub with his knuckles but she did not flinch. "What's her name?"

"Madeline Barghouti."

"Does she have any medical problems?"

"High blood pressure."

"She take her meds today?"

"Yes, yes, yes."

Psycho Sal checked for a pulse in three different places but found none. He hit the shoulder-mic on his portable and said, "Rescue 1 to Fire Alarm. This is not a woman ill. Code 99. Witnessed arrest. Get me an engine company."

"Roger." Fire Alarm hit the Alert Tone and urgently stated, *"Attention Engine 1, Special Signal. Assist Rescue 1 with a Code 99 at 178 Abbington Road..."*

"Everybody clear out!" Sal yelled, "You're not gonna want to see this."

The man was suddenly terrified. "What is it? What's happened?"

"She's in cardiac arrest, sir."

The relatives wailed and hugged one another. Some left the room while others did not, but Sal was out of time. Normally, with enough firemen on-scene, they would have thrown her on the stretcher and hauled ass for the rescue. But since they were alone, and the truck was half a block away, Sal just knelt down and abruptly tore open her shirt. He used a pair of trauma shears to snip away her bra and cut through both shirtsleeves so they could start IVs. Yoda arrived with the gear as Sal said, "We're gonna need the Lifepack, man. No Engine means no AED."

Yoda sprinted to the truck and returned with the Lifepack 12-lead cardiac monitor. It was heavy and the size of an old school boom-box. It did everything from blood pressures to SpO2 readings and defibrillation. None of this seemed to phase Yoda. It was why he was here. He stuck one defibrillator pad above her right breast, and the other on the left flank so the electricity, if called for, could flow directly through the heart. They hit the Analyze button and a soothing female voice said, *"No shock advised. Continue CPR."*

People cried and gasped once Psycho Sal started full-blown CPR. It was one thing to see it done on a practice dummy, quite another on a half-naked 78-year-old grandmother in front of her whole family. Ribs, never designed to withstand this kind of two-inch thrusting, grotesquely snapped. Saliva and worse oozed from her mouth and nose. Her eyes, alive just minutes before, were already opaque.

Yoda readied the bag-valve mask to pump oxygen into her lungs.

"Yo." Sal slammed up and down like a piston. "We need a line, bro."

Due to the original miscommunication between the family and 911, which caused the lack of personnel, it was easy to become overwhelmed. Yoda bounced between bagging the patient and trying to set up for the IV, but it took a 12-year-old kid to save the day.

"Can I help?" he asked.

Both Psycho Sal and a woman who must have been the kid's mother, yelled "No!" at the same time

But with too much to do, Yoda scanned the kid like the teacher he used to be. "How old are you?"

"Twelve."

"What's your name?"

"Andre. Andre Barghouti."

"Think you can hold this mask and pump this bag, Andre Barghouti?"

"Yes."

No one else stepped forward.

Yoda looked at Sal who looked at the woman who may or may not have been his mom, but she said nothing.

"I'll help grandma." Andre was too intrigued to be scared. He knelt next to Yoda. "This will help her too."

Yoda said, "See how simple this is? Just like this, every five seconds. See where my hands are? One holds the mask, the other pumps the bag, okay?"

"Okay."

"No one should be in here," Sal said, sweating. "Please go in the other room."

Nobody listened.

Starting IVs on healthy people was never a given, but on people with no pulse it was equal parts skill and miracle. Yoda's growing reputation as an excellent stick-man was definitely on the line. He tied off a tourniquet and hunted for a vein. Through the violence of Sal's CPR, Yoda was operating on a wave-tossed boat. He found a target, used his left hand to lock the arm against the floor, and lined up the 18-gauge needle like a junkie desperate for the flash. He sunk it into her left elbow and the backfilling blood told him he was in. "Got it."

"Strong work, man." Sal was sweating as he pumped her chest. "Game changer."

Yoda hooked up a bag of saline. Then he dove into the drug bag searching for epinephrine. He drew up 1 mg of 1-10,000 and slammed it into the IV port. "Epi's on board."

"Nice, kid. Hit the analyze button." Psycho Sal stopped CPR and dripped sweat as the Lifepack device swept her for any signs of a shockable rhythm. That lovely female voice said, *"No shock advised. Continue CPR."*

"Let me take a turn." Yoda pushed Sal out of the way and started hammering her chest. He tried to avoid staring at the flattened gyrating sacks her breasts had become and had no idea how the family could watch this. Andre, however, seemed fascinated by it all.

"Okay, kid," Sal said, "thanks for the help. Let me slide in." He took over managing the airway. There was no time to intubate her, so he inserted an oropharyngeal device. Shaped like a plastic U, it was designed to keep her tongue from flopping over and blocking her epiglottis. Then he continued bagging her.

"Engine 1 to Rescue 1. What do you need in there?"

Psycho Sal answered, "Backboard and a stretcher to the door."

"Roger."

Psycho Sal stopped bagging her just long enough to inject another round of epinephrine. "Clear out. I'm hitting the analyze button."

Yoda was now dripping sweat. The female voice said, *"No shock advised. Continue CPR."*

Engine 1 appeared with a backboard and straps. They placed the backboard next to her as Yoda banged out the CPR.

"Here..." Psycho Sal handed the IV bag to Mike Suzchecki. Nicknamed "Bugsy" after a bed-bug infested patient he dropped off caused the shutdown of St. Elizabeth's entire Emergency Department, he and Kevin Finnegan, the privates on Engine 1, were both accomplished EMTs. Finnegan had spent five years each working for both Capt. LeClaire and Lt. Killmoor and was regarded as one of the most medically knowledgeable guys on the job. Quiet and circumspect, his punk rock past as a top-step drummer for national hardcore bands was completely impossible to discern. Now balding, and with two kids of his own, he looked like a regular dad, but this dad had superpowers if a drum-set was nearby. Anyone present would then stand in awe of the sudden and violent onslaught furiously unleashed.

They got her on the backboard and strapped her down. They made sure the IV and oxygen lines were accounted for and then carried her out.

Psycho Sal paused a second to scan the room. The mess that got left behind included all the packing ripped off the equipment they had just used, and the family now shattered by everything they never should have seen. He locked eyes with Andre on the way out the door and wished he had not.

In the truck, Sal resecured the 12-lead monitor into its holder and re-checked the pads. He grabbed another round of epinephrine and drew it into the syringe. They hung the IV bag and continued CPR.

"Third epi going in. Clear to analyze."

Again, the monitor swept her for a shockable rhythm, finally found one, and the soothing female voice said, *"Shock advised. Stand clear of the patient."*

"Well, fuck me standing. Everybody clear?" Psycho Sal hit the shock button. Unlike TV or the movies, where the whole body dramatically lifted and flopped, in real time a momentary body-wide twitch and sizzle was the only evidence the electricity left behind.

The soothing voice said, *"Attempt unsuccessful. Continue CPR."*

Psycho Sal said, "Looks like she might've switched into V-fib for a second. Let's get 300 of amiodarone ready just in case." He looked at Kevin Finnegan. "What do you think, Finn?"

"Man, I don't know. You've done everything. You check her sugar?"

Yoda grabbed the glucometer and ten seconds later said, "BG 113."

"Doesn't get any better than that," Finnegan said.

"I doubt she OD'd."

"You can push some Narcan. Nothing can hurt you when you're already dead."

Two minutes later, Bugsy was knocking out the CPR when the monitor said, *"Analyze rhythm."*

Sal said, "Everybody clear."

"Shock advised," the monitor said.

"Stand back." Sal hit the button and she twitched and sizzled again. He watched the monitor and said, "Holy shit, look at that beautiful thing." Sal watched a healthy P-wave and QRS complex continuously scroll across the screen. He grabbed her wrist and felt for a pulse. "There she is. Holy fuck, she's back."

"Hot damn." Yoda, drenched in sweat even though it was twenty degrees outside, high-fived everyone in the truck.

"Bugsy," Sal said. "Get us out of here, man."

"Roger." Bugsy jumped out and got behind the wheel. He grabbed the mic and said, "Rescue 1 to Fire Alarm. Transporting to Saint E's with two men from the engine."

"Rescue 1's transporting with two men from Engine 1 at 1512."

They got a round of vital signs before Psycho Sal triggered his mic and said, "Rescue 1 to Fire Alarm. Notify Saint E's we're coming in with a 78-year-old female found in witnessed cardiac arrest. IV established, three rounds of epi on board, shocked twice, we now have a sinus rhythm. BP 90/60, pulse 98, SpO2 98%, BG 113. We're four minutes out."

"Roger, Rescue 1, notifying them now."

"Hang on, grandma," Psycho Sal told her. "We're almost there."

Three minutes later they backed into St. Elizabeth's. Thirty seconds after that they sped her into Critical Care One where the crash team was gloved up and ready. Sal gave them the story while Bugsy, Yoda, and Finnegan transferred her to the bed and switched over the oxygen and cardiac monitor to the hospital equipment. Once they withdrew, the doctors and nurses surged forward.

When Psycho Sal finished giving his report, he stepped out into the cold for a much-needed cigarette and ran right into the just arriving Barghouti family.

"Please!" her son cried out. "How is she?"

"What's your name?"

"Solomon Barghouti."

"Okay, Solomon, I'm Sal. Before we left we got a pulse back—"

"Praise God!"

"Wait. This doesn't mean—"

"Thank you, Sal!"

Psycho Sal winced when Solomon Barghouti wrapped him in a joyous hug before turning to his family and exclaiming, "She's alive!"

"Praise God!" everyone yelled.

"Please, I've seen this before," Sal shook his head. "Even with a pulse she's a very sick woman. There are never guarantees."

"Can we see her?"

"They're working on her now, so I would go to the front desk through those doors and ask them. Once it's okay they'll let you through."

"Thank you, Sal! May God bless you!"

"Yeah, thanks. You too." Psycho Sal greedily sucked on the cigarette as if it might be the last one he would ever have.

***

Because of the severity of the call, it took forty-five minutes to restock the rescue and complete a detailed run report.

Back in the truck, Psycho Sal said, "Don't think we're gonna catch the end of Goodfellas."

"I'd say not." Yoda steered them through the beginning of the evening rush hour. "I can't believe the sun's already setting and it ain't even four o'clock."

"Winter blows."

"Wanna get a coffee at Soléil?"

"Yes, please. That place is always stacked with yummy mommies." Sal was texting someone as he said, "I feel bad for that family."

"Why?"

"Because that kid's gonna grow up to be a serial killer. Could you have done that to your own grandma?"

"Probably not. But why serial killer? Maybe he'll become a doctor."

"Sure he will. He'll become the next serial killing doctor."

"Jesus..."

"Even if she somehow pulls through, which she probably won't, she's gonna wake up to a chest-full of broken ribs."

"I didn't even think of that."

"It won't matter. They say 8% survive, but nine times out of ten we're just creating organ donors." Psycho Sal lit a cigarette. "You know, for the last couple of months, I've been riding you pretty hard..."

"And...? Wait a second. Were you about to compliment me?"

"I really didn't want to."

"This must be killing you. To not be an asshole for even one minute?"

Psycho Sal could receive as good as he gave, so he only smiled and said, "You're doing it right. Tomorrow you might turn into a total bag of shit, but enjoy it for now."

"That's the worst compliment I've ever heard. Even when you're trying to be nice you're a complete douche."

Sal laughed and returned to his phone.

Soléil Coffeehouse was just across the Providence line. An upscale clientele unfolded after work, warming up from the cold.

They got online for coffee as Sal said, "What a racket. Five bucks for a freaking cup of coffee..."

"Why don't you say that a little louder, that way they can take a dump in our coffee."

"In some countries that's considered a delicacy."

The lady behind them burst out laughing. "I'm sorry. I was trying not to eavesdrop."

"Looks like you failed." Psycho Sal, with that one drop of blood in the water, zeroed in. He was a good-looking guy with a series of disastrous relationships behind him. "You feel like buying one of America's heroes a five-dollar cup of coffee?"

"What about me?" Yoda asked.

"You're married. Buy your own."

Sal switched places with Yoda to get closer to the woman. "What's your name?"

"Melissa." She was in a pants-suit and had long black hair. "You?"

"They call me Tri-pod, but you'll never guess why—"

"Somebody help!" The scream came from the front of the store.

"Please no." Psycho Sal closed his eyes. "I just wanted a cup of coffee."

"He collapsed! Somebody help!"

Sal shielded his eye and turned away as if trying to hide himself from view.

Disgusted, Yoda said, "You really are an asshole."

Outside on the slushy sidewalk, Psycho Sal could not believe his eyes. *"Pete?"*

"Ah-ha-ha-ha! You cocksuckas!" Laying on the ground was Pete DeAngelis, the DUI victim with the head injury.

Psycho Sal said, "This can't be happening."

"Bus pass!" Pete slurped out of the right side of his mouth. "I have a bus pass! Ah-ha-ha!"

Any of the bystanders convinced this was an actual emergency suddenly felt used.

"God help me." Psycho Sal looked to the heavens as if summoning strength. "This must be a test. I even have to pick you up in freaking *Providence*!"

"I want to go to Galilee! That's where all the Jews are!"

Yoda laughed before he could stop himself because no one in the crowd was smiling.

"C'mon, dude." Psycho Sal reached down and grabbed Pete's good hand. "We're gonna get you on your feet, okay? You hurting anywhere?"

"No."

"Okay. Here we go. On three…"

They got him up but he immediately buckled and yelped, "My knee!"

"Okay, all right, we're gonna set you down and get the stretcher."

Fortunately, the rescue was illegally parked on the corner, but they had to pull the stretcher around a snowbank.

"Okay, Pete, cross your arms. We're gonna head-to-toe you." Sal reached under both armpits. Yoda grabbed his feet and they lifted him onto the stretcher.

Yoda said, "He's soaked from the slush."

"We'll get a blanket on him after we get him in the bus." Sal grabbed Pete's cane before they wheeled him to the truck. "Besides, Saint E's is right around the corner."

Psycho Sal splinted the leg and cued the mic on his portable radio. "Rescue 1 to Fire Alarm."

"Go Rescue 1."

"We are in and out of service. We cleared Saint E's and were flagged down by passersby for a man down. We are now transporting back to Saint E's."

"Rescue 1 transporting at 1602."

"The Jews will fix me!"

"We're not going to Galilee, Pete, so calm down with all the Jew talk, will ya?"

They backed into the ER two minutes later. Preoccupied, Psycho Sal was scribbling out the run report on the back of the stretcher as they wheeled it in. But when the doors whooshed open it was already too late. Critical Care One was the room closest to the door. Inside, a sheet was pulled over her body as the Barghouti family cried and hugged each other.

Psycho Sal just wanted to disappear. Instead, he locked eyes with Solomon Barghouti but blinked first, unable to absorb anymore pain.

***

Neither one of them were expecting to go home anytime soon. Yoda especially. As one of the junior men in the Second Battalion, he was getting held and ordered to stay after nearly every shift. And with both Cadillac Frank and Super-Wop out tonight, Yoda and Psycho Sal were preparing to spend another twenty-four hours together on Rescue 1.

The Alert Tone hit and Fire Alarm announced, *"Attention Rescue 1. Still Alarm. 15 Conway Drive. Male with abdominal pain..."*

Psycho Sal got into the truck. "So it begins."

"More like never ends."

"Ten hours down. Twenty-four more to go." Sal grabbed the mic. "Rescue 1 responding."

"Rescue 1 responding at 1705."

Outside it was rush hour and 23-degrees. On Conway Drive, they found Alessio Moncrief, a professionally attired black man cradling his abdomen. His vitals were normal, he had no allergies to food or medication, and had not eaten anything immediately suspicious.

Psycho Sal said, "Show me where it hurts."

Moncrief, laying on the stretcher, pointed at his belly.

Psycho Sal snapped on gloves. "I'm gonna palpate it." He started at the navel and immediately felt a firm distension. Moncrief moaned in pain. Sal inched his hands up and felt the same mass. He was stumped. "You take a crap today?"

"Yes. This morning. Please, man, it really hurts."

"We'll have to let the doctors do their thing, buddy. I honestly have no idea what to tell you."

At St. Elizabeth's, he handed off care to Charge Nurse Mary Durando.

A salty sort, Durando had been a nurse for thirty years. She never said she had seen it all, but few had seen more. "C'mon, Sal. Belly pain? You're usually good for a stabbing or two."

"Careful what you wish for. I still got twenty-four more to go."

"Great. Thankfully, I only have ten more hours of this nonsense."

"I don't know. You felt it. His belly's all spasmed up, right?"

"Denies falling?"

"No traumatic mechanism at all."

"Any past-history?"

"None. No allergies, no meds, and took a dump this morning. What's the medical term for that?"

"Shitting."

"Right." Sal grinned. "You're like the only person left on this planet I don't want to kill."

"Speaking of killing. Your buddy Pete's back there driving us all nuts. He hasn't stopped insulting us since he got here."

"Stop shocking me. What's his story?"

"Doctors think he sprained his knee. I'll pay you twenty bucks if you take him to Ocean State next time."

He handed her the metal contractor case. The run report was on the front awaiting her signature. He detached her copy and said, "Please give him my regards."

"I'll be your friend forever if you bring me back an ice coffee next time."

"Promises, promises…"

Out in the truck, Yoda handed him a piece of paper. "Almost forgot. This was on the seat when we left the coffeeshop with Pete."

Psycho Sal laughed and read it aloud. "'Dear Tri-pod. I'm sorry we couldn't continue our conversation but, alas, duty calls. Speaking of calls, here's my number. Melissa.'"

"Can't say she doesn't have a sense of humor."

Sal balled up the note and tossed it out the window. "Figured I just saved her from wrecking her own life."

"Talk about dodging bullets. She doesn't even know how lucky she just got."

Psycho Sal said into the mic, "Rescue 1 back in."

"Rescue 1's back in service at 1735."

"Where to now?" Yoda asked.

"Store. I gotta get some smokes. Murphy's is coming up on the left."

"That's a liquor store..."

"So what?"

"So we're in uniform driving a freaking ambulance."

"Don't be such a dork." Psycho Sal zipped up his black bomber jacket and hopped out.

Yoda frowned. Sal had been coming apart for weeks, but drinking on the clock was only the most recent nightmare.

When Sal exited the store, he was on his cellphone. Chain-smoking allowed him to avoid eye contact. It was only 5:45 P.M. but already black outside. After he got into the truck, he said, "Spring can't come soon enough."

Yoda said nothing. He started heading back to the station.

As Psycho Sal smacked the fresh pack against his palm, he flared smoke from both nostrils like a dragon. "Any idea what the engine guys are cooking for dinner?"

Yoda stared at the road.

"Okay..." Ignored again, Sal scrolled through his phone.

Yoda said, "You know how they say you can't smell vodka on someone's breath?"

"I told you I needed smokes—"

"My name's on that run report too, you know. You ever think about that?"

"First of all, mind your own business. Second, fuck off."

"Great. That's great. Some partner—"

"I'm your *boss*." Psycho Sal flicked away the cigarette. "That's probably something you shouldn't forget."

***

They got back to the station and immediately blew each other off. The engine guys had no idea what had happened and did not ask, so they ate dinner without them. In close quarters, with crews that spent months and years together, these ruptures occasionally occurred. Some were harmless and quickly resolved. But others could take down whole stations, especially if other shifts started choosing sides.

They hid in their rooms until Fire Alarm hit the Alert Tone and announced, *"Attention Rescue 1, Engine 2. Still alarm. Armistice Tower. 136 Eisenhower Avenue..."*

Through the decades, Sachem City had built five high-rise buildings to house the indigent, the elderly, the handicapped, and others in need of assistance. At eighteen-stories, the Armistice Tower was the tallest in the city. Medically, for the fire department, these were very busy buildings.

"Engine 2 to Rescue 1. Use caution. Frequent flyer."

Inside Rescue 1, nothing was said on the way over, nothing as they pulled out the stretcher, and nothing during the long elevator ride up to the twelfth-floor.

Engine 2 was looking to bust balls until they saw the dour faces approaching down the long hallway.

"Whaddaya got?" Psycho Sal asked.

"Flying Freddy." Lt. Salamanca held open the apartment door.

Frederick Wolitznaya was the son of two Polish émigrés who arrived in Boston in 1958. Accomplished Olympic gymnasts, they were also broke, so they immediately went to work. The father got a job on a concrete gang pouring foundations, and the mother became a seamstress. Neither job suited them, so when the circus came to town, they saw a different way to prosper. Husband and wife became, in less politically correct days, 'The Flying Pollacks,' and specialized in various highwire acts.

Psycho Sal said, "Thought I recognized the apartment number. Hey, Fred, what's going on, man?"

Frederick Wolitznaya was balding in front but had a long grey ponytail. He was only 50-years-old yet already in failing health. He, too, had been a highwire performer until a fall ten years ago paralyzed him from the waist down. He had lived such a well-traveled life, the firefighters always loved hearing his obscene stories.

"They switched up my heart meds," he now said, squinting into the hallway light. "Something ain't right."

Yoda asked, "Do you have any chest—"

"If you don't mind, private, I'll triage the patient." Psycho Sal let the reprimand linger. "So when did they switch up your heart meds?"

"Yesterday. I got home with the new pills, but something ain't been right since."

"Well, you're already on meds for CHF, high blood pressure, edema, diabetes... maybe they're just not playing nice together with this new drug. Any chest pain with the pressure?"

"Just a heaviness."

"Not related to the CHF?"

"Doesn't feel like it."

Psycho Sal turned to Lt. Salamanca and said, "We're all set."

"Sure?"

"Yeah, man. Like Killmoor says, 'low stress EMS.'"

Engine 2 headed for the elevators.

Sal said, "Okay, my friend, we're gonna load you up. Everything off in your apartment?"

"Yes."

"You got your cellphone and keys?"

"Yes."

They pushed the stretcher down the hall. The elevator made for tight quarters.

The silence grew uncomfortable, so Yoda asked, "Why do they call you Flying Freddy?"

"You must be new. I used to be in the circus. I was born in a railcar somewhere between Cleveland and Kansas City." Despite his discomfort, Frederick Wolitznaya smiled a yellow-toothed grin. "You ever hear of Sam Patch?"

"No."

"He was America's first daredevil. Grew up right here in Sachem City. Born 1807. Back then, they sent the kids to work in the mills. He and the other kids spun cotton twelve hours a day. Got their fingers and arms sometimes ripped off because of it, which is how the unions came to be. But anyway, those kids led dreary lives, so after work, Patch would jump off the Blackstone Mill into the Massasoit River just to entertain his friends. Eventually, he traveled across the whole northeast jumping off dams, bridges, and ship masts."

The elevator opened onto a lobby filled with the retired, the infirm, and those medicated into zombies.

Flying Freddy continued, "He became known as the 'Yankee Leaper—'"

"Are you busting our balls?" Sal asked as they wheeled him out. "You've never told me this story before."

"The Yankee Leaper. Look it up. He became famous in 1829 when he jumped off Niagara Falls in front of 10,000 people and survived."

"So he just traveled around jumping off shit for money?"

"Yup. And drinking. He was known for his legendary thirst."

"I can almost picture how this ends. Hang on, we're gonna load you in."

As a practiced routine, Yoda lifted the stretcher as Sal lifted its legs. They joined him in the back and began gathering his vital signs.

"You have to remember," Freddy said, "back then there were only newspapers and word of mouth, but news still traveled fast. When the Yankee Leaper came to town, people would make a whole day of it because that was their entertainment. The traveling shows and circuses were all they had. He would sometimes make two or three jumps in a single day."

Psycho Sal said, "Sounds like a total nutcase. Listen, my partner's gonna start an IV, okay?"

"Sure."

"So..." Yoda got out the materials needed to start the IV and tied off the tourniquet. He searched for a vein and said, "So how does he jump off Niagara Falls? Did he just go over the edge?"

"No. Hell no. They rigged a platform forty-feet in the air. That made his actual jump 120-feet. He walked out to the edge of this swaying nightmare and just jumped."

"Dear Jesus."

"Yeah, he didn't care. Had zero fear. He even jumped off a hotel in Baltimore and landed in the Patapsco River. He was only 19-years-old when his three-year reign as the Yankee Leaper began."

"IV's done," Yoda said without looking at his boss. "Twenty-gauge in the left AC."

Psycho Sal said, "Guess boozing, jumping off shit, and banging chicks is better than getting his fingers ripped off in a loom. So what happened?"

"Well, he ended up in Rochester, New York, for a jump, but didn't make enough money. He scheduled another for a week later. 8,000 people showed up for that one. He even built a twenty-five-foot stand above the 100-foot falls. 125 feet. But spectators there that day said something went wrong. He either tripped or fell, so he didn't enter feet first. They never saw him again."

"How old was he when he died?"

"Twenty-two."

"What a nutbag."

"I don't know," Yoda added. "There's something to be said about getting paid to travel the country, and the only thing you have to do is nearly commit suicide once a week."

Sal said, "Okay, Fred, don't move. All those pads we stuck to your chest are gonna take a picture of your heart."

The 12-lead printed out the verdict. Psycho Sal read the strip and said, "Good news is that you're not having a heart attack. The pressure you're describing is probably related to your CHF. But right now you're

96% on room air." He looked at Yoda for the first time since their disagreement. "Maybe put him on a nasal cannula for comfort?"

"Roger." Yoda affixed it to Freddy's face. "So you were in the circus. Is that how you got injured?"

"Nope. Jumped off the Hernando De Soto Bridge in Memphis, Tennessee, for no good reason. At the time I was dating a woman named Sad Sue, and we'd been drinking all day. We were in town for a bunch of shows. Anyway, same thing happened to me. Broke the surface at a bad angle and that was that."

"You're a freaking madman," Psycho Sal said. "I love it."

"Die how you live, you know? Punish that shit."

Yoda finally made eye contact with Sal. "Anything else?"

"Naw, man, good to go. Saint E's it is."

"You got it." Yoda opened the door and jumped down. He said to Flying Freddy, "Riding in the back of one of these things might make you think bridge diving's safer."

"You're a funny guy."

Yoda slammed the door and hopped behind the wheel.

"Cheers." Psycho Sal pulled out two vodka nips and handed one to Freddy. "Die how you live."

They clinked bottles and Sal drained his out in one swallow. Then he slowly smiled.

***

Charge Nurse Mary Durando was eagerly awaiting their arrival at St. Elizabeth's. After Flying Freddy was processed, she dragged them both into X-Ray and said, "Remember Mr. Belly Pain?"

Psycho Sal was chomping gum. "Yeah..."

She killed the lights. The X-Ray on the wall displayed a pelvis and ribcage.

"What's..." Sal squinted.

"That," Mary said, "is a can of Aqua Net."

"What're you talking about." Yoda stepped closer. "You mean he—"

"Shoved it up his ass, yup, right up the ass. He finally came clean. Said it got sucked right in when he lost his grip from all the lube."

"A can of *Aqua Net?*" Sal grinned. "That's probably the biggest aerosol can on the market. Sick prick."

"How is that even possible?" Yoda was captivated by the image. It looked like a missile silo shoved inside a sock. "But there it is. Right in black and white. This guy lubed up a giant can of hairspray and somehow jammed it up his own ass. Incredible."

Psycho Sal said, "He definitely knows how to party."

Mary's laugh was distinctive and contagious. "I'm no doctor, but experience dictates that 30-year-old men with sudden onset 'unknown' belly pain usually equals something shoved up the ass every time."

"He did," Sal said, "he lied right to our faces."

"Well, wouldn't you?" Yoda asked. "If two strangers showed up at my house after I shoved God knows what up my ass, you can bet I'm gonna take the fifth."

"What room's he in?" Sal asked. "There's no way I can see this guy and not burst out laughing."

"That," Mary said, "will not be happening."

"Are they gonna operate?"

"Don't know. But I would say they almost have to. Dilating the sphincter that much...?"

"This dude's in for a bad couple of hours. Speaking of which." He looked at Yoda. "You hungry? We kind of missed dinner."

"How can you talk about dinner and sphincters at the same time?"

"It's a gift." Psycho Sal winked at Mary. "See what I do for you? You asked for a stabbing but instead got a guy with a submarine shoved up his ass. I just made your whole night."

She called out after them, "I'd rather you bring me back that ice coffee!"

"It's past eight o'clock. I don't want to keep you up all night."

"Jerk! I'm gonna be up all night anyway!"

"This isn't good-bye, Mary. The night's way too young for that."

"I hate you, Sal Giametti!"

"Huh," Yoda deadpanned, "bet you never heard that before."

The automatic doors whooshed open as Sal's cackle turned to smoke in the frozen night.

***

By the time they ate dinner it was nine o'clock. This post rush-hour lull usually lasted until the intoxicated started making bad decisions. Some nightshifts did not really begin until midnight and then ran until dawn. As always, the rescue played no favorites and accepted no excuses.

"Mind if we stop by my place?" Psycho Sal asked. "Gotta let the dog out."

"We've been partners for seven months and I didn't even know you had a dog."

"You never asked."

The Downtown Feeder, as it was called, had been built in 1868, forty years before the first automobile. It was originally designed as a half-mile trolley loop through downtown. Rents were always high as businesses competed for this limited store-front space. After church, families would spend Sunday afternoons having lunch, strolling, and shopping. But once the mills and their supporting businesses closed, the Feeder became an abandoned loop to nowhere. The trolley was long gone, the street was too small for most trucks and two-way traffic, so this limited one-way access with no parking doomed any future redevelopment. Now, multi-story ornate brick buildings stood like sentinels filled with ghosts. This left the homeless and the addicted to scuttle amongst the doorways like shadowy creatures trying to feed.

With rents so cheap, some of these spaces were illegally occupied. Hearty souls put up with spotty electrical service and plumbing that barely worked.

Psycho Sal said, "Just park it here."

"Here? Right on the corner?"

"Put it on the sidewalk. No one cares."

"Don't take this the wrong way, but this is where you live?"

"Guess you've never been divorced. Twice."

Yoda locked the rescue and followed him in. The sound of dripping water echoed down the dark hallways. The first-floor was all abandoned office space. Gold leaf descriptions of the small businesses they used to contain had a distinctive 1950's feel.

"Reminds me of Mad Men," Yoda said. "Except they had lights that worked."

"Don't be such a snob."

They started climbing an open stairway to the fifth-floor.

"It's freezing in here." Yoda ran his flashlight across the ornate wood-work. "What a shame. Shit like this will never be built again."

"Hey, Bob Villa, who gives a fuck?"

"This is your floor?" Yoda stepped around parts of the ceiling. "This place is like a horror movie. There's like one bulb down the whole hallway."

"Works out perfect, since I'm the only one up here."

"There's exposed wiring..."

"Come on, princess, we're almost there."

"I can't imagine what you're paying for rent."

"Three-hundred cash."

"That's two-hundred-and-ninety-nine too much."

Behind three deadbolts, the apartment had two bedrooms, a kitchen, and a wide-open common space. The windows were from 1872 and completely custom. Knee-height to ceiling, they afforded a panoramic view of downtown once considered spectacular.

Yoda looked around. "I don't see any dog."

"Oh yeah, my ex-wife has the dog tonight."

"Sal—"

"Just let me grab some socks and boxers. We might be working straight through."

"Why didn't you just say that?"

"Because I like to fuck with you."

Yoda looked around and saw a couch and the largest flat-screen TV he had ever seen. That was it for furniture. Everything else was strewn across the floor. He called out, "Place looks great. You really went all out."

"That's what everybody tells me." He reappeared with a plastic grocery bag. "Good to go."

"How can you live like this?"

"Like what? Like a 38-year-old who's lost everything twice?"

"You must have a horrible lawyer."

"You ain't kidding. What about you and the wife? Got a pre-nup?"

"No. We met in high school and have been together since."

"Huh. Good thing I have plenty of floor space. We'll have to get you a mattress for after your divorce."

"I don't know what's worse—the thought of losing the love of my life, or sleeping on your floor."

Sal opened the refrigerator and pulled out two beers. "Come on."

"Where we—"

"Just follow me."

The roof access was at the top of the stairwell. It was not even locked, so Sal just kicked it open. The frozen night instantly blew through. From here they could see City Hall and, behind that, the Massasoit River. The rhythmic rumble of I-95 and the S-curves were two blocks away. "What a view," Yoda said.

"Here." Psycho Sal handed him a beer. "For safety, everyone must be in on the conspiracy."

"I'm not drinking, dude. Forget it."

"Then just a sip."

"No. But I'm no rat, so stop worrying."

"One sip."

"I appreciate it, but I worked too hard to get here, man. Besides, I'm the one driving."

A frozen wind forced them both to shudder.

"Suit yourself." Sal pounded the beer.

"You know how this ends, right?"

"Where?"

"On the front page. Or in handcuffs. Or both."

"You're more dramatic than any chick I've ever known."

Yoda slowly shook his head. He looked at all the lights whizzing by on the highway. "You're a grown man. Half our job is picking up addicts and drunks—"

"I'm not a drunk."

"Semantics, man."

"What's a semantic?"

"It means confusion from different words describing the same thing."

"Easy, Webster, I'm just going through some shit. That's all."

"We're fucking partners. If you can't talk to me—"

"Things ain't good with my family, all right? My mom's been sick."

"Okay, take it easy."

"I don't like talking about this shit. Ever."

"Fire Alarm to Rescue 1."

Psycho Sal finished the beer and crushed it into the gravel roof. He toggled the mic and said, "Rescue 1."

"Are you available for a run?"

"That's a roger."

"158 Balkcom Street. Possible heart."

"Roger."

Fire Alarm hit the Alert Tone and said, *"That's Rescue 1, Engine 2. Still Alarm. 158 Balkcom Street..."*

"Let's go, junior, time to save the world."

Yoda took one last look around. "This city's got a helluva lot of ghosts."

"And new ones get added every day." Sal held the door open. "Isn't this run for a possible heart?"

"Aw, man, don't jinx the poor guy."

Inside, the stairwell was dark and cold.

***

Because it was after ten o'clock and the stations were on night mode, Fire Alarm called the rescue phones at Station 1 and said, "143 Needham. Well-being check. Police are on-scene. Possible forced entry. We're sending the 2's with you."

Psycho Sal said, "Don't bother. We'll call for the engine if we need them."

When they arrived, they saw a darkened police car parked in front of a brick apartment building.

Sal said into the mic, "Rescue 1 on-scene with police."

"Rescue 1 on-scene with police at 2342."

Like the fire trucks, the rescues carried master keys to access all Knox Boxes. By city ordinance, to assure the public that illegal entry and searches were off the table, the police had no access to the Knox Box without the fire department. Psycho Sal opened it and removed the keys to the building. "Can't believe it ain't even midnight yet."

The policeman, Sergeant Karmic Lansdowne, met them in the lobby. While most cops were by the book disciplinarians, Lansdowne did not fit this mold at all. He often said he had taken the wrong test and should have been a firefighter. Stuck in a patrol car because he could not pass the detective's test, his legendary black humor was known to lighten even the most awful scenes.

"What's up, kid?" Psycho Sal slapped his hand. "How's Cindy doing?"

"Great, man. Kids are great, too. You know Alice is gonna be ten this year?"

"That's incredible."

"Seems like just yesterday we were all hanging out by the fire."

Psycho Sal looked at Yoda and then pointed at Officer Lansdowne. "Friends before divorce number one."

"Yeah..." Lansdowne appeared wistful. "That first divorce was something special. A total and complete bloodbath, only to be out-done by your second."

"Yeah, man, number two was a total *bruiser*. So what do we got?"

"Explaining will do it no justice. Follow me." Lansdowne headed for the stairs. "The call came in as a noise complaint from the neighbor. I've been smashing on the door for the last ten minutes. Nothing."

"How do you know there's even someone in there?"

"Just wait. Seriously, you're not gonna believe this."

When they got to the third-floor, Sal frowned. "Is that..."

"Sounds like two people humping," Yoda said.

At 4K, the wails of fornication were loudly confirmed.

A neighbor appeared in a bathrobe and said, "It's been going on for an hour. He usually works second-shift, so I'm used to him being up late, but this is a little ridiculous."

"Someone's getting absolutely pounded in there." Psycho Sal knocked one last time before inserting the master key. "Sachem City Fire Department! We're coming in!"

The door swung open. Lansdowne went first, hand on his gun. "Hello! Police! Oh, God..."

A pornographic film was playing on a flat screen across from a white man with a purple face. He was kneeling, naked, and well-built. One end of a cord was tied around his neck, the other was knotted around a doorknob. Leaning forward, all the force was in his neck.

"Oh holy Jesus Christ." The neighbor had walked in too far. "Is he *dead*?"

Psycho Sal felt the neck. It was ice cold and the skin was already mottled.

Officer Lansdowne said, "You see the crank on this guy?"

Sal grinned. "What a waste."

"That thing's gotta be a foot long."

"It's impressive."

"I mean I don't even want my own dick after seeing this one."

The neighbor had wide eyes. "You guys are terrible."

"Really?" Lansdowne nodded at it. "*Really?*"

A woman suddenly yelped. She, too, wore a matching bathrobe.

The neighbor yelled, "Honey! Don't look! He's dead!"

"Is that..." She squinted. "Oh my."

"See?" Lansdowne said.

"What?" She clinched her robe closed and blushed.

Psycho Sal said, "Both of you need to get out of here."

They left.

Psycho Sal said, "Rescue 1 to Fire Alarm."

"Go Rescue 1."

"This is going to be a police matter. Time on-scene?"

"2342."

"Roger." He turned to Yoda. "Can you find the remote and turn down all this fucking?"

"Yeah, please hurry," Lansdowne said. "I'm starting to get all horned out."

"You see a wallet anywhere? Who is this guy?"

"Don't touch anything."

"Easy, Quincy, this ain't foul play. Dude choked himself out smashing the clown."

Lansdowne said, "I just don't understand this fetish. I mean does everything have to kill you in order for it to be enjoyable?"

"I think he has a butt-plug. Tonight must be ass-play night. Earlier we had a guy with a can of Aqua Net shoved up his ass."

"The indecency of death."

"Oh, he wasn't dead, but he probably wishes he was."

Yoda had seen enough. "I'll be in the truck."

"Yeah, man, we're out of here."

Lansdowne frowned. "You guys are just gonna leave me here alone with *this*?"

"Figured you could use some time for reflection before the M.E. gets here."

Out in the truck, Yoda could only stare ahead. "It would be hard to imagine a worse way to be found dead."

"Oh, lighten up. What's he care? He's never gonna see this hellhole again." Psycho Sal grabbed the mic. "Rescue 1's back in service. Police matter."

"Rescue 1 back in at 2358."

"All of this ass-play does not bode well for the rest of the night. We might be in for a real shafting."

"Please, can we go five minutes without any ass or penis references?"

"No promises." Psycho Sal lit a cigarette. "But it pays to be an optimist."

INTO THIN AIR

January 8, 2010

In the four days since Governor Carvalho's phone call, Receiver Till-inghast had been concerned with only one thing—finding a way to save face. More troublesome, however, were the governor's veiled threats dictating the parameters of the increasingly shrinking cage in which he was left to maneuver.

When he awoke Friday morning to news that federal prosecutors would be formally indicting the mayor of Providence, three state repre-sentatives, noted private businessmen, and various political operatives in a "pay-to-play" employment scheme, his chance finally appeared. Kick-backs and graft were nothing new to the Ocean State, but the implosion of the Providence mayor, a charismatic wonder-kid already being touted for a Congressional seat, provided a blinding distraction. Right after the eleven o'clock news Friday night, Receiver Tillinghast released a two-sentence statement. "With the best interests of the citizens of Sachem City in mind, it has been determined that current conditions preclude experimentations with vital city services. Considering this conclusion, the privatization of city 911 medical responses is no longer in consideration."

STRANGE BEDFELLOWS

January 9, 2010

Union President Lt. Ahearn was on the phone with Association of Rhode Island Firefighters President Vinny Szceriack the following morning. He said to him, "No idea whatsoever. This guy operates in a total vacuum."

Szceriack said, "Carvalho must've squeezed him. She's the only one he answers to."

"Absolutely."

"He can't even ask you for anything in return, either, because he's the one who voided all the contracts."

"Right? She bitch-slapped him for us—for free."

"Imagine that? You guys might even have to support her next year."

"You're a really funny guy."

Szceriack chuckled. "Our Receiver informed us yesterday he was cutting minimum-manning. We go from nine guys on shift to seven. And if two guys are out on a rescue run, we show up at a house fire with four guys and a B.C."

"At least you know what your life's worth."

"A private makes $200 a shift."

"400 bucks."

Szceriack said, "Make sure you tell them that at my memorial service."

"I love how he waited until midnight on a Friday. After all the protests, after all the arrests, now everything's just gonna disappear and blow away."

"Like it never happened."

"Like it never happened." Lt. Ahearn was still digesting the news. "Good thing it ain't April 1, because no one would've ever believed this."

YOU CAN'T SAVE THEM ALL

January 12, 2010

"Attention Rescue 2, Engine 4, still alarm. Big Burger Restaurant, 1253 John Adams Boulevard, possible overdose..."

Lt. Killmoor met T-Bag at the truck. They were parked in the ambulance bay at St. Elizabeth's. Lt. Killmoor said, "Time to raise the dead."

"Praise Jesus..."

"Rescue 2 responding from Saint Elizabeth's." Lt. Killmoor hung up the mic. "Not a good omen at the start of the nightshift."

"Especially not at Big Burger."

"That's reverse racism. White folks need their drugs too."

T-Bag floored it down John Adams Boulevard, a main artery that ran north/south from East Providence all the way to Attleboro. Its four lanes and dense surrounding population made it one of the busiest roads in the state. It also had no shoulders or middle lane for turning, so the ensuing car wrecks were spectacular. And for those foolhardy enough to ride a bicycle on a shoulder-less thoroughfare, another despicable human trait became quickly revealed—the hit and run. The utter disregard for human life by normal people was still something the newbies were adjusting to. They saw that in order to survive, most veterans had seared away their disgust and shock long before.

"Easy..." Lt. Killmoor braced himself between the door and armrest. "We're not gonna be helping anybody out by dying ourselves."

"You know, for a guy named *Kill-more*, you certainly are kind of a wuss."

"I'm the kind of wuss that wants to see his wife at the end of the shift."

"Lieutenant Wuss-more."

"Oh sorry, I actually have something to live for."

T-Bag cackled loudly as they slalomed lane to lane. "Is it Irish?"

"Scotch-Irish."

"Great name if you're a cop, but not so reassuring for a rescue lieutenant."

"Engine 4 to Rescue 2."

Lt. Killmoor grabbed the mic. "Go ahead."

"We have a 26-year-old female. Pinpoint pupils. Cyanotic with agonal breathing. Narcan's going on-board."

"Roger. Two minutes out." Lt. Killmoor looked at T-Bag and said, "Was that Chunks using all those big words?"

"What is it with OD'ing in the bathroom? This happens all the time."

"Anything near I-95 is fair game. Providence has enough heat already, so most of the drugs coming up from New York or south from Boston get broken down for distribution in Sachem City and C.F. Gangs meet up with cartel couriers and sell out of abandoned houses. Then the addicts take the drugs into the nearby restaurant bathrooms and shoot up." He grabbed the mic. "Rescue 2 on-scene."

"Rescue 2's on-scene at 1806."

It was the height of the dinner crush, so Big Burger was packed. Inside, Engine 4 had the bathroom door propped open. Curious bystanders ate their burgers standing up.

"Let's go, people," Lt. Killmoor said, "make a hole."

They pulled the stretcher through the crowd.

Inside the bathroom, Harry "Chunks" Paulson was transferred in charge of Engine 4 with Mikey Doneen and Cheeseburger.

"Look at this crew." Lt. Killmoor nodded. "What's up with the patient, Doctor Harry? Did I hear you say pinpoint and cyanotic in the same sentence?"

Chunks laughed. "Da fuck, right? I can't take credit for any of that. Mikey and Cheese got this all squared away. I'm just the monkey with the radio."

"What do we got, Mikey?"

"Two milligrams of Narcan intra-nasal. We were gonna go for a line and give her more because she was circling the drain. Pulse was 32, SpO2 was 62%. Once we started bagging her O2 came up to 92%. Her breathing and color are coming back. I've had her before but I can't remember her name."

"That her needle there? Be careful. Let's pull her out of the stall."

They grabbed her feet and dragged her out by the sinks.

Mikey Doneen and Cheeseburger got the IV while T-Bag drew up more Narcan.

Lt. Killmoor went through her purse until he found her license. "Deborah Paddington. 10/4/84."

"Cute girl," Cheeseburger said.

"Not for long." Looking for a vein, Mikey Doneen got a flash, backed the needle out, and took the line from Cheeseburger. "Right, Lou? Doesn't take long."

"No, it does not." Lt. Killmoor handed the license to the policewoman that had just arrived. "Remember Grace?"

Mikey Doneen nodded. "I caught the tail end of Grace. Guys said she used to be a freaking knockout."

"She was. She was such a good kid, too. How much you loading in?"

"Another deuce?"

"Sounds good."

Mikey Doneen pushed two more milligrams of Narcan into one of the ports on the IV line.

T-Bag asked, "What happened to Grace?"

Lt. Killmoor said, "First time I had her she was OD'd near Asshole Tree, 18-years-old. She was from the suburbs until the guy she was dating started partying hard. Six months later she was strung out on the street. We watched her slowly die for a decade. By the end she was a diseased mess."

"That's being kind. Here comes Deb." Mikey Doneen pointed at her fluttering eyelids. "Pulse is back up, 68."

"Give her a sternum rub."

Doneen took his knuckles and ran them up and down her breast plate. Her eyes sprang open as her left hand shot out and closed around Doneen's throat. She screamed and vomited all over Cheeseburger. When she swung her right hand to join her left on Doneen's throat, the IV line ripped out. It happened in seconds, too fast for anyone to react until they realized a bleeding junkie had sprung back to life with such force she was nearly on top of one of the department's strongest men. Narcan made some people cry, some vomit, but others came back looking to fight. Returning from death became a sloppy affair against zombies oblivious to it all. By the time it was over, Lt. Killmoor, T-Bag, and Cheeseburger had to lay across her on the floor as she vomited, writhed and fought.

"Flip her over!" Lt. Killmoor turned to the cop. "Gimme your cuffs."

The policewoman obliged, thankful she did not have to wrestle in the vomit.

It took three grown men to get the 100-pound junkie onto her stomach. They pinned her down.

Lt. Killmoor cuffed her, bent her ankles back to meet her wrists, and then he just picked her up and carried her out to the stretcher like a piece of luggage. She was placed face down and tightly strapped so she could not move.

"Check yourselves for blood."

The crowd recoiled from the statement. Cellphones recorded the action.

Cheeseburger was covered in puke. T-Bag and Doneen had it on their pants and gloves. Luckily, there was no blood because in the struggle her shirt had fallen over the torn-out IV site.

"Back up, people!" the female cop shouted. "Make a hole!"

But Mikey Doneen was having none of it. He took one look around at all the cameras and became disgusted. "Ain't none of you ever heard of HIPAA? She's a freaking patient, man, have some respect."

On the stretcher, Deborah Paddington twitched and cursed but could not move. They wheeled her out and loaded her in. She tolerated the oxygen mask they placed over her face, and then she seemed to drift away.

"She might be OD'ing again." Lt. Killmoor was loathe to release her restraints. He sat on the bench-seat and said, "Deb, can you hear me?"

Her eyelids blinked open. Her long blond hair was clogged with chunks of vomit, and it was smeared across her chin and chest as well. Her Holy Cross sweatshirt was unwashed and ripe. Facedown, her watery blue eyes spilled over. "Where am I?"

"You're in an ambulance." Lt. Killmoor gathered another round of vital signs. "At least your color's back. When we found you, you were blue." She started crying and the oxygen mask steamed up. "Where's Preston?"

"Who?"

"My boyfriend."

"Lady, we've been in that bathroom working on you for ten minutes and no one said a thing."

She kept crying.

Lt. Killmoor said, "What do you remember?"

"I've been feeling sick all day..."

"Stop." Lt. Killmoor held up the empty vial of Narcan. "The only reason you and I are even speaking is because of this stuff. And this only works on one thing—heroin. So please don't waste anymore of our time. Your freaking needle was next to you on the floor."

"Why am I upside down?"

"You're facedown because you attacked us. Then you puked on us. Then you attacked us some more."

She blinked and the tears returned. "I'm sorry."

"Don't be. I've been puked on before. Same with these guys. Question is, if I take these restraints off, are you gonna act like an adult?"

She slowly nodded.

"Let her up."

The cop took back her handcuffs. They unbuckled the restraints and allowed her to flip onto her back.

Mikey Doneen held up the peace sign and said, "This makes two. For me alone. I don't know how many other times you've OD'd—"

"Only twice, I swear—"

"Regardless, wake the fuck up. You almost died in a bathroom and your so-called boyfriend couldn't give two fucks neither."

She scrunched her eyes closed and gasped.

Lt. Killmoor said, "Thanks, guys. Get cleaned up."

They snapped off their gloves and jumped out.

Lt. Killmoor watched her sob and said, "It's wake up time, Deb. Only cats have nine lives."

T-Bag called from the frontseat, "You ready to roll back there?"

"Yes, sir. Saint E's, please."

T-Bag toggled the mic and said, "Rescue 2's transporting to Saint Elizabeth's."

"Rescue 2 transporting to Saint Elizabeth's at 1828."

She pointed to the mask. "Can I take this off?"

"Sure." He killed the oxygen feed. "Because of our exposure to your vomit and blood, the hospital's gonna test you. For everything."

"I'm clean—"

"I'm not saying you're not, I'm just saying we now have a right to know. And so do our families. As part of the protocol, you're gonna have to be tested again in thirty days. No exceptions. Do you understand that? If not, it's cuffs and cops."

"Yes." She laid on the stretcher, dazed, staring at the IV bag swaying back and forth. "How do I do this?"

"Do what? You just go to the hospital—"

"No. How do I get clean?"

"When you decide you'd rather live than get high. Other than that, there is no quitting."

"But how do you know when you've hit bottom?"

"Take a look around and tell me what you see..."

***

"Fire Alarm to Rescue 2?"

"Rescue 2."

"Are you available for a run?"

Two hours later, they had not even seen the station, much less eaten dinner.

"That's a roger, Fire Alarm, where we headed?"

"216 Filigree Street. Lift Assist. Be advised, this is a Lifeline activation."

"Roger. On the way."

"That's the one thing I'll never understand." T-Bag flipped on the lights. "I know they send the rescue because the person might end up being hurt, but aren't we busy enough? Can't they just send an engine and then call for a rescue if the person's injured?"

"It's because everyone hates the rescue. So they just turn it into a garbage truck for everything they don't want to do."

"A shitbox."

"Yes." Killmoor laughed before he could catch himself. "I shouldn't laugh at that."

"Shitbox!"

"Will you please watch the road?"

"Shiiitttttbbbooxxxx!"

"God help me."

They crossed the eastside into residential District 6. Filigree Street was filled with nice homes and large yards. T-Bag killed the siren as he searched for the address. "This is gonna be that old couple, right?"

"Yeah. The McCluskeys. Henry and Julianne. Three more up on the left."

"I don't know how these people still live alone."

"You'll never see another generation like this one. Tough as stones."

"Fire Alarm to Rescue 2?"

"Rescue 2."

Since these were public airways, Fire Alarm said, *"Contact Fire Alarm by cell for a key location."*

"Negative, Fire Alarm, we know where it is. You can show us on-scene."

"Rescue 2's on-scene at 2043."

Lt. Killmoor pointed. "Just put it in the driveway and kill the lights."

To the left of the front door was a planter. Lt. Killmoor dug out a key-box and unlocked the door.

"Hello! Fire Department!"

A feeble voice called out, "In the kitchen!"

The house was in perfect order, the stately furniture pristine. Marble floors led them to the kitchen where they found both husband and wife piled on the floor.

"Oh, geez." Lt. Killmoor rushed over and untangled their walkers from their limbs. "What happened?"

"Well," Henry said, "I heard her fall, came to help, and then fell myself."

"Does anything hurt?"

"I'm ninety-two. Everything hurts."

His wife chuckled. "We've been through worse."

"I was at the Battle of the Bulge," Henry said. "Laying on the floor ain't nothing compared to that."

"And sixty-two years of marriage," Julianne said, chuckling again. "Four kids, sixteen grandkids, and eight great-grandchildren. This ain't nothing."

"How about you, ma'am?" Lt. Killmoor asked. "Are you hurt?"

"Only my pride. Be a dear and just help me up."

"Do either one of you want to go to the hospital?"

"For what? Being old?"

Lt. Killmoor and T-Bag got Julianne up first. They made sure she could use her walker without losing her balance. They stood Henry up next and did the same.

"How we doing?" Lt. Killmoor asked.

"Fine. We're fine." Henry nodded down the hall. "We were just getting ready for bed."

"Well, don't hesitate to call us back. Marble floors and 90-year-old bodies are a tough mix."

"Thank you, gentlemen. Sorry to bother you with this nonsense."

"We'll let ourselves out and lock the door."

They put the key back and hurried to the truck.

Lt. Killmoor clapped his hands and cranked the heat. "It's getting colder by the second."

"Gonna be a long night. Supposed to start snowing, too."

Lt. Killmoor grabbed the mic and said, "Rescue 2's back in service. Lift assist only."

"2052, Rescue 2."

Lt. Killmoor asked, "You think private ambulance would ever do lift assists for free?"

"No chance. This whole thing was just a huge circle-jerk to nowhere. And then the guy just packs up shop in the middle of the night like nothing ever happened?"

"That was a hit. Pure and simple. Carvalho whacked him. Her big money union donors squeezed her until she had to make a move. Question is, what'd she get in return?"

"That's kind of gross... I've never watched politics up close because I was never in a union."

"Where the big boys play, there ain't no mercy."

They weaved their way back to John Adams Boulevard. The four-lane road was busy. At a stoplight, multiple sirens abruptly rang out.

Since their radio frequency was silent, Lt. Killmoor said, "Must be the cops."

The intersection became frozen since no one knew what to do. Two police cars suddenly screamed past heading west and, further down the boulevard, two more did the same in the same direction.

T-Bag said, "Those guys were hauling ass."

"Yeah. Somebody's about to get fucked up."

They made it another block before the Alert Tone hit and Fire Alarm announced, *"Attention Rescue 2 and Engine 4. 516 Columbia Road for a possible shooting. Stage for police..."*

"Great." T-Bag hit the lights and sirens. "We're never gonna eat dinner." He turned and saw his boss' expression. "What's up?"

"That's Delmar Higgins' address."

"Oh shit."

T-Bag practically had the truck on two wheels taking corners. They were on-scene one minute after the police. Neighbors were still fleeing down the block.

"Rescue 2's on-scene." Lt. Killmoor looked at T-Bag. "Park it here. Let's get the trauma and airway bags loaded onto the stretcher and wait for the cops to lock things down."

"I say we just run down there and see what happens."

"That," Lt. Killmoor said, "is why you have the worst instincts of anyone I've ever met. Honestly, I don't know how you're ever going to survive this job."

They loaded bags onto the stretcher as Engine 4 pulled up.

"Da fuck," Chunks said. "It's too cold for this shit."

But Mikey Doneen and Cheeseburger looked psyched. They were in their turnout gear and ready for a bloodbath.

One of the cops abruptly whistled. "Fire! Down here!"

Lt. Killmoor led the way, telling Engine 4, "This guy's got PTSD."

"I know the Sachem City Five," Chunks said. "True heroes."

A policeman met them halfway down the block and hurriedly said, "We got one upstairs bleeding out. The shooter is on the roof next door."

"Goddamnit." Lt. Killmoor picked up the pace. "He finally killed him. Can't you shut that shit off?"

"We're trying. But he's got the whole room in his scope."

As they neared, they heard an endless loop of machine-gun fire and hand grenades blaring from the dying neighbor's house.

The cop said, "Shooter can't see the front door, so we're gonna sneak you guys in through there. Once you're in the house, stay out of his line of sight."

"We know," Lt. Killmoor said. "He used to be a sniper."

For cover, they hugged the houses. In the street, six cops hid behind opened car doors. They spot-lit the roof. Guns drawn, they called for Delmar Higgins to clear and drop his weapon off the roof.

The firemen entered the neighbor's house. Upstairs, they found two more grim-faced cops, guns drawn, nervously standing on either side of a bedroom door. Now, the sounds of war were deafening.

One cop yelled, "You're gonna have to crawl in! He's around the bed! Stay low! He owns the window!"

"Has he fired since?"

"Negative!"

Lt. Killmoor turned to T-Bag. "Me and you only. Grab the trauma bag."

The two of them crawled around the bed. Lt. Killmoor found the sound system and yanked the power cord on the gunfire. Then he found the body. He searched the blood-splattered wrist for a pulse. The force of the bullet had thrown the neighbor against the bed, so he was partially sitting up. There was an ugly hole bored through his center-chest, the blood a red flower soaked into the rug around him. His head hung there, eyes wide and sightless.

"Naw, man, he's a goner." Lt. Killmoor made a slicing motion across his own throat. "Let's get out of here."

"He must have some kind of canon up there to punch a hole like that."

"This idiot had it coming." Lt. Killmoor turned and yelled to the cops, "He's dead! We're coming out!"

They re-grouped downstairs. Outside, the police were all business. One demoralizing blow of the budget cuts was the dissolution of the city SWAT Team. Now, if needed, four of the seven cars on-shift were "gun-cars" manned by officers who had completed a week-long course run by the State Police on the M-4 rifle. Red dots from these laser sights currently danced and twitched across Delmar's torso.

The fire and police radios were not compatible, so no one knew what anyone was doing. This meant they could only communicate through their respective dispatchers or by yelling across the scene.

Lt. Killmoor and T-Bag inched along the front of the house. At the corner, they peeked and saw Delmar Higgins straddling the peak of his roof with the long gun slung across his lap.

T-Bag whispered, "So much for low stress EMS."

Lt. Killmoor grunted. "If he even twitches that gun, they'll blow him right off the roof."

"What happens if he gets stuck up there instead?"

"Good point." Lt. Killmoor's dislike of ladders or heights or any combination of the two quickly made treating a gunshot victim on a roof a nightmare scenario. "Rescue 2 to Fire Alarm."

"Go ahead, Rescue 2."

"Dispatch Ladder 2. Have them stage on the corner of Littleton."

"Roger." Fire Alarm hit the Alert Tone and said, *"Attention Ladder 2. Special signal. Assist companies on-scene at 516 Columbia Drive..."*

"Delmar Higgins!" a metallic voice announced over a PA system. "My name is Sergeant Hastings of the Sachem City Police Department!"

"You all know my dad!" Delmar's breath released frozen clouds into the night air. "I want to talk to him! I ain't trying to have no problem with y'all."

"We're trying to get in touch with Captain Higgins right now, but will you please just come down?"

"I'm sorry he's dead!" Delmar shook his head. "Never wanted it to come to this, man."

"We know the history here, Delmar. There'll be time to sort all of this out. Right now, we just want you safely on the ground. You gotta come down. If not for your sake, then do it for your family."

"Man, this ain't got nothing to do with that. Nothing's the same anymore."

"Delmar—"

"And now it's never gonna be again."

"We have people you can talk to, real professionals—"

"I'm done talking. Just ask homeboy. He was all talk too. Thought he could get away with pressing up on me. Well, he won't be making that mistake again."

"What if—"

"I don't want to talk to you no more."

The block fell silent.

Lt. Killmoor whispered, "If something doesn't give, this is the beginning of the end."

"You should talk to him," T-Bag hissed back. "He actually likes you."

"What do you mean, 'actually?'"

"Just saying."

"Don't be hurtful. Plenty of people like me."

They retreated across the street. They found the policeman with the bullhorn and explained the situation.

"No," Sgt. Hastings immediately replied. "No chance."

"All he's seeing are guns and spotlights. Give him a reason—"

"We're trying to get his old man here but he's at some law enforcement conference in Boston. Mass Staties are driving him down lights and sirens but he's still thirty minutes out."

"We can—"

"I am not allowing unarmed, untrained firemen into the middle of an active shooter crime scene. Anything happens to you they'd fry my ass forever."

"Shooting dead a war hero ain't gonna look too good either."

"Well, if he hadn't just blown that guy's lungs out the back of his body, we wouldn't even be having this conversation, now would we?"

Rebuffed, Lt. Killmoor was not about to give up. "Just give us a chance if you decide to flex back. At that point, what's the difference?"

Sgt. Hastings barely nodded before huddling up with the remaining members of the Hostage Negotiation Team.

Lt. Killmoor tapped T-Bag on the shoulder. "Let's go. He's right. If someone told us how to do our jobs, we'd tell them to get fucked."

Just as they crossed the darkened street, when the HNT ignited their 1000-watt scene lights, the pair suddenly appeared mid-stride in the wide open.

"Hey, Lou!" Delmar Higgins yelled from the roof.

Lt. Killmoor stopped. He looked back at Sgt. Hastings who only shrugged.

Resigned, Lt. Killmoor nodded and lifted his gaze. "Delmar! You got a lot of people down here concerned!"

No answer.

Lt. Killmoor continued, "Since I hate treating people I know, is there any way I can talk you into coming down before anyone else gets hurt?"

"I ain't gonna hurt anybody!"

"How do we know that?"

"You want the gun?"

Stunned, Lt. Killmoor said, "Yes?"

"Then come around back. The ladder's waiting."

"You know I don't like heights!"

"I ain't throwing my baby off this roof. You can stay on the ladder. I'll slide it down to you, but I ain't going with it."

Lt. Killmoor whispered to T-Bag, "What do you think?"

"I think I believe him."

"Which part?"

"The gun. His dad's a cop, right? And they're the only thing left out here to shoot. Besides, it's 28-degrees. Marine or no Marine, he'll be down eventually."

"Goddamnit…" In the back of the house, Lt. Killmoor stared up at the ladder with trepidation. "All right! I'm coming up!" He kicked the snow off his boots and looked at T-Bag. "Tell my wife I love her."

"Easy. He wants to come down."

"We'll see."

"I'm right behind you, boss."

Lt. Killmoor made the sign of the cross and started climbing. One policeman footed the ladder. Another lit up their ascent with her flashlight.

"Slow and steady," Lt. Killmoor said aloud, climbing the rungs. "How's my ass look from down there?"

"Oh, it's a sight, all right."

"Guess I should do more squats."

"Just don't look down and keep climbing. Almost there."

"With my luck I'll pop my head above the gutter and take one to the melon."

"Dome. The kids these days call it a dome."

"I shouldn't have just looked down."

"I told you. Concentrate on what's above you. That's the only thing you can control."

"If I fall I'm taking you with me."

"Don't threaten me with a good time."

They got to the gutter and stopped.

"Delmar!" Lt. Killmoor slowly raised his head above the roofline.

Delmar Higgins was sitting on the ridge drinking whiskey. He was a faceless silhouette backlit from the police floodlights on the other side of the house. Lt. Killmore said, "We've got to stop meeting like this."

"Some habits are hard to break, Lou."

"I'm sorry it's going down like this."

"But not surprised, right?"

"No. That guy was a piece of shit. Like you said, he pushed up on the wrong guy."

"I knew it was wrong the second I did it, but man, it did feel good."

"No one can control who moves in next door, right? We don't get to pick our neighbors."

"I never wanted this to happen. But I wasn't about to move, either. He was never gonna get over on me like that."

"Look. The Mass Staties are driving your dad down here lights and sirens. Probably twenty minutes out."

"Did the family a favor though. Least they can have an open casket."

"Listen. You've got an awful lot of lead aimed your way. Can you give me that gun so no one finds an excuse or does something by mistake?"

"Deal's a deal." Delmar cleared the chamber, set the safety, and left the bolt locked open. "Only brought one bullet anyway." He slid the rifle down the roof.

"Thank you." Lt. Killmoor glanced at Delmar like he did not want this to be the last time they ever saw each other. "I really wish you'd come with us."

"Sorry, L-T. If I'm going down for murder, I'm gonna keep sipping on this whiskey. After pops gets here, we can talk again."

"Fair enough. Be careful up here, will ya?"

"I ain't gonna let you down."

"Give a shout if you change your mind."

T-Bag took the rifle from his boss and slung it over a shoulder. "Same thing going down, Lou. Slow and smooth."

"I really hate ladders."

At the bottom, T-Bag handed the rifle to the female cop and said, "No ammo, just the gun."

"Roger."

"Mother Earth at last." Lt. Killmoor stepped off the final rung. "Anywhere else is vastly overrated."

"Hey," the female cop said. "Sgt. Hastings wants a debrief."

"Tell him he ain't coming down until he speaks with his father."

"Roger."

Twenty minutes later a blacked-out Massachusetts State Police cruiser arrived. A frantic Capt. Higgins jumped out and bee-lined for the Command Post. Sgt. Hastings briefed him and then Capt. Higgins ran around to the rear of the house. Negotiations went back and forth until the police radios echoed, "He's coming down. Check your background, watch your target."

"Thank God," Lt. Killmoor said.

Sgt. Hastings added, "Miracles do happen."

Activity pooled around the back of the house.

Out front, Lt. Killmoor and T-Bag were re-securing their medical bags onto the stretcher when a single shot rang out. People screamed and scattered.

"10-71! 10-71! Shots fired!"

The police converged on the backyard. Anguished screams could be heard, but there was no more gunfire.

"Fire!" someone yelled.

Lt. Killmoor and T-Bag grabbed the bags and ran. When they turned the corner, blood was pumping from Delmar's temple. The bullet had gone right to left across his brain. Broken skin and bone became a macabre flower hung above his left ear.

Capt. Higgins cradled his son's shattered skull. The father's pain, as he rocked back and forth, made him produce an awful mewling noise.

Lt. Killmoor was ready to work a full code until he saw the amount of brain matter still oozing out. He said, "Cap, please, I got to get in here."

Two other policemen pulled Capt. Higgins away.

Lt. Killmoor checked for pulses but found none. EMT's were allowed to call death in the field only if certain criteria were met—rigor mortis, fixed lividity, obvious injury incompatible with life, and decomposition with skin slippage or bloating. The severity of the head wound was definitely incompatible with life, but after Lt. Killmoor took one look at the dozen cops and grief-stricken father, he changed his mind completely.

"Engine 4! Grab the stretcher!" Lt. Killmoor started doing CPR.

T-Bag was all business. "What's first, Lou?"

"Let's get his jacket off and cut his shirt open."

T-Bag used the trauma shears and then took over CPR. With every pump of the chest, he saw blood and cerebral spinal fluid oozing from Delmar's ears. It was hard to watch, so he just closed his eyes and banged out chest compressions.

Engine 4 appeared with the stretcher. Mikey Doneen took one look at was going on and said, "Yo, man, what're we doing?"

"Not now, Mike." Lt. Killmoor squatted by Delmar's shoulders. "Grab his feet."

They loaded Delmar onto the stretcher and took off for the ambulance. T-Bag rode the rails still doing CPR.

Chunks had backed the rescue down the street, so they quickly loaded him in. Cheeseburger was already inside getting ready for the IV.

After the doors closed, Mikey Doneen said, "Guys, this ain't right. Look at this poor fuck."

"It's a trauma code, Mike." Lt. Killmoor had other things to do. "You can either help or get out of the way. You choose."

"L-T, I didn't mean it like that, but this guy's fucking dead, yo."

Lt. Killmoor whirled and pointed. "I got twenty fucking cops out there, Mike, so you know what? We're gonna put on the whole show, with all the bells and whistles, so no one can say the fire department just stood around and watched a cop's kid die."

"I didn't—"

"His father's standing right there covered in his freaking blood."

"My bad, Lou, I got the CPR." Mikey Doneen stepped up so T-Bag could step back and help his boss intubate Delmar.

"I think we're in." Lt. Killmoor attached the bag-valve mask to the ET tube. "Halt CPR. Checking for chest rise." He pumped the bag and watched it rise and fall. Then he listened with a stethoscope over the belly to make sure they were not in the esophagus by mistake. "All good. Back on the CPR and let's get the epi. Cheese, how we looking on that line?"

"Got an eighteen-gauge in the right AC. Going for the left one now."

"Get a sixteen in there, please." Lt. Killmoor yelled through the access window, "Who's on the wheel?"

"Wrong Way."

"Punch it."

"Where to?"

"The State."

"Roger." Wrong Way toggled the mic. "Rescue 2 transporting to Ocean State. Two men from Engine 4, one from Ladder 2."

"Roger, Rescue 2."

Lt. Killmoor said into the mic, "Rescue 2 to Fire Alarm. Advise OSH we're inbound with a late twenties-aged male. GSW through and through both temples. No pulse. Patient's intubated. Two IVs established. Epi's on board. We're four minutes out."

"Roger that, Rescue 2."

Lt. Killmoor asked, "Anybody know what happened?"

Mikey Doneen was sweating doing CPR. "I heard a cop say he grabbed a gun off one of the HNT guys. Told his dad he loved him and then pulled the trigger."

"Dear God..."

"I can't look at this anymore." Mikey Doneen let Cheeseburger take over.

On the stretcher, Delmar's opaque eyes watched the ceiling. The compressions forced brain matter to steadily drain from the head wounds into the bandages. His blood-crusted lips gaped around the ET tube inserted into his trachea. His chest rose and fell as Cheeseburger cracked whatever ribs T-Bag and Doneen had missed.

"The last ride of Delmar Higgins." Out of decency, Lt. Killmoor further cocooned his head in gauze. "Semper Fi."

THE OPPOSITION CONVENES

February 24, 2010

Two days after Receiver Tillinghast announced an additional $100 dollar a month increase for all city workers healthcare coverage, a rebellion gathered at Connolly's Revenge. In attendance were ex-City Council President Carlito Perreira, ex-City Solicitor Fallon Duggan, the presidents of the five municipal unions, and the eight other members of the City Council. Except for the union presidents, everyone else had been fired when Chapter 9 was declared.

"My people can't take anymore hits," Lt. Ahearn said. "Another hundred bucks a month is really gonna hurt."

"Oh, is the poor DPS feeling pain?" Donnie Teagues was president of the City Workers Union. As a young man he had failed the fire department boards three different times. "The Department of Public Sleepers—"

"Bad timing, Donnie." Lt. Ahearn stared him down.

"Prima donnas." Teagues was not done. "Cops, too. The chosen few. We lost seventy fucking guys!"

"So what? We're down fifty-four firefighters and pulling seventy to ninety-hour weeks."

"Enough." Police Major Landis, the ex-merchant marine, always wore a severe flat-top. "We can't take anymore hits either, Donnie. Help us fix this or just agree to stay out of the way."

"Is the mayor coming?" one of the city councilors hopefully asked.

"Negative." Lt. Ahearn's cigarette-stained mustache bent into a frown. "I tried. He told me it would set a bad precedent to challenge the constitutional process. What can I say? He's so delusional his ethical code borders on naivete."

"What about the other guy? What's it gonna take to get him out of here?" Ex-City Council President Carlito Perreira was an ambitious man. Having spent twenty years amassing power, he was no fan of having it all stolen by Receiver Tillinghast. "He's sucking the life out of everything around him."

"There's only one way." Fallon Duggan, as the Ex-City Solicitor, used to represent Sachem City in all legal matters. His office provided legal advice and representation to the mayor, the city council, all department heads, employees, commissions, and boards. It also defended them against any litigation arising from their day-to-day activities. He was a third-generation attorney well-versed in contract law, and before his appointment as City Solicitor, was a familiar face in the federal U.S. District Court, District of Rhode Island. He said, "The word around One Exchange Terrace is that Lorio is looking for a five-year plan."

"What's the catch?"

"Total solvency, a real plan. And even if at some point civilian leadership is elected and restored, Judge Lorio and the court can step back in at any time if said plan is deviated or amended in any way."

"Well, how long can that take?" Donnie Teagues was incredulous. "Nine months in and this guy can't do simple math? What's left to cut?"

"They're all feeding." Police Major Landis smirked. "There's a consulting agency, a pension study group, a management company—that's ten million right there—and we're not even through year one."

"I heard the sanitation contract went to L and R," ex-City Council President Perreira said. "A strange coincidence indeed. Turns out the owner is a former college roommate of our esteemed Madame Governor Carvalho."

Because of his thick neck, Lt. Ahearn had to swivel his shoulders to share an incredulous expression. "Are you freaking kidding me?"

"The Ivy League mafia strikes again."

"We lose half our pensions and work seventy-hour weeks to provide welfare for the wealthy." Lt. Ahearn had his back to the door, so he could not see why everyone suddenly smiled.

"Friends and colleagues!"

"Mr. Mayor." Major Landis stood up and shook his hand.

Mayor Houlinik, like every great politician/magician, reversed their enthusiasm into a celebration of themselves. He warmly shook hands with everyone at the table. "I decided my thirst for a cold beer trumped any of my misgivings."

"It's good to see you, Charles." Ex-City Council President Perreira poured him a beer from the pitcher.

Mayor Houlinik raised his glass. "As a better man than I once said, 'Never contend with a man that has nothing to lose!'"

"Here, here!"

They sat down and got to work.

NOW WE FIGHT

March 17, 2010

March in Rhode Island was like March everywhere else in New England—either cold and snowy or cold and rainy. This made St. Patrick's Day, after the long winter, a cherished waypoint on the long journey toward summer. But for the fire department, it was also a high holiday on par with Christmas. Marching season meant the Honor Guard participated in parades throughout the state. The Newport parade, filled with departments from as far away as New York City, was by far the largest. It was always held on the Saturday before, and even though it did not start until 11:00 A.M., the bars on Thames Street and Broadway were usually packed with a thousand firefighters by eight o'clock in the morning.

This year, the actual St. Patrick's Day fell on a Friday. By noon, Connolly's Revenge was jammed with off-duty guys and their families. A Dropkick Murphy cover band was playing in the parking lot even though it was raw and windy.

But when word of the City Hall press conference spread, the band was silenced. Inside the bar, TVs were commandeered. Murmurs went through the crowd when Lt. Ahearn appeared at the podium and said, "I want to thank you all for coming on such short notice..."

It was hard to hear him until Mikey Doneen hopped up on a barstool and yelled, "Yo! Everybody shut up!"

Because the TVs were so old and unclean, Lt. Ahearn looked like an orange blob with a brown mustache. He continued, "... I also want to thank the proud men and women standing behind me. If not for them, this fight would've already been lost. Ex-City Council President Perreira, members of the city council, union presidents and department heads. All of us, from both sides of the aisle, have come together with only one objective—returning elected officials to their proper offices and ending this state-run occupation. Without further ado, I would like to re-introduce the once and hopefully future mayor of Sachem City, Mr. Charles Houlinik."

The crowd at Connolly's Revenge abruptly cheered, but Mayor Houlinik could not hear them. He faced those cameras in front of City Hall with his cherubic face gleaming. His contagious optimism was his greatest weapon, so he said, "For those who know me best, this suit has been a long running joke. After my first campaign, I was convinced it made me look thinner on TV. So I've worn it on every election night ever since. It's always brought me luck. Which is why, considering the events of this past year, I decided to break it out today. We are here to humbly propose a plan that will return this city to its rightful owners— its people. How we got to this point is for the historians to debate. Quite frankly, it doesn't even matter. We will learn our lessons to insure it never happens again and then move on. There is no alternative. But time is not our ally. Everyday we stagger through this bankruptcy is another dollar added to the tab our children will have to repay. Litigation costs have so far topped $3,000,000. Buckland Consulting, which provided the pension study plan, billed out at $623,000. Harmore Group completed a comprehensive safety plan for $243,000. Pinnacle Associates, the management company in charge of day-to-day city operations—$10.3 million to date. Not to mention all the outside staff and hangers on accompanying the Receiver, whose $275,000 salary, I might add, is $195,000 more than I made as mayor.

"Initially I had misgivings about what we are now proposing. That's why I want to stress that this is in no way an attack upon this due process or Receiver Tillinghast himself. We made this mess and shame on us. This aftermath is our cost for failure. But going forward this occupation is not an option any freedom-loving individual could ever truly embrace. So myself, the city council, the department heads and union presidents, have come up with a plan we think is unbiased and equitable." Mayor Houlinik held up a binder. Copies got passed out to all the reporters. "Believe me when I tell you it's not perfect. It calls for unimaginable bloodletting. We know this. We tried to be fair where we could, and compassionate where we could not. But make no mistake. Things will get worse before they get better. We might lose another 200 homes to foreclosure in the next six months. Businesses are still closing and relocating elsewhere. More will go before we prove that Sachem City should be their home again. But for the people and businesses that remain, get ready, because you will all be witness to a great city's return.

"Another reason for urgency is that in the short time since the crash of 2008, the total property value of all land and structures within the city limits has fallen from \$5.6 billion to \$3.66 billion. That's a \$1.9 billion-dollar loss. Our bond rating is still in freefall. A quarter of our people live in poverty. To survive the long road ahead, sacrifice will become the new normal. Sadly, the public library, which opened in 1843, will be closed. There will also be massive cuts across the board in every department. They're all listed line by line in this plan. Property taxes will rise 4% each of the next five years, and our business tax rate will also increase 3% every year for the next five years as well. But the worst news is that even our children are not exempt. Since we could not in good conscience rob the next generation to pay for their parents' failure, we left most of the education budget alone. Except for sports. Regrettably, for the foreseeable future, all sports programs will be cancelled. There simply was nothing else to cut.

"Let me just say this. Going forward, we are hoping Judge Lorio and Receiver Tillinghast will adopt some form of these proposals. We want all state officials and our fellow Rhode Islanders to see how serious we are about this five-year plan. And in return we ask only one thing—elections to restore a fair and democratic order. Thank you!"

"Mr. Mayor!" a reporter shouted. "Forgive me for stating the obvious, but none of you have any real power. Why should Receiver Tillinghast or Judge Lorio heed this call?"

"Because the citizens of this state should not have to carry Sachem City indefinitely. We were told a five-year plan to solvency was required before Judge Lorio might sign off on an ending for this receivership."

"Can I jump in here for a second?" Lt. Ahearn stepped forward. "The former mayor is a kind and decent man. I am not. So I will tell you what he cannot. We need this to end because the buzzards are tearing apart our carcass. We've been inundated with consultants and lawyers and accountants. Everyone is lined up at the trough looking to get paid, which means old-school cronyism is back. After the Department of Sanitation got dissolved, the private contractor hired for waste removal turned out to be a former college roommate of Governor Carvalho. Receiver Tillinghast is not exempt either. He has business or professional ties to many of the firms brought in to quote/unquote 'help us.' And while our bones are being picked clean, everyday things get a little more dangerous. The police are down thirty-six officers. The fire department has fifty-four vacancies and being held together with duct tape. You know what this is?" He held up a sheaf of papers. "Before Christmas, the powers-that-be hired Vulcan Corporation to come in and rubber stamp the Receiver's claim that public safety was not impacted by these ridiculous cuts. However, the exact opposite occurred. A retired Baltimore Battalion Chief with thirty-one years on the line promptly labeled this the most dangerous situation he's ever seen. So they spent $62,000 on a report they then tried to bury. Imagine this? With the safety of our citizens and the people hired to protect them on the line, the powers-that-be were only worried about one thing—their agenda. Well, our agenda is pretty simple. Give us back our city or expect a street-fight on every corner."

The crowd at Connolly's Revenge roared and cheered. People thrust their drinks into the air and high-fived one another. For the day, at least, the future did not seem forsaken.

THE KNIVES ARE OUT
March 20, 2010

Two days later, even though a snowstorm slowed down Monday morning's commute, Receiver Tillinghast was early for work as usual. Like a magic trick, his silver hair, even after he pulled off his hat, quickly re-acquired its perfect edge. He had budget meetings at 9:00 A.M. and 11:00 A.M., so he told Fire Chief Fishbakke to be there at 10:30. That time came and went because the Chief was running late.

After his second budget meeting, Receiver Tillinghast froze when he returned to his office. His secretary tried to stifle her laughter because Chief Fishbakke was so asleep he was snoring.

"Dear lord." Receiver Tillinghast nudged his shoulder. "Chief?"

"Agh." He snorted awake. "Oh, hey. Must've dozed off. Had a busy weekend with the grandkids."

"Is that so? How delightful. I hope to be a grandfather one day as well. Come on in. Can I get you something to drink?"

"No, I'm fine, thank you."

"Have a seat. Hope your Saint Patrick's Day was fun."

"Certainly was. Gave me and the men some time to bond."

"Is that what goes on at Connolly's? 'Bonding'?"

"Absolutely. We are a tight knit group."

"I'd say." Receiver Tillinghast leaned back in his chair. He pulled off his glasses and said, "You know what, Chief? Leadership has its rewards, am I right?"

"It certainly does. Without it there's only chaos."

"Someone must lead. It can be a joy, or it can be a curse, especially after tough times gather on the horizon. As you and I have found out over these last nine months, heavy is the head that wears the crown."

"It is. Crowns are heavy." Chief Fishbakke looked around, completely lost.

"Can I get you a tissue, Chief?"

"No, I'm fine." He wiped his face. "Think I might be coming down with something."

"That would be unfortunate. It is cold and flu season after all."

Chief Fishbakke shifted in his seat. "So what was it you wanted to see me about?"

"Well, Chief, as you can imagine, that press conference last Friday created quite a stir."

"How so?"

"Seriously? You did see the press conference, right?"

"Yes. For the most part..."

"Well, let's just say afterwards I got phone calls from people that really matter. People who don't necessarily appreciate having their business dealings and names sullied in the press. Needless to say, the information that was divulged has proven to be politically toxic. And I'm having a hard time connecting these dots. See, you and I had an understanding. An agreement, if you will. There were only two copies of that report, and I can assure you I did not leak it."

"Me? You think it was me?"

"Well, who else could it be, Chief? I explicitly asked you to delete that email."

"I did!"

"When?"

"After you asked me. I think it was the next day."

"You think? I phoned B.C. Fastow in Baltimore and he swears he didn't leak it either. Besides, he has no skin in this game. But the fire department sure does."

"Well, I had nothing to do with that."

"Does anyone else have access to your account?"

"No." Chief Fishbakke was growing upset.

"What about your secretary? I've heard she's an unseen force behind the scenes."

"Ma Dukes? She would never do that. No way. She loves this department."

"That's exactly my point. God loves a martyr. Unless Lieutenant Ahearn or one of his minions broke into your office—"

"Don't be ridiculous."

Receiver Tillinghast's smile froze. "Well then. Going forward we are looking at a vast restructuring involving all departments. Cost cutting, if you will. Part of this re-organization will be hiring a Director of Public Safety to oversee both the police and fire departments."

"I'm sure I'll be able to work with whoever you've—"

"I'm afraid you've misunderstood me. Instead of paying two chiefs, there will now be one Public Safety Director. Guess you haven't read this yet?" Receiver Tillinghast held up a copy of ex-Mayor Houlinik's proposals for solvency. "I can't take credit for someone else's idea. And it seems the president of your own union signed off on your demise as well."

"There's been a fire chief for two hundred—"

"It's a new day, Chief, I am very sorry." He paused long enough to be polite and then said, "And I'm afraid I'm going to have to ask for your resignation."

"That's preposterous!"

"Or we can do it the other way." Receiver Tillinghast held out his hands. "Your choice."

"You're a piece of work, all right." Chief Fishbakke stood up. "Your kind are all the same. Vipers, the whole lot of you."

"So, is that a yes on the resignation letter?"

"Hell no." For the first time in thirty years, there was no political future to reconsider. "You can kiss my ass."

After the door slammed closed, Receiver Tillinghast slowly smiled. He opened the next file on his desk and picked up the phone. "Karen, please tell the Chief of Police one o'clock works for me."

It was going to be a busy afternoon.

***

After work that same day, Lt. Ahearn headed to a bar in District 3. The locals called it "John's" but its full name was "Gentleman John Cassidy's Ale and Plate." Opened in 1883, it became such a neighborhood staple, the myriad owners since never changed the name.

District 3 was a hybrid. The mill owners had once built stately wood mansions near their beloved Viri Club before everything collapsed in the 1970's. Sadly, these massive dis-repaired structures were now turned into group homes or cut into apartments. There were also two public housing projects and a trailer park known for violence. When crack arrived in the 1980's, the projects traded atrocities in a battle for control so heinous, the cops started calling it the Days of the Cocaine Cowboys. Nobody went in there without a police escort, not even the fire department.

In a ten-square-block section of District 3 that bordered the Massasoit River, a holdout of working-class German and Polish remained. It was also where Margaret "Ma Dukes" Duquesne lived.

Inside the bar, Lt. Ahearn found her sipping on her customary scotch and soda. She was an attractive woman and fending off a would-be suitor who quickly fled from Lt. Ahearn's glare. Then he ordered a Guinness and said, "Heard we lost Car 1 today."

"Indeed, we did." Age may have deepened a few wrinkles since her arrival in 1975, but Ma Dukes still retained her impish smile. For the former 22-year-old hippy girl, like the generation before her, hard work and reputation were not dirty words. "He was not a happy camper when he returned from City Hall."

"Heard he was blaming everybody for everything."

"He certainly was not amused that the police and fire unions recommended handing over their own chiefs for execution."

"Sucks to be them." Lt. Ahearn clinked her glass with his own and said, "I'm sure the man next door was none too happy with what went down last Friday."

"That certainly was part of it. The Chief said he was accused of being the leak..."

"I don't know who leaked what. But whoever did it sure had a sense of humor. The envelope that arrived at my house had a City Hall return address on it."

"That is funny."

Lt. Ahearn pulled the envelope from his pocket and laid it on the bar. "Is it just me, or does that look like a woman's handwriting?"

Ma Dukes smiled again, stirring her drink.

He said, "If I was a betting man—"

"A rebellion that turns into a just cause sometimes means choosing sides, lieutenant." She finished her scotch. "After all, without each other, what has any of this been for?"

Lt. Ahearn lit the envelope on fire. As the flames crawled toward his hand, he reached over the bar and dropped it into the sink. He finished his Guinness, laid down two twenty-dollar-bills, and told the bartender, "She drinks for free tonight."

Then he walked out the door.

KILLMAUGH MILL

April 11, 2010

Master Box 429 was struck at 2:39 P.M. on a dangerously windy Saturday afternoon. Downtown in Fire Alarm, the Vision 21 system suddenly blinked, chirped, and then went into full alarm.

All the vacancies meant Super-Wop and Cheeseburger were the dispatchers on duty. Super-Wop was reading a workout magazine while Cheeseburger watched television and exchanged angry texts with his already inebriated father. When the alarm popped, neither one knew the worst day of their lives had just arrived. Box Alarms happened all the time. Hospitals, schools, industrial buildings, apartments, high-rises—any business or high-occupancy structure had to be directly connected to the Vision 21 downtown. Since a master box could be triggered for any number of reasons—smoke alarms, heat detectors, or water pressure changes in the sprinkler system—responding to them became routine.

At the same time, a passing motorist was banging on the door at Station 4.

When Lt. Stokes opened the door, the man jerked a thumb over his shoulder and said, "I think you guys got a problem."

The tones hit. *"Attention Engines 4,2,6, Ladder 2, Battalion 1, Box Alarm. 516 Miller Avenue..."*

Inside Fire Alarm, before Super-Wop could even finish dispatching the run, the 911 phone suddenly rang.

Cheeseburger nonchalantly answered, "Sachem City Fire Department, Firefighter Rialto, how can I help you?"

"Sachem City, this is 911. We've just received about thirty calls for a possible mill fire..."

Completely frozen, Cheeseburger almost stroked out. Super-Wop saw the look, finished the dispatch, and said, "What?"

"911's saying it's a mill fire."

"Bullshit."

Engine 4 did not even pull out of the station before the Dude said, "Engine 4 to Fire Alarm. Confirmed Code Red. The place is roaring. Dump the city."

"Roger, Engine 4. Fire Alarm to Battalion 1?"

"Battalion 1 receives that. Strike a second alarm and a third for out-of-town companies."

The tones hit again. *"Attention Engine 5, Ladder 1, Rescue 2..."*

Black smoke poured into the blue sky from a humongous building only one block away from Station 4. Engine 4, Ladder 2, and Rescue 2 exited the station, took a left, and rolled up on the Killmaugh Mill Complex. Now owned by a Boston company that renovated old mills into luxury condominiums, this 500,000 square-foot structure was built in 1896 by Augustus Killmaugh, an Irish immigrant who foresaw the future. Killmaugh Mills would go on to eventually produce most of the wire used to create America's first telephone network. It was four-stories tall and longer than three football fields. The exterior was all brick. The interior had tree trunk-sized wood posts supporting massive wood beams that were covered by an ocean of hardwood floors. Because of the huge machinery, the wood floors were also soaked in a hundred years of oil, diesel, kerosene, and hydraulic fluid. Like most abandoned mills, it was a propellent-soaked kiln just waiting for a spark on a windy day. Once upon a time, these behemoths were packed with raw materials, thousands of workers, and the dreams of a country becoming an economic superpower. But once the jobs disappeared, everything that got left behind became toxic.

Lt. Stokes said, "Engine 4 to Battalion 1."

"Go ahead."

"Chief, we've got heavy fire showing on the first two-floors of side-two."

"Roger that."

Within one minute of the original dispatch, every truck in the city was screaming toward Miller Avenue. They all knew without a quick stop no one was going home for days.

Mikey Doneen was the chauffeur of Engine 4. Because the entire complex was ringed by a half-mile of continuous chain-link fence, he turned to Lt. Stokes and said, "Now what, Dude? Where's the gate?"

"Who cares. Blow the fence."

"Roger that."

After Engine 4 crashed through the ten-foot-high fence, Ladder 2 and Rescue 2 plowed in right behind them. Riding back-step on Engine 4 was Yoda. He got held on Engine 4 between his nightshifts on Rescue 1. He was in total awe. The mill itself was shaped like a rectangle. One of its shorter sides, where the fire had started, was westward facing. This meant it was also directly downwind. 50 MPH winds were now pouring through its broken windows. Lt. Stokes saw this and told Doneen to park near the front door of side-one halfway down the building. These industrial-sized infernos were nothing new to the SCFD. From day one of every fire academy for the last 150 years, the basics never varied because the math was simple. They had one shot to cut off the fire before it got blown through the rest of the complex. "Yoda! Grab the high-rise pack! Mikey, grab extra hose!"

Yoda's pulse was pounding through his neck. The high-rise pack was two 100-foot shots of hose and a bag of nozzles and adapters weighing fifty pounds. Instead of dragging half a mile of hose into the building from the engine, these short-shots could be hooked up to stand-pipes inside the building. Lt. Stokes and Yoda each shouldered a shot of hose and grabbed axes and Halligan tools to break down doors if needed. Wearing and carrying over 150-pounds of gear and tools, they hustled to the side-one main entrance. Lt. Stokes dropped the hose. He pitched his cigarette and jammed a Halligan behind the padlock. "Crush it, kid."

Yoda swung the reversed flat-head axe.

"Harder!"

Yoda smashed the lock free on the second shot. They both strained to roll back the giant steel door. They re-shouldered their hoses and tools just as Ladder 2 joined them in the seeping smoke.

Lt. Stokes said, "We gotta find the standpipe, dudes. Fire your bottles but don't go live until you absolutely need it."

They all nodded, opening their tanks.

"Stay connected. If anyone gets lost, find a window and bail. Otherwise, you'll never find your way out in the smoke." Lt. Stokes toggled his mic. "Fire Alarm, Engine 4 and Ladder 2 are making entry side-one, main door."

"Roger. Engine 4 and Ladder 2 entering side-one, level 1."

Inside, there was only smoke and heat. They could hear an ominous distant hum and knew that was the fire ripping apart the building. Even though it was three o'clock on a sunny day, inside it was already a haze-filled dusk. After an eerie walk through the increasing smoke, Lt. Stokes' helmet light caught another steel door. Guys started coughing. Lt. Stokes was hopeful that beyond this point, the building's sprinkler system was keeping the fire in check. "All right, boys, here we go. Mask up." He grabbed a lever on the massive sliding steel door. Built and installed a hundred years ago to protect against this very thing, these fire-doors were the last line of defense. "Push!"

It took three of them to roll it back.

"Holy shit..." Lt. Stokes stared at a world turned to fire. It was rolling up columns and across walls and floors, fiending for the fuel. But with the door now open, this many-headed hydra felt the pull of fresh air and, like a prehistoric monster, instantly lurched in their direction. "Engine 4 to Fire Alarm! We have no working sprinklers! Repeat, the sprinkler system is not working!" He turned to Yoda. "Get to that standpipe! It might be dead too, but we gotta try!"

Yoda nodded but then froze. It was a totally normal response he had not yet learned to suppress. Human beings were not wired to run toward infernos, and this one was rapidly advancing. He hesitated a second too long because Matt Biggio grabbed the hose instead.

"No." Yoda checked his banging pulse. The heat started to feel like he was standing in front of a giant forge. "I got this."

He took the line and ran thirty yards to the stand-pipe and connected the hose.

Meanwhile, the open door was serving as a chimney for the wind blowing in through side-two. Waves of heat and flame surged forward.

Yoda shouted, "All set!"

"Open it up!"

Yoda spun the valve but nothing happened. The hose hung there like a piece of empty spaghetti.

"Goddamn it!" Lt. Stokes tossed the nozzle. "Let's go! Everybody get the fuck out of here!"

By now, Mother Nature had created a giant bellows. The wind was a constant 50 MPH, with 60 MPH gusts. This, along with the small forest cut down to construct this giant place, had created a perfect four-story blowtorch now turned inward on itself.

Lt. Stokes was waiting for Yoda. Already, the super-heated gasses and smoke were racing him to the door.

"C'mon, dude!"

Once Yoda made it through, Biggio and Wrong Way rolled the door closed.

They all started jogging.

"Keep going." Lt. Stokes pointed with his light. "That's the door. After that it's two rights and a left to get out." He toggled his mic. "Engine 4 to Fire Alarm."

"Go, Engine 4."

"Tell Command the standpipes are dry. Repeat, there's no water to the sprinklers or standpipes."

"Command has that, Engine 4, get outta there."

"Roger, Chief."

"Command to Fire Alarm. I do not want any other companies inside that building."

"Roger, Command."

"Command to Ladder 2."

By chance, Engine 5's Matt Biggio had been transferred in-charge of Ladder 2. An Air Force veteran with three small daughters at home, Biggio loved two things—racing his beloved Ducati and putting out fires. He grabbed his lapel mic and said, "Go ahead, Chief."

"Get the saws and meet Ladder 1 on the roof. We're gonna try a trench-cut to gap the fire."

"Roger that."

The fire department was a spot-specific organization. On the fire-ground, every position on every truck had a designated job. Biggio, as a career engine guy, had little experience on roofs. He could drive a motorcycle at 180 MPH, but heights were not his thing. Since none of that mattered, he grabbed Wrong Way and headed up the stick. It was a long climb. Ladder 2 was full boom, 110 feet out and fifty-feet high. They were wearing sixty pounds of gear and each carried a saw—Biggio had the chainsaw and Wrong Way the K-12. They held axes in their other hands, so balancing the climb was tricky.

At the top, Biggio looked left and saw the wind had already driven the fire up the outside wall and over the parapet. Now the roof was catching fire. It was an acre of 100-year-old asphalt and rubber. Across the way, two guys from Ladder 1 waved hello through the blowing smoke. The B.C. wanted both crews to cut a three-foot trench across the entire roof to try and stop the advancing flames.

From the ladder, Biggio saw the asphalt bubbling and figured the fire was already trying to eat through from below. "I'm not stepping out there, man, fuck that."

Wrong Way, whose unkempt hair and mustache were a 1970's throwback, was a roof guy. "Bubbles ain't good, bro, but we can't stay here."

"Who's on Ladder 1?"

"A-Poc and T-Bag."

"Oh great."

"Apocalypse" was Lt. Tim Hurst, an otherwise quiet man with a penchant for risky behavior some truly feared. According to legend, Lt. Hurst had once stated he wanted to die in a fire, not exactly reassuring words for any potential crew-mates. Even worse, he was involved in a slew of close calls and near misses that almost got people injured. The veterans always told any newbies on his truck to watch out for themselves. But another hard truth was that even his most strident detractors considered A-Poc one of the best roof guys on the job. He was a master of ropes and repel, could tie almost any knot, and was a member of the New England Urban Search and Rescue Team deployed to Manhattan on 9/11. He had even struck up a friendship with a Chinese firefighter and ended up traveling to Beijing to train. On his down time, he studied videos of roof teams from across the country. Ladder guys only talked about three things—saws, forcible entry, and ventilation techniques, because if burning structures got improperly vented, that's how people died. He was also a renegade when it came to training since he seemed to think it could occur anywhere at any time. Business owners would call up headquarters and wonder why there was a ladder company on the roof of their building if it was not on fire. At the Armistice Tower downtown, a woman on the tenth-floor suddenly screamed when T-Bag swung across her kitchen window while waving from the tip of Ladder 1. And then there was the time the Battalion Chief lost his mind when he found A-Poc, Clownfeet, and T-Bag practicing bail out maneuvers from the fourth-floor window of an abandoned mill with no one else providing any type of safety or backup ropes whatsoever.

The roof was three football fields laid end to end. Biggio, completely out of his element, toggled his mic and said, "Ladder 2 to Ladder 1. Whaddaya got?"

"We've been sounding it. Still feels pretty solid."

Biggio watched them pounding the roof with their axes before taking each step. "Ladder 2 to Ladder 1, we got bubbling asphalt."

"Us too. No worries. We'll make it over and start from there."

"Man..." Wrong Way was still standing behind Biggio on the ladder. "Dude, we gotta get out there. They're making us look like pussies."

"Yeah, well, I'd like to see my kids tonight..." But Biggio knew he was right. He reached down with the axe and tested the roof. "I guess living's overrated anyway."

Wrong Way waited for him to jump, handed down both saws, and then jumped himself. There was plenty to be scared about.

A-Poc and T-Bag made it across.

"What's up, fellas?" A-Poc was actually smiling. "Nice day for a weenie roast, right?"

"You guys are fucking tapped." Biggio nodded to where the first quarter of roof was now fully engulfed. Choking black smoke made acrid by the burning asphalt washed across all four. "I'm an engine monkey. What's the plan?"

"Trench-cut." Apocalypse revved the chainsaw. "All the way across."

"Great."

"Do you mind?" T-Bag, who had a K-12, motioned for Biggio's chainsaw. This gesture, however, was not appreciated.

Biggio said, "Oh yeah? What's up, newbie?"

"Nothing, man." T-Bag was only trying to do the right thing. "This is what I did for years, bro."

Biggio held out his saw. "Well, have at it, hotshot."

"Sweet." T-Bag revved the Husqvarna and looked at A-Poc. T-Bag always tried working Ladder 1 on B-Shift because no one wanted that spot. As some guys said, they would rather go home to their families instead of rolling the dice with Lt. Apocalypse in-charge. But he had a lot to teach, which for some justified the gamble.

Apocalypse said to Biggio and Wrong Way, "After we cut, you guys mind smashing everything open?"

"Sure." Biggio picked up an axe. "Whatever we do, let's just hurry the fuck up."

A-Poc and T-Bag plunged their chainsaws straight down into the roof. Three-feet apart, they walked backwards, paralleling each other all the way across. The saws screamed and spat out the roof. Every few feet they made crosscuts to create sections that Biggio and Wrong Way smashed out with their axes. Once they reached the far side, all four choked in the venting smoke as the fire now rolled across the roof.

A-Poc toggled his mic. "Ladder 1 to Command. Trench-cut's complete."

"Great. Now get out of there. We're losing the building."

Biggio and Wrong Way ran back to retrieve their tools. As Biggio stepped from the parapet to the ladder, he saw the battle being lost below. Crews were firing 2½-inch master-streams through windows halfway down either side to try and stop the fire, but Mother Nature had different plans. Her 60 MPH gusts and superheated gasses were creating a Hollywood-style inferno. The temperature reached flashover and, suddenly, the giant windows exploded on all four floors in a spectacular succession that raced down the block.

Biggio held on as the blasts buffeted the ladder. If he had been two feet further down, glass from the fourth-floor windows would have sprayed his face. He leaned over and took the saws from Wrong Way before helping him up to the ladder just as the fire leapt across the trench-cut.

Wrong Way saw Biggio's face and got nervous. "What's up, dude?"

"That..." Biggio pointed at something he hoped he would never see again. The wind, after entering side-two and ripping through three-hundred yards of accelerant-soaked fuel, exploded out of side-four as if a seal between hell and earth had ruptured. Like NASA rockets tipped horizontal, the turbines of fire shooting out of each floor were thirty-feet long and six-feet wide. The fire had grown so large so fast, it ruthlessly spewed out pieces of the same building it was in the process of killing. Football-sized embers were being driven across the neighborhood like waves of planes turned Kamikaze. Roofs on close-by houses ignited, got blowtorched by the wind, and then shot more sparks and embers onto other homes downwind. Atop Ladder 2, Biggio caught a bird's eye view of a catastrophe unfolding.

***

"There! Put the stream in there!" Bullet Head Romine was bouncing between both sides of the building. Since no one was going in again, a full-scale exterior attack was underway. He had four hose teams on either side shooting 4-inch lines through the windows. That equaled more than 6000 gallons of water a minute. Along with the trench-cut on the roof, the original hope was to stop the fire at the building's midpoint. But the four massive hoses, which would have doused any other fire, were accomplishing nothing. In fact, the fire was so hot it was vaporizing the water into steam the second it crossed any flame-filled threshold. Even worse was the wind, which did two horrible things at once—feed the fire oxygen while also scattering the hose-streams into useless patterns blown sideways in the gusts. Yet somehow, in the rear of the mill, an even bigger nightmare was occurring. As Capt. Romine watched a cyclone of flaming debris napalm houses two blocks away, he had finally seen enough. "Shut 'em down!"

The hose teams threw him puzzled expressions.

He made a slashing motion across his own throat and toggled his mic. "Engine 5A to Command."

"Command, go."

"Yeah, Chief, the wind is killing us. The four-inch ain't even touching this thing. I don't think this building's worth it. The out-of-town companies can surround and drown. But the neighborhood behind us is starting to light up from all this debris."

"Captain—"

"Recommending we fall back and take up defensive positions

around the neighborhood, leave the ladder trucks here with their master-streams—"

"Captain, you will remain..."

Unfortunately for the men of A-Shift, B.C. McLoud was not about to shine. Like Chief Fishbakke, McLoud had largely avoided his entire career by being a good test-taker while acquiring minimal skills. Instead, he hid out on some of the slowest trucks in the city and waited to be promoted.

Capt. Romine had no time for this nonsense. He knew the cavalry was coming, because the one thing B.C. McLoud had done right was break a record by declaring a General Alarm nine minutes into the fire. This meant all sixty-seven off-duty firefighters were being recalled back to work.

B.C. McLoud had set up the Command Post before the wind shifted, so he was now choking in the smoke.

As Capt. Romine approached, he saw McLoud feverishly thumb through a giant Sachem City map-book. Spread across the opened back hatch of the B.C.'s SUV, it contained every hydrant on every street in the city. B.C. McLoud was monitoring the radios with a look of pure panic that he shared with Capt. Romine, saying, "Jesus Christ, Gary, the entire mill—"

"Fuck the mill." Capt. Romine reigned himself in. What he wanted to do was disembowel McLoud and sling his intestines across the street. In situations such as this, the guy was an outright danger to everyone. But seniority could not be the reason for failure, so they huddled over the map as the mill roared behind them. Capt. Romine pointed at the tightly packed streets settled over 300 years before and said, "If we don't get a stop by Argyle Street, we're gonna lose the whole neighborhood. And beyond that..." He tapped a finger on the corner. "Westman awaits."

"Oh Jesus Christ."

Westman Mills was as big as Killmaugh and in even worse disrepair. Inside it, giant vats of hazardous waste had been leaking for thirty years.

Capt. Romine had toured the place with his crew just last summer and already knew it was one spark away from catastrophe.

"You're right." B.C. McLoud mopped his brow. "I already called a General Alarm—"

"Oh, we're way beyond that now. Tell Fire Alarm to get with Metro Control. We need everybody—Providence, C.F., Attleboro—whoever they got." Metro Control was run by the Providence Fire Department. It coordinated cross-community emergencies when cities got overwhelmed.

A police car came crashing through the fence. The officer inside did not bother to hide his panic. "You guys need to get over to Everett Street right now."

"Which house?"

"All of them. We're gonna start evacuating everything north of that. From Argyle on up."

"Roger that."

The cop left in a screech of tires.

"Please listen to me." Capt. Romine pointed at the useless hose teams. "We have to move right now. This place ain't worth dying for. Let's save what we can save. I'm taking all of these guys and falling back into the neighborhood. The calvary's on the way. Let them handle this."

"Okay." B.C. McLoud grabbed his radio. "Command to Fire Alarm."

"Go, Command."

"I'm declaring a civil emergency. Contact Metro Control and have them activate the Major Disaster Protocols. We need anyone they can send."

Capt. Romine tapped his shoulder. "Have them roll the gas company, too. If enough of these houses go up together, we could start backfilling lines until this whole grid turns into one giant bomb."

"Fire Alarm, we also need the gas and electric companies immediately."

"Roger, Command."

As B.C. McLoud turned and saw Capt. Romine shouting orders through the smoke, his only hope was that no one would die today.

***

Muncy Street was directly behind Killmaugh Mills and six houses were fully involved. The wind was already driving embers northeast onto homes blocks away. Police cars went street by street shouting evacuation orders over their P.A.'s. The residents who refused to leave sprayed useless garden hoses at their homes while choking through continuous waves of smoke. This futility also siphoned off precious water pressure. The smarter ones just piled their pets and kids into their cars and fled. But those without vehicles struggled through the smoky streets like refugees with clothing knotted into makeshift masks over their mouths and noses.

Off-duty firefighters reported to their stations, grabbed their gear, and headed for Miller Avenue. It had been forty-five minutes since the master box tripped. The path of the fire was like an upside-down triangle starting from Killmaugh.

Capt. McCarrick swung into Dutch Carrigan's driveway.

"Whaddawe got, Cap?"

Capt. McCarrick's cigarette was sticking out of his overgrown mustache like a twitching appendage. It flopped back and forth as he said, "Fucking Hiroshima, Dutchie, pack a lunch."

"Fucking A. The wife says it's already on CNN."

"Yeah, well, if Westman catches, the BBC will see the fucking smoke from England."

"Ah-ha-ha-ha!"

"This is gonna be fucking beautiful."

They tore off towards the fire like a couple of kids headed to the beach.

***

Muncy Street was getting blowtorched by the rockets shooting from Killmaugh. The wind was tearing houses apart and spewing flaming shingles onto Everett, the next street up. Eight houses on Everett were already fully involved. Linden Avenue was the third street after that, and ten houses were either close to or completely engulfed with flame. Next came Sea Street, Argyle, and then the disaster of Westman Mills awaited. In this ten-by-ten square block area, it looked like war had broken out. Trees were bent forty-five degrees in the ripping wind and shooting flaming pieces of themselves into the sky.

When their phones rang, Jimmy Rowdell and Brian Fonseco were packing the jeep with beer and their girlfriend nurses. They were headed to Newport until Super-Wop called from Fire Alarm. At first, they thought he was kidding. But then the chaos from the radios echoed in the background.

Afterward, Rowdell said to Fonzie, "Did you hear all that madness going on?"

"Dude." Fonzie started unpacking the coolers. "I'm so fucking glad I'm not in that room right now."

"Right? For a mill fire? Fuck me in the face."

"Excuse me?" Annie Sadler rounded the corner just in time to be offended by both that awful imagery, and the fact that they were unpacking the jeep. "What's going on?"

"That." Rowdell pointed toward a giant black plume suddenly scrawling across the perfect blue sky. "Killmaugh Mill is ripping. We gotta go."

"Just like that?"

Flustered, Rowdell shouldered his backpack and tried to maintain his composure. "Do you remember where I work?"

"But... Newport. And we have tickets for tonight—"

"Annie, please. What am I supposed to do?"

"No, I get it. It's just, so sudden."

"I hear you."

Fonzie already had everything dumped out of the jeep. He turned to tiny Molly Bish and gave her a hug, saying, "You guys can chill here as long as you want. Just lock it up when you go."

"Yes, darling." She stared up at him with a look of happiness. "Be careful."

"I will." He leaned down a foot to kiss her. "Call you when I can."

"Okay, Big Boo." She blinked. "Am I your Little Boo?"

"If he answers that," Rowdell said, smirking, "I'm gonna bust his balls forever."

She said, "Fuck you, Jimmy."

Fonzie kissed her again and then joined Rowdell in the Jeep. They backed out of the driveway and waved good-bye.

"What's up, man?" Fonzie asked. "Everything okay?"

"Naw, man, she just doesn't get it. But I guess in her defense, every time we make plans I'm getting held at work. And today, the one day off I've had all week, we catch a General Alarm. I mean what are the fucking chances?"

"I hear ya."

"I keep telling her this ain't the Water Department, it's the Fire Department. You can't say no. Besides..." Rowdell shot him a grin. "This is gonna rock."

"Our first one, bro."

"Fucking A."

They bumped fists and hauled ass for Station 4.

***

There were only enough radios for twenty-nine people, so the rest had no communication. There also were not enough air-packs.

As off-duty firefighters kept arriving, they were told to just hook up with companies on-scene. By this point, FOX News was reporting visible smoke for sixty miles in any direction. Meteorologists reported the fires were producing so much heat and gas, they actually began altering weather conditions above Sachem City. As it tried to breathe and spread, the fire needed more oxygen, so it created 80 MPH wind gusts just to feed itself.

Since he was practically their own age, Mikey Doneen was always a magnet for the newbies. They felt more comfortable following him than some salty old-timer waiting to feast on their mistakes. Rowdell and Fonzie found him in the front yard of a raging inferno on Muncy Street, directly behind Killmaugh. Trees, cars, houses—everywhere Rowdell looked seemed to be on fire. For a veteran fireman, this would be one of many career events. But for a newbie with no experience on which to draw, their choice of profession now seemed extremely shortsighted.

Mikey Doneen was literally sitting on a 2½-inch attack line alone, a feat in and of itself. The normal 1¾-inch hoses were having no effect against the volume of fire spewing across Muncy Street. But the 2½, which weighed 500 pounds, threw so much water it usually could not be manned or moved alone. Doneen was sitting splay-legged with the nozzle clutched between his thighs and hands. He was eating so much smoke he could barely breathe. "Row! Fonzie! Help me drag this thing left!"

The oven of Killmaugh Mills was 200 feet away and spitting waves of fire sixty feet into the sky. Rowdell and Fonzie started coughing and did not stop until the smoke and soot had seared away whatever caused the cough in the first place. They crouched down behind Doneen and backed him up. Through watery eyes, they watched ropes of fire whip the sky. Cyclones of flames roared from the rear of the mill. Every now and then a pocket of clarity appeared through the impenetrable smoke, and when this occurred, as it did now, they suddenly saw Capt. McCarrick and Dutch Carrigan on a hose-line fifty feet away. They all spotted each other at the same time, so Capt. McCarrick waved and screamed, "We can't stay here! We gotta—"

Killmaugh Mills could take no more. At first, there was a loud groaning and a whooshing sound that felt like a terrible pause. Then the full acre of roof collapsed. As it fell, it sucked the air and smoke back into itself before the blast wave returned it tenfold into their faces. Flames roared across the surrounding streets. Guys ducked behind parked cars that now ignited. With fire devouring so much oxygen, it was even hard to breathe.

But Capt. McCarrick knew they could not eat much more heat and smoke. He screamed, "Fuck Muncy Street! Fall back to Everett!" He yelled into his mic. "Engine 3! Cut the water to both deuce-and-a-halves!"

They followed the hoses back through the smoke. Engine 3 waited on Everett Street. Johnny Swistak was at the pump panel munching on a half-chewed cigar. He was not even wearing his coat. A thirty-year man, he had survived the fiery 1970's, so this was just another day at the office. At sixty-two, Swistak still had melon-sized biceps. His helmet looked like a scorched beak welded to his head. A man of extremes, he smoked too much, drank too much, and, in consequence, fought too much. Once he saw Capt. McCarrick and the other four falling back to his truck, he was disgusted. It said something about his reputation and standing that he could look Capt. McCarrick directly in the face and say, "Fucking pussies."

"Swiss, we can't survive that—"

"This thing ain't gonna put itself out!"

Rowdell and Fonzie were stunned. Even amid this chaos, witnessing a private waste a captain, and Capt. McCarrick no less, brought everything to a halt. On opposing shifts, Rowdell had only met Swistak once. Before he did, the warnings had been vigorous and unanimous to not fuck with the guy in any way. A salty old-schooler, Swistak once had half his ear bitten off in a bar fight. Since he was now the senior private on the entire job, no one with any common sense took him lightly.

He grabbed his jacket and yelled at Fonzie, "You! Man this pump!" Then he stalked around Engine 3 and disappeared into the smoke.

They followed the hose-lines, found the nozzles, and lurched forward into the heat. It seemed futile, like trying to hold back the tide by using a spoon. Conditions had also noticeably worsened. With everything burning, there was nowhere to turn, so trying to shield their heat-seared faces was pointless. As before, a wind shift sucked the heat and smoke back into the mill, and they all knew what was coming next.

"Everybody duck!" Capt. McCarrick screamed. They dove behind the already burnt-out cars parked along the street. This time, to protect themselves, they dialed their nozzles onto fog-stream and aimed the 2½-inch lines straight into the sky above them. The third-floor, already loaded with the burning roof, collapsed onto the second-floor, which instantly failed as well. With thousands of tons smashing into the first-floor simultaneously, the ensuing explosions sent so much fire into the streets, their hose-lines were the only reason they were not incinerated. Waves of fire rolled over their heads and tugged the oxygen from their lungs. The surging flames even consumed the smoke to reveal a humbling sight. In this split-second of clarity, they all saw each other, because Bullet Head Romine and his hose teams were strung down Miller Avenue. Before this, sealed inside the walls of smoke, they might have thought they were fighting alone. But now, even though this visibility would not last, they gave a cheer and rose to fight again.

***

By 4:45 P.M., two hours into the fire, Station 4 had been transformed into a staging area for out-of-town crews. Companies from as far away as New Bedford were pulling up and horrifically told to just pick a fire and put it out. Thirty homes and businesses were now involved as the path of flames marched northeast toward where Westman Mills awaited.

With hundreds of firemen now on-scene, the counter attack started to contain the perimeter. But Muncy Street and Miller Avenue were lost, and since Killmaugh had already collapsed into a roaring acre of shooting fire, saving the east side took priority. Everyone fell back into the neighborhood.

Despite their best attempts, Everett Street was soon lost as well. Fonzie had to shut down the lines and drive Engine 3 two blocks up to Sea Street. It was here and on Argyle that their last stand would occur. If not, and Westman Mills ignited, the fire might chase them all the way to Attleboro.

The Massachusetts State Police arrived with their Mobile Command Vehicle, which was basically an RV with next generation video and communication capabilities. It was parked in the parking lot of Westman Mills. From there, Capt. Romine hoped to coordinate this final defense.

On a white board, he drew out a rough map of the surrounding streets. Then he marked the positions of the incoming companies. He tried to line the forward perimeter with battle-tested crews, so Central Falls, Providence, and Fall River were digging in. Since the Sachem City water system was already overwhelmed, crews from smaller towns were laying 4-inch feeder lines all the way from Attleboro. These massive hoses were laid across streets, through people's yards, and looked like veins strung throughout the neighborhoods.

Capt. Romine stepped to the door. Visibility was awful. Day was turning to night through the waves of smoke. Even though Westman Mills was only feet away, he could barely make out the black coats of the Providence firefighters standing on its roof. Elsewhere, he had dispatched Warwick, Cranston, and Woonsocket to secure two schools and the looming disaster of the National Electric substation. Also of concern were the Amtrak lines behind Westman Mills. Those lines carried 24,000 volts along the entire Northeast corridor. Since trains were still trying to flee, they were yet to be shut down. But Capt. Romine did not care either way because, barring a disaster, no one was going out there for any reason.

Through the blowing smoke, Engine 1 D-Shift suddenly appeared like a magic trick. Lieutenant Menard and Privates Daviau and Lefebvre were soot-smeared and smiling. Hardworkers, they were called the "French Connection" because of their last names.

Bullet Head Romine said, "Look at you glorious fucks."

"Captain." Lt. Menard peeled off a crisp salute. Physically, he was the largest man in the department, a 6'6" 360-pounder renowned for smashing in dead-bolted exterior doors with only his size-sixteen boots. And while he could have been a terrorizing menace, he was likely the nicest guy on the whole job. He had only been in one fight his entire life, and after throwing his opponent through a door, profusely apologized before helping him up. He was a born teacher, so the newbies loved him. But he was also a stickler on station protocol and camaraderie, so laptops and cellphones were forbidden before lunch.

Behind him were Reno Daviau and Leo Lefebvre. Daviau was an ex-embassy Marine who later traveled the world as a private contractor. He was also nicknamed Shit-Gut because he could eat almost anything. His partner, Leo Lefebvre, was shaped like a block and dense to the touch. Since his whole family was from Brooklyn, he became a Yankee loving New Yorker surviving in Red Sox country after falling in love with a girl from Warwick. As far as skills and instincts, Engine 1 D-Shift was considered put together.

Bullet Head said, "How you feeling, Lou?"

"Salty." Lt. Menard smacked his giant blackened hands. "Heard you were looking for us?"

"Yeah, I got a real shit-burger for you guys. Police dispatch is saying their substation on Van Ness is 'starting to smoke,' whatever the fuck that means. But that's where their primary armory is. All the stuff from the SWAT guys and cabinet after cabinet of concussion grenades and armor piercing bullets."

"Yeah, we might not want that to catch fire."

"It might already be. Who knows? Leicester Engine 4 just pulled up and they want nothing to do with that place. They'll give you their truck. We got a portable water supply on Camber."

"Fucking A. Let's do it."

"Billy, listen to me. If that place starts cooking off rounds, we're gonna have to pull everyone out of the area, and that means good-bye to Westman and everything north. How's that for pressure?"

"No worries, Cap. I'll let you know what I find."

"Amen. Here." Capt. Romine handed them each one small bottle of water. "It's all I got. You're gonna have to hoof it from here because there's no one left to send."

"I'm taking this in case we need a key." Lt. Menard grabbed a 'married set,' which was a flathead axe and Halligan. He merely slung the heavy tools over his massive shoulder as if they were toys. "You got your cellphone on you? I got no radio."

"Hey!" Capt. Romine stuck two fingers into his mouth and whistled at a passing cop. "Can you give these guys a lift?"

The cop car swung around. "Where to?"

"Van Ness."

"Oh, great. Nothing like putting out a fire in a gun store, right?"

Daviau, the ex-Marine, only smiled. "Embrace the suck."

They piled in and the cruiser took off lights and sirens into the smoke.

***

In the streets leading up to Capt. Romine's last line of defense, strange alliances spontaneously occurred. Cadillac Frank and Psycho Sal, sworn blood enemies, dragged a charged 1¾-inch line 150 feet and entered a house by themselves. They hauled in more hose than they needed because charged lines weighed 250 pounds, and pulling them around corners was impossible without assistance. They might have been Rescue Lieutenants, but both were former line guys. Psycho Sal was on-shift and had an air-pack and radio, but Cadillac Frank had responded to the General Alarm from an afternoon concert and did not. They kicked in three interior doors before realizing the fire was in the basement.

"Fuck me, man." Psycho Sal felt the heat behind the door. Then he turned and aimed his tank at Cadillac Frank. "How much air I got?"

Cadillac Frank squinted at the gauge. "Twenty-five."

"Fuck. Just feed me the line—"

"You ain't going down there alone."

"Listen, you half-ass lounge singer, you have no air—"

"I'll back out then. C'mon, man, we gotta do this."

The houses on either side were barely feet apart. The wind was doing two things—catching roofs on fire, and blowing flaming debris along the ground until it hit foundations and crawled into the first-floor system and basements. This was the first house of five about to burn down if they did not get a stop.

"Fuck it." Psycho Sal whipped open the door and immediately disappeared down into the smoke. It took both to drag the hose into the basement. With no mask or air-pack, Cadillac Frank was instantly coughing and spitting and barely able to blink fast enough to clear the tears.

Psycho Sal said, "Dude—"

"Go!"

They pulled the hose further into the basement. Psycho Sal knew the fire was close but had zero visibility. Behind him, all he heard was horrendous coughs and retching. "That's it." He shut the nozzle and grabbed Cadillac Frank. After he half-dragged him up the stairs and dropped him in the hallway, he shoved a gloved finger into his coughing face and said, "Do not go down there again!"

"You can't—"

"You wanna help? Feed me line, bro." Psycho Sal resealed his mask, reset his helmet, and disappeared down the stairs. He followed the hose, found the nozzle, found the fire, and saw the gas line just feet away. "Oh, fuck me, man!" He levered the nozzle wide open to prevent the gas line from exploding. The force of holding the hose alone left him panting. His arms began to cramp. He chased the fire back into the floor where it had originally burned through from outside. He sprayed water everywhere, totally freaked out. There was still fire somewhere, but he got turned around and confused. He pushed into the darkness, feeling for heat. He found another batch of smoldering flames crawling upside down across the ceiling and put it out. Then he got caught on something and tripped. But he did not just fall. He landed in a step-down and rolled into something that felt like hanging clothes. When he hit the ground his helmet light went dead. Just to make things worse, the vibe-alert on his mask started going off, signaling he only had a quarter tank of air remaining. He searched for the hose but could not find it, and that's when he really panicked. He reached for his radio before realizing that was what had gotten caught and ripped away when he fell. He spun and bumped into a thousand things, tripping again. Desperate and freaked out, he got to a wall and searched for a window. After he found one, he had no tool to smash it, so he pounded with his fist until the tiny window exploded.

"Help! I'm trapped! Anybody out there?"

A passing Seekonk firefighter swiveled her head, confused.

Psycho Sal screamed, "Hey! I'm over here!"

Inside the house, Cadillac Frank had no idea what was going on until he heard the screaming. Since he was off-shift, he had no radio to call for help. Half-conscious, he was drooling mucous and coughing when the Seekonk firefighter came flying through the door. She saw Cadillac Frank retching and gasping and said, "Aw, fuck." She switched on her air and toggled her mic. "Seekonk Engine 2 to Fire Alarm. Mayday, Mayday, Mayday. We have a fireman trapped in the basement of—" She looked at Cadillac Frank. He coughed and spit and said, "We're on Sea Street. That's all I know."

"Standby." She stuck her head out the front door and saw the number on the wall. "67. 6-7 Sea Street. Repeat, 67 Sea Street."

She masked up and switched on her lights. Then she descended into the smoke. Smart firefighters carried a personal fifty-foot shot of rope to self-extricate if they had to bail from windows on upper floors. But it could also be used as a lifeline in a disaster. She clipped her carabiner to the banister and followed the hose, screaming, "Hello! Hello!"

"Over here!"

She could hear the vibe-alert and man-down beacon somewhere to her left. She tripped and crashed into a shelf that tipped over.

Psycho Sal, yelled, "I see you! My light's dead!"

"Let's go, man. I gotta line hooked up." She held the rope in one hand and Psycho Sal in the other. They would not be lost again.

"Aw, man, I'm starting to suck face!"

"Don't pull off that mask!"

Psycho Sal was gasping as he ran out of air. It was a feeling akin to drowning. When he pulled the last puffs from his tank, he knew this was it. The mask was coming off next or he would pass out anyway. Then they found the stairs.

"Go, go, go!"

Psycho Sal made it to the first-floor and collapsed next to Cadillac Frank. They lay there, exhausted. The Seekonk firefighter cleared the Mayday just as the front door banged open. Capt. McCarrick, Dutch Carrigan, Swistak, Mikey Doneen, Fonzie, and Rowdell piled in.

"What da fuck." Capt. McCarrick was panting. "You scared the shit out of us."

From the floor, Cadillac Frank gave them a thumbs up. His soot-caked skin made his eyes and teeth glow.

Psycho Sal, elated at being alive, just started laughing. "Nothing like a two-man basement fire."

"Nobody cares." With everyone safe, the real ball-busting could now commence. Capt. McCarrick said, "What do you guys want? The Medal of fucking Honor? Get up, you lazy fucks."

"Yeah." Swistak was actually grinning. "I'm old enough to be your fucking grandpa and you don't see me laying on the floor."

"Ah-ha-ha-ha!" Dutch Carrigan leaned over to help them up. "Don't listen to these guys. We all know you rescue cunts can't hang."

They all laughed until the radios grew chaotic, because on Argyle Street the worst was coming true.

***

By 8:00 P.M., more than five hours since the first alarm, major resources started arriving. The National Guard was mobilized for two reasons—to secure the disaster zone against looters, and the eventual cleanup. Since the fire was incinerating everything, the electric, cable, and telephone companies were staging crews from across New England to re-set new poles and re-string every line once the fire was declared under control. The gas company had teams scouring neighborhoods with sniffer-meters in case an unknown leak lurked in the path of the flames. No one was taking any chances, so the electric and gas to the whole east side had been terminated hours before.

Temporary shelters were established in schools thrown open on a Saturday night. The Red Cross deployed a small army to set up cots and feed the estimated 1,000 people who had fled their homes. Since the EPA was reporting elevated levels of hydrogen cyanide, hydrogen sulfide, carbon monoxide, and hydrochloric acid as the toxic soup blew sideways across the city, evacuations downwind continued. The FBI and ATF arrived with accelerant sniffing dogs. They began the official investigation in conjunction with the Sachem City Arson Unit, the State Fire Marshal's Office, and the State Police Major Crimes Division.

All this staging happened in the background, because the fire suppression operation was still ongoing. Forecasts had the winds blowing until midnight.

At Station 4, a small city had formed. By protocol, when companies from one city were sent out-of-town on Mutual Aid, their Battalion Chief went with them. So there were basically twenty-seven Battalion Chiefs organizing different parts of the fight. Sixty engine companies, twenty-eight ladder trucks, and twenty-three rescues were somewhere out there battling in the night. Massive lights were brought in to illuminate this makeshift basecamp. News crews from as far away as New York arrived to film the destruction. The smoke was so bad, I-95 was shut down in both directions, forcing 300,000 vehicles into the streets of surrounding towns. Even veteran reporters were taken aback by the sheer violence of the winds. Things were burning so fast it seemed like a cloud of gasoline had rained across the city.

Nightfall made the glowing and twisting flames even more spectacular. In the command vehicle at Westman Mills, Capt. Romine would have taken a moment for reflection if he had one to spare. With Muncy, Everett, Linden, and Sea Streets incinerated, only a hundred yards remained between them and the fire. Argyle Street was filling up with crews forced to retreat from the onslaught. Exhausted companies dug in next to where Central Falls, Providence, and Fall River hoped to ambush the advancing flames, because if the fire broke through the zero barrier of Argyle Street, Westman Mills, the Amtrak lines, I-95, and Attleboro would be devoured next.

Capt. Romine could not sit in the RV any longer. Even though it had access to all of the cameras strung throughout the city, every screen was filled with smoke. Besides, there was nothing left to orchestrate. They either stopped the fire right here or all of them would be chased two miles north into Massachusetts.

There were no streetlights because the power had been cut, so the night was filled with blowing smoke and voices yelling in the dark. Every now and then a helmet light would pop a hole through the black curtain, but otherwise sixty exhausted firefighters hunkered down with charged hose-lines waiting for the marching flames.

As he approached the line, Bullet Head Romine found himself entranced by the growling hum the burning city produced. He crossed Argyle and poked his head onto Sea Street, which was filled with flames. The wind was ripping apart a dozen houses as if they were toys in front of a blowtorch. It was even worse than he thought, so he ran back to Argyle and shouted, "Here it comes!"

The warning got yelled down the line. Tucked behind cars, trees, and this last row of houses, they braced for impact. Bullet Head joined Dutch Carrigan, Capt. McCarrick, Swistak, and Rescue Captain LeClaire, who had just appeared out of nowhere. They were alongside twenty other Sachem City firefighters. Since Argyle Street was on a curve, they would be the first point hit.

Ominously, the wind suddenly filled with even more heat. Everyone shuddered. The guys with packs had run out of air long ago, so all of them were coughing through the choking smoke. Argyle Street had houses on one side and Westman Mills on the other. Bullet Head's hope was that the fifty-foot gap of concrete between the houses and mill would provide them one last chance. As all the houses ignited simultaneously, the wall of fire had finally arrived. Dutch Carrigan and

Swistak cracked their 4-inch master-stream first, and then the other cannons opened up as well. These monster hoses weighed 700 pounds and could flow a 1000 gallons per minute. There were fourteen of them hooked up to eight screaming engine companies two blocks back. The water from these massive hoses rose up like their last hope. Smaller 2½ and 1¾-inch attack lines filled in around these cannons. At first, things seemed grim. Some even looked over their shoulder to mark a path for retreat. But then the massive high-low water curtain Capt. Romine had devised blunted the first attack. When they saw this, they suddenly knew they had a chance.

"Stay in your lanes!" Capt. Romine ran down the line. "Steady pressure, don't let it flank us!"

He grabbed the last hose team and had them protect the corner of Westman Mills in case the fire rolled right. That was the gamble. With the sheer volume of wind and flame, even if they stonewalled the initial assault, all that energy had to flow somewhere. That's why he had held back six engine companies as an emergency reserve. Not wanting to panic and deploy them to the wrong side, he was first waiting to see if the assault could even be stopped. If not, those six companies were coming right to the front.

Bullet Head Romine had been on the job for twenty-six years and seen his share of big fire. And while mill fires were always dynamic events, no one in the last hundred years had ever seen anything like Killmaugh. The 60 MPH continuous winds tornadoed ribbons of fire fifty-feet into the night. As he headed back to where Sachem City was dug in on Argyle Street, Bullet Head scanned across the dozen other departments risking their lives trying to save a place they did not even live or work in. Three-man teams manned each 4-inch hose as the flames roared right at them. The fire, unhappy to have encountered this organized opposition, hissed and belched flaming scythes out of the cyclone. Everyone ducked. Capt. Romine could feel the intensity of the fight. With fourteen lines fueling this wall of water, 40,000 gallons were used in the first five minutes.

"White smoke!" Dutch Carrigan screamed.

A cheer went up. It was the first good news Capt. Romine had received all day. White smoke meant things were being cooled, extinguished. But as he stepped back, what he had originally feared was coming true. With the frontal assault blunted, the wind drove the fire left and right seeking both fuel and another way through. Capt. Romine grabbed a passing East Providence guy and said, "Get back to the mill. Tell those six engine companies to deploy on our flanks. Three on each. You got that?"

The guy looked completely freaked out but seemed happy to run an errand in order to escape this nightmare.

"Keep it up, boys!" Capt. Romine went down the line. "It's already giving up and trying to flank us!"

In the face of a three-story wall of fire, he wondered if they believed him.

***

By midnight, the Sachem City firefighters had been working for nine hours straight. Dehydrated, hungry, and exhausted, they were replaced by out-of-town companies and sent back to rehab at Station 4. Once there, they found a hundred people gathered. Some were friends and family relieved to see them. Others manned the makeshift cafeteria that had been hastily erected in the apparatus bay. Local restaurants were dropping off food and bottled water. It seemed everyone realized the gravity of this event after a photo was posted online of guys sleeping on the asphalt parking lot. Evans Furniture sent a truck loaded with mattresses, and Greyhound dispatched buses to shuttle men and supplies back and forth from the front. Off-duty nurses from St. Elizabeth's started IVs and monitored their CO and cyanide levels. Smoke-choked, all anyone could hear was a hundred people coughing.

"My fucking feet..." Capt. McCarrick rubbed his swollen, purple toes. "They're killing me."

"Whaddaya expect?" Dutch Carrigan wrapped a wet towel around his head. They were sitting on the already soot-destroyed mattresses strewn across the parking lot. "You don't take care of yourself, ya diabetic fuck."

T-Bag wasted no time. He made a horrific face and drag-walked one leg behind him like a cripple. He did his best Wilford Brimley impersonation. "I got the dia-beatus. They done gonna saw me off one piece at a time!"

"Ah-ha-ha-ha!" Dutch's laugh rolled across the night.

Capt. McCarrick said, "Fuck you, T-Bag. You couldn't make—"

"—a pimple on a fireman's ass. Yeah, Cap, that was funny the first hundred times."

"If I wasn't in so much pain, I would chase you down—"

"You can't rape what you can't catch!" T-Bag sprinted to the food line.

"Ah-ha-ha-ha-ha!"

"Fuck you too, Dutchy."

"Ha-ha! You are one salty old prick, you know that?"

"I fucking love you. I'd give you a hug if I could stand up." He lit two cigarettes and passed one to Dutch. "I don't know about you, but I ain't in the mood for sleeping."

"Me neither, boss."

"Let's grab some food, maybe catch another smoke, and then head back out."

"Sounds good." Dutch stood up and then laughed because Capt. McCarrick was motioning for assistance like a little kid too tired to stand on his own. But Dutch had no mercy. "Come on, ya fat fuck, get up."

"Gimme a hand, Dutchy, for Christ's sake."

"Ha-ha!" Dutch, who was eight-inches shorter and eighty-pounds lighter, yanked him to his feet. "You think they got any spaghetti and meatballs?"

"I fucking hope so, man, I'm freaking starving."

They had shed their jackets but still wore their "night-hitches," the bunker pants and boots. From so many years on the line, each now had a limp or ache or two. They headed for the buffet as Dutch said, "After this, what do you figure?"

"Probably try and find Bullet Head. If he still has the perimeter contained, maybe we can actually start to put this fucking thing out."

"We're eating dinner at one in the morning."

"I know." Capt. McCarrick could not stop smiling. "Any place you'd rather be?"

"Nope." Dutch handed him a paper plate and spork after the line inched forward. Everywhere around them soot-smeared firefighters dumped heaping spoons of food on bending plates. Some passed around a garden hose in-between mouthfuls to clean themselves and cool down. Others were getting IVs and flirting with the nurses. Still more posed for the news cameras like weary old-school jakes on a break from an epic battle.

The buses kept coming and going. This continued all night into the dawn. With the perimeter holding, they were able to concentrate their efforts on a block-by-block attack to douse the remaining fires in the incinerated neighborhoods. On Sunday morning, the carnage could be quantified. Killmaugh Mills, two schools, and fifty-three homes and businesses had been destroyed. Another nineteen had been seriously damaged and were uninhabitable. 285 people were left homeless or temporarily displaced. Twenty-seven firefighters were hospitalized for smoke inhalation and a variety of injuries. With fourteen of these firemen from Sachem City, an already understaffed job was placed under even more duress.

The first alarm at Killmaugh was struck at 2:45 P.M. on Saturday afternoon. It would not be until noon Sunday that the last structure fires were finally declared extinguished. The remains of Killmaugh Mills, however, would be smoking and smoldering for the next week. Ladder crews with their master streams were left behind to soak these hot-spots and flare-ups until the demolition guys could come in and truck it all away. Sadly, another proud piece of city history was headed into the dumpster.

AFTERMATH

April 13, 2010

Monday morning forced everyone into a new reality. Restoring order and basic services to the whole east side became the paramount objective in a list of 10,000 things to do. Along with the Red Cross, FEMA was organizing the humanitarian relief, while the National Guard was in the process of protecting and clearing fifteen-square-blocks of utter devastation. Blowtorched cars resembled hollowed skulls tossed into the gutter. Everything smelled like ash.

Until this point, Receiver Tillinghast had not held a joint meeting with all branches of the city government at the same time. For obvious reasons, it was not an audience he was about to win over. But faced with the unprecedented, Receiver Tillinghast had to relent.

In the three weeks since the police and fire chiefs had been dismissed, the Public Safety Director had yet to be hired, so seniority created interim chiefs by default. Police Major Hollenbach and Acting Battalion Chief Theodore Etchel, who was actually a captain, became the de facto representatives of their departments. "Etch" did not even want to be a Battalion Chief, much less Chief of Department. He was 60-years-old and had gone to high school with Dutch and Capt. LeClaire.

He was in his dress blues. Since he had not earned the two ranks he was now forced to supersede, he still wore the captain's double bugle insignia on his white officer's hat. His full head of shockingly white hair belied the fact that he was an immature prankster of the highest order.

The Chief of Police finished his summation of the weekend disaster—three police cars destroyed by fire, four policemen injured during operations and evacuations, two of which remained hospitalized.

Acting Fire Chief Etchel spoke next. He despised Receiver Tillinghast with a palpable hate, so he made himself stick to the facts. "Two engines—Engine 1 and Engine 3—have broken pumps. Ladder 1's down until next week at the earliest. We've borrowed replacement apparatus from surrounding cities because there are not enough mechanics left to fix our own. The ATF has so far found no source of ignition. They are surmising an unseen spark was created by the demolition teams working inside that morning. They were using saws and torches, so best guess is that a spark got squirreled away somewhere and festered until ignition. We suffered fourteen injuries—a couple of sprained backs, a dislocated shoulder, a fractured leg, one broken arm, assorted burns with smoke inhalation across the board." Chief Etchel pulled off his glasses. "The E.P.A. got some horrendous readings that day. We're talking about extreme levels of everything—cyanide, hydrogen sulfide, carbon monoxide, on top of whatever else was burning in that mill. My men, and this is no exaggeration, some of them were covered in so much soot you could only see them because of the whites of their eyes. The fourteen injuries have also tipped us over the edge—"

"Chief—"

"I'm not done yet." Chief Etchel stared directly at the Receiver. "We are down to seventy-six firefighters. That's cataclysmic. This morning we instituted a minimum ninety-six-hour work week, meaning once you walk in the door on your first day you're not leaving until four days later. Period. Some might even be ordered in a day early or held a day late. We're not too sure how this is all gonna shake out. More retirements and resignations are rumored to be in the pipeline because, quite honestly, who needs this? That's it. I'm done."

"Chief—"

"Stop calling me that. You've turned that position into a mockery. No Car 1, Car 2, and me, a captain, forced into the Chief's—"

"That's quite enough—"

"Guess you forgot one thing. You can't touch me. I'm still in the union, loud and proud Local 1-2-1."

"Sit down!"

"I don't think so. I'm only doing this job because there's no one left to do it. Pick up a phone, find your Public Safety Director, and let them be the one on the hook. I've made it my whole career without seeing a line of duty death, much less being responsible for one. Who wants to be promoted onto the bridge of the Titanic?"

"How dare—"

"Yeah, I'm all set with this."

"We're going to start the recruiting process for the next fire academy."

"How many?"

"Well, twenty-five to start—"

"Don't even waste my time."

"Chief—Captain! How dare you walk away!"

"You're a disgrace. That's what makes this so easy." Capt. Etchel pushed open the door but could not stop himself. "See you in hell."

Receiver Tillinghast, simultaneously startled and aghast, somehow kept his smile perfectly in place.

***

That afternoon, because he could not be fired, Capt. Etchel was returned to his position of Acting Battalion Chief on C-Shift. The next senior captain was promoted to Chief, and the reaction was predictable.

"Fucking Donut?" Bullet Head Romine was in disbelief. He and B.C. Etchel were at Connolly's Revenge after work.

"That's Chief Donut to you." B.C. Etchel smirked. "My reign as Chief lasted twenty-three days."

"You're leaving quite a legacy. Only half the city burned down."

B.C. Etchel laughed. Even though they were in a bar, only Etchel was drinking. "In thirty years, I don't think I've ever seen you in here."

"I hate these places. They're stuffed with losers fleeing their own pathetic lives."

"Jesus, I'm sitting right here."

"Too close to home?"

"I'll let you know after I get a refill."

The door swung open and Capt. McCarrick strolled in. His massive handlebar mustache seemed to be vibrating as he said, "Please tell me it's not true."

"Chief Donut is for real—"

"Not that. The fact that Bullet Head just made B.C."

"That," B.C. Etchel said, "is an unfortunate truth as well."

"B.C. Bullet Head." Capt. McCarrick peeled off a mocking salute.

"Yeah, thanks. What an honor. If you're gonna crash, you might as well be driving, right?"

"Absolutely." Capt. McCarrick turned to B.C. Etchel. "Heard you pretty much told the Receiver to get his face fucked this morning. See you in hell? Not very good for job security."

"Nope. The phone was ringing before I even got back to the office."

"Must've been a short conversation."

"It was. 'Thank you for your service, but you're being written up for insubordination."

"Around here that's now a badge of honor."

Etchel smirked. "Guess they decided to go in a different direction."

"Yeah, backwards. Considering how awful Chief Fishfuck was, I didn't even think that was possible."

"Can you imagine Donut facing the media?"

"It's going to be a complete disaster."

"I'll drink to that." B.C. Etchel raised his glass. "I can't lie. I've been thinking some pretty selfish thoughts lately."

"Please don't." Bullet Head was actually concerned. "This place is dangerous enough without anymore experience walking out the door."

"Besides," Capt. McCarrick added, "you're already screwed, so you might as well stay. Help us ride this bitch into the ground."

Bullet Head ordered another Coke.

Capt. McCarrick deadpanned, "Hope you're not driving."

"I'm in the minor leagues compared to you two boozebags."

"Yeah, well, maybe one day your nuts will drop."

They shared a few more insults but not a laugh, because none of this was funny anymore.

RAINING BLOOD

April 28, 2010

Seventeen days after the Killmaugh Mill fire, the phone rang in Fire Alarm at 11:03 A.M. A woman could be heard screaming before the line went dead. The 911 operator immediately cut in and said, "Sachem City, this is 911. We're receiving multiple calls for a structure fire at 312 Burgeon Avenue."

At the extreme west edge of the city, Burgeon was almost in North Providence. But since Engine 5 was already on the highway for a car crash, and Engine 1 was closed for the day, Engine 2 and Ladder 1 were first-due coming all the way from downtown.

"Lou!" Yoda was driving Engine 2 and getting saltier by the second. "We got hangers!"

"Fuck me." Lt. Salamanca grabbed the mic. "Engine 2 to Fire Alarm. Four-story multi-unit. Fire showing level two. People waving from windows on side-two, level two. We're making grabs."

"Roger, Engine 2. Battalion 1 receive?"

"Roger. Strike a second alarm for us and a third for out-of-town companies. Establishing command on side-one." In the fifteen days since Bullet Head had been made Acting Battalion Chief, the hardest part was checking his ultra-aggressive mentality in favor of other people's safety. As an officer on Engine 5, overseeing two people was stressful enough. But now, as B.C., he was responsible for the health and safety of twenty-five firefighters and 80,000 civilians. He took one look at the four-story behemoth and knew they did not have enough manpower.

"There's people trapped up there!" a woman screamed at him from across the street. "There's a handicap woman with three kids—"

"Which apartment?"

"Twenty-two! Near the main staircase!"

"Excuse me!" A frantic man approached. "My mother's missing!"

"Which apartment?"

"Forty-four."

"Does anybody know how many people live here?"

There was no answer.

B. C. Romine did not have to do the math. On average it took four firefighters to affect one rescue. Already, five people were unaccounted for. "Fire Alarm, strike a fourth alarm. Make note, we have reports of people trapped in apartments twenty-two and forty-four."

"Roger, Command."

"Roll the gas and electric companies and get someone from the Red Cross down here."

"Roger, Command."

"Command to Engine 3."

When Lt. Brodie clicked open the mic, Engine 3's siren pedal was pinned to the floor. "Go ahead, Chief!"

"We got four people missing in apartment twenty-two. When you get here, take a line into the center stairwell. After the search I need you to protect that main staircase."

"Roger!"

B.C. Romine went around the corner and saw twenty-four electric meters on the wall. Divided by four, that meant there was six apartments per floor. But he still had no idea how many people lived here and who was missing. This was not the way he ever imagined his first in-charge fire transpiring.

***

Sprinting for side-two, Lt. Salamanca fired his bottle after he saw a screaming woman about to drop a baby into an old woman's shaky hands.

"Wait!" He pushed her out of the way just as the baby fell into his arms. He handed it to the old lady and then helped his backstep man—who was actually a woman, Rescue Lt. Pelly Monet—set the ladder she had shouldered over alone. Suddenly, a chair flew through a first-floor window as more people suddenly screamed, so Lt. Salamanca sprinted over to help whoever was trying to survive.

Lt. Monet never strayed far from her military roots. Always in shape, she shot up the ladder just as the mother shoved a second screaming toddler out the window.

"Hang on!" Lt. Monet reached for the terrified kid. "Take my hand."

Then the frantic mother, with black smoke choking her out, handed over a third shrieking kid. Mom seemed to know what was coming, because civilians never launched themselves headfirst out of windows unless they were about to die. She made it onto the ladder two seconds before the room flashed over.

Lt. Monet had a kid under each arm. The effort and balance required to descend no-handed might have been possible if she was an Olympic gymnast, but she was not, so she smashed her face and chin into every rung the whole way down. She broke her nose and sprayed blood on the kids. Every muscle in her legs and back were screaming.

The mother, burnt and singed, was only relieved her kids were alive. She crawled headfirst down the ladder toward them while cooing reassurances like only a mother in the middle of a catastrophe could.

***

The last time Lt. Brodie was on Engine 3, Useless and Blister had turned Christmas Day into a fiasco. Today, at least he had Cheeseburger, whose reputation was growing. Useless was driving and completely freaked out. The radio was going crazy with reports of people trapped, so it was easy to become distracted.

"Jesus Christ!" Lt. Brodie shouted after they caught air going over the Faulk Street Bridge. "Remember we got twenty tons—"

"Hang on!" Useless cringed as they smashed over two potholes the size of small craters. "The check engine light just popped on!"

"So what? Calm down, will ya? We ain't gonna be doing anyone any good arriving in body bags." He cinched on his air-pack and shouted into the backseat, "Cheese! We're going straight in. I want the fog nozzle, so stretch the yellow line and I'll grab the irons."

"Roger!"

"Take this left!" Lt. Brodie screamed, bracing against the door. "All kidding aside, you do know how to run this pump, right?"

"Yes," Useless croaked, blinking back the sweat. "Oh God, hang on!"

"Watch that cop car, goddamnit!"

Blocking access to the fire scene, the officer inside visibly flinched when Engine 3 missed him by inches.

Jumping out, Lt. Brodie and Cheeseburger fired their air-packs, grabbed the line, and with one last look at the completely freaked out Useless, Lt. Brodie said, "Without water, we die."

They made entry into the smoke-choked front door and headed up.

***

When Lt. Salamanca saw Useless stumbling around Engine 3's pump panel, he envisioned a disaster in the making, so he shouted to his own chauffeur, "Yoda! Grab a hydrant for the 3's! Me and Pelly are heading in!"

"Roger, Lou!"

Lt. Salamanca toggled his mic. "Engine 2 to Fire Alarm. Four people pulled out of side-two, level two. Ask Command where he wants us."

B.C. Romine wasted no time. "Sal, get me a line into the first-floor."

"Roger."

B.C. Romine surveyed the dying building. Engine 2 was on the first-floor, Engine 3 was heading up to search apartment twenty-two, Engine 6 was just entering the back staircase to the third-floor, and Ladder 1 was heading to apartment forty-four on the fourth-floor. Time, like the building, was rapidly disappearing.

***

Engine 3 dragged extra line up to the second-floor landing. The door was hot. Lt. Brodie looked at Cheeseburger's wide eyes and yelled through his mask, "Good to go?"

"Hell yeah, boss."

Lt. Brodie toggled the mic and yelled, "3A to 3C! Charge the line!"

They heard the water snapping the hose against the walls all the way up to where it violently slammed against the nozzle in Cheeseburger's hands.

Lt. Brodie saw Cheeseburger's mixture of excitement and dread and said, "Remember! Stay low, aim high, figure-eight that shit, okay? Twenty-two is supposed to be the first apartment on the right. You got this." Lt. Brodie punched his shoulder and then faced the door. "Going hot!"

He swung it open and fire immediately launched into their faces. Cheeseburger threw open the bale. The water smashed into the flames, but the flames hissed and spit steam and debris across their masks. The black smoke, in a wraith-like counter-punch, instantly banked down and blinded them. With his seven-foot wingspan, Lt. Brodie was hauling line so Cheeseburger could inch down the hall. Fire and flames leapt through the roiling darkness like errant fists. Lt. Brodie chalked open the door and hunkered down behind Cheeseburger.

"Talk about a bad hair day!" Cheeseburger shouted through his mask. "This ain't gonna be too good for your toupee!"

"Real funny! What's that on the right?"

"I think it's a door!"

Lt. Brodie unslung the irons in case he needed to force entry. His light caught the number twenty-two. "Hold the hallway! Let me check it out!"

"Roger."

Try before you pry, Lt. Brodie told himself. The door was open. He took a quick peek and only saw thick smoke. "Hello! Fire department! Anybody in here?"

There was no answer. He crawled room to room, quickly checking everything. "Engine 3 to Command! Made entry. Twenty-two is empty!"

"We're getting conflicting information, lieutenant. Someone else is claiming it's apartment twenty-six."

"Twenty-six. Roger. The hallway's filled with fire but we're gonna punch through." He re-joined Cheeseburger and immediately had to duck down. The heat was so bad he just wanted to melt through the floor to escape it. On their knees, they took a beating but could barely press ahead.

"I don't like this." Lt. Brodie sensed a trap. He was six-inches from Cheeseburger and could not even see him. "Stop right here. My earlobes get any hotter we're bailing the fuck out."

"Old school!" Cheeseburger loved it, swinging the nozzle, but Lt. Brodie's words made him nervous.

Engrossed, whatever lurked behind them became disregarded.

***

On Ladder 1, Lt. Paul Kaczmarek was in charge, the Kid was driving, and Beef Dumas was gearing up in the back-step.

"Uh-oh." The Kid had just summed up what all three were thinking when they turned the corner. "Guess we're heading in."

"Lemme talk to Bullet Head." Barely 5'8", Lt. Kaczmarek was a self-described stubborn Pollack. This was also why he and his ex-wife destroyed everything they owned in one of the worst divorces in department history. Nonetheless, he had a cerebral disposition that left his peers thinking he would one day make B.C. He grabbed the mic. "Ladder 1 to Command. What's your pleasure?"

"Get a ladder around back and make entry on the fourth-floor. We're looking for an elderly woman in apartment forty-four first and then a primary search of everything else."

"Roger." Lt. Kaczmarek turned to the Kid. "Park us on the 1-4 corner. That'll give us a clear shot for the roof if he wants a hole later."

"You got it, Dad."

Search and rescue meant all three were going in. Around back, they threw a massive thirty-five-foot ladder up to the fourth-floor and smashed out a window. Inside, the smoke was bad but the growing heat was alarming, especially since there were still no flames. Stumbling room-to-room, they whacked their knees and shins on obstacles unseen in the dense smoke. They checked where unconscious people were most often found—under windows, near doors, in closets, bathtubs, and under beds.

"Ladder 1 to Command. Fourth-floor searched and empty. Increasing heat, smoke is banked down. No visible fire yet."

"All right, Kaz, come on out and cut me a hole."

"Roger."

"Command to Ladder 2."

"Ladder 2!" the lieutenant screamed through his mask.

"Status?"

"Third-floor's half searched! It's bad up here, Chief. Fire's starting to break through from the second-floor."

"Where's Engine 6?"

"Haven't seen them. Chief, you should know, the other half of the floor is starting to really rip."

"Command to Engine 6."

When the mic opened, it sounded like a riot in a bathroom. "6!"

"Where are you?"

"No idea, Chief! We went left with the hose! Maybe side-three?"

"Talk to me, Ray. We got a chance up there?"

"Not without more help!"

"The out-of-town companies are coming right now, man, hang on. Command to Ladder 1."

"Yeah, Chief!"

"Try and put that hole near the peak on the backside above the 2-3 corner."

"Roger!"

B.C. Romine considered the schools of thought on fully involved buildings. Better to orchestrate an aggressive interior attack to get a quick stop and save life and property? Or a safer exterior attack and containment before risking lives to make entry? A mother and three kids were missing, and an old woman was still nowhere to be found. Who knew who else was up there? Until B.C. Romine heard otherwise, the risk was justifiable.

***

On Ladder 1, Kaz kept climbing. He looked over his shoulder to check on Beef who was right behind him. Kaz said, "Who says fat men can't fly?"

Beef Dumas revved the chainsaw to keep it running. "I'm thick but nimble."

"Too true."

Even twenty-feet away they could feel the heat. Smoke was chugging out of opened windows and slithering through seams of siding. When Kaz got to the tip, he plucked the axe and ten-foot pike pole from pre-staged hangers on the side rails of the ladder. He sounded the roof with the axe. "Feels okay." He stepped onto the roof and waited for Beef. Then they walked the ridge to the other side of the house. Because the roof was a six-pitch, and not steep like an eight, ten, or twelve pitch, they did not waste time with the roof ladder.

"It feel hot up here to you?" Kaz kept sounding the roof with the axe.

"Look at this." Beef lifted his boot and pointed at the melted asphalt shingle.

"Great." Facing the ridge, Kaz cut a four-foot square and traded the saw for an axe. After he smashed in the roof—plywood, shingles and all—a black cauldron of smoke and searing heat roared through. With this portal suddenly opened, everything bad began to happen simultaneously. With too many companies out of service, and too long a response time getting there, zero hour had finally arrived. Too much heat meant volatile gases were now gathering and looking to explode.

Kaz was about to slam the pike-pole through the drywall ceiling below when a tornado of fire suddenly spun up through the hole.

"Oh no." Beef started backing up. "Lou, I think the attic's flashed!"

"It came up through the walls." Kaz scampered up to the ridge. Below, he could see the B.C. and everyone scurrying around. He clicked the mic and said, "Ladder 1 to Command. Hole is cut but attic has flashed. We are bailing out."

Beef was already heading across the roof. But Kaz must have screamed when he fell, because Beef turned just as Kaz's helmet bounced twice before sailing off the roof.

"Kaz!"

"Stay back!" Arms thrashing, Kaz fought to pull himself out of the hole. After he did, it quickly filled with fire. His boots and pants were scorched and smoking but he did not even notice. He crawled headfirst down the roof toward Beef whose eyes suddenly widened.

"Hurry, Lou!" he shouted. "Don't look back!"

The chimney, which was near the hole they just cut, collapsed. When it did a domino effect of failing trusses dropped half the roof into the fourth-floor with a building shuddering crash.

Beef jumped onto the ladder and then turned with an outstretched hand. He pulled Kaz onboard before yelling to the Kid, "Get us out of here!"

Down below, somehow, even worse things were occurring.

***

After Ladder 1 cut the hole, several windows on the third and fourth-floors exploded.

"Engine 3 to Command!"

"Command, go."

"We've pushed halfway through the second-floor—"

B.C. Romine had seen enough. They had never gotten to apartment twenty-six, and half the third-floor was not even searched. But conditions were now so bad he knew any civilians in street clothes stood zero chance. "Evacuate the building, lieutenant, we now have fire above and below you. Copy?"

"Roger."

"Command to Fire Alarm. I want all companies evacuated from this building."

Dispatch triggered the Evacuation Tone, and a series of urgent beeps chirped across everyone's radios. *"Fire Alarm to all companies. Evacuate the building. Per order of Command, evacuate the building."*

In case those inside had not heard their radios, firefighters outside jumped into the trucks and wailed the airhorns to deliver this universal message. That was before Kaz's helmet suddenly smashed into the street. When B.C. Romine looked up and saw half of him hanging inside the inferno, there was no worse nightmare. Watching Kaz die was not an option, not even for a gearless Battalion Chief, so Bullet Head Romine sprinted for Ladder 1. He got there as the chimney dropped the roof and the fourth-floor exploded. He was a quarter-way up the ladder when Beef and Kaz jumped onboard.

At the turntable, the Kid was already swinging them away from the dying building.

Used to being the aggressor, B.C. Romine had never felt this helpless. Hanging onto the ladder, he said into the mic, "Fire Alarm, get me an immediate accountability."

"Roger, Command." Fire Alarm hit the Alert Tone. *"Fire Alarm to all companies. Standby for accountability. Fire Alarm to Engine 2."*

"Engine 2," Lt. Salamanca answered. "All present on side-one."

"Ladder 2?"

"All present side-four."

"Engine 3?"

Silence.

"Fire Alarm to Engine 3? Status?"

Silence.

"Fire Alarm to—"

"Command to all companies..." B.C. Romine was not used to feeling this level of panic. "Prepare for R.I.T."

The Rapid Intervention Team was usually comprised of fresh firefighters standing outside in case they needed to be sent in to make a rescue. But there were barely enough firemen to fight the fire, much less stand outside doing nothing, so a dozen exhausted guys were already gathering at the front door with tools and bottles and fresh hose-lines in case those left behind had burnt through. Inside, Engine 3 was missing.

***

Cheeseburger was fatiguing on the line. "Tell that idiot to dial back the pressure, man, he's killing us up here!"

"Shut it down!"

"What?"

"Shut it down!" Lt. Brodie yelled. "The radios are going crazy. Kaz almost just died on the roof. They're pulling everyone out."

"Thank God." Cheeseburger dropped the hose as the air-horns wailed outside.

"Stay on my heels." Lt. Brodie started crawling back the way they had entered. Or at least he thought he was. He reached left to keep in contact with the hose. It was so hot he thought the back of his neck was literally beginning to cook.

"It's right behind us!" Cheeseburger screamed.

With the hose-line shut down, the fire inhaled fresh gases and oxygen. Like a bellows refueling itself, the hallway then spit even more fire against their fleeing heels.

"Stairway!" Lt. Brodie crawled in and pulled Cheeseburger in behind him. He removed his chalk from the door but the charged hose-line kept the door from fully closing. Hungrily, the fire tried to lick them through this seam.

They knelt and caught their breath, leaning against the wall.

"You good?" Lt. Brodie's helmet light caught Cheeseburger's sweaty puzzlement through his mask. "What's wrong?"

"You feel that?"

"Naw, man, let's go. The front door's right below us."

They stood up and took two steps before everything turned to black.

BURN UNIT

April 30, 2010

Changing shades of light were the first thing he remembered. Like drifting through a shifting mist that only ended after his eyelids fluttered open. Then came the pain.

"Brodie?"

Lt. Brodie rolled his head until Bullet Head Romine crept into view. He was not smiling. "Can you hear me?"

Lt. Brodie slowly nodded. "Where am I?"

"Boston. The burn unit at Mass. General."

Lt. Brodie ran a thick tongue across dry lips. "I'm in a lot of pain."

"Believe it or not, that's the good news. They were originally worried about paralysis."

"Can you give me a drink of water?"

B.C. Romine stood up and poured him a glass. Then he held the cup so Lt. Brodie could slurp it through a straw.

Brodie drained it dry and leaned back. "What's wrong with my legs?"

B.C. Romine pulled his chair closer. "There's a lot to tell you."

"I didn't ask you that, Gary."

"You know, our academy was twenty-six-years ago—"

"What time is it?"

"It's two days later, Russ."

"Two *days...*?"

"Everyone's been really worried—"

"Where's Cheeseburger?"

"As far as your legs are concerned—"

"I respect the fact that you can't lie to me."

"Russ..."

"I used to be the Safety Officer. I know they tell you to shield the injured from further trauma."

"Apparently, but you won't even let me do that."

"Why should I? Would you?"

"No." Bullet Head Romine could not look at him when he said, "Cheeseburger's dead, Russ, he died right beside you."

"Please... Oh God." Lt. Brodie blinked. "Dear Jesus Christ..."

"We found you guys in the basement after the stairwell collapsed. The beams broke your legs. The third-degree burns came from that burning timber. From the mid-thighs down, the docs are very concerned about infection. The orthos put rods and screws in your calves, and then the burn team came second. They're saying partial to full recovery, but obviously, it will be a long road. De-braiding the wounds every day, skin grafts, PT, further surgeries..."

"Dead."

"Russ..."

"How come I didn't die?" He was crying.

"Russ—"

"If he was right beside me—"

"NIOSH and the State Fire Marshal's Office are doing a full investigation, including the autopsy. The only thing we can figure is that your mask stayed on. By the time we got to you guys, you were out cold but you were still breathing. Cheeseburger... his mask must've got dislodged by all the falling debris. There was a ton of it. The whole stairway collapsed. The out-of-town companies had just arrived, so they took over suppression while we came after you two. And while all the meatheads were digging from above, Monet was the only one who could fit through the basement window. She's the one who crawled in there and hooked you up to the RIT pack. That kept you breathing until we could remove enough crap to drag you both out."

"Pelly, huh?" Lt. Brodie stared ahead. "She's got more balls than half these fucks put together."

"At the time, things were still collapsing, too. She didn't even flinch. That chick's got balls as big as my head." The silence extended. "If it's any consolation, Russ, she said Cheeseburger was already dead by the time she got there."

"Fuck me."

"You know," B.C. Romine said, "Since the bankruptcy I've been running around here screaming about how everyone's out of position and acting out of rank, and that eventually someone was gonna get jammed up. I just never thought it'd be me."

"You did nothing wrong. People trapped on multiple floors? That sums up our whole profession."

"Yeah, well, it turns out there was no one even in the goddamn building."

"That doesn't matter. How could it? You can't do this job in reverse."

"Cheeseburger's fucking dead, Russ. A kid with barely a year-and-a-half on the job—"

"You don't have to tell me that. Like I don't know?"

"And now, whether or not he ever should've been in there will haunt me to my grave."

"That fire had a ten-minute head start, and the first engine was actually making grabs. We never had a chance."

"I called up Chief Donut. I'm turning in my command. I can't be in charge of a suicide mission anymore, because that's all this is now."

"That's not—"

"Let the next guy bury the bodies, Russ. I just want to go back to my truck and play captain again."

"I can respect that."

"Cheeseburger. Or Cheese. It's been so long since he was called anything else, I totally forgot his first name was Lenny."

"That's because the place where we work is filled with merciless assholes."

"He's getting the full send-off. IAFF is estimating 10,000 firefighters. The city's closing all the streets between his church and the cemetery. Guys are all taking turns at the house with his family. His poor mom... she's still in a wheelchair."

"What a mess, man. It must be awful."

"The whole place is exhausted and traumatized."

"I meant you. Having to deal with this."

"I..."

"I've never seen you speechless. Fucking Bullet Head, man, they named you that for a reason, right?"

"I ain't laughing, Russ."

"I hear ya. But at the end of the day, after you sign on the dotted line, it doesn't really matter anymore, does it? Twenty-six years later and I can tell you one thing that's truer now than it ever was before—we only owe God one death."

"What about you? You're still here. Feeling guilty about that yet?"

"No."

"Yeah, right. That kid died right beside you."

"He sure did, the glorious bastard. And that's how I'm gonna remember him. He fought like hell up in that hallway, man, it sucked up there."

"Just wait. After the exhilaration of being alive wears off, the guilt comes next."

"That's a pretty shitty thing to say."

"Yeah, well, I'm in a pretty shitty mood."

"I was in charge of him, you were in charge of me. Split the blame if you have to, just don't be a fucking asshole about it."

"Then stop fantasizing. It's insulting. This sucks. Just admit it and stop trying to convince me it was unavoidable."

"What's that? You not being an asshole? Yeah, clearly there ain't no avoiding that."

"You'll get yours, believe me. I haven't slept in two days."

"Just get out of here, Gary. Only you would show up in someone's sick room looking to make them feel even worse."

Bullet Head Romine stood up and left.

BAGPIPES
May 4, 2010

Firefighters from across America and Canada started arriving days before the funeral. The preparations for a Line of Duty Death were extensive and closely guarded by tradition, so every aspect had to be precise. Capt. McCarrick led a team of ten mapping out the logistics. Accommodations had to be made for attendees that would include Governor Carvalho, both state senators, congressmen, state representatives, local politicians, the public, and 10,000 firefighters. Receiver Tillinghast, however, was informed his presence would not be required. Lt. Ahearn even publicly stated the safety of the Receiver could not be guaranteed.

The Police Department helped by setting up for the public ceremony, which would be held at the minor league baseball stadium downtown. They also handled all the transportation, traffic details, and road closures.

***

At 8 A.M. the day of the funeral, members of Class 61 gathered at Fonzie's house. They were all in their Class A winter dress uniforms and hats. In the garage, they drank beers and passed flasks while the wives and girlfriends stayed inside. Stunned pain seemed to be the shared emotion.

That Cheeseburger was gone forever was still too new a reality for anyone to process.

"I can't wait for this to be over," Super-Wop said. "I'm getting flash-backs from the service. These things are brutal."

"We got a long way to go." Fonzie cracked another beer. "We gotta be downtown by nine, so everybody drink up."

Fresh beers popped open.

T-Bag said, "This is gonna be a bloodbath."

"It sure is." Rowdell fired up a cigarette. "You know how they say amputees can still feel their phantom limb? That's what this feels like."

No one said anything.

"It's gross." Yoda sipped off his flask. "No one ever thinks about it, because if they did, they'd never take the job."

Fonzie added. "The gift of this place just got torched."

"Listen," T-Bag said. "What're we gonna do about his mom?"

"We'll set up a rotation," Rowdell answered. "Have somebody go over once a day in case she needs groceries or anything."

A fire department van pulled into the driveway. Capt. McCarrick and Dutch Carrigan joined them in the garage. Their dress blues were adorned with all kinds of medals. They had different color bars for heroism on their left chest, and slashes sewn onto their forearms for every three years of service. Only Capt. McCarrick cracked a beer since Dutch had not touched alcohol in twenty years.

"To Cheese," Capt. McCarrick toasted. "Bastard died on his feet instead of living on his knees."

T-Bag said, "Who'd you steal that from?"

"Fuck you, T-Bag."

"Emiliano Zapata," Yoda said. "He was a Mexican revolutionary."

T-Bag grinned. "God, how I love your giant brain..."

Fonzie said, "You got everything all squared away, Cap?"

"All set. We're gonna send him off like a Norse god."

"Absolutely."

"Can't believe you fucks only have eighteen months on the job."

"Ain't that awful?" Dutch asked. "Some guys go their whole careers without losing any of their friends, and you guys didn't even make it two years."

"Like anything else about this place," Capt. McCarrick added, "just stick together and you'll find your way through. Or you can sit around whining and crying like a bunch of twats. You choose."

Dutch nodded. "That's exactly right."

"You mean you're not gonna give us a shoulder to cry on?" T-Bag asked. "Shocking."

Capt. McCarrick grinned and guzzled the rest of his beer. "What do you say, guys? You ready to send Cheese to Valhalla?"

They refilled their flasks, grabbed their hats, and braced for the worst.

***

The State Police had closed four square blocks of downtown to traffic. News helicopters hovered overhead as thousands of firefighters poured out of buses and swarmed the staging area. From here, for the full eight blocks it took to reach the minor league baseball stadium, they stood at attention on both sides of the street. As much a celebration of the life that was lost, en masse they would now accompany Cheeseburger this last mile.

Downtown at headquarters, Yoda, Super-Wop, Rowdell, Fonzie, T-Bag, and Mikey Doneen were in charge of the casket. In front of City Hall, the Honor Guards from dozens of police and fire departments from around the country stood crisply at attention. There were so many flags flying along Blackstone Avenue, it made City Hall look like an adjunct office for the United Nations. Once the bagpipes started braying, even the civilians quieted down.

Outside fire departments were covering the Sachem City stations so all members could attend the funeral. The eighty-nine firefighters that remained were lined up and down the street. Recent injuries left some in wheelchairs and slings.

Capt. McCarrick shouted, "Detail! Present arms!"

They saluted and held it.

The casket was pulled from the back of the hearse. The six of them carried it over and carefully lifted it onto the hose-bed of Engine 3. Washed and waxed, Engine 3 was draped in black bunting. Cheeseburger's scorched helmet was zip-tied to the front bumper with a black wreath hung directly above it. His wrecked and bloody turnout gear was hung with zip-ties across the back of the truck like a scarecrow. His mangled boots stood on the back bumper, reversed, to symbolize him witnessing his own funeral procession.

"Detail! Order arms!"

They finished the salute in unison.

"Detail! Fall in!"

What was left of the Sachem City Fire Department lined up by rank in three columns behind Engine 3.

The long-retired Engine 1, a classic 1952 Maxim used for parades, was the lead vehicle. Behind that were ten limousines loaded with Cheeseburger's family and dignitaries. Next were the marching ranks of the Rhode Island Professional Pipes and Drums, and then came the endless honor guards from across New England. Engine 3 followed in front of the marching SCFD.

"Present arms!" was barked out every hundred feet as firefighters lining the street snapped to attention and solemnly saluted as the caravan approached. No one spoke. They were all in their dress uniforms. Those from volunteer departments that could not afford dress blues wore their turnout gear and helmets instead.

The civilians wore looks of stunned appreciation. Some had stumbled upon this scene on a beautiful Saturday morning entirely by mistake. Most had never seen anything like it. But when Engine 3 crawled by with the casket on top, people started crying. They had never met Cheeseburger, but that a perfect stranger could die just doing his job on their behalf was a horrible thing to witness.

The column of vehicles wound through downtown. The sun popped in and out of the clouds as they approached the stadium. Little kids snuck in behind the wall of firefighters and saluted as well.

Inside the stadium, the limousines stopped on the infield grass. Cheeseburger's mom was helped into her wheelchair by her ex-husband, sister, and aunts. In the last two months she had had a stroke and now lost her only son, so she was barely coherent. She could not stop crying, and no one tried to stop her, so she just sagged into her chair.

The stadium had seating for 12,000 people, and between the firefighters and public, nearly every seat was taken. The style of hats and dress uniforms might have varied, but the color did not—a sea of dark navy blue had washed ashore.

Engine 3 was pulled in and parked. The dignitaries took their seats on a dais to the right.

Capt. McCarrick was at the podium and filled with the importance of the moment. Even his enormous mustache conveyed this point, that there was no other job he could have ever done. When he thanked everyone for attending, his voice boomed across the stadium. "They say you can judge a man by who shows up for his funeral. Weddings are fun. Birthdays are easy. Saying good-bye is neither of those things. Firefighters swear an oath, so we know moments like this are possible. When they appear, we turn to each other for support. A solemn tradition as old as the fire service itself—no one goes anywhere alone. Especially not today.

"Father James Burnell has been the pastor for the Sachem City Fire Department for the last forty years. He's going to say a few words..."

The priest spent twenty minutes offering platitudes and support. He said his peace and finished by leading them through the Lord's Prayer.

Capt. McCarrick thanked him and said, "As most of you know, Private Leonard Rialto was only on our job for eighteen months. This makes a tragic situation exponentially worse. His academy classmate, Glenn St. Pierre, will now say a few words."

Yoda stepped forward. At the podium he unfolded his notes and readied to speak. But when he looked up, the 12,000 faces staring back nearly froze him. He cleared his throat and said, "William Shakespeare once wrote, 'Cowards die many times before their deaths, the valiant never taste of death but once.' In his short career, Leonard Rialto had already demonstrated courage and fortitude. His first day on a fire truck he caught a double-fatal motor vehicle accident. Soon after, when a limousine loaded with a bridal party overturned in the S-curves, he was first on-scene with Engine 2, helping the grievously wounded with the patience and care of a twenty-year veteran. Then came Terrace Street. At 11:15 A.M. last August 18th, the basement of a triple-decker with only one working smoke detector on the third-floor, caught fire. Engine 4 was out of service due to the blackouts, and Engine 3 was involved in an accident on the way to the fire. By the time third-due Engine 2 turned the corner, the place was roaring. People were hanging out of windows screaming for help. Lenny never missed a beat. He shot up that ladder and rescued two kids and their mother seconds before the room flashed over. The footage from that fire was so dramatic it was on the news for days. When I heard about it, I asked him what it was like to be a star and he just shrugged. That was him. He was a worker. Never in a bad mood, he accepted every challenge. He liked to say that he wasn't the fastest or the smartest, but no one outworked him. And that was the case in everything he did. He was invaluable around the station, cooking meals and doing chores. A great cook, he considered Chef Anthony Bourdain a personal hero. Which I found ironic, because Mr. Bourdain once said, "Firefighters, in my experience, are a lot like the Marines I've met through the years. No matter how badly led, how ridiculously underequipped, underappreciated, no matter how doomed their mission, they take a bizarre and quite beautiful pride in at least being screwed more than everybody else and doing it with style... It's not a job, it's a calling.'" Yoda choked up and could not continue. "Rest easy, Cheese. We'll take it from here."

Capt. McCarrick re-took the podium. He stood and stared out into the sea of blue and barked, "Detail! Present arms!"

10,000 firefighters rose as one and saluted.

***

After the funeral, Governor Carvalho wasted no time. Flanked by her aides, she swept into City Hall and called on Receiver Tillinghast unannounced.

"Marissa?" Tillinghast tried to cover up his surprise with kindness. "And to what do I owe the honor on this grim day?"

Governor Carvalho wore a black pants suit, black heels, and a carnivorous look. She kicked everyone out, locked the door, and strolled over to the window. She watched the Massasoit River tumble over the rocks as she said, "There are few duties I detest more than presiding over the deaths of civil servants. The optics are horrible. Someone employed by the city or state has died at work. People want to know it was not in vain. This is when they need to see the chain of command in action. To ensure anyone and everyone involved in these fateful decisions is held responsible, accountable."

"I totally concur."

"Accountability. Both you and I know that at the end of the day, the public has to see the buck stop somewhere."

"Forgive me, Madame Governor, but I'm not following you."

"Really, Arthur? I would've thought you'd be more discerning. I guess I have to spell it out?"

"I see." He tried not to audibly swallow. "Collateral damage, so to speak?"

"It can't be thought of as personal if this is the business we have voluntarily chosen."

"So you won't even let me see it through to the end? All my hard work, at the end of the day, doesn't even buy me a second chance?"

"I tried to warn you. Politics, at this level, doesn't allow for that." Governor Carvalho looked at him from the window. "I'm offering you the chance to resign with dignity. Draft some drivel about how you need to spend more time with your family, your pets, your golf game—whatever."

"Or else?"

Her black eyes flashed. "I need a neck for the noose, Arthur. This was your baby. I told you in the beginning that with great risk could come great reward. But I also told you you would swing alone if the roof came crashing down."

"It was a tragic accident—"

"Public opinion is a pendulum. Unfortunately for you, it has swung too far away to save you."

"I respectfully disagree. The taxpayers in this city know the sacrifices that have been made on their behalf are only a part of the cost of doing business. When we re-emerge from this bankruptcy, Sachem City will be poised for the comeback of the century. Mark my words."

"That may be the case. But that's a far future neither you nor I will be around to see."

"With all due respect, Madame Governor..." He peeled off his glasses and placed them on his desk. "I have a real problem quitting. I am no quitter. It's just not in my DNA. Besides, it will destroy my reputation. Not to mention any future political aspirations I may have."

"Is that your final answer?"

"Can't we meet halfway? Where does the compromise lie?"

"When public opinion is lost, leadership must be changed."

"I believe the public will rally to my defense."

"Seriously? This from a man whose own safety can't be guaranteed at a funeral?"

"I believe that to be a by-product of our hysterical firefighters. Once emotions have cooled down, I'll make it right with them or anybody else affected by my policies."

"Of course you will." Governor Carvalho extended a sad smile. As she headed for the door, she said, "Please tell your lovely wife I said hello."

"Madame Governor—"

The mahogany door clicked closed behind her.

FADE TO BLACK
May 10, 2010

Five days later, Arthur Tillinghast was at his kitchen table drinking coffee. He was already immaculately dressed for work. The newspaper was spread before him like a giant napkin.

He was biting into a bagel when the house phone rang. After his wife did not answer, he got up and said, "Yes, hello?"

"Dad?"

"Lizzy?"

"Dad, what is going on? You're all over the news! Why aren't you answering your cell phone?"

"It's upstairs in my office... what do you mean I'm on the news?"

"How could you be such a monster! You've made all of us live this lie *together*?"

The line went dead. He clicked on the television and that's when his stomach quickly dropped.

A reporter said, "... As stated, we are following developing news out of Newport, where cold-case detectives, after receiving new information, have abruptly re-opened a 30-year-old investigation into the disappearance of Molly Bennington, a 21-year-old debutante when she disappeared the night of May 3, 1979. Originally, speculation centered around a group purported to be comprised of the sons of Rhode Island elites. Molly was alleged to have been in their company at the Arkmore Country Club the night she disappeared. But the case remained unsolved and eventually faded from public view. Police have said in the past that this group was renowned for parties that at times included prostitutes and illicit drug use. The biggest name so far revealed in this investigation, which we have also just now confirmed, is retired Supreme Court Justice Arthur Tillinghast. Other names are sure to follow, as the Washington County District Attorney has just released a statement saying further indictments are on the horizon..."

He knew every word was gone but one.

Carvalho.

The assassin had struck again.

ACKNOWLEDGEMENTS

The following books and websites provided invaluable research:

- "A Social History of Samuel Slater's Pawtucket, 1790-1830." Brendan Francis Gilbane. Doctoral thesis published in 1969
- "The History of Pawtucket, 1635-1986." Susan Marie Boucher.
- "Sam Patch; The Famous Jumper." Paul E. Johnson. Hill and Wang Publishers, New York, New York. 2004.

Quote on page 541: "Never contend with a man that has nothing to lose," is attributed to Baltasar Gracian Y Morales.

Page 363-364 song lyrics excerpted from Jerry Lee Lewis, "Great balls of Fire," Sun Records, 1957.

All of the illustrations were drawn and published with permission by Leila Trabulsi.

The photograph of ladder operations was reprinted with the permission of Captain Ken Labelle.

The map of Sachem City was made by Tom Trabulsi.

The cover photo is what Pine Street looked like when we pulled up at 0330 on March 14, 2020.

ABOUT THE AUTHOR

Tom Trabulsi was born in the Midwest and attended high school in Rhode Island. After college, he worked as a bike courier in Boston and New York City. He moved to Colorado and worked construction throughout the Rocky Mountains. *Sandaman's Riposte* was his first novel. *Forked Head Pass*, a story about the Colorado land rush in the late 1990s, followed six years later. Currently, he is a firefighter in a northeast city. *The Fire Service of Sachem City* is his third novel.